D1594008

THE LOEB CLASSICAL LIBRARY

FOUNDED BY JAMES LOEB

AELIAN

HISTORICAL MISCELLANY

(VARIA HISTORIA)

LCL 486

AELIAN

HISTORICAL MISCELLANY

EDITED AND TRANSLATED BY

N. G. WILSON

HARVARD UNIVERSITY PRESS
CAMBRIDGE, MASSACHUSETTS
LONDON, ENGLAND
1997

Library of Congress Cataloging-in-Publication Data

Aelian, 3rd cent.
[Varia historia. English]
Historical miscellany / Aelian; edited and translated by N.G. Wilsc
p. cm. — (Loeb classical library; 486)
Includes index.
ISBN 0–674–99535–X
1. History, Ancient. I. Wilson, Nigel Guy. II. Title.
III. Title: Aelian: historical miscellany IV. Series.
PA3821.A4 1997 96–38637 938—dc20

*Typeset in ZephGreek and ZephText
by Chiron, Inc, North Chelmsford, Massachusetts.
Printed in Great Britain by St Edmundsbury Press Ltd,
Bury St Edmunds, Suffolk, on acid-free paper.
Bound by Hunter & Foulis Ltd, Edinburgh, Scotland.*

CONTENTS

ACKNOWLEDGEMENTS

Editors are usually indebted to friends and colleagues for their willingness to share knowledge and give advice, and I am no exception. Apart from certain specific acknowledgements made in the notes I should like to record here my warmest gratitude to the following for substantial help and kindness, which has saved me from error and guided me towards numerous improvements: Claudio Bevegni, Mervin Dilts, Rudolf Kassel, and Donald Russell. I should also like to thank Jan Fredrik Kindstrand, who allowed me to see his forthcoming survey article on Aelian for *Aufstieg und Niedergang der römischen Welt* II 34.4, and the Classics Department of the University of Michigan at Ann Arbor, who enabled me to consult the unpublished translation of the *Varia Historia* by Warren Blake. Last but not least the editors of the Loeb Classical Library have earned my gratitude by their prompt acceptance of my suggestion that this work should figure in the series and by their assistance at later stages of the enterprise.

INTRODUCTION

The *Varia Historia* is a miscellaneous collection of anecdotes and historical material, with the addition of a few slightly longer pieces of narrative or description in very elegant prose. It is the work of an educated Roman of whom very little is known, and was put together in the early third century. It belongs therefore to a period of antiquity which was one of the least productive of first-class literature either in Greek or in Latin. Other authors who were approximate contemporaries of Aelian and wrote works that have come down to us—such as the gastronome Athenaeus, the philosophy professor Alexander of Aphrodisias, the historians Dio Cassius and Herodian, and the sophist Flavius Philostratus—are of interest to professional scholars but have little claim on the attention of a wider public today. Though it cannot be claimed that Aelian wrote a great masterpiece, his book has a certain attraction and tells us something about the tastes of the reading public in the later Roman Empire.

By the time that Aelian wrote there was already a quantity of literature of the type represented by his *Historical Miscellany*. The best known example is in Latin, the *Attic Nights* of Aulus Gellius, published about A.D. 180. These books served the needs of cultivated readers in search of literary and historical facts. Since the mass of

Greek, and to a lesser extent Latin, literature had grown to unmanageable proportions it was handy to have a ready-made selection.[1] The reader thus acquired some pleasant and instructive material; the facts were set down haphazardly, often with no obvious link between one chapter and the next. They offered variety without making undue demands on the reader's intelligence, and satisfied a need that is now met in other ways, for instance by novels, biographies, and accounts of travel. The first two of these genres, if not the third, were already well established in Aelian's day. Plutarch's *Lives* had been written about a century earlier and were clearly known to Aelian. Since the first century the novel had been slowly asserting its place as a recognised form of literature—a tentative hypothesis would make Longus' *Daphnis and Chloe* and Heliodorus' *Aethiopica* contemporary with Aelian; but it is far from certain that he and his circle would have taken any interest in them. Though it is not clear whether Aelian is the last in a long line of compilers of miscellanies, his work is of a type that was about to lose some of its popularity in an age of changing tastes.

Aelian was born in Praeneste, the modern Palestrina, probably ca. A.D. 170, and died ca. 235. He seems to have lived in Rome; he may conceivably have been the owner of a house in the outskirts of the city beyond the Basilica of San Paolo at Tre Fontane where in the sixteenth century two stones were found inscribed with Greek epigrams in honour of Homer and Menander.[2] For reasons

[1] L. Holford-Strevens, *Aulus Gellius* (London, 1988) pp. 20–22, offers a good brief survey.

[2] *Inscriptiones graecae* XIV 1183.

which they do not reveal to us the antiquarians Fulvio Orsini and Pirro Ligorio identified the villa as that of Aelian. Certainly it would have been appropriate for our author to have statues of such famous figures in his house and to compose epigrams about them, and the indifferent quality of the verses is no argument against the identification. At all events Aelian thought of himself as a Roman and took pride in the fact, as is shown by several remarks in the *Historical Miscellany.*[3]

But he wrote in Greek, and for Greeks. In his day Greek culture was dominated, as it had been for a century or more, by the nostalgic vision of a great past, in which the achievements of Athens took pride of place. One result of this admiration for an ancient culture so evidently in contrast with the impoverishment of Greece under Roman rule was that intellectuals imitated as best they could the language of the great writers of the fourth century B.C.; at least in this respect they could try to equal the great men of the past. Aelian like other authors wrote in a somewhat archaic language, as can be seen by comparison with the New Testament and the private letters found among the papyri from Egypt.[4]

Not all writers were equally skilled in the art of imitation, and there are a number of passages where a translator may feel that Aelian has failed to make his meaning explicit. In his case there is an obvious additional factor at work: Aelian was a Roman, and even if he was bilingual to a degree that elicited the admiration of Philostratus, a

[3] Cf. 2.38, 12.25, 14.45.

[4] At 1.25, 4.3, and 13.44 he even uses dual forms, also found in fr. 86.

younger contemporary who was probably the best Greek writer of his generation,[5] it is not rare for a bilingual person to exhibit occasional shortcomings in handling the finest nuances. Aelian is no exception: there are a few places where his Greek may reflect Latin idiom. To a modern reader the phenomenon of a writer aiming at literary success in a language which is not his mother tongue is unusual—the outstanding example is Joseph Conrad, and even he had to admit that the critics spotted faults in his English. But in antiquity things were different: Romans of the upper classes were brought up to be bilingual. Quintilian says that some young children concentrated on Greek to such an extent that their pronunciation and command of idiom suffered.[6] Many Romans could write Greek, notable cases being Cicero and Marcus Aurelius; but how many achieved a perfect command of style and idiom is not clear. Philostratus' praise is that of a connoisseur, but it needs to be analysed with care. He says that Aelian was as expert in Attic Greek as the inhabitants of the inland area of Attica, regarded as the place where the best Attic was spoken, as Philostratus himself had explained earlier in his biography of Herodes Atticus. This has been taken to mean that Aelian wrote as well as the natives, but as the general view of modern scholars is much less flattering, one should at least consider the possibility that Philostratus referred simply to his command of the spoken language. However that may be, Philostratus admired him for his linguistic skill and for the fact that though he was awarded the title of sophist he had reservations about his capacity as a rhetorician and so decided to write history instead.

[5] *Lives of the Sophists* 2.31 (624–625).

[6] *Institutio oratoria* 1.1.12–14.

Philostratus also records an episode from the year 222 or soon after which is not entirely flattering to Aelian. One day, soon after the death of the unpopular emperor Elagabalus, he called on Aelian and found him holding a book in his hand from which he was reading in a vehement and powerful voice. Philostratus asked what he was doing, and he replied "I have composed an indictment of Gunnis—that is my name for the tyrant who died recently—because he was a disgrace to Rome." Philostratus then said "I should have admired you if you had denounced him during his lifetime." Being concerned with rhetoricians rather than writers of other genres Philostratus does not bother to tell us much more about Aelian. Among the few details he adds it may be worth mentioning the statement that Aelian never travelled outside Italy. This, if true, is *prima facie* in conflict with a passage in Aelian's other major surviving work, *On the Characteristics of Animals* (*De Natura Animalium*), which appears to claim that he had seen in Alexandria animals with teratogenic deformities (11.40). The conflict of evidence has to be explained by assuming that Philostratus was wrong or that in the passage in question Aelian absent-mindedly copied out his source, an oversight which seems extraordinarily careless in what is otherwise a finished work.[7]

In the epilogue to that work Aelian makes it clear that though he could have lived at court he chose to avoid public life and the opportunities of making money. This

[7] Near the beginning of the chapter Apion is cited by name as a source and some facts are reported from him. *Pace* M. Wellmann in *RE* s.v. Aelianus (11) col. 486, it is not likely that Aelian would suddenly at the end of the chapter fail to convert a first person verb into the third person.

induces us to think of him as a scholarly recluse; but a passage in the *Historical Miscellany* (3.17) is expressed in a way that might imply substantial public duties. We are told by the *Suda* lexicon that he was a priest, and perhaps this position occupied him more than we might assume. Yet he managed to find time to write a good deal. The longest extant work is *On the Characteristics of Animals,* a miscellany of information in seventeen books which collects facts and fables about the animal kingdom with the aim of inviting thought about the contrast between human and animal behaviour. A much slighter extant work is a set of twenty short fictitious letters supposedly written by farmers. Two lost books—or perhaps they are one, quoted by an alternative title, *De providentia* (Περὶ προνοίας) and *De signis divinis* (Περὶ θείων ἐναργειῶν)—dealt with the operation of divine providence in human affairs. The *Historical Miscellany* was presumably Aelian's last production; its clearly unfinished state invites the inference that he died before completing it, but left it in a state which his executors thought good enough to allow publication. Many chapters, if not most, look as if they are now in their final form.

In its present state the *Historical Miscellany* lacks a prologue and a conclusion, both of which are found in *Characteristics of Animals;* it also exhibits numerous repetitions; and the first fifteen chapters of Book I seem inappropriately placed—they should have been distributed randomly throughout the text, and one must suspect that they are material collected for the *Characteristics of Animals* and then rejected as unsuitable. But it is not absolutely certain that Aelian's work was unknown to the

public during his lifetime. He might have availed himself of the time-honoured means of preliminary publication by reading parts of it to friends. This practice, known as *recitatio*, had been quite normal about a century before—indeed there were complaints about the excessive use made of it—and it may be inferred that it continued; an admittedly unreliable source says that the emperor Severus Alexander (222–233) often went to the Athenaeum, a lecture hall built by Hadrian, to hear Greek and Latin poets and rhetoricians.[8] Although we have no external evidence that Aelian was one of them, we may note that in three places (1.28, 2.4, 3.16) he addresses his readers in the plural, in a way which would hardly be natural unless he thought of himself reading the text to an audience. However, recitation could only benefit a local audience. A travelling sophist could overcome that difficulty, but Aelian is said not to have travelled abroad. Yet some of his work can only be aimed at a Greek audience; the brief remarks which now constitute 7.11 and 7.16, even if they are abridgements, would be of no interest to an Italian public. In its written form the work would have circulated throughout the empire. So far no papyrus has been found to prove that it reached Egypt, and there is no reliable indication of Aelian's popularity. He may have aimed to reach a fairly wide public, if we are entitled to take a hint from the wording of 13.4. There Agathon is described as "the tragic poet" in a context which has already mentioned Euripides. The highly educated would hardly have needed that description. But one must also allow for the possibility that Aelian is here indulging in an affected simplicity, which is a feature of his style.

[8] *Historia Augusta, Severus Alexander* 35.4.

Aelian lived in a world dominated by the vision of a glorious Greek past. Athens was particularly prominent in that vision, and Aelian's admiration for the Athenians of the fifth and fourth centuries is not to be doubted. But he has to admit their failings at times. In 2.7 he comments on the defeat of Euripides by a nonentity at the dramatic festival competition, and finds both the possible explanations for this surprising event equally unpalatable. In the next chapter he expresses his dismay at three of the unpleasant decisions taken by the Athenian democracy in its dealings with its so-called allies. Curiously he does not bother to say that the most horrifying of the three was not carried out, thanks to a change of mind.

Other leading cities and their heroes are well represented, and Alexander the Great figures frequently. There are also anecdotes about the Hellenistic age, but one has the impression that his acquaintance with the literature of that period was not extensive. Certainly at 3.40 he writes as if he had not heard of, still less read, the *Silloi* of Timon of Phlius, satirical pieces about philosophers and others in hexameters of Homeric stamp, while at 13.20 he gives the impression of not knowing that the politician Cercidas was also an author. Perhaps he would have defended himself by saying that he deliberately withheld these facts in the belief that they were not relevant to his purpose at the time.

Though Aelian was much nearer to the classical past than we are, his historical perspective was not always sound. In several passages he creates the impression that ancient customs were still in force when it is quite certain that they were not. In 3.12 he speaks of Spartan customs in the present tense, and one wonders if he had the slight-

est idea of what contemporary Sparta was like. Similar criticisms can be made of 3.9, the second half of 3.10, and 4.1. At 5.21 he refers to a religious rite in Corinth which cannot have been carried out since the destruction of the city by the Romans in 146 B.C. In 8.10 he speaks of some laws of Solon as being still in force in Athens. There are also anachronisms: at 9.29 Socrates is made to put questions to members of the not yet extant Lyceum and Academy. In 5.13 he is hopelessly vague about Athenian constitutional history, and in 2.13 his misunderstanding of Aristophanes' *Clouds* is gross. There is a great deal of anecdote which is unreliable or worse, e.g. the account in 3.19 of the origins of the estrangement between Plato and Aristotle. But it would hardly be fair to blame him on this account; it is only in recent years that scholars have come to realise just how sceptical they ought to be in their attitude to all biographical material relating to figures from the classical period.[9]

Another criticism which might be made of his work is that he does not show much capacity to generalise about the history of the classical city-states; but to this charge he could at least have replied by pointing to 6.13, where he makes the good observation—perhaps not his own—that the dynasties of the so-called Greek tyrants did not normally survive long.

But whatever his shortcomings he had one great advantage over us, in that he could appreciate a wider range of ancient art. We are impressed above all by Greek architecture, vase painting, and sculpture. Aelian shows awareness of the last of these, while neglecting the other

[9] M. R. Lefkowitz, *The Lives of the Greek Poets* (London, 1981), *passim*.

two; but he is able to pay tribute to one aspect of Greek art almost entirely denied to us. Painting from the classical period seems to have survived in considerable quantity down to his day, and wealthy Romans were in a position to form private collections. So Aelian's references to works by the great masters do not have to be treated as an empty display of learning; at least he had probably seen some paintings by the great masters he mentions, even if not the particular paintings that he writes about. That he and others were right to prize Greek painting highly seems now to be confirmed by the wonderful specimens recovered from the fourth century Macedonian tombs at Vergina. It may be worth adding that the famous painters were not Athenians, and so Aelian's admiration for their work is another sign that his gaze did not focus too much on Athens at the expense of other Greek cities.

Where did Aelian get his material from? Is his book a collection formed in the course of his reading over a period of many years or has he availed himself of the work of previous compilers of the same kind? Probably it is a mixture, in proportions which we cannot now determine because of the loss of so much ancient literature. Many chapters coincide closely with passages in other authors such as Plutarch. A particularly close relation seems to exist between Aelian and Athenaeus; most of the chapters in question appear in the same order in both authors, and a close comparison of the wording, especially of the details omitted or simplified by Aelian, makes it extremely plausible to suppose that Aelian is borrowing from the *Deipnosophists.* But Athenaeus was quite a recent writer; exactly how recent is disputed—certainly

he published after 193, but the attempt to date him after 228 seems misguided; and if Athenaeus' work was still relatively recent, decency and caution might have been a deterrent to open borrowing. Some modern scholars prefer to think that both were drawing on a common source, now lost but obviously of great attractions. Without wishing to be too severe it has to be said that if more of the literature of the early Roman empire were extant we should almost certainly extend the list of chapters in Aelian that depend directly on other anthologists. On the other hand the ancients took a less severe view than we do in judging plagiarism, and for them imitation was a form of honourable competition, in which one attempted to offer variations on a known theme. The new treatment of the theme was judged a success if it could be thought an improvement in some respect. No ordinary reader would have criticised Aelian for his aims in the *Historical Miscellany;* but we cannot say how much such a reader would have found to praise.[10]

But is the *Historical Miscellany* just a compilation of information? Not quite. Although the majority of the chapters fit that description, there are some exceptions. We find a few longer chapters, designed as examples of formal prose. There are just five of these. The longest

[10] The difficult question of Aelian's sources was discussed three times by F. Rudolph, who changed his mind within a few years of his original publication, *De fontibus quibus Aelianus in Varia Historia componenda usus sit* (Leipzig, 1884); see "Die Quellen und die Schriftstellerei des Athenaios," in *Philologus, Supplementband* 6 (1891): 109–162, esp. 127–132, and "Zu den Quellen des Aelian und Athenaios," in *Philologus* 52 (1894): 652–663.

(12.1) is the story of Aspasia the Younger, which fills seven printed pages in a modern edition. One of the five, the tale told by Silenus to Midas (3.18), opens with the admission that Theopompus is the source being used. Thanks to a quotation by an obscure ancient rhetorician we know that Theopompus was also the source for the description of Tempe (3.1). The sources of the others cannot now be identified; but there is good reason to suppose that in each case Aelian was following a model quite closely. It would be interesting to make a comparison with the original if one had survived. Presumably Aelian aimed in each case to produce a piece of prose which by the standards of his day would seem superior to the original. Towards the end of 13.1 he lets slip a remark which throws some light on his practice: it will do no harm, he says, to describe Atalanta's appearance since the attempt may improve one's experience and skill as a writer. But in his effort to achieve fine effects his taste sometimes let him down; at the end of the same paragraph he mixes his metaphors in a most unfortunate way, comparing Atalanta to a star and to lightning in the same clause.

In general Aelian's style can be described as one of studied simplicity. He was not writing history or composing pieces of epideictic oratory, even if he may have given some public readings; so Thucydides and the orators were not the models to follow. The plain style, unpretentious and with a touch of naiveté, was appropriate. It is not possible for us to say whether a single author served as his principal model; but it is likely that the early annalistic historians and Xenophon exerted influence on him. Since we know that in two of his longer and carefully polished pieces Aelian drew upon Theopompus it is tantalising that

we cannot comment on the stylistic changes he made; but as it is known that Theopompus was a pupil of Isocrates one may suspect that he normally used an elaborate periodic style quite different from what Aelian offers us. One may speculate—but this is no more than a risky hypothesis, since we do not know to what extent Theopompus was capable of stylistic diversity—that the originals offered a challenge to Aelian to transform the descriptions into the simple style that he felt more appropriate.

A modern translator can give some idea of Aelian's manner. While it is not feasible to reproduce the archaising vocabulary and syntax—one modern translator of Herodotus into English made the unfortunate decision to render him in the language of the King James Bible—the simplicity of the syntax, with its many brief clauses and rare use of subordination, can be reflected in a version. The effect tends towards monotony; though Aelian offers a great variety of subject matter he fails to match this with sufficient variation of style.

There is, however, an obstacle which prevents us from doing full justice to the text. At some unknown date, probably in the early Byzantine period, it has been subjected to a process of abbreviation. This is not to say that what we now read is merely an epitome; but it is clear that a certain number of chapters cannot now be read in the form that Aelian intended them to have. There are various indications of this fact. Certain chapters—the first is 3.13—begin with a word meaning "note that," which is a regular sign of epitomisation. Others have been abbreviated in a more subtle way; we are only aware of it because they are quoted in the fifth-century anthology of Johannes Stobaeus in a slightly longer and more stylish form.

It looks as if abbreviation may have affected a third group of chapters, which seem much too brief as they stand; but as they are not quoted by Stobaeus or anyone else we cannot be sure of the original wording.

Apart from a certain monotony of style and the effects of abbreviation there are occasional blemishes or other oddities which are not likely to be visible to the reader of a translation. Aelian's handling of some of the demonstrative pronouns does not seem to conform to classical practice, and the translator does not find it easy to avoid a rather free version. In two passages he appears to contravene the rules for final clauses; at 4.15 he is unaware that in Attic Greek a purpose which remained unrealised is expressed with a verb in the indicative mood, and at 14.45 he uses the optative in primary sequence. And there are a few passages where one may even suspect him of being influenced by Latin idiom, notably in his liking for a particular adverb used in the superlative, ἀνδρειότατα, which looks like a calque of *fortissime.* In four of the passages I have noted the word might perhaps be acceptable as an imitation of a usage seen occasionally in Plato, where it is jocular or metaphorical.[11] In such contexts the word has positive connotations; but in a fifth passage that is not the case: in 14.25 the adverb is used to describe the disease of civil war, and so here it is hard to escape the conclusion that a Latin usage has crept into Aelian's writing.

Other passages which arouse suspicion of the same kind are 2.41 where the words ἀπὸ τούτων τάττειν do

[11] The four passages are in 4.19, 6.7, 9.1, and 12.1; the Platonic examples are at *Cratylus* 440 d 4, *Euthydemus* 294 d 5, and *Politicus* 262 a 5.

not look idiomatic and suggest some phrase like *ab his seponere,* and 2.42 where the phrase *σὺν τῇ ἀνωτάτω σπουδῇ* is very odd, since *πάσῃ σπουδῇ* would have been natural, but Aelian may have had in mind *summo studio.*[12] At 3.12 he uses a peculiar word to describe a punishment (*θερμότερον*), and one wonders whether he had incautiously made a literal translation from Latin (*acrius*). Some doubt also attaches to his use of *τὰ ἴδια δίκαια καρποῦσθαι* at 2.4, as if he were thinking of *ius suum obtinere; ἄνωθεν . . . γράφειν* at 2.13, perhaps induced by the use of *scribere* by officials to mean "enlist, register" or in wills to mean "list (beneficiaries)"; and *ἄδικος ὁρμή* at 2.42, where the choice of adjective may have been prompted by the Latin *improbus.* A strange use of *τοὺς αὐτοὺς* in 12.1 may conceivably reflect Latin *et eosdem.*

Despite Aelian's inclusion of several longer passages designed to show off his talent as a stylist, these constitute only a small proportion of the work. They receive little attention from the modern scholar, who usually thinks of the *Historical Miscellany* as a selection of material drawn from a wide variety of sources, most of them now lost, so that we have no option but to accept what Aelian offers us. His choice gives us some idea of the culture of the educated classes at the time when the Roman Empire was in its first phase of decline. As we read Aelian we should also bear in mind that he lived in a world which was experiencing an important change in its spiritual and cultural life. Though he shows no sign whatever of being aware of

[12] W. Schmid, *Der Atticismus* vol. III (Stuttgart, 1893) p. 259, also noted the usage *ἀθροίζειν ἑαυτὸν* in *N.A.* 9.43 and 10.48, which presumably reflects *se colligere.*

it—and perhaps as a priest he had a closed mind in all such matters—there is evidence to suggest that his lifetime coincided with the growth of Christianity from a tiny sect on the fringe of society to a substantial force in the religious life of the empire. The new faith soon produced writers of note, whose works included defences of their beliefs and attempts to win the allegiance of pagans. One such writer was Hippolytus, an almost exact contemporary of Aelian who spent most of his career in Rome and died soon after being exiled by the emperor Maximinus in 235. Another was Clement of Alexandria, who died between 211 and 216, presumably before Aelian began work on the *Historical Miscellany.* Nevertheless, his main work, the *Stromateis* (*Miscellanies*) has some features of interest to the reader of Aelian. Being a large collection of material designed to appeal to the pagan it draws on the usual stock of literary and historical anecdote and quotation. Occasionally there are surprising similarities: *Historical Miscellany* 4.16 is very like *Stromateis* VII.101.4. But more important is that the fashion for miscellaneous anthologies was so strong that Clement claimed in more than one passage to be following in the footsteps of earlier writers who deliberately avoided systematic presentation of their subject matter. Needless to say, this claim by Clement is disingenuous, but it shows the force of a literary tradition, and it is worth quoting two of the passages in question, because Clement says almost exactly what we would expect Aelian to have said if he had written a preface with a statement of his intentions. At *Stromateis* IV.4.1 we find the following disclaimer: "Because of inexperienced and unsystematic readers our treatise, as we have often said, is to be haphazardly composed with vari-

ation of material as the technical term has it, continually changing from one topic to another, and conveying one meaning by the sequence of its arguments, but demonstrating something else." The strength of the literary tradition is made clear at VI.2.1: "In a meadow the various flowers in bloom, and in a park the fruit trees, are not separated each according to their species. Just so learned men have compiled collections, making varied anthologies called *Leimones* ("meadows"), *Helicones*, *Ceria* ("honeycombs"), and *Peploi* ("embroidered cloths"). And our presentation in the *Stromateis* ("patchwork") is variegated like a meadow, with material as it chanced to come to mind, not organised or stylistically embellished, but deliberately tossed out in no particular order." This passage, however, continues in a way that marks the difference between the two cultures: "In fact my treatise, given its present form, could serve as a spark. The person who has the capacity to achieve true knowledge, if he chances to light upon it, will make strenuous efforts in his search for what is valuable and beneficial. For it is not right to think only of our daily bread; true knowledge is far more important for those taking the narrow and painful road of the Lord towards the eternal blessing of salvation." If Aelian had seen his book as providing sparks, presumably he would have expected them to induce in his readers a heightened belief in the moral values of paganism, many of them little different from Christianity—indeed the Christians regularly accused the pagans of unacknowledged borrowings from the teachings of Moses; but the concept of salvation might not have found any counterpart in his statement.

When Aelian died his book was still in need of final revision. The executors nevertheless allowed it to be copied and circulated. It may have lacked a definitive title; when it is first cited in the fifth-century anthology of classical wisdom put together by Johannes Stobaeus it is referred to by two titles, neither of which is the one we now use. Stobaeus' quotations are of interest in another respect; he quotes five fragments not transmitted in the medieval manuscripts. There are other short fragments, of much less certain attribution, preserved in the tenth-century compilation known as the *Suda*. At some stage this extra material was lost, and certain parts of the remaining text were abbreviated, as has already been mentioned.

We cannot follow the fortunes of Aelian's book at all closely through late antiquity and the early middle ages.[13] But it may be worth noting a curious fact; the most voracious reader of Byzantine times, the patriarch Photius, who would certainly have derived great pleasure from the *Historical Miscellany*, seems not to have known it. He does not mention it in the *Bibliotheca*, and the one passage in his correspondence which might be taken to prove that he knew it can in fact be explained adequately as an allusion to a different classical text.[14]

Nor was the Italian Renaissance quick to ensure the circulation of the *Historical Miscellany* in print. Although Politian, *Miscellanea* 2.6, had spoken of Aelian as

[13] Such evidence as we have is collected in the article by M. R. Dilts, "The Testimonia of Aelian's Varia Historia," *Manuscripta* 15 (1971): 3–12.

[14] A passage in *Letter* 276 can be taken as a quotation of Plutarch, *Moralia* 229 B.

"a Roman who wrote much in very elegant Greek," it first appeared in Rome in 1545, edited by Camillo Peruschi, Rector of the university in Rome and a friend of Pope Paul III, to whom the book is dedicated with a three-page letter in Greek. Peruschi recommends the work as a store of useful historical information. Soon translators set to work. Giacobo Laureo issued an Italian version at Venice in 1550. In a preface addressed to Marietta Giustiniana he explains that he had rendered the text into Latin but now offers it "in the vernacular," because women do not enjoy a knowledge of Latin and Greek, this being the result of "custom, a most powerful tyrant." An English version soon followed, produced by Abraham Fleming in 1576. His title page describes the work as "A register of histories containing martial exploits of worthy warriors, politic practices of civil magistrates, wise sentences of famous philosophers, and other matters manifold and memorable."

One might have expected Aelian to figure in Montaigne's essays or even in *Scaligerana*, but he appears not to have been of interest to either of those great figures of the late sixteenth century. English antiquarian writers of the next century found him congenial. He is named from time to time in Burton's *Anatomy of Melancholy* and Sir Thomas Browne's *Pseudodoxia Epidemica*. Browne has this to say of him (Book I, ch. 8): "Claudius Aelianus . . . an elegant and miscellaneous author, he hath left two books which are in the hands of everyone, his History of Animals and his *Varia Historia*, wherein are contained many things suspicious, not a few false, some impossible; he is much beholding unto Ctesias, and in many uncertainties writes more confidently than Pliny."

In 1805 the Greek scholar and patriot Adamantios Korais published in Paris the text of the *Historical Miscellany* with brief notes. The volume is interesting; it also contains the fragments of two much more obscure Greek authors, Heraclides Ponticus and Nicolaus of Damascus, and it is designed as the first volume in a series offering the public the best literary productions of the ancient world. The choice of Aelian, accompanied by two less well known writers, rouses curiosity. Korais tells us that he had been asked by friends, the brothers Zosimas, what they could do to promote the Renaissance of Greece which was beginning. He suggested publishing a library of classical texts which would be unencumbered by the excessive scholarly apparatus of most editions. Despite this he rather surprisingly indicated his intention of printing the ancient scholia on the texts, if there were any. He hoped the series would serve the needs of readers in Greece. At the end of a very long preface he devotes a few pages to Aelian, taking him to task for stylistic infelicity, including Latinisms, and the derivative nature of his subject matter. Since he evidently did not have a very high opinion of our author it was a little odd to give him pride of place in a new series that was to present the classics to a wide public.

The somewhat critical judgements expressed by figures as diverse as Browne and Korais make it clear that, once the debate between the Ancients and the Moderns had ceased to be an issue in intellectual circles, Aelian had little hope of attracting readers. He became at best a quarry for scholars hoping to fill the many gaps in our information about the ancient world. The commentary in Perizonius' Leiden edition of 1701, though occasionally

revised, has not been replaced. But recently the *Historical Miscellany* has enjoyed fresh popularity, and versions have appeared in German, Russian, French, and Italian.

Since the first printing of the *Varia Historia* the text has been edited frequently—some might say more frequently than its merits appear to justify. Of these various editions the most important are those of C. Gesner (1556), J. Scheffer (1647, 1662), T. Faber (1668), J. Kühn (1685), J. Perizonius (1701), A. Gronovius (1731), A. Korais (1805) and R. Hercher (1858, 1866, 1870). All these editors made useful contributions to textual criticism or assembled material towards a commentary. No modern scholar has attempted a commentary, and as my notes can only supply a bare minimum of information it may be as well to remind readers that some of the old variorum editions, for example those of Gronovius and C. G. Kühn (1780), however antiquated in certain respects, do contain a fair amount of relevant material.

The standard modern text is that prepared by M. R. Dilts for the Teubner series (Leipzig, 1974). I have not thought it necessary to make any fresh inquiry into the manuscript tradition, since Dilts established that the text depends on two main sources: (1) V = Paris, supplément grec 352, formerly in the Vatican Library, datable probably to the late 12th or early 13th century; (2) x = a lost manuscript which is traceable in the Vatican between 1475 and 1522, and may be reconstructed from its various apographs d, g, a, b (Florence, Laur. 60.19; Milan, Ambr. C 4 sup.; Paris, gr. 1693 and 1694; and Leiden, Voss. gr. qu. 18). There is in addition an epitome found in Vaticanus gr. 96 of the 12th century (Φ). This is the sole

source of the correct reading in four passages (in 4.1, 4.27, 13.1 ad fin., and 14.31), and while these points do not earn a mention in my limited apparatus, there is a further passage (6.12) where the epitome offers an extra clause that is worth recording. For further details see Dilts' paper in *Transactions and Proceedings of the American Philological Association* 96 (1965): 57–72.

In a number of passages I have deviated from Dilts' text, either in introducing emendations published after his work had gone to press or preferring different solutions to problems indicated in his apparatus criticus.

Though the text presents few if any unintelligible passages, it cannot be said that it is very well preserved. Even chapters which have not been abbreviated are sometimes obscure. Apart from the hazards that affect all ancient texts there were three other factors at work in this case: Aelian's modest intellectual capacity, the unrevised state of his draft, and not least his use of an archaising language in which he was less at home than he imagined.

Some notes on textual difficulties are therefore a necessity; but the conventions of the Loeb Classical Library require that they should be restricted and not on the scale that one expects to find in an Oxford Classical Text or a Teubner edition. For detailed information the user of this book is referred to Dilts. Nevertheless I have tried to ensure that the reader is not misled into thinking of the *Varia Historia* as a text without problems. Necessary emendations are recorded in all but trivial cases, and a number of other attractive suggestions have been included if they have a bearing on the meaning of the Greek. In a number of passages it has been possible to trace emendations back to an earlier source than that

recorded in Dilts. As to the so-called "anonymus" of 1733, this is my way of referring to proposals made in a series of articles in the journal *Miscellaneae observationes*, volumes 2 and 3, and attributed to "Thom. S.," "D.C.," and "C.D." In his 1780 edition C. G. Kühn conjectured that the first of these was Thomas Smith, of whom I can find no other trace.

By way of appendix I have added a few short fragments of text ascribed to Aelian, in all cases except one attributed to the *Varia Historia.* If such ascriptions are correct, it would appear to follow that the original text extended beyond 14.48 or that in the process of epitomisation some chapters were completely omitted. There is a recent Teubner edition of the fragments by D. Domingo-Forasté (Stuttgart-Leipzig, 1994).

In the notes to the translation sources are mentioned when they are identifiable with certainty or a high degree of probability. But it did not seem feasible to record all the numerous passages in other authors which furnish much the same information or anecdotal material, and I have limited myself to noting a few that are particularly illuminating. Nor have I listed passages in later authors who cite or are dependent upon Aelian.[15]

In my critical notes Kühn refers to the editor who published his text in 1685, not his more recent namesake. I have abbreviated the names of the three scholars who have contributed most to the improvement of the text: Per(izonius), Kor(ais), and Her(cher).

[15] See Dilts in *Manuscripta* 15: 3–12.

ΑΙΛΙΑΝΟΥ

ΠΟΙΚΙΛΗ ΙΣΤΟΡΙΑ

A

1. Δεινοὶ κατὰ κοιλίαν εἰσὶν οἱ πολύποδες καὶ πᾶν ὁτιοῦν φαγεῖν ἄμαχοι. πολλάκις οὖν οὐδὲ ἀλλήλων ἀπέχονται, ἀλλὰ τῷ μείζονι ὁ βραχύτερος ἁλοὺς καὶ ἐμπεσὼν τοῖς ἀνδρειοτέροις θηράτροις τοῖς καλουμένοις τοῦ ἰχθύος πλοκάμοις, εἶτα αὐτῷ γίνεται δεῖπνον. ἐλλοχῶσι δὲ οἱ πολύποδες καὶ τοὺς ἰχθῦς τὸν τρόπον τοῦτον· ὑπὸ ταῖς πέτραις κάθηνται καὶ ἑαυτοὺς εἰς τὴν ἐκείνων μεταμορφοῦσι χροιὰν καὶ τοῦτο εἶναι δοκοῦσιν ὅπερ οὖν καὶ πεφύκασιν αἱ πέτραι. οἱ τοίνυν ἰχθῦς προσνέουσιν οἱονεὶ τῇ πέτρᾳ τοῖς πολύποσιν, οἱ δὲ ἀφυλάκτους ὄντας αὐτοὺς περιβάλλουσι ταῖς ἐξ ἑαυτῶν ἄρκυσι ταῖς πλεκτάναις.

2. Ὑφαντικὴν καὶ ὑφαίνειν,[1] [καὶ][2] δῶρα Ἐργάνης δαίμονος, οὔτε ἴσασιν αἱ φάλαγγες οὔτε εἰδέναι βούλονται. ἢ τί ποτ᾽ ἂν καὶ χρήσαιτο τῷ τοιῷδε ἐσθήματι τὸ τοιοῦτον θηρίον; τὸ δὲ ἄρα <***>[3] πάγη καὶ οἱονεὶ κύρτος ἐστὶ τοῖς ἐμπίπτουσι. καὶ ἡ μὲν ἀρκυωρεῖ πάνυ σφόδρα ἀτρεμοῦσα, καὶ ἔοικεν

[1] καὶ ὑφαίνειν fortasse delenda [2] del. Bernhardy
[3] lacunam statuit Her.: <ἀράχνιον> Slothouwer

BOOK ONE

1. Octopuses have remarkable stomachs and are unsurpassed in their ability to eat anything. Frequently they even attack each other: a small one is caught by a larger one, falling into its more powerful clutches, the so-called tentacles of the fish, and then becomes a meal for it. Octopuses also ambush fish in the following way: they sit under the rocks and change their colour to match and so they appear to be indistinguishable from the rocks. The fish then swim towards the octopuses, as if they were the rocks, and are caught off their guard; the octopuses entangle them in their own form of net, their tentacles.[a]

2. Spiders neither know nor wish to know the art and practice of weaving, the gifts of the goddess Ergane.[b] To what use would an animal of this kind put such clothing? Its web would seem to be a trap, a kind of snare for objects that fall into it. The spider watches the net, keep-

[a] Chapters 1–15 of this book are untypical, because they all deal with a single basic idea, the intelligence of animals, and fail to offer the variety of theme appropriate to a miscellany such as the *V.H.*

[b] Ergane was the cult title of Athena as patron deity of crafts, especially weaving. The opening sentence is contradicted by Aelian in *N.A.* 6.57.

ἀκινήτῳ· καὶ τὸ μὲν ἐνέπεσεν,[1] ὅ τί ποτέ ἐστι τὸ ἐμπεσόν,[2] ἡ δὲ ἔχει δαῖτα. τοσοῦτον δ' ἐμπίπτει, ὅσον καὶ τὸ ὕφασμα κατέχειν δυνατόν ἐστι καὶ ἐκείνῃ δειπνεῖν ἀπόχρῃ.

3. Σοφόν τι ἄρα χρῆμα ἦν γένος βατράχων Αἰγυπτίων, καὶ οὖν καὶ τῶν ἄλλων ὑπερφέρουσι κατὰ πολύ. ἐὰν γὰρ ὕδρῳ περιπέσῃ Νείλου θρέμματι βάτραχος, καλάμου τρύφος ἐνδακὼν πλάγιον φέρει καὶ ἀπρὶξ ἔχεται καὶ οὐκ ἀνίησι κατὰ τὸ καρτερόν. ὁ δὲ ἀμηχανεῖ καταπιεῖν αὐτὸν αὐτῷ καλάμῳ· οὐ γάρ οἱ χωρεῖ περιλαβεῖν τοσοῦτον τὸ στόμα, ὅσον ὁ κάλαμος διείργει. καὶ ἐκ τούτου περιγίνονται τῆς ῥώμης τῶν ὕδρων οἱ βάτραχοι τῇ σοφίᾳ.

4. Καὶ ἐκεῖνο δὲ κυνὸς Αἰγυπτίου τι[3] σοφόν· οὐκ ἀθρόως οὐδὲ ἀνέδην οὐδὲ ἐλευθέρως ἐκ τοῦ ποταμοῦ πίνουσιν ἐπικύπτοντες ἅμα καὶ ὅσον διψῶσι λάπτοντες· ὑφορῶνται γὰρ τὰ ἐν αὐτῷ θηρία. παραθέουσι δὲ τὴν ὄχθην καὶ παρακλέπτοντες πίνουσιν ὅσον ἁρπάσαι, <πάλιν>[4] καὶ πάλιν. εἶτα οὕτως ἐκ διαλειμμάτων ἐκορέσθησαν, οὐ μὴν ἀπώλοντο, καὶ οὖν καὶ ἠκέσαντο τὸ δίψος.

5. Ἡ ἀλώπηξ, οὐ μόνον τὸ χερσαῖον θηρίον δολερόν ἐστιν, ἀλλὰ καὶ ἡ θαλαττία πανοῦργός ἐστι. τὸ μὲν γὰρ δέλεαρ οὐχ ὑφορᾶται οὐδὲ μὴν φυλάττεται διὰ τὴν ἀκρασίαν τοῦτο,[5] τοῦ δὲ ἀγκίστρου καταφρονεῖ καὶ πάνυ ἡ ἀλώπηξ. πρὶν ἢ γὰρ τὸν ἀσπαλιέα σπάσαι τὸν κάλαμον ἡ δὲ ἀνέ-

ing quite still and looking motionless; the object falls in, whatever it is, and the spider has its feast. Just so many objects fall in as the net can hold and are sufficient for the spider's meals.

3. The species of frog found in Egypt is clever, it appears, and therefore much superior to the others. If a frog encounters the water snake that lives in the Nile, it bites off a piece of reed, which it carries at an angle and holds tightly, doing its best not to lose its grip. The water snake cannot swallow the frog, reed and all, because its mouth cannot open as wide as the length of the reed. As a result the frogs by their skill overcome the strength of the water snakes.

4. Egyptian dogs also have a clever habit. They do not drink their fill from the river carelessly and freely, bending down to lap up as much water as will satisfy their thirst. As they are suspicious of the animals that live in it, they run along the bank and surreptitiously steal a sip, again and again. In this way they are eventually satisfied by drinking at intervals; they do not lose their lives and they deal with their thirst.[a]

5. The fox is cunning, not only the land animal, but also the fox shark is astute. It does not treat bait as suspect, and in its greed does not take precautions. The shark is quite contemptuous of the hook, because it leaps up and cuts the line before the fisherman can pull in his

[a] The content of this ch. is almost identical with *N.A.* 6.53.

---

[1] ἐνέπεσεν Davis: ἔπεσεν codd.

[2] τὸ ἐμπεσόν aut delenda (Russell) aut post δαῖτα transponenda [3] τι Per.: τὸ codd.

[4] suppl. Kühn [5] τοῦτο del. Her.

θορε καὶ ἀπέκειρε τὴν ὁρμιὰν καὶ νήχεται αὖθις. πολλάκις γοῦν[1] καὶ δύο καὶ τρία κατέπιεν ἄγκιστρα, ὁ δ' ἁλιεὺς ἐκείνην οὐκ ἐδείπνησε προϊοῦσαν τῆς θαλάσσης.

6. Αἱ χελῶναι αἱ θαλάττιαι ἐν τῇ γῇ τίκτουσι, τεκοῦσαι δὲ παραχρῆμα κατέχωσαν ἐν τῇ γῇ τὰ ᾠά, εἶτα ὑποστρέψασαι ὀπίσω εἰς ἤθη τὰ ἑαυτῶν νήχονται. εἰσὶ δὲ εἰς τοσοῦτον λογιστικαί, ὥστε ἐφ' ἑαυτῶν ἐκλογίζεσθαι τὰς ἡμέρας τὰς τετταράκοντα, ἐν αἷς τὰ ἔγγονα αὐταῖς τῶν ᾠῶν συμπαγέντων ζῷα γίνεται. ὑποστρέψασαι οὖν αὖθις εἰς τὸν χῶρον, ἐν ᾧ κατέθεντο κρύψασαι τὰ ἑαυτῶν βρέφη, ἀνώρυξαν τὴν γῆν, ἣν ἐπέβαλον, καὶ κινουμένους ἤδη τοὺς νεοττοὺς <καὶ>[2] ἕπεσθαι δυναμένους αὐταῖς ἀπάγουσιν.

7. Ἦσαν ἄρα οἱ σῦς οἱ ἄγριοι καὶ θεραπείας ἅμα καὶ ἰατρικῆς οὐκ ἀπαίδευτοι. οὗτοι γοῦν ὅταν αὑτοὺς λαθόντες ὑοσκυάμου φάγωσι, τὰ ἐξόπισθεν ἐφέλκουσι, παρειμένως ἔχοντες [οὕτως][3] αὐτῶν.[4] εἶτα σπώμενοι ὅμως ἐπὶ τὰ ὕδατα παραγίνονται, καὶ ἐνταῦθα τῶν καρκίνων ἀναλέγουσι καὶ ἐσθίουσι προθυμότατα. γίνονται δὲ αὐτοῖς οὗτοι τοῦ πάθους φάρμακον καὶ ἐργάζονται ὑγιεῖς αὐτοὺς αὖθις.

8. Φαλάγγιον ἐλάφοις τοσοῦτόν ἐστι κακὸν ὅσον καὶ ἀνθρώποις, καὶ κινδυνεύουσιν ἀπολέσθαι διὰ ταχέων. ἐὰν μέντοι κιττοῦ γεύσωνται, ἐλύπησεν αὐτοὺς τὸ δῆγμα οὐδέν. δεῖ δὲ εἶναι τὸν κιττὸν ἄγριον.

rod, and then swims away. Often it will swallow two or three hooks and the fisherman fails to catch it for his dinner when it emerges from the sea.[a]

6. Sea turtles give birth to their young on land. When they have done so they immediately bury their eggs in the earth. Then they turn back to their usual habitat and swim away. But they are good enough at calculation to be able by their own unaided efforts to keep a count of the forty days at the end of which their offspring are hatched, having taken shape within the eggs. So they go back once more to the place where they deposited and hid their young, dig away the earth which they had used as a covering, and lead away the young ones, who are already moving and capable of following.

7. Wild boars, it seems, are not ignorant of medical skill and methods of treatment. At any rate, when they have inadvertently eaten henbane they lose their vigour and drag their hind quarters along; but despite muscular spasms[b] they reach water and there catch crabs, eating them with great gusto. These serve as a medicine against the symptoms, and so the boars are restored to health.

8. The poisonous spider is as much a danger to deer as it is to men, and they risk a speedy death. But if deer eat some ivy, the spider's bite has no effect on them; the ivy must, however, be wild.[c]

[a] Cf. *N.A.* 9.12; also Aristotle, *Historia animalium* 621 a 12.
[b] The participle used by Aelian here is ambiguous; it could also mean "dragging themselves."
[c] Cf. 13.35.

---

[1] γοῦν Russell: δ' οὖν codd. [2] suppl. Kühn
[3] del. Her. [4] αὐτῶν Her.: ἑαυτῶν codd.

9. Λέοντα δὲ νοσοῦντα τῶν μὲν ἄλλων οὐδὲν ὀνίνησι, φάρμακον δέ ἐστιν αὐτῷ τῆς νόσου βρωθεὶς πίθηκος.

10. Οἱ Κρῆτές εἰσι τοξεύειν ἀγαθοί, καὶ οὖν καὶ τὰς αἶγας βάλλουσιν ἐπ' ἄκροις νεμομένας τοῖς ὄρεσιν. αἱ δὲ βληθεῖσαι παραχρῆμα τῆς δικτάμνου βοτάνης διέτραγον, καὶ ἅμα τῷ γεύσασθαι ὅλα ἐκείναις[1] τὰ βέλη ἐκπίπτει.

11. Ἦσαν δ' ἄρα μαντικώτατοι τῶν ζῴων καὶ μύες· γηρώσης γὰρ οἰκίας ἤδη καὶ μελλούσης κατολισθαίνειν αἰσθάνονται πρῶτοι, καὶ ἀπολιπόντες τὰς μυωπίας τὰς αὐτῶν καὶ τὰς ἐξ ἀρχῆς διατριβάς, ᾗ ποδῶν ἔχουσιν ἀποδιδράσκουσι καὶ μετοικίζονται.

12. Ἔχουσι δὲ καὶ οἱ μύρμηκες, ὡς ἀκούω, μαντικῆς τινα αἴσθησιν. ὅταν γὰρ μέλλῃ λιμὸς ἔσεσθαι, δεινῶς εἰσι φιλόπονοι πρὸς τὸ θησαυρίσαι καὶ ἑαυτοῖς ἀποταμιεύσασθαι[2] τοὺς πυροὺς καὶ τὰ λοιπὰ τῶν σπερμάτων, ὅσα μυρμήκων δεῖπνόν ἐστιν.

13. Ὁ Συρακούσιος Γέλων ὄναρ ἐβέβλητο κεραυνῷ καὶ διὰ τοῦτο ἐβόα οὐκ ἀμυδρὸν οὐδ' ἀσθενὲς ὡς ἐν ὀνείρῳ, ἀλλ' ἀνδρικῶς ἅτε δεινῶς ἐκπλαγεὶς ὑπὸ τοῦ δέους. ὁ δὲ κύων, ὅσπερ οὖν αὐτῷ παρεκάθευδεν, ἐκ τῆς βοῆς διεταράχθη καὶ περιβὰς αὐτὸν ὑλάκτει πάνυ σφοδρῶς ἀπειλητικὸν καὶ σύντονον, καὶ ἐκ τούτων ὁ Γέλων ἅμα τε ἀφυπνίσθη καὶ τοῦ δέους ἀφείθη.

[1] ἐκείναις Slothouwer: -να codd.

[2] ἀποταμιεύσασθαι Stephanus: -ειώσασθαι codd.

9. When a lion is ill, no other remedy helps it, but a cure for the illness is to eat a monkey.

10. The Cretans are expert archers. They shoot goats grazing on mountain peaks. The wounded animals at once eat the plant called dittany, and as soon as they taste it, all the arrows fall out of their wounds.[a]

11. Mice are among the animals most gifted with prescience, it appears. When a house is old and on the verge of collapse, they are the first to notice. They leave their holes and their former haunts, running as fast as they can, and make a home elsewhere.[b]

12. Ants also, I hear, have some prophetic powers. When famine is about to occur, they are very active in storing provisions. They put aside for themselves a stock of corn and all the other seeds that form the diet of ants.

13. Gelon of Syracuse[c] had a dream that he had been struck by lightning. This made him cry out, not in a weak or unclear voice as happens in dreams, but vigorously, since he was quite overcome by fear. The dog sleeping beside him was disturbed by his shout and stood by him, barking very loudly in a threatening and energetic way. As a result Gelon woke up and at once recovered from his fright.

[a] The medicinal properties of the herb dittany are mentioned by Aristotle, *Historia animalium* 612 a 3, and many subsequent writers.

[b] Aelian gives an example in *N.A.* 11.19, which deals with the earthquake that destroyed the city of Helice in 373 B.C. Cf. also *N.A.* 6.41.

[c] Tyrant of Syracuse 485–478 B.C., mentioned again at 4.15, 6.11, and 13.37. The same story is told in *N.A.* 6.62.

14. Λέγει Ἀριστοτέλης τὸν κύκνον καλλίπαιδα εἶναι καὶ πολύπαιδα, ἔχειν γε μὴν καὶ θυμόν. πολλάκις γοῦν εἰς ὀργὴν καὶ μάχην προελθόντες καὶ ἀλλήλους ἀπέκτειναν οἱ κύκνοι. λέγει δὲ ὁ αὐτὸς καὶ μάχεσθαι τοὺς κύκνους τοῖς ἀετοῖς· ἀμύνεσθαί γε μὴν αὐτούς, ἀλλ' οὐκ ἄρχειν ἀδίκων. ὅτι δέ εἰσι φιλῳδοί, τοῦτο μὲν ἤδη καὶ τεθρύληται. ἐγὼ δὲ ᾄδοντος κύκνου οὐκ ἤκουσα, ἴσως δὲ οὐδὲ ἄλλος· πεπίστευται <δ'>[1] οὖν ὅτι ᾄδει. καὶ λέγουσί γε αὐτὸν μάλιστα <κατ'>[2] ἐκεῖνον εἶναι τὸν χρόνον εὐφωνότατόν τε καὶ ᾠδικώτατον, ὅταν ᾖ περὶ τὴν καταστροφὴν τοῦ βίου. διαβαίνουσι δὲ καὶ πέλαγος, καὶ πέτονται [καὶ][3] κατὰ θαλάσσης, καὶ αὐτοῖς οὐ κάμνει τὸ πτερόν.

15. Ἐκ διαδοχῆς φασιν ἐπῳάζειν τὰς περιστεράς. εἶτα τῶν νεοττῶν γενομένων ὁ ἄρρην ἐμπτύει αὐτοῖς, ἀπελαύνων αὐτῶν τὸν φθόνον, φασίν, ἵνα μὴ βασκανθῶσι· δέδιε γὰρ[4] τοῦτο. τίκτει δὲ ᾠὰ δύο ἡ θήλεια, ὧν τὸ μὲν πρῶτον ἄρρεν ποιεῖ πάντως, τὸ δὲ δεύτερον θῆλυ. τίκτουσι δὲ αἱ περιστεραὶ κατὰ πᾶσαν ὥραν τοῦ ἔτους· ἔνθεν τοι καὶ δεκάκις τοῦ ἔτους ὠδίνουσι. λόγος δέ τις περίεισιν Αἰγύπτιος λέγων δωδεκάκις τὰς ἐν Αἰγύπτῳ τίκτειν.

Λέγει δὲ Ἀριστοτέλης καὶ διάφορον εἶναι τῆς περιστερᾶς τὴν πελειάδα· τὴν μὲν γὰρ περιστερὰν εἶναι μείζονα, τὴν δὲ πελειάδα βραχυτέραν, καὶ τὴν

[1] suppl. Kor.
[2] suppl. Her.

14. Aristotle says [fr. 344 R.] that swans have beautiful young in large numbers, but that they are bad-tempered. At any rate swans are often angry and fight, killing each other. The same author tells us that swans also fight against eagles, warding off their attack;[a] but they are not the aggressors. Their love of song has long been notorious. But I have not heard a swan sing, nor perhaps has anyone else. There is a belief that it sings, and people say that its voice is best and most tuneful at the time when it is about to end its life. The swan also crosses the sea, and it flies over the waves; its wings do not tire.

15. They say that pigeons take it in turn to hatch out eggs. Then, when the chicks emerge, the male bird spits on them, to protect them from envy, so that—as the saying goes—the evil eye cannot be cast on them; for that is what he fears.[b] The female produces two eggs, the first of which is invariably male, the second female. Pigeons produce young at all seasons of the year, which means that they give birth as often as ten times a year. In Egypt a report circulates which says that Egyptian pigeons produce young twelve times a year.

Aristotle says [544 b 1] that the pigeon is different from the wild pigeon—the pigeon is bigger, the wild pigeon smaller, and the one is domesticated, the other

[a] The tendency of swans to fight eagles is mentioned in *N.A.* 17.24.

[b] This passage is discussed by U. Albini in *Studi italiani di filologia classica* 3 (1985): 264; I have made a slight adjustment to the emendation he proposes there.

---

[3] del. Her.

[4] δέδιε γὰρ scripsi post Albini: δι' ἄρα codd.

μὲν περιστερὰν τιθασὸν γίνεσθαι, τὴν δὲ οὔ. λέγει δὲ ὁ αὐτὸς μὴ πρότερον ἀναβαίνειν τὸν ἄρρενα τὴν θήλειαν[1] πρὶν ἢ φιλῆσαι[2] αὐτήν· μὴ γὰρ ἀνέχεσθαι τὰς θηλείας τὴν τῶν ἀρρένων ὁμιλίαν τοῦ φιλήματος ἔρημον. προστίθησι[3] τούτοις καὶ ἐκεῖνα, ὅτι καὶ αἱ θήλειαι ἀλλήλας ἀναβαίνουσιν, ὅταν τῆς πρὸς ἄρρενα μίξεως ἀτυχήσωσι· καὶ οὐδὲν μὲν εἰς ἀλλήλας προΐενται, τίκτουσι δὲ ᾠά, ἐξ ὧν νεοττοὶ οὐ γίνονται αὐταῖς.[4] εἰ δέ τι Καλλιμάχῳ χρὴ προσέχειν, φάσσαν καὶ πυραλλίδα καὶ περιστερὰν καὶ τρυγόνα φησὶ μηδὲν ἀλλήλαις ἐοικέναι. Ἰνδοὶ δέ φασι λόγοι περιστερὰς ἐν Ἰνδοῖς γίνεσθαι μηλίνας τὴν χρόαν.

Χάρων δὲ ὁ Λαμψακηνὸς περὶ τὸν Ἄθω φανῆναι περιστερὰς λευκὰς λέγει, ὅτε ἐνταῦθα ἀπώλοντο αἱ τῶν Περσῶν τριήρεις περικάμπτουσαι τὸν Ἄθω.

Ἐν Ἔρυκι δὲ τῆς Σικελίας ἔνθα ἐστὶν ὁ τῆς Ἀφροδίτης νεὼς σεμνός τε καὶ ἅγιος, [ἔνθα][5] κατά τινα καιρὸν θύουσιν οἱ Ἐρυκινοὶ τὰ Ἀναγώγια καὶ λέγουσι τὴν Ἀφροδίτην εἰς Λιβύην ἐκ Σικελίας ἀνάγεσθαι. <τότ᾽ οὖν>[6] ἀφανεῖς ἐκ τοῦ χώρου αἱ περιστεραὶ γίνονται, ὥσπερ οὖν τῇ θεῷ συναποδημοῦσαι. κατά γε μὴν τὸν λοιπὸν χρόνον πάμπολύ τι πλῆθος τῶνδε τῶν ὀρνίθων ἐπιπολάζειν τῷ νεῷ τῆς θεοῦ ὡμολόγηται.

[1] τὴν θήλειαν Dilts: τῇ -είᾳ codd.
[2] φιλῆσαι Kühn: -σει codd.
[3] προστίθησι <δὲ> Her.

not. He also says [560 b 25] that the male does not mount the female before he has kissed her, because the females cannot accept intercourse without a kiss. To these facts he adds another, that the females have intercourse with each other when they fail to have it with a male. They do not transmit any seed to each other, but they lay eggs from which no chicks are born. And if we are to accept Callimachus' authority [fr. 416 Pf.], the ringdove, the pyrallis,[a] the pigeon, and the turtledove are not at all similar. Indian traditions report that yellow pigeons are found in India.

Charon of Lampsacus says [FGrH 262 F 3 b] that white pigeons appeared near mount Athos when the Persian triremes were destroyed in that area, as they sailed round Athos.[b]

At Eryx in Sicily, where the holy and venerable temple of Aphrodite stands, the inhabitants of Eryx at a certain season of the year celebrate with sacrifice the Anagogia,[c] and they say that Aphrodite departs from Sicily for Libya. At that time the pigeons disappear from the locality as if they were departing with the goddess. For the rest of the year, however, it is a known fact that a great number of these birds are found at the temple.

[a] The meaning of the word *pyrallis* is uncertain.

[b] An episode from the Persian Wars, recounted by Herodotus 6.44.

[c] The term means "embarcation." In *N.A.* 4.2 Aelian tells us that there was also a festival called *Catagogia,* meaning "return." Remains of the great temple at Eryx, now Erice, are scanty.

---

[4] αὐταῖς Faber: -οῖς codd. [5] del. Her.

[6] ex Athenaeo suppl. Dilts post Her.

Ἀχαϊκοὶ δὲ αὖ πάλιν λέγουσι λόγοι καὶ τὸν Δία αὐτὸν μεταβαλεῖν τὴν μορφὴν εἰς περιστεράν, ἐρασθέντα παρθένου Φθίας ὄνομα. ἐν Αἰγίῳ δὲ ᾤκει ἡ Φθία αὕτη.

16. Ὅτε ἧκεν ἡ ναῦς ἡ ἐκ Δήλου καὶ ἔδει Σωκράτην ἀποθνῄσκειν, ἀφίκετο εἰς τὸ δεσμωτήριον Ἀπολλόδωρος ὁ τοῦ Σωκράτους ἑταῖρος, χιτῶνά τε αὐτῷ φέρων ἐρίων πολυτελῆ καὶ εὐήτριον καὶ ἱμάτιον τοιοῦτο. καὶ ἠξίου ἐνδύντα αὐτὸν τὸν χιτῶνα καὶ θοἰμάτιον περιβαλόμενον εἶτα οὕτω πιεῖν τὸ φάρμακον. ἔλεγε γὰρ αὐτῷ καλῶν ἐνταφίων μὴ ἀμοιρήσειν, εἰ ἐν αὐτοῖς ἀποθάνοι· καὶ γὰρ οὖν καὶ προκείσεσθαι[1] σὺν τῷ κόσμῳ τὸν νεκρὸν οὐ πάνυ τι ἀδόξως. ταῦτα τὸν[2] Σωκράτην ὁ Ἀπολλόδωρος· ὁ δὲ οὐκ ἠνέσχετο, ἀλλ᾽ ἔφη πρὸς τοὺς ἀμφὶ τὸν Κρίτωνα καὶ Σιμμίαν καὶ Φαίδωνα· "καὶ πῶς ὑπὲρ ἡμῶν καλῶς Ἀπολλόδωρος οὕτω δοξάζει, εἴ γε αὐτὸς πεπίστευκεν ὅτι μετὰ τὴν ἐξ Ἀθηναίων φιλοτησίαν καὶ τὸ τοῦ φαρμάκου πόμα ἔτι οὕτως[3] ὄψεται Σωκράτην; εἰ γὰρ οἴεται τὸν ὀλίγῳ[4] ὕστερον ἐρριμμένον ἐν ποσὶ καὶ κεισόμενόν γε εἶναι ἐμέ, δῆλός ἐστί με οὐκ εἰδώς."

17. Ταῦτα ἄρα ἐστὶ τὰ θαυμαζόμενα Μυρμηκίδου τοῦ Μιλησίου καὶ Καλλικράτους τοῦ Λακεδαιμονίου

[1] προκείσεσθαι Gesner: -κεῖσθαι codd.
[2] ταῦτα <πρὸς> τὸν Kühn
[3] οὕτως] ὄντως Gesner
[4] ὀλίγῳ Scheffer: -ον codd.

In addition, there are traditions in Achaea that even Zeus himself took on the appearance of a pigeon when he fell in love with a girl called Phthia. This Phthia lived in Aegium.[a]

16. When the ship came from Delos,[b] and Socrates was due to suffer the death penalty, Apollodorus the companion of Socrates arrived at the prison bringing him an expensive finely woven woollen tunic and a cloak of the same kind. He asked him to put on the tunic and wrap himself in the cloak before drinking the hemlock, saying that he would not lack the trappings of an elegant funeral if he died in these clothes—at any rate his body would lie ready for burial without any loss of dignity, thanks to its dress. That was Apollodorus' request to Socrates. But Socrates would not hear of it, and said to Crito, Simmias, and Phaedo: "How can Apollodorus be right to think of us in this way, if he is personally convinced he will still be able to see Socrates like this after the drinking of the poison, the loving-cup given by the Athenians? If he thinks that the person who will shortly lie in a heap at his feet is me, he clearly does not know me."

17. The following are the admired productions of Myrmecides the Milesian and Callicrates the Lacedae-

[a] Despite the references to Aristotle and other authorities this ch. appears to derive from Athenaeus 394 B–395 A, omitting a few details.

[b] In Plato's *Phaedo* 58 ac it is explained that the Athenians sent a ship to Delos each year with a delegation to the temple of Apollo. This was a celebration of the victory of Theseus over the Minotaur. Until the ship came back the city avoided any risk of pollution by ensuring that no public execution took place.

τὰ[1] μικρὰ ἔργα. τέθριππα μὲν ἐποίησαν ὑπὸ μυίας καλυπτόμενα, καὶ ἐν σησάμῳ δίστιχον ἐλεγεῖον χρυσοῖς γράμμασιν ἐπέγραψαν. ὧν, ἐμοὶ δοκεῖν, ὁ σπουδαῖος οὐδέτερον ἐπαινέσεται· τί γὰρ ἄλλο ἐστὶ ταῦτα ἢ χρόνου παρανάλωμα;

18. Πῶς δὲ οὐ διέρρεον ὑπὸ τρυφῆς πολλαὶ τῶν τότε[2] γυναικῶν; ἐπὶ μὲν γὰρ τῆς κεφαλῆς στεφάνην ἐπετίθεντο ὑψηλήν, τοὺς δὲ πόδας σανδάλοις ὑπεδοῦντο, ἐκ δὲ τῶν ὤτων αὐταῖς ἐνώτια μακρὰ ἀπεκρέμαντο, τῶν δὲ χιτώνων τὰ περὶ τοὺς ὤμους ἄχρι τῶν χειρῶν οὐ συνέρραπτον, ἀλλὰ περόναις χρυσαῖς καὶ ἀργυραῖς συνεχέσι κατελάμβανον. καὶ ταῦτα αἱ πάνυ παλαιαί· τῶν δὲ Ἀττικῶν γυναικῶν τὴν τρυφὴν Ἀριστοφάνης λεγέτω.

19. Ὁ μὲν δημώδης λόγος καὶ εἰς πάντας ἐκφοιτήσας λέγει Συβαρίταις καὶ αὐτῇ τῇ Συβάρει αἰτίαν τῆς ἀπωλείας γενέσθαι τὴν πολλὴν τρυφήν. ἃ δὲ οὐκ ἔστι τοῖς πολλοῖς γνώριμα, ταῦτα ἐγὼ ἐρῶ. Κολοφωνίους φασὶ καὶ αὐτοὺς διὰ τὴν πάνυ τρυφὴν ἀπολέσθαι· καὶ γάρ τοι καὶ οὗτοι ἐσθῆτι πολυτελεῖ ἐθρύπτοντο, καὶ τραπέζης ἀσωτίᾳ καὶ ὑπὲρ τὴν χρείαν χρώμενοι ὕβριζον. καὶ ἡ τῶν Βακχιαδῶν δὲ

[1] τὰ codd.: del. Her.
[2] τότε] πρὸ τοῦ A. Gronovius

---

[a] These two craftsmen are commonly mentioned together. Their date is quite uncertain. Varro, *De lingua latina* 7.1, speaks as if he had seen some works by Myrmecides, but he does not say where. One is tempted to speculate that the two were originally

monian, their miniature pieces:[a] they made four-horse chariots that were concealed beneath the wings of a fly, and they inscribed an elegiac couplet in gold letters on a sesame pod. Neither of these, in my opinion, will earn the approval of a serious person. What are these things except a waste of time?

18. Surely most women of antiquity indulged in extravagant habits. On their heads they wore tall diadems, their feet were clad in sandals. From their ears hung long earrings. The part of the jacket between the shoulder and the hand was not sewn but fastened with golden pins and silver brooches. These were the habits of women in very ancient times; as to the women of Attica, let Aristophanes tell of their luxury [fr. 332 K.-A.].[b]

19. A popular story which circulates everywhere lays the blame for the ruin of the Sybarites and the city of Sybaris itself on their extreme luxury.[c] But I will report what is not generally known. The inhabitants of Colophon,[d] it is said, were also destroyed by their extreme luxury. In fact they too prided themselves on their expensive clothing, their indulgence at table went beyond all need, and they committed excesses. In addition, the government of the Bacchiadae at Corinth, who

experts in carving cameos or sealstones and may even have used lenses. [b] A reference to a lost play, the *Second Thesmophoriazousae*, which Aelian apparently expected his readers to know. A fifteen-line fragment survives, quoted by Pollux 7.95 and Clement of Alexandria, *Paedagogus* 2.245.6. [c] Sybaris, founded ca. 720 B.C. on the gulf of Taranto, was destroyed in 510 B.C., and despite attempts at restoration never regained its importance. [d] An Ionian city situated between Smyrna and Ephesus, and birthplace of the poet Xenophanes.

τῶν ἐν Κορίνθῳ ἀρχή, ἐπὶ μέγα δυνάμεως προελθοῦσα, ὅμως διὰ τὴν τρυφὴν τὴν ἔξω τοῦ μέτρου καὶ αὐτὴ κατελύθη.

20. Διονύσιος ἐξ ἁπάντων τῶν ἐν Συρακούσαις ἱερῶν ἐσύλησε τὰ χρήματα. τοῦ δὲ ἀγάλματος τοῦ Διὸς περιεῖλε τὴν ἐσθῆτα καὶ τὸν κόσμον, ὃς ἦν, φασι, χρυσίου πέντε καὶ ὀγδοήκοντα[1] ταλάντων. ὀκνούντων δὲ τῶν δημιουργῶν ἅψασθαι, ὁ δὲ πρῶτος ἔκρουσε τὸ ἄγαλμα. καὶ τὸ ἄγαλμα δὲ τοῦ Ἀπόλλωνος περιεσύλησεν, ἔχον καὶ αὐτὸ χρυσοῦς βοστρύχους, κελεύσας ἀποκεῖραί τινα αὐτούς.[2] πλεύσας δὲ εἰς Τυρρηνούς,[3] τὰ τοῦ Ἀπόλλωνος καὶ τῆς Λευκοθέας ἅπαντα ἐσύλησε χρήματα, τὴν παρακειμένην ἀργυρᾶν τῷ Ἀπόλλωνι τράπεζαν κελεύσας ἀφελεῖν, ἀγαθοῦ δαίμονος τῷ θεῷ διδόντας[4] πρόποσιν.

21. Ἰσμηνίου τοῦ Θηβαίου σοφὸν ἅμα καὶ Ἑλληνικὸν οὐκ ἂν ἀποκρυψαίμην ἔργον. πρεσβεύων οὗτος ὑπὲρ τῆς πατρίδος πρὸς <τὸν>[5] βασιλέα τῶν Περσῶν ἀφίκετο μέν, ἐβούλετο δὲ αὐτὸς ὑπὲρ ὧν ἧκεν ἐντυχεῖν τῷ Πέρσῃ. ἔφατο οὖν πρὸς αὐτὸν ὁ χιλίαρχος ὁ καὶ τὰς ἀγγελίας εἰσκομίζων τῷ βασιλεῖ καὶ τοὺς δεομένους εἰσάγων· "ἀλλ', ὦ ξένε Θηβαῖε" (ἔλεγε δὲ ταῦτα περσίζων[6] δι' ἑρμη-

[1] ὀγδοήκοντα V: ἑβδομήκοντα x [2] αὐτούς J. D. van Lennep: αὐτό codd. [3] Τυρρηνούς ex Aristotele (1349 b 33) Faber post Scheffer: Τροιζηνίους codd.
[4] διδόντας] διδοὺς Scheffer: fortasse δόντας

achieved great power, was nevertheless destroyed by immoderate luxury, as in the other cases.[a]

20. Dionysius[b] stole objects from all the temples in Syracuse. From the cult statue of Zeus he removed the clothing and other ornaments, which amounted, it is said, to eighty-five talents of gold. When the workmen were hesitant to touch the statue, he dealt the first blow. He despoiled the statue of Apollo as well; it too had gold on the god's flowing hair, and he gave orders for someone to shear it off. He sailed to Etruria and stole all the property of Apollo and Leucothea, instructing his men to drink a toast to the Benevolent Deity as they removed a silver table that stood next to the statue of Apollo.[c]

21. I would not wish to conceal an action of Ismenias the Theban which was both ingenious and typically Hellenic. This man was an envoy for his country sent to the Persian king. On arrival he wished personally to meet the Persian to discuss the business for which he had come. The official who took messages in to the king and presented petitioners said to him "But there is, Theban visitor (he spoke in Persian, using an interpreter, and the

[a] The Bacchiadae were an oligarchy who dominated Corinth for a century or more until they were overthrown by the tyrant Cypselus in 657 B.C. [b] Dionysius I, tyrant of Syracuse (ca. 430–367 B.C.), mentioned several times later in the *V.H.* His behaviour was notorious; cf. e.g. Cicero, *De Natura Deorum* 3.83–84, and esp. ps-Aristotle, *Oeconomica* 2.41 (1353 b 20–26). [c] Dionysius compounded the gravity of his offence by the frivolous use of a formula regularly employed at dinner parties, whereby a toast was drunk at the end of a meal to the "Benevolent Deity" and the tables were removed.

---

[5] suppl. Her. [6] περσίζων Koen: παίζων codd.

νέως, Τιθραύστης δὲ ἦν ὄνομα τῷ χιλιάρχῳ), "νόμος ἐστὶν ἐπιχώριος Πέρσαις, τὸν εἰς ὀφθαλμοὺς ἐλθόντα τοῦ βασιλέως μὴ πρότερον λόγου μεταλαγχάνειν πρὶν ἢ προσκυνῆσαι αὐτόν. εἰ τοίνυν αὐτὸς δι' ἑαυτοῦ[1] συγγενέσθαι θέλεις αὐτῷ, ὥρα σοι τὰ ἐκ τοῦ νόμου δρᾶν· εἰ δὲ μή, τὸ αὐτό σοι τοῦτο καὶ δι' ἡμῶν ἀνυσθήσεται καὶ μὴ προσκυνήσαντι." ὁ τοίνυν Ἰσμηνίας "ἄγε με" εἶπε, καὶ προσελθὼν καὶ ἐμφανὴς τῷ βασιλεῖ γενόμενος, περιελόμενος τὸν δακτύλιον ὃν ἔτυχε φορῶν[2] ἔρριψεν ἀδήλως παρὰ τοὺς πόδας καὶ ταχέως ἐπικύψας, ὡς δὴ προσκυνῶν, πάλιν ἀνείλετο αὐτόν· καὶ δόξαν μὲν ἀπέστειλε τῷ Πέρσῃ προσκυνήσεως, οὐ μὴν ἔδρασεν οὐδὲν τῶν ἐν τοῖς Ἕλλησιν αἰσχύνην φερόντων. πάντα δ' οὖν ὅσα ἠβουλήθη κατεπράξατο, οὐδὲ ἠτύχησέ τι[3] ἐκ τοῦ Πέρσου.

22. Δῶρα τὰ ἐκ βασιλέως διδόμενα τοῖς παρ' αὐτὸν ἥκουσι πρεσβευταῖς, εἴτε παρὰ τῶν Ἑλλήνων ἀφίκοιντο εἴτε ἑτέρωθεν, ταῦτ' ἦν· τάλαντον μὲν ἑκάστῳ Βαβυλώνιον ἐπισήμου ἀργυρίου, ταλαντιαῖαι[4] δὲ φιάλαι δύο ἀργυραῖ. δύναται δὲ τὸ τάλαντον τὸ Βαβυλώνιον δύο καὶ ἑβδομήκοντα μνᾶς Ἀττικάς. ψέλλιά τε καὶ ἀκινάκην ἐδίδου καὶ στρεπτόν, χιλίων δαρεικῶν ἄξια ταῦτα, καὶ στολὴν ἐπ' αὐτοῖς Μηδικήν· ὄνομα δὲ τῇ στολῇ δωροφορική.

23. Ἐν τοῖς Ἕλλησι τοῖς πάλαι μακρᾷ τῇ δόξῃ

[1] δι' ἑαυτοῦ V: διὰ σαυτοῦ x [2] ὃν ἔτυχε φορῶν huc revocavi: post πόδας praebent codd.: del. Her. [3] τι] τινος Her.

official's name was Tithraustes), a national custom in Persia that a person who has audience with the king should not converse with him before kneeling in homage. So if you wish to meet him personally, this is the moment for you to do what custom prescribes. Otherwise, if you do not kneel, the same result will be achieved by us on your behalf." Ismenias said "Take me in." Entering and coming into full view of the king, he surreptitiously took off the ring he happened to be wearing and let it fall at his feet. Looking down quickly he knelt to pick it up, as if he were performing the act of homage. This gave the Persian king the impression of obeisance, but he had not done anything that causes Greeks a feeling of shame. He achieved everything he wished, and did not fail in any of his requests to the Persian king.[a]

22. The presents given by the king of Persia to envoys who came to see him, whether they came from Greece or elsewhere, were the following. Each received a Babylonian talent of silver coins and two silver cups weighing a talent each (the Babylonian talent is equivalent to 72 Attic minae).[b] He gave them bracelets, a sword, and a necklace; these objects were worth 1,000 darics.[c] In addition there was a Persian robe. The name of this robe was *dorophorikē*.

23. Among the ancient Greeks Gorgias of Leontini was

[a] Cf. Plutarch, *Artaxerxes* 22.8.

[b] The Attic mina was about 437 grammes. Pollux 9.86 says that the Babylonian talent was equivalent to seventy Attic minae.

[c] The daric was a Persian coin worth two gold drachmae.

---

4 *ταλαντιαῖαι* Kor. (-*ταῖαι* iam Faber): *τάλαντα* codd.

διέπρεπε Γοργίας ὁ Λεοντῖνος Φιλολάου καὶ Πρωταγόρας Δημοκρίτου, τῇ δὲ σοφίᾳ τοσοῦτον ἐλείποντο ὅσον ἀνδρῶν παῖδες. ἔοικε γάρ πως ἡ δόξα μὴ πάνυ τι ἀκριβὲς μήτε ὁρᾶν μήτε ἀκούειν· ἔνθεν τοι καὶ πολλὰ σφάλλεται, καὶ τὰ μὲν καταχαρίζεται, τὰ δὲ ψεύδεται.

24. Καύκωνος τοῦ Ποσειδῶνος καὶ Ἀστυδαμείας τῆς Φόρβαντος γίνεται παῖς Λεπρεύς, ὅσπερ οὖν συνεβούλευσε τῷ Αὐγέᾳ δῆσαι τὸν Ἡρακλῆ, ὅτε αὐτὸν ἀπῄτει τὸν ὑπὲρ τοῦ ἄθλου μισθὸν Ἡρακλῆς. ἦν οὖν οἷα εἰκὸς πολέμιος τῷ Ἡρακλεῖ ὁ Λεπρεὺς ἐκ τῆς τοιαύτης συμβουλῆς. χρόνῳ δὲ ὕστερον ὁ μὲν τοῦ Διὸς παῖς εἰς Καύκωνος[1] ἀφίκετο, δεηθείσης δὲ τῆς Ἀστυδαμείας διαλύεται τὴν πρὸς τὸν Λεπρέα ὁ Ἡρακλῆς ἔχθραν. φιλονεικία δ' οὖν αὐτοῖς ἐμπίπτει νεανικὴ καὶ ἐρίζουσιν ἀλλήλοις περὶ δίσκου καὶ ὕδατος ἀντλήσεως καὶ τίς καταδειπνήσει ταῦρον πρότερος· καὶ ἐν πᾶσι τούτοις ἡττᾶται Λεπρεύς. καὶ ὑπὲρ πολυποσίας ἀγὼν αὐτοῖς ἐγένετο καὶ ἐνταῦθα πάλιν ὁ Ἡρακλῆς ἐκράτει. διανιώμενος δὲ ὁ Λεπρεύς, λαβὼν ὅπλα εἰς μονομαχίαν προκαλεῖται τὸν Ἡρακλῆ. καὶ οὖν καὶ ἔτισε δίκας ὑπὲρ τῶν παρ' Αὐγέᾳ· μαχόμενος γὰρ ἀποθνῄσκει.

25. Ἀλέξανδρος ὁ Φιλίππου (εἰ δέ τῳ δοκεῖ, ὁ τοῦ Διός, ἐμοὶ γὰρ οὐδὲν διαφέρει) Φωκίωνι μόνῳ, φασί,

[1] Καύκωνος Scheffer: -νας codd.

---

[a] Of these four fifth-century philosophers and sophists Gorgias and Protagoras may have achieved greater fame than the

far more celebrated than Philolaus, and Protagoras than Democritus. But in wisdom they were inferior, in the same measure as children are to men.[a] Somehow Fame seems not to have very accurate sight or hearing. As a result she makes many mistakes, sometimes granting favours, at other times cheating men of their due.[b]

24. Caucon son of Poseidon and Astydamia daughter of Phorbas had a child called Lepreus. He advised Augeas to tie up Heracles when the latter asked him for the reward for his labour.[c] So Lepreus, as was to be expected, was disliked by Heracles after giving that advice. Some time later the son of Zeus arrived at Caucon's house. At Astydamia's request Heracles gave up his dislike of Lepreus. But they were overcome by a youthful spirit of quarrelsomeness, and competed with each other in throwing the discus, in bailing out water, in seeing who could first consume a bull for dinner. In all these matters Lepreus was defeated. They had a drinking competition, and here again Heracles won. Lepreus was very annoyed, took up his weapons and challenged Heracles to single combat. And so he paid the penalty for his misbehaviour at Augeas' house, because he died in the fight.[d]

25. Alexander son of Philip (if anyone thinks he was the son of Zeus, it makes no difference to me) added the

others because they were protagonists of Platonic dialogues. Aelian perhaps drew on a source hostile to Plato; he is unlikely to have read the writings of the four.

[b] The personification of the Greek term *doxa* reminds one of Vergil's description of Fama in *Aeneid* 4.173–188.

[c] The cleansing of the Augean stables.

[d] The story told in this ch. is also found in Athenaeus 412 AB, but the wording is not close enough to suggest that Aelian is copying him.

τῷ Ἀθηναίων στρατηγῷ γράφων προσετίθει τὸ χαίρειν· οὕτως ἄρα ᾑρήκει τὸν Μακεδόνα ὁ Φωκίων. ἀλλὰ καὶ τάλαντα αὐτῷ ἀργυρίου ἔπεμψεν ἑκατὸν καὶ πόλεις τέτταρας ὠνόμασεν, ὧν ἠξίου μίαν ἣν βούλεται προελέσθαι αὐτόν, ἵνα ἔχοι καρποῦσθαι τὰς ἐκεῖθεν προσόδους. ἦσαν δὲ αἱ πόλεις αἵδε Κίος Ἐλαία Μύλασα Πάταρα. ὁ μὲν οὖν Ἀλέξανδρος μεγαλοφρόνως ταῦτα καὶ μεγαλοπρεπῶς· ἔτι γε μὴν μεγαλοφρονέστερον ὁ Φωκίων, μήτε τὸ ἀργύριον προσέμενος[1] μήτε τὴν πόλιν. ὡς δὲ μὴ δοκοίη πάντῃ ὑπερφρονεῖν τοῦ Ἀλεξάνδρου, ἐτίμησεν αὐτὸν κατὰ τοῦτο· τοὺς ἐν τῇ ἄκρᾳ τῇ ἐν Σάρδεσι δεδεμένους ἄνδρας ἠξίωσεν αὐτὸν ἀφεῖναι ἐλευθέρους αὐτῷ, Ἐχεκρατίδην τὸν σοφιστὴν καὶ Ἀθηνόδωρον τὸν Ἴμβριον[2] καὶ Δημάρατον <καὶ Σπάρτωνα>.[3] ἀδελφὼ δὲ ἄρα ἤστην οὗτοι Ῥοδίω.

26. Γυναῖκα ἀκούω σαλπίσαι καὶ τοῦτο ἔργον ἔχειν ἅμα καὶ τέχνην, Ἀγλαΐδα ὄνομα, τὴν Μεγακλέους παῖδα· περίθετον δὲ εἶχε κόμην καὶ λόφον ἐπὶ τῆς κεφαλῆς. καὶ ὁμολογεῖ Ποσείδιππος ταῦτα. δεῖπνον δὲ ἦν ἄρα αὐτῇ κρεῶν μὲν μναῖ δώδεκα, ἄρτων δὲ χοίνικες τέτταρες· ἔπινε δὲ οἴνου χοᾶ.

[1] προσέμενος x: -ιέμενος V [2] Ἴμβριον e Plutarcho Frenshemius: Ἱμεραῖον codd. [3] e Plutarcho suppl. Scheffer

[a] Phocion, a successful Athenian general of the fourth century B.C., is one of Aelian's favourite heroes in the *V.H.*; he was notable for his honesty. For the stories in this ch. cf. Plutarch, *Phocion* 17.10–18.7.

formula of greeting to his letters, they say, only when writing to the Athenian general Phocion.[a] Such was the impression Phocion had made on the Macedonian. But Alexander also gave him a hundred talents of silver, and named four cities with the request that he should choose one of them according to his preference, in order to be able to enjoy revenues from it. The cities were Cios, Elaea, Mylasa, and Patara.[b] This was generous and high-minded on Alexander's part; but Phocion was even more high-minded, since he accepted neither the money nor the city. However, as it was not his wish to show open contempt for Alexander, he honoured him in the following way: he asked Alexander to release for him the prisoners held in the citadel at Sardis, Echecratides the sophist, Athenodorus of Imbros, Demaratus and Sparton—these two were brothers from Rhodes.

26. I learn that a woman called Aglaïs, daughter of Megacles, played the trumpet and was employed in this art. Her hair was covered by a wig and she wore a plume on her head; Poseidippus is the source of this information [fr. 3 Schott]. Her dinner consisted of twelve minae of meat, and four days' rations of bread, and she drank a jug of wine.[c]

[b] These four cities in Asia Minor were widely separated. Cios, later known as Prusias, was on the coast of the Propontis and became the port for Nicaea and Prusa; Elaea, insignificant in the fourth century, was a little south of Pergamum; Mylasa was in Caria, between Halicarnassus and Miletus; and Patara was on the coast of Lycia.

[c] This story probably derives from Athenaeus 415 AB, who gives it a context, a great parade in Alexandria in the third century B.C.

27. Ἀδηφάγους λέγουσιν ἀνθρώπους γεγονέναι Λιτυέρσαν[1] τὸν Φρύγα καὶ Κάμβλητα τὸν Λυδὸν καὶ Θῦν τὸν Παφλαγόνα καὶ Χαρίλαν καὶ Κλεώνυμον καὶ Πείσανδρον καὶ Χάριππον καὶ Μιθριδάτην τὸν Ποντικὸν καὶ Καλαμόδρυν τὸν Κυζικηνὸν καὶ Τιμοκρέοντα τὸν Ῥόδιον, τὸν ἀθλητὴν ἅμα καὶ ποιητήν, καὶ Καντίβαριν τὸν Πέρσην καὶ Ἐρυσίχθονα τὸν Μυρμιδόνος, ἔνθεν τοι καὶ Αἴθων ἐκλήθη οὗτος. λέγεται δὲ καὶ ἐν Σικελίᾳ Ἀδηφαγίας ἱερὸν εἶναι καὶ Σιτοῦς ἄγαλμα Δήμητρος. ὁμολογεῖ δὲ καὶ Ἀλκμὰν ὁ ποιητὴς ἑαυτὸν πολυβορώτατον γεγονέναι. καὶ Κτησίαν δέ φησί τινα Ἀναξίλας ὁ τῆς κωμῳδίας ποιητὴς πολλὰ ἐσθίειν.

28. Ἀλλὰ ἔγωγε ὑμῖν ἐθέλω εἰπεῖν Ῥοδίων[2] δόξαν. ἐν Ῥόδῳ φασὶ τὸν μὲν εἰς τοὺς ἰχθῦς ὁρῶντα καὶ θαυμάζοντα αὐτοὺς καὶ ὄντα τῶν ἄλλων ὀψοφαγίστατον, ἀλλὰ τοῦτόν γε ὡς ἐλευθέριον ὑπὸ τῶν δημοτῶν ἐπαινεῖσθαι· τόν γε μὴν πρὸς τὰ κρέα ἀπονεύοντα ὡς φορτικὸν καὶ γάστριν διαβάλλουσι Ῥόδιοι. εἴτε δὲ ἐκεῖνοι ὀρθῶς εἴτε οὗτοι φλαύρως,[3] ὑπερφρονῶ τοῦτο ἐξετάζειν.

29. Λέγουσι Κῴων παῖδες ἐν Κῷ τεκεῖν ἔν τινι ποίμνῃ Νικίου[4] τοῦ τυράννου ὄιν· τεκεῖν δὲ οὐκ ἄρνα ἀλλὰ λέοντα. καὶ οὖν καὶ τὸ σημεῖον τοῦτο τῷ Νικίᾳ τὴν τυραννίδα τὴν μέλλουσαν αὐτῷ μαντεύσασθαι ἰδιώτῃ ἔτι ὄντι.

[1] in hoc cap. pleraque nomina ex Athenaeo corrigenda sunt
[2] Ῥοδίων scripsi: -ιον codd.: -ίαν Her.
[3] ἐκεῖνοι . . . φλαύρως] ὀρθῶς ἐκεῖνοι τοῦτο εἴτε φλαύρως

27. They say that the following were gluttons: Lityersas the Phrygian, Cambles the Lydian, Thys the Paphlagonian, Charilas, Cleonymus, Pisander, Charippus, Mithridates of Pontus, Calamodrys of Cyzicus, Timocreon of Rhodes, who was both athlete and poet, Cantibaris the Persian, and Erysichthon the son of Myrmidon, who as a result was called "Fiery."[a] It is also said that there was a temple to Gluttony in Sicily, and a statue of Demeter the corn goddess. The poet Alcman [fr. 17 P.] confesses to having had an enormous appetite. And the comic poet Anaxilas [fr. 30 K.-A.] says that a certain Ctesias ate a great deal.[b]

28. Now I wish to report to you an opinion held by the Rhodians. In Rhodes, it is said, anyone who looks at the fish in the market and admires them and is much more of an epicure than other people—any such person is esteemed by his fellow citizens as a gentleman. But a man who shows a preference for meat is criticised by the Rhodians as vulgar and gluttonous. Whether they are right in this or mistaken, I shall not deign to discuss.

29. The inhabitants of Cos report that on their island a sheep belonging to the flocks of the tyrant Nicias gave birth, not to a lamb, but to a lion. This sign to Nicias, who was at that time still a private citizen, was a prophecy of his future tyranny.[c]

[a] As an adjective the same word is applied to the hunger which afflicted Erysichthon in Callimachus, *Hymn* 6.67.

[b] This ch. looks like an abridgement of Athenaeus 415 B–416 E. [c] Nicias was installed by Mark Antony in 41/0 B.C. It is rare for Aelian to mention relatively recent events.

Her. φλαύρως x: φαύλως V
[4] Νικίου Per.: Νικίππου codd.

30. Πτολεμαῖος ὁ βασιλεὺς ἐρώμενον εἶχε Γαλέστην ὄνομα, ἰδεῖν κάλλιστον. ἀμείνων δὲ ἦν ἄρα τούτῳ[1] τῷ μειρακίῳ ἡ γνώμη τῆς μορφῆς. πολλάκις γοῦν αὐτῷ καὶ ὁ Πτολεμαῖος ἐμαρτύρει καὶ ἔλεγεν· "ὦ ἀγαθὴ κεφαλή, κακοῦ μὲν οὐδεπώποτε οὐδενὶ γέγονας αἴτιος, πολλοῖς δὲ καὶ[2] πολλὰ ἀγαθὰ προὐξένησας." ὁ μὲν[3] ἵππευε σὺν τῷ βασιλεῖ τὸ μειράκιον· ἰδὼν δὲ πόρρωθεν ἀγομένους τινὰς ἐπὶ θανάτῳ, οὐ ῥᾳθύμως εἶδεν, ἀλλ' ἔφη πρὸς τὸν Πτολεμαῖον· "ὦ βασιλεῦ, ἐπεὶ κατά τινα δαίμονα τῶν ἀγομένων ἀγαθὸν ἐπὶ ἵππων[4] ἐτύχομεν[5] ὄντες, φέρε, εἴ σοι δοκεῖ, τὴν ἔλασιν ἐπιτείναντες καὶ συντονώτερον ἐπιδιώξαντες Διόσκοροι τοῖς δειλαίοις γενώμεθα,

σωτῆρες ἔνθα[6] κἀγαθοὶ παραστάται,

τοῦτο δὴ τὸ λεγόμενον ἐπὶ τῶν θεῶν τούτων." ὁ δὲ ὑπερησθεὶς αὐτοῦ τῇ χρηστότητι καὶ τὸ φιλοίκτιρμον ὑπερφιλήσας, καὶ ἐκείνους ἔσωσε καὶ ἐπὶ πλέον προσέθηκε τῷ φίλτρῳ τοῦ κατ' αὐτὸν ἔρωτος.

31. Νόμος οὗτος Περσικὸς ἐν τοῖς μάλιστα ὑπ' αὐτῶν φυλαττόμενος. ὅταν εἰς Πέρσας ἐλαύνῃ βασιλεύς, πάντες αὐτῷ Πέρσαι κατὰ τὴν ἑαυτοῦ δύναμιν ἕκαστός <τι>[7] προσκομίζει.[8] ἅτε δὲ ὄντες

[1] τούτῳ Her.: -του V: om. x [2] καὶ post πολλὰ traiecit Scheffer [3] μὲν <οὖν> Her. [4] ἵππων Per.: ἵππῳ codd.
[5] ἐτύχομεν] τυγχάνομεν Her.
[6] ἔνθα] ἐσθλοὶ Her.: alii alia
[7] suppl. Haupt [8] προσκομίζει] -ίζουσιν Her.

30. King Ptolemy was in love with a boy called Galestes, of most handsome appearance.[a] But the lad's judgement proved superior to his looks. Frequently Ptolemy recognised this and said to him, "Dear boy, you have never been the cause of misfortune to anyone, while you have brought many benefits to a lot of people." The young man was riding with the king, when he saw some men at a distance being led off to be executed. He watched with concern and said to Ptolemy, "Sire, since by a chance that is lucky for the condemned men we happen to be on horseback, if you are willing, let us increase our pace and make an effort to catch up with them, so as to be like Dioscuri to the poor wretches, 'saviours and benevolent guardians' [TrGF Adesp. 14], as those gods are commonly described."[b] The king was greatly delighted by his noble thought and much appreciated his wish to show mercy; so he spared the men and increased his feeling of devotion for the boy.

31. A custom most carefully maintained by the Persians, when the king drives to Persepolis,[c] is that each and every one of them, according to his means, brings an

[a] Galestes was a friend of Ptolemy VI Philometor, mentioned in Diodorus Siculus 33.20 and 22.

[b] Though the text of this iambic line is not entirely certain, the sense is clear. For the Dioscuri as saviours see the evidence assembled e.g. by W. Burkert, *Greek Religion* (Oxford and Cambridge, Mass., 1985), pp. 212–213.

[c] In support of this rendering see J. Wackernagel, *Glotta* 14 (1925): 40–42 (= *Kleine Schriften*, Göttingen, 1955, vol. 2, pp. 848–850).

ἐν γεωργίᾳ καὶ περὶ γῆν πονούμενοι καὶ αὐτουργοὶ πεφυκότες οὐδὲν τῶν ὑβρισμένων οὐδὲ τῶν ἄγαν πολυτελῶν προσφέρουσιν, ἀλλ' ἢ βοῦς ἢ ὄις, οἱ δὲ σῖτον, καὶ οἶνον ἄλλοι. παρεξιόντι δ' αὐτῷ καὶ παρελαύνοντι ταῦτα ὑπὸ ἑκάστου πρόκειται καὶ ὀνομάζεται δῶρα καὶ δοκεῖ [τούτῳ].[1] οἱ δὲ ἔτι τούτων ἐνδεέστεροι τὸν βίον καὶ γάλα καὶ φοίνικας αὐτῷ καὶ τυρὸν προσφέρουσι καὶ τρωκτὰ ὡραῖα καὶ τὰς ἄλλας ἀπαρχὰς τῶν ἐπιχωρίων.

32. Λόγος οὖν καὶ οὗτος Περσικός. φασὶν ἄνδρα Πέρσην, ᾧ ὄνομα ἦν Σιναίτης, πόρρω τῆς ἐπαύλεως τῆς ἑαυτοῦ ἐντυχεῖν Ἀρταξέρξῃ τῷ ἐπικαλουμένῳ Μνήμονι. ἀποληφθέντα οὖν θορυβηθῆναι δέει τοῦ νόμου καὶ αἰδοῖ τοῦ βασιλέως. οὐκ ἔχων δὲ ὅ τι χρήσεται τῷ παρόντι, ἡττηθῆναι τῶν ἄλλων Περσῶν μὴ φέρων μηδὲ ἄτιμος δόξαι τῷ μὴ δωροφορῆσαι βασιλεῖ,[2] ἀλλ' οὗτός γε πρὸς τὸν ποταμὸν τὸν πλησίον παραρρέοντα, ᾧ Κῦρός ἐστιν ὄνομα, ἐλθὼν σὺν σπουδῇ καὶ ᾗ ποδῶν εἶχε [μάλιστα],[3] ἐπικύψας ἀμφοτέραις ταῖς χερσὶν ἀρυσάμενος τοῦ ὕδατος "βασιλεῦ" φησιν "Ἀρταξέρξη, δι' αἰῶνος βασιλεύοις. νῦν μὲν οὖν σε ὅπῃ τε καὶ ὅπως ἔχω τιμῶ, ὡς ἂν μὴ ἀγέραστος τὸ γοῦν ἐμὸν [καὶ τὸ κατ' ἐμὲ][4] παρέλθῃς, τιμῶ δέ σε Κύρου ποταμοῦ ὕδατι· ὅταν δὲ ἐπὶ τὸν σταθμὸν τὸν σὸν παραγένῃ, οἴκοθεν,

[1] delevi: τοῦτο Faber
[2] βασιλεῖ Her.: -έα codd.
[3] del. Her.

offering. Since they are engaged in farming and toil on the land, living by what they produce, they bring no pretentious or unduly expensive gifts, but rather oxen, sheep, or corn, or in other cases wine. As the king passes and drives on his way these objects are laid out by each man, and are termed gifts; the king treats them as such. Men who are even poorer than these farmers bring him milk and dates and cheese, with ripe fruit and other first fruits of local produce.

32. Here is another story from Persia. They say that a Persian called Sinaetes, at some distance from his country estate, met Artaxerxes, who was known as Mnemon.[a] Caught unawares, he was disturbed, owing to fear arising from the local custom and his respect for the king. Not knowing what to do in the circumstances and dismayed at the thought of being outdone by the other Persians, or of appearing dishonourable by not presenting the king with a gift, he nevertheless went urgently, as fast as his feet could carry him, to the river that flowed nearby (called the Cyrus),[b] bent down, and drew up some water in both hands, saying "King Artaxerxes, may your reign be eternal. At this moment I honour you as best I can in the circumstances, in order that you shall not pass by unhonoured by me, so far as lies in my power. And I honour you with the water of the Cyrus. When you reach your

[a] This is Artaxerxes II (404–358 B.C.), also known as Ochus and Memnon, whereas the king in chh. 33 and 34 is Artaxerxes I (465–425 B.C.).

[b] The Kura, which flows into the Caspian.

[4] del. Faber; fortasse ipsius Aeliani altera locutio

ὡς ἂν [μάλιστα][1] ἐμαυτοῦ[2] κράτιστα καὶ πολυτελέστατα χορηγήσαιμι,[3] οὕτω τιμήσω σε, καὶ δὴ οὐδὲν <ἂν>[4] ἐλάττων γενοίμην τινὸς τῶν ἄλλων τῶν ἤδη σε δεξιωσαμένων τοῖς δώροις." ἐπὶ τούτοις ὁ Ἀρταξέρξης ἥσθη καὶ "δέχομαι ἡδέως" φησὶν "ἄνθρωπε, τὸ δῶρον καὶ τιμῶμαί γε αὐτὸ τῶν πάνυ πολυτελῶν καὶ ἰσοστάσιον ἐκείνοις λέγω· πρῶτον μέν, ὅτι ὕδωρ ἐστὶ τὸ πάντων ἄριστον, δεύτερον δέ, ὅτι Κύρου ὄνομα ἐν ἑαυτῷ φέρει. καὶ σὺ δέ μοι καταλύοντι ἐν τῷ σταθμῷ πάντως ἐπιφάνηθι." ταῦτα εἰπὼν προσέταξε τοὺς εὐνούχους λαβεῖν τὸ ἐξ αὐτοῦ δῶρον· οἱ δὲ τὴν ταχίστην προσδραμόντες εἰς χρυσῆν φιάλην ἐδέξαντο ἐκ τῶν χειρῶν αὐτοῦ τὸ ὕδωρ. ἐλθὼν δὲ ἔνθα κατέλυεν ὁ βασιλεὺς ἔπεμψε τῷ ἀνδρὶ [τῷ Πέρσῃ][5] στολὴν Περσικὴν καὶ φιάλην χρυσῆν καὶ χιλίους δαρεικούς, καὶ προσέταξε τὸν κομίζοντα αὐτὰ εἰπεῖν τῷ λαμβάνοντι· "κελεύει σε βασιλεὺς ἐκ μὲν τούτου τοῦ χρυσίου εὐφραίνειν τὴν σεαυτοῦ ψυχήν, ἐπεὶ καὶ σὺ τὴν ἐκείνου εὔφρανας, μὴ αὐτὴν[6] ἀγέραστον μηδὲ ἄτιμον ἐάσας, ἀλλ' ὡς ἤδη ἐχώρει ταύτῃ τιμήσας. βούλεται δέ σε καὶ τῇ φιάλῃ ταύτῃ ἀρυόμενον πίνειν ἐξ ἐκείνου τοῦ ὕδατος."

33. Ῥοιὰν ἐπὶ λίκνου μεγίστην Ὠμίσης[7] Ἀρταξέρξῃ τῷ βασιλεῖ ἐλαύνοντι τὴν Περσίδα προσεκόμισε. τὸ μέγεθος οὖν αὐτῆς ὑπερεκπλαγεὶς ὁ βασι-

[1] del. Her. [2] ἐμαυτοῦ Gesner: ἑαυτοῦ codd.
[3] χορηγήσαιμι Albini: χωρήσαιμι codd. [4] suppl. Her.
[5] delevi [6] αὐτὴν] -τὸν ed. Tornaesiana

destination, I will bring you from my home the very best and most expensive objects I have, and in that way I will honour you. So I shall not fall short by comparison with any of the others who have greeted you with their offerings." Artaxerxes was pleased with this and said, "My man, I am happy to accept your gift, I esteem it as one of the most valuable, and I declare it to be equal in value to those others: first of all because water is the best of all things,[a] secondly because it bears the name of Cyrus. You should certainly appear before me when I stay at my residence." With these words he instructed the eunuchs to accept the man's gift. They raced over as quickly as possible and received the water from his hands in a golden cup. When the king reached his staging post he sent his [Persian] subject a Persian robe, a golden cup, and a thousand darics. The man who brought the objects was instructed to say to the recipient "The king requests you to gladden your heart from this golden object, since you brought joy to his by not letting him pass without honour or reverence; instead you did him such honour as was possible, and he wishes you to draw water from the river in this cup."

33. As king Artaxerxes was travelling through Persia Omises brought him a very large pomegranate on a winnowing fan. The size of it caused the king great

[a] Aelian here adapts a famous quotation from Pindar, *Olympians* 1.1.

---

[7] Ὠμίσης e Plutarcho Scheffer et Faber: Ὀμίσης x: ὁ Μίθρας V

λεὺς "ἐκ ποίου παραδείσου" φησὶ "λαβὼν φέρεις μοι τὸ δῶρον τοῦτο;" τοῦ δὲ εἰπόντος ὅτι οἴκοθεν καὶ ἐκ τῆς αὐτοῦ γεωργίας, ὑπερήσθη καὶ δῶρα μὲν αὐτῷ βασιλικὰ ἔπεμψε καὶ ἐπεῖπε· "νὴ τὸν Μίθραν, ἀνὴρ οὗτος ἐκ τῆς ἐπιμελείας ταύτης δυνήσεται καὶ πόλιν κατά γε τὴν ἐμὴν κρίσιν ἐκ μικρᾶς μεγάλην ποιῆσαι." ἔοικε δὲ ὁ λόγος ὁμολογεῖν οὗτος ὅτι πάντα ἐκ τῆς ἐπιμελείας καὶ τῆς διαρκοῦς φροντίδος καὶ τῆς σπουδῆς τῆς ἀνελλιποῦς καὶ τῶν κατὰ φύσιν δύναιτο ἂν κρείττονα γενέσθαι.

34. Ἀνὴρ γένει Μάρδος, ὄνομα Ῥακώκης, παῖδας εἶχεν ἑπτά. ἀλλὰ τούτων ὁ νεώτατος ἐκαλεῖτο Καρτώμης, κακὰ δὲ πολλὰ τοὺς μείζους[1] εἰργάζετο. καὶ τὰ μὲν πρῶτα ἐπειρᾶτο αὐτὸν ὁ πατὴρ παιδεύειν καὶ ῥυθμίζειν λόγῳ· ἐπεὶ δὲ οὐκ ἐπείθετο, τῶν δικαστῶν τῶν περιχώρων ἀφικομένων ἔνθα ᾤκει ὁ τοῦ νεανίσκου πατήρ, ἀλλ' ἐκεῖνός γε συλλαβὼν τὸ παιδίον καὶ τὼ χεῖρε ὀπίσω περιαγαγὼν αὐτοῦ, πρὸς τοὺς δικαστὰς ἤγαγε καὶ ὅσα αὐτῷ τετόλμητο[2] πάντα ἀκριβῶς κατηγόρησε καὶ ᾔτει παρὰ τῶν δικαστῶν ἀποκτεῖναι τὸν νεανίσκον. οἱ δὲ ἐξεπλάγησαν καὶ αὐτοὶ μὲν ἐφ' ἑαυτῶν οὐκ ἔκριναν τὴν καταδικάζουσαν ἀγαγεῖν[3] ψῆφον, ἀμφοτέρους δὲ ἐπὶ τὸν βασιλέα τῶν Περσῶν τὸν Ἀρταξέρξην ἤγαγον. τὰ αὐτὰ δὲ λέγοντος τοῦ Μάρδου ὑπολαβὼν ὁ βασιλεὺς ἔφη· "εἶτα τολμήσεις τοῖς ὀφθαλμοῖς τοῖς ἑαυ-

[1] μείζους J. F. Gronovius: μάγους codd.: ἄλλους Cuper, haud male

amazement and he asked: "From what estate do you come with this offering?" When the other replied: "From my home, from my own farm" he was quite delighted and sent the man royal gifts, adding: "By Mithras, with care such as he displays this man will even be capable, as far as I can judge, of making a small city into a great one." This remark seems to acknowledge that by care, continuous thought, and unremitting enthusiasm anything may be improved beyond its natural state.[a]

34. A man called Rhacoces, of the Mardian tribe,[b] had seven children. The youngest of them was called Cartomes, who did a great deal of harm to his elder brothers. At first his father tried to correct and restrain him by admonition. But when this failed, the local magistrates arrived at the house of the young man's father, and the latter arrested the lad, tying his hands behind his back and taking him into the presence of the magistrates. He made a full and detailed denunciation of all his acts of misbehaviour and asked the magistrates to execute the young man. They were horrified, and decided not to pass sentence on their own authority; instead they brought both before Artaxerxes, the king of Persia. When the Mardian repeated his statement, the king replied: "Have you really the courage to witness with your own eyes the

[a] Cf. Plutarch, *Artaxerxes* 4.5.

[b] One of the constituent peoples of the Persian Empire, originally nomadic.

---

[2] τετόλμητο Kor.: -ται codd.

[3] ἀγαγεῖν] ἐνεγκεῖν Cobet

τοῦ τὸν υἱὸν ἀποθνήσκοντα ὑπομεῖναι;" ὁ δὲ ἔφη· "πάντων μάλιστα· ἐπεὶ καὶ ἐν τῷ κήπῳ ὅταν τῶν φυομένων θριδακινῶν τὰς ἐκφύσεις τὰς πικρὰς ἀποκλῶ καὶ ἀφαιρῶ, οὐδὲν ἡ μήτηρ αὐτῶν ἡ θριδακίνη λυπεῖται, ἀλλὰ θάλλει μᾶλλον καὶ μείζων καὶ γλυκίων γίνεται. οὕτω[1] καὶ ἐγώ, ὦ βασιλεῦ, τὸν βλάπτοντα τὴν ἐμὴν οἰκίαν καὶ τὸν τῶν ἀδελφῶν βίον [εἶπε][2] θεωρῶν ἀπολλύμενον καὶ τῆς κακουργίας τῆς εἰς αὐτοὺς παυόμενον, καὶ αὐτὸς αὐξηθήσομαι καὶ τοῖς λοιποῖς τοῖς κατὰ γένος συνείσομαι[3] τὰ αὐτὰ ἐμοὶ εὖ πάσχουσιν." ὧν ἀκούσας Ἀρταξέρξης ἐπῄνεσε μὲν τὸν Ῥακώκην καὶ τῶν βασιλικῶν δικαστῶν ἐποίησεν ἕνα, εἰπὼν πρὸς τοὺς παρόντας ὅτι ὁ περὶ τῶν ἰδίων παίδων οὕτω δικαίως ἀποφαινόμενος πάντως καὶ ἐν τοῖς ἀλλοτρίοις ἀκριβὴς ἔσται δικαστὴς καὶ ἀδέκαστος· ἀφῆκε δὲ καὶ τὸν νεανίαν τῆς παρούσης τιμωρίας, ἀπειλῶν αὐτῷ θανάτου τρόπον βαρύτατον, ἐὰν ἐπὶ τοῖς φθάσασιν ἀδικῶν φωραθῇ ἕτερα.

[1] οὕτω Gesner: ἅμα codd.

[2] del. Hercher: εἴ γε J. Gronovius possis etiam ἐπιθεωρῶν (Russell)

[3] συνείσομαι scripsi: συνέσομαι codd.: συνήσομαι Per. (rectius συνησθήσομαι)

death of your son?" "Quite certainly," said the man, "because in my garden, when I tear off and throw away the bitter shoots which grow on the lettuces, the parent lettuce shows no grief and flourishes all the more, becoming larger and sweeter. In the same way I too, your majesty," he said, "seeing the destruction of one who ruins my home and the lives of his brothers, seeing an end to the damage done to them, I myself shall be the gainer and I shall witness the other members of my family enjoying the same good fortune as myself." On hearing this Artaxerxes commended Rhacoces and made him one of the royal magistrates, observing to the assembled company that a man who showed himself so fair-minded in the case of his own children would certainly be accurate and incorruptible in his treatment of other people's affairs. He also annulled the sentence which the young man was about to suffer, threatening him with the direst form of death sentence if he should be found adding to his past record of crime.

B

1. Καὶ ταῦτα Σωκράτους πρὸς Ἀλκιβιάδην. ὁ μὲν ἠγωνία καὶ ἐδεδίει πάνυ σφόδρα εἰς τὸν δῆμον παρελθεῖν τὸ μειράκιον· ἐπιθαρσύνων δὲ αὐτὸν καὶ ἐγείρων ὁ Σωκράτης "οὐ καταφρονεῖς" εἶπεν "ἐκείνου τοῦ σκυτοτόμου;" τὸ ὄνομα εἰπὼν αὐτοῦ. φήσαντος δὲ τοῦ Ἀλκιβιάδου ὑπολαβὼν πάλιν ὁ Σωκράτης· "ἔτι δὲ ἐκείνου τοῦ ἐν τοῖς κύκλοις κηρύττοντος ἢ ἐκείνου τοῦ σκηνορράφου;" ὁμολογοῦντος δὲ τοῦ Κλεινίου μειρακίου[1] "οὐκοῦν" ἔφη ὁ Σωκράτης "ὁ δῆμος ὁ Ἀθηναίων ἐκ τοιούτων ἤθροισται· καὶ εἰ τῶν καθ' ἕνα καταφρονεῖς, καταφρονητέον ἄρα καὶ τῶν ἠθροισμένων," μεγαλοφρόνως ταῦτα ὁ τοῦ Σωφρονίσκου καὶ τῆς Φαιναρέτης τὸν τοῦ Κλεινίου καὶ τῆς Δεινομάχης διδάσκων.

2. Μεγαβύζου ποτὲ ἐπαινοῦντος γραφὰς εὐτελεῖς καὶ ἀτέχνους, ἑτέρας δὲ σπουδαίως ἐκπεπονημένας διαψέγοντος, τὰ παιδάρια τὰ τοῦ Ζεύξιδος <τὰ>[2] τὴν μηλίδα[3] τρίβοντα κατεγέλα. ὁ τοίνυν Ζεῦξις ἔφατο· "ὅταν μὲν σιωπᾷς, ὦ Μεγάβυζε, θαυμάζει σε τὰ παιδάρια ταῦτα· ὁρᾷ γάρ σου τὴν ἐσθῆτα καὶ τὴν θεραπείαν τὴν περὶ σέ· ὅταν γε μὴν τεχνικόν τι

BOOK TWO

1. And here is how Socrates advised Alcibiades. The latter was anxious and felt great diffidence as a young man about speaking in public. Socrates gave him encouragement and support by saying "Don't you despise that leather worker?" adding the man's name. When Alcibiades agreed Socrates continued: "And also the town crier who accosts the public; and that tent maker?" The young son of Clinias agreed. "Well, the Athenian public is composed of such people," said Socrates, "and if you despise them as individuals, you should despise them collectively." Such was the distinguished lesson given by the son of Sophroniscus and Phaenarete to the son of Clinias and Dinomache.[a]

2. One day when Megabyzus gave praise to some inferior and crude paintings, while being quite critical of others that displayed excellent technique, the slaves of Zeuxis who were grinding Melian earth began to laugh.[b] So Zeuxis remarked, "Megabyzus, when you keep silent, the slaves admire you, because they can see your dress and the attendants with you. But when you try to say

[a] Cf. Xenophon, *Memorabilia* 3.7.6–7, and O. Gigon, *Eranos* 44 (1946): 149–150. [b] Melian earth was a yellow pigment.

---

[1] Κλεινίου del. Her., μειρακίου del. Russell
[2] suppl. Her. [3] μηλίδα x, Plutarchus: μηλιάδα V

θέλῃς εἰπεῖν, καταφρονεῖ σου. φύλαττε τοίνυν σεαυτὸν εἰς τοὺς ἐπαινουμένους, κρατῶν τῆς γλώττης καὶ ὑπὲρ μηδενὸς τῶν μηδέν σοι προσηκόντων φιλοτεχνῶν."

3. Ἀλέξανδρος *θεασάμενος τὴν ἐν* Ἐφέσῳ *εἰκόνα ἑαυτοῦ τὴν ὑπὸ* Ἀπελλοῦ *γραφεῖσαν οὐκ ἐπῄνεσε κατὰ τὴν ἀξίαν τοῦ γράμματος. εἰσαχθέντος δὲ τοῦ ἵππου καὶ χρεμετίσαντος πρὸς τὸν ἵππον τὸν ἐν τῇ εἰκόνι ὡς πρὸς ἀληθινὸν καὶ ἐκεῖνον "ὦ βασιλεῦ" εἶπεν ὁ* Ἀπελλῆς *"ἀλλ' ὅ γε ἵππος ἔοικέ σου γραφικώτερος εἶναι κατὰ πολύ."*

4. Φαλάριδος *ὑμῖν ἔργον οὐ μάλα ἐκείνῳ σύνηθες εἰπεῖν ἐθέλω· τὸ δὲ ἔργον φιλανθρωπίαν ἄμαχον ὁμολογεῖ καὶ διὰ τοῦτο ἀλλότριον ἐκείνου δοκεῖ.* Χαρίτων *ἦν* Ἀκραγαντῖνος *φιλόκαλος ἄνθρωπος καὶ περὶ τὴν ὥραν τὴν τῶν νέων ἐσπουδακὼς δαιμονίως· διαπύρως δὲ ἠράσθη μάλιστα* Μελανίππου, Ἀκραγαντίνου *καὶ ἐκείνου, καὶ τὴν ψυχὴν ἀγαθοῦ καὶ τὸ κάλλος διαφέροντος. τοῦτον ἐλύπησέ τι* Φάλαρις *τὸν* Μελάνιππον· *δικαζομένῳ γὰρ αὐτῷ πρός τινα τῶν ἑταίρων αὐτοῦ τοῦ* Φαλάριδος *προσέταξεν ὁ τύραννος τὴν γραφὴν καταθέσθαι. τοῦ δὲ μὴ πειθομένου ὁ δὲ ἠπείλησε τὰ ἔσχατα δράσειν αὐτὸν μὴ ὑπακούσαντα. καὶ ἐκεῖνος μὲν παρὰ τὴν δίκην ἐκράτησεν τῇ*[1] *ἀνάγκῃ προστάξαντος τοῦ* Φαλάρι-

[1] *τῇ* V: *τοῦ* x: del. Per.

something about art, they despise you. So continue to be admired by holding your tongue and not discussing anything that is not your business."[a]

3. Alexander looked at Apelles' portrait of him in Ephesus and did not give it the praise which its artistry deserved. When his horse was brought along it whinnied at the horse in the picture as if it too were real, and Apelles said, "Your majesty, the horse certainly seems to have much better taste in art than you do."[b]

4. I want to mention to you an act of Phalaris which was not altogether like him.[c] The act indicates unsurpassed kindness and for this reason appears foreign to his nature. Chariton of Acragas, a lover of beauty, was specially susceptible to the charms of the young. He fell passionately in love with Melanippus, who was also from Acragas, a youth of noble character and exceptional beauty. Phalaris annoyed this Melanippus, because in a lawsuit the latter brought against one of the companions of the tyrant himself, Phalaris ordered him to stop his action. When he refused the tyrant threatened him with extremely severe punishment for disobedience. The defendant therefore won his case, unjustly, because Phalaris' orders amounted to compulsion, and the magis-

[a] The famous painter Zeuxis flourished ca. 435–390 B.C. Plutarch, *Moralia* 58 D and 471 F–472 A, tells this same story about Apelles, who was a contemporary of Alexander the Great. If Megabyzus could be identified, we should know which version is correct.

[b] Cf. Pliny, *Natural History* 35.95; the reference is to Bucephalus.

[c] Phalaris, tyrant of Acragas, 570–554 B.C., was a byword for cruelty.

δος, οἱ δὲ[1] ἄρχοντες τὴν γραφὴν τοῦ ἀγῶνος ἠφάνισαν. βαρέως δ᾽ ἐπὶ τούτοις ὁ νεανίσκος ἤνεγκεν ὑβρίσθαι λέγων, καὶ ὡμολόγει τὴν ὀργὴν τὴν ἑαυτοῦ πρὸς τὸν ἐραστὴν ὁ Μελάνιππος[2] καὶ ἠξίου κοινωνὸν αὐτὸν γενέσθαι τῆς ἐπιθέσεως τῆς κατὰ τοῦ τυράννου[3] καὶ ἄλλους δὲ ἔσπευδε προσλαβεῖν τῶν νεανίσκων, οὓς μάλιστα ᾔδει περὶ τὴν τοιαύτην πρᾶξιν θερμοτάτους. ὁρῶν δὲ αὐτὸν ὁ Χαρίτων ἐνθουσιῶντα καὶ ὑπὸ τῆς ὀργῆς ἀναφλεγόμενον καὶ γινώσκων ὅτι τῶν πολιτῶν οὐδεὶς αὐτοῖς συλλήψεται δέει τῷ ἐκ τοῦ τυράννου, καὶ αὐτὸς ἔφη πάλαι τοῦτο ἐπιθυμεῖν καὶ σπεύδειν ἐκ παντὸς τὴν πατρίδα ῥύσασθαι τῆς δουλείας τῆς καταλαβούσης· ἀσφαλὲς δὲ μὴ εἶναι πρὸς πολλοὺς τὰ τοιαῦτα ἐκφέρειν. ἠξίου δὴ τὸν Μελάνιππόν οἱ συγχωρῆσαι ἀκριβέστερον ὑπὲρ τούτων διασκέψασθαι καὶ ἐᾶσαι παραφυλάξαι τὸν χρόνον τὸν ἐπιτήδειον εἰς τὴν πρᾶξιν. συνεχώρησε τὸ μειράκιον. ἐφ᾽ ἑαυτοῦ τοίνυν ὁ Χαρίτων βαλόμενος τὸ πᾶν τόλμημα καὶ κοινωνὸν αὐτοῦ μὴ θελήσας παραλαβεῖν τὸν ἐρώμενον, ἵν᾽, εἰ καταφωραθείη, αὐτὸς ὑπέχοι τὴν δίκην, ἀλλὰ μὴ καὶ ἐκεῖνον εἰς ταὐτὰ ἐμβάλοι, ἡνίκα οἱ ἐδόκει καλῶς ἔχειν, ἐγχειρίδιον λαβὼν ὡρμᾶτο ἐπὶ τὸν τύραννον. οὐ μὴν ἔλαθε, κατεφωράθη δέ, πάνυ σφόδρα ἀκριβῶς[4] τῶν δορυφόρων τὰ τοιαῦτα φυλαττόντων. ἐμβληθεὶς δὲ ὑπὸ τοῦ Φαλάριδος εἰς τὸ δεσμωτήριον καὶ στρεβλούμενος ἵν᾽ εἴπῃ τοὺς συνεγνωκότας, ὁ δὲ ἐνεκαρτέρει καὶ ἐνήθλει ταῖς βασάνοις. ἐπεὶ δὲ

trates annulled the case. The young man was offended by this and complained of having been badly treated. He admitted to his lover his personal feelings of annoyance and asked him to join in a conspiracy against the tyrant. He also made efforts to enlist other young men whom he knew to be very keen to take part in such an enterprise. Chariton saw he was beside himself and blazing with anger, but he knew that none of the other citizens would join them, for fear of the tyrant. He said he himself had longed to take this action for some time and was anxious at all costs to free their country from the servitude that had overtaken it. But it would not be safe to reveal such thoughts to many people. He asked Melanippus to let him investigate the matter more closely, and to leave to him the choice of the right moment for action. The young man agreed. So Chariton took upon himself all the responsibility for the adventure, not wanting to engage his beloved as a partner, so that if he himself were caught and paid the penalty, at least he would not bring the same fate upon the boy. When the time seemed to be right he took a dagger and attacked the tyrant. But he did not escape detection, and was caught, as the bodyguards kept a very close watch against such attempts. He was put in prison by Phalaris and tortured in order that he should reveal who had conspired with him; but he held out and resisted the torture. When this had gone on for some time, Melanip-

---

[1] *οἱ δὲ* Per.: *δὲ οἱ* codd.
[2] ὁ Μελάνιππος del. Her.
[3] *κατὰ τοῦ τυράννου* Russell: *κατ' αὐτοῦ* codd.
[4] *ἀκριβῶς* hic Her.: post *δορυφόρων* praebent codd.

μακρὸν τοῦτο ἦν, ὁ Μελάνιππος ἧκεν ἐπὶ τὸν Φάλαριν καὶ ὡμολόγησεν οὐ μόνον κοινωνὸς εἶναι τῷ Χαρίτωνι [τῆς βουλῆς][1] ἀλλὰ καὶ αὐτὸς ἄρξαι τῆς ἐπιβουλῆς. τοῦ δὲ πυνθανομένου τὴν αἰτίαν, εἶπε τὸν ἐξ ἀρχῆς λόγον καὶ τὴν τῆς γραφῆς ἄρσιν, καὶ ἐπὶ τούτοις ὡμολόγει περιαλγῆσαι. θαυμάσας οὖν <ὁ Φάλαρις>[2] ἀμφοτέρους ἀφῆκε τῆς τιμωρίας, προστάξας αὐθημερὸν ἀπελθεῖν μὴ μόνον τῆς Ἀκραγαντίνων πόλεως ἀλλὰ καὶ τῆς Σικελίας· συνεχώρησε δὲ αὐτοῖς τὰ ἴδια δίκαια καρποῦσθαι. τούτους ὕστερον ἡ Πυθία καὶ τὴν φιλίαν αὐτῶν ὕμνησε διὰ τούτων τῶν ἐπῶν·

θείας ἡγητῆρες ἐφημερίοις φιλότητος
εὐδαίμων Χαρίτων καὶ Μελάνιππος ἔφυν,[3]

τοῦ θεοῦ τὸν ἔρωτα αὐτῶν θείαν ὀνομάσαντος φιλίαν.

5. Λακεδαιμόνιοι δεινὴν ἐποιοῦντο τοῦ χρόνου τὴν φειδώ, ταμιευόμενοι πανταχόθεν αὐτὸν εἰς τὰ ἐπειγόμενα καὶ μηδενὶ τῶν πολιτῶν ἐπιτρέποντες μήτε ῥᾳστωνεύειν μήτε ῥᾳθυμεῖν εἰς αὐτόν, ὡς ἂν μὴ πρὸς τὰ ἔξω τῆς ἀρετῆς ἀναλισκόμενος εἶτα μάτην διαφθείροιτο. μαρτύριον τούτου πρὸς τοῖς ἄλλοις καὶ τοῦτο. ἀκούσαντες οἱ ἔφοροι Λακεδαιμονίων τοὺς Δεκέλειαν καταλαβόντας περιπάτῳ χρῆσθαι

[1] del. Kor.
[2] suppl. Her.
[3] ἔφυν Her.: ἔφυ codd.

pus approached Phalaris and confessed not only to being an accomplice in Chariton's plan, but to having suggested the idea of a conspiracy. When Phalaris asked the reason, he told the whole story, beginning with the annulment of the lawsuit, and admitted his great annoyance at this. Phalaris was struck with admiration and released them both without punishment, with an order to leave not merely Acragas, but Sicily, that very day. But he allowed them to enjoy their own rights of property. The Pythian priestess later celebrated them and their friendship in these verses:

> Setting mortals an example of divine affection
> Chariton and Melanippus were blessed in fortune.

The god termed their love a divine friendship.[a]

5. The Spartans were most economical with time, saving it for urgent matters in every way possible and not allowing any citizen to be idle or careless in using it, so that it should not be spent on aims outside the scope of virtuous action and so be wasted to no purpose. Among other proofs of their principle is the following. The ephors[b] heard that the Spartans who had captured Decelea[c] were taking a walk in the afternoon, and sent

[a] The Pythian prophet was regarded as the mouthpiece of Apollo. This oracle is no. 327 in H. W. Parke and D. E. W. Wormell, *The Delphic Oracle* (Oxford, 1956). It is cited in Athenaeus 602 B and Eusebius, *Praeparatio evangelica* 5.35.1–3. See also J. Hammerstaedt, *Die Orakelkritik des Kynikers Oenomaus* (Frankfurt, 1988), pp. 13 n. 3 and 223.

[b] The board of five officials, elected annually, who effectively ran Sparta.

[c] Decelea was the fort 12 miles north of Athens occupied by the Spartans at a late stage of the Peloponnesian War in 413 B.C.

δειλινῷ, ἐπέστειλαν αὐτοῖς· "μὴ περιπατεῖτε," ὡς τρυφώντων αὐτῶν μᾶλλον ἢ τὸ σῶμα ἐκπονούντων. δεῖν γὰρ Λακεδαιμονίους οὐ διὰ τοῦ περιπάτου ἀλλὰ διὰ τῶν γυμνασίων τὴν ὑγείαν πορίζεσθαι.

6. Ἱππόμαχος, φασίν, ὁ γυμναστής, ἐπεὶ πάλαισμά τι ὁ ἀθλητὴς ὁ ὑπ' αὐτῷ γυμναζόμενος ἐπάλαισεν, εἶτα ὁ πᾶς ὄχλος ὁ περιεστὼς ἐξεβόησε, καθίκετο αὐτοῦ τῇ ῥάβδῳ ὁ Ἱππόμαχος[1] καὶ εἶπεν· "ἀλλὰ σύ γε κακῶς καὶ οὐχ ὡς ἐχρῆν ἐποίησας ὅπερ ἐχρῆν ἄμεινον γενέσθαι· οὐ γὰρ ἂν ἐπῄνεσαν οὗτοι τεχνικόν σε δράσαντά τι," αἰνιττόμενος ὅτι τοὺς εὖ καὶ καλῶς ἕκαστα δρῶντας οὐ τοῖς πολλοῖς ἀλλὰ τοῖς ἔχουσιν νοῦν θεωρητικὸν τῶν δρωμένων ἀρέσκειν δεῖ. ἔοικε δὲ καὶ Σωκράτης τὴν τῶν πολλῶν ἐκφαυλίζειν κρίσιν ἐν τῇ συνουσίᾳ τῇ πρὸς Κρίτωνα, ὅτε ἀφίκετο ὁ Κρίτων εἰς τὸ δεσμωτήριον καὶ δὴ ἔπειθεν αὐτὸν ἀποδρᾶναι καὶ τὴν τῶν Ἀθηναίων τὴν κατ' αὐτοῦ κρίσιν διαφθεῖραι.

7. Νόμος οὗτος Θηβαϊκὸς ὀρθῶς ἅμα καὶ φιλανθρώπως κείμενος ἐν τοῖς μάλιστα ὅτι οὐκ ἔξεστιν ἀνδρὶ Θηβαίῳ ἐκθεῖναι παιδίον οὐδὲ εἰς ἐρημίαν αὐτὸ ῥῖψαι θάνατον αὐτοῦ καταψηφισάμενον,[2] ἀλλ' ἐὰν ᾖ πένης εἰς τὰ ἔσχατα ὁ τοῦ παιδὸς πατήρ, εἴτε ἄρρεν τοῦτο εἴτε θῆλύ ἐστιν, ἐπὶ τὰς ἀρχὰς κομίζειν ἐξ ὠδίνων τῶν μητρῴων σὺν τοῖς σπαργάνοις αὐτό· αἱ δὲ παραλαβοῦσαι ἀποδίδονται τὸ βρέφος τῷ

[1] ὁ Ἱππόμαχος codd.: del. Her.

them the order "Do not go for walks" because they were indulging in a luxury instead of training their bodies. The Spartans were obliged to maintain their health not by walking but by gymnastic exercises.

6. Hippomachus the trainer,[a] it is said, when the athlete he was training had won a wrestling contest and the whole crowd of bystanders shouted applause, struck his pupil with a cane and said: "But you have performed badly, and have not done correctly what ought to have been managed better. These people would not have applauded if you had made some use of technique." He was hinting that if one is to do everything in right and proper fashion, one must give pleasure not to the crowd but to those who have a theoretical understanding of what is being done. Socrates too seems to show scant respect for the judgement of the crowd in his conversation with Crito, when Crito came to the prison and tried to persuade him to escape, so nullifying the judgement the Athenians had passed on him.[b]

7. It was a law at Thebes, just and at the same time extremely humane, that a Theban could not expose his child or leave it on waste land, condemning it to death. But if the father of the infant was extremely poor, whether the child was male or female, he had to take it immediately after the birth in its clothing to the magistrates. They took it and turned it over to the person who

[a] For Hippomachus see 14.8 below.
[b] An allusion to a famous passage in Plato, *Crito* 44 cd.

---

[2] *καταψηφισάμενον* x (de V non liquet): -*μένῳ* Her.

τιμὴν ἐλαχίστην λαβόντι.[1] ῥήτρα τε πρὸς αὐτὸν καὶ ὁμολογία γίνεται ἦ μὴν τρέφειν τὸ βρέφος καὶ αὐξηθὲν ἔχειν δοῦλον ἢ δούλην, θρεπτήρια αὐτοῦ τὴν ὑπηρεσίαν λαμβάνοντα.

8. Κατὰ τὴν πρώτην καὶ ἐνενηκοστὴν Ὀλυμπιάδα, καθ' ἣν ἐνίκα Ἐξαίνετος ὁ Ἀκραγαντῖνος στάδιον, ἀντηγωνίσαντο ἀλλήλοις Ξενοκλῆς καὶ Εὐριπίδης. καὶ πρῶτός γε ἦν Ξενοκλῆς, ὅστις ποτὲ οὗτός ἐστιν, Οἰδίποδι καὶ Λυκάονι καὶ Βάκχαις καὶ Ἀθάμαντι Σατυρικῷ. τούτου[2] δεύτερος Εὐριπίδης ἦν Ἀλεξάνδρῳ καὶ Παλαμήδει καὶ Τρωάσι[3] καὶ Σισύφῳ Σατυρικῷ. γελοῖον δὲ (οὐ γάρ;) Ξενοκλέα μὲν νικᾶν, Εὐριπίδην δὲ ἡττᾶσθαι, καὶ ταῦτα τοιούτοις δράμασι. τῶν δύο τοίνυν τὸ ἕτερον· ἢ ἀνόητοι ἦσαν οἱ τῆς ψήφου κύριοι καὶ ἀμαθεῖς καὶ πόρρω κρίσεως ὀρθῆς, ἢ ἐδεκάσθησαν. ἄτοπον δὲ ἑκάτερον καὶ Ἀθηναίων ἥκιστα ἄξιον.

9. Οἷα ἐψηφίσαντο Ἀθηναῖοι, καὶ ταῦτα ἐν δημοκρατίᾳ, Αἰγινητῶν μὲν ἑκάστου τὸν μέγαν ἀποκόψαι τῆς χειρὸς δάκτυλον τῆς δεξιᾶς, ἵνα δόρυ μὲν βαστάζειν μὴ δύνωνται, κώπην δὲ ἐλαύνειν δύνωνται· Μιτυληναίους δὲ ἡβηδὸν ἀποσφάξαι καὶ τοῦτο

[1] λαβόντι anonymus (1733): δόντι codd. (quod si recipias, possis τῳ pro τῷ temptare)

[2] τούτου Peruscus: -των V: om. x

[3] Τρωάσι Musgrave: Τρωσὶ codd.

---

[a] The most famous case of exposure in antiquity is the story of Oedipus, set in Thebes. Were the inhabitants of the city suffi-

accepted the lowest payment. A contract was made with the latter, an agreement whereby he pledged to foster the child, and retained it as a slave when it grew up, receiving its services as the reward for having reared it.[a]

8. In the year of the ninety-first Olympiad, when Exaenetus of Acragas won the foot race, Xenocles and Euripides competed against each other.[b] Xenocles, whoever he was, won first prize with his *Oedipus*, *Lycaon*, *Bacchae*, and *Athamas*, a satyr play. After him in second place was Euripides with his *Alexander*, *Palamedes*, *Trojan Women*, and *Sisyphus*, a satyr play. It is surely ridiculous that the result was not defeat for Xenocles and victory for Euripides, especially as he competed with such plays. So we have to accept one of two possibilities: either the men responsible for the decision were stupid, ignorant, and far from having sound judgement, or they were bribed. Yet both ideas are strange and unworthy of Athens.[c]

9. What decrees the Athenians passed, even though they were a democracy! They ordered that each Aeginetan should have his right thumb amputated so that he could not hold a spear but would be able to manage an oar. They ordered the execution of all adult Mytileneans.[d]

ciently impressed by it to respond by making this law? Or is the law a fiction? [b] The year is 416–415 B.C. Of the plays mentioned only Euripides' *Troades* is still extant. [c] Modern scholars are more willing than Aelian to concede that the so-called lesser tragedians may sometimes have reached the same level as their more famous colleagues. [d] The original spelling of the city, now generally adopted, was Mytilene, but Aelian's manuscripts suggest that he used the later form Mitylene.

ἐψηφίσαντο εἰσηγησαμένου Κλέωνος τοῦ Κλεαινέτου. τούς γε μὴν ἁλισκομένους αἰχμαλώτους Σαμίων στίζειν κατὰ τοῦ προσώπου καὶ εἶναι τὸ στίγμα γλαῦκα καὶ τοῦτο Ἀττικὸν ψήφισμα. οὐκ ἐβουλόμην δὲ αὐτὰ οὔτε Ἀθήνησι κεκυρῶσθαι οὔτε ὑπὲρ Ἀθηναίων λέγεσθαι, ὦ Πολιὰς Ἀθηνᾶ καὶ Ἐλευθέριε Ζεῦ καὶ [οἱ][1] Ἑλλήνων θεοὶ πάντες.

10. Τιμόθεον ἀκούω τὸν Κόνωνος τὸν Ἀθηναίων στρατηγόν, ὅτε ἐν ἀκμῇ τῆς εὐτυχίας ἦν καὶ ᾕρει τὰς πόλεις ῥᾷστα, καὶ οὐκ εἶχον Ἀθηναῖοι ὅποι ποτὲ αὐτὸν κατάθωνται ὑπὸ θαύματος τοῦ περὶ τὸν ἄνδρα, ἀλλὰ τοῦτόν γε Πλάτωνι τῷ Ἀρίστωνος περιτυχόντα βαδίζοντι ἔξω τοῦ τείχους μετά τινων γνωρίμων καὶ ἰδόντα σεμνὸν μὲν ἰδεῖν τὸν Πλάτωνα,[2] ἵλεων δὲ τῷ προσώπῳ, διαλεγόμενον δὲ οὐχὶ περὶ εἰσφορᾶς χρημάτων οὐδὲ ὑπὲρ τριήρων, οὐδὲ ὑπὲρ ναυτικῶν χρειῶν οὐδὲ ὑπὲρ πληρωμάτων, οὐδὲ ὑπὲρ τοῦ δεῖν βοηθεῖν οὐδὲ ὑπὲρ φόρου τοῦ τῶν συμμάχων, οὐδὲ ὑπὲρ τῶν νησιωτῶν ἢ ὑπὲρ ἄλλου τινὸς τοιούτου φληνάφου, ὑπὲρ ἐκείνων δέ, ὧν ἔλεγε Πλάτων καὶ ὑπὲρ ὧν εἴθιστο σπουδάζειν, ἐπιστάντα τὸν Τιμόθεον[3] τὸν τοῦ Κόνωνος εἰπεῖν· "<ὢ>[4] τοῦ

[1] del. Her.
[2] τὸν Πλάτωνα Her.: τὸ πλάτος codd.
[3] τὸν Τιμόθεον del. Her.
[4] suppl. Per.

[a] Aegina was conquered by Athens in 458 B.C. and treated severely; Mytilene rebelled in 428 B.C. (the events are narrated

They passed this proposal, made by Cleon, son of Cleaenetus. Captured prisoners from Samos were to be branded on the forehead, the mark being an owl; this too was an Athenian decree. By Athena Polias, by Zeus god of freedom and all the gods of the Greeks, I wish these measures had not been passed by the Athenians and that such things were not reported of them.[a]

10. I learn that Timotheus,[b] son of Conon and Athenian general, when he was at the height of good fortune, capturing cities with great ease, and the Athenians did not know what honour could do justice to their admiration for him[c]—Timotheus met Plato, son of Ariston, walking with some friends outside the city walls. He saw Plato was distinguished in appearance, had a calm expression, and was talking not about levies on income, not about triremes or the needs of the navy, the manning of ships, the need to mount an expedition, the taxes paid by the allies, nor about the islanders, or any other trifles of that kind. The conversation was of subjects which Plato used to talk about, in which he habitually took a serious interest. Timotheus, son of Conon, stopped and said: "What a

by Thucydides 3.2–50); the revolt of Samos against the Athenian Empire lasted from 441 to 439 B.C. Aelian strangely fails to note that the proposal to commit genocide at Mytilene was reversed by a second meeting of the assembly on the following day. He also fails to mention the Athenian massacre at Melos in 416 B.C.

[b] Timotheus, a pupil of Isocrates, was an intermittently successful Athenian general, first elected in 378 B.C. He died in 354 B.C. Aelian has six further references to him in the *V.H.*

[c] The Greek is not easy to translate here; it may have been Aelian's intention to say that the Athenians were erecting a statue of Timotheus.

βίου καὶ τῆς ὄντως εὐδαιμονίας." ἐκ τούτων οὖν δῆλον ὡς ἑαυτὸν οὐ πάνυ τι εὐδαίμονα ἀπέφαινεν ὁ Τιμόθεος, ὅτι μὴ ἐν τούτοις ἀλλ' ἐν τῇ παρ' Ἀθηναίων δόξῃ καὶ τιμῇ ἦν.

11. Σωκράτης ἰδὼν[1] κατὰ τὴν ἀρχὴν τῶν τριάκοντα τοὺς ἐνδόξους ἀναιρουμένους καὶ τοὺς βαθύτατα[2] πλουτοῦντας ὑπὸ τῶν τυράννων ἐπιβουλευομένους, Ἀντισθένει φασὶ περιτυχόντα εἰπεῖν· "μή τί σοι μεταμέλει ὅτι μέγα καὶ σεμνὸν οὐδὲν ἐγενόμεθα ἐν τῷ βίῳ καὶ τοιοῦτοι οἵους ἐν τῇ τραγῳδίᾳ τοὺς μονάρχας ὁρῶμεν, Ἀτρέας τε ἐκείνους καὶ Θυέστας καὶ Ἀγαμέμνονας καὶ Αἰγίσθους; οὗτοι μὲν γὰρ ἀποσφαττόμενοι καὶ ἐκτραγῳδούμενοι[3] καὶ πονηρὰ δεῖπνα δειπνίζοντες[4] καὶ ἐσθίοντες ἑκάστοτε ἐκκαλύπτονται· οὐδεὶς δὲ οὕτως ἐγένετο τολμηρὸς οὐδὲ ἀναίσχυντος τραγῳδίας ποιητής, ὥστε εἰσαγαγεῖν εἰς δρᾶμα ἀποσφαττόμενον χορόν."[5]

12. Θεμιστοκλέους τοῦ Νεοκλέους οὐκ οἶδα εἰ ἐπαινεῖν χρὴ τοῦτο. ἐπεὶ γὰρ τῆς ἀσωτίας ἐπαύσατο Θεμιστοκλῆς ἀποκηρυχθεὶς ὑπὸ τοῦ πατρός, καὶ ὑπήρχετό πως τοῦ σωφρονεῖν καὶ τῶν μὲν ἑταιρῶν ἀπέστη, ἤρα δὲ ἔρωτα ἕτερον τὸν τῆς πολιτείας

[1] Σωκράτης ἰδὼν] Σωκράτην ἰδόντα Gesner
[2] τοὺς βαθύτατα anonymus (1733): βαρύτατα τοὺς codd.
[3] ἐκτραγῳδούμενοι] ἐκτραχηλιζόμενοι dubitanter Russell
[4] δειπνίζοντες Albini: δειπνοῦντες codd.
[5] χορόν Holstenius: χοῖρον codd.: τὸν Ἶρον Faber

life, what true good fortune!" From this it is clear that Timotheus did not regard himself as completely fortunate, because he did not share that kind of existence, but enjoyed honour and glory from the Athenians.

11. During the rule of the Thirty[a] Socrates, who saw famous men being destroyed and the really wealthy a target for the tyrants, is said to have met Antisthenes[b] [fr. 167 D.C.] and remarked: "Do you regret that we have not become grand and important, like the kings we see in tragedy, men like Atreus, Thyestes,[c] Agamemnon, and Aegisthus? They are always portrayed as victims of murder, as figures to be lamented, as preparing and eating evil banquets. No tragic poet has had the audacity or lack of decency to introduce into his play the slaughter of the chorus."[d]

12. I do not know whether Themistocles, son of Neocles, should be praised for the following action. When Themistocles gave up his intemperate habits after being disowned by his father he began to behave somewhat more reasonably, abandoned his mistresses, and conceived another passion—for Athenian politics. He began

[a] The Thirty Tyrants imposed a short-lived dictatorship on Athens in 404 B.C. at the end of the Peloponnesian War.

[b] Antisthenes (ca. 445–360 B.C.) was considered the founder of the Cynic school of philosophy.

[c] Thyestes' sons were murdered by his brother Atreus, who cut them up, boiled them, and served them at dinner to Thyestes. Apart from Seneca's extant play *Thyestes* Aelian could in principle have read plays on the same macabre theme by numerous other writers, including Sophocles, Euripides, and Agathon.

[d] The chorus represent ordinary people who are not targets for disaster; Socrates expects to be safe in the same way.

τῶν Ἀθηναίων καὶ θερμότατα ἐπεχείρει ταῖς ἀρχαῖς καὶ ἑαυτὸν ἔσπευδεν εἶναι πρῶτον, ἔλεγε, φασί, πρὸς τοὺς γνωρίμους· "τί δ' ἂν ἐμοῦ[1] δοίητε, ὃς οὔπω φθονοῦμαι;" ὅστις δὲ ἐρᾷ φθονεῖσθαι, τοῦτο δή που τὸ τοῦ Εὐριπίδου, περιβλέπεσθαι σπεύδει. ὅτι δὲ τοῦτο ἔστι κενόν, ὁ αὐτὸς Εὐριπίδης φησίν.

13. Ἐπετίθεντο τῷ Σωκράτει καὶ ἐπεβούλευον οἱ ἀμφὶ τὸν Ἄνυτον ὧν χάριν καὶ δι' ἃς αἰτίας λέλεκται πάλαι. ὑφορώμενοι δὲ τοὺς Ἀθηναίους καὶ δεδιότες ὅπως ποτὲ ἕξουσι πρὸς τὴν κατηγορίαν τοῦ ἀνδρός (πολὺ γὰρ ἦν τὸ τοῦ Σωκράτους ὄνομα διά τε τὰ ἄλλα καὶ ὅτι τοὺς σοφιστὰς ἤλεγχεν οὐδὲν ὑγιὲς ὄντας οὐδέ τι σπουδαῖον ἢ εἰδότας ἢ λέγοντας), ἐκ τούτων οὖν ἐβουλήθησαν πεῖραν καθεῖναι ὑπὲρ τῆς κατ' αὐτοῦ διαβολῆς. τὸ μὲν γὰρ ἄντικρυς ἀπενέγκασθαι γραφὴν κατ' αὐτοῦ παραχρῆμα οὐκ ἐδοκίμαζον δι' ἃ προεῖπον καὶ δι' ἐκεῖνα δέ, μή ποτε ἄρα ἀγριάναντες οἱ φίλοι οἱ τοῦ Σωκράτους ἐξάψωσι κατ' αὐτῶν τοὺς δικαστάς, εἶτα <αὐτοί>[2] τι πάθωσι κακὸν ἀνήκεστον, ἅτε συκοφαντοῦντες ἄνδρα οὐ μόνον οὐδενὸς αἴτιον κακοῦ τῇ πόλει, ἐκ δὲ τῶν ἐναντίων καὶ κόσμον ταῖς Ἀθήναις ὄντα.

Τί οὖν ἐπινοοῦσιν; Ἀριστοφάνην τὸν τῆς κωμῳδίας ποιητήν, βωμολόχον ἄνδρα καὶ γελοῖον ὄντα καὶ εἶναι σπεύδοντα, ἀναπείθουσι κωμῳδῆσαι τὸν

[1] ἐμοῦ Casaubon: ἐμοὶ codd.
[2] supplevi

a most enthusiastic pursuit of office and tried to make himself the foremost citizen. According to reports he used to say to his acquaintances: "What esteem could you have for me, as I am not yet the subject of envy?" The man who likes to be envied, in the words of Euripides, seeks prominence;[a] and that is empty, as Euripides again tells us.[b]

13. Anytus and his associates attacked and plotted against Socrates; their motives and reasons have been stated long ago. But they were suspicious of the Athenians, and fearful of how they would respond to the accusation against him. Socrates had made a great name for himself, in a variety of ways, including his refutation of the sophists, men of no merit, without any serious knowledge or claims to be heard. These men they decided to exploit as an experiment for their attack upon him. The idea of a direct charge against him in court without delay was rejected, both for the reasons I have already given and because of a fear that Socrates' friends would be provoked into stirring up the jury against them and they might then suffer disaster, because they would have made malicious accusations against a man who not only had done no harm to the city but on the contrary was an ornament to Athens.

So what was their plan? They persuaded the comic poet Aristophanes, who was—and aimed to be—a vulgar and ridiculous humorist, to lampoon Socrates, making of

[a] *Iphigenia in Aulis* 428–429: "The great are famous and highly regarded by all mankind."

[b] *Phoenissae* 551: "Is admiration to be treasured? No, it is empty."

Σωκράτη, ταῦτα δήπου τὰ περιφερόμενα, ὡς ἦν ἀδολέσχης, λέγων τε αὖ καὶ τὸν ἥττω λόγον ἀπέφαινε κρείττονα, καὶ εἰσῆγε ξένους δαίμονας καὶ οὐκ ᾔδει[1] θεοὺς οὐδ' ἐτίμα, τὰ δὲ αὐτὰ ταῦτα καὶ τοὺς προσιόντας αὐτῷ ἐδίδασκέ τε καὶ εἰδέναι ἀνέπειθεν. ὁ δὲ Ἀριστοφάνης λαβόμενος ὑποθέσεως εὖ μάλα ἀνδρικῶς,[2] ὑποσπείρας γέλωτα καὶ τὸ ἐκ τῶν μέτρων αἱμύλον καὶ τὸν ἄριστον τῶν Ἑλλήνων λαβὼν ὑπόθεσιν (οὐ γάρ οἱ κατὰ Κλέωνος ἦν τὸ δρᾶμα, οὐδὲ ἐκωμῴδει Λακεδαιμονίους ἢ Θηβαίους ἢ Περικλέα αὐτόν, ἀλλ' ἄνδρα τοῖς τε ἄλλοις θεοῖς φίλον καὶ δὴ καὶ μάλιστα τῷ Ἀπόλλωνι), ἅτε οὖν ἄηθες πρᾶγμα καὶ ὅραμα παράδοξον ἐν σκηνῇ καὶ κωμῳδίᾳ Σωκράτης, πρῶτον μὲν ἐξέπληξεν ἡ κωμῳδία τῷ ἀδοκήτῳ τοὺς Ἀθηναίους, εἶτα [δὲ][3] καὶ φύσει φθονεροὺς ὄντας[4] καὶ τοῖς ἀρίστοις βασκαίνειν προῃρημένους,[5] οὐ μόνον τοῖς ἐν τῇ πολιτείᾳ καὶ ταῖς ἀρχαῖς ἀλλ' ἔτι καὶ πλέον τοῖς εὐδοκιμοῦσιν ἢ ἐν λόγοις ἀγαθοῖς ἢ ἐν βίου σεμνότητι, ἄκουσμα ἔδοξεν ἥδιστον αἵδε αἱ Νεφέλαι καὶ ἐκρότουν τὸν ποιητὴν ὡς οὔποτε ἄλλοτε καὶ ἐβόων νικᾶν καὶ προσέταττον τοῖς κριταῖς ἄνωθεν Ἀριστοφάνην ἀλλὰ μὴ ἄλλον γράφειν.[6] καὶ τὰ μὲν τοῦ δράματος τοιαῦτα.

[1] ᾔδει] ᾐδεῖτο Jacobs [2] ἀνδρικῶς Gesner: -ῆς codd.
[3] del. Her. [4] φθονεροὺς ὄντας] -οῖς οὖσι Gesner
[5] προῃρημένους x: προαιρουμένοις V
[6] γράφειν] κρίνειν Cobet

course the well-known charges against him, that he was a windbag, that when he talked he would make the weaker argument seem superior, that he introduced foreign deities, was an atheist and did not honour the gods; that he taught his associates these same doctrines and persuaded them to believe accordingly.[a] Aristophanes applied himself to the task with great energy, adding a little humour to it and some metrical versatility, and making the best man in Greece his theme. His play was not aimed at Cleon;[b] it was not a satire on the Spartans, the Thebans, or Pericles himself, but on a man loved by the gods as a whole and especially by Apollo. Since Socrates was an unusual subject, an odd figure on the stage in a comedy,[c] the play at first astounded the Athenians by its unexpected theme. Later, as they had a natural tendency to jealousy and made a habit of criticising the best people, not only those in political life and officeholders, but to an even greater degree men famous for their literary accomplishments or honourable behaviour, this play, *The Clouds*, was thought to be a very agreeable entertainment, and they applauded the poet. They shouted that he should win the prize, and they told the judges to put Aristophanes, and no one else, at the top of their list.

[a] This story was widely believed in antiquity and the Renaissance; see W. Süss, *Aristophanes und die Nachwelt* (Leipzig, 1911), p. 17. But it is chronologically absurd, as the *Clouds* was produced in 423 (winning third prize), and Socrates' trial took place in 399 B.C. Aelian has allowed himself to be unduly impressed by what Socrates is made to say in Plato's *Apology* 18 a.

[b] Aristophanes' *Knights* is largely an attack on Cleon.

[c] Here Aelian is quite wrong; Old Comedy was full of attacks on prominent or eccentric Athenians.

Ὁ δὲ Σωκράτης σπάνιον μὲν ἐπεφοίτα τοῖς θεάτροις, εἴ ποτε δὲ Εὐριπίδης ὁ τῆς τραγῳδίας ποιητὴς ἠγωνίζετο καινοῖς τραγῳδοῖς, τότε γε ἀφικνεῖτο. καὶ Πειραιοῖ δὲ ἀγωνιζομένου τοῦ Εὐριπίδου καὶ ἐκεῖ κατῄει· ἔχαιρε γὰρ τῷ ἀνδρὶ δηλονότι διά τε τὴν σοφίαν αὐτοῦ καὶ τὴν ἐν τοῖς μέτροις ἀρετήν. ἤδη δέ ποτε αὐτὸν ἐρεσχελῶν Ἀλκιβιάδης ὁ Κλεινίου καὶ[1] Κριτίας ὁ Καλλαίσχρου καὶ κωμῳδῶν ἀκοῦσαι παρελθόντα εἰς τὸ θέατρον ἐξεβιάσαντο. ὁ δὲ αὐτοῖς οὐκ ἠρέσκετο, ἀλλὰ δεινῶς κατεφρόνει, ἅτε ἀνὴρ σώφρων καὶ δίκαιος καὶ ἀγαθὸς καὶ ἐπὶ τούτοις σοφός, ἀνδρῶν κερτόμων καὶ ὑβριστῶν καὶ ὑγιὲς λεγόντων οὐδέν· ἅπερ ἐλύπει δεινῶς αὐτούς.

Καὶ ταῦτα οὖν τῆς κωμῳδίας ἦν αὐτῷ τὰ σπέρματα, ἀλλ᾽ οὐ μόνον ἃ παρὰ τοῦ Ἀνύτου καὶ Μελήτου ὡμολόγηται. εἰκὸς δὲ καὶ χρηματίσασθαι ὑπὲρ τούτων Ἀριστοφάνην. καὶ γὰρ βουλομένων, μᾶλλον δὲ ἐκ παντὸς συκοφαντῆσαι τὸν Σωκράτη σπευδόντων ἐκείνων, καὶ αὐτὸν [δὲ][2] πένητα ἅμα καὶ κατάρατον ὄντα, τί παράδοξον ἦν ἀργύριον λαβεῖν ἐπ᾽ οὐδενὶ ὑγιεῖ; καὶ ὑπὲρ μὲν τούτων αὐτὸς οἶδεν. εὐδοκίμει δ᾽ οὖν αὐτῷ τὸ δρᾶμα, καὶ γάρ τοι καὶ τὸ τοῦ Κρατίνου τοῦτο συνέβη εἴ ποτε ἄλλοτε καὶ τότε, τῷ θεάτρῳ νοσῆσαι τὰς φρένας. καὶ ἅτε ὄντων Διονυσίων πάμπολύ τι χρῆμα τῶν Ἑλλήνων σπουδῇ τῆς θέας ἀφίκετο. περιφερομένου τοίνυν ἐν τῇ σκηνῇ τοῦ Σωκράτους καὶ ὀνομαζομένου πολλάκις, οὐκ ἂν

[1] *καὶ* Kor.: ἢ codd. [2] del. Her.

That is the story of the play. But Socrates did not often go to the theatre. However, if the tragic poet Euripides was entering the competition with new plays, then he would go. If Euripides was competing at the Piraeus, he would even go down there, since he enjoyed his work, obviously because of its wisdom and poetic quality. Alcibiades son of Clinias and Critias son of Callaeschrus once teased him and cajoled him into going to the theatre to see comedies as well. He did not get any pleasure from them and, being a man of sound judgement, just, good, and in addition sagacious, was severe in his contempt for men who dealt in insults and abuse and had nothing sensible to say. These views annoyed them greatly.

These facts were the germ of the comedy written against him; it was not just the issues known to have been raised by Anytus and Meletus. Probably Aristophanes made money out of this; given that they wished, indeed were making every effort to bring malicious charges against Socrates, while the poet was both a poor man and morally depraved, is it implausible that he should have accepted money for an immoral purpose? About this he alone knows the truth. But his play was famous. In fact, if ever the remark of Cratinus [fr. 395 K.-A.] was a reality, it was then: the theatre audience lost its wits.[a] Since the Dionysia were being celebrated, a very large number of Greeks came out of interest to watch.[b] When Socrates was moving around on the stage and referred to fre-

[a] Cratinus was the first great master of Old Comedy, senior to Aristophanes by a generation.

[b] Although Aelian's historical perspective is often faulty, he is right in saying that many foreigners might be present at the Dionysia festival in the spring.

δὲ θαυμάσαιμι εἰ καὶ βλεπομένου ἐν τοῖς ὑποκριταῖς (δῆλα γὰρ δὴ ὅτι καὶ οἱ σκευοποιοὶ ἔπλασαν αὐτὸν ὡς ὅτι μάλιστα ἐξεικάσαντες), ἀλλ' οἵ γε ξένοι (τὸν γὰρ κωμῳδούμενον ἠγνόουν) θροῦς παρ' αὐτῶν ἐπανίστατο, καὶ ἐζήτουν ὅστις ποτὲ οὗτος ὁ Σωκράτης ἐστίν. ὅπερ οὖν ἐκεῖνος αἰσθόμενος (καὶ γάρ τοι καὶ παρῆν οὐκ ἄλλως οὐδὲ ἐκ τύχης, εἰδὼς δὲ ὅτι κωμῳδοῦσιν αὐτόν· καὶ δὴ καὶ ἐν καλῷ τοῦ θεάτρου ἐκάθητο), ἵνα οὖν λύσῃ τὴν τῶν ξένων ἀπορίαν, ἐξαναστὰς παρ' ὅλον τὸ δρᾶμα ἀγωνιζομένων τῶν ὑποκριτῶν ἑστὼς ἐβλέπετο. τοσοῦτον ἄρα περιῆν τῷ Σωκράτει τοῦ κωμῳδίας καὶ Ἀθηναίων καταφρονεῖν.

14. Γελοῖος ἐκεῖνος ὁ Ξέρξης ἦν εἴ γε θαλάσσης μὲν καὶ γῆς κατεφρόνει τῆς Διὸς τέχνης, ἑαυτῷ δὲ εἰργάζετο καινὰς ὁδοὺς καὶ πλοῦν ἀήθη, δεδούλωτο δὲ πλατάνῳ καὶ ἐθαύμαζε τὸ δένδρον. ἐν Λυδίᾳ γοῦν, φασίν, ἰδὼν φυτὸν εὐμέγεθες πλατάνου καὶ[1] τὴν ἡμέραν ἐκείνην κατέμεινεν οὐδέν τι δεόμενος καὶ ἐχρήσατο σταθμῷ τῇ ἐρημίᾳ τῇ περὶ τὴν πλάτανον. ἀλλὰ καὶ ἐξῆψεν αὐτῆς κόσμον πολυτελῆ, στρεπτοῖς καὶ ψελλίοις τιμῶν τοὺς κλάδους, καὶ μελεδωνὸν αὐτῇ κατέλιπεν, ὥσπερ ἐρωμένῃ φύλακα καὶ φρουρόν. ἐκ δὲ τούτων τί τῷ δένδρῳ καλὸν ἀπήντησεν; ὁ μὲν γὰρ κόσμος ὁ ἐπίκτητος καὶ μηδὲν αὐτῷ προσήκων ἄλλως ἐκρέματο καὶ συνεμάχετο εἰς ὥραν οὐδέν,

[1] καὶ del. Her.

quently (and I should not be surprised if he was also recognisable among the figures on stage, for it is clear that the makers of the masks had portrayed him with an excellent likeness) the foreigners, who did not know the person being satirised, began to murmur and ask who this man Socrates was. When he heard that—he was in fact present, not as a result of luck or chance, but because he knew that he was the subject of the play, and he sat in a prominent position in the theatre—at any rate, in order to put an end to the foreigners' ignorance, he stood up and remained standing in full view throughout the play as the actors performed it. So great was Socrates' contempt for comedy and the Athenians.

14. The famous king Xerxes was ridiculous, if it is true that he despised sea and land, the handiwork of Zeus, manufactured for himself novel roads and abnormal sea routes,[a] and yet was the devotee of a plane tree, which he admired.[b] In Lydia, they say, he saw a large specimen of a plane tree, and stopped for that day without any need. He made the wilderness around the tree his camp, and attached to it expensive ornaments, paying homage to the branches with necklaces and bracelets. He left a caretaker for it, like a guard to provide security, as if it were a woman he loved. What benefit accrued to the tree as a result? The ornaments it had acquired, which were quite inappropriate to it, hung on it without serving any pur-

[a] An allusion to two notorious episodes of the Persian Wars: in 480 Xerxes used his ships to form a makeshift bridge across the Hellespont, and some years before he had had a canal cut through Mount Athos; see Herodotus 7.22–24, 33–38.

[b] Herodotus refers briefly to the tree at 7.31.

ἐπεὶ τοῦ φυτοῦ κάλλος ἐκεῖνό ἐστιν· εὐγενεῖς οἱ κλάδοι καὶ ἡ κόμη πολλὴ καὶ στερεὸν τὸ πρέμνον καὶ αἱ ῥίζαι ἐν βάθει καὶ διασείοντες οἱ ἄνεμοι καὶ ἀμφιλαφὴς ἡ ἐξ αὐτοῦ σκιὰ καὶ ἀναστρέφουσαι αἱ ὧραι καὶ ὕδωρ τὸ μὲν διὰ τῶν ὀχετῶν ἐκτρέφον, τὸ δὲ ἐξ οὐρανοῦ ἐπάρδον· χλαμύδες δὲ αἱ Ξέρξου καὶ χρυσὸς ὁ τοῦ βαρβάρου καὶ τὰ ἄλλα δῶρα οὔτε πρὸς τὴν πλάτανον οὔτε πρὸς ἄλλο δένδρον εὐγενὲς ἦν.

15. Κλαζομενίων τινὲς εἰς τὴν Σπάρτην ἀφικόμενοι καὶ ὕβρει καὶ ἀλαζονείᾳ χρώμενοι τοὺς τῶν ἐφόρων θρόνους, ἔνθα εἰώθασι καθήμενοι χρηματίζειν καὶ τῶν πολιτικῶν ἕκαστα διατάττειν, ἀλλὰ τούτους γε τοὺς θρόνους ἀσβόλῳ κατέχρισαν. μαθόντες δὲ οἱ ἔφοροι οὐκ ἠγανάκτησαν, ἀλλὰ τὸν δημόσιον κήρυκα καλέσαντες προσέταξαν αὐτὸν[1] δημοσίᾳ κηρύξαι τοῦτο δὴ τὸ θαυμαζόμενον· "ἐξέστω Κλαζομενίοις ἀσχημονεῖν."

16. Φωκίωνος δὲ τοῦ Φώκου καὶ τοῦτο ἔγωγε ἔγνων καλόν· παρελθὼν γὰρ εἰς τοὺς Ἀθηναίους ἐκκλησίας οὔσης, ἐπεί τι αὐτοῖς ἐμέμφετο ἀγνωμονοῦσι, πάνυ σφόδρα πεπαιδευμένως καὶ πληκτικῶς εἶπε· "βούλομαι μᾶλλόν τι ὑφ' ὑμῶν παθεῖν κακὸν αὐτὸς ἢ αὐτός[2] τι ὑμᾶς κακῶς δρᾶσαι."

17. Ἡ τῶν ἐν Πέρσαις μάγων σοφία τά τε ἄλλα οἶδεν ὁπόσα αὐτοῖς εἰδέναι θέμις καὶ οὖν καὶ μαν-

[1] αὐτὸν] αὐτῷ Kor.
[2] αὐτός del. Her.

pose and made no contribution to its appearance, since the beauty of a tree consists of fine branches, abundant leaves, a sturdy trunk, deep roots, movement in the wind, shadow spreading all around, change in accordance with the passing of seasons, with irrigation channels to support it and rain water to sustain it. Xerxes' robes, barbarian gold, and the other offerings did not ennoble the plane or any other tree.

15. Some men from Clazomenae[a] who had gone to Sparta behaved in arrogant and insolent fashion. The seats of the ephors, in which they normally sit in order to perform their duties and deal with all state affairs, these seats the men covered with soot. When the ephors learned of this they were not annoyed. Instead they summoned the town crier and instructed him to make the following much admired public announcement: "Let the men of Clazomenae be given leave to misbehave."[b]

16. I have learned of the following fine act by Phocion son of Phocus. Appearing before the Athenians at an assembly, since he had some criticism to make of their poor judgement, he made his point in a very cultivated and effective way by saying: "I would rather suffer some harm at your hands than do you any harm myself."

17. The wisdom of the Persian magi[c] included a number of skills which it was their privilege to possess, and

[a] A city near Smyrna, birthplace of the philosopher Anaxagoras.

[b] Plutarch, *Moralia* 232 F–233 A, tells a similar story about a group of visitors from Chios.

[c] The caste of priests and wise men who interpreted dreams. The Persian kings are those mentioned above at 1.32–34.

τεύεσθαι. οἵπερ οὖν καὶ προεῖπον τὴν τοῦ Ὤχου περὶ τοὺς ὑπηκόους ἀγριότητα καὶ τὸ φονικὸν αὐτοῦ, διά τινων ἀπορρήτων συμβόλων καταγνόντες τοῦτο. ὅτε γὰρ Ἀρταξέρξου τοῦ πατρὸς αὐτοῦ τελευτήσαντος εἰς τὴν βασιλείαν τῶν Περσῶν ὁ Ὦχος παρῆλθεν, οἱ μάγοι προσέταξαν τῶν εὐνούχων τινὶ τῶν πλησίον παρεστώτων φυλάξαι τὸν Ὦχον τῆς τραπέζης παρατεθείσης τίνι πρῶτον τῶν παρακειμένων ἐπιχειρεῖ. καὶ ὁ μὲν εἱστήκει τηρῶν τοῦτο, ὁ δὲ Ὦχος τὰς χεῖρας ἐκτείνας τῇ μὲν δεξιᾷ τῶν μαχαιρίων τῶν παρακειμένων ἓν ἔλαβε, τῇ δὲ ἑτέρᾳ τὸν μέγιστον τῶν ἄρτων προσειλκύσατο, καὶ ἐπιθεὶς ἐπ' αὐτὸν τῶν κρεῶν, εἶτα τέμνων ἤσθιεν ἀφειδῶς. ἅπερ ἀκούσαντες οἱ μάγοι δύο ταῦτα ἐμαντεύσαντο, εὐετηρίαν τὴν ἐξ ὡρῶν καὶ εὐφορίαν [τὴν][1] παρὰ τὸν τῆς ἀρχῆς αὐτοῦ χρόνον καὶ πολλοὺς φόνους. καὶ οὐ διεψεύσαντο.

18. Τιμόθεος ὁ Κόνωνος <ὁ>[2] στρατηγὸς τῶν Ἀθηναίων ἀποστάς ποτε τῶν δείπνων τῶν πολυτελῶν καὶ τῶν ἑστιάσεων τῶν στρατηγικῶν ἐκείνων, παραληφθεὶς ὑπὸ Πλάτωνος εἰς τὸ ἐν Ἀκαδημίᾳ συμπόσιον καὶ ἑστιαθεὶς ἀφελῶς ἅμα καὶ μουσικῶς ἔφη πρὸς τοὺς οἰκείους ἐπανελθὼν ὅτι ἄρα οἱ παρὰ Πλάτωνι δειπνοῦντες καὶ τῇ ὑστεραίᾳ καλῶς διάγουσιν. ἐκ δὴ τούτου διέβαλλε[3] Τιμόθεος τὰ πολυτελῆ δεῖπνα καὶ φορτικὰ ὡς πάντως εἰς τὴν ὑστεραίαν οὐκ εὐφραίνοντα. λόγος δὲ καὶ ἐκεῖνος ἀδελφὸς τῷ προειρημένῳ καὶ ταὐτὸν νοῶν, οὐ μὴν

one of these was prophecy. It was they who predicted the ferocity of Ochus towards his subjects and his murderous tendencies, recognising them by means of some secret signs. When, on the death of his father Artaxerxes, Ochus became king of Persia, the magi ordered one of the eunuchs in his entourage to watch him and see which dish he would take first when dinner was served. The eunuch took up his position to observe and Ochus stretched out his hands; with the right hand he took one of the knives laid out on the table and with the other he picked up the largest piece of bread, put some meat on it, cut it up, and ate greedily. On hearing about this the magi made two prophecies, that there would be good seasons and rich crops during the period of his reign, and many murders. And they were not mistaken.

18. Timotheus son of Conon, the Athenian general, once gave up the luxurious dinners and well-known rich entertainments offered to generals. He was taken by Plato to a symposium in the Academy and given a dinner that was both simple and civilised. On returning to his family he said: "Those who dine with Plato are in good form the following day." After this experience Timotheus was critical of lavish and vulgar dinners because they certainly give no pleasure the next day. There is another story in circulation akin to the one I have just told, and with the same moral although not in the same words.

---

[1] del. Russell

[2] suppl. Her.

[3] διέβαλλε Kor.: -αλε codd.

τὰ αὐτὰ λέγων περίεισιν, ὅτι ἄρα τῇ ὑστεραίᾳ ὁ Τιμόθεος περιτυχὼν τῷ Πλάτωνι εἶπεν· "ὑμεῖς, ὦ Πλάτων, εὖ δειπνεῖτε μᾶλλον εἰς τὴν ὑστεραίαν ἢ εἰς τὴν παροῦσαν."

19. Ἀλέξανδρος ὅτε ἐνίκησε Δαρεῖον καὶ τὴν Περσῶν ἀρχὴν κατεκτήσατο, μέγα ἐφ᾿ ἑαυτῷ φρονῶν καὶ ὑπὸ τῆς εὐτυχίας τῆς περιλαβούσης αὐτὸν τότε ἐκθεούμενος, ἐπέστειλε τοῖς Ἕλλησι θεὸν αὐτὸν ψηφίσασθαι. γελοίως γε· οὐ γὰρ ἅπερ οὖν ἐκ τῆς φύσεως οὐκ εἶχε, ταῦτα ἐκ τῶν ἀνθρώπων αἰτῶν ἐκεῖνος ἐκέρδαινεν. ἄλλοι μὲν οὖν ἄλλα ἐψηφίσαντο, Λακεδαιμόνιοι δὲ ἐκεῖνα· "ἐπειδὴ Ἀλέξανδρος βούλεται θεὸς εἶναι, ἔστω θεός," Λακωνικῶς τε ἅμα καὶ κατὰ τὸν ἐπιχώριόν σφισι τρόπον ἐλέγξαντες τὴν ἔμπληξιν οἱ Λακεδαιμόνιοι τοῦ Ἀλεξάνδρου.

20. Ἀντίγονόν φασι τὸν βασιλέα δημοτικὸν καὶ πρᾶον γενέσθαι. καὶ ὅτῳ μὲν σχολὴ τὰ κατ᾿ αὐτὸν εἰδέναι καὶ αὐτὰ ἕκαστα ἐξετάζειν ὑπὲρ τοῦ ἀνδρός, εἴσεται ἑτέρωθεν· εἰρήσεται δ᾿ οὖν αὐτοῦ καὶ πάνυ πρᾶον καὶ ἄτυφον ὃ μέλλω λέγειν. ὁ Ἀντίγονος οὗτος ὁρῶν τὸν υἱὸν τοῖς ὑπηκόοις χρώμενον βιαιότερόν τε καὶ θρασύτερον "οὐκ οἶσθα," εἶπεν "ὦ παῖ, τὴν βασιλείαν ἡμῶν ἔνδοξον εἶναι δουλείαν;" καὶ τὰ μὲν τοῦ Ἀντιγόνου πρὸς τὸν παῖδα πάνυ ἡμέρως ἔχει καὶ φιλανθρώπως· ὅτῳ δὲ οὐ δοκεῖ ταύτῃ, ἀλλ᾿ ἐκεῖνός γε οὐ δοκεῖ μοι βασιλικὸν ἄνδρα εἰδέναι οὐδὲ πολιτικόν, τυραννικῷ δὲ συμβιῶσαι μᾶλλον.

According to it Timotheus met Plato on the following day and said: "Plato, you dine well, but with tomorrow in view rather than today."[a]

19. When Alexander had defeated Darius and taken over the Persian empire he was very proud of his achievement. Feeling himself raised to the level of divinity by the good fortune which had now overtaken him, he sent an instruction to the Greeks to vote him divine honours. This was ridiculous; he could not acquire on demand from the rest of mankind what nature had not endowed him with. The cities passed various decrees, and the Spartans resolved as follows: "Since Alexander wishes to be a god, let him be a god." In laconic fashion and in accordance with their own tradition the Spartans deflated Alexander's madness.[b]

20. They say that king Antigonus was popular and lenient.[c] Anyone who has leisure to learn about him and investigate all the details for himself will get information from other sources. But what I am about to report of him will serve as proof of his very mild and unpretentious character. This Antigonus saw his son treating their subjects in rather violent and overbearing fashion. "Don't you know, my boy," he said, "that our monarchy is a glorious form of servitude?" Antigonus' remark to his son is very mild and humane. A person who thinks otherwise seems to me not to know what makes a king or a politician, but to have lived instead under tyranny.

[a] This story is given in Athenaeus 419 CD in both versions; this may well be Aelian's source. [b] Cf. 5.12 below.

[c] Antigonus II Gonatas, king of Macedonia 276–239 B.C., mentioned again below at 3.5, 3.17, 7.14, 9.26, and 12.25. On his aphorism see H. Volkmann, *Historia* 16 (1967): 155–161.

21. Ἀγάθωνος ἤρα τοῦ ποιητοῦ Παυσανίας ὁ ἐκ Κεραμέων. καὶ τοῦτο μὲν διατεθρύληται· ὃ δὲ μὴ εἰς πάντας πεφοίτηκεν, ἀλλ' ἐγὼ ἐρῶ. εἰς Ἀρχελάου ποτὲ ἀφίκοντο ὅ τε ἐραστὴς καὶ ὁ ἐρώμενος οὗτοι. ἦν δὲ ἄρα ὁ Ἀρχέλαος ἐρωτικὸς οὐχ ἧττον ἢ καὶ φιλόμουσος. ἐπεὶ τοίνυν ἑώρα διαφερομένους πρὸς ἀλλήλους τόν τε Παυσανίαν καὶ τὸν Ἀγάθωνα πολλάκις, οἰόμενος τὸν ἐραστὴν ὑπὸ τῶν παιδικῶν παρορᾶσθαι, ἤρετο ἄρα τὸν Ἀγάθωνα ὁ Ἀρχέλαος τί βουλόμενος οὕτω πυκνὰ ἀπεχθάνεται τῷ πάντων μάλιστα φιλοῦντι αὐτόν. ὁ δὲ "ἐγώ σοι" ἔφη "φράσω, βασιλεῦ. οὔτε γάρ εἰμι πρὸς αὐτὸν δύσερις, οὔτε ἀγροικίᾳ πράττω τοῦτο· εἰ δέ τι καὶ ἐγὼ ἠθῶν ἐπαΐω τῇ τε ἄλλῃ καὶ ἐκ ποιητικῆς, ἥδιστον εὑρίσκω εἶναι τοῖς ἐρῶσι πρὸς τὰ παιδικὰ ἐκ διαφορᾶς καταλλάσσεσθαι, καὶ πεπίστευκα οὐδὲν αὐτοῖς οὕτως ἀπαντᾶν τερπνόν. τούτου γοῦν τοῦ ἡδέος πολλάκις αὐτῷ μεταδίδωμι, ἐρίζων πρὸς αὐτὸν πλεονάκις· εὐφραίνεται γὰρ καταλυομένου μου τὴν πρὸς αὐτὸν ἔριν συνεχῶς, ὁμαλῶς δὲ καὶ συνήθως προσιόντος οὐκ εἴσεται τὴν διαφορότητα." ἐπῄνεσε ταῦτα ὁ Ἀρχέλαος, ὡς λόγος.

Ἤρα δέ, φασι, τοῦ αὐτοῦ Ἀγάθωνος τούτου καὶ Εὐριπίδης ὁ ποιητής, καὶ τὸν Χρύσιππον τὸ δρᾶμα αὐτῷ χαριζόμενος λέγεται διαφροντίσαι. καὶ εἰ μὲν σαφὲς τοῦτο, ἀποφήνασθαι οὐκ οἶδα, λεγόμενον δ' οὖν αὐτὸ οἶδα ἐν τοῖς μάλιστα.

21. Pausanias from the Cerameis[a] was the lover of the poet Agathon. This fact is notorious, but I will say something that is not universally known. The two lovers once went to visit Archelaus.[b] It turned out that he was as much interested in love as in the arts. So when he saw Pausanias and Agathon frequently in disagreement, thinking the lover neglected by his favourite, Archelaus asked Agathon what his intention was in giving such frequent offence to the man who loved him above all others. "I will tell you, your majesty," he replied. "I am not quarrelsome with him, nor am I uncouth in what I do. But if I know anything about human behaviour from poetry or from other sources, I have found that lovers like best of all reconciliation with their beloved, and I am sure that nothing gives them so much pleasure. At any rate I often give him this pleasure by arguing with him repeatedly. He cheers up at once when I stop being argumentative. But if I approach him in my usual equable manner he will not appreciate the difference."[c] Archelaus applauded these views, according to the story.

They say the poet Euripides was also in love with this same Agathon. He is said to have composed the play *Chrysippus*[d] in his honour. I am not able to state this as a fact, but I can say that it is very frequently asserted.

[a] The name of an Attic deme, part of the tribe Acamantis.

[b] King of Macedon 413–399 B.C. Both Euripides and Agathon were said to have taken up residence at his court. See also 13.4 below.

[c] Cf. Terence, *Andria* 555: *amantium irae amoris redintegratio est* (no. 1402 in R. Tosi, *Dizionario delle sentenze latine e greche*, Milan, 1991, p. 634).

[d] A lost play, produced along with the extant *Phoenissae* in the period 411–409 B.C.

22. Εὐνομωτάτους[1] γενέσθαι καὶ Μαντινέας ἀκούω οὐδὲν ἧττον Λοκρῶν οὐδὲ Κρητῶν οὐδὲ Λακεδαιμονίων αὐτῶν οὐδ᾽ Ἀθηναίων· σεμνὸν γάρ τι χρῆμα καὶ τὸ Σόλωνος ἐγένετο, εἰ καὶ μετὰ ταῦτα Ἀθηναῖοι κατὰ μικρὸν τῶν νόμων τινὰς τῶν ἐξ αὐτοῦ γραφέντων αὐτοῖς διέφθειραν.

23. Νικόδωρος δὲ ὁ πύκτης ἐν τοῖς εὐδοκιμωτάτοις Μαντινέων γενόμενος, ἀλλὰ ὀψὲ τῆς ἡλικίας καὶ μετὰ τὴν ἄθλησιν νομοθέτης αὐτοῖς ἐγένετο, μακρῷ τοῦτο ἄμεινον πολιτευσάμενος τῇ πατρίδι τῶν κηρυγμάτων τῶν ἐν τοῖς σταδίοις. φασὶ δὲ αὐτῷ Διαγόραν τὸν Μήλιον συνθεῖναι τοὺς νόμους ἐραστὴν γενόμενον.

Εἶχον <δέ>[2] τι καὶ περαιτέρω ὑπὲρ Νικοδώρου εἰπεῖν· ὡς δ᾽ ἂν μὴ δοκοίην καὶ τὸν ἔπαινον τὸν τοῦ Διαγόρου προσπαραλαμβάνειν, εἰς τοσοῦτον διηνύσθω τὰ τοῦ λόγου. θεοῖς γὰρ ἐχθρὸς Διαγόρας, καὶ οὔ μοι ἥδιον ἐπὶ πλέον[3] μεμνῆσθαι αὐτοῦ.

24. Ἤδη τινὲς τὴν Μίλωνος τοῦ Κροτωνιάτου περιφερομένην ῥώμην ἐξέβαλον, τοιαῦτα ὑπὲρ αὐτοῦ λέγοντες. Μίλωνος τούτου τὴν ῥοιάν, ἣν ἐν τῇ χειρὶ κατεῖχεν, οὐδεὶς τῶν ἀντιπάλων ἑλεῖν[4] ἐδύνατο· ἡ δὲ ἐρωμένη αὐτοῦ ῥᾳστα αὐτὴν ἐξῄρει, φιλονικοῦσα πρὸς αὐτὸν πολλάκις. ἐκ δὴ τούτου νοεῖν ἔσται ὅτι

[1] Εὐνομωτάτους Eustathius 1860.52: Ἐνν- codd.
[2] suppl. Her.
[3] πλέον Cobet: πλεῖστον codd.
[4] ἑλεῖν] ἐξελεῖν Kor.

22. I learn that the Mantineans also had excellent laws, no less than the Locrians, the Cretans, even the Spartans and the Athenians. Solon's constitution was an object of veneration, even if later the Athenians gradually spoiled[a] some of the laws he had drafted for them.[b]

23. The boxer Nicodorus, one of the most famous citizens of Mantinea, late in his life and after his athletic achievements, became a legislator, thus performing much greater services to his native land than he had by being proclaimed victor in the sports arena. They say that Diagoras of Melos, who had become his lover, drafted the laws for him.

I had something further to report about Nicodorus, but in order not to give the impression of introducing praise of Diagoras, let me say no more, because Diagoras was an enemy of the gods and it does not give me pleasure to mention him at length.[c]

24. In the past some people have belittled the celebrated physical strength of Milo of Croton. They have told stories of him such as the following: when this Milo held a pomegranate in his hand none of his competitors could remove it, but his girl friend very easily extracted it, challenging him frequently. From this one can tell that

[a] The verb could be translated "annulled."

[b] The legislation of Solon, archon in 594–3 B.C., was outstandingly successful in resolving acute economic and social problems. He was included in the list of the Seven Sages.

[c] But he figures in the list in ch. 31 below. Diagoras was one of the few atheists of antiquity; he was sufficiently well known for Aristophanes to make jokes about him (*Birds* 1073, and cf. *Clouds* 830). He is the subject of a monograph by F. Jacoby, *Diagoras ὁ ἄθεος* (Berlin, 1959).

ὁ Μίλων ἰσχυρὸς μὲν τὸ σῶμα ἦν, ἀνδρεῖος δὲ τὴν ψυχὴν οὐκ ἦν.

25. Τὴν ἕκτην τοῦ μηνὸς τοῦ Θαργηλιῶνος πολλῶν καὶ ἀγαθῶν αἰτίαν γενέσθαι λέγουσιν οὐ μόνον τοῖς Ἀθηναίοις ἀλλὰ καὶ ἄλλοις πολλοῖς. αὐτίκα γοῦν Σωκράτης ἐν ταύτῃ ἐγένετο, καὶ Πέρσαι δὲ ἡττήθησαν τῇ ἡμέρᾳ ταύτῃ, καὶ Ἀθηναῖοι δὲ τῇ Ἀγροτέρᾳ ἀποθύουσι τὰς χιμαίρας τὰς τριακοσίας, κατὰ τὴν εὐχὴν τοῦ Μιλτιάδου δρῶντες τοῦτο. τοῦ δ' αὐτοῦ μηνὸς ἕκτῃ ἱσταμένου καὶ τὴν ἐν Πλαταιαῖς μάχην φασὶ γενέσθαι καὶ νικῆσαι τοὺς Ἕλληνας· τὴν γὰρ προτέραν ἧτταν αὐτῶν ἧς ἐμνήσθην [τὴν][1] ἐπ' Ἀρτεμισίῳ γεγονέναι. καὶ τὴν ἐν Μυκάλῃ δὲ τῶν Ἑλλήνων νίκην οὐκ ἄλλης ὡμολόγηται δῶρον ἡμέρας γενέσθαι ἢ ταύτης, εἴ γε κατὰ τὴν αὐτὴν ἐνίκων καὶ ἐν Πλαταιαῖς καὶ ἐν Μυκάλῃ. καὶ Ἀλέξανδρον δὲ τὸν Μακεδόνα, τὸν Φιλίππου παῖδα, τὰς πολλὰς μυριάδας τὰς τῶν βαρβάρων φθεῖραι καὶ αὐτὸν λέγουσιν ἕκτῃ ἱσταμένου, ὅτε καὶ Δαρεῖον καθεῖλεν Ἀλέξανδρος. [καὶ ὁμολογοῦσι τοῦ αὐτοῦ μηνὸς πάντα].[2] καὶ αὐτὸν δὲ τὸν Ἀλέξανδρον καὶ γενέσθαι καὶ ἀπελθεῖν τοῦ βίου τῇ αὐτῇ ἡμέρᾳ πεπίστευται.

26. Ἀριστοτέλης λέγει ὑπὸ τῶν Κροτωνιατῶν τὸν

[1] del. Per. et Jens
[2] del. Her. post πάντα suppl. ταῦτα Scheffer

---

[a] In the Athenian calendar Thargelion approximates to May.
[b] The defeat is the sea battle at Artemisium, mentioned a few

Milo was physically powerful but not strong in character.

25. They say that the sixth of Thargelion[a] brought much good fortune not only to Athens but to many other cities. It was for instance the date of Socrates' birth; the Persians were defeated on that day;[b] on it the Athenians sacrifice to the goddess Agrotera three hundred goats, acting in accordance with Miltiades' vow.[c] The sixth day at the beginning of the month is also said to be the date of the battle of Plataea, when the Greeks were victorious. The previous defeat of the Persians, which I have mentioned, was at Artemisium. The Hellenic victory at Mycale is also accepted as having been the gift of that day and no other, assuming that the victories of Plataea and Mycale were on the same day. Alexander of Macedon, son of Philip, is also reported to have crushed the many myriads of barbarians on the sixth of the month; that was when Alexander defeated Darius.[d] [It is agreed that all this took place in the same month.][e] And it is believed that Alexander himself was born and departed this life on the same day.

26. Aristotle [fr. 191 R.] says that Pythagoras was

lines below. [c] In 490 B.C. the Athenians, under Miltiades' command, vowed to sacrifice annually one goat for each Persian killed in the forthcoming battle; but the Persian dead at Marathon were so numerous that the number had to be limited to 500, according to Xenophon, *Anabasis* 3.2.12. Apart from giving a different figure Aelian is in error: the victory at Marathon was celebrated on the sixth of Boedromion, a day which happened also to be a festival in honour of Artemis. [d] A reference to the battle of Gaugamela; Darius was killed a few months later. [e] Aelian's concern in this ch. is with the day, not the month, and Hercher was almost certainly right to delete this sentence.

Πυθαγόραν[1] Ἀπόλλωνα Ὑπερβόρειον προσαγορεύεσθαι. κἀκεῖνα δὲ προσεπιλέγει ὁ τοῦ Νικομάχου, ὅτι τῆς αὐτῆς ἡμέρας ποτὲ <καὶ>[2] κατὰ τὴν αὐτὴν ὥραν καὶ ἐν Μεταποντίῳ ὤφθη ὑπὸ πολλῶν καὶ ἐν Κρότωνι, <καὶ ἐν Ὀλυμπίᾳ δὲ ἐν>[3] τῷ ἀγῶνι ἐξανιστάμενος, ἔνθα[4] καὶ τῶν μηρῶν ὁ Πυθαγόρας παρέφηνε τὸν ἕτερον χρυσοῦν. λέγει δὲ ὁ αὐτὸς καὶ[5] ὅτι ὑπὸ τοῦ Κόσα[6] ποταμοῦ διαβαίνων προσερρήθη· καὶ πολλούς φησιν ἀκηκοέναι τὴν πρόσρησιν ταύτην.

27. Ἀννίκερις ὁ Κυρηναῖος ἐπὶ [τῇ][7] ἱππείᾳ μέγα ἐφρόνει καὶ ἁρμάτων ἐλάσει. καὶ οὖν ποτε καὶ ἐβουλήθη Πλάτωνι ἐπιδείξασθαι τὴν τέχνην. ζεύξας οὖν τὸ ἅρμα περιήλασεν ἐν Ἀκαδημίᾳ δρόμους παμπόλλους, οὕτως ἀκριβῶς φυλάττων τοῦ δρόμου τὸν στίβον,[8] ὡς μὴ παραβαίνειν τὰς ἁρματοτροχιάς, ἀλλ' ἀεὶ κατ' αὐτὸν[9] ἰέναι. οἱ μὲν οὖν ἄλλοι πάντες ὥσπερ εἰκὸς ἐξεπλάγησαν, ὁ δὲ Πλάτων τὴν ὑπερβάλλουσαν αὐτοῦ σπουδὴν διέβαλεν εἰπών· "ἀδύνατόν ἐστι τὸν εἰς μικρὰ οὕτω καὶ οὐδενὸς ἄξια τοσαύτην φροντίδα κατατιθέμενον ὑπὲρ μεγάλων τινῶν σπουδάσαι· πᾶσαν γὰρ αὐτῷ τὴν διάνοιαν εἰς ἐκεῖνα

[1] Πυθαγόραν Gesner: Πύθιον codd.
[2] suppl. Her.
[3] suppl. Rose post Per.; cf. 4.17 infra
[4] ἔνθα] ἐν τῷ θεάτρῳ Rose
[5] καὶ hic Kor.: ante ὁ praebent codd.
[6] Κόσα V: Κῶσα x: Κάσα Burkert
[7] del. Kor.
[8] στίβον Dilts: στίχον V: στοῖχον x

addressed by the citizens of Croton as Apollo Hyperboreus.[a] The son of Nicomachus adds that on one occasion, on the same day and at the same hour, he was seen not only in Metapontum, by many witnesses, but in Croton and Olympia, where he rose to his feet during the competition. It was there that he revealed that he had one thigh of gold. The same authority tells us that he was greeted by the river Cosas[b] as he forded it, and many people are said to have heard this greeting.

27. Anniceris of Cyrene was proud of his horsemanship and skill in driving chariots. On one occasion he even wished to give a display of his ability to Plato. So he prepared his chariot and drove it many times round the Academy, following the path so accurately that he never deviated from his own tracks but always followed them precisely. Everyone else was amazed, as was to be expected; but Plato was critical of his excessive meticulousness and said: "It is impossible for a man who devotes such care to petty things of no value to be serious about important matters. When his mind is entirely occupied

[a] Pythagoras of Samos set up his school in Croton at the end of the sixth century B.C. Aelian is not the only ancient author to cite from the lost works of Aristotle on the subject of Pythagoras. On Pythagoras as a deity and as a shaman see W. Burkert, *Lore and Science in Ancient Pythagoreanism* (Oxford and Cambridge, Mass., 1972), pp. 141–144. On this ch. see also P. Corssen in *Rheinisches Museum* 67 (1912): 29–38.

[b] The river Cosas is mentioned in Bacchylides 11.119; hence Burkert's conjecture, *Lore and Science*, p. 144 n. 122. The modern name is Basento.

---

9 κατ' αὐτὸν] fortasse κατὰ τὸ αὐτὸ

ἀποτεθεῖσαν[1] ἀνάγκη ὀλιγωρεῖν τῶν ὄντως θαυμάζεσθαι δικαίων."

28. Μετὰ τὴν κατὰ τῶν Περσῶν νίκην Ἀθηναῖοι νόμον ἔθεντο ἀλεκτρυόνας ἀγωνίζεσθαι δημοσίᾳ ἐν τῷ θεάτρῳ μιᾶς ἡμέρας τοῦ ἔτους· πόθεν δὲ τὴν ἀρχὴν ἔλαβεν ὅδε ὁ νόμος ἐρῶ. ὅτε Θεμιστοκλῆς ἐπὶ τοὺς βαρβάρους ἐξῆγε τὴν πολεμικὴν[2] δύναμιν, ἀλεκτρυόνας ἐθεάσατο μαχομένους· οὐδὲ ἀργῶς αὐτοὺς εἶδεν, ἐπέστησε δὲ τὴν στρατιὰν καὶ ἔφη πρὸς αὐτούς· "ἀλλ' οὗτοι μὲν οὔτε ὑπὲρ πατρίδος οὔτε ὑπὲρ πατρῴων θεῶν οὐδὲ μὴν ὑπὲρ προγονικῶν[3] ἠρίων κακοπαθοῦσιν οὐδὲ ὑπὲρ δόξης οὐδὲ ὑπὲρ ἐλευθερίας οὐδὲ ὑπὲρ παίδων, ἀλλ' ὑπὲρ τοῦ μὴ ἡττηθῆναι ἑκάτερος μηδὲ εἶξαι θατέρῳ τὸν ἕτερον." ἅπερ οὖν εἰπὼν ἐπέρρωσε τοὺς Ἀθηναίους. τὸ τοίνυν γενόμενον αὐτοῖς σύνθημα τότε εἰς ἀρετὴν ἐβουλήθη διαφυλάττειν καὶ εἰς τὰ ὅμοια ἔργα ὑπόμνησιν.

29. Πιττακὸς ἐν Μιτυλήνῃ κατεσκεύασεν <ἐν>[4] τοῖς ἱεροῖς κλίμακα εἰς οὐδεμίαν μὲν χρῆσιν ἐπιτήδειον,[5] αὐτὸ δὲ τοῦτο ἀνάθημα[6] εἶναι, αἰνιττόμενος τὴν ἐκ τῆς τύχης ἄνω καὶ κάτω μετάπτωσιν, τρόπον τινὰ τῶν μὲν εὐτυχούντων ἀνιόντων, κατιόντων δὲ τῶν δυστυχούντων.

[1] ἀποτεθεῖσαν] ἀποταθ- Gesner [2] πολεμικὴν Kassel: πολιτικὴν codd.; cf. Ar. *Rhet.* 1360 a 36, F. J. Bast, *Commentatio palaeographica* (Leipzig, 1811), pp. 834, 934

[3] προγονικῶν Faber: γονικῶν codd. [4] suppl. Her.

with such things he is bound to neglect all that truly deserves admiration."[a]

28. After their victory over the Persians the Athenians passed a law that the state should organise cock fighting in the theatre one day each year. How this law originated I will now reveal. While Themistocles was leading his military force against the Persians he saw some cocks fighting. He did not look on idly, but halted his troops and said to them: "These birds are not fighting for their country or their fathers' gods; they are not enduring pain to defend the tombs of their ancestors, their reputation, freedom, and children; each of the pair aims to avoid defeat and not to yield to the other." These words gave strength to the Athenians, and so he wanted to retain, as a reminder for similar occasions, the symbol of courage seen by them on that day.

29. Pittacus[b] made a ladder for the temples in Mytilene, not to serve any useful purpose but simply as an offering. His intention was to hint that fortune moves up and down, with the lucky as it were climbing up and the unlucky coming down.

[a] Plato's riposte is ungenerous, since Anniceris allegedly ransomed him after he had been sold into slavery; see Diogenes Laertius 3.20. He was the great-grandfather of the poet Callimachus. See F. Williams, *Zeitschrift für Papyrologie und Epigraphik* 110 (1996): 40–42.

[b] Pittacus was the ruler of Mytilene ca. 600 B.C.; he is the target of hostile remarks in Alcaeus, e.g. fr. 348 P.

---

[5] κλίμακα . . . ἐπιτήδειον] -κας . . . -είους ex Eustathio 1669.39–41 Her.

[6] ἀνάθημα] -ματα Eustathius

30. Πλάτων ὁ Ἀρίστωνος τὰ πρῶτα ἐπὶ ποιητικὴν ὥρμησε καὶ ἡρωϊκὰ ἔγραφε μέτρα· εἶτα αὐτὰ κατέπρησεν ὑπεριδὼν αὐτῶν, ἐπεὶ τοῖς Ὁμήρου αὐτὰ ἀντικρίνων ἑώρα κατὰ πολὺ ἡττώμενα. ἐπέθετο οὖν τραγῳδίᾳ καὶ δὴ καὶ τετραλογίαν εἰργάσατο καὶ ἔμελλεν ἀγωνιεῖσθαι, δοὺς ἤδη τοῖς ὑποκριταῖς τὰ ποιήματα. πρὸ τῶν Διονυσίων δὲ παρελθὼν ἤκουσε Σωκράτους, καὶ ἅπαξ αἱρεθεὶς ὑπὸ τῆς ἐκείνου σειρῆνος, τοῦ ἀγωνίσματος οὐ μόνον ἀπέστη τότε, ἀλλὰ καὶ τελέως τὸ γράφειν τραγῳδίαν ἀπέρριψε καὶ ἀπεδύσατο ἐπὶ φιλοσοφίαν.

31. Καὶ τίς οὐκ ἂν ἐπῄνεσε τὴν τῶν βαρβάρων σοφίαν; εἴ γε μηδεὶς αὐτῶν εἰς ἀθεότητα ἐξέπεσε, μηδὲ ἀμφιβάλλουσι περὶ θεῶν ἆρά γέ εἰσιν ἢ οὔκ εἰσιν, καὶ ἆρά γε ἡμῶν φροντίζουσιν ἢ οὔ. οὐδεὶς γοῦν ἔννοιαν ἔλαβε τοιαύτην οἵαν Εὐήμερος ὁ Μεσσήνιος ἢ Διογένης ὁ Φρὺξ ἢ Ἵππων ἢ Διαγόρας ἢ Σωσίας ἢ Ἐπίκουρος οὔτε Ἰνδὸς οὔτε Κελτὸς οὔτε Αἰγύπτιος. λέγουσι δὲ τῶν βαρβάρων οἱ προειρημένοι καὶ εἶναι θεοὺς καὶ προνοεῖν ἡμῶν καὶ προσημαίνειν τὰ μέλλοντα καὶ[1] διὰ ὀρνίθων καὶ διὰ συμβόλων καὶ διὰ σπλάγχνων καὶ δι' ἄλλων τινῶν μαθημάτων τε καὶ διδαγμάτων, ἅπερ οὖν ἐστι τοῖς ἀνθρώποις διδασκαλία ἐκ τῆς παρὰ[2] τῶν θεῶν εἰς

[1] καὶ del. Her. [2] παρὰ del. Kühn

---

[a] The only poetry to have come down to us under Plato's name is a handful of epigrams in elegiac couplets in the *Greek*

30. Plato son of Ariston first turned his hand to poetry and wrote in the metre of epic. Then he burned his work, not thinking well of it because he saw that in comparison with Homer it was much inferior. So he attempted tragedy and composed a tetralogy. He was on the point of competing and had given the parts to the actors, when he went to hear Socrates just before the Dionysia. He was immediately captivated by that Siren voice, and not only withdrew from the contest but entirely abandoned the writing of tragedy and devoted himself to philosophy.[a]

31. Who could fail to admire the wisdom of the barbarians? None of them has lapsed into atheism, and none argue about the gods—whether they exist or do not exist, and whether they have any concern for us or not. None of them has had the same kind of notion as Euhemerus of Messene,[b] Diogenes the Phrygian, Hippon, Diagoras, Sosias, or Epicurus[c]—neither the Indian, nor the Celt, nor the Egyptian. The barbarians I have just mentioned say that gods exist, that they provide for us, that they indicate the future by omens and signs, by entrails[d] and by other forms of instruction and teachings. These indeed are a lesson for men which derives from the gods' fore-

Anthology; their authenticity is very doubtful.

[b] Euhemerus (fl. ca. 300 B.C.) was the inventor of the notion that the gods were originally human beings, whose achievements led to their achieving first royal and then divine status.

[c] Epicurus and his followers were not atheists, but many people in antiquity believed that they were.

[d] The barbarians are here credited with a standard Greco-Roman belief, namely that future events could be predicted by inspection of various internal organs, especially the liver, of sacrificial animals.

αὐτοὺς προνοίας. καὶ δι' ὀνείρων δὲ λέγουσι καὶ δι' αὐτῶν τῶν ἀστέρων πολλὰ προδηλοῦσθαι. καὶ ὑπὲρ τούτων ἰσχυρὰν ἔχοντες τὴν πίστιν θύουσί τε καθαρῶς καὶ ἁγνεύουσιν ὁσίως, καὶ τελετὰς τελοῦσι καὶ ὀργίων φυλάττουσι νόμον, καὶ τὰ ἄλλα πράττουσιν ἐξ ὧν ὅτι τοὺς θεοὺς ἰσχυρῶς καὶ σέβουσι καὶ τιμῶσιν ὡμολόγηται.

32. Λέγουσί τινες λόγοι Πυθικοὶ τὸν Ἡρακλῆ τὸν Διὸς καὶ Ἀλκμήνης παῖδα ἀπὸ γενεᾶς Ἡρακλῆ μὲν οὐ[1] κεκλῆσθαι, χρόνῳ δὲ ὕστερον ἐλθόντα εἰς Δελφοὺς διά τινα αἰτίαν δεόμενον χρησμοῦ, μήτε ὧν ἧκε χάριν ἀμοιρῆσαι, προσακοῦσαί τε[2] ἐκείνοις καὶ ἰδίᾳ παρὰ τοῦ θεοῦ ταῦτα·

Ἡρακλῆ δέ σε Φοῖβος ἐπώνυμον ἐξονομάζει·
ἦρα γὰρ ἀνθρώποισι φέρων κλέος ἄφθιτον ἕξεις.

33. Τὴν τῶν ποταμῶν φύσιν καὶ τὰ ῥεῖθρα αὐτῶν ὁρῶμεν· ὅμως δὲ οἱ τιμῶντες αὐτοὺς καὶ τὰ ἀγάλματα αὐτῶν ἐργαζόμενοι οἱ μὲν ἀνθρωπομόρφους αὐτοὺς ἱδρύσαντο, οἱ δὲ βοῶν εἶδος αὐτοῖς περιέθηκαν. βουσὶ μὲν οὖν εἰκάζουσιν οἱ Στυμφάλιοι μὲν τὸν Ἐρασῖνον καὶ τὴν Μετώπην, Λακεδαιμόνιοι δὲ τὸν Εὐρώταν, Σικυώνιοι δὲ καὶ Φλιάσιοι τὸν Ἀσωπόν, Ἀργεῖοι δὲ τὸν Κηφισόν· ἐν εἴδει δὲ ἀνδρῶν Ψωφίδιοι[3] τὸν Ἐρύμανθον, τὸν δὲ Ἀλφειὸν Ἡραιεῖς, Χερρονήσιοι δὲ οἱ ἀπὸ Κνίδου καὶ αὐτοὶ τὸν αὐτὸν ποταμὸν ὁμοίως, Ἀθηναῖοι δὲ τὸν Κηφισὸν ἄνδρα

[1] Ἡρακλῆ μὲν οὐ Russell (-ῆν οὐ iam J. Gronovius): Ἡρακλείδην codd.: Ἀλκαῖον Scheffer

thought on their behalf. They also say that much is revealed in advance by dreams and by the stars themselves. In these matters their faith is strong. They sacrifice with purity, they piously avoid pollution, performing rites and preserving custom in ceremony, and have other practices as a result of which it is agreed that they respect and worship the gods with conviction.

32. Some Pythian traditions report that Heracles son of Zeus and Alcmene was at the time of his birth not called Heracles; but later, when he came to Delphi, needing an oracle for some reason, he was not disappointed in his mission and in addition heard the god say this to him privately: "Phoebus gives you the name of Heracles; for by doing favours to mankind you will win undying glory."[a]

33. The nature of rivers, and their streams, are visible to us. But men who honour them, and have statues made of them, in some cases set up anthropomorphic statues, while others give them bovine form. A likeness to cattle is attributed by the Stymphalians to the Erasinus and Metope, by the Spartans to the Eurotas, by the Sicyonians and Phliasians to the Asopus, and by the Argives to the Cephisus. The form of a man is adopted by the Psophidians for the Erymanthus, and by the Heraeans for the Alpheus; the Chersonesians from Cnidus treat the same river in the same way. The Athenians portray the

[a] The god's words consist of two hexameters which aim to etymologise Heracles' name; the second element is correctly derived from κλέος "glory," but the first is generally linked with the goddess Hera, despite the short alpha, rather than ἦρα "favour, kindness."

---

[2] τε Her.: δὲ codd.

[3] Ψωφίδιοι Faber: -ίλιοι codd.

μὲν δεικνύουσι ἐν προτομῇ,[1] κέρατα δὲ ὑποφαίνοντα. καὶ ἐν Σικελίᾳ δὲ Συρακούσιοι μὲν τὸν Ἄναπον ἀνδρὶ εἴκασαν, τὴν δὲ Κυάνην πηγὴν γυναικὸς εἰκόνι ἐτίμησαν· Αἰγεσταῖοι δὲ τὸν Πόρπακα καὶ τὸν Κριμισὸν καὶ τὸν Τελμησσὸν ἀνδρῶν εἴδει τιμῶσιν. Ἀκραγαντῖνοι δὲ τὸν ἐπώνυμον τῆς πόλεως ποταμὸν παιδὶ ὡραίῳ εἰκάσαντες θύουσιν. οἱ δὲ αὐτοὶ καὶ ἐν Δελφοῖς ἀνέθεσαν ἐλέφαντος διαγλύψαντες ἄγαλμα, καὶ ἐπέγραψαν τὸ τοῦ ποταμοῦ ὄνομα· καὶ παιδός ἐστι τὸ ἄγαλμα.

34. Ἐπίχαρμόν φασι πάνυ σφόδρα πρεσβύτην ὄντα, μετά τινων ἡλικιωτῶν ἐν λέσχῃ καθήμενον, ἐπεὶ ἕκαστος τῶν παρόντων ἔλεγεν, ὁ μέν τις· "ἐμοὶ πέντε ἔτη ἀπόχρη βιῶναι," ἄλλος δέ· "ἐμοὶ τρία," τρίτου δὲ εἰπόντος· "ἐμοί γε τέτταρα," ὑπολαβὼν ὁ Ἐπίχαρμος "ὦ βέλτιστοι," εἶπε, "τί στασιάζετε καὶ διαφέρεσθε ὑπὲρ ὀλίγων ἡμερῶν; πάντες γὰρ οἱ συνελθόντες κατά τινα δαίμονα ἐπὶ δυσμαῖς ἐσμεν· ὥστε ὥρα πᾶσιν ἡμῖν τὴν ταχίστην ἀνάγεσθαι πρὸ τοῦ καί τινος[2] ἀπολαῦσαι κακοῦ πρεσβυτικοῦ."[3]

35. Γοργίας ὁ Λεοντῖνος ἐπὶ τέρματι ὢν τοῦ βίου καὶ γεγηρακὼς εὖ μάλα ὑπό τινος ἀσθενείας καταληφθείς, κατ' ὀλίγον εἰς ὕπνον ὑπολισθαίνων ἔκειτο. ἐπεὶ δέ τις <εἰς>[4] αὐτὸν παρῆλθε τῶν ἐπιτηδείων ἐπισκοπούμενος καὶ ἤρετο τί πράττοι, ὁ Γοργίας

[1] ἐν προτομῇ Kor.: ἐν τιμῇ codd.: ἐντελῇ Faber
[2] καί τινος scripsi: τινος καὶ codd.
[3] πρεσβυτικοῦ Oudendorp: πρεσβυτιδίου codd.

Cephisus as a human bust but with horns just showing. And in Sicily the Syracusans represented the Anapus as a man, whereas they honoured the spring Cyane with the statue of a woman. The Egestans honour the Porpax, Crimisus, and Telmessus in the form of men. The inhabitants of Acragas portray the river of the same name as a handsome boy and make sacrifice to him. They also made an offering at Delphi, carving an ivory statue with the river's name inscribed on it, and the statue is of a boy.[a]

34. At a very advanced age Epicharmus,[b] they say, sat in conversation with some of his contemporaries. One of the company said: "I am content to live five years"; another: "For me three are enough"; a third: "For me four." Epicharmus replied: "My good friends, why are you in dispute and disagreement about a few days? All of us who by chance are gathered here are at the evening of our lives; so it is time for us all to depart as quickly as possible before experiencing some evil connected with old age."

35. At the end of his life, having reached a very great age, Gorgias of Leontini was overcome by weakness and lay gradually slipping away into sleep.[c] When one of his friends came to see him and asked how he was, Gorgias

[a] This ch. is the best ancient source for the worship of river gods. Many of the details can be confirmed from coins and other works of art. See C. Weiss, *Griechische Flussgottheiten in vorhellenistischer Zeit* (Würzburg, 1984).

[b] Sicilian writer of comedy, active in the early fifth century B.C. Exactly how long he lived is uncertain.

[c] The ancient sources suggest that Gorgias reached the age of 100 (ca. 480–380 B.C.).

---

[4] suppl. Her.

ἀπεκρίνατο·[1] "ἤδη με ὁ ὕπνος ἄρχεται παρακατατίθεσθαι τῷ ἀδελφῷ."

36. Ἰσοκράτης[2] δὲ καὶ αὐτὸς βαθύτατα γηρῶν εἶτα νόσῳ περιπεσών, ἐπεί τις αὐτὸν ἠρώτησε πῶς ἔχει, "καλῶς" εἶπε "πρὸς ἀμφότερα· ἐὰν μὲν γὰρ ζῶ, ζηλωτὰς ἕξω πλείονας· ἐὰν δὲ ἀποθάνω, ἐπαινέτας πλείονας."

37. Ζαλεύκου τοῦ Λοκροῦ πολλοὶ μέν εἰσι καὶ ἄλλοι νόμοι κάλλιστα καὶ εἰς δέον κείμενοι, καὶ οὗτος δὲ οὐχ ἥκιστα. εἴ τις Λοκρῶν τῶν Ἐπιζεφυρίων νοσῶν ἔπιεν οἶνον ἄκρατον, μὴ προστάξαντος τοῦ θεραπεύοντος, εἰ καὶ περιεσώθη, θάνατος ἡ ζημία ἦν αὐτῷ, ὅτι μὴ προσταχθὲν αὐτῷ ὁ δὲ ἔπιεν.

38. Νόμος καὶ οὗτος Μασσαλιωτικός, γυναῖκας μὴ ὁμιλεῖν οἴνῳ, ἀλλ' ὑδροποτεῖν πᾶσαν γυναικῶν ἡλικίαν. λέγει δὲ Θεόφραστος καὶ παρὰ Μιλησίοις τὸν νόμον τοῦτον ἰσχύειν καὶ <μὴ>[3] πείθεσθαι αὐτῷ τὰς Ἰάδας, ἀλλὰ[4] τὰς Μιλησίων γυναῖκας. τί δὲ οὐκ ἂν εἴποιμι καὶ τὸν Ῥωμαίων νόμον; καὶ πῶς οὐκ ὀφλήσω δικαίως ἀλογίαν, εἰ τὰ μὲν Λοκρῶν καὶ Μασσαλιωτῶν καὶ τὰ Μιλησίων διὰ μνήμης ἐθέμην, τὰ δὲ τῆς ἐμαυτοῦ πατρίδος ἀλόγως[5] ἐάσω; οὐκοῦν καὶ Ῥωμαίοις ἦν ἐν τοῖς μάλιστα νόμος ὅδε ἐρρωμέ-

[1] ἀπεκρίνατο Stobaeus 4.51.22: ἔφη codd.

[2] Ἰσοκράτης scripsi: Σωκράτης codd. [3] suppl. d

[4] locus obscurus: fortasse supplendum τὰς <ἄλλας> Ἰάδας vel ἀλλὰ <μόνας>

[5] ἀλόγως del. Hercher

said: "Sleep is now beginning to hand me over to his brother."[a]

36. Isocrates too, at a very advanced age, fell ill, and when someone asked him how he was he said: "Well, in either event: if I live, I shall have more admirers, if I die, more people to praise me."[b]

37. Among many excellent and essential laws devised by Zaleucus of Locri[c] this is one of the best. If anyone among the Epizephyrian Locrians fell ill and drank unmixed wine without his doctor's orders, even if he survived, the penalty for him was death, because he had drunk something without having received the order to do so.

38. There was a law at Massilia that women should not touch wine, but drink water at all ages. Theophrastus [fr. 579A F.-H.-S.] says this law was also in force at Miletus, and while Ionian women in general did not adhere to it, at least the Milesians did. Why should I not mention the Roman law as well? I should rightly be thought unreasonable if I recorded facts about Locri, Massilia and Miletus, and at the same time failed, without reason, to mention my own country. At any rate one of the best enforced laws

[a] Thanatus. Sleep and Death are described as brothers in *Iliad* 14.231, 16.672.

[b] According to the MSS. this story is about Socrates, who probably lived 469–399 B.C. and therefore did not reach extreme old age. For this reason, and because of the speaker's words, the name of Isocrates has to be restored.

[c] The author of what may have been the earliest written law code in Greece, traditionally dated 663–2 B.C. This ch. and the next are similar in content to Athenaeus 429 AB.

νος. οὔτε ἐλευθέρα γυνὴ ἔπιεν ἂν οἶνον οὔτε οἰκέτις, οὐδὲ μὴν τῶν εὖ γεγονότων οἱ ἀφ' ἥβης μέχρι πέντε καὶ τριάκοντα ἐτῶν.

39. *Κρῆτες δὲ τοὺς παῖδας τοὺς ἐλευθέρους μανθάνειν ἐκέλευον τοὺς νόμους μετά τινος μελῳδίας, ἵνα ἐκ τῆς μουσικῆς ψυχαγωγῶνται καὶ εὐκολώτερον αὐτοὺς τῇ μνήμῃ παραλαμβάνωσι καὶ ἵνα μή τι τῶν κεκωλυμένων πράξαντες ἀγνοίᾳ πεποιηκέναι ἀπολογίαν ἔχωσι. δεύτερον δὲ μάθημα ἔταξαν τοὺς τῶν θεῶν ὕμνους μανθάνειν, τρίτον τὰ τῶν ἀγαθῶν ἀνδρῶν ἐγκώμια.*

40. *Πᾶν μὲν ὅσον ἄλογόν ἐστιν ἀλλοτρίως πρὸς οἶνον πέφυκε, μάλιστα δὲ τῶν ζῴων ἐκεῖνα, ὅσα σταφυλῆς ἢ γιγάρτων ὑπερπλησθέντα μεθύει. καὶ οἱ κόρακες δὲ τὴν καλουμένην οἰνοῦτταν*[1] *βοτάνην ὅταν φάγωσι, καὶ οἱ κύνες δὲ καὶ αὐτοὶ βακχεύονται. πίθηκος δὲ καὶ ἐλέφας ἐὰν οἴνου πίωσιν, ὁ μὲν τῆς ἀλκῆς ἐπιλανθάνεται ὁ ἐλέφας, ὁ δὲ τῆς πανουργίας· καί εἰσιν αἱρεθῆναι πάνυ ἀσθενεῖς.*

41. *Φιλοπόται δὲ λέγονται γενέσθαι Διονύσιος ὁ Σικελίας τύραννος, καὶ Νυσαῖος*[2] *καὶ οὗτος τύραννος, καὶ Ἀπολλοκράτης ὁ Διονυσίου τοῦ τυράννου υἱός,*[3] *καὶ Ἱππαρῖνος Διονυσίου ὢν υἱὸς*[4] *καὶ οὗτος, καὶ Τιμόλαος ὁ Θηβαῖος καὶ Χαρίδημος ὁ Ὠρείτης καὶ Ἀρκαδίων καὶ Ἐρασίξενος καὶ Ἀλκέτας ὁ*

[1] *οἰνοῦτταν* Scheffer: *σινοῦτ(τ)αν* codd.

[2] Νυσαῖος] in hoc c. pleraque nomina ex Athenaeo 435D–440D corrigenda sunt

in Rome was that neither free women nor slaves would drink wine, nor did the men in good families between adolescence and the age of thirty-five.

39. The Cretans ordered the children of free citizens to learn the laws with a musical accompaniment, so that they should receive pleasure from the music and register the laws in their memory more easily, and if they committed some forbidden act they would not be able to plead ignorance. As a second subject for study, the Cretans insisted that hymns to the gods should be learned, and as a third, encomia of brave men.

40. All brute animals reject wine, especially those animals which become intoxicated on a surfeit of grapes and pips. When crows eat the grass called *oinoutta*—and the same is even true of dogs—they behave excitedly. If a monkey or an elephant drinks wine, the elephant loses its strength, and the monkey its cunning, so that both are easy to capture.[a]

41. The following are said to have been heavy drinkers: Dionysius the tyrant of Sicily; Nysaeus, another tyrant; Apollocrates the son of Dionysius the tyrant; Hipparinus, another son of Dionysius; Timolaus of Thebes;[b] Charidemus of Oreus; Arcadion,[c] Erasixenus and Alcetas

[a] Athenaeus 429 D conveys much the same information as this ch.

[b] Timolaus is named in Demosthenes 18.295.

[c] For an epigram on him see D. L. Page, *Further Greek Epigrams* (Cambridge, 1981), p. 444.

---

[3] *ὁ . . . υἱός*] *οἱ . . . υἱοί* ex Athenaeo Per.

[4] *ὢν υἱὸς*] *ἀνεψιὸς* codd.

Μακεδὼν καὶ Διότιμος ὁ Ἀθηναῖος. οὗτός τοι καὶ Χώνη ἐπεκαλεῖτο· ἐντιθέμενος γὰρ τῷ στόματι χώνην ἀδιαλείπτως ἐχώρει τὸν εἰσχεόμενον οἶνον. Κλεομένης δὲ ὁ Λακεδαιμόνιος οὐ μόνον φασὶν ὅτι πολυπότης ἦν, ἀλλὰ γὰρ προστιθέασιν αὐτῷ καὶ τοῦτο δήπου τὸ Σκυθικὸν κακόν, ὅτι ἀκρατοπότης ἐγένετο. καὶ Ἴωνα δὲ τὸν Χῖον τὸν ποιητὴν καὶ αὐτόν φασι περὶ τὸν οἶνον ἀκρατῶς ἔχειν.

Καὶ Ἀλέξανδρος δὲ ὁ Μακεδὼν ἐπὶ Καλανῷ τῷ Βραχμᾶνι, τῷ Ἰνδῶν σοφιστῇ, ὅτε ἑαυτὸν ἐκεῖνος κατέπρησεν, ἀγῶνα μουσικῆς καὶ ἱππικῶν[1] καὶ ἀθλητῶν διέθηκε. χαριζόμενος δὲ τοῖς Ἰνδοῖς καί τι ἐπιχώριον αὐτῶν ἀγώνισμα εἰς τιμὴν τοῦ Καλανοῦ συγκατηρίθμησε τοῖς ἄθλοις τοῖς προειρημένοις. οἰνοποσίας γοῦν ἀγωνίαν προὔθηκε, καὶ ἦν τῷ μὲν τὰ πρῶτα φερομένῳ τάλαντον τὸ γέρας, τῷ δὲ δευτέρῳ τριάκοντα μναῖ, τῷ γε μὴν τρίτῳ δέκα. ὁ δὲ τὰ νικητήρια ἀναδησάμενος ἐν αὐτοῖς ἦν Πρόμαχος. καὶ ἐκ Διονυσίου[2] δὲ τῇ τῶν Χοῶν ἑορτῇ προὔκειτο ἆθλον τῷ πιόντι πλέον[3] στέφανος χρυσοῦς. καὶ ἐνίκησε Ξενοκράτης ὁ Χαλκηδόνιος, καὶ τὸν στέφανον λαβών, ὅτε ἐπανῄει μετὰ τὸ δεῖπνον, τῷ Ἑρμῇ τῷ πρὸ τῶν θυρῶν ἑστῶτι ἐπέθηκεν αὐτὸν κατὰ τὸ ἔθος τῶν ἔμπροσθεν ἡμερῶν· καὶ γὰρ καὶ τοὺς ἀνθεινοὺς καὶ τοὺς ἐκ τῆς μυρρίνης καὶ τὸν ἐκ τοῦ κιττοῦ καὶ τὸν ἐκ τῆς δάφνης ἐνταῦθα ἀνέπαυσε καὶ ἀπέλιπε.

[1] ἱππικῶν] -ικὸν J. F. Gronovius: ἱππέων Her.

[2] ἐκ Διονυσίου ex Athenaeo Battierius et Scheffer: ἐν Διονύσου codd.

the Macedonian; and Diotimus of Athens. This man was nicknamed "the funnel," because he put a funnel in his mouth and swallowed without interruption the wine that was poured in. Cleomenes the Spartan was not only a heavy drinker, according to reports, but they also say of him that he acquired the bad Scythian habit of drinking wine undiluted.[a] The poet Ion of Chios is also said to have been an immoderate drinker.

When Calanus the Brahmin, an Indian sage, set fire to himself, Alexander of Macedon arranged a competition for music, horse racing and athletics. As a favour to the Indians he included among the contests just mentioned one that was traditional among them, in honour of Calanus. This was a drinking contest, and the prize for the winner was a talent; the runner-up won thirty minae, and the third prize was ten. The person who celebrated victory was Promachus. Dionysius offered a prize of a golden crown at the festival of the Choes for the man who drank most.[b] It was won by Xenocrates of Chalcedon.[c] He took his crown, went home after dinner and put it on the statue of Hermes by his front door, following the custom he had observed during the preceding days—in fact he had rested there crowns made from flowers, myrtle, ivy, and laurel and left them.

[a] It was a generally held view in antiquity that wine should be drunk diluted with a substantial quantity of water. Aelian seems to exploit Athenaeus 435 D–440 D in this paragraph.

[b] The second day of the Athenian festival Anthesteria.

[c] Successor of Plato and Speusippus as head of the Academy (339–312 B.C.). Cf. also 14.9 below.

---

[3] πλέον] πλεῖστον Her.

Καὶ Ἀνάχαρσις δὲ πάμπολυ, φασίν, ἔπιε παρὰ Περιάνδρῳ, τοῦτο μὲν καὶ οἴκοθεν ἑαυτῷ ἐπαγόμενος τὸ ἐφόδιον· Σκυθῶν γὰρ ἴδιον τὸ πίνειν ἄκρατον. καὶ Λακύδης δὲ καὶ Τίμων οἱ φιλόσοφοι, καὶ τούτους φασὶ πάμπολυ πιεῖν. καὶ Μυκερῖνος δὲ ὁ Αἰγύπτιος, ὅτε αὐτῷ τὸ ἐκ Βουτοῦς[1] μαντεῖον ἀφίκετο προλέγον τὴν τοῦ βίου στενοχωρίαν, εἶτα ἐβουλήθη σοφίσασθαι τὸ λόγιον ἐκεῖνος, διπλασιάζων τὸν χρόνον καὶ ταῖς ἡμέραις προστιθεὶς τὰς νύκτας, διετέλει καὶ αὐτὸς ἀγρυπνῶν καὶ πίνων ἅμα. τίθει μετὰ τούτων καὶ Ἄμασιν τὸν Αἰγύπτιον, ἐπεί τοι καὶ[2] Ἡρόδοτος ἱκανὸς τεκμηριῶσαι.

Καὶ Νικοτέλην δὲ τὸν Κορίνθιον οὐ χρὴ ἀπὸ τούτων τάττειν, καὶ Σκόπαν τὸν Κρέοντος υἱόν. καὶ Ἀντίοχον τὸν βασιλέα φασὶν οἰνεραστὴν γενέσθαι. διὰ ταῦτά τοι καὶ τὴν βασιλείαν αὐτῷ διῴκουν Ἄριστός τε καὶ Θεμίσων οἱ Κύπριοι, αὐτὸς δὲ διὰ τὴν πολυποσίαν ἐπεγέγραπτο τῇ ἀρχῇ ἄλλως. καὶ ὁ Ἐπιφανὴς δὲ κληθεὶς Ἀντίοχος ὁ Ῥωμαίοις δοθεὶς ὅμηρος, καὶ οὗτος ἀκρατῶς ἐδίψη οἴνου πίνειν. καὶ ὁ ὁμώνυμος δὲ τούτου Ἀντίοχος ὁ <ἐν>[3] Μήδοις πρὸς Ἀρσάκην πολεμήσας, καὶ οὗτος ἦν τοῦ πίνειν δοῦλος. καὶ ὁ Μέγας δὲ καλούμενος Ἀντίοχος, καὶ οὗτος σὺν τούτοις τετάχθω.

[1] Βουτοῦς Holstenius: Βούτης codd.
[2] ἐπεί τοι καὶ] εἴ τῳ Her.
[3] ex Athenaeo suppl. Scheffer

They say that Anacharsis[a] drank a great deal when he was with Periander; this was a habit he brought with him from home, as it is characteristic of the Scythians to drink wine undiluted. Lacydes[b] and Timon[c] the philosophers are also reported to have been heavy drinkers. Mycerinus the Egyptian, on receiving the prophecy from Buto which predicted for him a short life, was anxious to outwit the oracle; so he doubled his time by adding the nights to his days, staying awake all the time and drinking.[d] Add to these examples Amasis of Egypt, since Herodotus' testimony [2.174] is sufficient.

Nor should one leave out of this category Nicoteles of Corinth or Scopas the son of Creon. They say that king Antiochus too was a lover of wine, which is why the Cypriots Aristus and Themison administered his kingdom, whereas he himself owing to his heavy consumption was ruler only in name.[e] The Antiochus who was known as Epiphanes and became a hostage of the Romans also had an uncontrollable thirst for wine. His namesake Antiochus who fought among the Medes against Arsaces was another slave to drink. Antiochus the Great should also be included alongside the others.

[a] A Scythian prince who visited Greece and was occasionally counted as one of the Seven Sages. Plato, *Republic* 600 a, mentions him alongside Thales as an inventor.

[b] Lacydes of Cyrene was head of the Academy ca. 241/0–216/5 B.C.

[c] Timon of Phlius, ca. 320–230 B.C., sceptical philosopher and author of satires called *Silloi*.

[d] This story derives from Herodotus 2.133 and 174.

[e] This and the other Antiochi are all Hellenistic kings of Syria.

Καὶ Ἄγρωνα δὲ τὸν Ἰλλυριῶν βασιλέα ἀπέκτεινεν ἡ πρὸς τὸν οἶνον ἄδικος[1] ὁρμή, καὶ αὐτῷ πλευρῖτιν ἐνειργάσατο.[2] καὶ ἕτερος Ἰλλυριῶν βασιλεὺς Γένθιος, πίνειν καὶ οὗτος εἴθιστο[3] ἀκρατῶς. τόν γε μὴν Καππαδόκων βασιλέα Ὀροφέρνην τί τοῦτον ἐάσομεν,[4] καὶ ἐκεῖνον πιεῖν γενόμενον δεινόν;

Εἰ δὲ χρὴ καὶ γυναικῶν μνημονεῦσαι, ἄτοπον μὲν γυνὴ φιλοπότις, καὶ πολυπότις ἔτι μᾶλλον,[5] εἰρήσθω δ' οὖν καὶ περὶ τούτων. Κλεώ, φασιν,[6] εἰς ἅμιλλαν ἰοῦσα οὐ γυναιξὶ μόναις ἀλλὰ καὶ τοῖς ἀνδράσι τοῖς συμπόταις δεινοτάτη πιεῖν ἦν, καὶ ἐκράτει πάντων, αἴσχιστόν γε τοῦτο φερομένη τὸ νικητήριον ὥς γε ἐμοὶ[7] κριτῇ.

42. Ἡ Πλάτωνος δόξα καὶ ὁ τῆς κατ' αὐτὸν ἀρετῆς λόγος καὶ εἰς Ἀρκάδας ἀφίκετο καὶ Θηβαίους, καὶ οὖν καὶ ἐδεήθησαν αὐτοῦ πρέσβεις ἀποστείλαντες σὺν τῇ ἀνωτάτω σπουδῇ ἀφικέσθαι σφίσι τὸν ἄνδρα οὐκ ἐπὶ μόνῃ τῇ τῶν νέων προστασίᾳ, οὐδ' ἵνα αὐτοῖς συγγένηται ἐπὶ τοῖς λόγοις τοῖς κατὰ φιλοσοφίαν, ἀλλὰ γὰρ καὶ τὸ ἔτι τούτων μεῖζον νομοθέτην αὐτὸν ἐκάλουν. οὔκουν ἔμελλον ἀτυχήσειν τοῦ ἀνδρός· καὶ γὰρ ἥσθη ὁ τοῦ Ἀρίστωνος τῇ κλήσει καὶ δὴ καὶ ἔμελλεν ὑπακούσεσθαι. ἤρετο μέντοι τοὺς ἥκοντας πῶς ἔχουσι πρὸς τὸ ἴσον ἔχειν

[1] ἄδικος] an voluit *improbus*? malim ἄκριτος: ἄσχετος Faber [2] ἐνειργάσατο Kor.: εἰργ- codd. [3] εἴθιστο Kor. (εἴωθεν iam A. Gronovius): ἑαυτῷ codd. [4] ἐάσομεν Her.: δράσομεν codd. plerique [5] μᾶλλον x: πλέον V

Agron the king of Illyria was killed by his unreasonable desire for wine, which brought on pleurisy.[a] Another Illyrian king, Genthius, drank immoderately.[b] And why should we omit the Cappadocian king Orophernes, who was a great drinker?[c]

And if it is our duty to mention women—it is odd for a woman to be fond of drink, and still more so for her to be a tippler—at any rate let us say something of them. Cleo, they say, competed not only with women but even with men at drinking parties. She was formidable and could defeat anyone, carrying off a victory which in my judgement at least was most unbecoming.

42. The reputation of Plato, and word of his merits,[d] reached both the Arcadians and the Thebans. They sent delegations to him with the most urgent request that he should visit them, not simply so that he could give guidance to the young, nor even that he should take part in philosophical discussions with them, but in addition—and this was more important—they invited him as a legislator. They were about to secure their man—the son of Ariston was flattered by the invitation and was about to accept—but he asked the men who had come to see him how they all felt about equality. When he heard from

[a] Agron (fl. ca. 230 B.C.) is mentioned by Polybius 2.2.4.

[b] Genthius was king of Illyria 180–168 B.C.

[c] Orophernes ruled Cappadocia 158–156 B.C.

[d] One could also translate "the fame of his conception of virtue."

[6] φασιν Peruscus: φησιν codd.

[7] <παρ'> ἐμοὶ I. Vossius

ἅπαντας.[1] ἐπεὶ δὲ ἔμαθε παρ' αὐτῶν ὅτι καὶ πάνυ ἀλλοτρίως οὐδὲ πείσει[2] αὐτοὺς τιμᾶν τὴν ἰσονομίαν, ἀπείπατο τὴν πρὸς αὐτοὺς ἐπιδημίαν.

43. Πενέστατοι ἐγένοντο οἱ ἄριστοι τῶν Ἑλλήνων· Ἀριστείδης ὁ Λυσιμάχου[3] καὶ Φωκίων ὁ Φώκου καὶ Ἐπαμεινώνδας ὁ Πολύμνιδος[4] καὶ Πελοπίδας ὁ Θηβαῖος καὶ Λάμαχος ὁ Ἀθηναῖος καὶ Σωκράτης ὁ Σωφρονίσκου καὶ Ἐφιάλτης δὲ ὁ Σοφωνίδου καὶ ἐκεῖνος.[5]

44. Θέωνος τοῦ ζωγράφου πολλὰ μὲν καὶ ἄλλα ὁμολογεῖ τὴν χειρουργίαν ἀγαθὴν οὖσαν, ἀτὰρ οὖν καὶ τόδε τὸ γράμμα· ὁπλίτης ἐστὶν ἐκβοηθῶν, ἄφνω τῶν πολεμίων εἰσβαλλόντων καὶ δῃούντων ἅμα καὶ κειρόντων τὴν γῆν· ἐναργῶς δὲ καὶ[6] πάνυ ἐκθύμως ὁ νεανίας ἔοικεν ὁρμῶντι εἰς τὴν μάχην, καὶ εἶπες ἂν αὐτὸν ἐνθουσιᾶν, ὥσπερ ἐξ Ἄρεος μανέντα. γοργὸν μὲν αὐτῷ βλέπουσιν οἱ ὀφθαλμοί, τὰ δὲ ὅπλα ἁρπάσας ἔοικεν ᾗ ποδῶν ἔχει ἐπὶ τοὺς πολεμίους ᾄττειν. προβάλλεται δὲ ἐντεῦθεν ἤδη τὴν ἀσπίδα καὶ γυμνὸν ἐπισείει τὸ ξίφος φονῶντι ἐοικὼς καὶ σφαγὴν[7] βλέπων καὶ ἀπειλῶν δι' ὅλου τοῦ σχήματος ὅτι μηδενὸς φείσεται. καὶ πλέον οὐδὲν περιείργασται

[1] ἅπαντας Per.: -τες codd. [2] πείσει Kor.: -ειν codd.

[3] Λυσιμάχου Scheffer: Νικομάχου codd. et Stobaeus 4.32.10

[4] Πολύμνιδος Scheffer: Πολυμάτιδος codd.: Πολύμωδος Stobaeus

[5] καὶ ἐκεῖνος codd.: om. Stobaeus

them that they were quite opposed to it and that he would not be able to persuade them to respect the concept of equality before the law, he abandoned his idea of visiting them.[a]

43. The best of the Greeks were very poor—Aristides son of Lysimachus, Phocion son of Phocus, Epaminondas son of Polymnis, Pelopidas of Thebes, Lamachus of Athens, Socrates son of Sophroniscus, and even Ephialtes son of Sophonides.[b]

44. Many works attest the fine technique of the painter Theon,[c] and in particular the painting of a hoplite coming to the rescue when the enemy suddenly invade and bring death and destruction to the land. The young man clearly looks as if he is about to do battle with great spirit; you would say he was inspired, as if he were possessed by Ares. His eyes have a fiery look. Having snatched his weapons, it appears, he makes for the enemy as fast as his feet will carry him. Already he holds his shield in position on one side, and brandishes a drawn sword, with a blood-thirsty look and ready to kill, and shows by his whole bearing that he will spare no one. Theon has added nothing

[a] The presentation of Plato as an egalitarian is unexpected, and perhaps the story was originally told of someone else.

[b] An almost identical list is given at 11.9 below; in a revised version of his text Aelian would doubtless have omitted the present ch.

[c] A fourth-century painter from Samos. J. Six, *Mitteilungen des deutschen archäologischen Instituts (Römische Abteilung)* 32 (1917): 190, suggested that the figure represented Achilles.

---

[6] *καὶ* del. Russell

[7] *σφαγὴν* Valckenaer: *σφάττειν* codd.

τῷ Θέωνι, οὐ λοχίτης οὐ ταξίαρχος οὐ λοχαγὸς[1] οὐχ ἱππεὺς οὐ τοξότης, ἀλλ' ἀπέχρησέν οἱ καὶ ὁ εἷς ὁπλίτης οὗτος πληρῶσαι τὴν τῆς εἰκόνος ἀπαίτησιν. οὐ πρότερόν γε μὴν ὁ τεχνίτης ἐξεκάλυψε τὴν γραφὴν οὐδὲ ἔδειξε τοῖς ἐπὶ τὴν θέαν συνειλεγμένοις πρὶν ἢ σαλπιγκτὴν παρεστήσατο καὶ προσέταξεν αὐτῷ τὸ παρορμητικὸν ἐμπνεῦσαι μέλος διάτορόν τε καὶ γεγωνὸς ὅτι μάλιστα καὶ οἷον εἰς τὴν μάχην ἐγερτήριον. ἅμα τε οὖν τὸ μέλος ἠκούετο τραχὺ καὶ φοβερὸν καὶ οἷον εἰς ὁπλιτῶν ἔξοδον ταχέως ἐκβοηθούντων μελῳδοῦσι σάλπιγγες,[2] καὶ ἐδείκνυτο ἡ γραφὴ καὶ ὁ στρατιώτης ἐβλέπετο, τοῦ μέλους ἐναργεστέραν τὴν φαντασίαν τοῦ ἐκβοηθοῦντος ἔτι καὶ μᾶλλον παραστήσαντος.

[1] λοχαγὸς Faber: λόχος codd.

[2] μελῳδοῦσι σάλπιγγες G. G. Kühn: -ούσῃ . . . -ιγγι codd.: -ούσης . . . -ιγγος Gesner

else to the picture—no comrades, no commanding officer, no subaltern, no cavalry or archers; this one hoplite was enough to satisfy the demands of the picture. However, the artist did not reveal the picture, or show it to the public that had come to look at it, before he had summoned a trumpeter. He ordered the man to play the call to attack as loud and clear as possible, as if it were a summons to battle. The strident, terrifying notes rang out just as trumpets summon the infantry to immediate action, and at once the picture was revealed; the soldier could be seen, and the music made the impression of the man dashing into battle even more vivid.

Γ

1. Φέρε οὖν καὶ τὰ καλούμενα Τέμπη τὰ Θετταλικὰ διαγράψωμεν τῷ λόγῳ καὶ διαπλάσωμεν· ὡμολόγηται γὰρ καὶ ὁ λόγος, ἐὰν ἔχῃ δύναμιν φραστικήν, μηδὲν ἀσθενέστερον ὅσα βούλεται δεικνύναι τῶν ἀνδρῶν τῶν κατὰ χειρουργίαν δεινῶν.

Ἔστι δὴ χῶρος μεταξὺ κείμενος τοῦ τε Ὀλύμπου καὶ τῆς Ὄσσης. ὄρη δὲ ταῦτά ἐστιν ὑπερύψηλα καὶ οἷον ὑπό τινος θείας φροντίδος διεσχισμένα, κατὰ μέσον δ' ἔχεται[1] χωρίον, οὗ τὸ μὲν μῆκος ἐπὶ τετταράκοντα διήκει σταδίους, τό γε μὴν πλάτος τῇ μέν ἐστι πλέθρου, τῇ δὲ καὶ μεῖζον ὀλίγῳ. διαρρεῖ δὲ μέσου αὐτοῦ ὁ καλούμενος Πηνειός. εἰς τοῦτον δὲ καὶ οἱ λοιποὶ ποταμοὶ συρρέουσι, καὶ ἀνακοινοῦνται τὸ ὕδωρ αὐτῷ καὶ ἐργάζονται τὸν Πηνειὸν ἐκεῖνοι μέγαν.

[1] κατὰ . . . δ' ἔχεται Radermacher: καὶ . . . δέχεται codd.: καὶ μέσον περιέχεται Russell

---

[a] This elegant description of a landscape in northern Greece is not the result of travel by Aelian in those parts; it is almost certainly an attempt to improve upon a similar description in Book 9

BOOK THREE

1. Well now, let us give an account of the Thessalian region called Tempe and create a picture of it.[a] For there is agreement that the spoken word, if it has descriptive power, is no less effective than the work of artists.

It is a district lying between Olympus and Ossa; these are two extremely high mountains, divided as it were by divine dispensation, and they have between them a space which in length stretches about forty stades, and as to the width, in some places it is one plethron, elsewhere a little more.[b] Through the middle of it runs the river called Peneus; the other rivers flow into it and share their water with it, and so they create the great Peneus.

of Theopompus' *History*, the opening words of which are cited in a handbook of rhetoric, Theon's *Progymnasmata* (ed. L. Spengel, *Rhetores graeci*, Leipzig, 1853–6, vol. 2, p. 68 lines 12–16). This acute observation is due to E. L. De Stefani, *Berliner philologische Wochenschrift* 31 (1914): 92 (perhaps anticipated by Gronovius in his edition). Another elegant description of Tempe, by Dio Chrysostom, is mentioned by Synesius, *Dio* 3 C, but nothing is known of it. Tempe was so famous that the emperor Hadrian landscaped an area of his villa at Tivoli so as to resemble it, and Aelian was presumably acquainted with this.

[b] The stade measured about 185 metres, the plethron about 30.

Διατριβὰς δ' ἔχει ποικίλας καὶ παντοδαπὰς ὁ τόπος οὗτος, οὐκ ἀνθρωπίνης χειρὸς ἔργα, ἀλλὰ φύσεως αὐτομάτως[1] εἰς κάλλος τότε φιλοτιμησαμένης, ὅτε ἐλάμβανε γένεσιν ὁ χῶρος. κιττὸς μὲν γὰρ πολὺς καὶ εὖ μάλα λάσιος ἐνακμάζει καὶ τέθηλε καὶ δίκην τῶν εὐγενῶν ἀμπέλων κατὰ τῶν ὑψηλῶν δένδρων ἀνέρπει καὶ συμπέφυκεν αὐτοῖς, πολλὴ δὲ σμίλαξ [ἡ μὲν][2] πρὸς αὐτὸν τὸν πάγον ἀνατρέχει καὶ ἐπισκιάζει τὴν πέτραν· καὶ ἐκείνη μὲν ὑπολανθάνει, ὁρᾶται δὲ τὸ χλοάζον πᾶν, καὶ ἔστιν ὀφθαλμῶν πανήγυρις. ἐν αὐτοῖς[3] δὲ τοῖς λείοις καὶ καθημένοις ἄλση τέ ἐστι ποικίλα καὶ ὑποδρομαὶ συνεχεῖς, ἐν ὥρᾳ θέρους καταφυγεῖν ὁδοιπόροις ἥδιστα καταγώγια, ἃ καὶ δίδωσιν ἀσμένως ψυχάσαι.[4] διαρρέουσι δὲ καὶ κρῆναι συχναί, καὶ ἐπιρρεῖ νάματα ὑδάτων ψυχρῶν καὶ πιεῖν ἡδίστων. λέγεται δὲ τὰ ὕδατα ταῦτα καὶ τοῖς λουσαμένοις ἀγαθὸν εἶναι καὶ εἰς ὑγίειαν αὐτοῖς συμβάλλεσθαι. κατᾴδουσι δὲ καὶ ὄρνιθες ἄλλος ἄλλῃ διεσπαρμένοι, καὶ μάλιστα οἱ μουσικοί, καὶ ἑστιῶσιν εὖ μάλα τὰς ἀκοὰς καὶ παραπέμπουσιν ἀπόνως καὶ σὺν ἡδονῇ, διὰ τοῦ μέλους τὸν κάματον τῶν παριόντων ἀφανίσαντες. παρ' ἑκάτερα δὲ τοῦ ποταμοῦ αἱ διατριβαί εἰσιν αἱ προειρημέναι καὶ αἱ ἀνάπαυλαι.

Διὰ μέσων δὲ τῶν Τεμπῶν ὁ Πηνειὸς ποταμὸς ἔρχεται, σχολῇ καὶ πράως προϊὼν ἐλαίου δίκην. πολλὴ δὲ κατ' αὐτοῦ σκιὰ ἐκ τῶν παραπεφυκότων δένδρων καὶ τῶν ἐξηρτημένων κλάδων τίκτεται, ὡς

This locality has a variety of different spots to linger in that are not the result of human handiwork but are the artless product of nature, which showed its urge to produce beauty when the region was created. A quantity of very luxuriant ivy grows and flourishes there; it climbs up the tall trees and clings to them like noble vines. Abundant honeysuckle rises towards the peak itself and casts its shadow over the rock, which is half hidden under it, while all the foliage is visible, and is a feast for the eye. In the flat low-lying area there are a variety of woods and a succession of arbors, delightful spots for the traveller to take refuge in during the summer, as they give him a welcome chance to cool off. There are many springs, and streams of cold water, delicious to drink, flow down. These waters are said to be good for people who wash in them, and to be beneficial for health. Here and there birds sing, especially those noted for their song; they provide a feast for the ear and escort the traveller effortlessly and with pleasure, their song dissipating the fatigue of the passer-by. On each side of the river are the arbors mentioned already and resting-places.

The river Peneus runs through the middle of Tempe, making its leisurely and gentle progress like olive oil.[a] It is well shaded by the trees growing alongside with their overhanging branches, so that for the greater part of the

[a] This comparison is taken from Homer, *Iliad* 2.753.

---

[1] αὐτομάτως Vb: -του g: -τα Kühn
[2] del. Her.
[3] αὐτοῖς del. Her.
[4] ψυχάσαι Kor.: -ᾶσθαι codd.

ἐπὶ πλεῖστον τῆς ἡμέρας αὐτὴν προήκουσαν ἀποστέγειν τὴν ἀκτῖνα καὶ παρέχειν τοῖς πλέουσι πλεῖν κατὰ ψῦχος. πᾶς δὲ ὁ περίοικος λεὼς συνίασιν ἄλλοι σὺν ἄλλοις, καὶ θύουσι καὶ συνουσίας ποιοῦνται καὶ συμπίνουσιν. ἅτε οὖν πολλῶν ὄντων τῶν θυόντων καὶ τῶν καθαγιζόντων συνεχῶς, εἰκότως καὶ τοῖς βαδίζουσι καὶ τοῖς πλέουσιν ὀσμαὶ συμπαρομαρτοῦσιν ἥδισται· οὕτως ἄρα ἡ τιμὴ ἡ διαρκὴς ἡ περὶ τὸ κρεῖττον ἐκθεοῖ τὸν τόπον.

Ἐνταῦθά τοί φασι παῖδες Θετταλῶν καὶ τὸν Ἀπόλλωνα τὸν Πύθιον καθήρασθαι κατὰ πρόσταγμα τοῦ Διός, ὅτε τὸν Πύθωνα τὸν δράκοντα κατετόξευσεν φυλάττοντα τοὺς Δελφούς, τῆς Γῆς ἔτι[1] ἐχούσης τὸ μαντεῖον. στεφανωσάμενον οὖν ἐκ [ταύτης][2] τῆς δάφνης τῆς Τεμπικῆς καὶ λαβόντα κλάδον εἰς τὴν δεξιὰν χεῖρα [ἐκ τῆς αὐτῆς δάφνης][3] ἐλθεῖν εἰς Δελφοὺς καὶ παραλαβεῖν τὸ μαντεῖον τὸν Διὸς καὶ Λητοῦς παῖδα. ἔστι δὲ καὶ βωμὸς ἐν αὐτῷ τῷ τόπῳ, ἐν ᾧ καὶ ἐστεφανώσατο καὶ τὸν κλάδον ἀφεῖλε. καὶ ἔτι καὶ νῦν δι' ἔτους ἐνάτου οἱ Δελφοὶ παῖδας εὐγενεῖς πέμπουσι καὶ ἀρχιθέωρον ἕνα σφῶν αὐτῶν. οἱ δὲ παραγενόμενοι καὶ μεγαλοπρεπῶς θύσαντες ἐν τοῖς Τέμπεσιν ἀπίασι πάλιν στεφάνους ἀπὸ τῆς αὐτῆς δάφνης διαπλέξαντες, ἀφ' ἧσπερ ἑλὼν[4] καὶ τότε ὁ θεὸς ἐστεφανώσατο. καὶ τὴν ὁδὸν ἐκείνην ἔρχονται, ἣ καλεῖται μὲν Πυθιάς, φέρει δὲ διὰ Θετταλίας καὶ Πελασγίας[5] καὶ τῆς Οἴτης καὶ τῆς Αἰνιάνων χώρας καὶ τῆς Μηλιέων καὶ Δωριέων

day the shadow is enough to give protection from the penetrating rays of the sun, and those who are navigating the river can do so in cool conditions. All the surrounding population meets here for sacrifice, assembly, and drinking parties. As there are many who offer sacrifice and perform rites regularly, it follows that the sweetest smells accompany the traveller, whether he be on foot or in a boat. The honours continuously offered to superior powers render the place divine.

Here, as the people of Thessaly report, Pythian Apollo purified himself on the orders of Zeus, when he had slaughtered the snake Pytho that still guarded Delphi, the oracle still being in the control of Earth. He made himself a crown from the laurel of Tempe, and carrying a branch [from the same laurel] in his right hand he went to Delphi to take over the oracle as the son of Zeus and Leto. There is an altar at the very spot where he put on the crown and removed the branch. Even now, every eight years the Delphians send here the children of noble families accompanied by someone to head the delegation. They arrive, make a lavish sacrifice in Tempe, and return with crowns woven from the same laurel from which the god took branches for his crown on the earlier occasion. They take the route known as the Pythian which carries them through Thessaly, Pelasgia, Oeta, and the territory of the Aenianes, the Melieis, the Dorians, and the Western

---

[1] ἔτι huc traiecit Her.: ante φυλάττοντα praebent codd.

[2] delevi

[3] del. Per.

[4] ἑλὼν scripsi: ἐρῶν codd.

[5] Πελασγίας Ortelius: Πελαγονίας codd.

καὶ Λοκρῶν τῶν Ἑσπερίων. οὗτοι δὲ καὶ παραπέμπουσιν αὐτοὺς σὺν αἰδοῖ καὶ τιμῇ οὐδὲν ἧττον ἤπερ οὖν ἐκεῖνοι, οἳ τοὺς ἐξ Ὑπερβορέων τὰ ἱερὰ κομίζοντας τῷ αὐτῷ θεῷ τούτῳ τιμῶσι. καὶ μὴν καὶ τοῖς Πυθίοις ἐκ ταύτης τῆς δάφνης τοὺς στεφάνους τοῖς νικῶσι διδόασιν. ὑπὲρ μὲν οὖν τῶν ἐν Θετταλίᾳ Τεμπῶν καὶ ἐμοὶ νῦν τοσαῦτα εἰρήσθω.

2. *Ἀναξαγόρᾳ τις τῷ Κλαζομενίῳ σπουδάζοντι πρὸς τοὺς ἑταίρους προσελθὼν ἔφη τεθνηκέναι οἱ τοὺς δύο παῖδας οὕσπερ οὖν καὶ εἶχε μόνους ὁ Ἀναξαγόρας. ὁ δὲ μηδὲν διαταραχθεὶς εἶπεν· "ᾔδειν θνητοὺς γεγεννηκώς."*

3. *Ξενοφῶντι θύοντι ἧκέ τις ἐκ Μαντινείας ἄγγελος, λέγων τὸν υἱὸν αὐτῷ τὸν Γρύλλον τεθνάναι· κἀκεῖνος ἀπέθετο μὲν τὸν στέφανον, διετέλει δὲ θύων. ἐπεὶ δὲ ὁ ἄγγελος προσέθηκε <τῷ πρότερον λόγῳ>*[1] *καὶ ἐκεῖνον <τὸν λέγοντα> ὅτι νικῶν <μέντοι> τέθνηκε, πάλιν ὁ Ξενοφῶν ἐπέθετο <τῇ κεφαλῇ> τὸν στέφανον. ταῦτα μὲν οὖν δημώδη καὶ εἰς πολλοὺς ἐκπεφοίτηκεν.*

4. *Δίων δὲ ὁ Ἱππαρίνου μὲν παῖς, Πλάτωνος δὲ ὁμιλητής, ἔτυχε μὲν χρηματίζων ὑπέρ τινων δημοσίων καὶ κοινῶν πραγμάτων, ὁ δὲ παῖς αὐτῷ ἐκ τοῦ τέγους κατενεχθεὶς εἰς τὴν αὐλὴν τὸν βίον κατέστρεψεν. οὐδὲν οὖν ἐπὶ τούτοις μετεβάλετο ὁ Δίων, ἀλλ' ὅπερ οὖν ἐξ ἀρχῆς ἔπραττε, τοῦτο καὶ δρῶν διετέλεσεν.*

Locrians. The latter escort them with respect and honour equal to that accorded to the delegation bringing sacred offerings to this same god from the Hyperboreans.[a] In addition the crowns given to victors at the Pythian games are from this laurel. On the subject of Tempe in Thessaly that is all I wish to say now.

2. Anaxagoras of Clazomenae was engaged in serious discussion with some companions when someone came up to him with the news that his two children were dead—these were in fact Anaxagoras' only children. But he was unperturbed and replied: "I knew I had created mortal beings."[b]

3. While Xenophon was sacrificing, a messenger arrived from Mantinea with the news that his son Gryllus had died. Xenophon removed the garland from his head and continued the sacrifice. When the messenger added to his initial report the extra fact that Gryllus had at least died victorious, Xenophon put the garland back on his head. This is an anecdote in general circulation, recurring persistently in many sources.

4. Dion, son of Hipparinus and pupil of Plato, happened to be dealing with some public business of general concern when his son fell off the roof into the courtyard and died. Dion was unaffected by the accident and continued to handle the business he had been dealing with.

[a] Herodotus 4.33 reports that offerings came from the Hyperboreans to Apollo's shrine at Delos, not directly but conveyed by a series of messengers. The identity of the Hyperboreans remains a mystery. [b] The anecdotes in chs. 2–5 are part of a series found also in ps.-Plutarch, *Moralia* 118 D–119 D.

---

[1] in hoc c. verba uncinis inclusa praebet Stobaeus 4.44.63: om. codd.

5. Ἀντίγονόν γε μήν φασι τὸν δεύτερον ἐπεί τινες τὸν υἱὸν αὐτῷ ἐκ τῆς παρατάξεως ἐκόμισαν νεκρόν, εἶδε μὲν αὐτόν, οὐδὲν δὲ τρέψας τοῦ χρωτός, οὐδὲ μὴν ἐπιδακρύσας, ἐπαινέσας δὲ ὡς ἀγαθὸν στρατιώτην, θάπτειν προσέταξεν.

6. Κράτης ὁ Θηβαῖος τά τε ἄλλα μεγαλόφρων ὢν πεφώραται καὶ καταφρονητικὸς τῶν ὑπὸ τοῦ πλήθους θαυμαζομένων, ἀτὰρ οὖν καὶ χρημάτων καὶ πατρίδος. ὅτι μὲν οὖν τῆς οὐσίας ἀπέστη τοῖς Θηβαίοις, τοῦτο μὲν καὶ εἰς πάντας ἐξεφοίτησε· τὸ δὲ ἕτερον αὐτοῦ οὐ πᾶσι γνώριμον, ἔστι δὲ ἐκεῖνο. ἀπαλλαττόμενος τῶν Θηβῶν οἰκισθεισῶν πάλιν ἔφη· "οὐ δέομαι πόλεως, ἣν Ἀλέξανδρος κατασκάψει [ἢ][1] ἄλλος."

7. Δημοχάρης ὁ τοῦ Δημοσθένους ἀδελφιδοῦς ἐπιδεῖξαι βουλόμενος ὅτι τῆς ἐκ τῶν πολλῶν κακοφημίας ὑπερφρονεῖ, θεασάμενός τινας καθεζομένους ἐν ἰατρείῳ ψογεροὺς καὶ κακῶς ἀγορεύειν ἐκ παντὸς τρόπου διψῶντας, "τί φατε ὑμεῖς," εἶπε "Δυσμενίδαι;" τὸ ἦθος αὐτῶν ἅμα ἐκκαλύψας διὰ τούτου τοῦ ὀνόματος.

8. Φρύνιχον Ἀθηναῖοι στρατηγὸν εἵλοντο οὔτε κατὰ σπουδὰς οὔτε κατὰ τὴν τοῦ γένους ἀξίαν οὐδὲ μὴν ὅτι ἦν πλούσιος· πολλάκις γὰρ καὶ ἐκ τούτων ἐθαυμάζοντο ἐν ταῖς Ἀθήναις, καὶ τῶν ἄλλων προῃροῦντο. ἀλλ' ἐπεὶ τοῖς πυρριχισταῖς ἔν τινι τραγῳ-

[1] del. Menagius (cf. Diog. Laert. 6.93)

5. Antigonus II,[a] according to the reports, when his son's dead body was brought to him from the battlefield, looked at him and without changing colour or shedding a tear praised him for being a brave soldier and ordered the funeral.

6. Crates of Thebes gave many proofs of his lofty spirit. In particular he had contempt for what the masses admired, including money and one's native city. Everyone knows that he turned his property over to the Thebans, but another fact about him is not generally known. It is that he left Thebes after it had been rebuilt, saying "I have no need of a city which a second Alexander will raze to the ground."[b]

7. Demochares the nephew of Demosthenes wished to prove his contempt for popular slander. Seeing that some sharp-tongued people, men anxious to be critical at all costs, were sitting in a doctor's surgery, he said "What are you talking about, Dysmenidae?"[c] By this form of address he revealed their character.

8. The Athenians elected Phrynichus general not because of his political connections or the distinction of his family or even for his wealth. At Athens people were often admired for these reasons and elected in preference to others. But he had composed for a tragedy suitably

[a] This is the Antigonus of 2.20 above.

[b] Thebes had been destroyed by Alexander after an abortive rebellion against Macedonian rule in 335 B.C. Cf. 13.7 below.

[c] This neologism meaning "malevolent" is coined by analogy with Eumenides meaning "Furies," as in the title of Aeschylus' play.

δίᾳ ἐπιτήδεια μέλη καὶ πολεμικὰ ἐξεπόνησεν, οὕτως ἄρα κατεκτήσατο τὸ θέατρον καὶ ἐκράτησε τῶν παρόντων, ὥστε παραχρῆμα αὐτὸν εἵλοντο στρατηγεῖν, πιστεύσαντες ὅτι τῶν πολεμικῶν ἔργων ἡγήσεται καλῶς καὶ εἰς δέον, ὅπου μὴ ἀπᾴδοντα τοῖς ἐνόπλοις ἀνδράσιν εἰργάσατο τὰ ἐν τῷ δράματι μέλη τε καὶ ποιήματα.

9. Ἐρῶντι ἀνδρί τις οὐκ ἐρῶν [ὅπλοις],[1] ἐπειγούσης τῆς μάχης καὶ συνάγοντος τοῦ πολέμου, οὐκ ἂν συμμίξειεν. ὁ γὰρ ἀνέραστος φεύγει καὶ ἀποδιδράσκει τὸν ἐρωτικόν, ἅτε βέβηλος καὶ ἀτέλεστος τῷ θεῷ καὶ τοσοῦτον ἀνδρεῖος ὅσον αὐτῷ καὶ ἡ ψυχὴ χωρεῖ καὶ τὸ σῶμα ῥώμης ἔχει· δέδοικε δὲ τὸν ἕτερον, ἅτε ἐκ θεοῦ κατόχως ἐνθουσιῶντα καὶ οὐ μὰ Δία τοῦτο τὸ κοινὸν ἐξ Ἄρεος ἀλλ' ἐξ Ἔρωτος μανέντα. οἱ μὲν γὰρ ἐκ τοῦ ἑτέρου τῶν θεῶν κατειλημμένοι, ὧν ἕνα φησὶν Ὅμηρος ὅμοια τῷ Ἄρει μαίνεσθαι, ἀλλ' ἐκεῖνοί γε ἐξ ἑνὸς περιειλημμένοι δαίμονος εὖ καὶ καλῶς ἀγωνίζονται τοσοῦτον ὅσον ἐνθουσιᾶν αὐτοὺς ἅπαξ· οἱ δὲ Ἔρωτος Βάκχοι πολεμοῦντες καὶ ὑπὸ τῆς Ἄρεος ὁρμῆς καὶ ὑπὸ τῆς Ἔρωτος ἐκκαύσεως διπλῆν τὴν λατρείαν ὑπομένοντες εἰκότως κατὰ τὴν Κρητῶν ἔννοιαν καὶ κατορθοῦσι διπλᾶ. οὔκουν τῷ ἐξ Ἄρεος καὶ Ἔρωτος φονῶντι αἰτιάσαιτο ἄν τις εἰ μὴ ὑπομένοι ὁπλίτης

[1] del. Her.

---

[a] This refers to a dance by soldiers wearing armour. For Phrynichus see 13.17 below.

martial songs to accompany a pyrrhic dance,[a] and this so won over the audience, captivating everyone present, that he was immediately appointed general. They were confident that his sound leadership on campaign would meet all requirements because he had written for his play lyrics and poetry well suited to men in armour.

9. In the heat of battle when war brings men into combat, a man who is not in love could not match one who is. The man untouched by love avoids and runs away from the man who loves, as if he were an outsider uninitiated into the god's rites, and his bravery depends on his character and physical strength. He fears the other man because the latter is in the grip of divine possession and this inspiration, by Zeus, derives not from Ares, as is common, but from Eros. Those who are in the grip of the former of the two gods—Homer says [*Iliad* 15.605] that one of them was struck by madness like Ares—they are possessed by a single deity, and they fight well and bravely as far as the inspiration of a single divinity allows. But those who fight under the inspiration of Eros are in the service of two gods, stimulated by Ares and fired by Eros, and it is not surprising, as the Cretans believe, that they in fact achieve a double success.[b] No one would criticise a hoplite for not withstanding the assault of a man fired by

[b] Crete and Sparta were peculiar among Greek societies in having a male population organised as a military force, and it is often thought that homosexual behaviour, taken for granted in the army, was more acceptable in those areas of Greece than elsewhere. See K. J. Dover, *Greek Homosexuality* (London and Cambridge, Mass., 1978), pp. 185–186, 192–194. Aelian's interest in this topic is presumably antiquarian, not addressed to the military authorities of his own day.

ἀνταγωνίσασθαι ὑφ' ἑνὶ τεταγμένος θεῷ, ἀλλ' οὐχ ὑπὸ τοῖς δύο.

10. Περὶ τῶν ἐν Λακεδαίμονι ἐφόρων πολλὰ μὲν καὶ ἄλλα εἰπεῖν καλὰ ἔχω, ἃ δ' οὖν προῄρημαι νῦν ἐρῶ ταῦτα. ὅτε τις τῶν παρ' αὐτοῖς καλῶν πλούσιον ἐραστὴν εἵλετο[1] τοῦ[2] χρηστοῦ πένητος, ἐπέβαλον αὐτῷ χρήματα, κολάζοντες ὡς ἔοικε τὴν φιλοχρηματίαν τῇ τῶν χρημάτων ζημίᾳ. ἄλλον δέ τινα ἄνδρα καλὸν κἀγαθὸν οὐδενὸς ἐρῶντα τῶν[3] καλῶς πεφυκότων καὶ τοῦτον ἐζημίωσαν, ὅτι χρηστὸς ὢν οὐδενὸς ἤρα· δῆλον γὰρ ὡς ὅμοιον ἂν ἑαυτῷ κἀκεῖνον ἀπέφηνεν, ἴσως δ' ἂν καὶ ἄλλον. δεινὴ γὰρ ἡ τῶν ἐραστῶν πρὸς τὰ παιδικὰ εὔνοια ἀρετὰς ἐνεργάσασθαι, ὅταν αὐτοὶ σεμνοὶ ὦσιν· ἐπεί τοι Λακωνικὸς καὶ οὗτος νόμος, ὅταν ἁμάρτῃ μειράκιον, τῇ μὲν ἀφελείᾳ τοῦ τρόπου καὶ τῷ νεαρῷ τῆς ἡλικίας συγγινώσκουσι, τὸν δὲ ἐραστὴν ὑπὲρ αὐτοῦ κολάζουσιν, ἐπιγνώμονας αὐτοὺς καὶ ἐξεταστὰς ὧν ἐκεῖνοι πράττουσι κελεύοντες εἶναι.

11. Οἱ περιπατητικοί φασι μεθ' ἡμέραν θητεύουσαν τὴν ψυχὴν τῷ σώματι περιπλέκεσθαι καὶ μὴ δύνασθαι καθαρῶς τὴν ἀλήθειαν θεωρεῖν· νύκτωρ δὲ διαλυθεῖσαν τῆς περὶ τοῦτο λειτουργίας καὶ σφαιρωθεῖσαν ἐν τῷ περὶ τὸν θώρακα τόπῳ μαντικωτέραν γίνεσθαι, ἐξ ὧν τὰ ἐνύπνια.

12. Οὔκ εἰσι θρυπτικοὶ πρὸς τοὺς ἐραστὰς οἱ Λακεδαιμόνιοι καλοὶ οὐδὲ ἀλαζόνες, ἐπεὶ τοὐναντίον

Ares and Eros; a hoplite is the servant of one god, not two.

10. Though I have many other good things to report of the Spartan ephors, there is one I have chosen to mention now. When one of the handsome young men in their society chose a rich lover in preference to one who was poor but of good character, they imposed a fine, punishing, it would seem, the desire for possessions by a monetary penalty. And any man of good appearance and character who did not fall in love with someone well-bred was also fined, because despite his excellence he did not love anyone. It was clear that he could have made his beloved, and perhaps even another man, similar to himself. Lovers' affection for their beloved has a remarkable power of stimulating the virtues, if the former are themselves worthy of respect. In fact there is also a Spartan law, that when a young man commits a misdemeanour, the ephors are indulgent to a naive character and to the inexperience of youth, but they punish his lover instead, because they require lovers to watch and control what the young do.

11. The Peripatetics say that during the day the soul is enveloped by the body and is a slave to it, unable to see the truth clearly; but at night it is freed from this servitude and, taking the form of a sphere in the parts around the chest, it becomes more prophetic. As a result we have dreams.

12. Spartan boys are not overbearing or arrogant towards their lovers. It is possible to see that they behave

---

[1] *εἵλετο*] *προείλετο* Gesner, sed cf. Soph. *Phil.* 1100, Gow ad Theocr. 11.49 [2] *τοῦ*] *του* Russell: del. Her.

[3] *τῶν* x: *τῶν οὐ* V: *τῶν εὖ* <*καὶ*> Per.

ἢ παρὰ τοῖς ἄλλοις ὡραίοις [τὰ][1] ἐκ τούτων καταμαθεῖν ἔστιν. αὐτοὶ γοῦν δέονται τῶν ἐραστῶν εἰσπνεῖν αὐτοῖς· Λακεδαιμονίων δέ ἐστιν αὕτη ἡ φωνή, ἐρᾶν δὴ[2] λέγουσα. Σπαρτιάτης δὲ ἔρως αἰσχρὸν οὐκ οἶδεν· εἴτε γὰρ μειράκιον ἐτόλμησεν ὕβριν ὑπομεῖναι εἴτε ἐραστὴς ὑβρίσαι, ἀλλ' οὐδετέροις ἐλυσιτέλησε τὴν Σπάρτην καταμιᾶναι·[3] ἢ γὰρ τῆς πατρίδος ἀπηλλάγησαν ἢ καὶ τὸ ἔτι θερμότερον [καὶ][4] τοῦ βίου αὐτοῦ.

13. Ὅτι φιλοινότατον ἔθνος τὸ τῶν Ταπύρων τοσοῦτον ὥστε ζῆν αὐτοὺς ἐν οἴνῳ καὶ τὸ πλεῖστον τοῦ βίου ἐν τῇ πρὸς αὐτὸν ὁμιλίᾳ καταναλίσκειν. καὶ οὐ μόνον εἰς πόμα καταχρῶνται αὐτῷ, ἀλλὰ γὰρ καὶ χρῖσμά ἐστιν αὐτοῖς ὁ οἶνος, ὥσπερ ἄλλοις τὸ ἔλαιον.

14. Βυζαντίους δὲ δεινῶς οἰνόφλυγας ὄντας ἐνοικεῖν τοῖς καπηλείοις λόγος[5] ἔχει, τῶν οἰκιῶν τῶν ἰδίων καὶ τῶν δωματίων[6] ἐξοικισθέντας καὶ τοῖς ξένοις τοῖς ἐνεπιδημοῦσι τῇ πόλει ἀπομισθώσαντας αὐτά, καὶ οὐ μόνον ἐκείνων ἀλλὰ καὶ τῶν γυναικῶν αὐτοῖς ἀποστάντας, ὡς ἐν ταὐτῷ τοὺς Βυζαντίους διπλῆν αἰτίαν φέρεσθαι καὶ οἰνοφλυγίας καὶ προαγωγείας. ἅτε δὲ ὑπὸ τῆς μέθης καὶ τοῦ οἴνου διαρρέοντες, αὐλοῦ μὲν ἀκούοντες χαίρουσι, καὶ τὸ ἔργον αὐτοῖς αὐλεῖσθαί ἐστι· σάλπιγγα δὲ οὐδὲ

[1] del. Faber [2] δὴ Gesner: δεῖν x: δοεῖν V

[3] τὴν Σπάρτην καταμιᾶναι Bruhn: τῇ -ῃ καταμεῖναι codd. (<ἐν> τῇ Faber, ἐγκαταμεῖναι Her.)

in the opposite way to attractive young men in other societies, from this evidence. They themselves ask their lovers to inspire them; this is a Spartan word, meaning precisely "to love."[a] Spartan love has nothing shameful about it. For whether a boy is rash enough to submit to abuse or a lover dares to go too far, neither of them profits by having brought dishonour to Sparta. They either abandon their country or, what is more serious, life itself.

13. Note that the Tapyri as a nation are very fond of wine, to such an extent that they live on wine and pass most of their time in contact with it. They do not use it simply as a drink; for them wine is something to rub on the skin, as olive oil is for others.[b]

14. The inhabitants of Byzantium, who are formidable tipplers, are reported to live in bars, moving out of their own houses and dwellings, which they let to foreigners visiting the city. They abandon to the visitors not simply their homes, but also their wives; and so the Byzantines by this one act lay themselves open to the double charge of drunkenness and prostitution. As wine and drunkenness lead them into extravagance, they enjoy listening to the aulos, and it is their daily business to be serenaded;

[a] Dover, *Greek Homosexuality*, p. 202, refers to this passage. The word εἰσπνεῖν used by Aelian seems unremarkable, but there is also evidence of a rare derivative εἴσπνηλος used in Doric dialect.

[b] The Tapyri were an Indian people. Much the same information is given by Athenaeus 442 B. This is the first of many chs. beginning with ὅτι, which is a sign of abbreviation.

---

[4] del. Her. [5] ante λόγος add. ὁ x

[6] δωματίων Kor.: -των codd. (καὶ τῶν δωμάτων del. Her.)

ἀρχὴν ὑπομένουσι. καὶ ἐκ τούτων ἔξεστι νοεῖν ὅτι καὶ πρὸς ὅπλα καὶ πρὸς πολέμους ἀλλοτριώτατα διάκεινται Βυζάντιοι.

Διὰ ταῦτά τοι καὶ Λεωνίδης ὁ στρατηγὸς αὐτῶν ἐν πολιορκίᾳ ἰσχυρᾷ, ἐπεὶ τῶν πολεμίων τοῖς τείχεσι προσβαλόντων ἐκεῖνοί γε τὰς φρουρὰς ἐκλιπόντες διημέρευον ἐν ταῖς συνήθεσι διατριβαῖς, προσέταξε τὰ καπηλεῖα ἐπὶ τῶν τειχῶν διασκηνωθῆναι αὐτοῖς. Καὶ τοῦτο τὸ σόφισμα ἀνέπεισεν αὐτοὺς ὀψὲ καὶ βραδέως τὴν τάξιν μὴ καταλιπεῖν, ἅτε τῆς προφάσεως αὐτοῖς περιῃρημένης. λέγει δὲ ταῦτα ὑπὲρ αὐτῶν Δάμων. ὁμολογεῖν δὲ τούτοις ἔοικε καὶ ὁ Μένανδρος, ὅταν λέγῃ·

μεθύσους τοὺς ἐμπόρους
ποιεῖ τὸ Βυζάντιον· ὅλην ἐπίνομεν[1]
τὴν νύκτα.

15. Καὶ Ἀργεῖοι δὲ καὶ Τιρύνθιοι κεκωμῴδηνται καὶ οὗτοι ἀκρατέστερον τῷ οἴνῳ προσιόντες. τό γε μὴν ὑπὲρ τῶν Θρᾳκῶν, ἀλλὰ τοῦτο μὲν καὶ διαβεβόηται ἤδη καὶ διατεθρύληται, ὡς εἰσὶ πιεῖν δεινότατοι. οὐ διαπεφεύγασι δὲ ταύτην τὴν αἰτίαν οὐδὲ Ἰλλυριοί, ἀλλ' ἐκεῖνοί γε προσειλήφασι κἀκεῖνο τὸ ἐπίκλημα, ὅτι ἐφεῖται τοῖς ἐν τῷ συνδείπνῳ παροῦσι ξένοις προπίνειν ταῖς γυναιξὶν ἕκαστον, ἐὰν[2] βούληται, κἂν μηδὲν προσήκῃ ἡ γυνὴ αὐτῷ.

16. Εἶτα τίς ἀμείνων ἦν στρατηγεῖν, Δημήτριος ὁ πολιορκητὴς ἢ Τιμόθεος ὁ Ἀθηναῖος; ἐγὼ μὲν ἐρῶ

but they cannot endure the trumpet. One can infer that the Byzantines find war and military matters utterly uncongenial.

That is why their general Leonides, during a severe siege, when the enemy were attacking the walls, and the garrison abandoned their posts to pass the day in their usual haunts, gave instructions to have bars set up for them on the walls. This device gradually and after some long time persuaded them not to abandon their posts of duty, as their pretext had been removed.

This report about them comes from Damon [FGrH 389 F 1]. Menander [fr. 61 K.] seems to be in agreement when he says "Byzantium turns merchants into drunkards—we drank all night long."[a]

15. The Argives and Tirynthians were also ridiculed in comedy for their addiction to wine. As to the Thracians, it is now a well established commonplace that they are great drinkers. The Illyrians do not escape the same criticism; but they have been accused of something else in addition—it is permissible at their dinners for each of the guests, if he wishes, to toast the women, even if the woman in question is no relation.[b]

16. Who then was the better general, Demetrius Poliorcetes[c] or Timotheus the Athenian? I will describe

[a] This ch. probably derives from Athenaeus 442 CD.

[b] This ch. looks like an abridgement of Athenaeus 442 D–443 A.

[c] Demetrius Poliorcetes was king of Macedon 293–287 B.C.

---

[1] ἐπίνομεν ex Athenaeo Scheffer: ἔπινε codd.

[2] ἐὰν] ᾗ ἂν Her. post Kor.

τὸν τῶν ἀμφοτέρων τρόπον· ἔνεστι δ' ὑμῖν προτιμῆσαι τὸν ἕτερον. Δημήτριος μὲν βίᾳ καὶ πλεονεξίᾳ καὶ λυπῶν τὰ μέγιστα καὶ ἀδικῶν ᾕρει τὰς πόλεις μηχανὰς προσάγων καὶ κατασείων καὶ ὑπορύττων τὰ τείχη, Τιμόθεος δὲ πείθων καὶ διδάσκων λόγῳ ὅτι λυσιτελέστερόν ἐστι τῶν Ἀθηναίων ἀκούειν.

17. Ἐπολιτεύσαντο οὖν καὶ φιλόσοφοι ἢ[1] αὐτὸ τοῦτο μόνον τὴν διάνοιαν ἀγαθοὶ γενόμενοι ἐφ' ἡσυχίας κατεβιώσαν. ἐπηνώρθωσαν γὰρ τὰ κοινὰ Ζάλευκος μὲν τὰ ἐν Λοκροῖς, Χαρώνδας δὲ τὰ ἐν Κατάνῃ καὶ τὰ ἐν Ῥηγίῳ, ὅτε ἐκ Κατάνης ἔφευγε. Ταραντίνοις δὲ ἐγένετο ἀγαθὸν Ἀρχύτας, Σόλων δὲ Ἀθηναίοις. Βίας δὲ καὶ Θαλῆς τὴν Ἰωνίαν πολλὰ ὤνησαν, Χίλων δὲ Λακεδαιμονίους, Μιτυληναίους γε μὴν Πιττακός, Κλεόβουλος δὲ Ῥοδίους. καὶ Ἀναξίμανδρος δὲ ἡγήσατο τῆς εἰς Ἀπολλωνίαν ἐκ Μιλήτου ἀποικίας. ἀλλὰ καὶ Ξενοφῶν στρατιώτης ἀγαθὸς ἦν καὶ ἀμείνων στρατηγός, ὅτε Κύρῳ συνανέβη· καὶ Κῦρος μὲν καὶ οἱ σὺν αὐτῷ ἀπέθανον, καλούσης δὲ τῆς χρείας τὸν δυνησόμενον σῶσαι τοὺς Ἕλληνας καὶ ἀγαγεῖν τὴν ὀπίσω εἰς τὰ οἰκεῖα, οὗτος ἐκεῖνος ἦν. Πλάτων δὲ ὁ Ἀρίστωνος Δίωνα κατήγαγεν εἰς Σικελίαν, καὶ δι' ὧν αὐτῷ συνεβούλευε καὶ ἐδίδασκε, διὰ τούτων τὴν τυραννίδα τὴν Διονυσίου κατέλυσε. Σωκράτης δὲ τῇ μὲν Ἀθηναίων πολιτείᾳ οὐκ ἠρέσκετο· τυραννικὴν γὰρ καὶ μοναρχικὴν ἑώρα τὴν δημοκρατίαν οὖσαν, καὶ διὰ

the methods of both, and it will be for you to choose one of them. Demetrius captured cities by force and aggression, causing great pain and injustice, bringing up siege machines, knocking down walls or undermining them. Timotheus did so by persuasion and expounding reasons why it was more profitable to be subject to the Athenians.

17. Philosophers too have engaged in politics rather than confining themselves to intellectual excellence and living a sheltered life. Zaleucus restored society at Locri, as did Charondas at Catane, and later in Rhegium when he had gone into exile from Catane. Archytas brought benefit to Tarentum, Solon to Athens,[a] Bias and Thales performed great services in Ionia, Chilon in Sparta, Pittacus for Mytilene, Cleobulus for Rhodes. Anaximander led the party of colonists from Miletus to Apollonia.[b] Xenophon was a good soldier, and better general, when he joined Cyrus' expedition;[c] and when Cyrus and his companions had lost their lives, the need of the moment called for a man who could save the Greeks and lead them back to their homes, and he was the man. Plato the son of Ariston restored Dio to power in Sicily; by his advice and teaching Dio subverted the tyranny of Dionysius.[d] Socrates was dissatisfied with the Athenian state; he saw the democracy as tyrannical or monarchical. That is why

[a] Aelian here begins a list of the Seven Sages, who are first named as a group in Plato, *Protagoras* 343 a.

[b] Now Sozopol. [c] As narrated in the *Anabasis*.

[d] The story of Plato, Dion, and Dionysius is given in Plato's *Seventh Letter.*

---

[1] ἢ] οἳ Russell dubitanter: an <μᾶλλον> ἢ?

ταῦτα οὔτε ἐπεψήφισεν[1] Ἀθηναίοις τὸν τῶν δέκα στρατηγῶν θάνατον, ἀλλ' οὐδὲ τοῖς τριάκοντα ἐκοινώνει τῶν ἀσεβημάτων. ἔνθα δὲ ἐχρῆν ὑπὲρ τῆς πατρίδος ἀγωνίζεσθαι, ἀλλ' ἐνταῦθά γε ἀπροφάσιστος ἐκεῖνος στρατιώτης ἦν. ἐστρατεύσατο γοῦν ἐπὶ Δηλίῳ[2] καὶ εἰς Ἀμφίπολιν καὶ εἰς Ποτίδαιαν. Ἀριστοτέλης δὲ τὴν ἑαυτοῦ πατρίδα, οὐ τὸ λεγόμενον δὴ τοῦτο εἰς γόνυ πεσοῦσαν, ἀλλ' ἐπὶ στόμα ἀνέστησεν αὖθις. Δημήτριος δὲ ὁ Φαληρεὺς καὶ Ἀθήνησιν ἐπιφανέστατα ἐπολιτεύσατο, ἔστ' [ἂν][3] αὐτὸν ὁ συνήθης Ἀθηναίοις φθόνος ἐξέωσε, καὶ ἐν Αἰγύπτῳ δὲ συνὼν τῷ Πτολεμαίῳ νομοθεσίας ἦρξε. τίς δὲ ἀντιφήσει καὶ Περικλέα τὸν Ξανθίππου φιλόσοφον γενέσθαι καὶ Ἐπαμεινώνδαν τὸν Πολύμνιδος καὶ Φωκίωνα τὸν Φώκου καὶ Ἀριστείδην τὸν Λυσιμάχου καὶ Ἐφιάλτην τὸν Σοφωνίδου καὶ ἔτι κάτω τοῦ χρόνου Καρνεάδην καὶ Κριτόλαον, εἴ γε καὶ[4] εἰς τὴν Ῥώμην ἀφίκοντο [καὶ][5] ἐκεῖνοι ὑπὲρ τῶν Ἀθηναίων πρεσβεύοντες καὶ αὐτοῖς[6] σωτηρίαν εὕραντο; οἵπερ οὖν εἰς τοσοῦτον ἐνέτρεψαν τὴν σύγκλητον βουλὴν ὡς εἰπεῖν αὐτούς· "ἔπεμψαν Ἀθηναῖοι πρεσβεύοντας οὐ τοὺς πείσοντας ἀλλὰ γὰρ τοὺς βιασομένους ἡμᾶς δρᾶσαι ὅσα θέλουσιν." ἐγὼ δὲ πολιτείαν φαίην <ἂν>[7] καὶ τὸ Περσαίου, εἴ γε

[1] *ἐπεψήφισεν* J. A. Ernesti: *ἐψήφισεν* codd.
[2] *Δηλίῳ* e Plat. *Apol.* 28 e Dilts: *Δῆλον* codd.
[3] del. Her. [4] *καὶ* x: om. V [5] del. Kor.
[6] *αὐτοῖς* Gesner: *-τοὶ* codd. [7] suppl. Kor.

he did not put before the Athenians the motion proposing the death penalty for the ten generals[a] or associate himself with the monstrous acts of the Thirty.[b] When there was a duty to fight on behalf of his country, then he made no excuses and served as a soldier. He was a member of the expeditions to Delium, to Amphipolis, and to Potidaea. Aristotle restored his native city when it was not, as the saying is, on its knees, but had collapsed. Demetrius of Phalerum [fr. 65 W.] not only had a most distinguished career at Athens, until the typical jealousy of the Athenians ousted him; he then took charge of legislation in Egypt as an associate of Ptolemy. Who will deny that Pericles son of Xanthippus, Epaminondas son of Polymnis, Phocion son of Phocus, Aristides son of Lysimachus, and Ephialtes son of Sophonides were philosophers? And, in later times, Carneades and Critolaus [fr. 7 W.]? They came to Rome in a delegation on behalf of Athens and ensured its safety.[c] Indeed, they made such an impression on the senate that its members said: "The Athenians have sent a delegation not to persuade but to compel us to do whatever they want." I would also class as political the activity of Persaeus[d] [fr. 439 v. Arn.], who was tutor to

[a] Socrates happened to be in the chair when the Council had to decide whether to prosecute the Athenian generals for not rescuing their men during a storm after the battle of Arginusae in 406 B.C.

[b] Socrates' previous association with some of the Thirty Tyrants is likely to have influenced the jury at his trial.

[c] They were members of an embassy sent in 156/5 B.C.

[d] Stoic philosopher who accepted an invitation to the court of Antigonus Gonatas in 276 B.C.; he was also active as a leader of Antigonus' army.

Ἀντίγονον ἐπαίδευσε, καὶ τὸ Ἀριστοτέλους, ἐπεὶ καὶ αὐτὸς σὺν Ἀλεξάνδρῳ τῷ Φιλίππου νέῳ ὄντι φιλοσοφῶν ἦν δῆλος. καὶ Λῦσις δὲ ὁ γνώριμος ὁ Πυθαγόρου καὶ αὐτὸς Ἐπαμεινώνδαν ἐξεπαίδευσεν. εἴ τις οὖν ἀπράκτους λέγει τοὺς φιλοσόφους, ἀλλὰ εὐήθη γε αὐτοῦ καὶ ἀνόητα ταῦτα· ἐγὼ μὲν γὰρ τὴν σὺν αὐτοῖς ἀπραγμοσύνην καὶ τὸν τῆς ἡσυχίας ἔρωτα κἂν[1] ἁρπάσαιμι ἐπιδραμών.

18. Περιηγεῖταί τινα Θεόπομπος συνουσίαν Μίδου τοῦ Φρυγὸς καὶ Σειληνοῦ. νύμφης δὲ παῖς ὁ Σειληνὸς οὗτος, θεοῦ μὲν ἀφανέστερος τὴν φύσιν, ἀνθρώπου δὲ κρείττων, εἰ[2] καὶ ἀθάνατος ἦν. πολλὰ μὲν οὖν καὶ ἄλλα ἀλλήλοις διελέχθησαν, καὶ ὑπὲρ τούτων ὁ Σειληνὸς ἔλεγε πρὸς τὸν Μίδαν, τὴν μὲν Εὐρώπην καὶ τὴν Ἀσίαν καὶ τὴν Λιβύην νήσους εἶναι, ἃς περιρρεῖν κύκλῳ τὸν Ὠκεανόν, ἤπειρον δὲ εἶναι μόνην ἐκείνην τὴν ἔξω τούτου τοῦ κόσμου. καὶ τὸ μὲν μέγεθος αὐτῆς ἄπειρον διηγεῖτο, τρέφειν δὲ[3] τὰ ἄλλα ζῷα μεγάλα, καὶ τοὺς ἀνθρώπους δὲ τῶν ἐνταυθοῖ διπλασίονας τὸ μέγεθος, καὶ χρόνον ζῆν αὐτοὺς οὐχ ὅσον ἡμεῖς, ἀλλὰ καὶ ἐκείνου[4] διπλοῦν. καὶ πολλὰς μὲν εἶναι καὶ μεγάλας πόλεις καὶ βίων ἰδιότητας, καὶ νόμους αὐτοῖς τετάχθαι ἐναντίως κειμένους τοῖς παρ᾽ ἡμῖν νομιζομένοις. δύο δὲ εἶναι πόλεις ἔλεγε μεγέθει μεγίστας, οὐδὲν δὲ ἀλλήλαις ἐοικέναι· καὶ τὴν μὲν ὀνομάζεσθαι Μάχιμον, τὴν δὲ Εὐσεβῆ. τοὺς μὲν οὖν Εὐσεβεῖς ἐν εἰρήνῃ τε διάγειν καὶ πλούτῳ βαθεῖ, καὶ λαμβάνειν τοὺς καρποὺς ἐκ τῆς γῆς[5] χωρὶς ἀρότρων καὶ βοῶν, γεωργεῖν δὲ

Antigonus, and of Aristotle, who clearly lived as a philosopher with the young Alexander son of Philip. Lysis the disciple of Pythagoras was tutor to Epaminondas. So if anyone says that philosophers are inactive, his comment is naive and stupid. I would grasp with alacrity the leisure they enjoy and their love of tranquillity.

18. Theopompus[a] [FGrH 115 F 75c] describes a meeting between Midas the Phrygian and Silenus—this Silenus was the son of a nymph, less illustrious than a god, but superior to a man, since he was immortal. There was a long conversation between them, and Silenus spoke to Midas on the following themes.

Europe, Asia, and Libya are islands, around which the ocean flows, and the only continent is the one surrounding the outside of this world. He explained how infinitely big it is, that it supports other large animals and men twice the size of those who live here. Their lives are not the same length as ours, but in fact twice as long. There are many large cities, with various styles of life, and laws in force among them are different from those customary among us. He said there were two very big cities, not at all like each other, one called Warlike and the other Pious. The inhabitants of Pious live in peace and with

[a] Theopompus, the fourth-century historian from Chios, was the unacknowledged source for ch. 1 of this book. Ch. 18 reflects another piece of fine writing which may have been intended to compete with Plato's account of the lost civilisation of Atlantis. See E. Rohde, *Der griechische Roman* (3rd ed., Leipzig, 1914), pp. 204–208.

---

[1] *κἂν* Kor.: *καὶ* codd. [2] *εἰ* V: *ἢ* x: *ἐπεὶ* Her.: *εἴ* <*γε*> Russell [3] *δὲ* Per.: *τε* codd.

[4] *ἐκείνου* H. Richards: *ἐκεῖνον* codd.

[5] post *γῆς* add. *φασι* codd. praeter a (unde *φησι* Per.)

καὶ σπείρειν οὐδὲν αὐτοῖς ἔργον εἶναι. καὶ διατελοῦσιν, ἦ δ' ὅς, ὑγιεῖς καὶ ἄνοσοι, καὶ καταστρέφουσι τὸν ἑαυτῶν βίον γελῶντες εὖ μάλα καὶ ἡδόμενοι. οὕτω δὲ ἀναμφιλόγως εἰσὶ δίκαιοι ὡς μηδὲ[1] τοὺς θεοὺς πολλάκις ἀπαξιοῦν ἐπιφοιτᾶν αὐτοῖς. οἱ δὲ τῆς Μαχίμου πόλεως μαχιμώτατοί γέ εἰσι καὶ αὐτοὶ καὶ γίνονται μεθ' ὅπλων, καὶ ἀεὶ πολεμοῦσι, καὶ καταστρέφονται τοὺς ὁμόρους, καὶ παμπόλλων ἐθνῶν μία πόλις κρατεῖ αὕτη. εἰσὶ δὲ οἱ οἰκήτορες οὐκ ἐλάττους δισχιλίων[2] μυριάδων. ἀποθνήσκουσι δὲ τὸν μὲν ἄλλον χρόνον νοσήσαντες· σπάνιον δὲ τοῦτο, ἐπεὶ τά γε πολλὰ ἐν τοῖς πολέμοις ἢ λίθοις ἢ ξύλοις παιόμενοι· ἄτρωτοι γάρ εἰσι σιδήρῳ. χρυσοῦ δὲ ἔχουσι καὶ ἀργύρου ἀφθονίαν ὡς ἀτιμότερον εἶναι παρ' αὐτοῖς τὸν χρυσὸν τοῦ παρ' ἡμῖν σιδήρου. ἐπιχειρῆσαι δέ ποτε καὶ διαβῆναι τούτους εἰς τάσδε τὰς ἡμεδαπὰς νήσους ἔλεγε, καὶ διαπλεύσαντάς γε τὸν Ὠκεανὸν μυριάσι χιλίαις ἀνθρώπων ἕως Ὑπερβορέων ἀφικέσθαι, καὶ πυθομένους τῶν παρ' ἡμῖν τούτους εἶναι τοὺς εὐδαιμονεστάτους, καταφρονῆσαι ὡς φαύλως καὶ ταπεινῶς πράττοντας, καὶ διὰ ταῦτα ἀτιμάσαι προελθεῖν περαιτέρω.

Τὸ δὲ ἔτι θαυμασιώτερον προσετίθει· μέροπάς τινας οὕτω καλουμένους ἀνθρώπους οἰκεῖν παρ' αὐτοῖς ἔφη πόλεις πολλὰς καὶ μεγάλας, ἐπ' ἐσχάτῳ δὲ τῆς χώρας αὐτῶν τόπον εἶναι καὶ ὀνομάζεσθαι Ἄνοστον, ἐοικέναι δὲ χάσματι, κατειλῆφθαι δὲ

great wealth; they obtain the fruits of the earth without the plough and oxen, and they have no need to farm and cultivate. They remain healthy and free of disease, he said, and end their lives full of laughter and contented. They are indisputably just, so that even the gods frequently deign to visit them. The citizens of Warlike are for their part very bellicose; they are born with weapons, they are always fighting, and they subdue their neighbours; this one city controls a great many nations. The inhabitants are not less than twenty million. Sometimes they die of illness, but this is rare, since for the most part they lose their lives in battle, wounded by stones or wooden clubs (they cannot be harmed by iron). They have an abundance of gold and silver, so that to them gold is of less value than iron is to us. He said they had once tried to cross over to these islands of ours, and sailed over the ocean with a force of ten million until they reached the Hyperboreans. Learning that the latter were the richest of our peoples, they felt contempt for them as inferior beings of lowly fortunes, and for that reason dismissed the idea of travelling further.

He added an even more remarkable fact. He said that some men called Meropes live among them in numerous large cities, and on the edge of their territory is a place named Point of No Return, which looks like a chasm and

---

[1] μηδὲ Her.: μήτε codd.
[2] δισχιλίων Kor.: διακοσίων codd.

οὔτε ὑπὸ σκότους οὔτε ὑπὸ φωτός, ἀέρα δὲ ἐπικεῖσθαι ἐρυθήματι μεμιγμένον θολερῷ. δύο δὲ ποταμοὺς περὶ τοῦτον τὸν τόπον ῥεῖν, καὶ τὸν μὲν Ἡδονῆς καλεῖσθαι τὸν δὲ Λύπης· καὶ παρ' ἑκάτερον τούτων ἑστηκέναι δένδρα τὸ μέγεθος πλατάνου μεγάλης. φέρειν δὲ καρποὺς τὰ μὲν παρὰ τὸν τῆς Λύπης ποταμὸν τοιαύτην ἔχοντας[1] τὴν φύσιν· ἐάν τις αὐτῶν ἀπογεύσηται, τοσοῦτον ἐκβάλλει δακρύων[2] ὥστε κατατήκεσθαι πάντα τὸν ἑαυτοῦ βίον τὸν λοιπὸν θρηνοῦντα καὶ οὕτω τελευτᾶν. τὰ δὲ ἕτερα τὰ παραπεφυκότα τῷ τῆς Ἡδονῆς ποταμῷ ἀντίπαλον ἐκφέρειν καρπόν. ὃς γὰρ ἂν γεύσηται τούτων, τῶν μὲν ἄλλων τῶν πρότερον ἐπιθυμιῶν παύεται, ἀλλὰ καὶ εἴ του ἤρα καὶ αὐτοῦ λαμβάνει λήθην, καὶ γίνεται κατὰ βραχὺ νεώτερος καὶ τὰς φθανούσας ἡλικίας καὶ τὰς ἤδη διελθούσας ἀναλαμβάνει ὀπίσω. τὸ μὲν γὰρ γῆρας ἀπορρίψας ἐπὶ τὴν ἀκμὴν ὑποστρέφει, εἶτα ἐπὶ τὴν τῶν μειρακίων ἡλικίαν ἀναχωρεῖ, εἶτα παῖς γίνεται, εἶτα βρέφος, καὶ ἐπὶ τούτοις ἐξαναλώθη. καὶ ταῦτα εἴ τῳ πιστὸς ὁ Χῖος λέγων, πεπιστεύσθω· ἐμοὶ δὲ δεινὸς εἶναι δοκεῖ μυθολόγος καὶ ἐν τούτοις καὶ ἐν ἄλλοις δέ.

19. Λέγεται τὴν διαφορὰν Ἀριστοτέλους πρὸς Πλάτωνα τὴν πρώτην ἐκ τούτων γενέσθαι. οὐκ ἠρέσκετο αὐτοῦ τῷ βίῳ ὁ Πλάτων οὐδὲ τῇ κατασκευῇ τῇ περὶ τὸ σῶμα. καὶ γὰρ ἐσθῆτι ἐχρῆτο περιέργῳ ὁ Ἀριστοτέλης καὶ ὑποδέσει, καὶ κουρὰν δὲ ἐκείρετο καὶ ταύτην ἀηδῆ[3] Πλάτωνι, καὶ δακτυλίους δὲ πολ-

is filled neither by light nor darkness, but is overlaid by a haze of a murky red colour. Two rivers run past this locality, one named Pleasure, the other Grief. Along the banks of both stand trees the size of a large plane. Those by the river Grief bear fruit, which has this quality: if someone tastes it he sheds so great a quantity of tears that he melts into laments for all the rest of his life and dies in this condition. The other trees, growing by the river Pleasure, produce a fruit that is quite the opposite. The person who tastes it loses all his previous desires; and if he had any love, he forgets it as well, and is slowly rejuvenated, recovering the previous stages of life that he has passed through. Casting off his old age he returns to his prime and finds his way back to the years of adolescence; then he becomes a child and an infant, after which he dies. If someone is prepared to believe the author from Chios, let this tale be credited; but to me he seems a clever inventor of stories, both in this and in other cases.

19. The first difference between Aristotle and Plato is said to have arisen in the following way. Plato did not like the way he lived or his physical appearance. Aristotle wore elaborate clothes and shoes; he also had his hair cut in a style that displeased Plato; he wore many rings and

---

[1] ἔχοντας Faber: -τα codd.
[2] δακρύων Brunner: -υον codd.
[3] ἀηδῆ scripsi: ἀήθη codd.

λοὺς φορῶν ἐκαλλύνετο ἐπὶ τούτῳ· καὶ μωκία δέ τις ἦν αὐτοῦ περὶ τὸ πρόσωπον, καὶ ἄκαιρος στωμυλία λαλοῦντος κατηγόρει καὶ αὕτη τὸν τρόπον αὐτοῦ. πάντα δὲ ταῦτα ὡς ἔστιν ἀλλότρια φιλοσόφου, δῆλον. ἅπερ οὖν ὁρῶν ὁ Πλάτων οὐ προσίετο τὸν ἄνδρα, προετίμα δὲ αὐτοῦ Ξενοκράτην καὶ Σπεύσιππον καὶ Ἀμύκλαν καὶ ἄλλους, τῇ τε λοιπῇ δεξιούμενος αὐτοὺς τιμῇ καὶ οὖν καὶ τῇ κοινωνίᾳ τῶν λόγων.

Ἀποδημίας δὲ γενομένης ποτὲ τῷ Ξενοκράτει εἰς τὴν πατρίδα, ἐπέθετο τῷ Πλάτωνι ὁ Ἀριστοτέλης, χορόν τινα τῶν ὁμιλητῶν τῶν ἑαυτοῦ περιστησάμενος, ὧν ἦν Μνάσων τε ὁ Φωκεὺς καὶ ἄλλοι τοιοῦτοι. ἐνόσει δὲ τότε ὁ Σπεύσιππος καὶ διὰ ταῦτα ἀδύνατος ἦν συμβαδίζειν τῷ Πλάτωνι. ὁ δὲ Πλάτων ὀγδοήκοντα ἔτη ἐγεγόνει καὶ[1] ὁμοῦ τι διὰ τὴν ἡλικίαν ἐπιλελοίπει τὰ τῆς μνήμης αὐτόν. ἐπιθέμενος οὖν αὐτῷ καὶ ἐπιβουλεύων ὁ Ἀριστοτέλης καὶ φιλοτίμως πάνυ τὰς ἐρωτήσεις ποιούμενος καὶ τρόπον τινὰ καὶ ἐλεγκτικῶς, ἀδικῶν ἅμα καὶ ἀγνωμονῶν ἦν δῆλος· καὶ διὰ ταῦτα ἀποστὰς ὁ Πλάτων τοῦ ἔξω περιπάτου, ἔνδον ἐβάδιζε σὺν τοῖς ἑταίροις.

Τριῶν δὲ μηνῶν διαγενομένων ὁ Ξενοκράτης ἀφίκετο ἐκ τῆς ἀποδημίας καὶ καταλαμβάνει τὸν Ἀριστοτέλη βαδίζοντα οὗ κατέλιπε τὸν Πλάτωνα. ὁρῶν δὲ αὐτὸν μετὰ τῶν γνωρίμων οὐ πρὸς Πλάτωνα ἀναχωροῦντα ἐκ τοῦ περιπάτου, ἀλλὰ καθ' ἑαυτὸν ἀπιόντα εἰς τὴν πόλιν, ἤρετό τινα τῶν ἐν τῷ περιπάτῳ ὅπου[2] ποτὲ εἴη ὁ Πλάτων· ὑπώπτευε γὰρ αὐτὸν

prided himself upon this. There was a look of mockery on his face, and an inappropriate garrulity as he talked created an unfavourable impression of his character. Obviously all these traits are alien to a philosopher. Seeing them, Plato was not attracted to the man, and he preferred Xenocrates, Speusippus, Amyclas, and others, according them all kinds of respect and access to discussion with him.

One day when Xenocrates had gone back to his home town, Aristotle attacked Plato, surrounding him with a group of his own companions. They included Mnason of Phocis and others like him. At the time Speusippus was ill and so could not accompany Plato. Plato was eighty years old, and owing to his age had suffered some loss of memory. It was clear that Aristotle had aggressive designs, as he put very arrogant questions to him, to some extent in a spirit of refutation, which was unjust and unfair. As a result Plato abandoned his walk out of doors and strolled with his companions inside.

After three months had passed Xenocrates returned from his travels and found Aristotle taking a walk where he had left Plato doing the same thing. Noticing that he and his friends did not go in to see Plato after their stroll and that he made off for the city by himself,[a] Xenocrates asked one of the people walking around where Plato was. He suspected Plato might be unwell, but the reply was:

[a] The Academy was on the outskirts of Athens.

---

[1] καὶ huc traiecit Her.: post τι praebent codd.
[2] ὅπου Her.: ὅποι codd.: fortasse ὅπῃ

μαλακίζεσθαι. ὁ δὲ ἀπεκρίνατο· "ἐκεῖνος μὲν οὐ νοσεῖ, ἐνοχλῶν δὲ αὐτὸν Ἀριστοτέλης παραχωρῆσαι πεποίηκε τοῦ περιπάτου, καὶ ἀναχωρήσας ἐν τῷ κήπῳ τῷ ἑαυτοῦ φιλοσοφεῖ." ὁ δὲ Ξενοκράτης ἀκούσας παραχρῆμα ἧκε πρὸς Πλάτωνα, καὶ κατέλαβε διαλεγόμενον τοῖς σὺν ἑαυτῷ· ἦσαν δὲ μάλα συχνοὶ καὶ ἄξιοι λόγου καὶ οἱ μάλιστα δοκοῦντες τῶν νέων ἐπιφανεῖς. ἐπεὶ δὲ ἐπαύσατο τῆς ὁμιλίας, ἠσπάσατό τε ὡς τὸ εἰκὸς τὸν Ξενοκράτην φιλανθρώπως καὶ αὖ πάλιν ὁ Ξενοκράτης ἐκεῖνον ὁμοίως. διαλυθείσης δὲ τῆς συνουσίας οὐδὲν οὔτε εἰπὼν πρὸς τὸν Πλάτωνα ὁ Ξενοκράτης οὔτε ἀκούσας, συναγαγὼν τοὺς ἑταίρους καὶ[1] τῷ Σπευσίππῳ πάνυ ἰσχυρῶς ἐπέπληξε παραχωρήσαντι τοῦ περιπάτου Ἀριστοτέλει, αὐτός τε ἐπέθετο τῷ Σταγειρίτῃ κατὰ τὸ καρτερὸν καὶ εἰς τοσοῦτον προῆλθε[2] φιλοτιμίας, ὡς ἐξελάσαι αὐτὸν καὶ ἀποδοῦναι τὸ σύνηθες χωρίον τῷ Πλάτωνι.

20. Λυσάνδρῳ τῷ Σπαρτιάτῃ εἰς Ἰωνίαν ἀφικομένῳ οἱ κατὰ τὴν Ἰωνίαν ξένοι πολλὰ μὲν καὶ ἄλλα ἀπέπεμψαν ἀτὰρ οὖν καὶ βοῦν καὶ πλακοῦντα. ὁ δὲ ἀπιδὼν εἰς τὸν πλακοῦντα ἤρετο· "τί βούλεται τὸ πέμμα ἐκεῖνο εἶναι;" ὁ δὲ κομίζων ἀπεκρίνατο ὅτι ἐκ μέλιτος καὶ τυροῦ καὶ ἄλλων τινῶν ἐσκεύασται.[3] ὁ δὲ Λύσανδρος "ἀλλὰ τοῦτο μὲν" εἶπε "τοῖς Εἵλωσι[4] δότε· ἐλευθέρου γὰρ οὐκ ἔστι βρῶμα." τὸν δὲ βοῦν προσέταξε κατὰ τὰ πάτρια σκευασθῆναι καὶ ἐδείπνησεν ἡδέως.

"He is not ill, but Aristotle has irritated him and caused him to abandon his stroll. He has retreated to his own garden and devotes himself to philosophy there." When Xenocrates heard that he immediately went in to see Plato and found him in conversation with his followers. They were fairly numerous and important, young men reckoned to be quite outstanding. When Plato stopped talking and gave Xenocrates the expected cordial greeting, Xenocrates replied in kind. The company dispersed, and without any exchange between himself and Plato Xenocrates criticised Speusippus harshly for having ceded the promenade to Aristotle, and he personally attacked the Stagirite vigorously with such determination that he drove him away and restored Plato to his usual haunts.

20. When Lysander the Spartiate[a] arrived in Ionia his hosts there sent him many gifts, including an ox and a cake. Taking a look at the cake he asked: "What is that baked object?" The person who brought it to him replied: "It is prepared with honey, cheese, and other ingredients." "You can give that to the Helots," said Lysander, "it is not food for a free man." But he gave orders to prepare the ox in traditional fashion, and had an enjoyable dinner.

[a] Spartan commander who won the final victory in the Peloponnesian War. Athenaeus 657 BC reports a similar tale about Agesilaus.

---

[1] καὶ x: ἐν V: del. Her.: εἰς ἓν olim Her.
[2] προῆλθε Kor.: περι- codd.
[3] ἐσκεύασται Her.: διεσκ- codd.
[4] Εἵλωσι editio Tornaesiana: εἰδόσι codd.

21. Ἐπανῄει ποτὲ ἐκ διδασκαλείου παῖς ἔτι ὢν Θεμιστοκλῆς. εἶτα προσιόντος Πεισιστράτου ὁ παιδαγωγὸς ἔφη τῷ Θεμιστοκλεῖ μικρὸν ἐκχωρῆσαι τῆς ὁδοῦ προσάγοντος τοῦ τυράννου. ὁ δὲ καὶ πάνυ ἐλευθερίως ἀπεκρίνατο· "αὕτη γὰρ" εἶπεν "αὐτῷ οὐχ ἱκανὴ ὁδός;" οὕτως ἄρα εὐγενές τι καὶ μεγαλόφρον ἐνεφαίνετο τῷ Θεμιστοκλεῖ καὶ ἐξ ἐκείνου.

22. Ὅτε ἑάλω τὸ Ἴλιον, οἰκτείραντες οἱ Ἀχαιοὶ τὰς τῶν ἁλισκομένων τύχας καὶ πάνυ Ἑλληνικῶς τοῦτο ἐκήρυξαν· ἕκαστον τῶν ἐλευθέρων ἓν ὅ τι καὶ βούλεται τῶν οἰκείων ἀποφέρειν ἀράμενον. ὁ οὖν Αἰνείας τοὺς πατρῴους θεοὺς βαστάσας ἔφερεν, ὑπεριδὼν τῶν ἄλλων. ἡσθέντες οὖν ἐπὶ τῇ τοῦ ἀνδρὸς εὐσεβείᾳ οἱ Ἕλληνες καὶ δεύτερον αὐτῷ κτῆμα συνεχώρησαν λαβεῖν· ὁ δὲ τὸν πατέρα πάνυ σφόδρα γεγηρακότα ἀναθέμενος <τοῖς>[1] ὤμοις ἔφερεν. ὑπερεκπλαγέντες οὖν καὶ ἐπὶ τούτῳ οὐχ ἥκιστα, πάντων αὐτῷ τῶν οἰκείων κτημάτων ἀπέστησαν, ὁμολογοῦντες ὅτι πρὸς τοὺς εὐσεβεῖς τῶν ἀνθρώπων καὶ τοὺς θεοὺς καὶ τοὺς γειναμένους δι' αἰδοῦς ἄγοντας καὶ οἱ φύσει πολέμιοι ἥμεροι γίνονται.

23. Καλὰ μὲν οὖν Ἀλεξάνδρου τὰ ἐπὶ Γρανίκῳ καὶ τὰ ἐπὶ Ἰσσῷ καὶ ἡ πρὸς Ἀρβήλοις μάχη καὶ Δαρεῖος ἡττημένος[2] καὶ Πέρσαι δουλεύοντες Μακεδόσι, καλὰ δὲ καὶ <τὰ>[1] τῆς ἄλλης ἁπάσης Ἀσίας νενικημένης, καὶ Ἰνδοὶ δὲ καὶ οὗτοι Ἀλεξάνδρῳ πει-

[1] suppl. Kor. [2] ἡττημένος Her.: ᾑρημένος codd.

21. One day during his childhood Themistocles was coming home from school when Pisistratus approached, and the slave in charge of the boy told Themistocles to stand a little to one side of the road as the tyrant drove along. The boy's reply was very much in the spirit of freedom: "Isn't this road big enough for him?" he asked, and from this moment onwards Themistocles' great and noble qualities began to make themselves apparent.[a]

22. When Troy was captured the Greeks felt pity at the fate of the captives and issued a typically Greek proclamation: that each free citizen should take away with him one of his possessions, whichever he wanted. Aeneas disregarded everything else and picked up the ancestral deities to carry away. The Greeks were enchanted by his display of piety and allowed him to take a second object. He raised his very aged father on to his shoulders and carried him away. This too caused no small amazement, and they granted him all his private property, demonstrating that even traditional enemies become mild in the face of pious men who respect the gods and their parents.[b]

23. Alexander's achievements—at the Granicus, at Issus, the battle of Arbela, the defeat of Darius, Persia enslaved by Macedon—were splendid. So too was the conquest of all the rest of Asia, with the Indians also becoming subjects of Alexander. So again were his

[a] The story is dubious on chronological grounds; Themistocles was born about the time of Pisistratus' death.

[b] Aelian here follows Xenophon, *Cynegeticus* 1.15, in all essentials; but to us, as to Romans of his day, the standard version of the story is the one given by Vergil, *Aeneid* 2.705–725.

θόμενοι· καλὸν <δὲ>[1] καὶ τὸ πρὸς τῇ Τύρῳ καὶ τὰ ἐν Ὀξυδράκαις καὶ τὰ ἄλλα αὐτοῦ. τί γὰρ δεῖ νῦν στενοχωρίᾳ λόγου περιλαμβάνειν τοσαύτην ἀνδρὸς εἰς ὅπλα ἀρετήν; ἔστω δὲ καὶ τῆς Τύχης Ἀλέξανδρον ἀγαπώσης τὰ πλεῖστα, εἴ τις εἴη δύσερις. καλὸς δ' οὖν Ἀλέξανδρος μὴ ἡττώμενος τῆς Τύχης μηδὲ πρὸς τὴν ἐξ αὐτῆς εἰς αὐτὸν προθυμίαν ἀπαγορεύων.

Ἐκεῖνα δὲ οὐκέτι καλὰ Ἀλεξάνδρου. Δίου[2] μηνός, φασι, πέμπτῃ ἔπινε παρ' †Εὐμαίῳ,†[3] εἶτα ἕκτῃ ἐκάθευδεν ἐκ τοῦ πότου, καὶ τοσοῦτον ἐκείνης τῆς ἡμέρας ἔζησεν ὅσον ἀναστὰς χρηματίσαι τοῖς ἡγεμόσιν ὑπὲρ τῆς αὔριον πορείας, λέγων ὅτι ἔσται πρωΐ. καὶ ἑβδόμῃ εἱστιᾶτο παρὰ Περδίκκᾳ καὶ ἔπινε πάλιν καὶ ὀγδόῃ ἐκάθευδε. πέμπτῃ δὲ ἐπὶ δέκα τοῦ αὐτοῦ μηνὸς καὶ ταύτῃ ἔπινε καὶ τῇ ἑπομένῃ τὰ εἰθισμένα ἔδρα τὰ ἐκ τοῦ πότου. παρὰ Βαγώᾳ δὲ ἐδείπνησε τετράδι μετὰ εἰκάδα (ἀπεῖχε <δὲ>[4] τῶν βασιλείων ὁ Βαγώα οἶκος δέκα σταδίους), εἶτα τῇ τρίτῃ ἐκάθευδε. δυοῖν οὖν θάτερον, ἢ Ἀλέξανδρος κακῶς τοσαύτας τοῦ μηνὸς ἡμέρας ἑαυτὸν ζημιοῖ διὰ τὸν οἶνον ἢ οἱ ταῦτα ἀναγράψαντες ψεύδονται. ἔξεστι δὲ ἐκ τούτων ἐννοεῖν καὶ τοῦ

[1] suppl. Her.
[2] Δίου Gesner: δι' οὗ codd.
[3] Εὐμαίῳ x: Εὐλαίῳ V: Πτολεμαίῳ Geier: Εὐμένει Scheffer
[4] suppl. Kor.

---

[a] An Indian people noted for military prowess.

exploits at Tyre and against the Oxydracae,[a] and elsewhere. I do not need to describe within a narrow compass such great military talent. Let most of it be put down to Fortune who favoured Alexander, if one wishes to be captious. But Alexander was great because he was not defeated by Fortune and did not give up in the face of her persistent attentions to him.[b]

The following behaviour of Alexander was not good. On the fifth of the month of Dius[c] he was drinking with Eumaeus,[d] they say; then on the sixth he slept because of the amount he had drunk. During that day he was conscious only long enough to get up and discuss with his generals the following day's march, saying that it would start early. On the seventh he banqueted with Perdiccas and drank again; on the eighth he slept. On the fifteenth of the same month he drank once more, and on the following day did what he would normally do after a party. He had dinner on the twenty-seventh with Bagoas—the distance from the palace to Bagoas' house was ten stades—and on the twenty-eighth he slept. One of two alternatives follows: either Alexander damaged himself with wine by drinking so often within the month, or the authors of these stories are telling lies. From them one

[b] It was probably a regular theme for students of declamation to discuss whether Alexander owed more to fortune or to his talents. In Plutarch's *Moralia* there are two incomplete declamations of this kind (326 B–345 D).

[c] Dius was the eleventh month in the Macedonian calendar and began at the autumn equinox.

[d] The name is probably in need of correction, as one expects to find some well known companion of Alexander mentioned here.

λοιποῦ χρόνου τὰ ὅμοια αὐτοὺς λέγοντας, ὧν καὶ Εὐμένης ὁ Καρδιανὸς καὶ ἐκεῖνός ἐστι.[1]

24. Ξενοφῶντι ἔμελε τῶν <τε>[2] ἄλλων σπουδαίων καὶ οὖν καὶ ὅπλα καλὰ ἔχειν. νικῶντι γὰρ ἔλεγε τοὺς πολεμίους τὴν καλλίστην στολὴν ἁρμόττειν καὶ ἀποθνήσκοντι ἐν τῇ μάχῃ κεῖσθαι καλῶς ἐν καλῇ τῇ πανοπλίᾳ· τῷ γὰρ ἀνδρὶ τῷ γενναίῳ ταῦτα εἶναι τὰ ἐντάφια τὰ ὡς ἀληθῶς κοσμοῦντα αὐτόν. λέγεται οὖν ὁ τοῦ Γρύλλου τὴν μὲν ἀσπίδα Ἀργολικὴν ἔχειν, τὸν δὲ θώρακα Ἀττικόν, τὸ δὲ κράνος Βοιωτιουργές, τὸν δὲ ἵππον Ἐπιδαύριον. φιλοκάλου δὲ ἔγωγε ἂν φαίην εἶναι ἀνδρὸς τὰ τοιαῦτα καὶ ἀξιοῦντος ἑαυτὸν τῶν καλῶν.

25. Ὁ Λεωνίδης ὁ Λακεδαιμόνιος καὶ οἱ σὺν αὐτῷ τριακόσιοι τὸν μαντευόμενον αὐτοῖς θάνατον εἵλοντο ἐν Πύλαις, καὶ ὑπὲρ τῆς Ἑλλάδος εὖ καὶ καλῶς ἀγωνισάμενοι τέλους ἔτυχον εὐκλεοῦς, καὶ δόξαν ἑαυτοῖς ἀθάνατον ἀπέλιπον καὶ φήμην ἀγαθὴν δι' αἰῶνος.

26. Πίνδαρος ὁ Μέλανος υἱός, Ἀλυάττου δὲ θυγατριδοῦς τοῦ Λυδοῦ, διαδεξάμενος τὴν Ἐφεσίων τυραννίδα πρὸς μὲν τὰς τιμωρίας πικρὸς ἦν καὶ ἀπαραίτητος, τά γε μὴν ἄλλα ἐδόκει φιλόπατρις[3] εἶναι καὶ σώφρων, καὶ τοῦ μὴ δουλεῦσαι τὴν πατρίδα τοῖς βαρβάροις πολλὴν πρόνοιαν ἔθετο.

[1] ἐκεῖνός ἐστι] Διόδοτος ὁ Ἐρυθραῖος Jacoby post Kor. (cf. Athen. 434B) [2] suppl. Kor.

[3] φιλόπατρις J. F. Gronovius: φιλόπαις codd.

can infer that such writers, who include Eumenes of Cardia [FGrH 117 F 2a], tell similar tales on other occasions.

24. Xenophon had a number of serious interests, including the ownership of fine weapons. He used to say that if one defeated the enemy it was appropriate to have the finest equipment; and, if one died in battle, to lie honourably in a fine suit of armour. For the noble warrior this was the funerary decoration that truly brought distinction.[a] It is said that the son of Gryllus possessed a shield made in Argos, a breastplate from Attica, a helmet of Boeotian manufacture, and a horse from Epidaurus. I would say that such objects indicate a man of taste who thinks himself entitled to the best.

25. Leonidas the Spartan and his force of three hundred accepted the death that was prophesied for them at Pylae.[b] After a brave and noble struggle on behalf of Greece they met a glorious end and left behind them an immortal reputation and a good name for eternity.[c]

26. Pindar, son of Melas and grandson of the Lydian Alyattes on his mother's side, became tyrant of Ephesus by succession.[d] In his punishments he was stern and unyielding, but in other respects he seemed to be reasonable and patriotic, and he was thought to take many precautions to prevent his country being enslaved by the

[a] At *Anabasis* 3.2.7 Xenophon (the son of Gryllus) expounds the same principle himself.

[b] Pylae was used as an alternative name for Thermopylae.

[c] The point of this ch. is unclear; perhaps it is incomplete.

[d] Despite his distinguished family connections Pindar of Ephesus remains an obscure figure.

ἔδειξε ταῦτα οὕτως ἔχειν ἐκεῖνα δήπου. ἐπεὶ γὰρ Κροῖσος ὁ πρὸς μητρὸς αὐτοῦ θεῖος καταστρεφόμενος τὴν Ἰωνίαν καὶ πρὸς τὸν Πίνδαρον πρεσβείαν ἀπέστειλεν ἀξιῶν Ἐφεσίους ὑπ' αὐτῷ γενέσθαι, ὁ[1] δ' οὐκ ἐπείσθη, ἐπολιόρκει τὴν πόλιν Κροῖσος. ἐπεὶ δέ τις τῶν πύργων ἀνετράπη ὁ κληθεὶς ὕστερον Προδότης, καὶ ἐν ὀφθαλμοῖς ἑωρᾶτο[2] τὸ δεινόν, συνεβούλευεν ὁ Πίνδαρος Ἐφεσίοις ἐκδήσαντας ἐκ τῶν πυλῶν καὶ τῶν τειχῶν θώμιγγας συνάψαι τοῖς κίοσι τοῦ τῆς Ἀρτέμιδος νεώ, οἱονεὶ τὴν πόλιν ἀνάθημα ἐῶντας εἶναι τῇ Ἀρτέμιδι, ἀσυλίαν διὰ τούτων ἐπινοῶν τῇ Ἐφέσῳ· ὁ[3] δὲ συνεβούλευε προσελθόντας δεῖσθαι τοῦ Λυδοῦ. προβαλλομένων δὲ τὴν ἱκετηρίαν τῶν Ἐφεσίων γελάσαντά φασι τὸν Κροῖσον καὶ δεξάμενον πράως τὸ στρατηγηθὲν τοῖς μὲν Ἐφεσίοις συγχωρῆσαι τὴν μετ' ἐλευθερίας ἀσφάλειαν,[4] τῷ δὲ Πινδάρῳ προστάξαι τῆς πόλεως ἀπαλλάττεσθαι. ὁ δὲ οὐκ ἀντεῖπε, τῶν φίλων δὲ τοὺς συναπαίρειν αὐτῷ βουληθέντας παραλαβών, τὸν υἱὸν καὶ τῆς οὐσίας τὸ πλεῖστον τῇ πόλει παρακαταθέμενος καὶ ἕνα τῶν συνήθων Πασικλέα ἀποδείξας ἐπίτροπον καὶ τοῦ παιδὸς καὶ τῶν χρημάτων, ἀπῆρεν εἰς Πελοπόννησον, τυραννικοῦ βίου φυγὴν αὐθαίρετον ἀλλαξάμενος ὑπὲρ τοῦ μὴ ποιῆσαι τὴν πατρίδα ὑποχείριον Λυδοῖς.

27. Πέπυσμαι καὶ τοῦτον τὸν λόγον· εἰ δὲ ἀληθής ἐστιν οὐκ οἶδα· ὃ δ' οὖν πέπυσμαι, ἐκεῖνό ἐστι· Πλάτων ὁ Ἀρίστωνος ὑπὸ πενίας, φασί, καταπονού-

barbarians. The following appears to show that this was true. When his maternal uncle Croesus was conquering Ionia and had sent envoys to Pindar to demand that Ephesus submit to him, the request was refused and Croesus began a siege of the city.[a] When one of the fortification towers was destroyed—it was later known as the Tower of Treason—and he could see disaster looming, Pindar advised the Ephesians to attach cords from the city gates and towers to the columns of the temple of Artemis as if they were consecrating the city to Artemis. He hoped by this means to ensure that Ephesus would not be captured. He advised them to go to plead with the Lydian. When the Ephesians displayed their credentials as suppliants, Croesus is said to have laughed and accepted the stratagem in good part, allowing the Ephesians unmolested freedom, while he ordered Pindar to leave the city. He raised no objection, collected those of his friends who wanted to go with him, and entrusted his son, along with most of his property, to the city. He nominated Pasicles, one of his close friends, to be guardian of his son and the property, left for the Peloponnese, and willingly accepted exile in exchange for the position of tyrant in order not to put his city under the control of the Lydians.

27. I have heard this story as well, but whether it is true I do not know. Anyway, what I have heard is as follows. Plato, son of Ariston, was on the point of leaving for

[a] Croesus reigned in Lydia 560–546 B.C.

---

[1] ὅ Jens: ὡς codd. [2] ἑωρᾶτο Her.: ἑώρα codd.
[3] ὅ] τότε Per. [4] ἀσφάλειαν Toup: φυγὴν codd.

μενος ἔμελλεν ἐπὶ στρατείαν ἀποδημῆσαι· καταληφθεὶς δὲ ὑπὸ Σωκράτους ὠνούμενος ὅπλα ὁ Πλάτων ἀνεστάλη τῆς ὁρμῆς,[1] διαλεχθέντος αὐτῷ τοῦ Σωκράτους ἃ εἰκὸς ἦν καὶ πείσαντος φιλοσοφίας ἐπιθυμῆσαι.

28. Ὁρῶν ὁ Σωκράτης τὸν Ἀλκιβιάδην τετυφωμένον ἐπὶ τῷ πλούτῳ καὶ μέγα φρονοῦντα <ἐπὶ τῇ περιουσίᾳ καὶ ἔτι πλέον>[2] ἐπὶ τοῖς ἀγροῖς, ἤγαγεν αὐτὸν εἴς τινα <τῆς πόλεως> τόπον ἔνθα ἀνέκειτο πινάκιον ἔχον γῆς περίοδον, καὶ προσέταξε <τῷ Ἀλκιβιάδῃ> τὴν Ἀττικὴν ἐνταῦθ' ἀναζητεῖν. ὡς δ' εὗρε, προσέταξεν <αὐτῷ καὶ> τοὺς ἀγροὺς τοὺς ἰδίους αὐτοῦ διαθρῆσαι. τοῦ δὲ εἰπόντος· "ἀλλ' οὐδαμοῦ γεγραμμένοι εἰσίν," "ἐπὶ τούτοις <οὖν>" εἶπε "μέγα φρονεῖς, οἵπερ οὐδὲν μέρος τῆς γῆς εἰσιν;"

29. Διογένης ὁ Σινωπεὺς συνεχῶς ἐπέλεγεν ὑπὲρ ἑαυτοῦ ὅτι τὰς ἐκ τῆς τραγῳδίας ἀρὰς αὐτὸς ἐκπληροῖ καὶ ὑπομένει· εἶναι γὰρ

πλάνης ἄοικος πατρίδος ἐστερημένος
πτωχὸς δυσείμων βίον ἔχων [τὸν][3] ἐφήμερον.

καὶ ὅμως ἐπὶ τούτοις μέγα ἐφρόνει οὐδὲν ἧττον ἢ Ἀλέξανδρος ἐπὶ τῇ τῆς οἰκουμένης ἀρχῇ, ὅτε καὶ Ἰνδοὺς ἑλὼν εἰς Βαβυλῶνα ὑπέστρεψεν.

[1] τῆς ὁρμῆς Her.: τὴν ὁρμὴν codd.
[2] in hoc c. verba uncinis inclusa e Stobaeo 3.22.33 suppleta sunt
[3] del. Jacobs

military service abroad[a] owing to (they say) his financial difficulties. He was found by Socrates buying his weapons, but lost his enthusiasm when Socrates put the right considerations to him and persuaded him to fall in love with philosophy.

28. When Socrates saw Alcibiades made arrogant by his wealth and proud of his property, in particular of his large estates, he took him to a spot in the city where a board had been set up showing a map of the earth. He asked him to look for Attica on it. When Alcibiades found it, he asked him to locate his own properties. In response to the comment "They are not marked anywhere" he replied "Are you then proud of properties which are not a fraction of the earth?"[b]

29. Diogenes of Sinope regularly said of himself that he suffered and endured to the full the curses of tragedy, for he was "a wanderer without a home, deprived of his native land, a beggar, ill-dressed, living from one day to the next" [TrGF adesp. 284].[c] Yet he took no less pride in these facts than Alexander in his rule over the world, at the time when he had captured India and returned to Babylon.

[a] I.e. as a mercenary.

[b] This anecdote may have been inspired by a scene in Aristophanes' *Clouds* (206–217), where a pupil of Socrates shows Strepsiades a map that includes Attica; but the purpose of that scene is quite different.

[c] These verses from an unidentified tragedy may have been spoken by Oedipus, in exile from Thebes.

30. Ἀμοιβεὺς[1] ὁ κιθαρῳδὸς σωφρονέστατος ἐλέγετο καὶ γυναῖκα ὡραιοτάτην ἔχων μὴ ὁμιλεῖν αὐτῇ, καὶ Διογένης ὁ τῆς τραγῳδίας ὑποκριτὴς <* * *>.[2] Κλειτόμαχος δὲ ὁ παγκρατιαστὴς εἴ ποτε καὶ κύνας εἶδε συμπλεκομένους, ἀπεστρέφετο· καὶ ἐν συμποσίῳ εἴ τις ἀφροδίσιος λόγος παρερρύη, ἀναστὰς ἀπηλλάττετο.

31. Νικίας ὁ ζωγράφος τοσαύτην περὶ τὸ γράφειν σπουδὴν εἶχεν, ὡς ἐπιλαθέσθαι πολλάκις αὐτὸν τροφὴν προσενέγκασθαι προστετηκότα τῇ τέχνῃ.

32. Ἀλέξανδρος ὁ Φιλίππου, παῖς ὢν οὔπω πρόσηβος, ἐμάνθανε κιθαρίζειν. τοῦ δὲ διδάσκοντος κροῦσαι κελεύσαντος χορδήν τινα σὺν μέλει[3] καὶ ἣν ἀπῄτει τὰ κιθαρίσματα, "καὶ τί διοίσει" ἔφη "ἐὰν ταύτην κρούσω;" ἑτέραν δείξας. ὁ δὲ οὐδὲν ἔφη διαφέρειν τῷ μέλλοντι βασιλεύσειν ἀλλὰ τῷ[4] ἐπὶ τέχνῃ κιθαρίσειν[5] μέλλοντι. ἔδεισε δὲ ἄρα οὗτος μὴ ὢν ἀπαίδευτος τὸ τοῦ Λίνου πάθος·[6] τὸν γὰρ Ἡρακλῆ ὁ Λίνος ἔτι παῖδα ὄντα κιθαρίζειν ἐπαίδευσεν, ἀμουσότερον δὲ ἁπτομένου τοῦ ὀργάνου, ἐχαλέπηνε πρὸς αὐτὸν ὁ Λίνος. ὁ δὲ ἀγανακτήσας ὁ Ἡρακλῆς τῷ πλήκτρῳ τοῦ Λίνου καθίκετο καὶ ἀπέκτεινεν αὐτόν.

[1] Ἀμοιβεὺς Scheffer: -έας codd.
[2] lacunam statuit Per.
[3] σὺν μέλει] συμμελῆ dubitanter Russell
[4] τῷ Her.: οὐκ codd.
[5] κιθαρίσειν (vel -ιεῖν) Her.: -ίζειν codd.
[6] πάθος V: πάθοι x

30. Amoebeus the cithara player was said to be a man of the utmost self-restraint. Though he had a very beautiful wife he would have no intercourse with her. Diogenes the tragic actor absolutely avoided all sexual relations.[a] Clitomachus the all-in wrestler[b] would turn away whenever he saw dogs mating, and if at a party the conversation turned to love he would get up and leave.

31. The artist Nicias was so devoted to painting that he often forgot to eat because he was concentrating on his art.

32. When he was a boy, not yet an adolescent, Alexander the son of Philip learned to play the cithara. The teacher told him to touch a string in tune and in accordance with the melody. "What difference will it make if I touch that one?" he asked, pointing to another. The teacher replied that it made no difference to a man destined to be king; it was otherwise for anyone who would practise the art of the cithara. But the man, not being uneducated, was afraid that he might suffer the fate of Linus.[c] Linus was teaching the child Heracles the cithara, and when he handled the instrument clumsily Linus was annoyed with him. Heracles was angry, attacked Linus with his plectrum and killed him.[d]

[a] A lacuna in the text here can be filled by using the similar passage in *N.A.* 6.1.

[b] The pancratiast practised a sport which combined features of boxing and wrestling.

[c] A variant reading in the MSS. could be translated: "he was afraid of suffering the fate of Linus for his bad behaviour."

[d] Whereas the modern plectrum is small, this was not always so in antiquity; Daremberg and Saglio, *Dictionnaire des antiquités grecques et romaines*, vol. 3, p. 1446, plate 4725, shows one shaped like a small hammer.

33. Σάτυρος ὁ αὐλητὴς Ἀρίστωνος τοῦ φιλοσόφου πολλάκις ἠκροᾶτο, καὶ κηλούμενος ἐκ τῶν λεγομένων ἐπέλεγεν

<αὐτίκ' ἔπειτ' ἀπ' ἐμεῖο κάρη τάμοι ἀλλότριος φώς>[1]
εἰ μὴ ἐγὼ τάδε τόξα φαεινῷ ἐν πυρὶ θείην,

τοὺς αὐλοὺς αἰνιττόμενος καὶ τρόπον τινὰ τὴν τέχνην ἐκφαυλίζων παραβολῇ τῇ πρὸς φιλοσοφίαν.

34. Ὅτι Λάκωσι καὶ Ῥωμαίοις νόμος ἦν μὴ ἐξεῖναί τινι ὀψωνεῖν μήτε ἃ βούλεται μήτε ὅσα βούλεται· προσέταττον γὰρ διά τε τῶν ἄλλων σωφρονεῖν τοὺς πολίτας καὶ διὰ τῆς τραπέζης οὐχ ἥκιστα.

35. Λόγος δέ τις διαρρεῖ καὶ οὗτος Ἀττικός, ὃς λέγει πρότερον ἐν Ἀκαδημίᾳ μηδὲ γελάσαι ἐξουσίαν εἶναι· ὕβρει γὰρ καὶ ῥαθυμίᾳ ἐπειρῶντο τὸ χωρίον ἄβατον φυλάττειν.

36. Ἀριστοτέλης ὅτε ἀπέλιπε τὰς Ἀθήνας δέει τῆς κρίσεως, πρὸς τὸν ἐρόμενον αὐτὸν τίς ἐστιν ἡ τῶν Ἀθηναίων πόλις ἔφη· "παγκάλη· ἀλλ' ἐν αὐτῇ

[1] supplevi

---

[a] The quotation of *Iliad* 5.215, where Pandarus threatens to destroy his weapons, is incomplete as it stands, and the previous line needs to be supplied (I can find no evidence that the passage was so well known that even a partial quotation would have been understood).

[b] Spartan rules about food are mentioned below at 14.7;

33. Satyrus the aulos player frequently went to lectures by the philosopher Ariston [fr. 337 v. Arn.]. Enchanted by his words, he commented [*Iliad* 5.214–215] "<Then may some stranger at once cut off my head> if I do not put these arrows in the shining fire."[a] He alluded to his instruments, and to some extent depreciated his art in comparison with philosophy.

34. Note that the Laconians and the Romans had a law that one was not allowed to buy food according to one's own taste or as much as one wished. They gave instructions that the citizen body should exercise moderation in a number of ways, and not least at table.[b]

35. There is a story circulating—it again is Athenian—which says that formerly in the Academy laughter was not allowed.[c] They tried to keep the place untouched by arrogance and idleness.

36. When Aristotle left Athens because of his fear of a prosecution[d] someone asked him "What sort of place is Athens?" and he replied "Very fine. But in it [*Odyssey*

Roman sumptuary laws are well known from such texts as Aulus Gellius, *Noctes Atticae* 2.24.

[c] For another pagan example of this characteristic see Porphyry, *Vita Pythagorae* 35: "no one ever saw him laugh or weep." It was not confined to would-be sages of pagan antiquity: church fathers could be equally severe, especially Jerome; see the discussion of various passages by N. Adkin, *Orpheus* 6 (1985): 149–152. John Chrysostom in the sixth of his *Homilies on Matthew* (*Patrologia graeca* 57.69) claimed on the evidence of the Gospels that Jesus did not laugh or even smile gently.

[d] After Alexander's death Aristotle's position in Athens became difficult, as he was too closely identified with Macedon; so he went to live in Chalcis on the island of Euboea and died soon afterwards.

ὄγχνη ἐπ' ὄγχνῃ γηράσκει, σῦκον δ' ἐπὶ σύκῳ,"

τοὺς συκοφάντας λέγων. καὶ πρὸς τὸν ἐρόμενον διὰ τί ἀπέλιπε τὰς Ἀθήνας, ἀπεκρίνατο ὅτι οὐ βούλεται Ἀθηναίους δὶς ἐξαμαρτεῖν εἰς φιλοσοφίαν, τὸ περὶ Σωκράτην πάθος αἰνιττόμενος καὶ τὸν καθ' ἑαυτὸν κίνδυνον.

37. Νόμος ἐστὶ Κείων, οἱ πάνυ παρ' αὐτοῖς γεγηρακότες, ὥσπερ ἐπὶ ξένια παρακαλοῦντες ἑαυτοὺς ἢ ἐπί τινα ἑορταστικὴν θυσίαν, συνελθόντες[1] καὶ στεφανωσάμενοι πίνουσι κώνειον, ὅταν ἑαυτοῖς συνειδῶσιν ὅτι πρὸς τὰ ἔργα τὰ τῇ πατρίδι λυσιτελοῦντα ἄχρηστοί εἰσιν, ὑπολη ρούσης ἤδη τι αὐτοῖς καὶ τῆς γνώμης διὰ τὸν χρόνον.

38. Ὅτι ἐν Ἀθήναις εὑρεθῆναι λέγουσι πρῶτον τὴν ἐλαίαν καὶ τὴν συκῆν, ἃ καὶ πρῶτον[2] ἡ γῆ ἀνέδωκε. δίκας τε δοῦναι καὶ λαβεῖν εὗρον Ἀθηναῖοι πρῶτοι. καὶ ἀγῶνα τὸν διὰ τῶν σωμάτων πρῶτοι ἐπενόησαν καὶ ἀπεδύσαντο καὶ ἠλείψαντο. καὶ ἵππους ἔζευξε πρῶτος Ἐριχθόνιος.

39. Ὅτι βαλάνους Ἀρκάδες, Ἀργεῖοι δ' ἀπίους, Ἀθηναῖοι δὲ σῦκα, Τιρύνθιοι δὲ ἀχράδας δεῖπνον

[1] συνελθόντες 'interpretis codex' ap. Fabrum: ἀνελθ- codd.
[2] πρῶτον] πρῶτα Her.

---

[a] The joke is lost in translation because in Greek "fig" is the first element in the word meaning "informer."

[b] Strabo, 10.5.6 (486), records a law obliging the inhabitants of the city of Ioulis on Ceos to drink hemlock on reaching the age

7.120–121] the pear grows old on the pear tree, the fig on the fig tree," by which he referred to the informers.[a] To someone else who asked him why he was leaving Athens he replied that he did not want the Athenians to commit two offences against philosophy, alluding to the fate of Socrates and his own danger.

37. There is a law at Ceos that those who are extremely elderly invite each other as if going to a party or to a festival with sacrifices, meet, put on garlands and drink hemlock. This they do when they become aware that they are incapable of performing tasks useful to their country, and that their judgement is by now rather feeble owing to the passing of time.[b]

38. Note the story that the olive and the fig, the first plants produced by the earth, were first discovered at Athens. The Athenians were the first to institute legal action. They first invented physical contests, for which they stripped and rubbed themselves down with oil. Erichthonius first yoked horses.[c]

39. Note that the Arcadians ate acorns, the Argives pears, the Athenians figs, the Tirynthians wild pears, the

of sixty. Similar themes occur below in 4.1 in the passages dealing with Sardinia and the Derbiccae. It is not surprising to find such usages recorded of barbarian tribes; cf. Herodotus 1.216 on the Massagetae and 3.99 on the Padaei in India. Modern anthropologists can cite plenty of cases; see e.g. those listed by G. Minois, *History of Old Age* (Cambridge, 1989), p. 10. The Latin phrase *senex depontanus* has suggested to some scholars that in the distant past the Romans had followed a similar practice.

[c] The Athenian contribution to civilisation was a theme that occurred naturally to all Atticist writers; one famous and detailed encomium of Athens is the *Panathenaicus* of the second-century writer Aelius Aristides.

εἶχον, Ἰνδοὶ καλάμους, Καρμανοὶ φοίνικας, κέγχρον δὲ Μαιῶται καὶ Σαυρομάται, τέρμινθον δὲ καὶ κάρδαμον Πέρσαι.

40. Ὅτι οἱ συγχορευταὶ Διονύσου Σάτυροι ἦσαν οἱ ὑπ' ἐνίων Τίτυροι ὀνομαζόμενοι. ἔσχον δὲ τὸ ὄνομα ἐκ τῶν τερετισμάτων οἷς χαίρουσι [Σάτυροι].[1] Σάτυροι δὲ ἀπὸ τοῦ σεσηρέναι. Σιληνοὶ δὲ ἀπὸ τοῦ σιλλαίνειν· τὸν δὲ σίλλον ψόγον λέγουσι μετὰ παιδιᾶς δυσαρέστου. ἐσθὴς δ' ἦν τοῖς Σιληνοῖς ἀμφίμαλλοι χιτῶνες. αἰνίττεται δὲ ἡ στολὴ τὴν ἐκ τοῦ Διονύσου φυτείαν καὶ τὰ τῶν οἰνάδων[2] [καὶ τὰ τῶν κλημάτων δάση].[3]

41. Ὅτι τὸ πολυκαρπεῖν οἱ ἀρχαῖοι ὠνόμαζον φλύειν. ἐντεῦθεν[4] τὸν Διόνυσον Φλεῶνα ἐκάλουν καὶ Προτρύγαιον[5] καὶ Σταφυλίτην καὶ Ὀμφακίτην καὶ ἑτέρως πως διαφόρως.

42. Ἐλέγη καὶ Κελαινὴ Προίτου θυγατέρες. μάχλους δὲ αὐτὰς ἡ τῆς Κύπρου βασιλὶς εἰργάσατο. ἐπὶ μέρους δὲ τῆς Πελοποννήσου [καὶ][6] ἔδραμον, φασί, γυμναὶ μαινόμεναι, ἐξεφοίτησαν δὲ καὶ εἰς ἄλλας χώρας τῆς Ἑλλάδος, παράφοροι οὖσαι

[1] del. Kor.
[2] *οἰνάδων*] *οἰνάρων* I. Vossius: *οἰναρίδων* Her.
[3] del. Her. [4] *ἐντεῦθεν* V: *ὅθεν* x
[5] *Προτρύγαιον* Scheffer: -*γὸν* V: -*γην* x
[6] del. Her.

---

[a] The translation "pistachio" seems justified by Theophrastus, *Historia plantarum* 4.4.7, and the commentators ad loc.

Indians reeds, the Carmanians dates, the Maeotae and Sauromatae millet, the Persians pistachio[a] and watercress.

40. Note that Dionysus' companions in the dance were Satyrs, called by some Tityri.[b] They received this name from the trills which the Satyrs enjoy, and the Satyrs got their name from the word "to grimace," the Sileni from the word "to mock"—they say that *sillos* is criticism with disagreeable humour.[c] The Sileni wore cloaks with wool on both sides. Their dress recalls Dionysus' vegetation, the thick foliage of the vines [and the vine twigs].[d]

41. Note that the ancients used the word *phlyein* [to luxuriate] of an abundant yield of fruit. So they called Dionysus Phleon [luxuriant], Protrygaios [the first at the vintage], Staphylites [the god of the grape], Omphacites [the god of the unripe grape], and various other epithets.

42. Elege and Celaene were daughters of Proetus. The queen of Cyprus had made them oversexed.[e] Naked and out of their minds, they raced across part of the Peloponnese, according to the story. Maddened by their disease, they travelled to other parts of Greece. I hear that the

[b] Tityrus occurs as a shepherd's name in Vergil's *Eclogues* and Theocritus' *Idylls*.

[c] Sileni were also companions of Dionysus; the name may have been applied to older Satyrs. *Silloi* is the title of some satirical poems in hexameters by the Hellenistic writer Timon of Phlius, of which scanty fragments survive.

[d] The point of the comparison is not clear, and no satisfactory emendation of the Greek has been proposed.

[e] Aphrodite, who rose out of the sea off the coast of Cyprus and was often associated with the island. Other versions of the story state that the offended deity was Hera or Dionysus.

ὑπὸ τῆς νόσου. ἀκούω δὲ ὅτι καὶ ταῖς Λακεδαιμονίων γυναιξὶν ἐπέπεσέ τις οἶστρος βακχικὸς καὶ ταῖς τῶν Χίων. καὶ αἱ τῶν Βοιωτῶν δὲ ὡς ἐνθεώτατα[1] ἐμάνησαν καὶ ἡ τραγῳδία βοᾷ. μόνας δὲ ἀφηνιάσαι τῆς χορείας ταύτης λέγουσι τοῦ Διονύσου τὰς Μινύου[2] θυγατέρας Λευκίππην καὶ Ἀρσίππην[3] καὶ Ἀλκιθόην. αἴτιον δὲ ὅτι ἐπόθουν τοὺς γαμέτας, καὶ διὰ τοῦτο οὐκ ἐγένοντο τῷ θεῷ μαινάδες. ὁ δὲ ὀργίζεται, καὶ αἱ μὲν περὶ τοὺς ἱστοὺς εἶχον καὶ ἐπονοῦντο περὶ τὴν Ἐργάνην εὖ μάλα φιλοτίμως· ἄφνω δὲ κιττοί τε καὶ ἄμπελοι τοὺς ἱστοὺς περιεῖρπον, καὶ τοῖς ταλάροις ἐνεφώλευον δράκοντες, ἐκ δὲ τῶν ὀρόφων ἔσταζον οἴνου καὶ γάλακτος σταγόνες. τὰς δὲ οὐδὲ ταῦτα ἀνέπειθεν ἐλθεῖν εἰς τὴν λατρείαν τοῦ δαίμονος. ἐνταῦθά τοι καὶ πάθος εἰργάσαντο ἔξω Κιθαιρῶνος, οὐ μεῖον τοῦ ἐν Κιθαιρῶνι· τὸν γὰρ τῆς Λευκίππης παῖδα ἔτι ἁπαλὸν ὄντα καὶ νεαρὸν διεσπάσαντο οἷα νεβρὸν τῆς μανίας ἀρξάμεναι αἱ Μινυάδες, εἶτα ἐντεῦθεν ἐπὶ τὰς ἐξ ἀρχῆς ᾖξαν μαινάδας·[4] αἱ δὲ ἐδίωκον αὐτὰς διὰ τὸ ἄγος. ἐκ δὴ τούτων ἐγένοντο ὄρνιθες, καὶ ἡ μὲν ἤμειψε τὸ εἶδος εἰς κορώνην, ἡ δὲ εἰς νυκτερίδα, ἡ δὲ εἰς γλαῦκα.

43. Ἐν Συβάρει κιθαρῳδοῦ ᾄδοντος ἐν τῇ ἀγωνίᾳ,

[1] ἐνθεώτατα Kor. -ται codd.

[2] Μινύου N. Heinsius: -ύων codd.

[3] Ἀρσίππην ex Antonino Liberali Verheyk: Ἀριστίππην codd.

[4] μαινάδας Cuper: Μινυάδας Vx: γυναῖκας Φ

women of Sparta were also attacked by a bacchic frenzy, as were the women of Chios. The divinely inspired madness of the Boeotian women has been made notorious by tragedy.[a] They say that only the daughters of Minyas, Leucippe, Arsippe, and Alcithoe, rebelled against the dance in honour of Dionysus, and they did so for love of their husbands; for this reason they did not become maenads of the god. He was angry. They sat at their looms and toiled industriously in honour of Ergane,[b] and suddenly ivy and vines began to envelop the looms and snakes made their lair in the baskets of wool. Wine and milk dripped down from the ceiling. But not even these events persuaded the women to join in the worship of the god. Then they committed a terrible act, not on Cithaeron, but no less serious than the one perpetrated on Cithaeron.[c] The daughters of Minyas tore to pieces, as if he were a fawn, the young child of Leucippe, a boy still of tender years. This was their first act of madness, and then they rushed off to join the women who had been maenads from the first. The latter chased them away because of their pollution, and they then became birds, one changing herself into a crow, the second into a bat, and the third an owl.

43. At Sybaris a cithara player was singing in the con-

[a] Aelian refers here to Euripides' *Bacchae;* he may also have had in mind Aeschylus' *Lycurgeia,* a tetralogy in which resistance to the cult of the new god Dionysus was probably the main theme.

[b] For Ergane see 1.2 above.

[c] In *Bacchae* 1118–1136 there is a terrifying description of the dismemberment of Pentheus by his mother Agave and her fellow maenads on Cithaeron.

ἣν ἐπετέλουν τῇ Ἥρᾳ, στασιασάντων ὑπὲρ αὐτοῦ τῶν Συβαριτῶν καὶ τὰ ὅπλα λαβόντων ἐπ' ἀλλήλους, φοβηθεὶς ὁ κιθαρῳδὸς σὺν[1] αὐτῇ στολῇ κατέφυγεν εἰς τὸν τῆς Ἥρας βωμόν· οἱ δὲ οὐδὲ ἐνταῦθα ἐφείσαντο τοῦ κιθαρῳδοῦ. ὀλίγῳ δὲ ὕστερον αἷμα ἐδόκει ἐν τῷ τῆς Ἥρας ναῷ ἀναβρύειν οὐδὲν ἔλαττον πηγῆς ἀενάου, Συβαρῖται δὲ ἔπεμψαν εἰς Δελφούς. ἡ δὲ Πυθία ἀπεκρίνατο·

> βαῖν' ἀπ' ἐμῶν τριπόδων, ἔτι τοι φόνος ἀμφὶ
> χέρεσσι
> πουλὺς ἀποστάζων ἀπὸ λαΐνου οὐδοῦ ἐρύκει.
> οὔ σε θεμιστεύσω· Μουσῶν θεράποντα κατέκτας
> Ἥρης πρὸς βωμοῖσι, θεῶν τίσιν οὐκ ἀλεείνας.
> τοῖς δὲ κακῶς ῥέξασι δίκης τέλος οὐχὶ χρονιστὸν
> οὐδὲ παραιτητόν,[2] οὐδ' εἰ Διὸς ἔγγονοι εἶεν,
> ἀλλ' αὐτῶν κεφαλῇσι καὶ ἐν σφετέροισι τέκεσσιν
> εἰλεῖται, καὶ πῆμα δόμοις ἐπὶ πήματι βαίνει.

ἡ δὲ δίκη οὐκ ἐβράδυνε· Κροτωνιάταις γὰρ ἐναντία <τὰ>[3] ὅπλα θέμενοι ἀνάστατοι ὑπ' ἐκείνων ἐγένοντο καὶ ἡ πόλις αὐτῶν ἠφανίσθη.

44. Νεανίσκοι τρεῖς εἰς Δελφοὺς ἀφικόμενοι θεωροὶ συμπολῖται κακούργοις περιτυγχάνουσιν. ὁ οὖν εἷς ἀπέδρα τοὺς λῃστάς, ὁ δὲ δεύτερος αὐτῶν συνεπλάκη τῷ λοιπῷ τῶν κακούργων, τῶν ἄλλων προαναλωθέντων, καὶ <ὁ τρίτος αὐτῷ βοηθῶν>[4] τοῦ μὲν λῃστοῦ ἥμαρτεν, ὦσε δὲ τὸ ξίφος κατὰ τοῦ φίλου. τῷ ἀποδράντι οὖν ἡ Πυθία ἀνεῖλε τάδε·

test they held in honour of Hera, when the Sybarites began to riot on his account, taking up weapons against each other. The player was frightened and took refuge in full dress at the altar of Hera. But even here they did not spare him. Not long after it seemed that blood welled up in the temple of Hera, in the same way as a perpetual spring. The Sybarites sent a delegation to Delphi and the Pythia responded: "Go away from my tripods, there is still blood on your hands, pouring down in quantity, to keep you from the stone threshold. I shall not deliver oracles to you; you have killed a servant of the Muses by the altars of Hera, without respect for the vengeance of the gods. For evildoers the fulfilment of justice is not long in coming, nor can it be put off, even if they should be descendants of Zeus. It hovers over their heads and among their children; misfortune after misfortune stalks in their homes."[a] Justice was not slow; for having taken up arms against the men of Croton they were overwhelmed by them, and their city disappeared.[b]

44. Three young men, fellow townsmen, arrived in Delphi as a delegation to consult the oracle and ran into some criminals. One of them ran away from the robbers, the second wrestled with the one remaining robber after all the others had been killed, while the third <,helping his friend,> missed the robber and drove his sword into his friend's body. The Pythia gave the following oracle to

[a] This oracle is no. 74 in Parke and Wormell, *The Delphic Oracle.* [b] For Sybaris see above on 1.19.

---

[1] σὺν del. Her.
[2] παραιτητόν Faber: ἀπαρ- codd.
[3] suppl. Eberhard [4] suppl. van Groningen

ἀνδρὶ φίλῳ θνῄσκοντι παρὼν πέλας οὐκ ἐβοήθεις.
οὔ σε θεμιστεύσω· περικαλλέος ἔξιθι νηοῦ·

καὶ τῷ ἑτέρῳ δὲ ἀνεῖλε τάδε ἐρομένῳ τὴν Πυθίαν·

ἔκτεινας τὸν ἑταῖρον ἀμύνων· οὔ σ' ἐμίανεν
αἷμα, πέλεις δὲ χέρας καθαρώτερος ἢ πάρος ἦσθα.

45. Φιλίππῳ φασὶ χρηστήριον ἐκπεσεῖν ἐν Βοιωτοῖς ἐν Τροφωνίου, φυλάττεσθαι δεῖν τὸ ἅρμα. ἐκεῖνον οὖν δέει τοῦ χρησμοῦ λόγος ἔχει μηδέποτε ἀναβῆναι ἅρμα. διπλοῦς οὖν ἐπὶ τούτοις διαρρεῖ[1] λόγος. ὁ μὲν γάρ φησι[2] τὸ τοῦ Παυσανίου ξίφος, ᾧ τὸν Φίλιππον διεχρήσατο, ἅρμα ἔχειν ἐπὶ τῆς λαβῆς διαγεγλυμμένον[3] ἐλεφάντινον· ὁ δὲ ἕτερος, τὴν Θηβαϊκὴν περιελθόντα λίμνην τὴν καλουμένην Ἅρμα ἀποσφαγῆναι. ὁ μὲν πρῶτος λόγος δημώδης, ὁ δὲ οὐκ εἰς πάντας ἐξεφοίτησεν.

46. Σταγειριτῶν νόμος οὗτος καὶ πάντῃ Ἑλληνικός· "ὃ μὴ κατέθου" φησὶ "μὴ λάμβανε."

47. Τιμόθεον τὰ μὲν πρῶτα ἐπῄνουν Ἀθηναῖοι· ἐπεὶ δὲ ἔδοξεν ἁμαρτεῖν ἃ ἔδοξεν,[4] ἡ φθάνουσα

[1] διαρρεῖ Her.: ὑπορρεῖ codd.
[2] ὁ . . . φησι Her.: οἱ . . . φασι codd.
[3] διαγεγλυμμένον x: -γεγραμμένον VΦ
[4] ἃ ἔδοξεν] textus vix sanus; an haec verba delenda (Russell)?

[a] These oracles are nos. 575 and 576 in Parke and Wormell.

the man who had run away. "When your friend was dying you stood by and did not help. I shall not give you an oracle; leave the beautiful temple." And when the other consulted the Pythian priestess she said: "You killed your friend while defending him; blood has not polluted you, and your hands are cleaner than before."[a]

45. They say Philip received an oracle in Boeotia at the shrine of Trophonius, to the effect that he must be on his guard against a chariot. The tradition has it that he was in fear of the oracle and never got up into his chariot. After this the story circulates in two versions. Some say that the sword of Pausanias, with which he killed Philip, had a chariot carved in ivory on the handle; the other version is that he was assassinated after walking round the lake at Thebes known as Harma [chariot].[b] The first story is popular, the second is not found everywhere.

46. A law from Stagira which is utterly Greek says "Do not claim what you did not put on deposit."[c]

47. Timotheus[d] at first received praise from the Athenians, but when he was found guilty of the mis-

[b] The lake was called Chariot, according to the ancients, because it was located where Amphiaraus, fleeing from Thebes in his chariot, was engulfed by the earth.

[c] This ch. is so brief as to be obscure; but cf. 4.1 below.

[d] The general already mentioned at 2.10 and elsewhere; his career came to an end after a second trial ca. 356 B.C. The next two figures in this ch. are heroes of the Persian Wars. Themistocles has already been the subject of 2.12 and 3.21, and the trick alluded to here is narrated by Thucydides 1.89–93. Pausanias was the Spartan king who defeated the Persians at Plataea and recovered Byzantium. With Phocion, already mentioned at 1.25, 2.16, and 2.43, Aelian comes back to the fourth century; but chronological order is not his concern.

αὐτὸν ἀνδραγαθία ἀλλ' οὐδὲ ὀλίγον ἔσωσεν, οὐδὲ μὴν αἱ τῶν προγόνων ἀρεταί.

Θεμιστοκλῆς δὲ οὐδὲν ὤνητο οὔτε ἐκ τῆς ναυμαχίας τῆς περὶ Σαλαμῖνα οὔτε ἐκ τῆς πρεσβείας τῆς εἰς Σπάρτην· λέγω δὲ ἣν ἐπρέσβευσε κλέπτων τὴν τῶν Ἀθηναίων τείχισιν. ἔφυγε γὰρ κἀκεῖνος οὐ τὰς Ἀθήνας μόνον, ἀλλὰ καὶ τὴν Ἑλλάδα πᾶσαν.

Καὶ Παυσανίαν δὲ τὸν Λακεδαιμόνιον οὐδὲν ὤνησεν ἡ ἐν Πλαταιαῖς νίκη· ὑπὲρ δὲ ὧν ἐν Βυζαντίῳ ἐκαινούργει καὶ ἐνόει[1] Περσικά, ὑπὲρ τούτων διέφθειρε καὶ τὴν χάριν τὴν ἐπὶ τοῖς πρώτοις.

Φωκίωνα δὲ ἡ εὐφημία ἡ καλοῦσα αὐτὸν Χρηστὸν οὐδὲν ὠφέλησεν, οὐδὲ τὰ πέντε καὶ ἑβδομήκοντα ἔτη, ἅπερ οὖν διεβίωσεν, οὐδὲν ἀδικήσας τοὺς Ἀθηναίους ἔμβραχυ·[2] ἐπεὶ δὲ ἔδοξεν Ἀντιπάτρῳ[3] τὸν Πειραιᾶ προδιδόναι, Ἀθηναῖοι κατέγνωσαν αὐτοῦ θάνατον.

[1] ἐνόει Her.: ἐνόσει codd.

[2] ἔμβραχυ Cobet: ἐν βραχεῖ codd.

[3] Ἀντιπάτρῳ] <Κασσάνδρῳ τῷ τοῦ> Ἀντιπάτρου Kor. post Per.

demeanours he appeared to have committed, his previous acts of bravery brought him no relief whatever, nor did his ancestors' noble acts.

Themistocles derived no advantage from the sea battle at Salamis or from his mission to Sparta—I refer to the mission which tricked them over the Athenian fortifications. He too went into exile, not just from Athens but from the whole of Greece.

Pausanias the Spartan did not benefit from victory at Plataea; his misbehaviour at Byzantium and his mania for things Persian nullified even the good will arising from his first exploits.

The good name which caused Phocion to be nicknamed "the honest" was of no advantage, nor the seventy-five years he had lived without harming anyone in the least; when he was found to have betrayed the Piraeus to Antipater, the Athenians condemned him to death.

Δ

1. Λέγει τις νόμος Λευκανῶν, ἐὰν ἡλίου δύναντος ἀφίκηται ξένος καὶ παρελθεῖν ἐθελήσῃ εἰς στέγην τινός, εἶτα <οὗτος>[1] μὴ δέξηται τὸν ἄνδρα, ζημιοῦσθαι αὐτὸν καὶ ὑπέχειν δίκας τῆς κακοξενίας ἐμοὶ δοκεῖ καὶ τῷ ἀφικομένῳ καὶ τῷ Ξενίῳ Διί.

Ὅτι Δαρδανεῖς τοὺς ἀπὸ τῆς Ἰλλυρίδος ἀκούω τρὶς μόνον λούεσθαι παρὰ πάντα τὸν ἑαυτῶν βίον, ἐξ ὠδίνων καὶ γαμοῦντας καὶ ἀποθανόντας.

Ἰνδοὶ οὔτε δανείζουσιν οὔτε ἴσασι δανείζεσθαι, ἀλλ' οὔτε θέμις ἄνδρα Ἰνδὸν οὔτε ἀδικῆσαι οὔτε ἀδικηθῆναι. διὸ οὐδὲ ποιοῦνται συγγραφὴν ἢ παρακαταθήκην.[2]

Νόμος ἐστὶ Σαρδῷος, τοὺς ἤδη γεγηρακότας τῶν πατέρων οἱ παῖδες ῥοπάλοις τύπτοντες ἀνῄρουν καὶ ἔθαπτον, αἰσχρὸν ἡγούμενοι τὸν λίαν ὑπέργηρων ὄντα ζῆν ἔτι, ὡς πολλὰ ἁμαρτάνοντος τοῦ σώματος τοῦ διὰ τὸ γῆρας πεπονηκότος. τῶν δὲ αὐτῶν ἐστι νόμος τοιοῦτος· ἀργίας ἦσαν δίκαι, καὶ τὸν εἰκῇ ζῶντα ἔδει κρίνεσθαι καὶ διδόναι τὰς εὐθύνας ἀποδεικνύντα ὁπόθεν ζῇ.

[1] supplevi [2] παρακαταθήκην] -θήκης δίκην Faber

BOOK FOUR

1. A law in Lucania declares: if a traveller arrives after sunset and wishes to enter someone's house but the latter declines to receive him, there is a punishment and the man pays the penalty for his bad hospitality, I presume both to the traveller and to Zeus Xenios.[a]

Note that the Dardanians of Illyria, as I hear, are washed only three times in the whole course of their lives, after birth, on marriage, and at death.

The Indians do not lend money, nor do they have any notion of accepting a loan. For an Indian it is not right to commit an injustice or to be the victim of one. Hence they make no written contracts or deposits.[b]

It was a custom in Sardinia that the children of aged parents beat them to death with clubs and buried them, in the belief that it was wrong for the excessively old to continue living, since the body, suffering through age, had many failings. The same community had the following law: there were trials for idleness, and a person who lived without a regular routine had to go to court and submit to an examination to prove the source of his income.

[a] Patron of travellers and guests. The Lucanians had ceased to exist as a separate nation by the end of the Roman Republic, but Aelian gives the impression of disregarding the fact.

[b] A literal translation; the meaning is not entirely clear.

Ἀσσύριοι τὰς ὡραίας γάμου παρθένους ἀθροίσαντες εἴς τινα πόλιν ἀγορὰν αὐτῶν προκηρύττουσι, καὶ ἕκαστος ἣν ἂν πρίηται ἀπάγει νύμφην.

Βύβλιος ἀνὴρ ἐν ὁδῷ περιτυχὼν οὐδὲν ὧν μὴ κατέθετο ἀναιρεῖται· οὐ γὰρ ἡγεῖται τὸ τοιοῦτον εὕρεμα ἀλλὰ ἀδίκημα.

Δερβίκκαι τοὺς ὑπὲρ ἑβδομήκοντα ἔτη βεβιωκότας ἀποκτείνουσι, τοὺς μὲν ἄνδρας καταθύοντες, ἀπάγχοντες δὲ τὰς γυναῖκας.

Κόλχοι δὲ τοὺς νεκροὺς ἐν βύρσαις θάπτουσι καὶ καταρράψαντες ἐκ τῶν δένδρων ἐξαρτῶσι.

Λυδοῖς ἦν ἔθος πρὸ τοῦ συνοικεῖν τὰς γυναῖκας ἀνδράσιν ἑταιρεῖν, ἅπαξ δὲ καταζευχθείσας σωφρονεῖν· τὴν δὲ ἁμαρτάνουσαν εἰς ἕτερον[1] συγγνώμης τυχεῖν ἀδύνατον ἦν.

2. Νικόστρατον τὸν κιθαριστὴν λόγος τις περίεισι λέγων Λαοδόκῳ τῷ κιθαρῳδῷ διαφερόμενον ὑπὲρ μουσικῆς εἰπεῖν ὅτι ἄρα ἐκεῖνος μέν ἐστιν ἐν μεγάλῃ τῇ τέχνῃ μικρός, αὐτὸς δὲ ἐν μικρᾷ μέγας. οὐ μόνον δὲ ἄρα ἐστὶ σεμνὸν οἰκίαν αὐξῆσαι καὶ πλοῦτον, ἀλλὰ γὰρ καὶ τέχνην, εἴ γέ τι δεῖ προσέχειν Νικοστράτῳ εὖ καὶ καλῶς τοῦτο εἰπόντι.

3. Πολύγνωτος ὁ Θάσιος καὶ Διονύσιος ὁ Κολοφώνιος γραφέε ἤστην. καὶ ὁ μὲν Πολύγνωτος ἔγραφε τὰ μεγάλα καὶ ἐν τοῖς τελείοις εἰργάζετο τὰ

[1] εἰς ἕτερον] ὕστερον Grasberger

The Assyrians collect in one city all the girls of marriageable age and announce a sale. Each man takes away as his bride the one he has bought.

A man from Byblus who finds an object in the street will not pick it up unless he put it there. He does not regard this as a find, but as an injustice.

The Derbiccae[a] kill those who are seventy years of age. They sacrifice the men and strangle the women.

The Colchians put the dead in leather skins; they sew them up and hang them from trees.[b]

It was the custom in Lydia for the women to live as courtesans before setting up house with their husbands; once married, they behaved correctly. The woman who misbehaved with another man had no chance of being forgiven.

2. A story circulates which says that Nicostratus the cithara player had an argument about music with Laodocus the singer and said that the latter was a minor exponent of a great art, whereas he himself was a great exponent of a minor art. Not only is it laudable to augment one's house and one's wealth, but also one's art, if we are to heed Nicostratus' apt and well-phrased comment.

3. Polygnotus of Thasus and Dionysius of Colophon were painters. Polygnotus painted on a large scale and won prizes for life-sized representations. The work of

[a] A large tribe living in the eastern part of Persia.

[b] This custom is attributed to the Colchians by Apollonius Rhodius, *Argonautica* 3.200–209, and some other ancient authorities. According to M. Marconi, *Rendiconti dell' Istituto Lombardo* 76 (1942–3): 309–320, it has been recorded in modern times among the Ossetians and other nationalities of the Caucasus.

ἆθλα, τὰ δὲ τοῦ Διονυσίου πλὴν τοῦ μεγέθους τὴν τοῦ Πολυγνώτου τέχνην ἐμιμεῖτο εἰς τὴν ἀκρίβειαν, πάθος καὶ ἦθος καὶ σχημάτων χρῆσιν[1] <καὶ>[2] ἱματίων λεπτότητας καὶ τὰ λοιπά.

4. Ἀκούω κεῖσθαι νόμον Θήβησι προστάττοντα τοῖς τεχνίταις καὶ τοῖς γραφικοῖς καὶ τοῖς πλαστικοῖς εἰς τὸ κρεῖττον τὰς εἰκόνας μιμεῖσθαι. ἀπειλεῖ δὲ ὁ νόμος τοῖς εἰς τὸ χεῖρόν ποτε ἢ πλάσασιν ἢ γράψασι ζημίαν τὸ τίμημα χιλίων δραχμῶν.[3]

5. Εὐεργεσιῶν ἀπεμνήσθησαν[4] καὶ χάριτας ὑπὲρ αὐτῶν ἀπέδοσαν, Θησεὺς μὲν Ἡρακλεῖ. Ἀιδωνέως γὰρ αὐτὸν τοῦ Μολοττῶν βασιλέως δήσαντος, ὅτε ἐπὶ τὴν γυναῖκα αὐτοῦ ἦλθε μετὰ Πειρίθου ἁρπασόμενος αὐτὴν ὁ Θησεύς (οὐχ ἑαυτῷ σπουδάζων τὸν γάμον, ἀλλὰ γὰρ τῇ τοῦ Πειρίθου χάριτι τοῦτο δράσας), Ἡρακλῆς εἰς τοὺς Μολοττοὺς ἀφικόμενος ἐρρύσατο τὸν Θησέα, καὶ διὰ ταῦτα ἐκεῖνος αὐτῷ βωμὸν ἀνέστησε.

Καὶ οἱ ἑπτὰ ἐπὶ Θήβας Πρώνακτι καὶ ἐκεῖνοι χάριτας ἀπέδοσαν. διὰ γὰρ αὐτοὺς ἀπολομένου τοῦ Πρώνακτος τὸν ἀγῶνα ἔθεσαν ἐπ᾽ αὐτῷ,[5] ὃν οἱ πολλοὶ οἴονται ἐπ᾽ Ἀρχεμόρῳ τεθῆναι ἐξ ἀρχῆς.[6]

Καὶ Ἡρακλῆς δὲ Νέστορι ἀπέδωκε χάριτας. Νηλέως γὰρ αὐτὸν οὐ βουλομένου καθῆραι, οἱ μὲν ἄλλοι παῖδες σύμψηφοι ἦσαν τῷ Νηλεῖ, ὁ δὲ

[1] χρῆσιν] fortasse χάριν (Russell) [2] suppl. Kor.
[3] χιλίων δραχμῶν Kor.: δρᾶν codd. [4] ἀπεμνήσθησαν V: ἐπ- x [5] αὐτῷ Cuper: αὐτόν codd.
[6] ἐξ ἀρχῆς Gesner: ἐξάρχῳ codd.: <κακῶν> ἐξάρχῳ Her.

Dionysius, except in its size, was an accurate imitation of Polygnotus in emotion and character, the treatment of gesture, the delicacy of the clothing, and so on.

4. I hear that in Thebes a law was in force which instructed artists—both painters and sculptors—to make their portraits flattering. As punishment for those who produced a sculpture or painting less attractive than the original the law threatened a fine of a thousand drachmae.

5. Benefits were remembered, and thanks for them given, by Theseus to Heracles. Aïdoneus king of the Molossians put Theseus in chains when he came with Pirithous to kidnap the king's wife. Theseus did not want to marry the woman himself but did this as a favour to Pirithous. Heracles came to the country of the Molossians and rescued Theseus, in return for which the latter set up an altar to him.

The Seven against Thebes also recorded their thanks to Pronax. As he had died in their cause they set up in his name the contest which most people think was established in the first instance for Archemorus.[a]

Heracles expressed his gratitude to Nestor. When Neleus did not wish to purify him, the other children were in agreement with Neleus, but not so Nestor.[b] For

[a] The Seven against Thebes were leaders of an army assembled by Polynices in Argos to recover control of Thebes from his brother Eteocles. Pronax was king of Argos. Archemorus, the young son of king Opheltes of Nemea, was killed by a snake. The contest referred to is the Nemean Games.

[b] Heracles might have needed purification for the crimes of murdering Iphitus or his own children; various versions of the myth circulated.

Νέστωρ οὐχί. καὶ διὰ ταῦτα ἑλὼν τὴν πόλιν[1] Ἡρακλῆς τὸν μὲν Νηλέα καὶ τοὺς ἄλλους αὐτοῦ παῖδας ἀπέκτεινεν, οὐ μόνον δὲ ἐφείσατο Νέστορος, ἀλλὰ καὶ τὴν βασιλείαν τὴν πατρῴαν ἔχειν ἔδωκε.

Καὶ Ἀθηναῖοι δὲ πανδημεὶ τοῖς Ἡρακλέους ἀπογόνοις ἀπέτισαν χάριτας. ἐπεὶ γὰρ καὶ ἐκείνων ὁ προπάτωρ εὐεργέτης ἐγένετο τοῦ Θησέως, οἱ Ἀθηναῖοι διὰ ταῦτα κατήγαγον αὐτοὺς εἰς Πελοπόννησον.

Καὶ Ἡρακλῆς δὲ ἀπέδωκε χάριτας τοῖς ἐκ Κλεωνῶν τριακοσίοις καὶ ἑξήκοντα. τούτοις γὰρ ἐπὶ τοῖς Μολιονίδαις[2] συστρατεύσασιν αὐτῷ καὶ ἀποθανοῦσιν εὖ καὶ καλῶς ἀπέστη τῶν ἐν Νεμέᾳ τιμῶν, ἃς ἔλαβε παρὰ τῶν Νεμέων,[3] ὅτε τὸν ἐπιχωριάζοντα αὐτοῖς καὶ λυμαινόμενον αὐτῶν τὰ ἔργα ἐχειρώσατο λέοντα.

Καὶ Μενεσθεὺς δὲ ὁ Πετεὼ[4] περὶ τοὺς Τυνδαρίδας οὐκ ἐγένετο ἀχάριστος. ἐκβαλόντες γὰρ ἐκεῖνοι τοὺς Θησέως υἱοὺς καὶ τὴν μητέρα τὴν Θησέως Αἴθραν αἰχμάλωτον λαβόντες ἔδωκαν τὴν βασιλείαν τῷ Μενεσθεῖ. διὰ ταῦτα πρῶτος ὁ Μενεσθεὺς Ἄνακτάς[5] τε καὶ Σωτῆρας ὠνόμασε.

Καὶ Δαρεῖος δὲ ὁ Ὑστάσπου παρὰ Συλοσῶντος λαβὼν ἱμάτιον ἔτι ἰδιώτης ὤν, ὅτε ἐγκρατὴς ἐγένετο τῆς βασιλείας, ἔδωκεν αὐτῷ τῆς πατρίδος τὴν ἀρχὴν τῆς Σάμου, χρύσεα χαλκείων φαίη τις ἄν.

[1] πόλιν] Πύλον Kühn
[2] τοῖς Μολιονίδαις] τοὺς . . . -ίδας anonymus

this reason Heracles captured the city[a] and killed Neleus and his other children. But he not merely spared Nestor; he installed him in his father's kingdom.

Athens as a community registered its gratitude to the descendants of Heracles. Since their ancestor had been the benefactor of Theseus, the Athenians restored them to the Peloponnese.[b]

Heracles displayed his gratitude to the three hundred and sixty men of Cleonae. They had joined him in his campaign against the Molionidae and met a noble death.[c] He transferred to them the honours from Nemea, honours he had received from that city when he had defeated the lion which lived nearby and damaged their farms.

Menestheus son of Peteos was not ungrateful to the children of Tyndareus.[d] The latter had expelled the children of Theseus, taken prisoner his mother Aethra, and given the kingdom to Menestheus. For this reason Menestheus was the first to call them Lords and Saviours.

Darius son of Hystaspes, while he was still a private citizen, received a coat from Syloson. On taking up the throne he gave Syloson command of his own country, Samos—gold for bronze, one might say.[e]

[a] The city is Pylos, and the name should perhaps be restored in the text. [b] See the opening paragraph of this ch.; J. Wilkins, *Euripides Heraclidae* (Oxford, 1993), pp. xi–xiv.

[c] The Molionidae were nephews of Augeas; Heracles killed them at Cleonae, in the vicinity of Nemea. [d] The Dioscuri; see n. on 1.30 above. [e] An allusion to *Iliad* 6.236.

---

[3] Νεμέων] -εαίων vel -εατῶν Her. post Gesner

[4] Πετεὼ e Plut. *Thes.* 32 Her.: -εὼν V: -εῶο x

[5] Ἄνακτάς] Ἄνακάς e Plut. Her.

6. Ὅτι ἡνίκα ἐβούλοντο Λακεδαιμόνιοι τὴν Ἀθηναίων ἀφανίσαι πόλιν, ἠρώτησαν τὸν θεόν, καὶ ἀπεκρίνατο τὴν κοινὴν ἑστίαν τῆς Ἑλλάδος μὴ κινεῖν.

7. Οὐκ ἦν ἄρα τοῖς κακοῖς οὐδὲ τὸ ἀποθανεῖν κέρδος, ἐπεὶ μηδὲ τότε ἀναπαύονται, ἀλλ' ἢ παντελῶς ἀμοιροῦσι ταφῆς ἢ καὶ ἐὰν φθάσωσι ταφέντες, ὅμως καὶ ἐκ τῆς τελευταίας τιμῆς καὶ τοῦ κοινοῦ πάντων σωμάτων ὅρμου καὶ ἐκεῖθεν ἐκπίπτουσι. Λακεδαιμόνιοι γοῦν Παυσανίαν μηδίσαντα οὐ μόνον λιμῷ ἀπέκτειναν, ἀλλὰ γὰρ καὶ τὸν νεκρὸν ἐξέβαλον αὐτοῦ ἐκτὸς τῶν ὅρων, φησὶν Ἐπιτιμίδης.

8. Εἶτα τίς οὐκ οἶδε τὰς τῆς τύχης μεταβολὰς ὀξυρρόπους καὶ ταχείας; Λακεδαιμόνιοι γοῦν Θηβαίων ἄρξαντες αὐτοὶ πάλιν ὑπ' ἐκείνων οὕτως ἐχειρώθησαν, ὡς τοὺς Θηβαίους μὴ μόνον εἰς Πελοπόννησον ἀφικέσθαι, ἀλλὰ γὰρ καὶ τὸν Εὐρώταν διελθεῖν καὶ τὴν τῶν Λακεδαιμονίων τεμεῖν χώραν. καὶ ὀλίγου καὶ τὴν πόλιν κατέλαβον, εἰ μὴ Ἐπαμεινώνδας ἔδεισε μὴ Πελοποννήσιοι πάντες συμπνεύσωσι καὶ ὑπὲρ τῆς Σπάρτης ἀγωνίσωνται.

Διονύσιος ὁ τύραννος καταστὰς ὑπὸ Καρχηδονίων εἰς πολιορκίαν, οὐδεμιᾶς αὐτῷ σωτηρίας ὑποφαινομένης, αὐτὸς μὲν ἄθυμος ἦν καὶ ἐπενόει[1] δρασμόν, τῶν δὲ ἑταίρων αὐτῷ τις, Ἑλλοπίδης ὄνομα, προσελθὼν ἔφατο· "ὦ Διονύσιε, καλὸν ἐντάφιον ἡ τυραννίς." αἰδεσθεὶς οὖν ἐπὶ τούτῳ ἀνερρώσθη τὴν γνώμην, καὶ σὺν ὀλίγοις παμπόλλους[2]

6. Note that when the Spartans wanted to destroy Athens,[a] they asked the god, and he replied that they should not disturb the hearth and home of all Greece.

7. Even death is of no advantage to the wicked, since they still have no relief. Either they are not buried at all, or if they are buried first, they still miss the final honours and the common haven of all bodies. The Spartans not only starved Pausanias to death for having sided with the Persians but cast his body outside the state's boundaries. So reports Epitimides [FGrH 566 F 159].[b]

8. Is there anyone unaware of the sharp and rapid turns of Fortune? The Spartans had ruled Thebes and were in turn defeated by them so severely that the Thebans did not just advance to the Peloponnese; they even crossed the Eurotas and devastated the Spartan countryside, and were close to capturing the city, had not Epaminondas been afraid that the whole of the Peloponnese would unite and make common cause with Sparta.[c]

The tyrant Dionysius was besieged by the Carthaginians without any prospect of survival.[d] In his despondency he contemplated flight, but one of his companions called Ellopides came and said to him, "Dionysius, tyranny is a fine shroud."[e] Shamed by this he recovered his spirits,

[a] After the defeat of Athens in 404 B.C. [b] Epitimides is otherwise unknown. [c] In the year after his victory at Leuctra in 371 B.C. Epaminondas invaded Sparta. [d] The reference is to a war between Dionysius I and Carthage in 397 B.C. [e] In other words, to die when one is ruler of a city is no cause for regret. This and the following paragraph derive from Isocrates 6.44–46.

---

[1] ἐπενόει Her.: ὑπενενόει codd.
[2] παμπόλλους] -ας Faber

μυριάδας κατηγωνίσατο, ἀλλὰ καὶ τὴν ἀρχὴν μείζω ἐποίησεν.

Καὶ Ἀμύντας δὲ ὁ Μακεδὼν ἡττηθεὶς ὑπὸ τῶν προσοίκων βαρβάρων καὶ ἀποβαλὼν τὴν ἀρχήν, γνώμην μὲν εἶχεν ὡς καὶ ἀπολείψων τὴν χώραν τελέως· ἠγάπα γὰρ εἰ δυνηθείη διασῶσαι αὑτὸν γοῦν μόνον. ἐπεὶ δὲ ἐν τούτοις ἦν, ἔφατό τις πρὸς αὐτὸν τὴν Ἑλλοπίδου φωνήν. καὶ μικρὸν χῶρον καταλαβὼν καὶ ἀθροίσας ὀλίγους στρατιώτας ἀνεκτήσατο τὴν ἀρχήν.

Ὅτι τὸν Ὦχον οἱ Αἰγύπτιοι τῇ ἐπιχωρίῳ φωνῇ Ὄνον ἐκάλουν, τὸ νωθὲς αὐτοῦ τῆς γνώμης ἐκ τῆς ἀσθενείας τοῦ ζῴου διαβάλλοντες. ἀνθ' ὧν ἐκεῖνος τὸν Ἆπιν πρὸς βίαν κατέθυσεν Ὄνῳ.

Δίων ὁ Ἱππαρίνου, φυγὰς ὢν ὑπὸ Διονυσίου, μετὰ δισχιλίων στρατιωτῶν αὖθις κατεπολέμησε, καὶ ὃ πρότερον αὐτὸς ἦν τοῦτο ἐκεῖνον εἰργάσατο, φυγάδα.

Συρακούσιοι δὲ ἐννέα τριήρεσι πρὸς ἑκατὸν καὶ πεντήκοντα τὰς τῶν Καρχηδονίων παραταξάμενοι κατὰ πολὺ ἐκράτησαν.

9. Πλάτων ὁ Ἀρίστωνος ἐν Ὀλυμπίᾳ συνεσκήνωσεν ἀγνῶσιν ἀνθρώποις, καὶ αὐτὸς ὢν αὐτοῖς ἀγνώς. οὕτως δὲ αὐτοὺς ἐχειρώσατο καὶ ἀνεδήσατο τῇ συνουσίᾳ, συνεστιώμενός τε αὐτοῖς ἀφελῶς καὶ συνδιημερεύων ἐν πᾶσιν, ὡς ὑπερησθῆναι τοὺς

---

[a] He ruled 385–382 B.C.

defeated an army of countless thousands with a small force, and enlarged his territories.

Amyntas of Macedon was defeated by his barbarian neighbours and lost his kingdom.[a] He was thinking of abandoning entirely his territories, happy to escape with his own safety. While he was in this mood someone reported to him Ellopides' remark. He occupied a small area, gathered a few soldiers and recovered his kingdom.

Note that the Egyptians called Ochus[b] "the ass" in their own language, mocking his slow wits by comparing him to the unintelligent animal. In response he enforced the sacrifice of Apis to an ass god.

Dion the son of Hipparinus, sent into exile by Dionysius, turned the tables on him with a force of two thousand soldiers and imposed on the tyrant the fate of exile which he had previously suffered himself.[c]

The Syracusans drew up nine triremes against a force of one hundred and twenty from Carthage and won a decisive victory.[d]

9. Plato the son of Ariston lodged at Olympia[e] with some men he did not know, and they in turn did not know him. He so won them over and gained their affection by his company, eating with them in unpretentious style and passing the days with them all, that the strangers were

[b] This is Artaxerxes III (358–337 B.C.). The episode is mentioned by Aelian at *N.A.* 10.28, where it is emphasised that Ochus suffered an appropriate penalty for his sacrilege; he had sacrificed a much revered Egyptian god.

[c] In 357 B.C.

[d] Ps.-Aristotle, *Rhetorica ad Alexandrum* 1429 b 18, attributes this victory to a Corinthian force.

[e] He was attending the festival as a spectator.

ξένους τῇ τοῦ ἀνδρὸς συντυχίᾳ. οὔτε δὲ Ἀκαδημίας ἐμέμνητο οὔτε Σωκράτους· αὐτό γε μὴν τοῦτο ἐνεφάνισεν αὐτοῖς, ὅτι καλεῖται Πλάτων. ἐπεὶ δὲ ἦλθον εἰς τὰς Ἀθήνας, ὑπεδέξατο αὐτοὺς εὖ μάλα φιλοφρόνως. καὶ οἱ ξένοι "ἄγε," εἶπον "ὦ Πλάτων, ἐπίδειξον ἡμῖν καὶ τὸν ὁμώνυμόν σου, τὸν Σωκράτους ὁμιλητήν, καὶ ἐπὶ τὴν Ἀκαδημίαν ἥγησαι τὴν ἐκείνου, καὶ ἀποσύστησον τῷ ἀνδρί, ἵνα τι καὶ αὐτοῦ ἀπολαύσωμεν." ὁ δὲ ἠρέμα ὑπομειδιάσας, ὥσπερ οὖν καὶ εἰώθει, "ἀλλ' ἐγώ" φησιν "αὐτὸς ἐκεῖνός εἰμι." οἱ δὲ ἐξεπλάγησαν εἰ τὸν ἄνδρα ἔχοντες μεθ' ἑαυτῶν τὸν τοσοῦτον ἠγνόησαν, ἀτύφως αὐτοῦ συγγενομένου καὶ ἀνεπιτηδεύτως αὐτοῖς καὶ δείξαντος ὅτι δύναται καὶ ἄνευ τῶν συνήθων λόγων χειροῦσθαι τοὺς συνόντας.

Ὅτι Πλάτων τὸν Ἀριστοτέλη ἐκάλει Πῶλον. τί δὲ ἐβούλετο αὐτῷ τὸ ὄνομα ἐκεῖνο; δηλονότι ὡμολόγηται τὸν πῶλον, ὅταν κορεσθῇ τοῦ μητρῴου γάλακτος, λακτίζειν τὴν μητέρα. ᾐνίττετο οὖν καὶ ὁ Πλάτων ἀχαριστίαν τινὰ τοῦ Ἀριστοτέλους. καὶ γὰρ ἐκεῖνος τὰ μέγιστα εἰς φιλοσοφίαν παρὰ Πλάτωνος λαβὼν σπέρματα καὶ ἐφόδια, εἶτα ὑποπλησθεὶς τῶν ἀρίστων καὶ ἀφηνιάσας, ἀντῳκοδόμησεν αὐτῷ διατριβὴν καὶ ἀντιπαρεξήγαγεν ἐν τῷ περιπάτῳ ἑταίρους ἔχων καὶ ὁμιλητάς, καὶ ἐγλίχετο ἀντίπαλος εἶναι Πλάτωνι.

10. Εἶτα οὐκ ἦν τοῦ δήμου τοῦ Ἀθηναίων θεραπευτικὸς ὁ Ξανθίππου Περικλῆς; ἐμοὶ μὲν δοκεῖ. ὁσάκις γοῦν ἔμελλεν εἰς τὴν ἐκκλησίαν παριέναι,

delighted by their chance encounter. He made no allusion to the Academy or Socrates, and declared to them the one fact that his name was Plato. When they came to Athens he received them very cordially, and the visitors said to him "Now, Plato, show us your namesake, the student of Socrates, take us to his Academy, and introduce us to the man, so that we can profit from his company." With a quiet smile, as was his usual habit, he replied "But I am that Plato myself." They were amazed at having had such a great man among them without recognising him. He had behaved towards them with modesty and simplicity, and had proved himself able to win the confidence of anyone in his company without the usual philosophical discussions.

Note that Plato called Aristotle Polus. What did he mean by that name?[a] Obviously it is a well known fact that when a foal has had enough of its mother's milk, it kicks its mother. So Plato was hinting at some ingratitude on the part of Aristotle. In fact the latter had acquired from Plato the essential seeds and guidance for philosophy; then, filled with the best ideas, he became rebellious, set up another school,[b] and in opposition took his companions and students out for a stroll, aspiring to be Plato's rival.

10. Is it not true that Pericles son of Xanthippus cultivated the Athenian public? In my opinion he did. At any rate, each time he was about to address the assembly he

[a] The word means "colt, foal" and was also used as a name, the famous example being the character in Plato's *Gorgias*.

[b] The Lyceum; see 3.19 above.

ηὔχετο μηδὲν αὐτῷ ῥῆμα ἐπιπολάσαι τοιοῦτον, ὅπερ οὖν ἔμελλεν ἐκτραχύνειν τὸν δῆμον, πρόσαντες αὐτῷ γενόμενον καὶ ἀβούλητον δόξαν.

11. Διογένης ἔλεγε καὶ τὸν Σωκράτην αὐτὸν τρυφῆσαι· περιειργάσθαι γὰρ καὶ τῷ οἰκιδίῳ καὶ τῷ σκιμποδίῳ καὶ ταῖς βλαύταις δὲ αἷσπερ οὖν ἐχρῆτο Σωκράτης ἔστιν ὅτε.

12. Ὁ Ζεῦξις ὁ Ἡρακλεώτης ὅτε τὴν Ἑλένην ἔγραψε, πολλὰ ἐχρηματίσατο ἐκ τούτου τοῦ γράμματος· οὐ γὰρ εἰκῇ καὶ ὡς ἔτυχε τοὺς βουλομένους ἀνέδην[1] εἴα ὁρᾶν αὐτήν, ἀλλ᾽ ἔδει ῥητὸν ἀργύριον καταβαλεῖν, εἶτα οὕτω θεάσασθαι. ὡς οὖν μίσθωμα τοῦ Ἡρακλεώτου λαμβάνοντος ὑπὲρ τῆς γραφῆς, ἐκάλουν οἱ τότε Ἕλληνες ἐκείνην τὴν Ἑλένην Ἑταίραν.

13. Ἐπίκουρος ὁ Γαργήττιος <ἐκεκράγει>[2] λέγων·[3] "ᾧ ὀλίγον οὐχ ἱκανόν, ἀλλὰ τούτῳ γε οὐδὲν ἱκανόν." ὁ αὐτὸς ἔλεγε[4] ἑτοίμως ἔχειν καὶ τῷ Διὶ ὑπὲρ εὐδαιμονίας διαγωνίζεσθαι μᾶζαν ἔχων καὶ ὕδωρ. ταῦτα μὲν οὖν ἐννοῶν ὁ Ἐπίκουρος τί βουλόμενος ἐπῄνει τὴν ἡδονήν, εἰσόμεθα ἄλλοτε.

14. Πολλάκις τὰ κατ᾽ ὀβολὸν μετὰ πολλῶν πόνων συναχθέντα χρήματα κατὰ τὸν Ἀρχίλοχον εἰς πόρνης γυναικὸς ἔντερον καταρρέει.[5] ὥσπερ γὰρ ἐχῖνον λαβεῖν μὲν ῥᾴδιον συνέχειν δὲ χαλεπόν, οὕτω καὶ τὰ

[1] ἀνέδην del. Her.
[2] e Stobaeo 3.17.29 suppl. Her.
[3] λέγων Stobaeus: ἔλεγε codd.

prayed that no thoughts should occur to him of a kind which might inflame the people by appearing objectionable to them and ill-considered.

11. Diogenes [fr. 263 M.] said that even Socrates himself indulged in luxuries, because he took undue care of his modest house, his small couch, and his sandals—which in fact Socrates sometimes wore.[a]

12. When Zeuxis of Heraclea painted Helen he made a lot of money from the picture. He did not simply allow anyone who wished to look at it as and when they pleased; a fixed fee had to be paid before they could examine it. But as the artist from Heraclea took a fee for his painting the Greeks of the day called this Helen "the courtesan."

13. Epicurus of the deme of Gargettus proclaimed that a man who is not satisfied with a little will not be satisfied with anything. He also said that he was ready to declare himself a match for Zeus in good fortune if he had bread and water. If Epicurus held these opinions, we shall learn on another occasion what he had in mind when he recommended pleasure.[b]

14. Hard-earned money, put together penny by penny, often finishes up in the intestines of a prostitute, as Archilochus said [fr. 302 W.]. Just as it is easy to catch a hedgehog but hard to keep hold of it, so with money. And

[a] Socrates' austere habits made him notorious. He is mentioned as (exceptionally) wearing sandals at Plato, *Symposium* 174 a.

[b] See Epicurus in Diogenes Laertius 10.131–132; H. Usener, *Epicurea* (Leipzig, 1887), p. 339.

---

[4] ὁ αὐτὸς ἔλεγε] ἔλεγε δὲ Stobaeus

[5] καταρρέει Jacobs post Scheffer: καταίρουσι codd.

χρήματα. καὶ Ἀνάξαρχος[1] ἐν τῷ Περὶ βασιλείας φησὶ χαλεπὸν χρήματα συναγείρασθαι, χαλεπώτερον δὲ φυλακὴν τούτοις περιθεῖναι.

15. Ἱέρωνά φασι τὸν Σικελίας τύραννον τὰ πρῶτα ἰδιώτην εἶναι καὶ ἀνθρώπων ἀμουσότατον, καὶ τὴν ἀγροικίαν ἀλλὰ μηδὲ κατ' ὀλίγον τοῦ ἀδελφοῦ διαφέρειν τοῦ Γέλωνος· ἐπεὶ δὲ αὐτῷ συνηνέχθη νοσῆσαι, μουσικώτατος ἀνθρώπων ἐγένετο, τὴν σχολὴν τὴν ἐκ τῆς ἀρρωστίας εἰς ἀκούσματα πεπαιδευμένα καταθέμενος. ῥωσθεὶς οὖν Ἱέρων συνῆν Σιμωνίδῃ τῷ Κείῳ καὶ Πινδάρῳ τῷ Θηβαίῳ καὶ Βακχυλίδῃ τῷ Ἰουλιήτῃ. ὁ δὲ Γέλων ἄνθρωπος ἄμουσος.

Μουσικώτατον δὲ λέγουσι καὶ Πτολεμαῖον γενέσθαι τὸν δεύτερον καὶ αὐτὸν νοσήσαντα. λέγει δὲ καὶ Πλάτων τὸν Θεάγην φιλοσοφῆσαι δι' οὐδὲν ἄλλο ἢ διὰ τὴν νοσοτροφίαν· εἴργουσα γὰρ αὐτὸν ἐκείνη τῶν πολιτικῶν συνήλασεν εἰς τὸν τῆς σοφίας ἔρωτα. τίς δὲ οὐκ ἂν νοῦν ἔχων συνηύξατο καὶ Ἀλκιβιάδῃ νόσον καὶ Κριτίᾳ καὶ Παυσανίᾳ τῷ Λακεδαιμονίῳ καὶ ἄλλοις; Ἀλκιβιάδῃ μὲν καὶ Κριτίᾳ, ἵνα μὴ ἀποδράντες Σωκράτους ὁ μὲν ὑβριστὴς γένηται καὶ ποτὲ μὲν φιλολάκων ᾖ, ποτὲ δὲ βοιωτιάζῃ τὸν τρόπον καὶ αὖ πάλιν θετταλίζῃ καὶ τοῖς Μήδων καὶ Περσῶν ἀρέσκηται ἐν Φαρναβάζου γενόμενος· τυραννικώτατος δὲ καὶ φονικώτατος ὁ Κριτίας γενόμενος καὶ τὴν πατρίδα ἐλύπησε πολλὰ

[1] Ἀνάξαρχος Her.: Ἀναξαγόρας codd.

Anaxarchus in his book on kingship said [D.-K. 72 B 2] it is hard to accumulate money, and harder still to protect it.[a]

15. Hieron the tyrant of Sicily,[b] they say, was originally an ordinary citizen of no culture, and in his boorishness did not differ in the least from his brother Gelon. When he became ill he turned into the most cultivated of men, using the free time resulting from his illness for cultural pursuits. After his recovery Hieron associated with Simonides of Ceos, Pindar of Thebes, and Bacchylides of Iulis. But Gelon was uncultured.

They say that Ptolemy II also became highly cultured after an illness. Plato says [*Republic* 496 bc] that Theages took up philosophy for no reason other than his poor health. This kept him out of politics and led him to a love of wisdom. What sensible man would not wish that Alcibiades, Critias, Pausanias the Spartan,[c] and others had suffered illness? Alcibiades and Critias would not have deserted Socrates—the former became arrogant, sometimes favouring Spartan customs, sometimes adopting Boeotian and Thessalian habits, or taking pleasure in the usages of the Medes and the Persians when he lived at the court of Pharnabazus. Critias turned into the worst of tyrants and murderers. He caused great distress to his

[a] Anaxarchus was a philosopher who accompanied Alexander the Great on his expedition; see 9.30 and 9.37 below. There is a study of him by J. Brunschwig in *Proceedings of the British Academy* 82 (1992): 59–88.

[b] Hieron was tyrant of Syracuse 478–466/5 B.C.

[c] For Pausanias see ch. 7 above. As Donald Russell points out to me, something may have been lost from this paragraph, as his fate is not followed up.

καὶ αὐτὸς μισούμενος τὸν βίον κατέστρεψε.[1]

Καὶ Στράτων δὲ ὁ Κορράγου εἰς δέον ἔοικε νοσῆσαι· εὖ[2] γὰρ γένους ἥκων εὖ δὲ καὶ πλούτου οὐκ ἐγυμνάζετο. καμὼν δὲ τὸν σπλῆνα καὶ θεραπείας δεηθεὶς τῆς ἐκ τῶν γυμνασίων, τὰ μὲν πρῶτα ὅσον εἰς τὸ ὑγιᾶναι ἐχρῆτο αὐτοῖς, χωρῶν δὲ εἰς τὸ πρόσω τῆς τέχνης καὶ ἐν ἔργῳ τιθέμενος αὐτήν, Ὀλυμπίασι μὲν ἐνίκησεν ἡμέρᾳ μιᾷ πάλην καὶ παγκράτιον, καὶ τῇ ἑξῆς Ὀλυμπιάδι, καὶ ἐν Νεμέᾳ δὲ καὶ Πυθοῖ καὶ Ἰσθμοῖ.

Δημοκράτης ὁ παλαιστὴς καὶ αὐτὸς νοσήσας τοὺς πόδας, παριὼν εἰς τοὺς ἀγῶνας καὶ στὰς ἐν τῷ σταδίῳ, περιγράφων ἑαυτῷ κύκλον προσέταττε τοῖς ἀντιπαλαισταῖς ἔξω τῆς γραμμῆς αὐτὸν προέλκειν· οἱ δὲ ἡττῶντο ἀδυνατοῦντες. ὁ δὲ εὖ διαβὰς ἐν τῇ στάσει καὶ ἐγκρατῶς, στεφανούμενος ἀπῄει.

16. Ἐὰν προσέχῃ τις Καλλίᾳ, φιλοπότην αὐτὸν ἐργάσεται ὁ Καλλίας·[3] ἐὰν Ἰσμηνίᾳ, αὐλητήν· ἀλαζόνα, ἐὰν Ἀλκιβιάδῃ· ὀψοποιόν, ἐὰν Κρωβύλῳ· δεινὸν εἰπεῖν, ἐὰν Δημοσθένει· στρατηγικόν, ἐὰν Ἐπαμεινώνδᾳ· μεγαλόφρονα, ἐὰν Ἀγησιλάῳ, καὶ χρηστόν, ἐὰν Φωκίωνι, καὶ δίκαιον, ἐὰν Ἀριστείδῃ, καὶ σοφόν, ἐὰν Σωκράτει.

[1] ἐλύπησε . . . κατέστρεψε] λυπήσῃ . . . καταστρέψῃ Kor.
[2] εὖ <μὲν> Her.
[3] αὐτὸν ἐργάσεται [ὁ Καλλίας] Russell

---

[a] According to Pausanias, *Periegesis* 5.21.9–10, this Straton

country, and was hated by the time of his death.

Straton the son of Corrhagus seems to have suffered illness for a purpose. Despite coming from a rich and noble family he did not take physical exercise. But he suffered an illness of the spleen and needed treatment through gymnastic exercise. At first he took as much as was required to regain health, but he made progress in this art and began to take it seriously. At Olympia he won the wrestling competition and the pancration on the same day, and repeated his success at the next Olympiad, and at the Nemean, Pythian, and Isthmian games.[a]

The wrestler Democrates also suffered an illness which affected his feet. He went to the competitions, stood in the stadium and drew a circle around himself. Then he challenged his rivals to pull him over the line. They could not do so and were defeated, and he left with the victor's crown as he had maintained his firm stance unshaken.[b]

16. If someone looks to Callias for guidance, Callias will turn him into a drinker. If to Ismenias, he will become an aulos player; if to Alcibiades, an arrogant cheat; if to Crobylus, a gourmet; if to Demosthenes, an orator; if to Epaminondas, a general; if to Agesilaus, a man of noble thoughts; if to Phocion, a good man; if to Aristides, a just man; if to Socrates, a wise man.

won a victory in the 178th Olympiad (68 B.C.); so he is one of the few relatively recent figures in Aelian.

[b] Democrates is mentioned in Pausanias, *Periegesis* 6.17.1 and named in an inscription found at Elis as a benefactor of the city (no. 425 in E. Schwyzer, *Dialectorum graecarum exempla epigraphica potiora*, Leipzig, 1923, pp. 218–219, probably to be dated ca. 200 B.C.).

17. Ἐδίδασκε Πυθαγόρας τοὺς ἀνθρώπους ὅτι κρειττόνων γεγένηται σπερμάτων ἢ κατὰ τὴν φύσιν τὴν θνητήν· τῆς γὰρ αὐτῆς ἡμέρας καὶ κατὰ τὴν αὐτὴν ὥραν ὤφθη[1] ἐν Μεταποντίῳ, φασί,[2] καὶ ἐν Κρότωνι, καὶ ἐν Ὀλυμπίᾳ δὲ παρέφηνε χρυσοῦν τὸν ἕτερον τῶν μηρῶν. καὶ Μυλλίαν δὲ τὸν Κροτωνιάτην ὑπέμνησεν ὅτι Μίδας ὁ Γορδίου ἐστὶν ὁ Φρύξ. καὶ τὸν ἀετὸν δὲ τὸν λευκὸν κατέψησεν ὑπομείναντα αὐτόν. ἀλλὰ καὶ ὑπὸ τοῦ Κόσα τοῦ ποταμοῦ διαβαίνων προσερρήθη, τοῦ ποταμοῦ εἰπόντος αὐτῷ· "χαῖρε, Πυθαγόρα."

Ἔλεγε δὲ ἱερώτατον εἶναι τὸ τῆς μαλάχης φύλλον. ἔλεγε δὲ ὅτι πάντων σοφώτατον ὁ ἀριθμός, δεύτερος δὲ ὁ τοῖς πράγμασι τὰ ὀνόματα θέμενος. καὶ τὸν σεισμὸν ἐγενεαλόγει οὐδὲν ἄλλο εἶναι ἢ σύνοδον [εἶναι][3] τῶν τεθνεώτων. ἡ δὲ Ἶρις, ἔφασκεν ὡς αὐγὴ τοῦ ἡλίου[4] ἐστί. καὶ ὁ πολλάκις ἐμπίπτων τοῖς ὠσὶν ἦχος, φωνὴ τῶν κρειττόνων. οὐχ οἷόν τε δὲ ἦν διαπορῆσαι ὑπέρ τινος αὐτῷ ἢ τοῖς λεχθεῖσί τι προσερωτῆσαι, ἀλλ' ὡς χρησμῷ θείῳ οὕτως οἱ τότε προσεῖχον τοῖς λεγομένοις ὑπ' αὐτοῦ. ἐπιστρεφομένου δὲ τὰς πόλεις αὐτοῦ διέρρει λόγος ὅτι Πυθαγόρας ἀφίκετο οὐ διδάξων ἀλλ' ἰατρεύσων.

Προσέταττε δὲ ὁ αὐτὸς Πυθαγόρας καρδίας ἀπέχεσθαι καὶ ἀλεκτρυόνος λευκοῦ καὶ τῶν θνησειδίων

[1] ὤφθη huc traiecit Her.: post ἡμέρας praebent codd.
[2] φασί Her.: φησί codd. [3] del. Peruscus
[4] αὐγὴ τοῦ ἡλίου Gesner: ἡ γῆ τοῦ Νείλου codd.

17. Pythagoras taught mankind that he came of a lineage superior to ordinary mortals. On the same day at the same hour, they say, he was seen both at Metapontum and at Croton. At Olympia, he revealed that he had one thigh made of gold.[a] He reminded Myllias of Croton that he was Midas the Phrygian, son of Gordias.[b] He stroked the white eagle, which allowed him to do so. He was addressed by the river Cosas as he forded it; the river said to him "Hail, Pythagoras."

He said that the most sacred object is the mallow leaf, and the wisest is number. Second to number is the person who first assigned names to things.[c] Earthquakes he traced back to nothing other than an assembly of the dead. The rainbow, he said, was the light of the sun; and the sound which often intrudes upon the ears is the voice of the gods. It was not possible to discuss a question with him or ask for further explanation of what he had said; the men of his day treated his words as if they were oracles from the god. As he toured cities word spread that Pythagoras had come not to teach but to heal.

The same Pythagoras gave instructions not to eat heart or white chicken, and above all to avoid eating dead

[a] See 2.26 above, and Burkert, *Lore and Science*, pp. 141, 168, 170, 181, 293.

[b] Metempsychosis was one of his doctrines.

[c] Strictly speaking this implies that there is only one language in the world, which accords well with Greek views about the inferior status of tongues spoken by other races. In Homer there are occasional references to the language of the gods, which was different from that of men.

παντὸς μᾶλλον καὶ μὴ χρῆσθαι βαλανείῳ μηδὲ βαδίζειν τὰς λεωφόρους· ἄδηλον γὰρ εἰ καθαρεύουσι καὶ αὐτὰ ἐκεῖνα.

18. Ὅτε κατῆλθε Πλάτων εἰς Σικελίαν[1] κλητός, πολλὰ ἐπὶ πολλοῖς ἐπιστείλαντος τοῦ Διονυσίου, καὶ ἀνήγαγεν αὐτὸν ἐπὶ τὸ ἅρμα ὁ [νέος][2] Διονύσιος, αὐτὸς μὲν ἡνιοχῶν, παραβάτην δὲ ποιησάμενος τὸν Ἀρίστωνος, τότε δή φασι Συρακούσιον ἄνδρα χαρίεντα καὶ τῶν Ὁμήρου μὴ ἀπαίδευτον, ἡσθέντα τῇ ὄψει ταύτῃ ἐπειπεῖν τὰ ἐξ Ἰλιάδος ἐκεῖνα, παρατρέψαντα ὀλίγον·

μέγα δ' ἔβραχε φήγινος ἄξων
βριθοσύνῃ· δεινὸν γὰρ ἄγεν βροτὸν ἄνδρα τ' ἄριστον.

Ὅτι ὑπόπτης ὢν εἰς πάντας ὁ Δονύσιος, ὅμως εἰς Πλάτωνα τοσαύτην ἔσχεν αἰδῶ, ὡς ἐκεῖνον μόνον εἰσιέναι πρὸς αὐτὸν μὴ ἐρευνώμενον, καίτοι Δίωνος αὐτὸν ἐπιστάμενος ἑταῖρον εἰς τὰ ἔσχατα εἶναι.

19. Φίλιππος ὁ Μακεδὼν οὐ μόνον ἐλέγετο εἶναι τὰ πολέμια ἀγαθὸς καὶ εἰπεῖν δεινός, ἀλλὰ καὶ παιδείαν ἀνδρειότατα ἐτίμα. Ἀριστοτέλει γοῦν χορηγήσας πλοῦτον ἀνενδεᾶ,[3] αἴτιος γέγονε πολλῆς καὶ ἄλλης πολυπειρίας, ἀτὰρ οὖν καὶ τῆς γνώσεως τῆς κατὰ τὰ ζῷα· καὶ τὴν ἱστορίαν αὐτῶν ὁ τοῦ Νικομάχου διὰ τὴν ἐκ Φιλίππου περιουσίαν ἐκαρπώσατο. καὶ Πλάτωνα δὲ ἐτίμησε καὶ Θεόφραστον.

1 εἰς Σικελίαν Faber: ἐν Σικελίᾳ codd.

animals; not to go to the baths and not to walk along public roads, because it was not clear whether these places were pure.

18. When Plato arrived by invitation in Sicily after persistent letters from Dionysius, he was conducted to a chariot by [the young] Dionysius, who drove it in person and placed the son of Ariston at his side.[a] On that occasion it is said that a witty Syracusan with some knowledge of Homer, delighted by the spectacle, quoted with slight alteration the famous verses of the *Iliad* [5.838–839]: "the beechwood axle groaned loudly under the weight, for it carried a remarkable mortal and the best of men."[b]

Note that although Dionysius was suspicious of everyone, he nevertheless had a great respect for Plato, so that the latter was the only person allowed to enter his presence without being searched, even though he knew Plato to be an extremely close friend of Dion.[c]

19. Philip of Macedon was said to be not merely a good soldier and powerful speaker but to have the highest respect for education. He provided resources unstintingly for Aristotle and so became responsible for many other facets of his wide learning, and in particular for his knowledge of zoology. The son of Nicomachus produced his *History of Animals* as the fruit of Philip's wealth. He also honoured Plato and Theophrastus.[d]

[a] Dionysius II was tyrant of Syracuse 367–344 B.C. This is the second of Plato's visits, in 366 B.C. [b] The original text refers to Athena and Diomedes. [c] In 366 B.C. Dion was accused of treason and exiled. [d] Theophrastus (ca. 372–286 B.C.) succeeded Aristotle as head of the Lyceum.

---

[2] del. Her. [3] ἀνενδεᾶ Her.: -εῆ codd.

20. Δημόκριτον τὸν Ἀβδηρίτην λόγος ἔχει τά τε ἄλλα γενέσθαι σοφὸν καὶ δὴ καὶ ἐπιθυμῆσαι λαθεῖν καὶ ἐν ἔργῳ θέσθαι πάνυ σφόδρα τοῦτο. διὰ ταῦτά τοι καὶ πολλὴν ἐπῄει γῆν. ἧκεν οὖν καὶ πρὸς τοὺς Χαλδαίους [καὶ][1] εἰς Βαβυλῶνα καὶ πρὸς τοὺς μάγους καὶ τοὺς σοφιστὰς τῶν Ἰνδῶν. τὴν παρὰ τοῦ Δαμασίππου τοῦ πατρὸς οὐσίαν εἰς τρία μέρη νεμηθεῖσαν τοῖς ἀδελφοῖς τοῖς[2] τρισί, τἀργύριον[3] μόνον λαβὼν ἐφόδιον τῆς ὁδοῦ, τὰ λοιπὰ τοῖς ἀδελφοῖς εἴασε. διὰ ταῦτά τοι καὶ Θεόφραστος αὐτὸν ἐπῄνει, ὅτι περιῄει κρείττονα ἀγερμὸν ἀγείρων Μενελάου καὶ Ὀδυσσέως. ἐκεῖνοι μὲν γὰρ ἠλῶντο, αὐτόχρημα Φοινίκων ἐμπόρων μηδὲν διαφέροντες· χρήματα γὰρ ἤθροιζον, καὶ τῆς περιόδου καὶ τοῦ περίπλου ταύτην εἶχον τὴν πρόφασιν.

Ὅτι οἱ Ἀβδηρῖται ἐκάλουν τὸν Δημόκριτον Φιλοσοφίαν,[4] τὸν δὲ Πρωταγόραν Λόγον. κατεγέλα δὲ πάντων ὁ Δημόκριτος καὶ ἔλεγεν αὐτοὺς μαίνεσθαι· ὅθεν καὶ Γελασῖνον αὐτὸν ἐκάλουν οἱ πολῖται. λέγουσι δὲ οἱ αὐτοὶ τὸν Ἱπποκράτην περὶ[5] τὴν πρώτην ἔντευξιν ὑπὲρ τοῦ Δημοκρίτου δόξαν λαβεῖν ὡς μαινομένου· προϊούσης δὲ αὐτοῖς τῆς συνουσίας εἰς ὑπερβολὴν θαυμάσαι τὸν ἄνδρα. λέγουσι δὲ Δωριέα ὄντα τὸν Ἱπποκράτην ἀλλ᾿ οὖν τὴν <τοῦ>[6]

[1] del. Per. [2] τοῖς x: δι᾿ αὐτοῦ τοῖς V
[3] τἀργύριον] ἀργύριον Kor.
[4] Φιλοσοφίαν] Σοφίαν Scheffer; cfr. Suda Δ 447
[5] περὶ] παρὰ Her. [6] suppl. Per. e cod. Voss. gr. O.4

20. Democritus of Abdera, according to tradition, was a man of wisdom in many respects, and in particular he was anxious to escape attention. He put this into practice with great determination. That is why he travelled very widely. He reached the Chaldaeans at Babylon, the Magi, and the Sophists of India. When the property of his father Damasippus was divided into three shares for the three brothers, he took only enough money for his expenses of travel and left the rest to his brothers. That is why Theophrastus praised him [fr. 513 F.-H.-S.] for collecting better possessions in the course of his travels than Menelaus or Odysseus.[a] They were just wanderers no different from Phoenician merchants, because they collected material possessions and made this the pretext for their journeys by land and sea.

Note that the Abderites called Democritus Philosophy and Protagoras Reason.[b] Democritus laughed at everyone and said they were all mad, which led his fellow citizens to call him "Gelasinus."[c] These same people say that at their first meeting Hippocrates got the impression that Democritus was mad; but as their acquaintance progressed he became a great admirer of the man.[d] They say that Hippocrates, who was a Dorian, nonetheless wrote

[a] An allusion to the adventures of the heroes in the *Odyssey* after the capture of Troy.

[b] Both philosophers were natives of Abdera.

[c] "Laughing."

[d] Tradition had it that Hippocrates was summoned by Abdera to cure Democritus of his apparent madness, and the episode became the subject of a set of letters circulating under Hippocrates' name (these are now to be read in the edition of Wesley D. Smith, *Hippocrates: Pseudepigraphic Writings*, Leiden, 1990).

Δημοκρίτου χάριν τῇ Ἰάδι φωνῇ συγγράψαι τὰ συγγράμματα.

21. Ὅτι παιδικὰ ἐγένετο Σωκράτους μὲν Ἀλκιβιάδης, Πλάτωνος δὲ Δίων. ὁ μέντοι Δίων καὶ ἀπώνητό τι τοῦ ἐραστοῦ.

22. Οἱ πάλαι Ἀθηναῖοι ἁλουργῆ μὲν ἠμπείχοντο ἱμάτια, ποικίλους δὲ ἐνέδυνον χιτῶνας· κορύμβους δὲ ἀναδούμενοι τῶν ἐν τῇ κεφαλῇ τριχῶν, χρυσοῦς ἐνείροντες αὐταῖς τέττιγας καὶ κόσμον ἄλλον πρόσθετον περιαπτόμενοι χρυσοῦ προῄεσαν. καὶ ὀκλαδίας αὐτοῖς δίφρους οἱ παῖδες ὑπέφερον, ἵνα μὴ καθίζωσιν ἑαυτοὺς εἰκῇ καὶ ὡς ἔτυχε. δῆλον δὲ ὅτι καὶ ἡ τράπεζα ἦν αὐτοῖς καὶ ἡ λοιπὴ δίαιτα ἁβροτέρα. τοιοῦτοι δὲ ὄντες τὴν ἐν Μαραθῶνι μάχην ἐνίκησαν.

23. Ὅτι Περικλέα καὶ Καλλίαν τὸν Ἱππονίκου καὶ Νικίαν τὸν Περγασῆθεν τὸ ἀσωτεύεσθαι καὶ ὁ πρὸς ἡδονὴν βίος εἰς ἀπορίαν περιέστησεν· ἐπεὶ γὰρ ἐπέλιπε τὰ χρήματα αὐτούς, οἱ τρεῖς κώνειον τελευταίαν πρόποσιν ἀλλήλοις προπιόντες ὥσπερ οὖν ἐκ συμποσίου ἀπέλυσαν.[1]

24. Λεωπρέπης ὁ Κεῖος ὁ τοῦ Σιμωνίδου πατὴρ ἔτυχέ ποτε ἐν παλαίστρᾳ καθήμενος· εἶτα μειράκια πρὸς ἀλλήλους οἰκείως διακείμενα ἤρετο τὸν ἄνδρα

[1] ἀπέλυσαν] -σαντο Her.

---

[a] Aelian expects a native of Cos to write in Doric; evidently he did not understand that in classical Greek literature the

his works in Ionic dialect to please Democritus.[a]

21. Note that Socrates' favourite boy was Alcibiades, and Plato's was Dion. But Dion did derive some benefit from his lover.

22. The ancient Athenians wore purple cloaks and embroidered jackets.[b] They gathered their hair on top of the head, fastening it with golden cicada brooches, and when they went out they put on additional gold jewellery. Slaves carried folding chairs for them so that they should not have to sit uncomfortably wherever they might be. Clearly their diet and the rest of their existence was quite luxurious. Such were the men who won the battle of Marathon.

23. Note that Pericles, Callias the son of Hipponicus, and Nicias of the deme Pergase were reduced to poverty by their drunken and hedonistic existence. When their money ran out, the three of them drank a final toast to each other in hemlock as if they were departing from a banquet.[c]

24. Leoprepes of Ceos, father of Simonides, was sitting in the gymnasium one day, when some boys who were on good terms with each other asked him how their

choice of dialect could be determined by precedent, and much early prose was composed in Ionic.

[b] Aelian's wording is very close to Athenaeus 512 BC, but both authors may be independently following Thucydides 1.6. The cicada-shaped brooch was a symbol of the Athenian claim to be autochthonous: the cicada larvae emerge from the ground, in which they were buried.

[c] This ch. is similar but not identical to Athenaeus 537 C. The information offered is partly or wholly erroneous. See F. Wehrli, *Heraclides Ponticus* (2nd ed., Basel-Stuttgart, 1969), p. 80.

πῶς ἂν αὐτοῖς ἡ φιλία διαμένοι μάλιστα. ὁ δὲ εἶπεν· "ἐὰν ταῖς ἀλλήλων ὀργαῖς ἐξιστῆσθε,[1] καὶ μὴ ὁμόσε χωροῦντες τῷ θυμῷ εἶτα παροξύνητε ἀλλήλους κατ' ἀλλήλων."

25. Θράσυλλος ὁ Αἰξωνεὺς παράδοξον καὶ καινὴν ἐνόσησε μανίαν. ἀπολιπὼν γὰρ τὸ ἄστυ καὶ κατελθὼν εἰς τὸν Πειραιᾶ καὶ ἐνταῦθα οἰκῶν τὰ πλοῖα τὰ καταίροντα ἐν αὐτῷ πάντα ἑαυτοῦ ἐνόμιζεν εἶναι καὶ ἀπεγράφετο αὐτὰ καὶ αὖ πάλιν ἐξέπεμπε καὶ τοῖς περισωζομένοις καὶ εἰσιοῦσιν εἰς τὸν λιμένα ὑπερέχαιρε· χρόνους δὲ διετέλεσε πολλοὺς συνοικῶν τῷ ἀρρωστήματι τούτῳ. ἐκ Σικελίας δὲ ἀναχθεὶς ὁ ἀδελφὸς αὐτοῦ παρέδωκεν αὐτὸν ἰατρῷ ἰάσασθαι, καὶ ἐπαύσατο τῆς νόσου οὕτως.[2] ἐμέμνητο δὲ πολλάκις τῆς ἐν μανίᾳ διατριβῆς καὶ ἔλεγε μηδέποτε ἡσθῆναι τοσοῦτον ὅσον τότε ἥδετο ἐπὶ ταῖς μηδὲν αὐτῷ προσηκούσαις ναυσὶν ἀποσωζομέναις.

26. Ξάνθος ὁ ποιητὴς τῶν μελῶν (ἐγένετο δὲ οὗτος πρεσβύτερος[3] Στησιχόρου τοῦ Ἱμεραίου) λέγει τὴν Ἠλέκτραν τοῦ Ἀγαμέμνονος οὐ τοῦτο ἔχειν τοὔνομα πρῶτον ἀλλὰ Λαοδίκην. ἐπεὶ δὲ Ἀγαμέμνων ἀνῃρέθη, τὴν δὲ Κλυταιμνήστραν ὁ Αἴγισθος ἔγημε καὶ ἐβασίλευσεν, ἄλεκτρον οὖσαν καὶ καταγηρῶσαν παρθένον Ἀργεῖοι Ἠλέκτραν ἐκάλεσαν διὰ τὸ ἀμοιρεῖν ἀνδρὸς καὶ μὴ πεπειρᾶσθαι λέκτρου.

[1] ἐξιστῆσθε Dilts: -ασθε codd.
[2] οὕτως Her.: οὗτος codd.

friendship might best be preserved. He replied: "If you give way in face of the annoyance of others instead of opposing with spirit, which will then inflame feelings between you."

25. Thrasyllus of the deme of Aexone suffered a strange new form of madness. He left the city and went down to live at the Piraeus. He imagined that all the ships coming into harbour there were his own. He made a list of them, attended when they departed once more, and was delighted when they returned safely to the harbour. For a long time he continued to suffer from this mania. But his brother, returning from Sicily, handed him over to a doctor to be cured, and in this way he recovered from the illness. He often recalled his mad hobby and used to say that he had never been so happy as when he rejoiced at the sight of ships which did not belong to him returning safely.[a]

26. The lyric poet Xanthus [fr. 2 P.], who was older than Stesichorus of Himera, says that Agamemnon's daughter Electra was not originally so called, but was named Laodice. When Agamemnon was murdered, and Aegisthus married Clytemnestra and became king, the Argives called the girl Electra because she was single and growing old, having no husband and no experience of marriage.[b]

[a] See Athenaeus 554 EF, and Wehrli, *Heraclides Ponticus*, p. 78.

[b] Aelian derives the name from the negative prefix a- and the word for "bed."

---

[3] πρεσβύτερος Casaubon: πρεσβευτὴς codd.

27. Ὅτι Παμφάης ὁ Πριηνεὺς Κροίσῳ τῷ Λυδῷ, τοῦ πατρὸς αὐτοῦ περιόντος, τριάκοντα μνᾶς ἐδωρήσατο. παραλαβὼν δὲ τὴν ἀρχήν, μεστὴν ἅμαξαν ἀργυρίου ἀπέπεμψεν αὐτῷ <Κροῖσος>.[1]

Ὅτι Διογένης λαβὼν παρὰ Διοτίμου τοῦ Καρυστίου νόμισμα ὀλίγον ἔφη·

σοὶ δὲ θεοὶ τόσα δοῖεν ὅσα φρεσὶ σῇσι μενοινᾷς,
ἄνδρα τε καὶ οἶκον.

ἐδόκει δέ πως ὁ Διότιμος μαλθακώτερος εἶναι.

28. Φερεκύδης ὁ Σύριος τὸν βίον ἀλγεινότατα ἀνθρώπων κατέστρεψε, τοῦ παντὸς αὐτῷ σώματος ὑπὸ [τῶν][2] φθειρῶν ἀναλωθέντος· καὶ γενομένης αὐτῷ αἰσχρᾶς τῆς ὄψεως τὴν ἐκ[3] τῶν συνήθων ἐξέκλινε συνουσίαν. ὁπότε δέ τις προσελθὼν ἐπυνθάνετο ὅπως διάγοι, διὰ τῆς ὀπῆς τῆς κατὰ τὴν θύραν διείρας τὸν δάκτυλον ψιλὸν γεγονότα τῆς σαρκὸς ἐπέλεγεν οὕτω διακεῖσθαι καὶ τὸ πᾶν αὐτοῦ σῶμα. λέγουσι δὲ Δηλίων παῖδες τὸν θεὸν τὸν ἐν Δήλῳ μηνίσαντα αὐτῷ τοῦτο ποιῆσαι. καθήμενον γὰρ ἐν Δήλῳ μετὰ τῶν μαθητῶν ἄλλα τε πολλά φασι περὶ τῆς ἑαυτοῦ σοφίας εἰπεῖν καὶ δὴ καὶ τοῦτο, μηδενὶ τῶν θεῶν θῦσαι, καὶ ὅμως οὐδὲν ἧττον ἡδέως βεβιωκέναι καὶ ἀλύπως, οὐ μεῖον τῶν ἑκατόμβας καταθυόντων. ὑπὲρ ταύτης οὖν τῆς κουφολογίας βαρυτάτην ζημίαν ἐξέτισεν.

29. Οὐ γὰρ δὴ δύναμαι πείθειν ἐμαυτὸν μὴ γελᾶν ἐπ' Ἀλεξάνδρῳ τῷ Φιλίππου, εἴ γε, ἀπείρους ἀκούων

27. Note that Pamphaes of Priene gave thirty minae to Croesus of Lydia while the latter's father was still alive. When Croesus assumed power he sent him a wagon loaded with silver.

Note that when Diogenes [fr. 264 M.] received a small coin from Diotimus of Carystus he said: "May the gods give you all your heart's desires, a husband and a home" [*Odyssey* 6.180–181]. Diotimus was thought to be rather effeminate.

28. Pherecydes of Syros ended his life in the most painful way a man can, because his whole body was consumed by lice. When his appearance became hideous he withdrew from ordinary society.[a] If anyone called to ask how he was, he would push a finger denuded of flesh through a hole in the door and say that his whole body was in a similar condition. The inhabitants of Delos say that the god of Delos[b] brought this upon him as an act of vengeance. He was sitting with a group of pupils on Delos, they say, and after making many other remarks about his wisdom he went so far as to say that he sacrificed to no god, but still had lived no less agreeably and painlessly than men who had sacrificed hecatombs. For this light-headed talk he paid the heaviest penalty.

29. I cannot persuade myself not to laugh at Alexander the son of Philip, if it is true that when he heard there

[a] His illness is recorded at greater length below at 5.2.
[b] Apollo.

---

[1] suppl. Per.
[2] del. Her.
[3] ἐκ] μὲν Scheffer

εἶναί τινας κόσμους λέγοντος Δημοκρίτου ἐν τοῖς συγγράμμασιν, ὁ δὲ ἠνιᾶτο μηδὲ τοῦ ἑνὸς καὶ κοινοῦ κρατῶν. πόσον δὲ ἐπ' αὐτῷ Δημόκριτος ἐγέλασεν <ἂν>[1] αὐτός, τί δεῖ καὶ λέγειν, ᾧ ἔργον τοῦτο ἦν;

[1] suppl. Kor.

were an infinite number of worlds—Democritus says this in his writings—he was pained at the thought of not even being the master of the one we all know. Need one say how much Democritus would have laughed at him, laughter being his stock-in-trade?[a]

[a] See ch. 20 above.

E

1. Ταχὼς ὁ Αἰγύπτιος ἕως μὲν ἐχρῆτο τῇ ἐπιχωρίῳ διαίτῃ καὶ εὐτελῶς διεβίω, ὑγιεινότατα[1] ἀνθρώπων διῆγεν· ἐπεὶ δὲ εἰς Πέρσας ἀφίκετο καὶ εἰς τὴν ἐκείνων τρυφὴν ἐξέπεσε, τὸ ἄηθες τῶν σιτίων οὐκ ἐνεγκών, ὑπὸ δυσεντερίας τὸν βίον κατέστρεψε, τῆς τρυφῆς ἀλλαξάμενος θάνατον.

2. Ὅτι Φερεκύδης <ὁ>[2] Πυθαγόρου διδάσκαλος ἐμπεσὼν εἰς τὴν ἀρρωστίαν πρῶτον μὲν ἴδρου ἱδρῶτα θερμὸν ἰξώδη ὅμοιόν πως[3] μύξαις, ὕστερον δὲ ἐθηριώθη,[4] μετὰ δὲ ἐφθειρίασε. καὶ διαλυομένων τῶν σαρκῶν εἰς τοὺς φθεῖρας ἐπεγένετο τῆξις, καὶ οὕτω τὸν βίον μετήλλαξεν.

3. Ἀριστοτέλης τὰς νῦν Ἡρακλείους στήλας καλουμένας, πρὶν ἢ κληθῆναι τοῦτο, φησὶ Βριάρεω καλεῖσθαι αὐτάς· ἐπεὶ δ' ἐκάθηρε γῆν καὶ θάλατταν Ἡρακλῆς καὶ ἀναμφιλόγως εὐεργέτης ἐγένετο τῶν ἀνθρώπων, τιμῶντες αὐτὸν τὴν μὲν Βριάρεω μνήμην παρ' οὐδὲν ἐποιήσαντο, Ἡρακλείους δὲ προσηγόρευσαν.

[1] ὑγιεινότατα Her.: -ότατος xΦ (de V non liquet)
[2] suppl. Her. [3] πως Charitonides: ὡς codd.
[4] ἐθηριώθη J. F. Gronovius: θηριώδη codd.

BOOK FIVE

1. The Egyptian Tachos enjoyed the best of health as long as he adhered to the customs of his country and lived modestly.[a] But when he moved to Persia and lapsed into its luxurious habits, he could not tolerate the unaccustomed diet and died of dysentery, exchanging luxury for death.

2. Note that Pherecydes the teacher of Pythagoras fell into poor health. At first he suffered from hot viscous sweat like mucus; then he was attacked by malignant sores and eventually by lice. As his flesh dissolved into verminous matter it began to rot, and in this way he ended his days.

3. Aristotle says [fr. 678 R.] that before the pillars of Hercules were so called they were known as the pillars of Briareus. But when Hercules purified both land and sea and became indisputably the benefactor of mankind, men honoured him, named the pillars after Hercules and ceased to honour the memory of Briareus.[b]

[a] Tachos, pharaoh 362–360 B.C., was ousted from power and took refuge in Persia.

[b] The ancients believed that by his labours Heracles had rid the world of various scourges that plagued mankind. Briareus, child of Ge and Uranus, was a monster with 50 heads and 100 hands. He came to be regarded as a typical giant.

4. Ὅτι ἀναθῆλαι λόγος ἐστὶ Δήλιος φυτὰ ἐν Δήλῳ ἐλαίαν καὶ φοίνικα, ὧν ἁψαμένην τὴν Λητὼ εὐθὺς ἀποκυῆσαι, τέως οὐ δυναμένην τοῦτο δρᾶσαι.

5. Ἐπαμεινώνδας ἕνα εἶχε τρίβωνα καὶ αὐτὸν ῥυπῶντα· εἴ ποτε δὲ αὐτὸν ἔδωκεν εἰς γναφεῖον, αὐτὸς ὑπέμενεν οἴκοι δι' ἀπορίαν ἑτέρου. ἐν δὴ τούτῳ[1] τῆς περιουσίας ὤν, τοῦ Περσῶν βασιλέως πέμψαντος αὐτῷ πολὺ χρυσίον, οὐ προσήκατο· καὶ εἴ γέ τι ἐγὼ νοῶ, μεγαλοφρονέστερος ἦν τοῦ διδόντος ὁ μὴ λαβών.

6. Ἄξιον δὲ καὶ τὸ Καλανοῦ τοῦ Ἰνδοῦ τέλος ἐπαινέσαι· ἄλλος δ' ἂν εἶπεν ὅτι καὶ ἀγασθῆναι. ἐγένετο δὲ τοιοῦτον· Καλανὸς ὁ Ἰνδῶν σοφιστὴς μακρὰ χαίρειν φράσας Ἀλεξάνδρῳ καὶ Μακεδόσι καὶ τῷ βίῳ, ὅτε ἐβουλήθη ἀπολῦσαι αὑτὸν ἐκ τῶν τοῦ σώματος δεσμῶν, ἐγεγένητο[2] μὲν ἡ πυρὰ ἐν τῷ καλλίστῳ προαστείῳ τῆς Βαβυλῶνος, καὶ ἦν τὰ ξύλα αὖα καὶ πρὸς εὐωδίαν εὖ μάλα ἐπίλεκτα κέδρου καὶ θύου[3] καὶ κυπαρίττου καὶ μυρσίνης καὶ δάφνης, αὐτὸς δὲ γυμνασάμενος γυμνάσιον τὸ εἰωθός (ἦν δὲ καὶ αὐτὸ δρόμος), ἀνελθὼν ἐπὶ μέσης τῆς πυρᾶς ἔστη ἐστεφανωμένος καλάμου κόμῃ. καὶ ὁ μὲν ἥλιος αὐτὸν προσέβαλλεν, ὁ δὲ αὐτὸν προσεκύνει, καὶ τοῦτο ἦν τὸ σύνθημα εἰς τὸ ἐξάπτειν τὴν πυρὰν τοῖς Μακεδόσι. καὶ τὸ μὲν δέδρατο,[4] ὁ δὲ περιληφθεὶς <ὑπὸ>[5] τῆς φλογὸς ἀτρέπτως[6] εἱστήκει καὶ οὐ πρό-

[1] τούτῳ Eberhard: -οις codd.

4. Note the Delian tradition that the trees which flourish on Delos are the olive and the palm.[a] When Leto took hold of them she immediately gave birth, which she had not been able to do before.

5. Epaminondas had just one coat, and a dirty one at that; and whenever he sent it to the cleaner's, he stayed at home because he did not have another. Though he lived in these comfortable circumstances, when he was sent a large quantity of gold by the Persian king, he did not accept it. If my judgement is worth anything, the refusal was nobler than the gift.

6. It is right to praise the death of Calanus;[b] one might even say, to marvel at it. This is how it happened. Calanus the Indian sage said goodbye to Alexander, the Macedonians and his life, wishing to free himself from the bonds of his body. The pyre was set up in the finest suburb of Babylon. The wood was dry, carefully selected for its fragrance, consisting of cedar, citron, cypress, myrtle, and laurel. Having taken his customary exercise—this was to run—he mounted to the middle of the pyre and stood there, his hair covered with a crown of reeds. The sun shone down upon him, and he knelt in respect for it. This was the cue for the Macedonians to light the pyre. When this was done the flames took hold of him, but he stood

[a] Leto's children were Apollo and Artemis. As early as the *Odyssey*, 6.162–163, it is stated that a palm tree stood in Apollo's sanctuary on Delos.

[b] For Calanus see 2.41 above.

---

[2] ἐγεγένητο] ἐνένηστο Kor. [3] θύον Gesner: θρύον codd.
[4] δέδρατο Her.: ἐδρᾶτο codd. [5] suppl. Kühn
[6] ἀτρέπτως V: ἀτρέστως x

τερον ἀνετράπη πρὶν ἢ διελύθη. ἐνταῦθά φασιν ἐκπλαγῆναι καὶ τὸν Ἀλέξανδρον καὶ εἰπεῖν ὅτι μείζονας ἀντιπάλους αὐτοῦ Καλανὸς κατηγωνίσατο. ὁ μὲν γὰρ πρὸς Πῶρον καὶ Ταξίλην καὶ Δαρεῖον διήθλησεν, ὁ δὲ Καλανὸς πρὸς τὸν πόνον καὶ τὸν θάνατον.

7. Οἱ μὲν Σκύθαι περὶ τὴν ἑαυτῶν πλανῶνται· Ἀνάχαρσις δὲ ἅτε ἀνὴρ σοφὸς καὶ περαιτέρω προήγαγε τὴν πλάνην. ἧκε γοῦν εἰς τὴν Ἑλλάδα, καὶ ὁ Σόλων ἐθαύμασεν αὐτόν.

8. Τὰ σκώμματα καὶ αἱ λοιδορίαι οὐδέν μοι δοκεῖ δύνασθαι. ἐὰν γὰρ στερεᾶς γνώμης λάβηται, καταλέλυται·[1] ἐὰν δὲ ἀγεννοῦς καὶ ταπεινῆς, ἴσχυσε καὶ οὐ μόνον ἐλύπησε πολλάκις, ἀλλὰ καὶ ἀπέκτεινε. τούτων ἀπόδειξις ἐκεῖνα ἔστω, Σωκράτης μὲν οὖν κωμῳδούμενος ἐγέλα, Πολίαγρος δὲ ἀπήγξατο.

9. Ἀριστοτέλης ἀσωτευσάμενος τὰ ἐκ τοῦ πατρὸς χρήματα ὥρμησεν ἐπὶ στρατείαν, εἶτα ἀπαλλάττων κακῶς ἐν τούτῳ, φαρμακοπώλης ἀνεφάνη. παρεισρυεὶς δὲ εἰς τὸν περίπατον καὶ παρακούων τῶν λόγων, ἀμείνων πεφυκὼς πολλῶν εἶτα ἕξιν περιεβάλετο, ἣν μετὰ ταῦτα ἐκτήσατο.[2]

[1] καταλέλυται Her.: -υνται codd.
[2] ἐκτήσατο] ἐκέκτητο Hackmann: num ἐπεδείξατο?

---

[a] For Anacharsis see 2.41 above.
[b] For Socrates and Old Comedy see 2.13 above. Poliagrus

there unflinching and did not fall over until he expired. Then, they say, even Alexander was astounded and said that Calanus had defeated more powerful enemies than he had himself. For Alexander had won his struggles against Porus, Taxila, and Darius, but Calanus against pain and death.

7. The Scythians are nomads in their own country. But Anacharsis, being an intelligent man, wandered further afield.[a] At any rate he reached Athens and Solon admired him.

8. Mockery and abuse seem to me to have no point. If they are directed at a strong mind, they are ineffectual; if at an ignoble and worthless one, they are powerful, and do not simply wound, which often happens, but even kill. Socrates was the butt of comedy and yet laughed, whereas Poliagrus hanged himself.[b]

9. Aristotle spent his inheritance on high living and went off to serve as a soldier. After a bad experience of this career he emerged as a druggist. He insinuated himself into the party that went for a walk and overheard the lectures.[c] Being more able than many he acquired the habits of mind which he later displayed.[d]

appears to have compelled his wife to earn money as a prostitute. See U. von Wilamowitz-Moellendorff, *Kleine Schriften*, vol. 4 (Berlin, 1962), pp. 551–552, on the bearers of this rare name (cf. fr. com. adesp. 708 K.-A.).

[c] If Aelian meant *peripatos* as a proper name, it is a mistake for Academy; if we take the word as an ordinary noun, the meaning is that Aristotle insinuated himself into the group who made the regular walk.

[d] This ch. is very similar to Athenaeus 354 BC, where Epicurus is named as the source.

10. Νηίτην στόλον Ἀθηναῖοι εἰργάζοντο ἑαυτοῖς ἀεὶ φιλοπόνως. κατὰ χρόνους δὲ τὰ μὲν κατορθοῦντες τὰ δὲ ἡττώμενοι ἀπώλεσαν τριήρεις μὲν ἐν Αἰγύπτῳ διακοσίας σὺν τοῖς πληρώμασι, περὶ Κύπρον δὲ πεντήκοντα καὶ ἑκατόν, ἐν Σικελίᾳ τετταράκοντα καὶ διακοσίας, ἐν δὲ Ἑλλησπόντῳ διακοσίας. ὁπλῖται δὲ ἀπώλοντο αὐτοῖς ἐν Σικελίᾳ μυριάδες τέτταρες, χίλιοι δὲ ἐν Χαιρωνείᾳ.

11. Ὁ Θρᾳκῶν βασιλεύς (τὸ δὲ ὄνομα λεγέτω ἄλλος), ὅτε ὁ Ξέρξης ἐπὶ τὴν Ἑλλάδα ἐστράτευσεν, εἰς Ῥοδόπην τὸ ὄρος ἀπέδρα. τοῖς δὲ ἓξ παισὶν αὐτοῦ συνεβούλευε μὴ στρατεύειν ἐπὶ τὴν Ἑλλάδα (δῆλον δὲ ὅτι φιλέλλην ἦν ὁ ἀνήρ). οἱ δὲ οὐκ ἐπείσθησαν· ὑποστρέψαντας δὲ αὐτοὺς πάντας ἐξετύφλωσε, μὴ ποιήσας Ἑλληνικά.

12. Οὐ δύναμαι δὲ Ἀθηναίων μὴ οὐ φιλεῖν ταῦτα. ἐκκλησίας οὔσης Ἀθηναίοις παρελθὼν ὁ Δημάδης ἐψηφίσατο θεὸν τὸν Ἀλέξανδρον τρισκαιδέκατον. τῆς δὲ ἀσεβείας ὁ δῆμος τὸ ὑπερβάλλον μὴ ἐνεγκών, ζημίαν ἐτιμήσαντο τῷ Δημάδῃ ταλάντων ἑκατόν, ὅτι θνητὸν αὐτὸν[1] δὴ τὸν Ἀλέξανδρον ὄντα ἐνέγραψε τοῖς Ὀλυμπίοις.

13. Ἦσαν δὲ ἄρα Ἀθηναῖοι δεινῶς εἰς τὰς πολιτείας εὐτράπελοι καὶ ἐπιτήδειοι πρὸς τὰς μεταβολὰς

[1] *αὐτὸν* del. Her.

---

[a] The source of this ch. is Isocrates, *On the Peace* 86. The first three episodes are described in Thucydides (1.110,

10. The Athenians always prepared their naval forces painstakingly. Over the years they were sometimes successful, sometimes defeated. They lost two hundred triremes in Egypt, crews and all; in Cyprus one hundred and fifty; in Sicily two hundred and forty; and two hundred in the Hellespont. They lost forty thousand hoplites in Sicily, and one thousand at Chaeronea.[a]

11. The king of Thrace—let others name him—ran away to mount Rhodope when Xerxes invaded Greece. He advised his six children not to invade Greece—obviously the man was a philhellene—but they refused to obey him. When they returned he blinded them all, an unhellenic act.[b]

12. I cannot suppress a liking for this act of the Athenians. Demades addressed the Athenian assembly and put forward a motion that Alexander be the thirteenth god.[c] The public found this an intolerable show of impiety and imposed a penalty of a hundred talents on Demades because he had included Alexander, a mortal, among the Olympians.[d]

13. The Athenians were strangely versatile in political matters and especially prone to revolutions. They ac-

1.112, and Books 6–7), while the fourth is the final disaster of the Peloponnesian War at Aegospotami in 405 B.C. The defeat of the Athenians and Thebans at Chaeronea in 338 marked the end of resistance to Philip of Macedon.

[b] Herodotus 8.116 also tells this story without giving the name of the king.

[c] See 2.19 above.

[d] Athenaeus 251 B gives the more plausible figure of ten talents.

παντὸς μᾶλλον. βασιλείαν μὲν γὰρ ἤνεγκαν σωφρόνως ἐπὶ Κέκροπος καὶ Ἐρεχθέως καὶ Θησέως καὶ τῶν Κοδριδῶν κάτω, τυραννίδος <δὲ>[1] ἐπειράθησαν ἐπὶ τῶν Πεισιστρατιδῶν, ἀριστοκρατίᾳ δὲ ἐχρήσαντο μέχρι τῶν τετρακοσίων· εἶτα ὕστερον δέκα τῶν πολιτῶν καθ' ἕκαστον ἔτος ἦρχον τῆς πόλεως, τελευταῖον δὲ ἐγένετο ἀναρχία περὶ τὴν τῶν τριάκοντα κατάστασιν. ταύτην δὲ τὴν οὕτως ἀγχίστροφον μεταβολὴν τοῦ τρόπου εἰ ἐπαινεῖν χρή, ἀλλὰ ἔγωγε τοῦτο οὐκ οἶδα.

14. Νόμος καὶ οὗτος Ἀττικός· ὃς ἂν ἀτάφῳ περιτύχῃ σώματι ἀνθρώπου, πάντως ἐπιβάλλειν αὐτῷ γῆν, θάπτειν δὲ πρὸς δυσμὰς βλέποντα. καὶ τοῦτο δὲ ἦν φυλαττόμενον παρ' αὐτοῖς· βοῦν ἀρότην καὶ ὑπὸ ζυγὸν πονήσαντα σὺν ἀρότρῳ ἢ καὶ σὺν τῇ ἁμάξῃ μηδὲ τοῦτον θύειν, ὅτι καὶ οὗτος εἴη ἂν γεωργὸς καὶ τῶν ἐν ἀνθρώποις καμάτων κοινωνός.

15. Ὅτι δικαστήρια ἦν Ἀττικὰ περὶ μὲν τῶν ἐκ προνοίας ἀποκτεινάντων ἐν Ἀρείῳ πάγῳ, περὶ δὲ τῶν ἀκουσίως ἐπὶ Παλλαδίῳ· περὶ δὲ τῶν κτεῖναι μὲν ὁμολογούντων, ἀμφισβητούντων δὲ ὅτι δικαίως, ἐπὶ[2] Δελφινίῳ ἐγίνοντο[3] αἱ εὔθυναι.

[1] suppl. Her. [2] ἐπὶ Gesner e Poll. *Onom.* 8.117–119: ἐν codd. [3] ἐγίνοντο Her.: γίνονται codd.

---

[a] This is a curious view of the Athenian democracy, perhaps influenced by Thucydides' opinion (2.65) that under Pericles it was really ruled by one man. The reference to the Four Hundred looks like an allusion to the events of 411 B.C.

cepted patiently the monarchy of Cecrops, Erechtheus, Theseus, and the Codridae who followed. They had experience of tyranny under the Pisistratids. They lived under aristocratic rule until the time of the Four Hundred.[a] After that ten citizens governed the city each year.[b] Finally there was anarchy during the regime of the Thirty.[c] Whether one should have praise for such extremes of change I myself do not know.

14. Another Athenian custom: anyone who came across an unburied body was obliged to cover it with earth, and to bury it facing west.[d] Another usage they preserved: a working ox that had been yoked to pull the plough or a wagon was not sacrificed, because it too could be thought of as a farmer and as one who shared man's labours.[e]

15. Note that the Athenian court for those who killed deliberately was in the Areopagus; for those who did so unintentionally, at the Palladium; for those who admitted killing but argued that they had acted justly, the hearings were held at the Delphinium.[f]

[b] The ten are perhaps the generals, who were *de facto* very powerful.

[c] After the fall of Athens in 404 B.C. the city was ruled for a few months by an extremist oligarchical clique.

[d] For another instance of burial facing west see 7.19 below. But there seems to be no supporting evidence in the material remains excavated in modern times. (I am grateful to M. Stamatapoulou for her advice on this matter.)

[e] The Athenian Bouphonia festival is mentioned below at 8.3.

[f] Lysias, *On the Murder of Eratosthenes,* will have been delivered before the Delphinium. All these courts were conducted in the open air in order to avoid pollution.

16. Ὅτι ἐκ τοῦ τῆς Ἀρτέμιδος στεφάνου πέταλον χρυσοῦν ἐκπεσὸν ἀνείλετο παιδίον, οὐ μὴν ἔλαθεν. οἱ οὖν δικασταὶ παίγνια καὶ ἀστραγάλους προὔθηκαν τῷ παιδὶ καὶ τὸ πέταλον· ὁ δὲ καὶ αὖθις ἐπὶ τὸν χρυσὸν κατηνέχθη. καὶ διὰ ταῦτα ἀπέκτειναν αὐτὸν ὡς θεοσύλην, οὐ δόντες συγγνώμην τῇ ἡλικίᾳ, ἀλλὰ τιμωρησάμενοι διὰ τὴν πρᾶξιν.

17. Ὅτι τοσοῦτον ἦν Ἀθηναίοις δεισιδαιμονίας, εἴ τις πρινίδιον ἐξέκοψεν ἐξ ἡρῴου, ἀπέκτειναν αὐτόν. ἀλλὰ καὶ Ἀτάρβην, ὅτι τοῦ Ἀσκληπιοῦ τὸν ἱερὸν στρουθὸν ἀπέκτεινε πατάξας, οὐκ ἀργῶς τοῦτο Ἀθηναῖοι παρεῖδον, ἀλλ' ἀπέκτειναν Ἀτάρβην καὶ οὐκ ἔδοσαν οὔτε ἀγνοίας συγγνώμην οὔτε μανίας, πρεσβύτερα τούτων ἀμφοτέρων τὰ τοῦ θεοῦ ποιησάμενοι. ἐλέγετο γὰρ ἀκουσίως, οἱ δέ, μεμηνὼς τοῦτο δρᾶσαι.

18. Ἡ ἐξ Ἀρείου πάγου βουλὴ ἐπεί τινα φαρμακίδα συνέλαβον καὶ ἔμελλον θανατώσειν, οὐ πρότερον[1] αὐτὴν ἀπέκτειναν πρὶν ἢ ἀπεκύησεν· ὅτε γὰρ συνελήφθη, ἔκυε. τὸ ἀναίτιον οὖν βρέφος ἀναλύοντες τῆς καταδίκης, τὴν αἰτίαν μόνην ἐδικαίωσαν τῷ θανάτῳ.

19. Αἰσχύλος ὁ τραγῳδὸς ἐκρίνετο ἀσεβείας ἐπί τινι δράματι. ἑτοίμων οὖν ὄντων Ἀθηναίων βάλλειν

[1] πρότερον Her.: πρῶτον codd.

[a] Ancient statues were often decorated with gold or other colours.

16. Note that a child picked up a golden leaf that fell from the crown of Artemis, but he was spotted.[a] The judges put toys and knucklebones in front of the child alongside the leaf. He again made for the golden object, and for this reason they executed him for sacrilege, not forgiving him on account of his age but exacting the penalty for his action.

17. Note that Athenian superstition was very great. If someone cut down a small oak tree from a hero's shrine, they executed him. Also, when Atarbes struck and killed the bird sacred to Asclepius,[b] the Athenians did not overlook the matter as trivial; they executed him and did not grant a pardon on grounds of ignorance or insanity, because they deemed the god's interest superior to both these considerations. He was in fact said to have acted involuntarily, or according to others to have been mad.

18. When the Areopagus had arrested a witch and were about to impose the death penalty on her, they did not execute her until she had given birth; for she was pregnant when arrested. Exempting the child from responsibility and punishment they inflicted the death penalty on the guilty party alone.

19. The tragedian Aeschylus was brought to trial on a charge of impiety arising from a play.[c] The Athenians

[b] I have not been able to identify this bird; perhaps the answer lies in Socrates' last words as reported by Plato, *Phaedo* 118 a: "we owe a cock to Asclepius."

[c] There was a tradition that Aeschylus was brought to trial for having revealed the Eleusinian mysteries; according to Aristotle, *Nicomachean Ethics* 1111 a 9, he defended himself by saying that he did not know that these were the secret doctrines.

αὐτὸν λίθοις, Ἀμεινίας ὁ νεώτερος ἀδελφὸς διακαλυψάμενος τὸ ἱμάτιον ἔδειξε τὸν πῆχυν ἔρημον τῆς χειρός. ἔτυχε δὲ ἀριστεύων ἐν Σαλαμῖνι ὁ Ἀμεινίας ἀποβεβληκὼς τὴν χεῖρα, καὶ πρῶτος Ἀθηναίων τῶν ἀριστείων ἔτυχεν. ἐπεὶ δὲ εἶδον οἱ δικασταὶ τοῦ ἀνδρὸς τὸ πάθος, ὑπεμνήσθησαν τῶν ἔργων αὐτοῦ καὶ ἀφῆκαν τὸν Αἰσχύλον.

20. Ταραντίνων πολιορκουμένων ὑπὸ Ἀθηναίων[1] καὶ μελλόντων ἁλῶναι λιμῷ, οἱ Ῥηγῖνοι ἐψηφίσαντο μίαν ἡμέραν ἐν ταῖς δέκα νηστεύειν καὶ ἐκείνης τὰς τροφὰς ἐκχωρῆσαι Ταραντίνοις. ἀποστάντων οὖν αὐτῶν ἐσώθησαν, καὶ μεμνημένοι τοῦ πάθους ἑορτὴν ἄγουσι τὴν καλουμένην Νηστείαν οἱ Ταραντῖνοι.

21. Λέγει τις λόγος τὴν φήμην τὴν κατὰ τῆς Μηδείας ψευδῆ εἶναι· μὴ γὰρ αὐτὴν ἀποκτεῖναι τὰ τέκνα ἀλλὰ Κορινθίους. τὸ δὲ μυθολόγημα τοῦτο ὑπὲρ τῆς Κολχίδος καὶ τὸ δρᾶμα Εὐριπίδην φασὶ διαπλάσαι δεηθέντων Κορινθίων, καὶ ἐπικρατῆσαι τοῦ ἀληθοῦς τὸ ψεῦδος διὰ τὴν τοῦ ποιητοῦ ἀρετήν. ὑπὲρ δὲ τοῦ τολμήματος, φασί, τῶν παίδων μέχρι τοῦ νῦν ἐναγίζουσι τοῖς παισὶ Κορίνθιοι, οἱονεὶ δασμὸν τούτοις ἀποδιδόντες.

[1] Ἀθηναίων x: Ῥωμαίων VΦ

---

[a] In Herodotus 8.93 Aminias of Pallene is not described as Aeschylus' brother. It is very hard to establish biographical facts about Greek writers; see M. Lefkowitz, *The Lives of the Greek Poets* (London, 1981), p. 69 on Aminias.

[b] This siege may be an episode in the Athenian expedition to

were prepared to stone him, but his younger brother Aminias rolled back his cloak and displayed the arm which had lost a hand; it happened that Aminias had performed an exploit at Marathon which cost him a hand, and he was the first of the Athenians to be decorated for valour.[a] When the jurors saw what the man had endured, they recalled his actions and let Aeschylus go free.

20. When Tarentum was besieged by the Athenians and on the point of surrendering because of famine, the inhabitants of Rhegium voted to fast one day in every ten and to give the food for that day to the Tarentines. The Athenians departed and Tarentum was saved.[b] In memory of their sufferings the inhabitants celebrate a festival called the Fast.

21. A tradition has it that the bad reputation of Medea is undeserved. It was not she who killed her children, but some Corinthians. The story about the woman from Colchis and the tragedy are said to be the invention of Euripides, at the request of the Corinthians, and falsehood ousted the truth because of the poet's talent.[c] But they say that on account of the crime against the children the Corinthians even today perform rites in their honour as if they were paying a debt to them.[d]

Sicily in 415–413 B.C., apparently not recorded elsewhere.

[c] Although this anecdote is implausible in the extreme, it is worth noting that many variant versions of the well known myths were offered to the Athenian theatre audience.

[d] Pausanias, *Periegesis* 2.3.7, writing about A.D. 160–180, records seeing a statue connected with this cult; he notes that after the sack of Corinth by the Romans in 146 B.C. it had been discontinued.

ϛ

1. Ἀθηναῖοι κρατήσαντες Χαλκιδέων κατεκληρούχησαν αὐτῶν τὴν γῆν εἰς δισχιλίους κλήρους, τὴν Ἱππόβοτον καλουμένην χώραν, τεμένη δὲ ἀνῆκαν τῇ Ἀθηνᾷ ἐν τῷ Ληλάντῳ ὀνομαζομένῳ τόπῳ, τὴν δὲ λοιπὴν ἐμίσθωσαν κατὰ[1] τὰς στήλας τὰς πρὸς τῇ βασιλείῳ στοᾷ ἑστηκυίας, αἵπερ οὖν τὰ τῶν μισθώσεων ὑπομνήματα εἶχον. τοὺς δὲ αἰχμαλώτους ἔδησαν, καὶ οὐδὲ ἐνταῦθα ἔσβεσαν τὸν κατὰ[2] τῶν Χαλκιδέων θυμόν.

Λακεδαιμόνιοι Μεσσηνίων κρατήσαντες, τῶν μὲν γινομένων ἁπάντων ἐν τῇ Μεσσηνίᾳ τὰ ἡμίση ἐλάμβανον αὐτοὶ καὶ τὰς γυναῖκας τὰς ἐλευθέρας εἰς τὰ πένθη βαδίζειν ἠνάγκαζον καὶ τοὺς ἀλλοτρίους καὶ μηδέν σφισι προσήκοντας νεκροὺς κλαίειν. τῶν δὲ ἀνδρῶν τοὺς μὲν[3] ἀπέλιπον γεωργεῖν, οὓς δὲ ἀπέδοντο, οὓς δὲ ἀπέκτειναν.

[1] *κατὰ* Meursius: *καὶ* codd. [2] *κατὰ* V: om. x
[3] *τῶν δὲ ἀνδρῶν τοὺς μὲν* scripsi post Dilts: *τοὺς μὲν τῶν ἀνδρῶν* codd.

---

[a] This episode occurred in 506 B.C. Herodotus 5.77 gives the number of colonists as 4,000, and says that he had seen on the

BOOK SIX

1. When the Athenians took control of Chalcis they divided the land into parcels for two thousand settlers; this was the area known as Hippobotus. They consecrated shrines to Athena in the place called Lelantum, and they leased out the rest of the land, according to the pillars which stand by the Stoa Basileios and carry a record of the leases. They put the prisoners in chains, and even then did not reduce their animosity against the Chalcidians.[a]

When the Spartans conquered the Messenians they took possession of half of all property found in Messenia, and they compelled the freeborn women to attend funerals to mourn over the corpses of men who had no connection or relation with them. Some men were left to farm the land, some were sold into slavery, and others killed.[b]

Acropolis the chains worn by the captives. Before there was a public record office it was standard practice in Athens to record decisions on stone pillars in the city centre; the Stoa Basileios, on the corner of the Agora, was the office of the *archon basileus*, built in the middle of the sixth century B.C. See J. Travlos, *Pictorial Dictionary of Ancient Athens* (London, 1971), pp. 527–533, 580.

[b] Sparta gradually acquired control over Messenia in the eighth and seventh centuries B.C. On this passage compare Tyrtaeus fr. 6 W.

Ἀθηναῖοι δὲ ὕβρισαν καὶ ἐκείνην τὴν ὕβριν· εὐτυχίας γὰρ λαβόμενοι τὴν εὐπραγίαν σωφρόνως οὐκ ἤνεγκαν. τὰς γοῦν παρθένους τῶν μετοίκων σκιαδηφορεῖν ἐν ταῖς πομπαῖς ἠνάγκαζον ταῖς ἑαυτῶν κόραις, τὰς δὲ γυναῖκας ταῖς γυναιξί, τοὺς δὲ ἄνδρας σκαφηφορεῖν.

Σικυώνιοι δὲ Πελλήνην ἑλόντες τάς τε γυναῖκας τῶν Πελληνέων καὶ τὰς θυγατέρας ἐπ' οἰκήματος ἔστησαν. ἀγριώτατα ταῦτα, ὦ θεοὶ Ἑλλήνιοι, καὶ οὐδὲ ἐν βαρβάροις καλὰ κατά γε τὴν ἐμὴν μνείαν.

Ἐπεὶ τὴν ἐν Χαιρωνείᾳ μάχην ἐνίκησεν ὁ Φίλιππος, ἐπὶ τῷ πραχθέντι αὐτός τε ἦρτο καὶ οἱ Μακεδόνες πάντες. οἱ δὲ Ἕλληνες δεινῶς αὐτὸν κατέπτηξαν καὶ ἑαυτοὺς κατὰ πόλεις ἐνεχείρισαν αὐτῷ φέροντες. καὶ τοῦτό γε ἔδρασαν Θηβαῖοι καὶ Μεγαρεῖς καὶ Κορίνθιοι καὶ Ἀχαιοὶ καὶ Ἠλεῖοι καὶ Εὐβοεῖς <καὶ>[1] οἱ ἐν τῇ Ἀκτῇ πάντες. οὐ μὴν ἐφύλαξε τὰς πρὸς αὐτοὺς ὁμολογίας ὁ Φίλιππος, ἀλλ' ἐδουλώσατο πάντας, ἔκδικα καὶ παράνομα δρῶν.

2. Ὁ Ἁρματίδου[2] τοῦ Θεσπιέως παῖς, παραγενόμενος σύμμαχος Λακεδαιμονίοις[3] μετὰ καὶ ἄλλων πολιτῶν, τὰ μὲν πρῶτα ἐμάχετο εὖ καὶ καλῶς· καταναλωθέντων δὲ αὐτοῦ τῶν ὅπλων ψιλαῖς ταῖς χερσὶ πρὸς καθωπλισμένους ἀγωνιζόμενος, εὐκλεῶς τὸν βίον ἐτελεύτα. πατρόθεν οὖν τὸν νεανίαν προσεῖπον, κυδαίνων αὐτὸν Ὁμηρικῶς. τὸ δὲ ὄνομα αὐτοῦ εἴ τῳ ἐπιμελὲς εἰδέναι, ἀλλαχόθεν εἴσεται.

[1] suppl. Per. [2] Ἁρματίδου Kor.: -ιδίου codd.

The Athenians committed another excess. Having had good fortune they failed to exploit their luck sensibly. They obliged the daughters of resident aliens to carry parasols to shade their own girls in processions, and similarly the wives for their own wives, while the men had to carry the trays with offerings.[a]

When the Sicyonians captured Pellene, they forced the wives and daughters of the inhabitants to prostitute themselves. By the gods of Greece, that was an extreme of cruelty, as far as I am aware unacceptable even among barbarian nations.

When Philip won the battle of Chaeronea he was buoyed up by his achievement, as were all the Macedonians. The Greeks were very frightened of him, and their cities surrendered individually; this was the decision of Thebes, Megara, Corinth, the Achaeans, Elis, Euboea, and the whole of Acte.[b] But Philip did not respect the agreements he had made with them, and enslaved them all unjustly and illegally.

2. The son of Harmatides of Thespiae, with some of his fellow citizens, joined the Spartan army and at first served with distinction. When his weapons were rendered useless he continued the struggle against his armed enemies with his bare hands and met a glorious death. I have named the young man by his patronymic, in Homeric style, as a compliment. If anyone wishes to know his name, he can obtain it from another source.[c]

[a] The Greek technical terms indicate that the reference is to the Panathenaea. [b] Acte is generally a poetic synonym for Attica; here it seems to refer to the coastline of the Argolid. [c] Herodotus 7.227 gives the name as Dithyrambus.

---

[3] Λακεδαιμονίοις ex Herodoto Kühn: Ἀθηναίοις codd.

3. Ὅτι Λακεδαιμόνιοι Ἰσάδαν ἔτι παῖδα ὄντα καὶ μήπω τοῦ νόμου καλοῦντος αὐτὸν εἰς ὅπλα, ὅτι ἐκ τοῦ γυμνασίου ἐκπηδήσας ἠρίστευσεν, ἐστεφάνωσαν μέν, ὅτι δὲ πρὸ τῆς ἀπαιτουμένης ἡλικίας καὶ μὴ τὰ ἐπιχώρια ἔχων ὅπλα ὥρμησεν εἰς τοὺς ἐχθρούς, ἐζημίωσαν.

4. Ὁ μὲν Λύσανδρος ἐτεθνήκει, ὁ δὲ τὴν θυγατέρα αὐτοῦ ἔτι ζῶντος ἐγγυησάμενος, ἐπεὶ καὶ ἡ παῖς ἐρήμη πατρὸς ἀπελείπετο καὶ ὁ Λύσανδρος μετὰ τὴν τοῦ βίου καταστροφὴν ἀνεφάνη πένης ὤν, ὁ δὲ ἀνεδύετο ὁ ἐγγυησάμενος καὶ οὐδὲ ἔφασκεν ἄξεσθαι γυναῖκα. ἐπὶ τούτοις οἱ ἔφοροι τὸν ἄνδρα ἐζημίωσαν· οὔτε γὰρ Λακωνικὰ ἐφρόνει οὔτε ἄλλως Ἑλληνικά, φίλου τε ἀποθανόντος ἀμνημονῶν καὶ τῶν συνθηκῶν τὸν πλοῦτον προτιμῶν.

5. Ὅτι Ἀθηναῖοι τοὺς εἰς Ἀρκαδίαν ἀποσταλέντας πρεσβευτάς, ἐπεὶ ἑτέραν ὁδὸν ἦλθον καὶ οὐ τὴν προστεταγμένην, καίτοι κατορθώσαντας, ὅμως ἀπέκτειναν.

6. Ἦ γὰρ οὐ καὶ ταῦτα Λακωνικά; νόμος ἐστὶ τοῖς Σπαρτιάταις τὸν παρασχόμενον υἱοὺς τρεῖς ἀτέλειαν ἔχειν φρουρᾶς, τὸν δὲ πέντε πασῶν τῶν λειτουργιῶν ἀφεῖσθαι, γαμεῖν δὲ ἀπροίκους ἔτι.

Βάναυσον δὲ εἰδέναι τέχνην ἄνδρα Λακεδαιμόνιον οὐκ ἐξῆν. φοινικίδα δὲ ἀμπέχεσθαι κατὰ τὰς

---

[a] See 10.15 below for the same story.

[b] This story seems quite untypical of the Athenians. Both the

3. Note that the Spartans honoured with a crown Isadas, who was still a boy not yet liable for military service, because he left the gymnasium and distinguished himself in battle. But they also fined him because he had attacked the enemy while still under the minimum age and not possessing the standard weapons.

4. Lysander had died, but during his lifetime a man had been engaged to his daughter. She was left as an orphan, and after Lysander's death it turned out that he had been poor. The man withdrew, saying that he would not take the girl as his wife. This led the ephors to impose a fine on him, because he did not live up to the Spartan or the general Greek ideal, having no regard for the memory of a friend and treating money as more important than the contract.[a]

5. Note that the Athenians executed the envoys sent to Arcadia because they had followed a different route from the one prescribed, even though they were successful in their mission.[b]

6. Is the following again typically Laconian? It was a Spartan law that the man who provided three sons for the state was exempt from garrison duty, and the father of five from all public obligations;[c] he could also marry off his daughters without a dowry.[d]

Spartan men were not allowed to practise banausic arts. They had to wear a purple coat for battle; the colour

reference to Arcadia and the first sentence of the following chapter are hints that the story was in fact told of the Spartans.

[c] On reading this sentence Aelian's original audience will have recalled legislation of the emperor Augustus which gave privileges to fathers of three children.

[d] See Aristotle, *Politics* 1270 b 3.

μάχας ἀνάγκη ἦν· ἔχειν γὰρ[1] τὴν χρόαν καὶ σεμνότητός τι· πρὸς ταύτῃ γε μὴν καὶ τὴν ῥύσιν τοῦ ἐπιγενομένου αἵματος ἐκ τῶν τραυμάτων ἔτι [δὲ][2] μᾶλλον ἐκπλήττειν τοὺς ἀντιπάλους, βαθυτέρας[3] τῆς ὄψεως γινομένης καὶ φοβερωτέρας μᾶλλον.

Ὅτι οὐκ ἐξῆν ἀνδρὶ Λάκωνι οὐδὲ σκυλεῦσαι τὸν πολέμιον. οἱ δὲ καλῶς ἀγωνισάμενοι καὶ ἀποθανόντες θαλλοῖς ἀνεδοῦντο καὶ κλάδοις ἑτέροις καὶ δι' ἐπαίνων ἤγοντο· οἱ δὲ τελέως ἀριστεύσαντες καὶ φοινικίδος αὐτοῖς ἐπιβληθείσης ἐνδόξως ἐθάπτοντο.

7. Ὅτε οἱ Λακεδαιμόνιοι τοὺς ἐκ Ταινάρου ἱκέτας παρασπονδήσαντες ἀνέστησαν καὶ ἀπέκτειναν (ἦσαν δὲ οἱ ἱκέται[4] τῶν εἱλώτων), κατὰ μῆνιν τοῦ Ποσειδῶνος σεισμὸς ἐπιπεσὼν τῇ Σπάρτῃ τὴν πόλιν ἀνδρειότατα κατέσεισεν, ὡς πέντε μόνας ἀπολειφθῆναι οἰκίας ἐξ ἁπάσης τῆς πόλεως.

8. Ἀρταξέρξην τὸν καὶ Ὦχον ἐπικληθέντα, ὅτε ἐπεβούλευσεν αὐτῷ Βαγώας ὁ εὐνοῦχος, ὃς ἦν Αἰγύπτιος, φασὶν ἀναιρεθέντα καὶ κατακοπέντα τοῖς αἰλούροις παραβληθῆναι· ἐτάφη δέ τις ἄλλος ἀντ' αὐτοῦ καὶ ἀπεδόθη ταῖς βασιλικαῖς θήκαις. [θεοσυλίαι μὴν τοῦ Ὤχου καὶ ἄλλαι μὲν λέγονται καὶ μάλιστα κατὰ τὴν Αἴγυπτον.][5] τῷ δὲ Βαγώᾳ οὐκ ἀπέχρησε τὸ ἀποκτεῖναι τὸν Ὦχον, ἀλλὰ γὰρ καὶ ἐκ τῶν μηρῶν αὐτοῦ λαβὰς μαχαιρῶν ἐποίησε, τὸ φονικὸν αὐτοῦ ἐνδεικνύμενος διὰ τούτων. ἐμίσησε δὲ αὐτόν, ἐπεὶ τὸν Ἆπιν ἐν Αἰγύπτῳ γενόμενος ἀπέκτεινε καὶ οὗτος, ὡς ὁ Καμβύσης πρότερον.

had something superior about it, and when the blood from wounds spread it terrified the enemy still more, as the spectacle was more sombre and frightening.

Note that a Spartan was not allowed to strip an enemy's corpse of its armour. Those who fought bravely and died were crowned with olive and other branches, and were eulogised; those who had been outstandingly brave were wrapped in a purple cloak and given special honours at burial.

7. When the Spartans broke the terms of an agreement by removing the suppliants from Taenarum and executing them—the suppliants were helots—the wrath of Poseidon brought an earthquake upon Sparta and shook the city so powerfully that only five houses were left standing in the whole city.[a]

8. Artaxerxes, known also as Ochus, was the victim of a plot planned by the Egyptian eunuch Bagoas. They say he was killed, cut to pieces and fed to the cats. Someone else was buried in his place and laid to rest in the royal mausoleum. [Ochus is said to have committed a number of acts of sacrilege, especially in Egypt.] But Bagoas was not content with killing Ochus; he even made knife handles out of his thigh bones, displaying in this way his murderous instincts. He hated him because, like Cambyses before him, he had killed Apis during a visit to Egypt.[b]

[a] This episode took place during a helot revolt earlier than 465 B.C. Our main source is Thucydides 1.128.2.

[b] See 4.8 above. The Persian king Artaxerxes Ochus had regained control of Egypt in 343 B.C.

---

[1] γὰρ Kor.: δὲ codd. [2] del. Kor. [3] βαθυτέρας] βαρυ- Faber [4] οἱ ἱκέται Per.: οἰκέται codd. [5] del. Her.

9. Ἐπεὶ καὶ ἐκ τῶν Ὁμήρου ποιημάτων ἧκεν εἰς Δελφοὺς λέγουσα δόξα παλαιόπλουτον εἶναι τὸ τοῦ Ἀπόλλωνος χωρίον ἐν τοῖς ἔπεσιν ἐκείνοις·

οὐδ' ὅσα λάινος οὐδὸς ἀφήτορος ἐντὸς ἐέργει
Φοίβου Ἀπόλλωνος Πυθοῖ ἐνὶ πετρηέσσῃ,

τοὺς Δελφοὺς ἐπιχειρῆσαι διασκάπτειν λόγος ἔχει τὰ περὶ τὴν ἑστίαν καὶ τὸν τρίποδα, γενομένων δὲ σεισμῶν περὶ τὸ μαντεῖον ἀνδρικῶν παύσασθαι σωφρονήσαντας.

10. Περικλῆς στρατηγῶν Ἀθηναίοις νόμον ἔγραψεν, ἐὰν μὴ τύχῃ τις ἐξ ἀμφοῖν ὑπάρχων ἀστῶν, τούτῳ μὴ μετεῖναι τῆς πολιτείας. μετῆλθε δὲ ἄρα αὐτὸν ἡ ἐκ τοῦ νόμου νέμεσις. οἱ γὰρ δύο παῖδες, οἵπερ οὖν ἤστην αὐτῷ, Πάραλός τε καὶ Ξάνθιππος, ἀλλὰ οὗτοι μὲν κατὰ τὴν νόσον τὴν δημοσίαν τοῦ λοιμοῦ[1] ἀπέθανον, κατελείφθη δὲ ὁ Περικλῆς ἐπὶ τοῖς νόθοις, οἵπερ οὖν οὐ μετέσχον τῆς πολιτείας κατὰ τὸν πατρῷον νόμον.

11. Γέλων ἐν Ἱμέρᾳ νικήσας Καρχηδονίους πᾶσαν ὑφ' ἑαυτὸν τὴν Σικελίαν ἐποιήσατο. εἶτα ἐλθὼν εἰς τὴν ἀγορὰν γυμνὸς ἔφατο ἀποδιδόναι τοῖς πολίταις τὴν ἀρχήν· οἱ δὲ οὐκ ἤθελον, δηλονότι πεπειραμένοι αὐτοῦ καὶ δημοτικωτέρου ἢ κατὰ τὴν τῶν μονάρχων ἐξουσίαν. διὰ ταῦτά τοι καὶ ἐν τῷ τῆς Σικελίας Ἥρας ναῷ[2] ἕστηκεν αὐτοῦ εἰκὼν γυμνὸν αὐτὸν δεικνῦσα καὶ ὁμολογεῖ[3] τὴν πρᾶξιν τοῦ Γέλωνος τὸ ἐπίγραμμα.[4]

9. From the Homeric poems Delphi acquired a reputation for being the shrine of Apollo that enjoyed ancient wealth. These are the verses [*Iliad* 9.404–405]: "Not even all the possessions held inside the stone threshold of the Archer, of Phoebus Apollo, at rocky Pytho." The story goes that the Delphians tried to dig up the area around the sacred hearth and tripod. But when powerful earthquakes shook the shrine they came to their senses and stopped.

10. As general Pericles proposed in Athens a law that unless both parents were citizens a man should not have citizenship.[a] But he was overtaken by the consequences of the law. The two sons he had, Paralus and Xanthippus, died in the epidemic of plague. Pericles was left with his illegitimate children, who could not be citizens owing to their father's law.

11. After his victory over the Carthaginians at Himera Gelon had the whole of Sicily under his control.[b] He then went unarmed into the main square[c] and declared that he was returning power to the citizens. They declined it, because they had learned by experience that he was more a friend of the people than is usual for a man with a monarch's powers. For this reason there is a statue of him in the temple of Sicilian Hera, which portrays him unarmed. The inscription attests his action.

[a] The law was passed in 451/0 B.C. See also 13.24 below.

[b] In 480 B.C. For another story about Gelon at Syracuse see 13.37. [c] I.e. the main square of Syracuse.

---

[1] *τοῦ λοιμοῦ* del. Her. [2] *Ἥρας ναῷ*] *ἡρῴῳ* A. Gronovius [3] *ὁμολογεῖ* Her.: *ὡμολόγει* codd.

[4] *ἐπίγραμμα* Per.: *γράμμα* codd.

12. Διονύσιος δὲ ὁ δεύτερος τὴν ἀρχὴν εἶχεν εὖ μάλα περιπεφραγμένην τοῦτον τὸν τρόπον. ναῦς μὲν ἐκέκτητο οὐκ ἐλάττους τῶν τετρακοσίων τετρήρεις[1] καὶ πεντήρεις, πεζῶν δὲ δύναμιν εἰς δέκα μυριάδας, ἱππεῖς δὲ ἐννεακισχιλίους. ἡ δὲ πόλις τῶν Συρακουσίων λιμέσιν ἐκεκόσμητο μεγίστοις, καὶ τεῖχος αὐτῇ περιεβέβλητο ὑψηλότατον, σκεύη δὲ εἶχεν ἕτοιμα ναυσὶν ἄλλαις πεντακοσίαις, τεθησαύριστο δὲ αὐτῇ καὶ σῖτος εἰς ἑκατὸν μεδίμνων μυριάδας καὶ ὁπλοθήκη νενησμένη ἀσπίσι καὶ μαχαίραις καὶ δόρασι. καὶ κνημῖδας περιττὰς καὶ θώρακας καὶ καταπέλτας <εἶχε>[2] (ὁ δὲ καταπέλτης εὕρημα ἦν αὐτοῦ Διονυσίου)· εἶχε δὲ καὶ συμμάχους παμπόλλους. καὶ τούτοις ἐπιθαρρῶν ὁ Διονύσιος ἀδάμαντι δεδεμένην ᾤετο τὴν ἀρχὴν κεκτῆσθαι.

Ἀλλ' οὗτός γε πρῶτον[3] μὲν ἀπέκτεινε τοὺς ἀδελφούς, εἶδε δὲ καὶ τοὺς υἱοὺς βιαίως ἀποσφαγέντας καὶ τὰς θυγατέρας καταισχυνθείσας εἶτα ἀποσφαγείσας γυμνάς. οὐδεὶς δὲ τῶν ἀπ' αὐτοῦ ταφῆς τῆς νομιζομένης ἔτυχεν· οἱ μὲν γὰρ ζῶντες κατεκαύθησαν, οἱ δὲ κατατμηθέντες εἰς τὸ πέλαγος ἐξερρίφησαν. τοῦτο δὲ ἀπήντησεν αὐτῷ, Δίωνος τοῦ Ἱππαρίνου ἐπιθεμένου τῇ ἀρχῇ. αὐτὸς δὲ ἐν πενίᾳ μυρίᾳ διάγων κατέστρεψε τὸν βίον γηραιός.

Λέγει δὲ Θεόπομπος ὑπὸ τῆς ἀκρατοποσίας τῆς ἄγαν αὐτὸν διαφθαρῆναι τὰς ὄψεις, ὡς ἀμυδρὸν

[1] *τετρήρεις* e Diod. Sic. Scheffer: *ἑξήρεις* codd.
[2] suppl. Gesner [3] *πρῶτον* Faber: *-ους* codd.

12. Dionysius II protected his power effectively in the following way. He had not less than four hundred ships, quadriremes and quinqueremes;[a] his infantry were not less than a hundred thousand, with nine thousand cavalry. The city of Syracuse was endowed with very large harbours, and an extremely high wall surrounded it. There was equipment in store for another five hundred ships. A million bushels of corn were stored away.[b] The armoury was piled high with shields, daggers, and spears, a great quantity of calf protectors, breastplates, and catapults—the catapult was an invention of Dionysius. He also had a large number of allies. All this gave him the confidence to believe his power was cast in steel.

But this man first assassinated his brothers, and then witnessed the violent death of his sons and the rape of his daughters, who were stripped and killed. None of his family was granted normal burial. Some were burned alive, others cut to pieces and thrown into the sea. This was the fate he met when Dion the son of Hipparinus laid claim to power. He himself lived in extreme poverty and died at an advanced age.[c]

Theopompus says [FGrH 115 F 283 b] that he damaged his sight by excessive indulgence in drinking

[a] Diodorus Siculus 14.42.2 confirms that in 398 B.C. Dionysius I began to build quadriremes and quinqueremes.

[b] The Greek term *medimnos* was usually about 50 litres, but not all cities used the same standard.

[c] The fall of Dionysius is recounted again at 9.8 below. At the end of this ch. the epitome adds a clause "and so he became an elementary school teacher in Corinth and died at an advanced age."

βλέπειν· ἀποκαθῆσθαι δὲ ἐν τοῖς κουρείοις καὶ γελωτοποιεῖν. καὶ ἐν τῷ μεσαιτάτῳ τῆς Ἑλλάδος ἀσχημονῶν διετέλει, βίον διαντλῶν ἀλγεινότατον.[1] καὶ ἦν δεῖγμα οὐ τὸ τυχὸν τοῖς ἀνθρώποις εἰς σωφροσύνην καὶ τρόπου κόσμον ἡ τοῦ Διονυσίου ἐκ τῶν τηλικούτων εἰς οὕτω ταπεινὰ μεταβολή.

13. Καλῶς τὸ δαιμόνιον ἐπὶ τριγονίαν τυραννίδας μὴ ἄγον, ἀλλὰ ἢ παραχρῆμα ἐκτρῖβον τοὺς τυράννους πίτυος δίκην ἢ παίδων ἐξισχῦον.[2] μνημονεύονται δὲ ὑφ' Ἑλλήνων ἐξ αἰῶνος καὶ εἰς ἐγγόνους διαρκέσαι αἵδε, ἥ τε Ἱέρωνος[3] ἐν Σικελίᾳ καὶ ἡ τῶν Λευκωνιδῶν[4] περὶ Βόσπορον καὶ ἡ τῶν Κυψελιδῶν ἐν Κορίνθῳ.

14. Ἡμερώτατον δὲ Δαρείου τοῦτο τὸ ἔργον ἀκούω τοῦ παιδὸς τοῦ Ὑστάσπου. Ἀρίβαζος ὁ Ὑρκανὸς ἐπεβούλευσεν αὐτῷ μετὰ καὶ ἄλλων ἀνδρῶν οὐκ ἀφανῶν [τῶν][5] ἐν Πέρσαις· ἦν δὲ ἡ ἐπιβουλὴ ἐν κυνηγεσίῳ. ἅπερ προμαθὼν ὁ Δαρεῖος οὐκ ἔπτηξεν, ἀλλὰ προστάξας αὐτοῖς λαβεῖν τὰ ὅπλα καὶ τοὺς ἵππους, ἐκέλευσεν αὐτοῖς διατείνασθαι τὰ παλτὰ καὶ δριμὺ ἐνιδὼν "τί οὖν οὐ δρᾶτε τοῦτο"

[1] post ἀλγεινότατον add. Φ καὶ γεγονὼς διὰ τοῦτο γραμματοδιδάσκαλος ἐν Κορίνθῳ ἐτελεύτα γηραιός

[2] ἐξισχῦον] στερίσκον Her. [3] Ἱέρωνος Per.: Γέλωνος codd. [4] Λευκωνιδῶν Scaliger: Λευκανίων V: Λακωνίων x

[5] del. Kor.

---

[a] The implication is that the pine, once cut down, does not

unmixed wine and had poor vision; that he sat in barbers' shops and played the buffoon, eking out a miserable existence and continually demeaning himself in full view of Greece. Dionysius' fall from such power to poverty served as a powerful warning to men to lead a disciplined and well-ordered life.

13. The divine power does well not to prolong tyrannies to the third generation; it either uproots tyrants at once like pine trees[a] or demonstrates its strength against the children. In the whole course of Greek history the tyrannies recorded as having passed to future generations are those of Hieron in Sicily,[b] of the Leuconidae at the Bosporus,[c] and of the Cypselidae at Corinth.[d]

14. I learn of this very kind act of Darius the son of Hystaspes. Aribazus the Hyrcanian plotted against him in alliance with other Persians of note. The plot was timed for a hunt. Darius learned of it in advance, but was not deterred; he ordered the men to make ready their equipment and horses and instructed them to hold their weapons at the ready. Looking at them severely he said:

grow fresh shoots again; the expression comes from Herodotus 6.37. [b] The reference is to Hieron II, who passed on control of Syracuse to his grandson in 215 B.C.; but his son had predeceased him.

[c] The Leuconidae are more often known as the Spartocidae; the first member of the dynasty ruled in the Crimean Bosporus from 438 to 433 or 431 B.C., and the family seem to have been in control as late as the third century.

[d] Cypselus came to power ca. 657, his son Periander ca. 625 B.C.; the last Corinthian tyrant was the latter's nephew Psammetichus. Aristotle, *Politics* 1315 b 11–39, notes that tyranny was a short-lived constitution; the longest he knew of was that of Sicyon, which lasted 100 years.

εἶπεν "ἐφ' ὃ καὶ ὡρμήσατε;" οἱ δὲ ἰδόντες ἄτρεπτον ἀνδρὸς βλέμμα ἀνεστάλησαν τῆς ὁρμῆς.[1] τὸ δέος δὲ αὐτοὺς κατέσχεν οὕτως, ὡς καὶ ἐκβαλεῖν τὰς αἰχμὰς καὶ ἀφάλασθαι[2] τῶν ἵππων καὶ προσκυνῆσαι Δαρεῖον καὶ ἑαυτοὺς παραδοῦναι ὅ τι καὶ βούλοιτο πράττειν. ὁ δὲ διέστησεν ἄλλους ἄλλῃ, καὶ τοὺς μὲν ἐπὶ τὰ τῆς Ἰνδικῆς ὅρια ἀπέπεμψε, τοὺς δὲ ἐπὶ τὰ Σκυθικά. καὶ ἐκεῖνοι ἔμειναν αὐτῷ πιστοί, διὰ μνήμης ἔχοντες τὴν εὐεργεσίαν.

[1] τῆς ὁρμῆς Dilts: τὴν -ὴν codd.

[2] ἀφαλάσθαι Faber post Gesner: ἀφελέσθαι codd.

"Why don't you do what you set out to do?" Seeing his unflinching gaze they abandoned their plan; fear gripped them to such an extent that they dropped their spears, jumped off their horses and knelt before Darius, surrendering unconditionally. He despatched them in various directions, sending some to the Indian frontier, others to the Scythian. They remained loyal to him, remembering his kindness.

Z

1. Σεμίραμιν τὴν Ἀσσυρίαν ἄλλοι μὲν ἄλλως ᾄδουσιν· ὡραιοτάτη δὲ ἐγένετο γυναικῶν, εἰ καὶ ἀφελέστερον ἐχρῆτο τῷ κάλλει. ἀφικομένη δὲ πρὸς τὸν τῶν Ἀσσυρίων βασιλέα κλητὴ κατὰ κλέος τῆς ὥρας, ὁ δὲ ἐντυχὼν τῇ ἀνθρώπῳ ἠράσθη αὐτῆς. ἡ δὲ ᾔτησεν ἐκ τοῦ βασιλέως τὴν βασίλειον στολὴν λαβεῖν [δῶρον][1] καὶ πέντε ἡμερῶν[2] τῆς Ἀσίας ἄρξαι καὶ <πάντας>[3] τὰ ὑπ' αὐτῆς[4] προστατττόμενα δρᾶσαι. καὶ οὐδὲ τῆς αἰτήσεως ἠτύχησεν. ἐπεὶ δὲ ἐκάθισεν αὐτὴν ὁ βασιλεὺς ἐπὶ τοῦ θρόνου καὶ ἔγνω διὰ χειρὸς καὶ γνώμης ἔχουσα πάντα, προσέταξε τοῖς δορυφόροις αὐτὸν τὸν βασιλέα κτεῖναι· καὶ οὕτω τὴν τῶν Ἀσσυρίων ἀρχὴν κατέσχε. λέγει δὲ ταῦτα Δείνων.

2. Στράτων ὁ Σιδώνιος λέγεται τρυφῇ καὶ πολυτελείᾳ ὑπερβάλλεσθαι[5] σπεῦσαι ἀνθρώπους πάντας. καὶ Θεόπομπος ὁ Χῖος παραβάλλει αὐτοῦ τὸν βίον τῇ τῶν Φαιάκων διαίτῃ, ἥνπερ καὶ Ὅμηρος κατὰ τὴν ἑαυτοῦ μεγαλόνοιαν, ὥσπερ εἴθιστο, ἐξετραγῴ-

[1] del. Her. [2] ἡμερῶν Vx: -ρας Φ
[3] suppl. Jacoby [4] ὑπ' αὐτῆς Her.: ἀπὸ ταύτης codd.

BOOK SEVEN

1. Semiramis of Assyria has been variously celebrated by different authors. She was the most attractive of women, even if she was rather careless of her appearance. When she appeared before the Assyrian king,[a] summoned because of her notorious beauty, he fell in love with her at their first encounter. She asked the king for royal dress and five days rule over Asia, with everyone carrying out her orders. She was not refused. When the king placed her on the throne and she realised that everything was in her hands and subject to her will, she instructed the bodyguards to kill the king, and in this way she acquired the kingdom of Assyria. This is the account of Dinon [FGrH 690 F 7].[b]

2. Straton of Sidon is said to have been intent on outdoing everyone in luxurious and expensive living.[c] Theopompus of Chios [FGrH 115 F 114] compares his existence to that of the Phaeacians, which Homer [*Odyssey* 8.248] celebrated with his customary magnifi-

[a] Ninus. [b] Dinon is an obscure historian, who probably lived ca. 360–330 B.C. Of his *Persica* in five books very few fragments survive.

[c] Athenaeus 531 AD appears to be the source of this ch.

---

[5] ὑπερβάλλεσθαι x: -βαλέσθαι V

δησεν. τούτῳ γε μὴν οὐχ εἷς παρῆν ᾠδὸς κατᾴδων αὐτοῦ τὸ δεῖπνον καὶ καταθέλγων αὐτόν, ἀλλὰ πολλαὶ μὲν παρῆσαν γυναῖκες[1] μουσουργοὶ καὶ αὐλητρίδες καὶ ἑταῖραι κάλλει διαπρέπουσαι καὶ ὀρχηστρίδες. διεφιλοτιμεῖτο δὲ ἰσχυρῶς καὶ πρὸς Νικοκλέα τὸν Κύπριον, ἐπεὶ καὶ ἐκεῖνος πρὸς αὐτόν. ἦν δὲ ἡ ἅμιλλα ὑπὲρ οὐδενὸς σπουδαίου, ἀλλ' ὑπὲρ τῶν προειρημένων. καὶ πυνθανόμενοι παρὰ τῶν ἀφικνουμένων τὰ παρ' ἀλλήλοις, εἶτα ἀντεφιλοτιμοῦντο ἑκάτερος ὑπερβάλλεσθαι[2] τὸν ἕτερον. οὐ μὴν εἰς τὸ παντελὲς ἐν τούτοις διεγένοντο· ἀμφότεροι γὰρ βιαίου θανάτου ἔργον ἐγένοντο.

3. Ὅτι Ἀρίστιππος, ἑταίρων αὐτῷ τινων ὀδυρομένων βαρύτατα, πολλὰ μὲν καὶ ἄλλα πρὸς αὐτοὺς εἶπε λύπης ἀνασταλτικά, καὶ ταῦτά γε ἐν προοιμίῳ· "ἀλλ' ἔγωγε ἥκω παρ' ὑμᾶς οὐχ ὡς συλλυπησόμενος, ἀλλ' ἵνα παύσω ὑμᾶς λυπουμένους."

4. Ὅτι Πιττακὸς πάνυ σφοδρῶς ἐπῄνει τὴν μύλην, τὸ ἐγκώμιον αὐτῆς ἐκεῖνο ἐπιλέγων, ὅτι ἐν μικρῷ τόπῳ διαφόρως ἔστι γυμνάσασθαι. ἦν δέ τι ᾆσμα ἐπιμύλιον οὕτω καλούμενον.

5. Καὶ Λαέρτης δὲ αὐτουργῶν ὑπὸ τοῦ παιδὸς πεφώραται καὶ φυτὸν ξύων, καίτοι γηράσκων βαθύτατα. ὁμολογεῖ δὲ καὶ Ὀδυσσεὺς αὐτὸς πολλὰ εἰδέναι καὶ τεχνίτης αὐτῶν εἶναι·

[1] γυναῖκες Her.: -κῶν codd.
[2] ὑπερβάλλεσθαι scripsi: -βαλέσθαι codd.

---

[a] Theopompus made this comparison in Book 15 of his

cence.[a] But Straton did not just have one singer to entertain at dinner and charm him; instead there were numerous women to sing and play the reed pipe, outstandingly beautiful courtesans and dancing girls. He was a keen rival of Nicocles of Cyprus, just as the latter competed with him; but the competition had no serious objective, and concentrated on what I have just mentioned. They would inquire from travellers what was going on in each other's houses, and then each would try to outdo the other. But they did not continue their rivalry indefinitely, for each became the victim of a violent death.

3. Note that when some of Aristippus' companions were deeply distressed, he gave them much advice aimed at reducing their grief, and said by way of preface [fr. 89 M.]: "I come to visit you not in order to grieve with you but so as to stop your grief."[b]

4. Note that Pittacus[c] had a great deal to say in favour of the millstone, and to his eulogy of it he added that it allows a great deal of exercise within a small area. There was also a song known as the millstone song.

5. Laertes was discovered by his son cultivating the land in person, trimming a plant, despite his very advanced age.[d] Odysseus also admits to having knowledge of many arts and to being skilled in them [*Odyssey*

Philippica. In *Odyssey* 8.248–9 the Phaeacians are described as living a life of luxury.

[b] Aristippus founded the Cyrenaic school of philosophy, based on the principal of hedonism. See also 14.6 below.

[c] For Pittacus see 2.29 and 3.17 above. Plutarch, *Moralia* 157 DE, cites the story of the philosopher Thales visiting Eresus and hearing a girl sing "Grind, mill, grind, for Pittacus also grinds, the monarch of great Mytilene."

[d] See *Odyssey* 24.226–227.

δρηστοσύνῃ [δ'][1] οὐκ ἄν μοι ἐρίσσειε βροτὸς ἄλλος,
πῦρ τ' εὖ νηῆσαι διά τε ξύλα δανὰ κεάσσαι.

καὶ τὴν σχεδίαν δὲ οὐ δεηθεὶς ναυπηγῶν, ἀλλὰ δι' ἑαυτοῦ τὴν ταχίστην εἰργάσατο. καὶ Ἀχιλλεὺς δέ, τρίτος ὢν ἀπὸ τοῦ Διός, αὐτὸς διακόπτει τὰ κρέα, δεῖπνον τοῖς παρὰ τῶν Ἀχαιῶν πρέσβεσιν ἀφικομένοις εὐτρεπίσαι σπεύδων.

6. Χιόνος ποτὲ πιπτούσης ἤρετο ὁ βασιλεὺς τῶν Σκυθῶν τινα εἰ ῥιγοῖ,[2] γυμνὸν διακαρτεροῦντα. ὁ δὲ αὐτὸν ἀντήρετο εἰ[3] τὸ μέτωπον ῥιγοῖ. τοῦ δὲ οὐ φήσαντος "οὐκοῦν" εἶπεν "οὐδὲ ἐγώ· πᾶς γὰρ μέτωπόν εἰμι."

7a. Ὅτι Πυθέας ἐπέσκωπτεν εἰς Δημοσθένην τὸν Δημοσθένους, ἐπιλέγων αὐτῷ τὰ ἐνθυμήματα ἐλλυχνίων ὄζειν, ὅτι ἐκεῖνος διὰ τῆς νυκτὸς πάσης ἠγρύπνει φροντίζων καὶ ἐκμανθάνων ἃ ἔμελλεν ἐρεῖν ἐλθὼν εἰς τοὺς Ἀθηναίους.

7b. Δημοσθένης ὁ Δημοσθένους, εἰ ἔμελλε τῆς ὑστεραίας ἔσεσθαι ἐκκλησία,[4] ἀλλὰ ἐκεῖνός γε διὰ τῆς νυκτὸς ἠγρύπνει πάσης, διαφροντίζων δηλονότι καὶ ἐκμανθάνων ταῦτα ἃ ἔμελλεν ἐρεῖν. ὁ τοίνυν Πυθέας ἐκ τούτων ἐμοὶ δοκεῖν ἀπέσκωπτεν εἰς αὐτόν, ἐπιλέγων αὐτοῦ τὰ ἐνθυμήματα ἐλλυχνίων ὄζειν.

[1] del. Her., qui alia quoque ex Homero correxit
[2] εἰ ῥιγοῖ post διακαρτεροῦντα traiecit Her.
[3] εἴ <οἱ> Per.
[4] ἐκκλησία Hirschig: -ίας codd.

15.321–322]: "In activity no other mortal could compete with me, in building up the fire and in cutting seasoned logs."[a] As to his raft, he did not need any shipbuilders, but made it by himself very quickly.[b] Achilles too, the third generation descendant of Zeus, himself carved the meat in his eagerness to prepare dinner for the ambassadors who had arrived from the Greeks.[c]

6. During a snowstorm the Scythian king asked someone who was braving the elements naked if he felt cold. The man asked him in turn if he felt the cold on his face. When the king said "No" he replied "Nor do I feel anything, because I am all face."

7a. Note that Pytheas mocked Demosthenes son of Demosthenes by saying that his reasoning smelled of midnight oil because he sat up all night meditating and learning by heart what he was going to say when he appeared before the Athenians.

7b. If there was to be an assembly on the following day, Demosthenes son of Demosthenes would stay up the whole night, because he was thinking about—and learning by heart—what he proposed to say. So that, I imagine, is why Pytheas mocked him by saying that his reasoning smelled of midnight oil.[d]

[a] Perhaps the text should also include the line that follows in Homer, which runs: "in carving and roasting meat, and in pouring wine."

[b] The construction of the raft is described in *Odyssey* 5.228–262. [c] See *Iliad* 9.206–221.

[d] Here we have a good example of the slight difference between the original text, as it could still be read in the fifth century A.D. by John of Stobi (3.29.60), and the text of our medieval manuscripts. For Pytheas see 14.28 below.

8. Ὅτε Ἡφαιστίων ἀπέθανεν, Ἀλέξανδρος ὅπλα αὐτῷ εἰς τὴν πυρὰν ἐνέβαλε, καὶ χρυσὸν καὶ ἄργυρον τῷ νεκρῷ συνέτηξε καὶ ἐσθῆτα τὴν μέγα τιμίαν ἐν Πέρσαις. ἀπέκειρε δὲ καὶ τοὺς πλοκάμους τοὺς ἑαυτοῦ,[1] Ὁμηρικὸν πάθος δρῶν καὶ μιμούμενος τὸν Ἀχιλλέα τὸν ἐκείνου. βιαιότερον δὲ καὶ θερμότερον ἐκείνου ἔδρασεν οὗτος, τὴν τῶν Ἐκβατάνων ἀκρόπολιν περικείρας καὶ τὸ τεῖχος αὐτῆς ἀφελόμενος.[2] μέχρι μὲν οὖν τῆς κόμης τῆς ἑαυτοῦ Ἑλληνικὰ ἐδόκει μοι δρᾶν· ἐπιχειρήσας δὲ τοῖς τείχεσιν, ἀλλ' ἐνταῦθα ἐπένθει βαρβαρικῶς Ἀλέξανδρος ἤδη, καὶ τὰ κατὰ τὴν στολὴν ἤμειψε, θυμῷ καὶ ἔρωτι ἐπιτρέπων πάντα καὶ δακρύοις.

Ὅτι Ἡφαιστίων εἰς Ἐκβάτανα ἀπέθανε.[3] διαρρεῖ δὲ λόγος Ἡφαιστίωνι μὲν ταῦτα εὐτρεπισθῆναι νεκρῷ, Ἀλέξανδρον δὲ αὐτοῖς ἀποθανόντα χρήσασθαι· μὴ γὰρ φθάσαι τὸ ἐπὶ τῷ μειρακίῳ τελεσθὲν πένθος, ἐπιλαβεῖν δὲ τὸν τοῦ Ἀλεξάνδρου θάνατον.

9. Εἶτα οὐκ ἔστι σωφροσύνη μεγάλη (ἐμοὶ μὲν δοκεῖ), εἴ γε καὶ ἡ Φωκίωνος γυνὴ τὸ Φωκίωνος ἱμάτιον ἐφόρει καὶ οὐδὲν ἐδεῖτο οὐ κροκωτοῦ οὐ Ταραντίνου οὐκ ἀναβολῆς οὐκ ἐγκύκλου[4] οὐ κεκρυφάλου οὐ καλύπτρας οὐ βαπτῶν χιτωνίσκων; ἠμπείχετο δὲ πρώτῃ μὲν τῇ σωφροσύνῃ, δευτέροις γε μὴν τοῖς παροῦσιν.

10. Τῇ Ξανθίππῃ δὲ ὁ Σωκράτης, ἐπεὶ οὐκ[5] ἠβούλετο τὸ ἐκείνου ἱμάτιον ἐνδύσασθαι <καὶ οὕτως>[6]

[1] πλοκάμους τοὺς ἑαυτοῦ Her.: πολεμικοὺς καὶ ἀγαθοὺς καὶ ἑαυτόν codd.

8. When Hephaestion died Alexander threw armour on to his pyre, and melted down with the corpse gold, silver, and clothing much prized by the Persians.[a] He cut off his own hair, a gesture in the Homeric manner, in imitation of the poet's Achilles.[b] But Alexander was more violent and hotheaded than Achilles: he destroyed the acropolis of Ecbatana and knocked down its walls. As far as his hair is concerned, I think he acted in accordance with Greek custom; but when he pulled down the walls, that was a barbaric expression of grief by Alexander. He changed his dress and allowed himself to be completely controlled by anger, love, and tears.

Note that Hephaestion died at Ecbatana. A story circulates that these ceremonies, while planned for Hephaestion, were carried out for Alexander on his death, because mourning for the young man was not yet completed when death overtook Alexander.

9. Is it not a sign of great modesty—so at least it seems to me—if it is true that Phocion's wife wore his coat? She felt no need for a yellow dress or a Tarentine dress, a cloak, a jacket, an upper garment, a hairnet, a veil, or dyed short frocks. She dressed first in modesty, and then with what she had available.

10. When Xanthippe refused to put on Socrates' cloak and go to watch the procession dressed in it, he said to

[a] Perizonius suggested that this is the dress worn by the Persian king, subsequently used by Alexander.

[b] See *Iliad* 23.141.

---

[2] *καὶ τὸ . . . ἀφελόμενος* del. Her.

[3] *ὅτι . . . ἀπέθανε* del. Per. [4] *ἐγκύκλου* Per.: -*κλίου* vel sim. codd. [5] *οὐκ* V (hoc cap. om. x): *οὖν* Faber

[6] suppl. Per.

ἐπὶ τὴν θέαν τῆς πομπῆς βαδίζειν, ἔφη· "ὁρᾷς ὡς οὐ θεωρήσουσα θεωρησομένη δὲ μᾶλλον βαδίζεις;"

11. Ῥωμαίων δὲ αἱ πολλαὶ γυναῖκες καὶ τὰ ὑποδήματα ταὐτὰ[1] φορεῖν τοῖς ἀνδράσιν εἰθισμέναι εἰσίν.

12. Δεῖ τοὺς παῖδας τοῖς ἀστραγάλοις ἐξαπατᾶν, τοὺς δὲ ἄνδρας τοῖς ὅρκοις. οἱ μὲν Λυσάνδρου εἶναι λέγουσι τὸν λόγον, οἱ δὲ Φιλίππου τοῦ Μακεδόνος. ὁποτέρου δ' ἂν ᾖ, οὐκ ὀρθῶς λέγεται κατά γε τὴν ἐμὴν κρίσιν. καὶ ἴσως οὐ παράδοξον εἰ μὴ τὰ αὐτὰ ἀρέσκει ἐμοὶ καὶ Λυσάνδρῳ· ὁ μὲν γὰρ ἐτυράννει, ἐγὼ δὲ ὡς φρονῶ δῆλον ἐξ ὧν μὴ τὸ λεχθὲν ἀρέσκει με.

13. Ἀγησίλαος ὁ Λακεδαιμόνιος γέρων ἤδη ὢν ἀνυπόδετος πολλάκις καὶ ἀχίτων προῄει, τὸν τρίβωνα περιβαλόμενος[2] αὐτόν, καὶ ταῦτα ἑωθινὸς ἐν ὥρᾳ χειμερίῳ. ᾐτιάσατο δέ τις αὐτὸν ὡς νεανικώτερα τῆς ἡλικίας ἐπιχειροῦντα· ὁ δὲ "ἀλλ' οἵ γε νέοι" φησὶ "τῶν πολιτῶν ὥσπερ οὖν πῶλοι πρὸς τὸν τέλειον ἀποβλέπουσιν ἐμέ."

14. Τί δέ; οὐκ ἦσαν καὶ οἱ φιλόσοφοι τὰ πολέμια ἀγαθοί; ἐμοὶ μὲν δοκοῦσιν, εἴ γε Ἀρχύταν μὲν εἵλοντο ἑξάκις στρατηγὸν Ταραντῖνοι, Μέλισσος δὲ ἐναυάρχησε, Σωκράτης δὲ ἐστρατεύσατο τρίς, Πλά-

[1] ταὐτὰ Her.: αὐτὰ V (hoc cap. om. x)
[2] περιβαλόμενος Faber: -βαλλόμενος codd.

---

[a] This story reminds one of Ovid, *Ars Amatoria* 1.99. If

her: "You see—you are not going as a spectator, but in order to be the object of attention."[a]

11. The majority of Roman women are in the habit of wearing the same shoes as their husbands.

12. Children have to be deceived with knucklebones, men with oaths. Some attribute this saying to Lysander, others to Philip of Macedon. Whoever it belongs to, it is wrong in my opinion. Perhaps it is not surprising if my views differ from Lysander's. He was a tyrant, and as to my views, it is obvious why the remark does not appeal to me.

13. When Agesilaus of Sparta reached an advanced age he often went out barefoot and without an overcoat, wearing just a tunic, even early in the morning on a winter's day. Someone criticised him for youthful behaviour inconsistent with his age, but he replied: "The young of this city look to me as colts do to a mature horse."

14. Well, were not philosophers also skilled in military matters?[b] It seems so to me, if Tarentum appointed Archytas as general six times, and Melissus[c] was commander of the fleet. Socrates served in the army three times,

Aelian had the Roman poet in mind, it would have been an error of taste to quote him, as Greeks took very little interest in Roman literature. The story is told in a different form in Marcus Aurelius 10.28, where Xanthippe does take Socrates' cloak. This would imply that it was a good quality garment, whereas Socrates was notoriously ill-dressed.

[b] Ch. 3.17 above is similar in content. For Socrates' military activities see I. Düring, *Herodicus the Cratetean* (Stockholm, 1941), p. 41.

[c] A pre-Socratic philosopher from Samos; see Diels and Kranz, *Die Fragmente der Vorsokratiker,* 30 A 3.

των δὲ καὶ αὐτὸς εἰς Τάναγραν καὶ εἰς Κόρινθον. τὴν δὲ Ξενοφῶντος στρατείαν καὶ στρατηγίαν πολλοὶ μὲν καὶ ἄλλοι ᾄδουσι καὶ αὐτὸς δὲ ὁμολογεῖ ἐν τοῖς περὶ Κύρου λόγοις. Δίων δὲ ὁ Ἱππαρίνου τὴν Διονυσίου τυραννίδα κατέλυσε. καὶ Ἐπαμεινώνδας βοιωταρχῶν ἐν Λεύκτροις ἐνίκησε Λακεδαιμονίους καὶ τῶν Θηβαίων[1] καὶ τῶν Ἑλλήνων πρῶτος ἐγένετο. πολλὰ δὲ καὶ Ζήνων ὑπὲρ Ἀθηναίων ἐπολιτεύσατο πρὸς Ἀντίγονον. οὐδὲν γὰρ διοίσει εἴτε[2] τις διὰ γνώμης ὤνησέ τινας εἴτε δι' ὅπλων.

15. Ἡνίκα τῆς θαλάσσης ἦρξαν Μιτυληναῖοι, τοῖς ἀφισταμένοις τῶν συμμάχων τιμωρίαν ἐκείνην ἐπήρτησαν, γράμματα μὴ μανθάνειν τοὺς παῖδας αὐτῶν μηδὲ μουσικὴν διδάσκεσθαι, πασῶν κολάσεων ἡγησάμενοι βαρυτάτην εἶναι ταύτην, ἐν ἀμουσίᾳ καὶ ἀμαθίᾳ καταβιῶναι.

16. Ὅτι Ῥώμη ὑπὸ Ῥώμου καὶ Ῥωμύλου ἐκτίσθη τῶν Ἄρεος καὶ Σιλβίας[3] παίδων. ἦν δὲ αὕτη μία τῶν Αἰνείου ἀπογόνων.

17. Ὅτε εἰς Σικελίαν ἧκεν Εὔδοξος, χάριν αὐτῷ πολλὴν ὁ Διονύσιος τῆς ἀφίξεως ᾔδει. ὁ δὲ οὐδέν τι πρὸς ταῦτα θωπεύσας οὐδὲ ὑποδραμὼν "ἀφικόμην"

[1] Θηβαίων Faber: Ῥωμαίων codd.
[2] εἴτε Gesner: εἰ V: οὔτε εἰ x
[3] Σιλβίας Kor.: Σερβίας codd.

---

[a] There are uncertainties about Plato's alleged military service; see A. S. Riginos, *Platonica: The Anecdotes Concerning the Life and Writings of Plato* (Leiden, 1976), pp. 51–52.

and so did Plato himself, at Tanagra and at Corinth.[a] Xenophon's expedition and command are celebrated by many other writers, and he himself is a witness in his account of Cyrus.[b] Dion the son of Hipparinus destroyed the tyranny of Dionysius. Epaminondas commanded the Boeotians at Leuctra and defeated the Spartans, making himself the outstanding figure both in Thebes and throughout Greece. Zeno conducted a good deal of business with Antigonus on behalf of the Athenians.[c] It does not make any difference whether a man serves others in battle or with his good judgement.

15. When Mytilene ruled the seas it imposed a penalty on allies who rebelled: that their children should not become literate or have a cultural education.[d] They reckoned it the most severe punishment to live in ignorance and have no acquaintance with the Muses.

16. Note that Rome was founded by Remus and Romulus, children of Ares and Silvia.[e] She was one of the descendants of Aeneas.

17. When Eudoxus reached Sicily Dionysius was very grateful to him for coming.[f] Eudoxus did not respond with flattery or subservience, and said "I have come here

[b] In the *Anabasis*. [c] Zeno is known to have been on good terms with Antigonus Gonatas.

[d] In his account of sea power in early Greece Thucydides (1.13–14) does not refer to Mytilene. [e] Rhea Silvia, otherwise known as Ilia, was the daughter of Aeneas in the old version of the saga; in another she was the daughter of Numitor.

[f] Eudoxus of Cnidus (ca. 391–338 B.C.) was a polymath with particular interests in geography, mathematics, and astronomy. His most significant contribution was the theory of concentric spheres to explain the motion of heavenly bodies.

εἶπεν "ὡσπερανεὶ πρὸς πανδοκέα ἀγαθόν, παρ' ᾧ κατήγετο Πλάτων," ὁμολογήσας ὅτι μὴ δι' ἐκεῖνον ἀλλὰ διὰ τοῦτον ἀφίκετο.

18. Αἰγυπτίους φασὶ δεινῶς ἐγκαρτερεῖν ταῖς βασάνοις, καὶ ὅτι θᾶττον τεθνήξεται ἀνὴρ Αἰγύπτιος στρεβλούμενος ἢ τἀληθὲς ὁμολογήσει.

Παρὰ Ἰνδοῖς δὲ αἱ γυναῖκες τὸ αὐτὸ πῦρ ἀποθανοῦσι τοῖς ἀνδράσιν ὑπομένουσι. φιλοτιμοῦνται δὲ περὶ τούτου αἱ γυναῖκες [τοῦ ἀνδρός]·[1] καὶ ἡ κλήρῳ λαχοῦσα συγκαίεται.[2]

19. Σόλων εἰς τὴν ὑπὲρ Σαλαμῖνος μάχην ἐστρατήγησε καὶ δύο νεῶν Μεγαρίδων κρατήσας μετεβίβασε ναυβάτας[3] Ἀττικοὺς εἰς αὐτὰς καὶ τὰ τῶν πολεμίων ὅπλα τοῖς οἰκείοις περιθεὶς καὶ μεθορμισθεὶς δι' ἀπάτης πολλοὺς τῶν Μεγαρέων κατέκοψεν ἀνόπλους.[4] ἐκράτησε δὲ καὶ τοῖς λόγοις αὐτῶν, οὐ λόγων δεινότητι ἀλλὰ δι' αὐτῶν τῶν ἐλέγχων τὸ πλέον ἐνεγκάμενος· ἀρχαίας γὰρ θήκας ἀνοίξας ἀπέδειξε πάντας Ἀθηναίους πρὸς δύσιν κειμένους κατὰ τὸ πάτριον αὐτοῖς ἔθος, τοὺς δὲ Μεγαρεῖς εἰκῇ καὶ ὡς ἔτυχε τεθαμμένους. ἔκριναν δὲ τὴν δίκην Λακεδαιμόνιοι.

20. Ἀνὴρ εἰς Λακεδαίμονα ἀφίκετο Χῖος,[5] γέρων ἤδη ὤν, τὰ μὲν ἄλλα ἀλαζών, ᾐδεῖτο δὲ ἐπὶ τῷ γήρᾳ καὶ διὰ ταῦτα τὴν τρίχα πολιὰν οὖσαν ἐπειρᾶτο βαφῇ ἀφανίζειν. παρελθὼν οὖν εἰς τοὺς Λακεδαιμο-

[1] del. Per.: τοῦ πυρὸς A. Gronovius
[2] συγκαίεται <τῷ ἀνδρί> Valckenaer

as if to live in a good hotel where Plato stayed," which was an admission that he came on Plato's account and not for Dionysius.

18. They say that Egyptians have a remarkable resistance to torture, and that an Egyptian will die on the rack before he confesses the truth.

In India the women submit to the same fire that burns their dead husbands. The wives of the dead man compete for this privilege, and the one who is selected by lot is burned with her husband.[a]

19. Solon was in command at the battle for Salamis. Having captured two Megarian ships he transferred to them an Athenian crew and fitted out his men with the armour of the enemy. He moved his ships and by a ruse killed a large number of unarmed Megarians. He also won a verbal battle, gaining the upper hand not by eloquence of language but simply by the force of the arguments. He had some old tombs opened and proved that all the Athenians lay facing west, in accordance with tradition, while the Megarians were buried randomly, in no consistent fashion.[b] The case was judged by the Spartans.

20. A man from Chios arrived in Sparta. He was elderly, vain in many ways, and ashamed of his age, and for this reason he tried to dye his white hair. He appeared

[a] Polygamy among the early Hindus is well attested, especially in the highest classes of society.

[b] Compare 5.14 above.

---

[3] *ναυβάτας* scripsi (*ναυηγοὺς* iam Per.): *στρατηγοὺς* codd.

[4] *ἀνόπλους* x: *ἀέθλους* V: *ἀέλπτους* Per.

[5] *Χῖος* Stobaeus 3.12.19, qui hoc cap. breviatum praebet: *Κεῖος* codd.

νίους καὶ τοιαύτην ὑποφαίνων τὴν κεφαλὴν ἐκεῖνα εἶπεν ὑπὲρ ὧν καὶ ἀφίκετο. ἀναστὰς οὖν ὁ Ἀρχίδαμος ὁ τῶν Λακεδαιμονίων βασιλεὺς "τί δ' ἂν" ἔφη "οὗτος ὑγιὲς εἴποι, ὃς οὐ μόνον ἐπὶ τῇ ψυχῇ τὸ ψεῦδος, ἀλλὰ καὶ ἐπὶ τῇ κεφαλῇ περιφέρει;" καὶ ἐξέωσε τὰ ὑπ' αὐτοῦ λεχθέντα, διαβάλλων τοῦ Χίου[1] τὸν τρόπον ἐξ ὧν ἑωρᾶτο.

21. Οὐκ ἀπηξίου Καῖσαρ ἐπὶ τὰς Ἀρίστωνος θύρας φοιτᾶν, Πομπήιος δὲ ἐπὶ τὰς Κρατίππου. οὐ γάρ, ἐπεὶ μέγα ἐδύναντο, ὑπερεφρόνουν τῶν τὰ μέγιστα αὐτοὺς ὀνῆσαι δυναμένων, ἀλλ' ἐδέοντο αὐτῶν, καίτοι τοσοῦτοι ὄντες τὴν ἀξίωσιν. οὐ γὰρ ἄρχειν ὡς ἔοικεν, ἀλλὰ καλῶς ἄρχειν ἐβούλοντο.

[1] Χίου Her.: Κείου codd.

before the Spartans, revealing his head as described, and explained the business for which he had come. Archidamus the Spartan king rose and said: "How could this man have anything sensible to say when he carries around falsehood not only in his soul but also on his head?" He rejected the proposals with a denunciation of the Chiot's character based on his appearance.

21. Caesar was not too proud to attend the school of Ariston, and Pompey that of Cratippus. Their great power did not cause them to despise men capable of conferring the greatest benefits on them. Instead, despite their standing, they came with a request. Their wish evidently was not to govern but to govern well.

Η

1. Ἔλεγε δήπου Σωκράτης περὶ τοῦ δαιμονίου τοῦ συνόντος αὐτῷ πρὸς Θεάγην καὶ Δημόδοκον καὶ πρὸς ἄλλους πολλούς. φωνὴν πολλάκις ἔφασκε ὁσίᾳ πομπῇ[1] ἐγκεκληρωμένην[2] αὐτῷ "ἥπερ ὅταν γένηται, ἀεί μοι" φησὶ "σημαίνει ὃ μέλλω πράττειν τούτου ἀποτροπήν, προτρέπει δὲ οὐδέποτε, καὶ αὖ πάλιν ἐάν τίς <μοι>"[3] φησὶ "τῶν φίλων ἀνακοινῶται ὑπέρ του,[4] καὶ ἐπιγένηται ἡ φωνὴ ἐκείνη, πάλιν ἀποτρέπει. καὶ ἐμοὶ μὲν αὕτη συμβουλεύει τοῦτο, ἐγὼ δὲ τῷ συμβουλευομένῳ μοι, καὶ οὐκ ἐῶ πράττειν, ἑπόμενος τῇ θείᾳ προρρήσει." παρείχετο δὲ μάρτυρα Χαρμίδην τὸν Γλαύκωνος· ἀνεκοινώσατο γὰρ αὐτῷ εἰ μέλλοι ἀσκήσειν <στάδιον>[5] εἰς Νεμέαν, καὶ εὐθὺς ἀπαρχομένου λέγειν <ἡ>[6] φωνὴ ἐπεγένετο. καὶ ὁ Σωκράτης τὸν Χαρμίδην διεκώλυσεν[7] ἔχεσθαι ὧν εἴχετο, [εἰπὼν][8] ὁ δὲ οὐκ ἐπείσθη· οὐ μὴν εἰς δέον ἀπήντησεν αὐτῷ ἡ σπουδή.

2. Ἵππαρχος ὁ Πεισιστράτου παῖς πρεσβύτατος ὢν τῶν Πεισιστράτου καὶ σοφώτατος ἦν Ἀθηναίων.

[1] ὁσίᾳ πομπῇ Faber: -ίαν -ὴν codd.
[2] ἐγκεκληρωμένην] συγκε- Wyttenbach

BOOK EIGHT

1. Socrates must have told Theages, Demodocus, and many others about the divine presence that kept him company. He often said that a sacred voice had been assigned to accompany him. "When this happens," he said, "it always tells me to avoid what I was proposing to do, but it never urges me to action. And on the other hand," he added, "if one of my friends confides in me about some matter and that voice speaks to me, once again it is a deterrent. It advises me in this way, and I pass on the advice to the friend who consulted me. I follow the divine instruction and forbid him to act." As an example he cited Charmides son of Glaucon, who had asked him if he should train for the Nemean games. As soon as he began to speak the voice intervened. Socrates tried to prevent Charmides from pursuing his project, but he would not listen and his efforts came to a disappointing end.[a]

2. Hipparchus son of Pisistratus was the oldest of his father's children and the wisest of the Athenians. He first

[a] This ch. follows Plato, *Theages* 128 de, closely.

[3] suppl. Kor. [4] *του* Per.: *τούτου* V: *τῶν* x
[5] suppl. Kühn [6] suppl. Her.
[7] *διεκώλυσεν*] *-νεν* Faber [8] del. Her.

οὗτος καὶ τὰ Ὁμήρου ἔπη πρῶτος ἐκόμισεν εἰς τὰς Ἀθήνας καὶ ἠνάγκασε τοὺς ῥαψῳδοὺς τοῖς Παναθηναίοις αὐτὰ ᾄδειν. καὶ ἐπ᾽ Ἀνακρέοντα δὲ τὸν Τήιον πεντηκόντορον ἔστειλεν, ἵνα αὐτὸν πορεύσῃ ὡς αὐτόν. Σιμωνίδην δὲ τὸν Κεῖον διὰ σπουδῆς ἄγων ἀεὶ περὶ αὐτὸν εἶχε, μεγάλοις δώροις ὡς τὸ εἰκὸς πείθων καὶ μισθοῖς· καὶ γὰρ ὡς ἦν φιλοχρήματος ὁ Σιμωνίδης, οὐδεὶς ἀντιφήσει. ἔργον δὲ ἦν ἄρα τούτῳ[1] τῷ Ἱππάρχῳ ἡ περὶ τοὺς πεπαιδευμένους σπουδή. καὶ ἐβούλετο ὑπὸ προσχήματι τῷ ἑαυτοῦ Ἀθηναίους παιδεύεσθαι καὶ βελτιόνων αὐτῶν[2] ὄντων ἄρχειν ἔσπευδεν· οὐκ ᾤετο γὰρ δεῖν οὐδενὶ φθονεῖν σοφίας, ἅτε ὢν καλὸς καὶ ἀγαθός. λέγει δὲ Πλάτων ταῦτα, εἰ δὴ ὁ Ἵππαρχος Πλάτωνός ἐστι τῷ ὄντι [μαθητής].[3]

3. Ὅτι Ἀττικὸν τοῦτο τὸ ἔθος, ὅταν ὁ βοῦς ἀποσφαγῇ, τῶν μὲν ἄλλων ἀποψηφίζονται, κρίνοντες ἕκαστον ἐν τῷ μέρει φόνου· καταγινώσκουσι δὲ τῆς μαχαίρας καὶ λέγουσι ταύτην ἀποκτεῖναι αὐτόν. καὶ ἐν ᾗ ταῦτα ἡμέρᾳ δρῶσι, Διπολίεια[4] τὴν ἑορτὴν καλοῦσι καὶ Βουφόνια.

4. Πολίαρχόν φασι τὸν Ἀθηναῖον εἰς τοσοῦτον προελθεῖν τρυφῆς, ὥστε καὶ κύνας καὶ ἀλεκτρυόνας

[1] τούτῳ] τοῦτο Faber [2] αὐτῶν] αὑτῶν Bevegni
[3] del. Faber [4] Διπολίεια Dilts: Διιπόλια codd.

[a] A common belief in antiquity was that Pisistratus deserved the credit for arranging performances of Homer at the Panathenaea; some held that he established a standard text.

introduced the poems of Homer to Athens and obliged the singers to perform them at the Panathenaea.[a] He also sent a ship for Anacreon of Teos, to transport him to Athens. He had a high regard for Simonides of Ceos and always had him in his circle, persuading him presumably with handsome gifts and rewards—for no one will deny that Simonides was keen on money. This Hipparchus made a point of seeking out cultivated men, and he wanted the Athenians to acquire culture through his own example, hoping to rule over an improved population. As he was a man of honour and good will, he did not think it right to begrudge anyone access to wisdom. Plato reports this, if indeed the *Hipparchus* is really by him.[b]

3. Note that the following is an Attic custom. When the ox is sacrificed,[c] they bring a case of murder against each participant and acquit them all but condemn the knife, saying that it killed the animal.[d] The day on which they perform these rites is known as the festival of Dipolieia and Bouphonia.[e]

4. The Athenian Poliarchus is reported to have lived so luxuriously that he arranged public burial for his favourite

[b] Modern critics also doubt the authenticity of the dialogue.

[c] The sacrifice took place on the 14th of Scirophorion.

[d] In Athenian law animals or inanimate objects which had caused death had to be tried at the Prytaneum, and if found guilty were expelled beyond the boundaries of Attica. See D. M. MacDowell, *Athenian Homicide Law in the Age of the Orators* (Manchester, 1963), pp. 85–89. Similar rules valid in other parts of Greece are reported by Pausanias, *Periegesis* 5.27.10 and 6.11.6.

[e] The names mean "festival of Zeus Polieus" (guardian of the city) and "sacrifice of the ox."

ἐκείνους οἷς ἔχαιρεν ἐκκομίζειν ἀποθανόντας δημοσίᾳ. καὶ ἐπὶ τὴν ἐκφορὰν αὐτῶν παρεκάλει τοὺς φίλους καὶ ἔθαπτεν αὐτοὺς πολυτελῶς καὶ ἐπιστήματα αὐτοῖς ἀναστήσας ἐπιγράμματα κατ' αὐτῶν ἐνεκόλαπτεν.

5. Ὅτι Νηλεὺς ὁ Κόδρου τῆς βασιλείας ἀμοιρήσας ἀπέλιπε τὰς Ἀθήνας διὰ τὸ τὴν Πυθίαν Μέδοντι τὴν ἀρχὴν περιάψαι εἰς ἀποικίαν στελλόμενος.[1] τῇ Νάξῳ δὲ προσωρμίσθη οὐχ ἑκών, ἀλλ' ὑπὸ χειμῶνος βιασθείς· ἀπᾶραι δὲ βουλόμενον καταπνέοντες ἐναντίοι ἄνεμοι διεκώλυον. ἀποροῦντι δὲ αὐτῷ ὑπὲρ τῶν ἐνεστώτων, οἱ μάντεις ἔφασαν δεῖν καθαρθῆναι τὸ στρατόπεδον, ὡς συμπλεόντων τινῶν[2] οὐ καθαρῶν τὰς χεῖρας. προσεποιήσατο δὴ καὶ αὐτὸς ἀποκτεῖναί τινα παῖδα καὶ δεῖσθαι καθαρμοῦ· καὶ αὐτὸς ἀνεχώρησε καὶ τοὺς ἄλλους ἔπεισε τοὺς συνειδότας ἑαυτοῖς. οὗ γενομένου καὶ γνωσθέντων ἐκείνων αὐτοὺς μὲν ἀπέλιπεν, οἱ δὲ ᾤκισαν τὴν Νάξον.

Νηλεὺς δὲ εἰς τὴν Ἰωνίαν ἀφίκετο, καὶ πρῶτον μὲν ᾤκισε Μίλητον, Κᾶρας ἐξελάσας καὶ Μυγδόνας καὶ Λέλεγας καὶ ἄλλους βαρβάρους . . .[3] ἀφ' ὧν αἱ δώδεκα πόλεις ἐκλήθησαν ἐν Ἰωνίᾳ. εἰσὶ δὲ αἵδε· Μίλητος Ἔφεσος Ἐρυθραὶ Κλαζομεναὶ Πριήνη Λέβεδος Τέως Κολοφὼν Μυοῦς Φώκαια Σάμος καὶ Χίος. καὶ ἄλλας δὲ πολλὰς ὕστερον ᾤκισε πόλεις ἐν τῇ ἠπείρῳ.

[1] στελλόμενος Scheffer: -μένῳ codd.

dogs and fighting cocks. He invited his friends to the funeral and buried the animals expensively, putting up tombstones in their honour and engraving inscriptions on them.[a]

5. Note that Neleus son of Codrus failed to become king and departed from Athens; as the Pythia had conferred power on Medon, he went off to found a colony. Involuntarily he put in at Naxos, forced by a storm, and when he wanted to leave, contrary winds blew to prevent him. The situation left him at a loss, and seers advised him to purify his force, on the ground that some people with unclean hands were sailing with the expedition. He personally pretended to have killed a child and to require purification. He himself withdrew and persuaded others with a bad conscience to do the same. When this was done and they were recognised he left them behind, and they settled on Naxos.

Neleus reached Ionia, and first of all settled in Miletus, driving out the Carians, Mygdones, Leleges, and other barbarians . . . after whom the twelve cities of Ionia were named. They are: Miletus, Ephesus, Erythrae, Clazomenae, Priene, Lebedos, Teos, Colophon, Myus, Phocaea, Samos, and Chios.[b] Later he founded many other cities on the mainland.

[a] Theophrastus, *Characters* 21.9, mocks the man of petty pride who sets up a tombstone in honour of his pet dog.

[b] The dodecapolis of Ionia is mentioned by Herodotus 7.95 and other sources. Its centre was on the promontory of Mycale, opposite Samos and not far from Priene.

---

[2] τινῶν x: πολλῶν V

[3] lacunam statuit Russell

6. Τῶν ἀρχαίων φασὶ Θρᾳκῶν μηδένα ἐπίστασθαι γράμματα· ἀλλὰ καὶ ἐνόμιζον αἴσχιστον εἶναι πάντες οἱ τὴν Εὐρώπην οἰκοῦντες βάρβαροι χρῆσθαι γράμμασιν. οἱ δὲ ἐν τῇ Ἀσίᾳ, ὡς λόγος, ἐχρῶντο αὐτοῖς μᾶλλον. ἔνθεν τοι καὶ τολμῶσι λέγειν μηδὲ τὸν Ὀρφέα σοφὸν γεγονέναι, Θρᾷκα ὄντα, ἀλλ' ἄλλως τοὺς μύθους αὐτοῦ κατεψεῦσθαι.[1] ταῦτα Ἀνδροτίων λέγει, εἴ τῳ πιστὸς ὑπὲρ τῆς ἀγραμματίας καὶ ἀπαιδευσίας Θρᾳκῶν τεκμηριῶσαι.

7. Ἀλέξανδρος ὅτε Δαρεῖον εἷλε, γάμους εἱστία καὶ ἑαυτοῦ καὶ τῶν φίλων. ἐνενήκοντα δὲ ἦσαν οἱ γαμοῦντες καὶ ἰσάριθμοι τούτοις οἱ θάλαμοι. ἦν δὲ ὁ ἀνδρὼν ὁ ὑποδεχόμενος καὶ ἑστιῶν αὐτοὺς ἑκατοντάκλινος· καὶ ἑκάστη κλίνη ἀργυρόπους ἦν, ἡ δὲ αὐτοῦ χρυσόπους, καὶ κεκόσμηντο πᾶσαι ἁλουργοῖς καὶ ποικίλοις ἱματίοις ὑφῆς βαρβαρικῆς μεγατίμου. συμπαρέλαβε δὲ εἰς τὸ συμπόσιον καὶ τοὺς ἰδιοξένους καὶ κατέκλινεν ἀντιπροσώπους ἑαυτῷ. ἐν δὲ τῇ αὐλῇ εἱστιῶντο αἵ τε ἄλλαι δυνάμεις, αἱ πεζαὶ καὶ αἱ ναυτικαὶ καὶ οἱ ἱππεῖς, καὶ αἱ πρεσβεῖαι δὲ εἱστιῶντο καὶ οἱ παρεπιδημοῦντες Ἕλληνες. καὶ ἐγένετο τὰ δεῖπνα πρὸς σάλπιγγα,[2] τὸ μὲν συγκλητικὸν μέλος ᾄδουσαν,[3] ὅτε αὐτοὺς ἐχρῆν παριέναι ἐπὶ τὴν δαῖτα, τὸ δὲ ἀνακλητικόν, ὅτε ἐσήμαινεν[4]

[1] κατεψεῦσθαι Per.: καταψεύσασθαι codd.

[2] πρὸς σάλπιγγα ex Athenaeo Scheffer: προσαλπιστά codd. [3] ᾄδουσαν scripsi: -σης x: ᾄδον V

[4] ἐσήμαινεν Kor.: -νον codd.

6. They say that among the ancient Thracians no one was literate. Indeed, all the barbarians inhabiting Europe thought it shameful to write. But, as tradition has it, those living in Asia were more inclined to do so. For this reason some people dare to maintain that even Orpheus was uncultured because he was a Thracian, and that the myths about him are idle falsehoods. This is stated by Androtion [FGrH 324 F 54 a], if he is a reliable guide to the illiteracy and lack of culture among the Thracians.[a]

7. When Alexander captured Darius he celebrated his own marriage and that of his friends. The number of people marrying was ninety, and the bridal chambers equal in number. The hall for the reception and banquet had a hundred couches. Each couch had silver feet, except his own, which had gold; they were all decorated with purple or embroidered cloth, of a weave much prized among the barbarians. He took his personal guests from foreign states to the banquet and had them seated facing him. In the courtyard there was a feast for the other forces, the infantry, marines, and cavalry. Ambassadors and Greeks resident locally were at the feast.[b] Dinner was regulated by trumpet calls; the signal for assembly was given when it was time to go in to dinner, and the signal for retreat

[a] Poems ascribed to Orpheus circulated in antiquity; it is perhaps surprising that this expression of scepticism by a fourth-century historian of Attica was not more widely shared.

[b] The general Greek contempt for barbarians can easily lead us into the mistaken view that Greeks would not consider living abroad. But a number of them had made their living in Persia in the fifth century B.C. See D. M. Lewis, *Sparta and Persia* (Leiden, 1977), p. 13.

ἀπαλλάσσεσθαι. πέντε δὲ ἡμέρας καθεξῆς τοὺς γάμους ἔθυεν. ἀφίκοντο δὲ καὶ μουσουργοὶ καὶ ὑποκριταί, οἱ μὲν κωμῳδίας οἱ δὲ τραγῳδίας, πάμπολλοι. ἦσαν δὲ καὶ ἐκ τῆς Ἰνδικῆς θαυματοποιοὶ διαπρέποντες, καὶ ἔδοξαν δὲ αὐτοὶ[1] κρατεῖν τῶν ἄλλων τῶν ἀλλαχόθεν.

8. Κίμων[2] ὁ Κλεωναῖος ἐξειργάσατο, φασί, τὴν τέχνην τὴν γραφικὴν ὑποφυομένην ἔτι καὶ ἀτέχνως ὑπὸ τῶν πρὸ αὐτοῦ καὶ ἀπείρως ἐκτελουμένην καὶ τρόπον τινὰ ἐν σπαργάνοις καὶ γάλαξιν οὖσαν. διὰ ταῦτά τοι καὶ μισθοὺς τῶν πρὸ αὐτοῦ πρῶτος ἔλαβεν ἁδροτέρους.

9. Ἀρχέλαον τὸν Μακεδόνων τύραννον (οὕτω γὰρ καὶ Πλάτων αὐτὸν ὀνομάζει, καὶ οὐ βασιλέα) τὰ παιδικὰ αὐτοῦ Κρατεύας ἐρασθεὶς τῆς τυραννίδος οὐδὲν ἧττον ἤπερ ἐκεῖνος τῶν παιδικῶν ἠράσθη, ἀπέκτεινε τὸν ἐραστήν [ὁ Κρατεύας Ἀρχέλαον],[3] ὡς τύραννός τε καὶ εὐδαίμων ἀνὴρ ἐσόμενος. τρεῖς δὲ ἢ τέτταρας ἡμέρας τὴν τυραννίδα κατασχὸν τὸ μειράκιον, πάλιν αὐτὸς ἐπιβουλευθεὶς ὑφ᾽ ἑτέρων ἐτελεύτησεν. εἴη δ᾽ ἂν[4] πρεπωδέστατον ἐπειπεῖν τῷδε τῷ Μακεδονικῷ δράματι τὸ ἔπος ἐκεῖνο·

τεύχων ὡς ἑτέρῳ τις ἑῷ κακὸν ἥπατι τεύχει.

[1] αὐτοὶ] οὗτοι Her.
[2] Κίμων e Plin. *N.H.* 35.36 Scheffer: Κόνων codd.
[3] del. Her.
[4] δ᾽ ἂν Kor.: δὲ codd.

when he gave instructions to leave. For five days in succession he celebrated the weddings. A great many artists and actors, of both tragedy and comedy, arrived; there were also outstanding Indian conjurers, and they were thought to be superior to the entertainers from elsewhere.[a]

8. Cimon of Cleonae, it is said, brought the art of painting to a high point.[b] It had been growing slowly, practised in simple and inexperienced style by his predecessors, one might say at the stage of a baby not yet weaned. That is how he was the first to receive greater rewards than his predecessors.

9. Archelaus the tyrant of Macedon—for that is what Plato calls him [*Alcibiades II,* 141 de], not king[c]—was killed by his favourite boy Crateuas, who fell in love with tyranny with the same intensity of feeling that Archelaus displayed to him as his favourite. Crateuas killed Archelaus on the assumption that he would become tyrant and enjoy great good fortune. But after three or four days in power the young man was in turn the victim of a plot and died at the hands of others. The most appropriate comment on this Macedonian episode would be "while preparing to hurt another man he dealt himself a blow to the liver."[d]

[a] The contents of this ch. may well derive from Athenaeus 538 BF.

[b] Cimon of Cleonae is thought to have worked ca. 500 B.C. One wonders whether Aelian and his contemporaries were in a position to see any of his work.

[c] Archelaus was king of Macedon 413–399 B.C.

[d] The verse is from Callimachus, *Aetia* I, fr. 2, line 5. Aelian does not often cite Hellenistic authors.

Ὅτι[1] διεψεύσατο αὐτῷ φασιν Ἀρχέλαος τῶν θυγατέρων μίαν δώσειν· ὅτε δὴ ἄλλῳ συνῴκισε τὴν παῖδα, ὑπεραγανακτήσας διέφθειρε τὸν Ἀρχέλαον.

10. Σόλωνα αἱρετὸν Ἀθηναῖοι προείλοντο ἄρχειν αὐτοῖς, οὐ γὰρ κληρωτὸν τοῦτον. ἐπεὶ δὲ ᾑρέθη, τά τε ἄλλα ἐκόσμησε τὴν πόλιν καὶ δὴ καὶ τοὺς νόμους τοὺς νῦν ἔτι φυλαττομένους συνέγραψεν αὐτοῖς. καὶ τότε ἐπαύσαντο οἱ Ἀθηναῖοι χρώμενοι τοῖς Δράκοντος· ἐκαλοῦντο δὲ ἐκεῖνοι θεσμοί. μόνους δὲ ἐφύλαξαν τοὺς φονικοὺς αὐτοῦ.

11. Οὐδὲν ἔτι θαυμάζομεν εἰ ἡ τῶν ἀνθρώπων φύσις θνητὴ οὖσα καὶ ἐφήμερος φθείρεσθαι αὐτοὺς ἀναγκάζει, ὅπου καὶ τοὺς ποταμοὺς ὁρῶμεν ἐπιλείποντας καὶ τῶν ὀρῶν δὲ τὰ ὑψηλότατα ἀκούομεν μειούμενα καὶ ἐκεῖνα. τὴν γοῦν Αἴτνην φασὶν οἱ πλέοντες ἐξ ἐλάττονος ὁρᾶν ἢ πρὸ τοῦ ἐβλέπετο· τὸ δὲ αὐτὸ τοῦτο καὶ τὸν Παρνασσὸν παθεῖν καὶ τὸν Ὄλυμπον τὸν Πιερικόν. οἱ δὲ ἔτι μᾶλλον δοκοῦντες τὴν τῶν ὅλων φύσιν κατεσκέφθαι λέγουσι καὶ τὸν κόσμον διαφθείρεσθαι αὐτόν.

12. Παράδοξόν γε, οὐ γάρ;[2] <ἀλλ'>[3] ἀληθές. ἐκπεσόντος Δημοσθένους ἐν Μακεδονίᾳ, Αἰσχίνης [δὲ][4] ὁ Ἀτρομήτου ὁ Κοθωκίδης καὶ ἐνευδοκίμει τοῖς Μακεδόσι καὶ πάμπολυ περιῆν τῶν πρέσβεων τῷ φρονήματι. αἰτία δὲ ἦν ἄρα τούτου τῷ Αἰσχίνῃ ἥ τε πρὸς Φίλιππον φιλία καὶ τὰ ἐξ αὐτοῦ δῶρα καὶ ὅτι

[1] <οἱ δὲ> ὅτι Kor.
[2] γὰρ] μὴν Gesner

They say that Archelaus had failed to honour a promise to let him marry one of his daughters; when Archelaus married the girl off to another man, Crateuas was enraged and killed him.

10. The Athenians elected Solon to govern them; he was not chosen by lot. After his election he attended to the affairs of the city in general and also drafted laws for it, which are still in force today.[a] It was then that the Athenians ceased to use the code of Draco; his laws were known as ordinances, and the only ones they retained related to murder.

11. We are no longer surprised that the nature of men, being mortal and ephemeral, compels them to perish. We see that rivers run dry, and we hear that even the highest mountains are reduced in height. Sailors report sighting Etna from a shorter distance than it used to be visible from. The very same thing is said about Parnassus and Pierian Olympus. Those who are credited with having investigated the nature of the world in more detail say that the cosmos itself is being destroyed.

12. Strange, is it not, but true. When Demosthenes lost his voice in Macedonia, Aeschines son of Atrometus, of the deme Cothocidae, was well regarded by the Macedonians and displayed far more confidence than the other members of the delegation.[b] The reason for this was his friendship with Philip, the gifts he received from him,

[a] An example of Aelian's lack of historical perspective, on which see the Introduction.

[b] The story of the embassy of 346 is narrated by Demosthenes' enemy Aeschines (2.34).

[3] suppl. Jens [4] del. Faber

πράως καὶ ἡδέως ἤκουεν αὐτοῦ ὁ Φίλιππος, μειλιχίῳ τῷ βλέμματι προσβλέπων καὶ ὑποφαίνων τὴν[1] ἐξ αὑτοῦ εὔνοιαν. ἅπερ οὖν πάντα ἐφολκὰ[2] ἦν εἰς τὴν παρρησίαν τῷ Αἰσχίνῃ καὶ τὴν τῶν λόγων εὔροιαν.

Οὐ μόνος δὲ τοῦτο ἔπαθε Δημοσθένης ἐν Μακεδονίᾳ, καίτοι δεινότατος ὢν εἰπεῖν, ἀλλὰ καὶ Θεόφραστος ὁ Ἐρέσιος. ἐξέπεσε γὰρ καὶ οὗτος ἐπὶ τῆς ἐξ Ἀρείου πάγου βουλῆς λέγων, καὶ ταύτην ἀπολογίαν προεφέρετο, ὅτι κατεπλάγη τὸ ἀξίωμα τοῦ συνεδρίου. πικρότατα οὖν ἀπήντησε καὶ ἑτοιμότατα πρὸς τοῦτον αὐτοῦ τὸν λόγον ὁ Δημοχάρης εἰπών· "ὦ Θεόφραστε, Ἀθηναῖοι ἦσαν ἀλλ' οὐχ οἱ δώδεκα θεοὶ οἱ δικάζοντες."

13. Ἀναξαγόραν τὸν Κλαζομένιόν φασι μὴ γελῶντά ποτε ὀφθῆναι μηδὲ[3] μειδιῶντα τὴν ἀρχήν. λέγουσι δὲ καὶ Ἀριστόξενον τῷ γέλωτι ἀνὰ κράτος πολέμιον γενέσθαι· Ἡράκλειτόν τε, ὅτι πάντα τὰ ἐν τῷ βίῳ ἔκλαεν.

14. Διογένης ὁ Σινωπεὺς ὅτε λοιπὸν ἐνόσει ἐπὶ θανάτῳ, ἑαυτὸν φέρων μόλις[4] ἔρριψε κατά τινος γεφυρίου πρὸς γυμνασίῳ ὄντος καὶ προσέταξε τῷ παλαιστροφύλακι, ἐπειδὰν αἴσθηται ἀποπεπνευκότα αὐτόν, ῥῖψαι εἰς τὸν Ἰλισσόν. οὕτως ἄρα ὀλίγον ἔμελε Διογένει καὶ θανάτου καὶ ταφῆς.

15. Ἐν Χαιρωνείᾳ τοὺς Ἀθηναίους ἡνίκα[5] ἐνίκησεν <ὁ>[6] Φίλιππος, ἐπαρθεὶς [δὲ][7] τῇ εὐπραγίᾳ ὅμως λογισμοῦ ἐκράτησε καὶ οὐχ ὕβρισε· καὶ διὰ ταῦτα ᾤετο δεῖν αὐτὸν ὑπομιμνήσκεσθαι ὑπό τινος

Philip's kind and patient willingness to listen to him; Philip's glance was sympathetic and displayed his good will. All these facts led Aeschines to speak freely and fluently.

Demosthenes in Macedonia was not the only person to have this experience, despite his great eloquence; it happened also to Theophrastus of Eresus. He failed in a speech before the Areopagus, and made the excuse that he was struck dumb by the prestige of the assembly. A tart and prompt reply was made by Demochares, who said "The jury were Athenians, Theophrastus, not the Twelve Gods."

13. They say that Anaxagoras of Clazomenae was never seen to laugh or to smile at all. Aristoxenus [fr. 7 W.] too was a determined opponent of laughter, while Heraclitus wept at the whole of human life.[a]

14. Diogenes of Sinope [fr. 301 M.], when suffering his last illness, dragged himself with difficulty to a bridge and threw himself down on it. This was near a gymnasium, and he told the guardian to throw his body into the Ilissus when he could see that he was dead. So little did Diogenes care about death and burial.

15. Philip had defeated the Athenians at Chaeronea. Encouraged by his success he nevertheless kept control of his faculties and did not become arrogant.[b] So he thought it necessary to be reminded by one of his slaves

[a] Compare 3.35 above, and for a philosopher of diametrically opposite habits 4.20. [b] Note the different story above at 6.1.

---

[1] τὴν huc traiecit Kor.: post αὐτοῦ (sic) codd. [2] ἐφολκὰ Gesner: ἐφόλκια codd. [3] μηδὲ Russell: μήτε codd. [4] μόλις Gesner: μόνον codd. [5] ἡνίκα Stobaeus 3.21.6: νίκῃ codd. [6] suppl. Stobaeus [7] δὲ om. Stobaeus, del. Her.

τῶν παίδων ἕωθεν ὅτι ἄνθρωπός ἐστι, καὶ προσέταξε τῷ παιδὶ τοῦτο ἔχειν ἔργον. καὶ οὐ πρότερον, φασίν, οὔτε αὐτὸς προῄει, οὔτε τις τῶν δεομένων αὐτοῦ παρ' αὐτὸν εἰσῄει, πρὶν τοῦτο αὐτῷ τὸν παῖδα ἑκάστης ἡμέρας ἐκβοῆσαι τρίς. ἔλεγε δὲ αὐτῷ· "Φίλιππε, ἄνθρωπος εἶ."[1]

16. Σόλων ὁ Ἐξηκεστίδου γέρων ἤδη ὢν ὑπώπτευε Πεισίστρατον τυραννίδι ἐπιθήσεσθαι, ἡνίκα παρῆλθεν εἰς τὴν ἐκκλησίαν τῶν Ἀθηναίων καὶ ᾔτει φρουρὰν ὁ Πεισίστρατος. ὁρῶν δὲ τοὺς Ἀθηναίους τῶν μὲν αὐτοῦ λόγων ῥᾳθύμως ἀκούοντας, προσέχοντας δὲ τῷ Πεισιστράτῳ, ἔφη ὅτι τῶν μέν ἐστι σοφώτερος, τῶν δὲ ἀνδρειότερος. ὁπόσοι μὲν[2] μὴ γινώσκουσιν ὅτι φυλακὴν λαβὼν περὶ τὸ σῶμα τύραννος ἔσται, ἀλλὰ τούτων μέν ἐστι σοφώτερος· ὁπόσοι δὲ γινώσκοντες ὑποσιωπῶσι, τούτων ἀνδρειότερός ἐστιν. ὁ δὲ λαβὼν τὴν δύναμιν τύραννος ἦν. καθεζόμενος δὲ Σόλων πρὸ τῆς οἰκίας, τὴν ἀσπίδα καὶ τὸ δόρυ παραθέμενος ἔλεγεν ὅτι ἐξώπλισται καὶ βοηθεῖ τῇ πατρίδι ᾗ δύναται, στρατηγὸς μὲν διὰ τὴν ἡλικίαν οὐκέτι ὤν, εὔνους δὲ διὰ τὴν γνώμην. ὅμως οὖν[3] Πεισίστρατος, εἴτε αἰδοῖ τῇ πρὸς τὸν ἄνδρα καὶ τὴν σοφίαν αὐτοῦ, εἴτε καὶ μνήμῃ τῶν ἐφ' ἡλικίας (λέγεται γὰρ αὐτοῦ[4] παιδικὰ γενέσθαι), οὐδέν γε ἔδρασε κακὸν Σόλωνα.

Ὁ δ' οὖν Σόλων ὀλίγῳ ὕστερον ὑπέργηρως ὢν τὸν βίον ἐτελεύτησεν, ἐπὶ σοφίᾳ καὶ ἀνδρείᾳ μεγάλην ἀπολιπὼν δόξαν. καὶ ἀνέστησαν αὐτῷ χαλκῆν

early in the morning that he was a human being, and he assigned this task to the slave. He would not go out himself, they say, or let any petitioner in to see him, until the slave had called out this daily message to him three times. The slave said "Philip, you are a human being."

16. In his old age Solon son of Execestides suspected Pisistratus of wishing to become tyrant when the latter entered the Athenian assembly and asked for a bodyguard. Seeing that the Athenians paid little attention to his own words, whereas they listened to Pisistratus, he described him as more intelligent than some and bolder than others. Whoever does not recognise that a man who obtains a bodyguard will become tyrant—the man is wiser than them; and as for those who do recognise the fact and say nothing—he is bolder than them. Pisistratus obtained power and was tyrant. Solon sat in front of his house with shield and spear and said that he had taken up arms in defence of his country to the best of his ability, being unable to command a force on grounds of age, but loyal in spirit. However, Pisistratus did Solon no harm, whether out of respect for the man and his wisdom, or because of recollections of youth—he is said to have been Solon's favourite boy.

Shortly afterwards Solon died at a very advanced age, leaving behind him a great reputation for wisdom and bravery. They put up a bronze statue of him in the main

---

[1] *ἑκάστης ἡμέρας* et *ἔλεγε . . . εἶ* del. Her.
[2] *μὲν* <*γὰρ*> Her.
[3] <*δ'*> *οὖν* Her.
[4] *αὐτοῦ* Faber: *αὐτὸν* codd.

εἰκόνα ἐν τῇ ἀγορᾷ· ἀλλὰ καὶ ἔθαψαν αὐτὸν δημοσίᾳ παρὰ τὰς πύλας πρὸς τῷ τείχει ἐν δεξιᾷ εἰσιόντων, καὶ περιῳκοδόμητο αὐτῷ ὁ τάφος.

17. Ὅτι Σκύθης ὁ Ἰνυκῖνος[1] ὁ τῶν Ζαγκλαίων μόναρχος ἀνέβη εἰς Ἀσίαν παρὰ βασιλέα Δαρεῖον. καὶ αὐτὸν ἐνόμισε <Δαρεῖος>[2] πάντων δικαιότατον ἀνδρῶν εἶναι, ὅσοι ἐκ τῆς Ἑλλάδος παρ᾽ αὐτὸν ἀνέβησαν, ὅτι παραιτησάμενος βασιλέα ἀφίκετο εἰς Σικελίαν καὶ πάλιν ἐκ Σικελίας παρὰ βασιλέα ὀπίσω. τοῦτο δὲ Δημοκήδης ὁ Κροτωνιάτης οὐκ ἐποίησε, καὶ διὰ τοῦτο Δαρεῖος ὑπὲρ αὐτοῦ φλαύρως ἔλεγεν, ἀπατεῶνα λέγων καὶ ἀνθρώπων κάκιστον. ὁ οὖν Σκύθης ἐν Πέρσαις μέγα ὄλβιος ὢν γήρᾳ κατέστρεψε τὸν βίον.

18. Εὔθυμος ὁ Λοκρὸς τῶν ἐν Ἰταλίᾳ πύκτης ἀγαθὸς ἦν, ῥώμῃ τε σώματος πεπίστευται[3] θαυμασιώτατος γενέσθαι· λίθον γὰρ μεγέθει μέγιστον δεικνύουσι Λοκροί, ὃν ἐκόμισε καὶ ἔθηκε πρὸ τῶν θυρῶν. καὶ τὸν ἐν Τεμέσῃ ἥρωα φόρους πραττόμενον παρὰ τῶν προσοίκων ἔπαυσεν· ἀφικόμενος γὰρ εἰς τὸ ἱερὸν αὐτοῦ, ὅπερ ἄβατον ἦν τοῖς πολλοῖς,

[1] Ἰνυκῖνος ex Herodoto Scheffer: ὁ νύκινος V: οἰνύκινος x
[2] ex Herodoto suppl. Per.
[3] πεπίστευται anonymus: -ευτο codd.

---

[a] According to Pausanias, *Periegesis* 1.16.1, there was a bronze statue of Solon in front of the Stoa Poikile.

[b] This ch. derives from Herodotus 6.24, except that the tale of Democedes is told by the same author at 3.130–137.

square, and buried him at public expense by the gates in the city wall, on the right as one enters.[a] A wall was built round the tomb.

17. Note that Scythes of Inycus, monarch of Zancle, travelled into Asia to see king Darius. The latter thought him the most equitable of all the Greeks who had come to visit him. He obtained permission from the king to go to Sicily and then returned again from Sicily to the court. But Democedes of Croton did not do this, and so Darius spoke unfavourably of him, calling him a cheat and the most evil of men. So Scythes lived out his old age in Persia in great wealth.[b]

18. Euthymus from Locri in Italy was a good boxer and is believed to have had the most remarkable physical strength.[c] The Locrians show an enormous stone which he carried and put down outside his front door. He put a stop to the hero of Temesa who exacted taxes from his neighbours.[d] Going to the sanctuary, which was out of

[c] At Locri archaeologists have discovered a cult centre in honour of Euthymus. He was an Olympic victor of the early fifth century B.C., and his story is told by Callimachus, *Aetia* IV, fr. 98–99 Pf., and by Pausanias, *Periegesis* 6.6.4–11; the base of the statue mentioned in that account is still extant. See P. M. Fraser, *Ptolemaic Alexandria* II (Oxford, 1972), p. 1072, n. 353.

[d] Strabo 6.1.5 (255) says that there was a temple at Temesa (Tempsa) near Locri in honour of the hero Polites, the companion of Odysseus who was treacherously murdered; he was thought of as a malign presence and the local inhabitants collected tribute for him. For the site see M. Manfredi Gigliotti, ΤΕΜΨΑ–ΤΕΜΗΣΗ, *Memorie storiche sull' antica città di Temesa, con particolare riguardo all' individuazione del suo sito* (Cosenza, 1994).

διηγωνίσατο πρὸς αὐτὸν καὶ ἠνάγκασεν ὧνπερ ἐσύλησεν ἀποτῖσαι πλείω. ἐντεῦθέν τοι καὶ διέρρευσεν[1] ἡ παροιμία ἡ λέγουσα ἐπὶ τῶν ἀλυσιτελῶς τι κερδαινόντων ὅτι αὐτοῖς ἀφίξεται ὁ ἐν Τεμέσῃ ἥρως. λέγουσι δὲ τὸν αὐτὸν Εὔθυμον καταβάντα ἐπὶ τὸν Καικῖνον ποταμὸν ὅς ἐστι πρὸ τῆς τῶν Λοκρῶν πόλεως ἀφανισθῆναι.

19. Ὅτι τοῦτο ἐπιγέγραπται Ἀναξαγόρᾳ·[2]

ἐνθάδ᾽ ὁ πλεῖστον ἀληθείας ἐπὶ τέρμα περήσας
οὐρανίου κόσμου κεῖται Ἀναξαγόρας.

Ὅτι καὶ βωμὸς αὐτῷ ἵσταται[3] καὶ ἐπιγέγραπται ᾗ μὲν Νοῦ ᾗ[4] δὲ Ἀληθείας.

[1] διέρρευσεν Her.: ἔρρ- codd.

[2] ὅτι . . . Ἀναξαγόρᾳ d: ἐπιτύμβιον Ἀναξαγόρου V: om. gab

[3] βωμὸς . . . ἵσταται] βωμὼ . . . ἵστατον Gesner

[4] ᾗ . . . ᾗ dubitanter scripsi: ὁ . . . ὁ codd.: <ὡς> οἱ . . . οἱ Kranz post Kor.

bounds to most people, he fought the hero and compelled him to repay with interest what he had plundered. This is the source of the proverb which describes those who make a useless profit: they will suffer[a] as the hero of Temesa. It is said that the same Euthymus went down to the river Caecinus,[b] which runs past the city of Locri, and disappeared.

19. Note that the epitaph of Anaxagoras runs: "Here lies Anaxagoras, the man who went furthest towards the frontier of truth about the celestial world."[c] Note that an altar was erected to him with an inscription: on one side "To Intellect," on the other "To Truth."[d]

[a] I have translated as the context requires; the Greek appears to say "will encounter the hero" and should probably be emended.

[b] Now the Portigliola.

[c] The couplet is also known from Diogenes Laertius 2.15 and the *Greek Anthology* 7.94.

[d] Aelian anachronistically imagines an altar (or, if Gesner was right, a pair of altars) inscribed with Anaxagoras' two nicknames "Mind" and "Truth." The interpretation of the passage is made very difficult by the uncertainty of the Greek text.

Θ

1. Ἱέρωνά φασι τὸν Συρακούσιον φιλέλληνα γενέσθαι καὶ τιμῆσαι παιδείαν ἀνδρειότατα. καὶ ὡς ἦν προχειρότατος εἰς τὰς εὐεργεσίας λέγουσι· προθυμότερον γὰρ αὐτόν φασι χαρίζεσθαι ἢ τοὺς αἰτοῦντας λαμβάνειν. ἦν δὲ καὶ τὴν ψυχὴν ἀνδρειότατος. ἀβασκάνως[1] δὲ καὶ τοῖς ἀδελφοῖς συνεβίωσε τρισὶν οὖσι, πάνυ σφόδρα ἀγαπήσας αὐτοὺς καὶ ὑπ' αὐτῶν φιληθεὶς ἐν τῷ μέρει. τούτῳ, φασί, καὶ Σιμωνίδης συνεβίωσε καὶ Πίνδαρος, καὶ οὐκ ὤκνησέ γε Σιμωνίδης βαρὺς ὢν ὑπὸ γήρως πρὸς αὐτὸν ἀφικέσθαι· ἦν μὲν γὰρ καὶ φύσει φιλάργυρος ὁ Κεῖος, προὔτρεπε δὲ αὐτὸν καὶ πλέον ἡ τοῦ Ἱέρωνος φιλοδωρία, φασίν.

2. Ὅτι ἐν Αἰγίνῃ ἐξ Ὀλυμπίας αὐθημερὸν διηγγέλη ἡ νίκη τοῦ Ταυροσθένους τῷ πατρὶ αὐτοῦ ὑπὸ φάσματος, φασίν. ἄλλοι δέ φασι περιστερὰν τὸν Ταυροσθένην ἐπαγαγέσθαι[2] ἀπολιποῦσαν τοὺς ἑαυτῆς νεοττοὺς ὑγροὺς ἔτι καὶ ἀπτῆνας, νικήσαντα δὲ ἀφεῖναι τὴν πελειάδα, προσάψαντα πορφύραν

[1] ἀβασκάνως Dilts: ἀβασανίστως codd.
[2] ἐπαγαγέσθαι Her.: ἐπάγεσθαι codd.

BOOK NINE

1. Hieron of Syracuse, they say, was a philhellene with a great enthusiasm for culture. And they say he was very quick to perform generous acts, being more anxious to confer favours than petitioners were to take them. In addition he was a man of very bold spirit. He lived with three brothers without strained relations, showing great affection for them and loved by them in turn.[a] Simonides and Pindar, they say, lived with him; and Simonides, weighed down by his years, did not hesitate to join him.[b] The man from Ceos was by nature keen to make money, but it is reported that Hieron's generosity was a greater inducement.

2. Note that, according to the story, the victory of Taurosthenes at Olympia was announced to his father in Aegina on the same day by a vision. Others say that Taurosthenes took with him a pigeon that had left its chicks, still moist and featherless, and when he won he released the bird, attaching to it a scrap of purple cloth. The bird

[a] Hieron's relations with his brothers were not in fact amicable at all times.

[b] For Hieron's ability to attract these poets see 4.15 above and 12.25.

αὐτῇ· τὴν δὲ ἐπειγομένην πρὸς τοὺς νεοττοὺς ἀπαυθημερίσαι ἐκ Πίσης εἰς Αἴγιναν.

3. Ὅτι διέθρυπτε τοὺς ἑταίρους Ἀλέξανδρος, τρυφᾶν ἐπιχωρῶν αὐτοῖς, εἴ γε καὶ Ἅγνων χρυσοῦς ἥλους ἐν ταῖς κρηπῖσιν ἐφόρει. Κλεῖτος δὲ εἴποτε μέλλοι τισὶ χρηματίζειν, ἐπὶ πορφυρῶν εἱμάτων βαδίζων[1] τοὺς δεομένους προσίετο. Περδίκκᾳ δὲ καὶ Κρατερῷ φιλογυμναστοῦσιν ἠκολούθουν διφθέραι σταδιαῖαι τὸ μέγεθος, ὑφ᾿ αἷς[2] περιλαμβάνοντες τόπον εὐμεγέθη ἐν ταῖς καταστρατοπεδείαις ἐγυμνάζοντο. εἵπετο δὲ αὐτοῖς καὶ πολλὴ κόνις δι᾿ ὑποζυγίων, εἰς τὰ γυμνάσια λυσιτελὴς οὖσα. Λεοννάτῳ δὲ καὶ Μενελάῳ φιλοθηροῦσιν αὐλαῖαι σταδίων ἑκατὸν ἠκολούθουν.

Αὐτῷ δὲ Ἀλεξάνδρῳ ἡ μὲν σκηνὴ ἦν κλινῶν ἑκατόν, χρυσοῖ δὲ κίονες πεντήκοντα διειλήφεσαν αὐτὴν καὶ τὸν ὄροφον αὐτῆς ἀνεῖχον, αὐτὸς δὲ ὁ ὄροφος διάχρυσος ἦν καὶ ἐκπεπόνητο ποικίλμασι πολυτελέσι. καὶ πρῶτοι μὲν Πέρσαι πεντακόσιοι οἱ καλούμενοι μηλοφόροι περὶ αὐτὴν ἐντὸς[3] εἱστήκεσαν πορφυρᾶς καὶ μηλίνας ἠσθημένοι στολάς· ἐπ᾿ αὐτοῖς δὲ τοξόται χίλιοι, φλόγινα ἐνδεδυκότες καὶ ὑσγινοβαφῆ· πρὸ δὲ τούτων οἱ ἀργυράσπιδες πεντακόσιοι[4] Μακεδόνες. ἐν μέσῃ δὲ τῇ σκηνῇ χρυσοῦς ἐτίθετο δίφρος καὶ ἐπ᾿ αὐτῷ καθήμενος Ἀλέξανδρος ἐχρη-

[1] *βαδίζων*] *διαπεριπατῶν* Athenaeus 539 E: *καθίζων* H. Richards [2] *ὑφ᾿ αἷς* ex Athenaeo Her.: *ἀφ᾿ ὧν* x (deficit V)

[3] *ἐντὸς* codd. et Athenaeus: *ἐκτὸς* Kor.

[4] *πεντακόσιοι* VΦ Athenaeus: *ἑκατὸν* x

made haste to return to its chicks and reached Aegina from Pisa within the day.[a]

3. Note that Alexander spoiled his friends by allowing them excessive luxury, if it is true that Hagnon had gold nails in his boots, and Clitus when about to transact business walked on purple cloth to receive petitioners. Perdiccas and Craterus were keen on exercise, and were equipped with tents of leather a stade in length, and with these they took over a substantial area in the camp in order to perform their exercises.[b] A great deal of sand, useful for gymnastics, was transported for them by pack animals. Leonnatus and Menelaus, who enjoyed hunting, had nets a hundred stades long.

Alexander's own tent could accommodate a hundred beds. Fifty gold pillars divided it and supported the roof, which was gilded and expensively embroidered. Inside it stood in line first of all five hundred Persians, called the apple bearers, wearing cloaks of purple and quince yellow;[c] then came a thousand archers dressed in flame colour and scarlet. In front of these were the five hundred Macedonians with silver shields. In the middle of the tent was a golden throne, on which Alexander sat to transact

[a] The victory of Taurosthenes, mentioned also by Pausanias, *Periegesis* 6.9.3, can be dated to 444 B.C. The distance between Olympia and Aegina is about 160 km. and the bird might have reached its destination in a few hours. This appears to be the first recorded use of the carrier pigeon in Greece.

[b] It may be that the skins were used to make a kind of fence, to ensure some privacy, rather than a complete tent.

[c] Athenaeus 514 B says that there were a thousand of these guards; they had a golden apple (or quince?) as an ornament on their spears.

μάτιζε, περιεστώτων αὐτῷ πανταχόθεν τῶν σωματοφυλάκων. περιῄει δὲ τὴν σκηνὴν περίβολος, ἔνθα ἦσαν Μακεδόνες χίλιοι καὶ Πέρσαι μύριοι. καὶ οὐδεὶς ἐτόλμα ῥᾳδίως προσελθεῖν αὐτῷ· πολὺ γὰρ ἦν τὸ ἐξ αὐτοῦ δέος ἀρθέντος ὑπὸ φρονήματος καὶ τύχης εἰς τυραννίδα.

4. Πολυκράτης ὁ Σάμιος ἐν Μούσαις ἦν καὶ Ἀνακρέοντα ἐτίμα τὸν Τήιον καὶ διὰ σπουδῆς ἦγε καὶ ἔχαιρεν αὐτῷ καὶ τοῖς ἐκείνου μέλεσιν. οὐκ ἐπαινῶ δὲ αὐτοῦ τὴν τρυφήν. Ἀνακρέων ἐπῄνεσε Σμερδίην θερμότερον τὰ παιδικὰ Πολυκράτους, εἶτα ἥσθη τὸ μειράκιον τῷ ἐπαίνῳ, καὶ τὸν Ἀνακρέοντα ἠσπάζετο σεμνῶς εὖ μάλα, ἐρῶντα τῆς ψυχῆς, ἀλλ᾿ οὐ τοῦ σώματος· μὴ γάρ τις ἡμῖν διαβαλλέτω πρὸς θεῶν τὸν ποιητὴν τὸν Τήιον, μηδ᾿ ἀκόλαστον εἶναι λεγέτω. ἐζηλοτύπησε δὲ Πολυκράτης ὅτι τὸν Σμερδίην ἐτίμησε καὶ ἑώρα τὸν ποιητὴν ὑπὸ τοῦ παιδὸς ἀντιφιλούμενον, καὶ ἀπέκειρε τὸν παῖδα ὁ Πολυκράτης, ἐκεῖνον μὲν αἰσχύνων, οἰόμενος δὲ λυπεῖν Ἀνακρέοντα. ὁ δὲ οὐ προσεποιήσατο αἰτιᾶσθαι τὸν Πολυκράτη σωφρόνως καὶ ἐγκρατῶς, μετήγαγε δὲ τὸ ἔγκλημα ἐπὶ τὸ μειράκιον ἐν οἷς ἐπεκάλει τόλμαν αὐτῷ καὶ ἀμαθίαν ὁπλισαμένῳ κατὰ τῶν ἑαυτοῦ τριχῶν. τὸ δὲ ᾆσμα τὸ ἐπὶ τῷ πάθει τῆς κόμης Ἀνακρέων ᾀσάτω· ἐμοῦ γὰρ αὐτὸς ἄμεινον ᾄσεται.

5. Θεμιστοκλῆς Ἱέρωνα ἥκοντα εἰς Ὀλυμπίαν,[1] Ὀλυμπίων ἀγομένων, ἵππους ἄγοντα εἶρξε τῆς ἀγω-

[1] Ὀλυμπίαν Kühn: -πια codd.

business, surrounded on all sides by bodyguards. An enclosure wall around the tent was manned by a thousand Macedonians and ten thousand Persians. No one dared approach him without good reason, as he aroused great fear; his pride and good fortune had raised him to the position of a tyrant.[a]

4. Polycrates of Samos was devoted to the Muses. He honoured Anacreon of Teos, and took him seriously, enjoying both his company and his poems. But I cannot applaud the tyrant's extravagant habits. Anacreon was warm in his praises for Smerdies, Polycrates' favourite boy. The youth was delighted by the compliments and greeted Anacreon, who was in love with his soul but not his body, in very formal style. Let no one, by the gods, utter in our hearing accusations against the poet from Teos or say that he was guilty of indecency. But Polycrates was jealous of his regard for Smerdies and because he could see the poet's friendship returned by the boy. Polycrates had the boy's hair cut off, which humiliated him and was intended to pain Anacreon. The latter displayed moderation and self-control by pretending not to criticise Polycrates; instead he blamed the youth and accused him of arrogance and bad behaviour, and of taking the shears to his own hair.[b] Let Anacreon [fr. 69 P.] sing his poem about the fate of the hair—he will sing it better than I can.

5. When Hieron came to Olympia for the festival, driving his horses, Themistocles excluded him from the

[a] Athenaeus 539 CF is probably the source of this ch.

[b] The Greek is difficult here; it seems to indicate that Smerdies brought disaster upon himself by being too attractive.

νίας εἰπὼν τὸν μὴ μεταλαβόντα τοῦ μεγίστου τῶν κινδύνων τῶν πανηγύρεων μεταλαμβάνειν μὴ δεῖν· καὶ ἐπῃνέθη Θεμιστοκλῆς.

6. Ὅτι Περικλῆς ἐν τῷ λοιμῷ τοὺς παῖδας ἀποβαλὼν ἀνδρειότατα τὸν θάνατον αὐτῶν ἤνεγκε καὶ πάντας Ἀθηναίους εὐθυμότερον ἔπεισε τοὺς τῶν φιλτάτων θανάτους φέρειν.

7. Ἡ Ξανθίππη ἔφη[1] μυρίων μεταβολῶν τὴν πόλιν <καὶ αὐτοὺς>[2] κατασχουσῶν ἐν πάσαις ὅμοιον τὸ Σωκράτους πρόσωπον καὶ προϊόντος ἐκ τῆς οἰκίας καὶ ἐπανιόντος ἀεὶ θεᾶσθαι·[3] ἥρμοστο γὰρ πρὸς πάντα ἐπιεικῶς, καὶ ἦν ἵλεως ἀεὶ τὴν διάνοιαν καὶ λύπης ὑπεράνω πάσης καὶ φόβου κρείττων παντὸς ὤν.[4]

8. Ὁ νέος Διονύσιος εἰς τὴν τῶν Λοκρῶν πόλιν παριὼν (εἴ γε [ἡ][5] Δωρὶς ἡ μήτηρ αὐτοῦ Λοκρὶς ἦν) τοὺς οἴκους τῶν μεγίστων τῶν ἐν τῇ πόλει καταλαμβάνων ῥόδοις καὶ ἑρπύλλοις καὶ ἄλλοις ἄνθεσι καταστρωννὺς τὰς τῶν Λοκρῶν θυγατέρας μετεπέμπετο καὶ συνῆν αὐταῖς ἀκολαστότατα. ὑπὲρ δὴ τούτου ἔτισε δίκην· ἐπειδὴ γὰρ αὐτοῦ ἡ τυραννὶς κατελύθη ὑπὸ Δίωνος, ἐνταῦθα οἱ Λοκροὶ τὴν γυναῖκα τοῦ Διονυσίου καὶ τὰς θυγατέρας κατεπόρνευσαν, καὶ ἀνέδην αὐταῖς ἐνύβριζον πάντες, μάλιστα οἱ προσήκοντες ταῖς παρθένοις ταῖς ὑπὸ Διονυσίου διεφθαρμέναις. ἡνίκα δὲ διακορεῖς ἐγένοντο ὑβρί-

[1] ἡ Ξανθίππη ἔφη Stobaeus 4.44.77: ἔλεγεν ἡ Ξανθίππη ὡς fere codd.

contest, saying that the man who had not shared the greatest dangers should not take part in the festivals. And Themistocles won approval.[a]

6. Note that Pericles, who lost his sons in the plague, bore their death very bravely, and persuaded all the Athenians to accept with better humour the deaths of their dearest friends.

7. Xanthippe used to say that, though innumerable vicissitudes had overtaken the city and themselves, she saw Socrates always with the same expression on his face both when he left the house and when he returned. He preserved an equable temperament in all circumstances and was always serene in spirit, superior to all pain and beyond the reach of any fear.

8. When Dionysius the Younger arrived in Locri—his mother Doris was a Locrian—he requisitioned the houses of the most important men in the town,[b] covered the floors with roses, tufted thyme, and other flowers, and summoned the daughters of the Locrians, with whom he behaved in the most abominable fashion. But he paid the penalty for this. When his tyranny was overthrown by Dion, the Locrians forced Dionysius' wife and daughters into prostitution. Everyone treated them with utter contempt, especially the relatives of the girls who had been raped by Dionysius. When they became bored with this

[a] Hieron had not contributed to the Greek effort in the wars against Persia. [b] In Athenaeus' version of this story we find instead "the biggest house in the city."

---

[2] praebet Stobaeus: malim <καὶ τοὺς ἀστοὺς>
[3] ἀεὶ θεᾶσθαι] θεάσασθαι Stobaeus
[4] ὢν del. Her. [5] del. Her.

ζοντες, κεντοῦντες αὐτὰς ὑπὸ τοῖς ὄνυξι τοῖς τῶν χειρῶν βελόναις ἀπέκτειναν. τὰ δὲ ὀστᾶ κατέκοψαν ἐν ὅλμοις, καὶ τὰ κρέα τῶν ὀστῶν ἀφελόντες ἐπηράσαντο τοῖς μὴ γευσαμένοις αὐτῶν· εἰ δέ τι περιελείφθη ἐξ αὐτῶν, κατεπόντωσαν. ὁ δὲ ἐν Κορίνθῳ πολλαῖς καὶ ποικίλαις χρησάμενος βίου μεταβολαῖς διὰ τὴν ὑπερβάλλουσαν ἀπορίαν, τελευταῖον δὲ μητραγυρτῶν καὶ κρούων τύμπανα καὶ καταυλούμενος τὸν βίον κατέστρεψεν.

9. Δημήτριος ὁ Φαληρεὺς[1] [ἥρει τὰς πόλεις καὶ][2] τῇ ἑαυτοῦ τρυφῇ καταχρώμενος χίλια μὲν καὶ διακόσια τάλαντα πρόσοδον ἑαυτῷ περιεποιήσατο καθ' ἕκαστον ἔτος καὶ ἐκ τούτων ὀλίγα μὲν εἰς τὸ στρατόπεδον ἐδαπάνα, τὰ δὲ λοιπὰ εἰς τὴν ἀκολασίαν τὴν ἑαυτοῦ. μύροις τε ἐρραίνετο [καὶ][3] αὐτῷ τὸ δάπεδον καὶ καθ' ἑκάστην ἔτους ὥραν τὰ ἐνακμάζοντα τῶν ἀνθέων [ταῦτα][4] ὑπεσπείρετο αὐτῷ, ἵνα κατ' αὐτῶν βαδίζῃ. ἦν δὲ καὶ πρὸς γυναῖκας ἀκόλαστος καὶ νεανικοῖς ἔρωσιν ἐπεχείρει. ἔμελε δὲ αὐτῷ καὶ καλῷ εἶναι εὐθετίζοντι τὴν τρίχα καὶ ξανθιζομένῳ καὶ ὑπαλειφομένῳ τὸ πρόσωπον παιδέρωτι. καὶ τοῖς ἄλλοις δὲ ἐχρίετο[5] ἀλείμμασι, προσφιλοτιμούμενος τῇ ῥᾳθυμίᾳ.

10. Ὁ Πλάτων, νοσεροῦ χωρίου λεγομένου εἶναι τῆς Ἀκαδημίας καὶ συμβουλευόντων αὐτῷ ἰατρῶν εἰς τὸ Λύκειον μετοικῆσαι, οὐκ ἠξίωσεν εἰπών· "ἀλλ' ἔγωγε οὐκ ἂν οὐδὲ εἰς τὰ ἄκρα τὰ τοῦ Ἄθω μετῴκησα ἂν ὑπὲρ τοῦ μακροβιώτερος γενέσθαι."

they killed them by pushing the pins of brooches under their fingernails.[a] They crushed their bones in mortars, stripping the flesh off the bones, and uttered a curse against anyone who would not eat it. Any remnants of the bodies were thrown into the sea. In Corinth Dionysius went through a great variety of experiences in extreme poverty, but ended his days as a mendicant priest of Cybele, playing the drums and accompanied by the aulos.[b]

9. Demetrius of Phalerum was given to very luxurious habits, and acquired an income of 1,200 talents a year. Of this he spent a little on his army, and the rest on his own extravagance. He had the floor sprinkled with perfume, and at each period of the year the flowers that were in season were scattered before him so that he could walk on them. He was uncontrollable in his behaviour to women and indulged in affairs with young men. He took care of his appearance, arranging his hair and dying it blond. He applied rouge to his face and used other cosmetics, taking a great deal of pride in his effeminacy.[c]

10. Though the Academy was said to be an unhealthy spot, and doctors advised a move to the Lyceum, Plato refused, saying "I would not even move to the summit of mount Athos in order to enjoy a longer life."[d]

[a] The death of the children was mentioned above at 6.12.

[b] The source of this ch. is apparently Athenaeus 541 CE.

[c] Athenaeus 542 CD is Aelian's source.

[d] The inhabitants of Athos enjoyed a reputation for longevity; see Lucian, *Macrobii* 5, and Pomponius Mela 2.2.32.

---

[1] *Φαληρεὺς* ex Athenaeo 542 C Dilts: *Πολιορκητὴς* codd.

[2] del. Dilts [3] del. Kor. [4] *ταῦτα* del. Her.: *πάντα* Kor.

[5] *ἐχρίετο* ex Athenaeo Kor.: *ἐχρῆτο* codd.

11. Παρράσιος ὁ ζωγράφος ὅτι μὲν πορφυρίδα ἐφόρει καὶ χρυσοῦν στέφανον περιέκειτο μαρτυροῦσι καὶ ἄλλοι καὶ τὰ ἐπιγράμματα δὲ ἐπὶ πολλῶν εἰκόνων αὐτοῦ· ἠγωνίσατο δέ ποτε ἐν Σάμῳ, συνέτυχε δὲ ἀντιπάλῳ [οὐ][1] κατὰ πολὺ ἐνδεεστέρῳ αὐτοῦ εἶτα ἡττήθη. τὸ δὲ γράμμα[2] ἦν αὐτῷ, ὁ Αἴας ὑπὲρ τῶν ὅπλων τῶν Ἀχιλλέως ἀγωνισάμενος πρὸς τὸν Ὀδυσσέα. ἡττηθεὶς δὲ εὖ μάλα ἀστείως ἀπεκρίνατο πρὸς τὸν συναχθόμενον αὐτῷ τῶν ἑταίρων ὁ Παρράσιος· ἔφη γὰρ αὐτὸς μὲν ὑπὲρ τῆς ἥττης ὀλίγον φροντίζειν, συνάχθεσθαι δὲ τῷ παιδὶ τοῦ Τελαμῶνος δεύτερον τοῦτο ὑπὲρ τῶν αὐτῶν ἡττηθέντι. κατεῖχε δὲ καὶ σκίπωνα χρυσᾶς ἕλικας ἔχοντα περιερπούσας, χρυσοῖς τε ἀνασπάστοις ἐπέσφιγγε τοὺς ἀναγωγέας τῶν βλαυτῶν. φασὶ δὲ αὐτὸν μήτε ἄκοντα μήτε[3] ἐπιπόνως τὰ ἐν τῇ τέχνῃ χειρουργεῖν, πάνυ δὲ εὐθύμως καὶ ῥᾳδίως· καὶ γὰρ καὶ ᾖδε καὶ ὑπομινυρόμενος[4] τὸν κάματον τὸν ἐκ τῆς ἐπιστήμης ἐπειρᾶτο ἐπελαφρύνειν. λέγει δὲ ταῦτα Θεόφραστος.

12. Ὅτι Ῥωμαῖοι Ἀλκαῖον καὶ Φίλισκον τοὺς Ἐπικουρείους ἐξέβαλον τῆς πόλεως, ὅτι πολλῶν καὶ ἀτόπων ἡδονῶν εἰσηγηταὶ τοῖς νέοις ἐγένοντο. καὶ Μεσσήνιοι δὲ ἐξέωσαν τοὺς Ἐπικουρείους.

13. Διονύσιον τὸν Ἡρακλεώτην, <τὸν>[5] Κλεάρχου τοῦ τυράννου υἱόν, ἀκούω ἐκ τῆς καθ' ἡμέραν ἀδηφαγίας καὶ τρυφῆς λαθεῖν ἑαυτὸν ὑπερσαρκήσαντα

[1] del. Scheffer [2] γράμμα Her.: ἐπίγραμμα codd.
[3] μήτε . . . μήτε Her.: μηδὲ . . . μηδὲ codd.

11. We know that the painter Parrhasius wore a purple cloak and a golden crown not only from various witnesses but also from inscriptions on a number of his works. He was once at a competition in Samos, met a rival much inferior to him, and was defeated. His picture showed Ajax after his contest with Odysseus for the armour of Achilles. After losing Parrhasius wittily remarked to a friend who was sympathising with him that he was not much worried by defeat but had sympathy for the son of Telamon, defeated twice in the same contest. He had a stick decorated with gold bands around it and he fastened the straps of his sandals with gold laces. They say he performed the manual part of his tasks without reluctance or effort, but quite cheerfully and easily; in fact he would sing or hum in the attempt to lighten the labour of his craft. This is the report of Theophrastus [fr. 552 A F.-H.-S.].[a]

12. Note that the Romans expelled from their city the Epicureans Alcaeus and Philiscus, because they had introduced the younger generation to many unnatural pleasures. The Messenians also expelled Epicureans.[b]

13. I learn that Dionysius of Heraclea, son of the tyrant Clearchus, did not realise that his daily gluttony and extravagance were causing him to put on weight and

[a] For this ch. Athenaeus 543 CF appears to be the source, and in some details is clearer. [b] Athenaeus 547 A is the source. He dates the expulsion of the Epicureans to the consulship of L. Postumius (173 or 154 B.C.). Messenians could be the inhabitants of Messene, but the *Suda* lexicon, s.v. Epicurus, shows that the Messenians of Arcadia are meant.

[4] ὑπομινυρόμενος West: ὑποκιν- codd.
[5] ex Athenaeo 549 A suppl. Dilts

καὶ καταπιανθέντα. τὰ ἐπίχειρα γοῦν τοῦ κατὰ τὸ σῶμα μεγέθους καὶ τοῦ περὶ τὰς σάρκας ὄγκου ἐκαρπώσατο δύσπνοιαν. φάρμακον οὖν αὐτῷ τοῦδε τοῦ πάθους συνέταξαν οἱ ἰατροί, φασι, βελόνας λεπτὰς κατασκευάσαι μηκίστας, εἶτα ταύτας διὰ τῶν πλευρῶν καὶ τῆς κοιλίας διωθεῖν, ὅταν εἰς ὕπνον τύχῃ βαθύτερον ἐμπεσών. ἦν δὲ ἄρα τοῦτο ἐπιμελὲς ἐκείνοις δρᾶν, ἔστε[1] ὅλη διὰ τῆς πεπωρωμένης καὶ τρόπον τινὰ ἀλλοτρίας αὐτοῦ σαρκὸς διεῖρπεν ἡ βελόνη· ἀλλ᾽ ἐκεῖνός γε ἔκειτο λίθου διαφέρων οὐδέν. εἰ δὲ ἀφίκετο τὸ βέλος ἔνθα λοιπὸν[2] ἦν αὐτῷ τὸ σῶμα ἐρρωμένον καὶ ἴδιον, ἀλλ᾽ οὐκ ἐκ τῆς ἄγαν πιμελῆς ἀλλότριον, τηνικαῦτα καὶ ἐκεῖνος ᾐσθάνετο, καὶ ἠγείρετο ἐκ τοῦ ὕπνου. τοὺς δὲ χρηματισμοὺς ἐποιεῖτο τοῖς βουλομένοις αὐτῷ προσιέναι, κιβωτὸν τοῦ σώματος προβαλλόμενος. οἱ δὲ οὐ κιβωτόν φασιν ἀλλὰ πυργίσκον, ἵνα τὰ μὲν λοιπὰ αὐτοῦ μέρη ἀποκρύπτοιτο, τὸ δὲ πρόσωπον μόνον ὑπερέχων[3] διαλέγοιτο,[4] πονηράν, ὦ θεοί, ταύτην ἐκεῖνος τὴν στολὴν περιαμπεχόμενος καὶ θηρίου φρουρὰν[5] μᾶλλον ἢ ἀνθρώπου ἐσθῆτα.

14. Φιλίταν λέγουσι τὸν Κῷον λεπτότατον γενέσθαι τὸ σῶμα. ἐπεὶ τοίνυν ἀνατραπῆναι ῥᾴδιος ἦν ἐκ πάσης προφάσεως, μολίβου, φασί, πεποιημένα εἶχεν ἐν τοῖς ὑποδήμασι πέλματα, ἵνα μὴ ἀνατρέπηται ὑπὸ τῶν ἀνέμων, εἴ ποτε σκληροὶ κατέπνεον. εἰ δὲ ἦν οὕτως ἀδύνατος ὥστε μὴ ἀντέχειν πνεύματι, πῶς οἷός τε ἦν τοσοῦτον φορτίον ἐπάγεσθαι; ἐμὲ μὲν

become obese. But the consequence of his physical size and corpulent body was difficulty in breathing. As a cure for this complaint the doctors, it is said, gave instructions to prepare very long, thin needles, which were then to be pushed into his ribs and belly when he had fallen into a deep sleep. Their object was to have the needle pass right through the flesh—it was insensitive and in a sense not part of him—while he lay there just like a stone. If the needle reached a point that was still healthy and part of his system, not transformed by the excess of fat, then he would notice and wake up. He held audience for those who wished to see him by placing a chest in front of his body—though other sources say it was a kind of small tower—in order that all the rest of his body should be hidden, and he could just hold his head above it during the conversation. This was a wretched way to cover himself, by the gods, more like the enclosure for a wild animal than the dress of a human being.[a]

14. Philitas of Cos is said to have been extremely thin. Since he could very easily be knocked over by anything, he wore shoes (they say) with soles made of lead, so as not to be blown over by the wind whenever it was gusty. But if he was so weak that he could not stand up against the wind, how was he able to carry such a burden around with

[a] This ch. derives from Athenaeus 549 AC.

---

[1] ἔστε Her.: ἔστ' ἂν codd.
[2] λοιπὸν del. Her.
[3] ὑπερέχων ex Athenaeo Scheffer: -έχον codd.
[4] διαλέγοιτο ex Athenaeo Her.: -λέγηται codd.
[5] φρουρὰν] φορίνην Grasberger

οὖν τὸ λεχθὲν οὐ πείθει· ὃ δὲ ἔγνων ὑπὲρ τοῦ ἀνδρός, τοῦτο εἶπον.

15. Ὅτι ποιητικῆς ἁπάσης Ἀργεῖοι τὰ πρῶτα Ὁμήρῳ ἔδωκαν, δευτέρους δὲ αὐτοῦ ἔταττον πάντας. ποιοῦντες δὲ θυσίαν, ἐπὶ ξένια ἐκάλουν τὸν Ἀπόλλωνα καὶ Ὅμηρον. λέγεται δὲ κἀκεῖνο πρὸς τούτοις, ὅτι ἄρα ἀπορῶν ἐκδοῦναι τὴν θυγατέρα, ἔδωκεν αὐτῇ προῖκα ἔχειν τὰ ἔπη τὰ Κύπρια. καὶ ὁμολογεῖ τοῦτο Πίνδαρος.

16. Τὴν Ἰταλίαν ᾤκησαν πρῶτοι Αὔσονες αὐτόχθονες. πρεσβύτατον δὲ γενέσθαι Μάρην τινὰ καλούμενον, οὗ τὰ μὲν ἔμπροσθεν λέγουσιν ἀνθρώπῳ ὅμοια, τὰ κατόπισθεν δὲ ἵππου·[1] καὶ αὐτὸ δὲ τοὔνομα εἰς τὴν Ἑλλάδα, φασίν,[2] ἱππομιγὴς δύναται. δοκεῖ δέ μοι πρῶτος ἵππον ἀναβῆναι καὶ ἐμβαλεῖν αὐτῷ χαλινόν, εἶτα ἐκ τούτου διφυὴς πιστευθῆναι. μυθολογοῦσι δὲ αὐτὸν καὶ βιῶναι ἔτη τρία καὶ εἴκοσι καὶ ἑκατόν, καὶ ὅτι τρὶς ἀποθανὼν ἀνεβίω[3] τρίς· ἐμοὶ δὲ οὐ πιστὰ δοκοῦσιν.

Ὅτι τὴν Ἰταλίαν φασὶν οἰκῆσαι ἔθνη πάμπολλα καὶ ὅσα οὐκ ἄλλην γῆν. τὸ δὲ αἴτιον, διὰ τὴν τῶν ὡρῶν εὐκρασίαν καὶ τὴν τῆς χώρας ἀρετὴν καὶ τὸ ἔνυδρον αὐτῆς καὶ τὸ πάμφορον καὶ τὸ εὔβοτον καὶ ὅτι ποταμοῖς ἐστι κατάρρυτος καὶ ὅτι θάλασσα ἀγαθὴ παράκειται αὐτῇ ὅρμοις πανταχόθεν διειλημ-

[1] ἵππου] -ῳ Scheffer [2] φασίν] φράσιν Scaliger
[3] ἀνεβίω Faber: ἐβίω codd.

him?[a] The story does not convince me, but I report what I have found out about him.

15. Note that the inhabitants of Argos accorded Homer the first place as a poet and made all others second to him. When they offered sacrifice they invited Apollo and Homer to their hospitality. In addition it is said that as he had no money when his daughter was married, he gave her as a dowry his epic the *Cypria*. Pindar [fr. 265 Sn.] is authority for this.[b]

16. Italy was originally inhabited by an indigenous people, the Ausones. The most ancient inhabitant was one Mares,[c] whose front parts, they say, were like those of a man, and his back that of a horse—and the name itself, it is said, means "horse-man" in Greek. I think he was the first man to mount a horse and to put a bit in its mouth, and because of this he was thought to have a hybrid nature. Legend has it that he lived a hundred and twenty-three years, dying three times and coming to life three times. But to me this is not plausible.

Note that Italy is said to have been settled by many races, more than any other country. The reason is the well-balanced climate, the excellence of the land, its supply of water, its fertility, the pastures; rivers flow through it, a beneficial sea stretches along its coast, with ports at

[a] The same fact about Philitas is reported by Athenaeus 552 B, who may be Aelian's source. For discussion of this ch. see A. Cameron, *Classical Quarterly* 85 (1991): 534–538.

[b] The *Cypria* formed part of the Epic Cycle. Not everyone in antiquity accepted that Homer was the author of it; among the sceptics was Herodotus 2.117.

[c] This may be the Etruscan god Maris, identified with Mars. See G. Hermansen, *Studi etruschi* 52 (1984): 147–166.

μένη καὶ καταγωγαῖς ἀφθόνοις καὶ καθάρσεσιν. ἀλλὰ καὶ τὸ τῶν οἰκητόρων ἥμερον καὶ πρᾶον ἐπῆρε πολλοὺς εἰς τὴν μετοίκησιν. καὶ ὅτι πόλεις ᾤκησαν τὴν Ἰταλίαν πάλαι ἑπτὰ καὶ ἐνενήκοντα καὶ ἑκατὸν πρὸς ταῖς χιλίαις.

17. Κουφότητα ἔοικε κατηγορεῖν οὗτος ὁ λόγος ὁ λέγων περὶ Δημοσθένους ὅτι ἄρα τύφου αὐτὸν ὑπεπλήρουν καὶ οἱ ὑδροφοροῦντες, εἴ ποτε παριόντος αὐτοῦ ὑπὲρ αὐτοῦ τι ψιθυρίσαιεν. ὃς γὰρ καὶ ὑπ' ἐκείνων ἐκουφίζετο καὶ ἐπαιρόμενος ἦν δῆλος, τίς ἦν, εἴ ποτε ὑπὸ τῆς ἐκκλησίας ἐκροτήθη;

18. Θεμιστοκλῆς ὁ Νεοκλέους ἑαυτὸν εἴκαζε ταῖς δρυσί, λέγων ὅτι καὶ ἐκείνας ὑπέρχονται οἱ ἄνθρωποι καὶ δέονται αὐτῶν, ὅταν ὕῃ, στέγην <τὴν>[1] ἐκ τῶν κλάδων ποθοῦντες· ὅταν δὲ οὔσης εὐδίας παρίωσι, τίλλουσιν αὐτὰς καὶ περικλῶσιν. <καὶ αὐτὸς οὖν ἔλεγεν ὑπὸ τοῦ δήμου τὰ αὐτὰ πάσχειν.>[1]

Ὁ αὐτὸς δὲ[2] ἔλεγεν· "εἴ μοί τις ὁδοὺς δύο δείξειε, τὴν μὲν εἰς ᾅδου φέρουσαν, τὴν δὲ ἐπὶ τὸ βῆμα, ἥδιον ἂν τὴν ἑτέραν ἦλθον τὴν εὐθὺ τοῦ ᾅδου."

19. Ἠρίστα ποτὲ Διογένης ἐν καπηλείῳ, εἶτα παριόντα Δημοσθένη ἐκάλει. τοῦ δὲ μὴ ὑπακούσαντος "αἰσχύνῃ," ἔφη "Δημόσθενες, παρελθεῖν εἰς καπηλεῖον; καὶ μὴν ὁ κύριός σου καθ' ἑκάστην ἡμέραν ἐνθάδε εἴσεισι," τοὺς δημότας λέγων καὶ τοὺς καθ' ἕνα, δηλῶν ὅτι οἱ δημηγόροι καὶ οἱ ῥήτορες δοῦλοι τοῦ πλήθους εἰσί.

20. Πλέων Ἀρίστιππος χειμῶνος ἐπιγενομένου

intervals all around it, an abundance of landing places and accommodation. The civilised and gentle character of the inhabitants tempted many people to settle. In ancient times there were 1,197 cities in Italy.

17. This story about Demosthenes seems to criticise him for vanity. He was apparently filled with pride if the water carriers whispered something about him as he passed. If he was flattered by them and obviously affected, what was he like when the assembly applauded him?

18. Themistocles son of Neocles likened himself to oak trees, saying that men take shelter under them and have need of them when it rains, longing for the protection of their branches; but when they walk by on a clear day they break off the leaves and branches. He said he had suffered in the same way at the hands of the people.

He also said "If someone showed me two roads, one leading to Hades and the other to the speaker's platform in the assembly, I would rather take the one leading straight to Hades."

19. Diogenes was having a meal in a bar one day, and called out to Demosthenes as he passed by. When the latter did not listen, he said "Demosthenes, are you ashamed to enter a bar? Yet your master comes in here every day," referring to the public and individual citizens. He was making it plain that politicians and public speakers are slaves of the people.

20. Aristippus [fr. 87 M.] became very alarmed when a

---

[1] suppl. Stobaeus 2.46.14
[2] αὐτὸς δὲ Her.: δὲ αὐτὸς codd.

πάνυ σφόδρα ἐταράττετο. ἔφη δέ τις τῶν συμπλεόντων· "ὦ Ἀρίστιππε, καὶ σὺ δέδοικας, ὡς οἱ πολλοί;" ὁ δέ· "καὶ μάλα γε εἰκότως· ὑμῖν μὲν γὰρ περὶ κακοδαίμονός ἐστι βίου ἡ σπουδὴ καὶ ὁ νῦν κίνδυνος, ἐμοὶ δὲ περὶ εὐδαίμονος."[1]

21. Θηραμένης ἔτυχεν ἐν οἰκίᾳ τινὶ διατρίβων, εἶτα ἐπεὶ προῆλθεν αὐτῆς, παραχρῆμα ἐκείνη κατηνέχθη. οἱ μὲν οὖν Ἀθηναῖοι ἄλλοι ἀλλαχόθεν αὐτῷ περιφύντες συνήδοντο ἐπὶ τῇ σωτηρίᾳ τῇ παραδόξῳ, ὁ δὲ παρὰ τὴν πάντων ἐλπίδα ἀπεκρίνατο· "ὦ Ζεῦ, εἰς τίνα με καιρὸν φυλάττεις;" καὶ μετ' οὐ πολὺν χρόνον ὑπὸ τῶν τριάκοντα ἀνῃρέθη, πιεῖν κώνειον κατακριθείς.

22. Λέγουσι τοὺς Πυθαγορείους πάνυ σφόδρα περὶ τὴν ἰατρικὴν σπουδάσαι τέχνην. καὶ Πλάτων δὲ φροντίδα εἰς αὐτὴν ἔσχε πλείστην καὶ Ἀριστοτέλης ὁ Νικομάχου καὶ ἄλλοι πολλοί.

23. Ἀριστοτέλης ἐνόσει ποτέ. προσέταξε δὲ αὐτῷ ὁ ἰατρὸς πρόσταγμά τι. καὶ ἐκεῖνος "μήτε ὡς βοηλάτην με" ἔφη "θεράπευε μήτε ὡς σκαπανέα, ἀλλὰ διδάξας πρότερον τὴν αἰτίαν, οὕτως ἕξεις ἕτοιμον πρὸς τὸ πείθεσθαι," διδάσκων ἐκ τούτων μηδὲν χωρὶς αἰτίας προσφέρειν.

24. Σμινδυρίδης ὁ Συβαρίτης εἰς τοσοῦτον τρυφῆς ἐξώκειλε· καὶ γάρ τοι Συβαρίταις πᾶσιν ἔργον ἦν τρυφᾶν καὶ τῷ βίῳ διαρρεῖν, ὁ δὲ Σμινδυρίδης καὶ πλέον. φύλλοις ῥόδων γοῦν ἐπαναπεσὼν καὶ κοιμηθεὶς ἐπ' αὐτῶν ἐξανέστη λέγων φλυκταίνας ἐκ τῆς

storm blew up during a voyage. One of the other passengers said "Aristippus, are you frightened just like most of us?" He replied "Yes, of course. Your concern in face of the present danger affects your miserable existence, but for me it is a question of true happiness at stake."

21. Theramenes had just come out of a house where he happened to be staying when it suddenly collapsed. The Athenians crowded round him on all sides to congratulate him on his miraculous escape. To their universal surprise he replied "Oh Zeus, for what fate have you preserved me?" Shortly after he was executed by the Thirty, condemned to drink hemlock.

22. They say the Pythagoreans took a great interest in medicine. Plato also devoted much thought to it, as did Aristotle son of Nicomachus, and many others.[a]

23. Aristotle was ill one day, and the doctor gave him an instruction. To which he replied "Don't treat me like a ploughman or labourer; tell me first the reason, and then you will have a patient willing to follow your advice." In this way he taught that one should not suggest anything without giving reasons.

24. Smindyrides of Sybaris fell into very effeminate habits (all Sybarites made it their business to live luxuriously and extravagantly, and Smindyrides more than most). He rested on rose petals, and after sleeping on them he got up and said his bed had given him blisters.

[a] Aristotle's father was a doctor at the Macedonian court.

---

[1] *εὐδαίμονος* d: *-ονίας* cett.

εὐνῆς ἔχειν. σχολῇ γ' ἂν οὗτος ἐπὶ χαμεύνης κατεκλίθη ἢ στιβάδος ἢ πόας ἐν προσάντει πεφυκυίας ἢ ταύρου δορᾶς, ὡς ὁ Διομήδης, πρεπούσης στρατιώτῃ σκληρῷ καὶ γενναίῳ·

ὑπὸ δ' ἔστρωτο ῥινὸν βοὸς ἀγραύλοιο.

25. Πεισίστρατος ὅτε τῆς ἀρχῆς ἐγκρατὴς ἐγένετο, μετεπέμπετο τοὺς ἐν ταῖς ἀγοραῖς ἀποσχολάζοντας, καὶ ἐπυνθάνετο τί δή ποτε εἴη τὸ αἴτιον τοῦ ἀλύειν αὐτούς. καὶ ἐπέλεγεν· "εἰ μέν σοι τέθνηκε ζεῦγος, παρ' ἐμοῦ λαβὼν ἄπιθι καὶ ἐργάζου· εἰ δὲ ἀπορεῖς σπερμάτων, παρ' ἐμοῦ σοι γενέσθω," δεδιὼς μὴ ἡ σχολὴ τούτων ἐπιβουλὴν τέκῃ.

26. Ζήνωνα τὸν Κιτιέα δι' αἰδοῦς ἄγαν καὶ σπουδῆς ἦγεν Ἀντίγονος ὁ βασιλεύς. καί ποτε οὖν ὑπερπλησθεὶς οἴνου ἐπεκώμασε τῷ[1] Ζήνωνι καὶ φιλῶν αὐτὸν καὶ περιβάλλων ἅτε ἔξοινος ὢν ἠξίου τι αὐτὸν προστάξαι, ὀμνὺς καὶ νεανιευόμενος σὺν ὅρκῳ μὴ ἀτυχήσειν αἰτήσαντα.[2] ὁ δὲ λέγει αὐτῷ· "πορευθεὶς ἔμεσον," σεμνῶς ἅμα καὶ μεγαλοφρόνως τὴν μέθην ἐλέγξας καὶ φεισάμενος αὐτοῦ, μήποτε διαρραγῇ ὑπὸ πλησμονῆς.

27. Ἀνδρὶ Λακωνικῷ μὲν χωριτικῷ δὲ ἐπέπληξέ τις πενθοῦντι πάνυ σφόδρα ἐκθύμως. ὁ δὲ ἀπλάστως ἀπεκρίνατο· "τί πάθω;" φησίν "οὐ γὰρ ἐγὼ αἴτιος τούτου, ἁ φύσις δέ μου ῥεῖ."

[1] τῷ Kor.: αὐτῷ codd.
[2] αἰτήσαντα scripsi: αἰτήσας codd.

He would scarcely have been able to lie on a camp bed, a straw mattress, a grassy slope, or like Diomedes on a bull's hide, as befitted a tough and noble warrior [*Iliad* 10.155]: "Beneath him was spread the skin of an ox from the farm."[a]

25. When Pisistratus acquired power, he summoned people who were standing idle in the main square and asked them why on earth they were doing nothing, adding "If your team of oxen is dead, take another from me and go away to plough; and if you have no seed, let me give you some." He was afraid that idleness would lead these men into conspiracy.[b]

26. Zeno of Citium [fr. 289 v. Arn.] was treated with great respect and consideration by king Antigonus. One day when the latter had drunk too much wine he burst in upon Zeno; in his drunken state he kissed and embraced him and invited him to give an instruction, swearing an oath with youthful enthusiasm that the request would not go unanswered. Zeno replied to him: "Go away and be sick," a stern and courageous reproof for drunkenness, which showed concern for the risk that he might be destroyed by his excesses.

27. A Laconian peasant was criticised by someone for mourning with extreme despondency. He replied unpretentiously: "What am I to do? I am not responsible for this; nature is taking its course."

[a] On this ch. see Wehrli on Chamaeleon, fr. 8.

[b] Aristotle, *Athenian Constitution* 16.2–4, interprets this episode as poor-relief rather than fear of conspiracy.

28. Ἐπῄνει Σπαρτιάτης τὸ ἔπος Ἡσιόδου τὸ λέγον·

οὐδ' ἂν βοῦς ἀπόλοιτ', εἰ μὴ γείτων κακὸς εἴη,

ἀκούοντος Διογένους· ὁ δὲ εἶπε· "καὶ μὴν Μεσσήνιοι καὶ οἱ βόες αὐτῶν ἀπολώλασι, καὶ ὑμεῖς αὐτῶν ἐστε οἱ γείτονες."

29. Τῆς νυκτὸς ἤδη προηκούσης ἐπάνεισί ποτε ἀπὸ δείπνου Σωκράτης. νεανίσκοι γοῦν ἀκόλαστοι προμαθόντες ἐνελόχησαν ἐπανιόντα, δᾷδας ἔχοντες ἡμμένας καὶ Ἐρινύων πρόσωπα. ἔθος δὲ ἦν αὐτοῖς καὶ ἄλλοις προσπαίζειν διὰ τὴν σχολὴν τὴν ἐπὶ τὰ χείρω. οὓς ἰδὼν ὁ Σωκράτης οὐ διεταράχθη, ἀλλ' ἐπιστὰς ἠρώτα οἷα καὶ τοὺς ἄλλους ἢ ἐν Λυκείῳ ἢ ἐν Ἀκαδημίᾳ.

Ἑορτῆς οὔσης παρὰ τοῖς Ἀθηναίοις[1] ἐφιλοτιμήσατο <ὁ>[2] Ἀλκιβιάδης δῶρα πολλὰ πέμψαι τῷ Σωκράτει. τῆς οὖν Ξανθίππης καταπλαγείσης καὶ τὸν Σωκράτην λαβεῖν αὐτὰ ἀξιούσης,[3] ὁ δὲ ἔφη· "ἀλλὰ καὶ ἡμεῖς τῇ φιλοτιμίᾳ τῇ τοῦ Ἀλκιβιάδου παραταξώμεθα, μὴ λαβεῖν τὰ πεμφθέντα ἀντιφιλοτιμησάμενοι." ἐπεὶ δέ τις ἔφη πρὸς αὐτὸν ὅτι μέγα ἐστὶν ὧν ἐπιθυμεῖ τις τούτων τυχεῖν, ὁ δέ· "ἀλλὰ μεῖζόν ἐστι τὸ μηδὲ ἐπιθυμεῖν τὴν ἀρχήν."[4]

30. Ἀνάξαρχος ὅτε σὺν Ἀλεξάνδρῳ ἐστρατεύετο, χειμῶνος ἐπιγενομένου προμαθὼν ὅτι μέλλει ὁ

[1] ἑορτῆς . . . Ἀθηναίοις Stobaeus 3.17.16: ὅτι codd.

28. A Spartiate cited with approval, in the presence of Diogenes, the verse of Hesiod [*WD* 348] "Nor would the ox die, if a neighbour were not evil." "But the Messenians and their oxen have died," said Diogenes [fr. 265 M.], "and you are their neighbours."[a]

29. One day Socrates came home from a dinner at a late hour of the night. Some badly behaved youths learned of his movements in advance and lay in wait for him. They carried lighted torches and wore masks of the Furies, it being their habit to misuse their leisure by playing tricks on other people. Socrates was not frightened when he saw them; he stopped and began asking them questions, as he would with other people at the Lyceum or Academy.[b]

When there was a festival at Athens Alcibiades made it a point of honour to send many presents to Socrates. Xanthippe expressed amazement and said they should be accepted, but Socrates replied: "No, we should match Alcibiades' sense of honour by having the courage not to accept." When someone said to him: "It is a great thing to obtain what one desires," he replied: "But it is still greater not to have desires in the first place."

30. Anaxarchus was on campaign with Alexander when winter began.[c] Knowing that Alexander would be pitching

[a] Messene had become independent again in 369 B.C. after a long period of subjugation to Sparta.

[b] A curious anachronism, since neither school existed in Socrates' day. [c] For Anaxarchus see on 4.14 above.

[2] <ὅ> add. Stobaeus [3] *καὶ . . . ἀξιούσης* Stobaeus: *τὰ πεμφθέντα καὶ ἀξιούσης λαβεῖν αὐτά* codd.

[4] *ἐπεὶ δὲ . . . ἀρχήν* codd.: om. Stobaeus

Ἀλέξανδρος ἐν ἀξύλῳ ποιεῖσθαι χωρίῳ τὴν στρατοπεδείαν, [εἰς τὸν σταθμὸν][1] ὅσα εἶχε σκεύη, ταῦτα ἐκρίψας,[2] τοῖς[3] σκευοφόροις ἐπέθηκε ξύλα. ἐπεὶ δὲ εἰς τὸν σταθμὸν ἀφίκοντο καὶ ἐνέδει ξύλων, Ἀλεξάνδρου[4] μὲν αἱ κλῖναι κατεκαίοντο, ἵνα ἑαυτὸν ἀλεᾶναι δυνηθῇ· ἐπεὶ δέ τις παρὰ Ἀναξάρχῳ πῦρ εἶναι ἤγγειλεν, ἀφίκετο παρ' αὐτὸν καὶ ηὐλίσατο[5] ἐν τῇ σκηνῇ τῇ Ἀναξάρχου. καὶ πυθόμενος τὴν προμήθειαν ὑπερεπῄνεσε, καὶ ὧν ἐξέρριψε[6] διπλάσιον ἔδωκε[7] καὶ σκεύη καὶ ἱμάτια ὑπὲρ τῆς τοῦ πυρὸς χρείας.

31. Ἀθλητὴς Κροτωνιάτης Ὀλυμπιονίκης ἀπιὼν πρὸς τοὺς Ἑλλανοδίκας, ἵνα λάβῃ τὸν στέφανον, ἐπίληπτος γενόμενος ἀπέθανε κατενεχθεὶς μετὰ πτώματος.

32. Φρύνην τὴν ἑταίραν ἐν Δελφοῖς ἀνέστησαν οἱ Ἕλληνες ἐπὶ κίονος εὖ μάλα ὑψηλοῦ. οὐκ ἐρῶ δὲ ἁπλῶς τοὺς Ἕλληνας, ὡς ἂν μὴ δοκοίην δι' αἰτίας ἄγειν πάντας, οὓς φιλῶ πάντων μάλιστα, ἀλλὰ τοὺς τῶν Ἑλλήνων ἀκρατεστέρους.[8] τὸ δὲ ἄγαλμα χρυσοῦν ἦν.

Καὶ αἱ Κίμωνος δὲ ἵπποι χαλκαῖ καὶ αὗται Ἀθήνησιν εἰκασμέναι ὅτι μάλιστα ταῖς[9] Κίμωνος ἵπποις εἱστήκεσαν.

33a. Μειράκιον Ἐρετρικὸν Ζήνωνι προσεφοίτησε πλείονα χρόνον. ἐπανελθὸν δὲ ἤρετο ὁ πατὴρ τί ἄρα μάθοι σοφόν. ὁ δὲ ἔφη δείξειν. χαλεπήναντος δὲ

[1] del. Her. [2] ἐκρίψας Kühn: ἐγκρύψας codd.

camp in a spot that had no timber, he disposed of all his equipment and loaded his pack animals with wood. When they got to the camp and there was a shortage of wood, Alexander's couches were burned in order to provide him with heat. But when someone reported that Anaxarchus had a fire, he called on him and stayed in Anaxarchus' tent. Learning of the latter's foresight he was very complimentary about it, and in return for the use of the fire he gave him twice as much equipment and clothing as he had thrown away.

31. An athlete from Croton, on winning at Olympia, went up to the presiding officials to receive his crown, and fell down dead from an attack of epilepsy.

32. The Greeks erected at Delphi, on top of a tall column, a statue of the courtesan Phryne. But I do not mean the Greeks as a whole, so as not to appear to be accusing all the people whom I like best—it was the more immoral ones among the Greeks. The statue was of gold.

The horses of Cimon, however, were bronze; they too, extremely lifelike, stood in Athens.[a]

33a. A boy from Eretria attended Zeno's school for quite a long time. When he went home his father asked him what wisdom he had learned. The boy said he would

[a] Herodotus 6.83 records that the horses with which Cimon had won his victories were buried near him.

---

[3] τοῖς Gesner: ταῖς codd. [4] Ἀλεξάνδρου] -ῳ Her.
[5] ηὐλίσατο Wilamowitz: ἠλείψατο codd.
[6] ὧν ἐξέρριψε Boivin: ἐξ ὧν ἔρριψε codd.
[7] ἔδωκε Her.: δέδωκε codd.
[8] τοὺς . . . ἀκρατεστέρους Her.: οἱ . . . -τεροι V: οἱ . . . -τατοι x [9] ταῖς Peruscus: τοῖς codd.

τοῦ πατρὸς καὶ πληγὰς ἐντείναντος, τὴν ἡσυχίαν ἀγαγὼν καὶ ἐγκαρτερήσας τοῦτο ἔφη μεμαθηκέναι, φέρειν ὀργὴν πατρός.

33b. Μειράκιον Ἐρετρικὸν προσεφοίτησε Ζήνωνι πλείονος χρόνου, ἔστ' [ἂν καὶ][1] εἰς ἄνδρας ἀφίκετο. ὕστερον οὖν εἰς τὴν Ἐρετρίαν ἐπανῆλθεν, καὶ αὐτὸν ὁ πατὴρ ἤρετο ὅ τι ἄρα μάθοι σοφὸν ἐν τῇ τοσαύτῃ διατριβῇ τοῦ χρόνου. ὁ δὲ ἔφη δείξειν, καὶ οὐκ εἰς μακρὰν ἔδρασε τοῦτο. χαλεπήναντος γὰρ αὐτῷ τοῦ πατρὸς καὶ τέλος πληγὰς ἐντείναντος, ὁ δὲ[2] τὴν ἡσυχίαν ἀγαγὼν καὶ ἐγκαρτερήσας τοῦτο ἔφη μεμαθηκέναι, φέρειν ὀργὴν πατέρων καὶ μὴ ἀγανακτεῖν.

34. Διογένης εἰς Ὀλυμπίαν ἐλθὼν καὶ θεασάμενος ἐν τῇ πανηγύρει Ῥοδιακούς τινας νεανίσκους πολυτελῶς ἠσθημένους, γελάσας "τῦφος" ἔφη "τοῦτό ἐστιν." εἶτα περιτυχὼν Λακεδαιμονίοις ἐν ἐξωμίσι φαύλαις καὶ ῥυπώσαις "ἄλλος" εἶπεν "οὗτος τῦφος."

35. Ὁ δὲ Σωκράτης ἰδὼν τὸν Ἀντισθένην τὸ διερρωγὸς τοῦ ἱματίου μέρος ἀεὶ ποιοῦντα φανερόν, "οὐ παύσῃ" ἔφη "ἐγκαλλωπιζόμενος ἡμῖν;"

36. Ψάλτης Ἀντιγόνῳ ἐπεδείκνυτο. τοῦ δὲ πολλάκις λέγοντος· "τὴν νήτην ἐπίσφιγξον," εἶτα πάλιν "τὴν μέσην," ὁ δὲ ἀγανακτήσας ἔφη· "μὴ γένοιτό σοι οὕτω κακῶς, ὦ βασιλεῦ, ὡς ἐμοῦ ταῦτα ἀκριβοῦν μᾶλλον."

show him. The father was annoyed and beat him; the son remained calm and patient, remarking that what he had learned was to endure his father's anger.

33b. A boy from Eretria attended Zeno's school over quite a long period, until reaching maturity. After that he returned to Eretria and his father asked him what wisdom he had learned in such a long time. The boy said he would show him, and soon did so. When his father became annoyed and finally beat him, he remained calm and patient and said that what he had learned was to endure the anger of parents and not to lose his temper.[a]

34. Diogenes [fr. 266 M.] went to Olympia and saw at the festival some young men from Rhodes in expensive clothing. He laughed and said: "That is pride." Then he met some Spartans, dressed in cheap and dirty jackets, and said: "This is another type of pride."

35. Socrates saw that Antisthenes [fr. 148 D.C.] always displayed the torn part of his cloak, and said: "Can't you stop preening yourself in front of us?"[b]

36. A cithara player was performing before Antigonus, who frequently gave him orders to tune first the lowest string, then the middle one. The man was annoyed and said: "Sire, I hope you are not overtaken by such an evil fate that you become more expert in these matters than I am."[c]

[a] This version of the ch., preserved in Stobaeus 4.25.39, is presumably Aelian's original wording. [b] Antisthenes was the founder of the Cynic school; this extravagantly ascetic behaviour would be in character. [c] Plutarch, *Moralia* 67 F, tells this story about Philip of Macedon.

---

[1] del. Her. [2] ὁ δὲ Her.: ὁδὶ codd.

37. Ἀνάξαρχος ὁ ἐπικληθεὶς Εὐδαιμονικὸς κατεγέλα Ἀλεξάνδρου ἑαυτὸν ἐκθεοῦντος. ἐπεὶ δὲ ἐνόσησέ ποτε Ἀλέξανδρος, εἶτα προσέταξεν αὐτῷ ὁ ἰατρὸς ῥόφημα σκευασθῆναι, γελάσας ὁ Ἀνάξαρχος "τοῦ μέντοι θεοῦ ἡμῶν" εἶπεν "ἐν τρυβλίου ῥοφήματι αἱ ἐλπίδες κεῖνται."

38. Ὁ μὲν Ἀλέξανδρος εἰς τὴν Ἴλιον ἦλθεν. ἀνασκοποῦντι δὲ αὐτῷ φιλοπόνως τῶν τις Τρώων προσελθὼν τὴν λύραν ἐδείκνυεν Ἀλεξάνδρου. ὁ δὲ ἔφη· "προτιμησαίμην ἂν μᾶλλον ἰδεῖν τὴν Ἀχιλλέως." ὑπέρευγε τοῦτο Ἀλέξανδρος· ἐπόθει γὰρ κτῆμα ἀγαθοῦ στρατιώτου, ᾧ προσῇδεν[1] ἐκεῖνος τὰ τῶν ἀγαθῶν ἀνδρῶν κλέα. τοῦ δὲ Πάριδος τί ἄρα ᾖσεν ἡ λύρα, εἰ μὴ μέλη μοιχικὰ καὶ οἷα αἱρεῖν γυναῖκας καὶ θέλγειν;

39. Πῶς δὲ οὐκ ἂν φαίη τις γελοίους ἅμα καὶ παραδόξους τούσδε τοὺς ἔρωτας; τὸν μὲν Ξέρξου, ὅτι πλατάνου ἠράσθη. νεανίσκος δὲ Ἀθήνησι τῶν εὖ γεγονότων πρὸς τῷ πρυτανείῳ ἀνδριάντος ἑστῶτος τῆς Ἀγαθῆς Τύχης θερμότατα ἠράσθη. κατεφίλει γοῦν τὸν ἀνδριάντα περιβάλλων, εἶτα ἐκμανεὶς καὶ οἰστρηθεὶς ὑπὸ τοῦ πόθου, παρελθὼν εἰς τὴν βουλὴν καὶ λιτανεύσας ἕτοιμος ἦν πλείστων χρημάτων τὸ ἄγαλμα πρίασθαι. ἐπεὶ δὲ οὐκ ἔπειθεν, ἀναδήσας πολλαῖς ταινίαις καὶ στεφανώσας τὸ ἄγαλμα καὶ θύσας καὶ κόσμον αὐτῷ περιβαλὼν πολυτελῆ εἶτα

[1] προσῇδεν Her.: συν- codd.

37. Anaxarchus, known as "the fortunate man," laughed at Alexander for declaring himself a god.[a] One day when Alexander was ill and the doctor ordered that some broth be prepared for him, Anaxarchus laughed and said: "The hopes of our god depend on a cup of broth."

38. Alexander arrived at Troy. As he looked around attentively, one of the Trojans came up to him and showed him the lyre belonging to Alexander.[b] "I should have preferred to see that of Achilles," he said. This was excellent from Alexander because he was keen to see something that had belonged to a good soldier, an object with which he had sung the deeds of famous men. What did Paris' lyre accompany except songs of adultery, the kind that attract and charm women?

39. One must admit that the following examples of love are ridiculous and bizarre. Xerxes conceived a passion for a plane tree.[c] A young man at Athens, from a noble family, fell deeply in love with a statue of Good Fortune standing near the Prytaneum.[d] He flung his arms round the statue and kissed it, and then, losing his head and spurred on by passion, he appeared before the Council declaring, with many an entreaty, that he was willing to buy the statue for a large sum. When he failed to persuade them, he put a large number of crowns and garlands on the statue, offered sacrifice, decorated it richly,

[a] Compare 4.14 and 9.30 above. The nickname implies "blessed with complete happiness."

[b] Alexander was the other name of Paris, and is much more frequently used by Homer. Achilles played the lyre in *Iliad* 9.186.

[c] Compare 2.14 above.

[d] The administrative centre of the city, where officials could also entertain.

ἑαυτὸν ἀπέκτεινε, μυρία προσκλαύσας.[1] Γλαύκης δὲ τῆς κιθαρῳδοῦ οἱ μέν φασιν ἐρασθῆναι κύνα, οἱ δὲ κριόν, οἱ δὲ χῆνα. καὶ ἐν Σόλοις δὲ τῆς Κιλικίας παιδός, Ξενοφῶντος, ἠράσθη κύων, ἄλλου δὲ ὡραίου μειρακίου ἐν Σπάρτῃ κολοιός.

40. Ὅτι Καρχηδόνιοι δύο κυβερνήτας εἰσῆγον εἰς τὴν ναῦν, ἄτοπον λέγοντες εἶναι δύο μὲν πηδάλια ἔχειν, τὸν δὲ λυσιτελέστατον τοῖς ἐμπλέουσι καὶ τὴν ἀρχὴν ἔχοντα τῆς νεὼς ἔρημον εἶναι καὶ μόνον[2] διαδόχου καὶ κοινωνοῦ.

41. Ἔν τινι, φασί, συνδείπνῳ παρῆν Σιμωνίδης ὁ Κεῖος καὶ Παυσανίας ὁ Λακεδαιμόνιος. προσέταξεν οὖν ὁ Παυσανίας τῷ Σιμωνίδῃ σοφόν τι εἰπεῖν, ὁ δὲ γελάσας ὁ Κεῖος "μέμνησο" εἶπεν "ἄνθρωπος ὤν." τοῦτο παραχρῆμα μὲν ἐξεφαύλισε Παυσανίας καὶ παρ' οὐδὲν ἔθετο, ὑποτυφόμενος ἤδη εἰς τὸν τοῦ μηδίζειν ἔρωτα καὶ μεγαλοφρονῶν ἐπὶ τῇ πρὸς βασιλέα ξενίᾳ, ἴσως δὲ καὶ ὑπὸ τοῦ οἴνου παραφερόμενος. ἐπεὶ δὲ ἦν πρὸς τῇ Χαλκιοίκῳ καὶ διεπάλαιε τῷ λιμῷ καὶ ἔμελλεν ἀποθνῄσκειν ἀνθρώπων ἀλγεινότατα, ἀλλὰ τηνικαῦτα ἐμνήσθη τοῦ Σιμωνίδου καὶ ἐξεβόησεν εἰς τρίς· "ὦ ξένε Κεῖε, μέγα τι ἄρα χρῆμα ἦν ὁ λόγος σου, ἐγὼ δὲ ὑπ' ἀνοίας οὐδὲν αὐτὸν ᾤμην εἶναι."

42. Ἀρταξέρξου ἀποκτείναντος τὸν πρεσβύτερον

[1] προσκλαύσας] προκλ- Abresch

[2] ἔρημον . . . μόνον] μόνον . . . ἔρημον Scheffer καὶ μόνον del. Faber

and killed himself, after uttering prolonged lamentation. Some say that the cithara player Glauce was loved by a dog, others by a ram or a goose. At Soli in Cilicia a boy called Xenophon was loved by a dog, and another handsome youth at Sparta was adored by a crow.[a]

40. Note that the Carthaginians put two steersmen on to their ships, saying that it was odd to have two rudders while the man who was most valuable for everyone on board and had control of the ship was alone, lacking any companion or replacement.

41. Simonides of Ceos and Pausanias the Spartan, they say, came to a dinner party. Pausanias asked Simonides to say something wise. The man from Ceos laughed and said: "Remember that you are human."[b] Pausanias immediately neglected this advice and treated it as of no importance, because he was already affected by a love of all things Persian and prided himself on the hospitality he had received from the king. He may also have been affected by the wine. But when he was in the temple of the Goddess of the Bronze House,[c] struggling against hunger and on the point of death, then he recalled Simonides and shouted three times: "Guest from Ceos, your words had great meaning after all, and I stupidly thought there was nothing to them."

42. When Artaxerxes executed his elder son Darius for

[a] The last few lines of the ch. are repeated almost verbatim from *N.A.* 1.6 (compare also *N.A.* 5.29 and 8.11).

[b] A similar point is made at 8.15 above.

[c] This temple of Athena was the main building in the city centre at Sparta.

υἱὸν Δαρεῖον ἐπιβουλεύοντα, ὁ δεύτερος ἀξιοῦντος τοῦ πατρὸς σπασάμενος τὸν ἀκινάκην ἑαυτὸν πρὸ τῶν βασιλείων ἀπέκτεινε.

conspiracy, the second son, on his father's instructions, drew his sword and killed himself in front of the palace.[a]

[a] Darius and Ariaspes were the two sons of Artaxerxes II (404–358 B.C.); Plutarch, *Artaxerxes* 30, gives a different account of the events.

I

1. Φερενίκη τὸν υἱὸν ἦγεν εἰς Ὀλύμπια ἀθλεῖν. κωλυόντων δὲ αὐτὴν τῶν Ἑλλανοδικῶν τὸν ἀγῶνα θεάσασθαι, παρελθοῦσα ἐδικαιολογήσατο πατέρα μὲν Ὀλυμπιονίκην ἔχειν καὶ τρεῖς ἀδελφοὺς καὶ ἄγειν[1] παῖδα Ὀλυμπίων ἀγωνιστήν· καὶ ἐξενίκησε τὸν δῆμον καὶ τὸν εἴργοντα νόμον τῆς θέας τὰς γυναῖκας, καὶ ἐθεάσατο Ὀλύμπια.

2. Εὐβάταν τὸν Κυρηναῖον ἰδοῦσα Λαῒς ἠράσθη αὐτοῦ θερμότατα καὶ περὶ γάμου λόγους προσήνεγκεν. ὁ δὲ φοβηθεὶς τὴν ἐξ αὐτῆς ἐπιβουλὴν ὑπέσχετο ταῦτα δράσειν· οὐ μὴν ὡμίλησεν αὐτῇ ὁ Εὐβάτας, σωφρόνως διαβιώσας. ἡ δὲ ὑπόσχεσις αὐτοῦ μετὰ[2] τὴν ἀγωνίαν ἦν. νικήσας οὖν ἵνα μὴ δόξῃ διαφθεῖραι[3] τὰς ὁμολογίας τὰς πρὸς τὴν ἄνθρωπον, εἰκόνα γραψάμενος τῆς Λαΐδος εἰς τὴν

[1] *ἄγειν* Cobet; cf. ps.-Aeschin., epist. 4.5: *αὐτὴ* codd.
[2] *μετὰ*] locus vix sanus; fortasse <*περὶ τὰ*> *μετὰ*
[3] *διαφθεῖραι* Kor.: -*είρας* codd.

---

[a] Eubatas' name is found on an inscription which records his victory in 408 B.C. It occurs again in another inscription of 364 B.C., which records victory in the four-horse chariot race; if this is

BOOK TEN

1. Pherenice brought her son to the Olympic festival to compete. The presiding officials refused to admit her as a spectator, but she spoke in public and justified her request by pointing out that her father and three brothers were Olympic victors, and she was bringing a son who was a competitor. She won over the assembly, the law excluding women as spectators was abolished, and she attended the Olympic festival.

2. When Lais saw Eubatas of Cyrene[a] she fell deeply in love with him and proposed marriage. He was afraid she might make trouble and promised to meet her wishes. But Eubatas had lived a chaste existence and did not make love with her. His promise, however, was made "after the contest."[b] And so, after winning, in order not to appear to be breaking his agreement with the woman, he had a portrait made of Lais and took it to Cyrene, saying

the same man, his career was uncommonly long. See L. Moretti, *Olympionikai, i vincitori negli antichi agoni olimpici* (Rome, 1957), nos. 347 and 421.

[b] A similar story is told of another athlete in Clement of Alexandria, *Stromateis* 3.6.50.4–51.1 (from Istros, FGrH 334 F 55). One would expect Aelian to say either that the promise was made before the contest or that it was to be honoured after the contest; but the Greek as transmitted cannot be so translated, and my version adopts a subterfuge.

Κυρήνην ἐκόμισε, λέγων ἄγειν Λαΐδα καὶ μὴ παραβῆναι τὰς συνθήκας. ἀνθ' ὧν ἡ γυνὴ ἡ νόμῳ γημαμένη αὐτῷ παμμέγιστον ἀνδριάντα ἐν Κυρήνῃ ἀνέστησεν, αὐτὸν ἀμειβομένη τῆς σωφροσύνης.

3. Τὰ τῶν περδίκων νεόττια ἐπειδὰν τάχιστα τοὺς πόδας ἔξω ποιήσῃ τοῦ λέμματος, ἐντεῦθεν ἤδη δρομικώτατά ἐστι. τὰ δὲ τῶν νηττῶν νεόττια, ὅταν ἴδῃ φῶς, παραχρῆμα ἐξ ὠδίνων νήχεται. καὶ οἱ τῶν λεόντων δὲ σκύμνοι καταγνάφουσι[1] τοῖς ὄνυξι τὰς μήτρας τῶν μητέρων πρὸς φῶς ἐπειγόμενοι.

4. Ἀλέξανδρος ὁ Φιλίππου τρὶς τετρακόσια στάδια ἐφεξῆς μεθ' ὅπλων ὁδοιπορήσας, συμβαλὼν τοῖς πολεμίοις, πρὶν ἀναπαῦσαι τὸ στρατόπεδον, ἐπεκράτησε τῶν ἐχθρῶν.

5. Φρύγιος οὗτος <ὁ>[2] λόγος· ἔστι γὰρ Αἰσώπου τοῦ Φρυγός. <ὁ δὲ λόγος φησὶ> τὴν ὗν, ἐάν τις ἅψηται αὐτῆς, βοᾶν καὶ μάλα γε εἰκότως· οὔτε γὰρ ἔρια ἔχειν[3] <οὔτε γάλα> οὔτε ἄλλο τι <πλὴν τῶν κρεῶν>. παραχρῆμα οὖν ὀνειροπολεῖν[4] τὸν θάνατον, εἰδυῖαν[5] εἰς ὅ τι τοῖς χρησομένοις <αὐτὴ πέφυκε> λυσιτελὴς[6] <εἶναι>. ἐοίκασι δὲ τῇ ὑὶ τῇ Αἰσώπου οἱ τύραννοι ὑποπτεύοντες καὶ δεδοικότες πάντα· ἴσασι γὰρ ὅτι ὥσπερ οὖν αἱ[7] ὗς ὀφείλουσι καὶ ἐκεῖνοι τὴν ψυχὴν πᾶσιν.

[1] καταγνάφουσι anonymus in exemplari ed. Hercherianae: -γράφουσι codd.

[2] in hoc cap. verba uncinis inclusa e Stobaeo 4.8.24 suppleta sunt

that he was bringing her[a] and was not breaking his agreement. In response to this his legitimate wife, in recognition of his fidelity, put up an enormous statue of him in Cyrene.

3. Partridge chicks, as soon as they get their feet outside the shell of the egg, are immediately able to run very fast. Young ducklings, when they see the light, can swim as soon as they have been born.[b] Lion cubs in their eagerness to see the light scratch their mother's womb with their claws.[c]

4. Alexander son of Philip, wearing full armour, completed three successive marches of four hundred stades. He then attacked the enemy before resting his army and defeated the opposing forces.

5. This is a story from Phrygia; it is from Aesop the Phrygian. It says that if one touches a pig, it squeals, and quite reasonably: it produces no fur or milk, nothing but meat, and it has visions of death because it knows in what way its nature is a source of profit to others. Tyrants are like Aesop's pig: they suspect and fear everything, because they know that they too, just like the pig, are at the mercy of everyone.

[a] There is a pun in the Greek verb *ἄγειν*, which can mean both "bring" and "marry."

[b] The same fact about ducklings is reported in *N.A.* 5.33.

[c] But this statement is rejected as false in *N.A.* 4.34.

---

[3] *ἔχειν* Her.: *ἔχει* codd.: *ἔχει ὗς* Stobaeus

[4] *παραχρῆμα . . . ὀνειροπολεῖν* Stobaeus: *καὶ ὀνειροπολεῖ εὐθὺς* codd. [5] *εἰδυῖαν* Stobaeus: *εἰδυῖα* codd.

[6] *λυσιτελὴς* Stobaeus: *-ελεῖ* codd.

[7] *αἱ* Stobaeus: *ἡ* codd.

6. Ἐκωμῳδοῦντο εἰς λεπτότητα Σαννυρίων ὁ κωμῳδίας ποιητὴς καὶ Μέλητος ὁ τραγῳδίας ποιητὴς καὶ Κινησίας κυκλίων χορῶν καὶ Φιλίτας ποιητὴς[1] ἑξαμέτρων. Ἀρχέστρατος δὲ ὁ μάντις ὑπὸ πολεμίων ἁλοὺς καὶ ἐπὶ[2] ζυγὸν ἀναβληθεὶς ὀβολοῦ ὁλκὴν εὑρέθη ἔχων, ὥς φασι. καὶ Πανάρετος δὲ λεπτότατος ἦν· διετέλεσε μέντοι ἄνοσος. λέγουσι δὲ καὶ Ἱππώνακτα τὸν ποιητὴν οὐ μόνον γενέσθαι μικρὸν τὸ σῶμα καὶ αἰσχρὸν ἀλλὰ καὶ λεπτόν. ἀλλὰ καὶ Φιλιππίδης, καθ᾽ οὗ λόγος ἐστὶν Ὑπερείδῃ, λεπτότατος ἦν. διὰ τοῦτο καὶ τὸ πάνυ κατισχνῶσθαι τὸ σῶμα πεφιλιππιδῶσθαι,[3] φασίν, ἔλεγον. μάρτυς Ἄλεξις.

7. Οἰνοπίδης ὁ Χῖος ἀστρολόγος ἀνέθηκεν ἐν Ὀλυμπίοις τὸ χαλκοῦν γραμματεῖον, ἐγγράψας ἐν αὐτῷ τὴν ἀστρολογίαν τῶν ἑνὸς δεόντων ἑξήκοντα ἐτῶν, φήσας τὸν μέγαν ἐνιαυτὸν εἶναι τοῦτον. ὅτι Μέτων ὁ Λευκονοιεὺς[4] ἀστρολόγος ἀνέστησε στήλας καὶ τὰς τοῦ ἡλίου τροπὰς κατεγράψατο καὶ τὸν μέγαν ἐνιαυτόν, ὡς ἔλεγεν, εὗρε καὶ ἔφατο αὐτὸν [ὡς ἔλεγεν][5] ἑνὸς δέοντα εἴκοσιν ἐτῶν.

[1] ποιητὴς del. Her. [2] ἐπὶ ex Athenaeo anonymus in exemplari ed. Gronovianae: ὑπὸ codd. [3] πεφιλιππιδῶσθαι Casaubon: -πῶσθαι codd. [4] Λευκονοιεὺς Rutgers: Λάκων x (deficit V) [5] del. Faber

---

[a] I.e. dithyrambs; the performing chorus is thought to have danced round an altar. [b] This ch. is perhaps an abridgement of Athenaeus 551 B–552 D. [c] Oenopides was a contemporary of Anaxagoras in the middle of the fifth century B.C. It was probably he who fixed at 24° the obliquity of the ecliptic, a figure

6. On the comic stage Sannyrion the writer of comedy, Meletus the tragedian, Cinesias the author of cyclical choruses,[a] and Philitas the hexameter poet were the butt of jokes because they were thin. When the seer Archestratus was captured by the enemy and put on the scales, he was found to weigh an obol, according to the story. Panaretus was also very thin, but he survived without illness. They say the poet Hipponax was not only small in stature and ugly, but thin. Philippides, also, the target of a speech by Hyperides, was very slim; as a result extreme emaciation of the body was known as "being philippidized." Alexis [fr. 148 K.-A.] is our evidence.[b]

7. The astronomer Oenopides of Chios dedicated at Olympia the famous bronze tablet on which he had inscribed the movements of the stars for fifty-nine years, what he called the Great Year.[c] Note that the astronomer Meton of the deme Leuconoe set up pillars and recorded on them the solstices. He claimed to have discovered the Great Year and said it was nineteen years.[d]

later refined by Eratosthenes. The Great Year was an attempt to calculate a lunisolar cycle. But the interpretation of the evidence about him is not easy; see O. Neugebauer, *A History of Greek Astronomy* (Berlin, 1975), p. 619, and I. Bulmer-Thomas in the *Dictionary of Scientific Biography* X (New York, 1981), s.v.

[d] Meton is a better known figure, who makes a famous appearance in Aristophanes' *Birds.* His nineteen-year cycle was calculated from 432 B.C.; it may have been an attempt to calculate a lunisolar cycle, but another view is that he published a calendar for nineteen years giving dates for solstices, equinoxes, and the risings and settings of constellations. See Neugebauer, *Greek Astronomy,* pp. 4 and 622–623, and G. J. Toomer in the *Dictionary of Scientific Biography* IX (New York, 1981) s.v. Note also an inscription from Crete, *SIG*[3] 1264, from a device for calculating the solstice.

8. Ἀριστοτέλης ὁ Κυρηναῖος ἔλεγε μὴ δεῖν εὐεργεσίαν παρά τινος προσίεσθαι· ἢ γὰρ ἀποδιδόναι πειρώμενον πράγματα ἂν ἔχειν ἢ μὴ ἀποδιδόντα ἀχάριστον φαίνεσθαι.

9. Φιλόξενος λίχνος ἦν καὶ γαστρὸς ἥττων. λοπάδος οὖν ποτε ἑψομένης ἐν καπηλείῳ, τέως μὲν εὐφραίνετο καὶ ἑαυτὸν εἱστία τῇ ὀσμῇ· ἐπεὶ δὲ αὐτῷ ἐπετείνετο ἡ ὄρεξις καὶ ἡττᾶτο τῆς φύσεως (κακῆς γε[1] οὔσης, ὦ θεοί), τηνικαῦτα οὐκ ἐνεγκὼν προσέταξε τὸν παῖδα πρίασθαι τὴν λοπάδα. ἐπεὶ δὲ ἔφατο πωλεῖν αὐτὴν τὸν κάπηλον πολλοῦ, "ταύτῃ μᾶλλον ἡδίων ἔσται" φησίν, "εἰ πλείονος αὐτὴν ὠνήσομαι." χρὴ δὲ καὶ τῶν τοιούτων μνημονεύειν, οὐκ εἰς ζῆλον αὐτῶν, ἀλλ' ὥστε φεύγειν αὐτά.

10. Ὅτε ὑπήρχετο ἡ γραφικὴ τέχνη καὶ ἦν τρόπον τινὰ ἐν γάλαξι καὶ σπαργάνοις, οὕτως ἄρα ἀτέχνως εἴκαζον τὰ ζῷα, ὥστε ἐπιγράφειν αὐτοῖς τοὺς γραφέας· "τοῦτο βοῦς, ἐκεῖνο ἵππος, ἐκεῖνο δένδρον."

11. Ἤλγει τὸν ὦμον Διογένης ἢ τρωθείς, οἶμαι, ἢ ἐξ ἄλλης τινὸς αἰτίας. ἐπεὶ δὲ ἐδόκει σφόδρα ἀλγεῖν, τῶν τις ἀχθομένων αὐτῷ κατεκερτόμει λέγων· "τί οὖν οὐκ ἀποθνῄσκεις, ὦ Διόγενες, καὶ σεαυτὸν ἀπαλλάττεις κακῶν;" ὁ δὲ εἶπε· "τοὺς εἰδότας ἃ δεῖ πράττειν ἐν τῷ βίῳ καὶ ἃ δεῖ λέγειν, τούτους γε ζῆν προσήκει," ὧν καὶ αὐτὸς ὡμολόγει εἶναι. "σοὶ μὲν οὖν" ἔφη "οὐκ εἰδότι τά τε λεκτέα καὶ τὰ

8. Aristoteles of Cyrene[a] used to say that one should not accept benefactions from anybody, because one would have difficulty when trying to reciprocate or else appear ungrateful by not reciprocating.

9. Philoxenus was greedy and a slave to his stomach. One day a dish was being cooked in a tavern, and for a time he was in good humour, as he feasted himself on the smell. But when his appetite was aroused and his nature got the better of him—it was disgraceful, by the gods—he could bear it no longer and ordered his slave to buy the dish. When the slave said that the tavern keeper wanted a high price for it, he replied: "It will taste all the better if I pay more for it." One should keep such behaviour in mind, not in order to imitate it, but so as to avoid it.

10. When the art of painting was in its early stages, as one might say not yet weaned or out of infant's clothing, animals were so crudely represented that the painters would write an inscription, "this is an ox, that is a horse, this is a tree."

11. Diogenes [fr. 267 M.] had a painful shoulder, because he had been wounded, I think, or for some other reason. When the pain seemed to be severe one of his enemies mockingly said to him: "Why not die, Diogenes, and free yourself from troubles?" To this he replied: "Men who know what to do with their lives, and what to say—they are the people who should live, and I count myself one of them. Now for you," he went on, "as you do not know what you should say or do, it is the right

[a] A fourth-century philosopher of little importance.

[1] γε Kor.: δὲ codd.: δὴ Faber

πρακτέα ἀποθανεῖν ἐν καλῷ ἐστιν· ἐμὲ δὲ τὸν ἐπιστήμονα ἐκείνων πρέπει ζῆν."

12. Ἀρχύτας ἔλεγεν· "ὥσπερ ἔργον ἐστὶν ἰχθὺν εὑρεῖν ἄκανθαν μὴ ἔχοντα, οὕτω καὶ ἄνθρωπον μὴ κεκτημένον τι δολερὸν καὶ ἀκανθῶδες."

13. Αἰτιᾶται Κριτίας Ἀρχίλοχον ὅτι κάκιστα ἑαυτὸν εἶπεν. "εἰ γὰρ μὴ" φησὶν "ἐκεῖνος τοιαύτην δόξαν ὑπὲρ ἑαυτοῦ εἰς τοὺς Ἕλληνας ἐξήνεγκεν, οὐκ ἂν ἐπυθόμεθα ἡμεῖς οὔθ' ὅτι Ἐνιποῦς υἱὸς ἦν τῆς δούλης, οὔθ' ὅτι καταλιπὼν Πάρον διὰ πενίαν καὶ ἀπορίαν ἦλθεν εἰς Θάσον, οὔθ' ὅτι ἐλθὼν τοῖς ἐνταῦθα ἐχθρὸς ἐγένετο, οὔτε μὴν ὅτι ὁμοίως τοὺς φίλους καὶ τοὺς ἐχθροὺς κακῶς ἔλεγε. πρὸς δὲ τούτοις" ἦν δ' ὃς "οὔθ' ὅτι μοιχὸς ἦν ᾔδειμεν ἂν εἰ μὴ παρ' αὐτοῦ μαθόντες, οὔθ' ὅτι λάγνος καὶ ὑβριστής, καὶ τὸ ἔτι τούτων αἴσχιον, ὅτι τὴν ἀσπίδα ἀπέβαλεν. οὐκ ἀγαθὸς ἄρα ἦν ὁ Ἀρχίλοχος μάρτυς ἑαυτῷ, τοιοῦτον κλέος ἀπολιπὼν καὶ τοιαύτην ἑαυτῷ φήμην." ταῦτα οὐκ ἐγὼ Ἀρχίλοχον αἰτιῶμαι, ἀλλὰ Κριτίας.

14. Σωκράτης ἔλεγεν ὅτι ἡ ἀργία ἀδελφὴ τῆς ἐλευθερίας ἐστί. καὶ μαρτύριον ἔλεγεν ἀνδρειοτάτους καὶ ἐλευθεριωτάτους Ἰνδοὺς καὶ Πέρσας, ἀμφοτέρους δὲ πρὸς χρηματισμὸν[1] ἀργοτάτους εἶναι· Φρύ-

[1] χρηματισμὸν Gesner: σχηματισμὸν codd.

moment to die; but for me it is right to live, as I understand these things."

12. Archytas said [p. 563 M]: "Just as it is hard to find a fish without bones, so too it is hard to find a man who does not have some deceptive and thorny qualities."

13. Critias [D.-K. 88 B 44] blames Archilochus [fr. 295 W.] for being very critical of himself.[a] If he had not spread this kind of opinion about himself among the Greeks, he notes, we should not have learned that he was the son of the slave woman Enipo, or that because of poverty and desperation he left Paros and went to Thasos; that, having arrived, he made enemies of the people there; and that he was equally rude about his friends and his enemies. In addition, he remarks, we should not have known of his adultery if we had not learned of it from him, nor of his sexual appetite and arrogance, and—what is a great deal worse—that he threw away his shield. So Archilochus was not a favourable witness in his own case, given that he left behind him such renown and reputation. These are not my accusations against Archilochus, they come from Critias.

14. Socrates said that idleness is the sister of freedom. As a proof he noted that the Indians and Persians are very brave and free, but both nations are quite idle in matters of commerce, whereas the Phrygians and Lydians are

[a] Critias (ca. 460–403 B.C.), pupil of Socrates and one of the Thirty Tyrants, was also a writer of prose and of tragedies. But it is not clear what kind of work could have contained these remarks on Archilochus, the seventh-century poet whose verses evidently gave a great deal of information about his life and personality. There is a danger that some of his utterances were taken out of context and used in support of facile inferences.

γας δὲ καὶ Λυδοὺς ἐργατικωτάτους, δουλεύειν δέ.

15. Τὰς Ἀριστείδου θυγατέρας ἔτι αὐτοῦ περιόντος ἐμνηστεύοντο οἱ τῶν Ἑλλήνων δοκοῦντες διαφέρειν. ἔβλεπον δὲ ἄρα οὐκ εἰς τὸν βίον Ἀριστείδου, οὐδὲ ἐθαύμαζον αὐτοῦ τὴν δικαιοσύνην, ἐπεὶ τούτων γε εἰ ἦσαν ζηλωταί, κἂν μετὰ ταῦτα ἐπέμειναν τῇ μνηστείᾳ. νῦν δὲ ὁ μὲν ἀπέθανεν, οἱ δὲ οὐδὲν ἡγήσαντο εἶναι πρᾶγμα κοινὸν[1] πρὸς τὰς κόρας· ἀποθανὼν γὰρ ἐγνώσθη ὁ παῖς Λυσιμάχου ὅτι πένης ἦν, ὅπερ καὶ ἀνέστειλεν ἐκείνους τοὺς κακοδαίμονας ἐνδόξου τε ἅμα καὶ σεμνοτάτου γάμου, παρ' ἐμοὶ κριτῇ. παραπλήσιον δὲ καὶ ἐπὶ Λυσάνδρου· μαθόντες γὰρ αὐτὸν εἶναι πένητα, τὸν γάμον ἀπέδρασαν.

16. Ἐπεὶ ὁ Ἀντισθένης πολλοὺς προὔτρεπεν ἐπὶ φιλοσοφίαν, οἱ δὲ οὐδὲν[2] αὐτῷ προσεῖχον,[3] τέλος ἀγανακτήσας οὐδένα προσίετο. καὶ Διογένην οὖν ἤλαυνεν ἀπὸ τῆς συνουσίας αὐτοῦ. ἐπεὶ δὲ ἦν λιπαρέστερος ὁ Διογένης καὶ ἐνέκειτο, ἐνταῦθα ἤδη καὶ τῇ βακτηρίᾳ καθίξεσθαι αὐτοῦ ἠπείλει· καί ποτε καὶ ἔπαισε κατὰ τῆς κεφαλῆς. ὁ δὲ οὐκ ἀπηλλάττετο, ἀλλ' ἔτι μᾶλλον ἐνέκειτο φιλοπόνως, ἀκούειν αὐτοῦ διψῶν, καὶ ἔλεγε· "σὺ μὲν παῖε, εἰ βούλει, ἐγὼ δὲ ὑποθήσω τὴν κεφαλήν· καὶ οὐκ ἂν οὕτως ἐξεύροις βακτηρίαν σκληράν, ὥστε με ἀπελάσαι τῶν διατριβῶν τῶν σῶν." ὁ δὲ ὑπερησπάσατο αὐτόν.

[1] κοινὸν del. Her.
[2] οὐδὲν Kor.: οὐδεὶς codd.
[3] προσεῖχον V: -εῖχε x

extremely active but live in slavery.[a]

15. The daughters of Aristides were courted during his lifetime by the most distinguished Greeks. It seems they were not interested in his conduct and were not impressed by his sense of justice, since if they had been admirers of these qualities, they would have persevered in their courtship afterwards. As it was, he died and they felt they had no bond linking them with the girls. For on his death it was realised that the son of Lysimachus[b] was poor, which deterred those miserable wretches from what would have been in my opinion a glorious and most distinguished marriage. Similarly with Lysander: when they learned he was poor, they rejected the marriage.[c]

16. When Antisthenes [fr. 138 D.C.] had pressed many people to take up philosophy and they paid no attention, he finally became angry and would receive no one. So he even dismissed Diogenes from his company. But when Diogenes became rather tenacious and insistent, he went so far as to threaten him with his stick, and once even struck him on the head. Diogenes did not go away, and persisted still more energetically, as he was very anxious to follow his lectures, saying: "Hit me if you wish, and I shall lay my head in front of you; but you will not find a stick hard enough to drive me away from your lectures." Antisthenes was delighted with him.

[a] This ch. is odd for two reasons: Socrates cannot have known much about India, and the Greek view of Persia in his day was not what is put into his mouth here. See Wehrli on Heraclides Ponticus, fr. 55. [b] Aristides.

[c] Compare 6.4 above. But it is possible, as D. A. Russell observes, that the final sentence of this ch. should be deleted: it may be a reader's note referring back to 6.4.

17. Λέγει Κριτίας Θεμιστοκλέα τὸν Νεοκλέους πρὶν ἢ ἄρξασθαι πολιτεύεσθαι, τρία τάλαντα ἔχειν τὴν οὐσίαν τὴν πατρῴαν· ἐπεὶ δὲ τῶν κοινῶν προέστη εἶτα ἔφυγε, καὶ ἐδημεύθη αὐτοῦ ἡ οὐσία, κατεφωράθη ἑκατὸν ταλάντων πλείω οὐσίαν ἔχων. ὁμοίως δὲ καὶ Κλέωνι[1] πρὸ τοῦ παρελθεῖν ἐπὶ τὰ κοινὰ μηδὲν τῶν οἰκείων ἐλεύθερον εἶναι· μετὰ δὲ πεντήκοντα ταλάντων τὸν οἶκον ἀπέλιπε.

18. Δάφνιν τὸν βουκόλον λέγουσιν οἱ μὲν ἐρώμενον Ἑρμοῦ, ἄλλοι δὲ υἱόν· τὸ δὲ ὄνομα ἐκ τοῦ συμβάντος σχεῖν. γενέσθαι μὲν[2] αὐτὸν ἐκ νύμφης, τεχθέντα δὲ ἐκτεθῆναι ἐν δάφνῃ. τὰς δ' ὑπ' αὐτοῦ βουκολουμένας βοῦς φασιν ἀδελφὰς γεγονέναι τῶν Ἡλίου, ὧν Ὅμηρος ἐν Ὀδυσσείᾳ μέμνηται. βουκολῶν δὲ κατὰ τὴν Σικελίαν ὁ Δάφνις,[3] ἠράσθη αὐτοῦ νύμφη μία, καὶ ὡμίλησε καλῷ ὄντι καὶ νέῳ καὶ πρῶτον[4] ὑπηνήτῃ, ἔνθα τοῦ χρόνου ἡ χαριεστάτη ἐστὶν ἥβη τῶν καλῶν μειρακίων, ὥς πού φησι καὶ Ὅμηρος. συνθήκας δὲ ἐποίησε μηδεμιᾷ ἄλλῃ πλησιάσαι αὐτόν, καὶ ἐπηπείλησεν ὅτι πεπρωμένον ἐστὶν αὐτὸν στερηθῆναι τῆς ὄψεως, ἐὰν παραβῇ· καὶ εἶχον ὑπὲρ τούτων ῥήτραν πρὸς ἀλλήλους. χρόνῳ δὲ ὕστερον βασιλέως θυγατρὸς ἐρασθείσης αὐτοῦ, οἰνωθεὶς ἔλυσε τὴν ὁμολογίαν καὶ ἐπλησίασε τῇ κόρῃ. ἐκ δὲ τούτου τὰ βουκολικὰ μέλη πρῶτον ᾔσθη καὶ εἶχεν ὑπόθεσιν τὸ πάθος τὸ κατὰ τοὺς ὀφθαλμοὺς αὐτοῦ. καὶ Στησίχορόν γε τὸν Ἱμεραῖον τῆς τοιαύτης μελοποιίας ὑπάρξασθαι.[5]

17. Critias says [D.-K. 88 B 45] that before beginning his political career Themistocles son of Neocles possessed family property to the value of three talents. After he had been prominent in public life, suffered exile and had his property confiscated, he was found to possess property worth more than a hundred talents. Similarly Cleon before entering public life owned nothing unencumbered by debt; later he left a house worth fifty talents.

18. Some say the herdsman Daphnis was the favourite boy of Hermes, others that he was his son. He acquired his name from something that happened to him: he was the child of a nymph, exposed after birth beside a laurel tree.[a] The cattle he looked after were said to be sisters of the Sun, recorded by Homer in the *Odyssey* [12.127]. While he was with his flock in Sicily a nymph fell in love with him; she made love to him—he was handsome, young, and just beginning to grow a beard, at the stage when good-looking young men show their youth in its most attractive form, as Homer himself remarks somewhere [*Iliad* 24.348]. She arranged that he should never approach any other woman and threatened him that he was fated to lose his sight if he transgressed. They made a solemn agreement with each other in these terms. Later, when a king's daughter fell in love with him, he got drunk, broke the agreement, and made advances to her. That was when pastoral songs were first sung and had as their subject his misfortune in being blinded. Stesichorus of Himera began this type of lyric poetry [fr. 279 P.-D.].

[a] The Greek word *daphne* means "laurel."

---

[1] Κλέωνι Per.: -να codd. [2] μὲν <γὰρ> Kor.
[3] βουκολῶν . . . Δάφνις] -οῦντος . . . -ιδος Jens
[4] πρῶτον Jens: πρώτῳ codd. [5] ὑπάρξασθαι V: ἀπ- x

19. Εὐρυδάμας ὁ Κυρηναῖος πυγμὴν ἐνίκησεν, ἐκκρουσθεὶς μὲν ὑπὸ τοῦ ἀνταγωνιστοῦ τοὺς ὀδόντας, καταπιὼν δὲ αὐτούς, ἵνα μὴ αἴσθηται ὁ ἀντίπαλος.

20. Ὅτι ὁ Πέρσης ἐπέστειλε πρὸς Ἀγησίλαον, φίλον αὐτὸν ἔχειν. ἀντεπέστειλε[1] δὲ Ἀγησίλαος ὅτι οὐ δυνατὸν φίλον αὐτὸν Ἀγησιλάου ἰδίᾳ εἶναι· εἰ δὲ εἴη Λακεδαιμονίοις κοινῇ φίλος, δῆλον ὅτι καὶ αὐτοῦ ἔσται· ἐφ' ἅπασι γὰρ καὶ ἐκεῖνον ἀριθμεῖσθαι.

21. Ὅτι τὸν Πλάτωνα ἡ Περικτιόνη ἔφερεν ἐν ταῖς ἀγκάλαις· θύοντος δὲ τοῦ Ἀρίστωνος[2] ἐν Ὑμηττῷ ταῖς Μούσαις ἢ ταῖς Νύμφαις, οἱ μὲν πρὸς τῇ ἱερουργίᾳ[3] ἦσαν, ἡ δὲ κατέκλινε Πλάτωνα ἐν ταῖς πλησίον μυρρίναις δασείαις οὔσαις καὶ πυκναῖς. καθεύδοντι δὲ ἐσμὸς μελιττῶν, Ὑμηττίου μέλιτος[4] ἐν τοῖς χείλεσιν αὐτοῦ καθεῖσαι,[5] ὑπῇδον τὴν τοῦ Πλάτωνος εὐγλωττίαν μαντευόμεναι ἐντεῦθεν.

22. Ὅτι Διώξιππος, παρόντος Ἀλεξάνδρου καὶ Μακεδόνων, ῥόπαλον λαβών, Κόρραγον τὸν Μακεδόνα ὁπλίτην μονομαχήσας[6] καὶ ἐκκρούσας αὐτοῦ τὸ ξυστὸν καὶ ἁρπάσας τὸν ἄνδρα σὺν τῇ πανοπλίᾳ, ἐπιβὰς ἐπὶ τὸν αὐχένα αὐτοῦ κειμένου τὴν μάχαιραν ἣν ὑπέζωστο ὑφαρπάσας ἀπέκτεινε τὸν ὁπλίτην. ἐμισήθη δὲ ὑπὸ Ἀλεξάνδρου. ὁ δὲ ἀπογνούς, ὡς μισηθεὶς ὑπὸ Ἀλεξάνδρου, καὶ ἀθυμήσας ἀπέθανεν.

[1] ἀντεπέστειλε Per.: ἀνταπ- codd.
[2] θύοντος . . . τοῦ Ἀρίστωνος Her.: -τι . . . τῷ -ωνι codd.

19. Eurydamas of Cyrene won a victory in boxing but had his teeth knocked out by his opponent. He swallowed them so that the other contestant should not notice.

20. Note that the Persian king wrote to Agesilaus, assuring him of his friendship. Agesilaus wrote back to say that it was not possible for him to be a friend of Agesilaus individually; if he were a friend of the Spartans as a whole, obviously he would be a friend of Agesilaus as well, since the latter was counted as one of them.

21. Note that Perictione was carrying Plato in her arms, and while Ariston sacrificed on Hymettus to the Muses or the Nymphs, the rest of the family attended to the ceremony, and she laid Plato in the myrtles nearby, which were thick and bushy. As he slept a swarm of bees laid some Hymettus honey on his lips and buzzed around him, prophesying in this way Plato's eloquence.

22. Note that Dioxippus, in the presence of Alexander and the Macedonians, took a club and fought a duel against the Macedonian hoplite Corragus. He broke the man's pike, seized hold of him in full armour, and stood on his neck as he lay on the ground. Then he pulled out the knife he carried in his belt and killed the man. But he was hated by Alexander, and despairing because of this hatred, he lost heart and died.

---

[3] *τῇ ἱερουργίᾳ* Eberhard: *τὴν -ίαν* codd.
[4] *Ὑμηττίου μέλιτος*] *-ιον μέλι* Dilts
[5] *καθεῖσαι* Charitonides
[6] *<κατα>μονομαχήσας* Her.

ΙΑ

1. Ὅτι Ὀρίκαδμος πάλης ἐγένετο νομοθέτης, καθ' ἑαυτὸν ἐπινοήσας τὸν Σικελὸν τρόπον καλούμενον <τοῦ>[1] παλαίειν.

2. Ὅτι ἦν Ὀροιβαντίου <τοῦ>[2] Τροιζηνίου ἔπη πρὸ Ὁμήρου, ὥς φασιν οἱ Τροιζήνιοι λόγοι. καὶ τὸν Φρύγα δὲ Δάρητα, οὗ Φρυγίαν Ἰλιάδα ἔτι καὶ νῦν ἀποσῳζομένην οἶδα, πρὸ Ὁμήρου καὶ τοῦτον γενέσθαι λέγουσι. Μελήσανδρος ὁ Μιλήσιος Λαπιθῶν καὶ Κενταύρων μάχην ἔγραψεν.

3. Ὅτι Ἴκκος ὁ Ταραντῖνος παλαιστὴς[3] ὑπήρξατο σωφρονέστερον τὸν τῆς ἀθλήσεως χρόνον διαζῆν[4] καὶ κεκολασμένῃ τροφῇ διαβιώσας καὶ Ἀφροδίτης ἀμαθὴς διατελέσας.

4. Ἀγαθοκλέα φασὶ τὸν Σικελίας τύραννον γελοιότατα <περὶ>[5] τὴν κεφαλὴν ἀσχημονεῖν. ψιλουμένης γὰρ αὐτῆς, κατὰ μικρὰ ὑπορρεουσῶν

[1] suppl. Per.
[2] suppl. Dilts
[3] παλαιστὴς Per.: πάλης codd.
[4] διαζῆν Kor.: -ζήσας codd.
[5] supplevi

BOOK ELEVEN

1. Note that Oricadmus fixed the rules for wrestling, and devised by himself what is called the Sicilian style.[a]

2. Note that the poems of Oroebantius of Troezen were earlier than Homer, as Troezenian tradition reports. Dares the Phrygian, whose *Iliad* is to my knowledge still preserved, is also said to have lived before Homer. Melesander of Miletus wrote on the battle of Lapiths and Centaurs.[b]

3. Note that Iccus the wrestler from Tarentum began the practice of living soberly during the period of training; he existed on a strict diet and remained without experience of sex.[c]

4. They say Agathocles the tyrant of Sicily behaved most ridiculously over his head, which became bald as his

[a] It is not clear what is meant by the Sicilian style of wrestling.

[b] The authors mentioned in this ch. are all fictitious (compare FGrH 607 F 2, 51 F 6). We do not know if Aelian had read works ascribed to Oroebantius or Melesander; as to Dares, a Latin text, *Historia de excidio Troiae,* circulated under his name and is still extant (ed. F. Meister, Leipzig, 1873); it is thought to be a product of the fifth century and to derive from a Greek original, presumably the text known to Aelian.

[c] This athlete is mentioned in *N.A.* 6.1, from which it emerges that Aelian's source is Plato, *Laws* 839 e–840 a.

αὐτῷ τῶν τριχῶν, ὁ δὲ αἰδούμενος προκάλυμμα κόμης ἐποιήσατο [τὸν][1] μυρρίνης στέφανον· καὶ ἦν πρόβλημα τῆς ψιλώσεως. ᾔδεσαν μέντοι τὸ φαλάκρωμα Συρακούσιοι καὶ τὴν εἰς αὐτὸν[2] τῶν τριχῶν ἐπιβουλὴν[3] οὐκ ἠγνόουν, ἐσιώπων δὲ διὰ τὸ τῶν τολμημάτων αὐτοῦ καὶ ἀσεβημάτων ἐμμανές.

5. Ἔθυόν τινες ἐν Δελφοῖς. τούτοις ἐπιβουλεύοντες Δελφοὶ εἰς τὰ κανᾶ, ἔνθα ἦν αὐτοῖς ὅ τε λιβανωτὸς καὶ τὰ πόπανα, ἐνέβαλον τῶν ἱερῶν χρημάτων λάθρᾳ. λαβόντες οὖν αὐτοὺς ὡς θεοσύλας ἀπήγαγον ἐπὶ τὴν πέτραν καὶ κατεκρήμνισαν κατὰ τὸν Δελφικὸν νόμον.

6. Συνέβη τινὰ μοιχὸν ἁλῶναι ἐν Θεσπιαῖς· εἶτα ἤγετο διὰ τῆς ἀγορᾶς δεδεμένος. ἀφείλοντο οὖν αὐτὸν οἱ ἑταῖροι. ἐξήφθη οὖν στάσις καὶ συνέπεσε γενέσθαι φόνους πολλούς.

7. Ἔλεγεν Ἐτεοκλῆς ὁ Λάκων δύο Λυσάνδρους τὴν Σπάρτην μὴ ἂν ὑπομεῖναι, καὶ Ἀρχέστρατος ὁ Ἀθηναῖος ἔλεγε δύο Ἀλκιβιάδας τὴν τῶν Ἀθηναίων. οὕτως ἄρα αὐτῶν [καὶ οἱ][4] ἑκάτεροι[5] ἦσαν ἀφόρητοι.

8. Ἵππαρχος ἀνῃρέθη ὑπὸ Ἁρμοδίου καὶ Ἀριστογείτονος, ὅτι ἐν τοῖς Παναθηναίοις[6] κομίσαι κανοῦν τῇ θεῷ κατὰ τὸν νόμον τὸν ἐπιχώριον οὐκ

[1] del. Kor. [2] αὐτὸν] αὐτὸ Russell
[3] ἐπιβουλὴν] ἀποβολὴν Gesner: ἐπιβολὴν Peruscus
[4] del. Gesner
[5] ἑκάτεροι Gesner: ἑταῖροι V: ἕτεροι x

hair gradually fell out. He was ashamed of this and put a garland of myrtle over his hair to cover it. It protected the bald patch, but the Syracusans knew of his baldness and were aware of the conspiracy of his hair against his appearance. However, they kept silent because of his mad audacity and impiety.

5. A party of men were sacrificing at Delphi. Some Delphians conspired against them and secretly put some sacred objects into the baskets which contained their incense and cakes for sacrifice. So they arrested the men for sacrilege, took them to the rock and pushed them off in accordance with Delphic law.[a]

6. An adulterer was caught in the act in Thespiae. He was bound and paraded through the main square. His friends rescued him. Civil war broke out and there were many deaths.

7. Eteocles the Laconian said that Sparta could not tolerate two Lysanders, while Archestratus the Athenian said that the city of Athens could not tolerate two Alcibiades. So intolerable were they both.[b]

8. Hipparchus was killed by Harmodius and Aristogiton because at the Panathenaea he would not let Harmodius' sister carry the basket in honour of the goddess

[a] In another version of the story the victim was Aesop; so Aristophanes, *Wasps* 1446, with the scholia ad loc. The name of the cliff was Hyampia.

[b] Here Aelian gives more information than Athenaeus 535 D, who is therefore not his source (unless the text of Athenaeus has been abridged at this point).

---

[6] Παναθηναίοις Kor.: *-ναικοῖς* codd.

εἴασε τὴν ἀδελφὴν τὴν Ἁρμοδίου, ὡς μὴ[1] ἀξίαν οὖσαν.

9. Οἱ τῶν Ἑλλήνων ἄριστοι πενίᾳ διέζων παρὰ πάντα τὸν βίον. ἐπαινείτωσαν οὖν πλοῦτόν τινες ἔτι μετὰ τοὺς τῶν Ἑλλήνων ἀρίστους, οἷς ἡ πενία παρὰ πάντα τὸν βίον συνεκληρώθη. εἰσὶ δὲ οὗτοι, οἷον Ἀριστείδης ὁ Λυσιμάχου, ἀνὴρ πολλὰ μὲν ἐν πολέμῳ κατορθώσας καὶ τοὺς φόρους δὲ τοῖς Ἕλλησι τάξας. ἀλλ' οὗτός γε ὁ τοιοῦτος οὐδὲ[2] ἐντάφια ἑαυτῷ κατέλιπεν ἱκανά.

Καὶ Φωκίων δὲ πένης ἦν. Ἀλεξάνδρου δὲ πέμψαντος αὐτῷ τάλαντα ἑκατὸν ἠρώτα· "διὰ τίνα αἰτίαν μοι δίδωσιν;" ὡς δ' εἶπον ὅτι μόνον αὐτὸν Ἀθηναίων ἡγεῖται καλὸν καὶ ἀγαθόν, "οὐκοῦν" ἔφη "ἐασάτω με τοιοῦτον εἶναι."

Καὶ Ἐπαμεινώνδας δὲ ὁ Πολύμνιδος πένης ἦν. Ἰάσονος δὲ αὐτῷ πέμψαντος πεντήκοντα χρυσοῦς, ὁ δὲ "ἀδίκων" ἔφη "ἄρχεις χειρῶν." δανεισάμενος δὲ παρά τινος τῶν πολιτῶν πεντήκοντα δραχμὰς ἐφόδιον εἰς Πελοπόννησον ἐνέβαλε. πυθόμενος δὲ τὸν ὑπασπιστὴν αὐτοῦ χρήματα εἰληφέναι παρά τινος τῶν αἰχμαλώτων, "ἐμοὶ μὲν" εἶπεν "ἀπόδος τὴν ἀσπίδα, σεαυτῷ δὲ πρίω καπηλεῖον, ἐν ᾧ καταζήσεις· οὐ γὰρ ἔτι κινδυνεύειν ἐθελήσεις, πλούσιος γενόμενος."

Πελοπίδας δὲ ἐπιτιμώντων αὐτῷ τῶν φίλων ὅτι χρημάτων ἀμελεῖ πράγματος εἰς τὸν βίον λυσιτε-

[1] ὡς μὴ Kor.: καὶ ἴσως codd.

according to local custom, on the ground that she was not worthy of the honour.[a]

9. The best of the Greeks lived in poverty throughout their lives. Let others find praise for wealth even after the best of the Greeks enjoyed poverty as their lot throughout their lives. These were men such as Aristides son of Lysimachus, who had many successes in war and imposed tribute on the Greeks. Yet he did not even leave enough for the expenses of his own funeral.[b]

Phocion too was poor. When Alexander sent him a hundred talents he asked: "Why does he give them to me?" When they said that Alexander considered him the only good and noble Athenian he remarked: "Then let him leave me in that condition."

Epaminondas son of Polymnis was another poor man. When Jason[c] sent him fifty gold pieces, he said: "You are provoking me unjustly." He borrowed fifty drachmae from a fellow citizen and used them as expenses for his invasion of the Peloponnese. On learning that his shield bearer had taken money from one of the prisoners he said: "Hand over the shield to me, and buy yourself a tavern to live in. You won't want to face danger any longer because you have made yourself rich."

Pelopidas, criticised by friends for neglecting money as a useful commodity in life, said: "Useful it is by Zeus,

[a] Here Aelian seems to depend on Thucydides 6.56. To carry the baskets in the procession at the Panathenaea was a great honour, as can be seen from such passages as Aristophanes, *Lysistrata* 646. [b] For the theme of this ch. compare 2.43 above. [c] Tyrant of Pherae in Thessaly ca. 380–370 B.C.

---

[2] *οὐδὲ* Her.: *οὔτε* codd.

λοῦς, "νὴ τὸν Δία" εἶπε "λυσιτελές, ἀλλὰ Νικομήδει τούτῳ," δείξας χωλόν τινα καὶ ἀνάπηρον.

Ὅτι Σκιπίων τέτταρα καὶ πεντήκοντα ἔτη βιώσας οὐδὲν οὔτε ἐπρίατο οὔτε ἀπέδοτο· οὕτως ἄρα ὀλίγων ἐδεῖτο, ἀσπίδα δὲ αὐτῷ τινος ἐπιδείξαντος εὖ κεκοσμημένην εἶπεν· "ἀλλὰ τόν γε Ῥωμαῖον ἄνδρα προσήκει ἐν τῇ δεξιᾷ τὰς ἐλπίδας ἔχειν, ἀλλ' οὐκ ἐν τῇ ἀριστερᾷ."

Ὅτι Ἐφιάλτης ὁ Σοφωνίδου πενέστατος ἦν. δέκα δὲ τάλαντα διδόντων αὐτῷ τῶν ἑταίρων, ὁ δὲ οὐ προσήκατο εἰπών· "ταῦτά με ἀναγκάσει αἰδούμενον ὑμᾶς καταχαρίσασθαί τι τῶν δικαίων, μὴ αἰδούμενον δὲ μηδὲ χαριζόμενον ὑμῖν ἀχάριστον δόξαι."

10. Ζωίλος ὁ Ἀμφιπολίτης ὁ καὶ εἰς Ὅμηρον γράψας καὶ εἰς Πλάτωνα καὶ εἰς ἄλλους, Πολυκράτους μὲν ἀκουστὴς ἐγένετο· οὗτος δὲ ὁ Πολυκράτης καὶ τὴν κατηγορίαν ἔγραψε τὴν κατὰ Σωκράτους. ἐκαλεῖτο δὲ <ὁ>[1] Ζωίλος οὗτος Κύων ῥητορικός. ἦν δὲ τοιοῦτος· τὸ μὲν γένειον αὐτῷ καθεῖτο, κέκαρτο δὲ ἐν χρῷ τὴν κεφαλήν, καὶ θοἰμάτιον ὑπὲρ τὸ γόνυ ἦν. ἤρα δὲ ἀγορεύειν κακῶς, καὶ ἀπεχθάνεσθαι πολλοῖς σχολὴν εἶχε, καὶ ψογερὸς ἦν ὁ κακοδαίμων. ἤρετο οὖν αὐτόν τις τῶν πεπαιδευμένων διὰ τί κακῶς λέγει πάντας· ὁ δέ· "ποιῆσαι γὰρ κακῶς βουλόμενος οὐ δύναμαι."

11. Ὅτι Διονύσιος ὁ Σικελὸς περὶ τὴν ἰατρικὴν

[1] suppl. Kor.

for Nicomedes here," pointing to a lame beggar.

Note that Scipio[a] in the fifty-four years of his life never bought or sold anything—so few were his needs. When someone showed him a nicely decorated shield he said: "But a Roman ought to have hope in his right hand, not his left."

Note that Ephialtes the son of Sophonides was very poor. His friends offered him ten talents, which he would not accept, saying: "This money will force me to do you some favour contrary to justice, out of respect towards you; and if I do not show that respect or do you the favour I shall appear ungrateful."

10. Zoilus of Amphipolis, who wrote against Homer, Plato and others, went to lectures by Polycrates; this Polycrates wrote a denunciation of Socrates. Rhetorical Hound was the name given to this Zoilus.[b] As to his appearance, he had a long beard, a close-shaven head, and a coat falling short of the knee. He was fond of criticising and made a point of picking quarrels with people—he was a captious, miserable wretch. When an educated man asked him why he spoke ill of everybody he said: "Because I can't do them any harm, though I want to."

11. Note that Dionysius the Sicilian took a personal

[a] P. Cornelius Scipio Aemilianus (185–129 B.C.). The facts given in this ch. are found in Plutarch, *Moralia* 199 F and 201 D.

[b] "Dog" in Greek allows a pun, since it implies "Cynic." Zoilus was known as Homeromastix, "the scourge of Homer," because of his carping criticism of an author generally regarded as beyond reproach.

ἔσπευδε[1] καὶ αὐτός, καὶ ἰᾶτο καὶ ἔτεμνε καὶ ἔκαε καὶ τὰ λοιπά.

12. Πλακοῦντα ὁ Ἀλκιβιάδης μέγαν καὶ ἐσκευασμένον κάλλιστα διέπεμψε Σωκράτει. ὡς οὖν ὑπὸ ἐρωμένου ἐραστῇ πεμφθὲν [τὸ][2] δῶρον ἐκκαυστικὸν τὸν πλακοῦντα διαγανακτήσασα κατὰ τὸν αὑτῆς τρόπον ἡ Ξανθίππη ῥίψασα ἐκ τοῦ κανοῦ κατεπάτησε. γελάσας δὲ ὁ Σωκράτης "οὐκοῦν" ἔφη "οὐδὲ σὺ μεθέξεις αὐτοῦ." εἰ δέ τις οἴεται περὶ μικρῶν με λέγειν λέγοντα ταῦτα, οὐκ οἶδεν ὅτι καὶ ἐκ τούτων ὁ σπουδαῖος δοκιμάζεται ὑπερφρονῶν αὐτῶν <ἐκείνων>[3] ἅπερ οὖν οἱ πολλοὶ λέγουσιν εἶναι κόσμον τραπέζης καὶ δαιτὸς ἀναθήματα.

13. Ἄνδρα φασὶ Σικελιώτην οἷον[4] βλέπειν ὀξὺ[5] γενέσθαι ἐν Σικελίᾳ,[6] ὥστε αὐτὸν ἐκ τοῦ Λιλυβαίου εἰς Καρχηδόνα τείναντα τοὺς ὀφθαλμοὺς μηδὲν τὰς ὄψεις[6] σφάλλεσθαι. καὶ ἀποδεῖξαι λέγουσι τὸν ἀριθμὸν τῶν νεῶν τῶν ἀναγομένων ἐκ Καρχηδόνος· καὶ οὐκ ἐψεύσατο οὐδεμίαν.

[1] ἔσπευδε V: ἔσπευσε x: ἐσπούδασε Scheffer
[2] del. Kor.
[3] supplevi
[4] οἷον] οὕτω Her.
[5] ὀξὺ Kühn: ὀξὺν codd.: ὀξύτατον Her.
[6] ἐν Σικελίᾳ et τὰς ὄψεις abesse malebat Her.

interest in medicine; he treated, operated, cauterised, and did other things.

12. Alcibiades sent Socrates a large and beautifully made cake. Xanthippe was annoyed in her usual way, treating the cake as a present sent by a favourite boy to his lover to reinforce his passion, so she emptied it out of the basket and trod on it. Socrates laughed and said: "Well, you won't get any of it either." If anyone thinks I am dealing in trivialities when I report this tale, he is unaware that the serious man is recognised by his disdain for things which most people say are an ornament to a table and add distinction to a dinner.[a]

13. They say that in Sicily there was an islander with eyesight so sharp that if he directed his gaze from Lilybaeum to Carthage nothing escaped his eye. They say he could specify the number of ships leaving Carthage, and never made a mistake.[b]

[a] The final phrase of the Greek is probably meant as an allusion to *Odyssey* 1.152.

[b] Other writers who tell this story give the name of the man as Strabo and set it in the time of the Punic Wars. But they leave a puzzle unexplained: even from the top of a mountain—and there is no high ground near Lilybaeum—the man could hardly have seen the nearest point on the African coast, 140 km. distant, let alone Carthage, 215 km. away. Strabo 6.2.1 (267) says the man watched from a lookout post, as if this could have given him sufficient altitude.

IB

1. Ἀσπασία ἡ Ἑρμοτίμου θυγάτηρ ἡ Φωκαῒς ἐτράφη [μὲν][1] ἐν ὀρφανίᾳ, τῆς μητρὸς αὐτῆς ἀποθανούσης ἐν ὠδῖσιν. ἐκ δὴ τούτων ἐν πενίᾳ μὲν ἐτράφη ἡ Ἀσπασία, σωφρόνως μέντοι καὶ ἐγκρατῶς.[2] ὄνειρος δὲ αὐτῇ συνεχῶς ἐπεφοίτα καὶ ἐμαντεύετο αὐτῇ χρηστόν,[3] τὴν μέλλουσαν αὐτῆς τύχην ὑπαινιττόμενος, ὅτι καλῷ καὶ ἀγαθῷ συνέσται ἀνδρί. παῖς δ' ἔτι οὖσα, γίνεται αὐτῇ κατὰ τοῦ προσώπου φῦμα ὑπ' αὐτὸ τὸ γένειον καὶ ἦν ἰδεῖν μοχθηρὸν καὶ ἐλύπει τόν τε πατέρα καὶ τὴν παῖδα. δείκνυσιν οὖν αὐτὴν ὁ πατὴρ ἰατρῷ· ὁ δὲ ὑπέσχετο ἰάσεσθαι,[4] εἰ λάβοι τρεῖς στατῆρας. ὁ δὲ ἔφατο μὴ ἔχειν, ὁ δὲ ἰατρὸς μηδὲ αὐτὸς εὐπορεῖν φαρμάκου φησί. καὶ ἠνιᾶτο ὥσπερ εἰκὸς ἐπὶ τούτοις ἡ Ἀσπασία καὶ ἀπελθοῦσα ἔξω ἔκλαεν· ἔχουσα <δ'>[5] ἐν τοῖς γόνασι κάτοπτρον καὶ ὁρῶσα ἑαυτὴν ἐν αὐτῷ σφόδρα ἤλγει. ἀδείπνῳ δὲ οὔσῃ ὑπὸ τῆς ἀνίας ἀφίκετό οἱ εὖ μάλα εὔκαιρος ὕπνος, καὶ ἅμα τῷ ὕπνῳ [ἡ][6] περιστερὰ παραγίνεται, καὶ γενομένη

[1] del. Her. [2] ἐγκρατῶς Her.: καρτερῶς codd.
[3] χρηστόν] -τά Her. [4] ἰάσεσθαι Her.: -ασθαι codd.

BOOK TWELVE

1. Aspasia of Phocaea, the daughter of Hermotimus, was brought up as an orphan, as her mother died in childbirth. After that Aspasia was brought up in poverty, but learning modesty and self-control. She regularly had a dream which prophesied good fortune for her, hinting at her future destiny, that she would live with a handsome and noble man. While she was still a child a growth developed right under the chin; it was unpleasant to look at and caused distress both to father and daughter. Her father took her to a doctor, who promised to cure her if he received three staters.[a] The father said he did not have the money, and the doctor said he did not have much of the medicine. Aspasia was naturally pained by this and went out in tears; putting a mirror on her lap and looking at herself in it she was very upset. In her distress she ate no dinner, and sleep came over her at a very timely moment. During her sleep a dove arrived,[b] which turned

[a] The Phocaean stater was for a time a widely accepted standard of about 15 grams. Perhaps the doctor here is demanding a high price, with payment in gold.

[b] Aphrodite's association with the dove is mentioned above at 1.15.

---

[5] suppl. Per. [6] ἡ del. Kor.: οἱ Kühn

γυνὴ "θάρρει" εἶπε "καὶ μακρὰ χαίρειν εἰποῦσα ἰατροῖς τε αὐτοῖς καὶ φαρμάκοις, σὺ δὲ τῶν τῆς Ἀφροδίτης στεφάνων τῶν ῥοδίνων ὅσοι ἂν ὦσιν ἤδη αὖοι τρίβουσα ἐπίπαττε τῷ φύματι." ταῦτα ἀκούσασα ἡ παῖς καὶ δράσασα, τὸ φῦμα ἠφανίσθη· καὶ ἡ Ἀσπασία καλλίστη τῶν συμπαρθένων ἦν αὖθις, παρὰ τῆς καλλίστης τῶν θεῶν τὴν ὥραν ἀπολαβοῦσα.

Καὶ χαρίτων μὲν ἀφθονίαν εἶχεν, ὡς οὐκ ἄλλη παρθένος τῶν τότε· ἦν δὲ καὶ τὴν κόμην ξανθὴ καὶ οὔλη τὰς τρίχας ἠρέμα, ὀφθαλμοὺς δὲ εἶχε μεγίστους, ὀλίγον δὲ ἦν καὶ ἐπίγρυπος, τὰ δὲ ὦτα εἶχε βραχύτερα. ἦν δὲ αὐτῇ καὶ δέρμα ἁπαλόν· ἐῴκει δὲ ἡ χροιὰ ἡ κατὰ τοῦ προσώπου ῥόδοις. διὰ ταῦτά τοι οἱ Φωκαεῖς ἔτι παιδίον οὖσαν ἐκάλουν Μιλτώ. ὑπέφαινε δὲ καὶ τὰ χείλη ἐρυθρά, καὶ οἱ ὀδόντες λευκότεροι χιόνος ἦσαν. ἦν δὲ καὶ τὰ σφυρὰ ἀγαθὴ καὶ οἵας Ὅμηρος λέγει τὰς ὡραιοτάτας γυναῖκας κατὰ τὴν ἑαυτοῦ φωνήν, καλλισφύρους ὀνομάζων. φώνημα δὲ εἶχεν ἡδὺ καὶ ἁπαλόν· εἶπεν ἄν τις, λαλούσης αὐτῆς, ἀκούειν Σειρῆνος. πολυπραγμοσύνης δὲ ἁπάσης γυναικείας καὶ περιεργίας ἀπήλλακτο. ὁ μὲν γὰρ πλοῦτος φιλεῖ χορηγεῖν καὶ τὰ τοιαῦτα, πενομένη δὲ ἐκείνη καὶ τρεφομένη ὑπὸ πατρὶ καὶ αὐτῷ πένητι περίεργον μὲν οὐδὲν οὐδὲ περιττὸν εἰς τὸ εἶδος ἠράνιζεν.

Ἀφίκετο δέ ποτε παρὰ Κῦρον τὸν Δαρείου καὶ Παρυσάτιδος ἡ Ἀσπασία τὸν ἀδελφὸν Ἀρταξέρξου,

into a woman and said: "Don't despair, say goodbye to the doctors and their drugs. Take all the garlands of roses offered to Aphrodite when they are withered, grind them up, and sprinkle the powder over the growth." The girl heard this and acted accordingly, and the growth disappeared. Aspasia was once again the most beautiful of her contemporaries, and had recovered her beauty from the most beautiful of the goddesses.

She had an abundance of charms, more than any girl of her day. She had blond hair with a gentle wave in it, very large eyes, a slightly aquiline nose, and rather small ears. Her skin was tender, and her complexion like roses. For this reason the Phocaeans called her Milto[a] while she was still a child. Her lips gleamed red, and her teeth were whiter than snow. She had pretty ankles, as Homer [*Iliad* 14.319] describes his most beautiful women, calling them "of the beautiful ankles." She had a pleasant, soft voice; one might have thought, when she was speaking, that one was listening to a Siren. She was quite free of all feminine fuss and refinement. Wealth brings with it habits of that kind, but she was poor, looked after by her father who was not rich, and she added nothing superfluous or artificial to her beauty.

One day Aspasia visited Cyrus,[b] son of Darius and Parysatis, the brother of Artaxerxes, against her will, and

[a] "Red paint."

[b] Cyrus as satrap held court at Sardis.

οὐχ ἑκοῦσα οὐδὲ ἑκόντος αὐτὴν τοῦ πατρὸς ἀποπέμψαντος, ἀλλὰ γὰρ πρὸς βίαν, οἷα[1] πολλάκις ἀπήντησεν[2] ἢ πόλεων ἁλουσῶν ἢ τυράννων βιασαμένων ἢ σατραπῶν [πολλάκις].[3] εἷς γοῦν[4] τῶν Κύρου σατραπῶν μετὰ καὶ ἄλλων παρθένων ἀνήγαγεν αὐτὴν πρὸς Κῦρον, καὶ τάχιστα τῶν ἄλλων παλλακίδων προετιμήθη διά τε ἤθους ἀφέλειαν καὶ τοῦ τρόπου τὸ αἰδῆμον καὶ ὅτι ἀπεριέργως καλὴ ἦν. συνεμάχετο δὲ πρὸς τὸ ὑπερφιλεῖσθαι καὶ ὅτι σύνεσιν εἶχε. πολλάκις γοῦν καὶ ὑπὲρ τῶν ἐπειγόντων ἐχρήσατο αὐτῇ συμβούλῳ Κῦρος, καὶ πεισθεὶς οὐ μετέγνω.

Ὡς δὲ ἦλθε τὸ πρῶτον πρὸς Κῦρον ἡ Ἀσπασία, ἔτυχε μὲν ἀπὸ δείπνου ὢν καὶ πίνειν ἔμελλε κατὰ τὸν τρόπον τὸν Περσικόν· μετὰ γὰρ τὸ ἐμπλησθῆναι τροφῆς οἱ Πέρσαι τῷ τε οἴνῳ καὶ ταῖς προπόσεσιν εὖ μάλα ἀποσχολάζουσιν, [οἱονεὶ][5] πρὸς τὸν πότον ὡς πρὸς ἀντίπαλον ἀποδυόμενοι. μεσοῦντος οὖν τοῦ πότου τέτταρες παρθένοι παράγονται τῷ Κύρῳ Ἑλληνικαί, ἐν δὲ ταῖς καὶ ἡ Φωκαῒς Ἀσπασία ἦν. ἦσαν δὲ κάλλιστα διεσκευασμέναι· αἱ μὲν γὰρ τρεῖς ὑπὸ τῶν οἰκείων γυναικῶν, αἳ ἔτυχον αὐταῖς συνανελθοῦσαι, διαπεπλεγμέναι τε ἦσαν τὰς κόμας καὶ διαπεποικιλμέναι τὰ πρόσωπα ἐντρίψεσι καὶ φαρμάκοις. ἦσαν δὲ καὶ ὑπὸ τῶν τροφέων[6] δεδιδαγμέναι ὅπως τε ὑποδραμεῖν χρὴ τὸν Κῦρον καὶ τίνα τρόπον θωπεῦσαι καὶ προσιόντα μὴ ἀποστραφῆναι καὶ ἁπτομένου μὴ δυσχερᾶναι καὶ φιλοῦντος ὑπομεῖναι,

her father had not wished to let her go; but she was compelled, as often happens when cities are captured or tyrants and satraps insist. At any rate one of Cyrus' satraps took her and other girls up to Cyrus, and she was very soon preferred to his other mistresses because of her natural manner, reserved disposition, and unstudied beauty. Her intelligence also contributed to the great affection felt for her; certainly Cyrus frequently sought her advice on urgent business, and after accepting it he did not change his mind.

When Aspasia first met Cyrus, he happened to have come from dinner and was about to have drinks in the Persian style; after eating a large meal the Persians spend a long time over wine, drinking toasts and preparing themselves as if the party were an athletic contest. Halfway through the party four Greek girls were brought before Cyrus, and the Phocaean girl Aspasia was one of them. They were splendidly turned out: three had had their hair groomed by their own maids who had travelled with them, and their faces were made up with powders and cosmetics. They had been instructed by their tutors on how to win Cyrus' favour, how to flatter him—not to turn away at his approach, not to be annoyed by his pet-

---

[1] *οἶα* e d A. Gronovius: *οἶαι* x: *εἰ* V

[2] *ἀπήντησεν* Her.: *-σαν* codd.

[3] del. Her.: *παλλακευσαμένων* Bruhn

[4] *γοῦν* V: *οὖν* x

[5] del. Dilts

[6] *τροφέων*] *τροφῶν* Gesner

ἑταιρικὰ εὖ μάλα μαθήματα καὶ διδάγματα <καὶ>[1] γυναικῶν καπηλικῶς τῷ κάλλει χρωμένων ἔργα. ἔσπευδον οὖν ἄλλη ἄλλην ὑπερβαλέσθαι τῷ κάλλει. ἡ δὲ Ἀσπασία οὔτε ἐνδῦναι πολυτελῆ χιτῶνα ἐβούλετο, οὔτε περίβλημα περιβαλέσθαι ποικίλον ἠξίου, οὔτε λούσασθαι ὑπέμενεν, ἀνευφημήσασα δὲ θεοὺς πάντας ἐκάλει Ἑλληνίους καὶ Ἐλευθερίους τοὺς αὐτούς, καὶ τὸ τοῦ πατρὸς ὄνομα ἐβόα καὶ κατηρᾶτο ἑαυτῇ καὶ τῷ πατρί, δουλείαν σαφῆ καὶ ὡμολογημένην ὑπομένειν πιστεύουσα τὴν ἔξω τῆς συνηθείας περὶ τὸ σῶμα στολήν τε ἅμα καὶ περίεργον κατασκεύην. ῥαπισθεῖσα δὲ πρὸς ἀνάγκην ἐνέδυ, καὶ εἶκε τοῖς ἐπιτάγμασιν, ἀλγοῦσα ὅμως <ὡς>[2] οὐ παρθενικὰ ἀλλ' ἑταιρικὰ πράττειν ἐβιάζετο. αἱ μὲν οὖν ἄλλαι παρελθοῦσαι ἀντέβλεπον τῷ Κύρῳ καὶ ὑπεμειδίων καὶ φαιδρότητα προσεποιοῦντο· ἥ γε μὴν Ἀσπασία ἑώρα κάτω, καὶ ἐρυθημάτων εὖ μάλα φλογωδῶν ἐνεπίμπλατο αὐτῆς τὸ πρόσωπον καὶ πεπλήρωντο οἱ ὀφθαλμοὶ δακρύων καὶ ἐκ παντὸς τοῦ τρόπου δήλη ἦν αἰδουμένη.[3] ἐπεὶ δὲ ἐκέλευσε πλησίον αὑτοῦ τὰς ἀνθρώπους καθίσαι, αἱ μὲν ἐπείσθησαν καὶ πάνυ εὐκόλως, ἡ δὲ Φωκαῒς τῷ προστάγματι οὐδὲν[4] προσεῖχεν, ἕως αὐτὴν ὁ ἀπαγαγὼν[5] σατράπης πρὸς βίαν ἐκάθισεν. ἁπτομένου δὲ τοῦ Κύρου καὶ διασκοποῦντος τοὺς ὀφθαλμοὺς αὐταῖς καὶ τὰς παρειὰς καὶ τοὺς δακτύλους, αἱ μὲν ἠνείχοντο, ἡ δὲ οὐχ ὑπέμενεν· ἄκρᾳ γὰρ τῇ χειρὶ μόνον τοῦ Κύρου προσαψαμένου ἐξεβόησέ τε καὶ ἔφατο αὐτὸν οἰμώ-

ting, to accept his kisses, all the tricks that are taught to courtesans and women who trade in beauty. But Aspasia did not wish to wear an expensive dress, did not ask for an embroidered coat, and could not be bothered to take a bath. With an invocation and a prayer to all the gods of Greece and of freedom—they are identical—she called out the name of her father and uttered a prayer that she and her father might die, feeling sure that to dress in abnormal clothes and to wear excessive makeup amounted to an open admission of slave status. But she was beaten and forced to submit; she obeyed instructions, pained nonetheless at the thought of being compelled to behave like a courtesan instead of a respectable young woman. The other girls came in and looked Cyrus in the face; they smiled and put on a semblance of good humour, whereas Aspasia looked down, her face quite covered by fiery blushes, her eyes full of tears, and quite obviously ashamed. When he told the women to sit by him, the others obeyed with a perfectly good grace, while the girl from Phocaea paid no attention to the order until the satrap took her and sat her down forcibly. When Cyrus petted them, looking at their eyes, cheeks, and fingers, the others accepted this and she refused to; when he merely touched her with the tip of his finger she gave a

---

[1] suppl. Scheffer
[2] suppl. Jens
[3] *αἰδουμένη* huc traiecit Her., post *παντὸς* praebent codd.
[4] *οὐδὲν* Kor.: *οὐδὲ* codd.
[5] *ἀπαγαγὼν* Dilts: *ἀπάγων* codd.

ξεσθαι τοιαῦτα δρῶντα. ὑπερήσθη τούτοις ὁ Κῦρος. ἐπανισταμένης τε αὐτῆς καὶ πειρωμένης φεύγειν, ἐπεὶ καὶ τῶν μαζῶν προσήψατο, ἀλλὰ ἐνταῦθα μὲν ὑπερηγάσθη τὴν εὐγένειαν οὐ Περσικῶς ὁ τοῦ Δαρείου, ἀλλὰ καὶ ἀποβλέψας πρὸς τὸν ἀγοραστὴν[1] "ταύτην μόνην" ἔφη "ἐλευθέραν καὶ ἀδιάφθορον ἤγαγες· αἱ δὲ λοιπαὶ καπηλικῶς ἔχουσι καὶ τοῦ εἴδους καὶ τοῦ τρόπου ἔτι[2] μᾶλλον." ἐκ δὴ τούτων ὁ Κῦρος πλέον ταύτην ἠγάπησεν <ἢ>[3] αἷς ὡμίλησέ ποτε ἀνθρώποις. χρόνῳ δὲ ὕστερον ὑπερηράσθη μὲν ταύτης ὁ Κῦρος, ἀντηρᾶτο δὲ καὶ ὑπ' ἐκείνης, καὶ εἰς τοσοῦτον ἀμφοῖν ἡ φιλία προῆλθεν, ὡς ἐγγὺς ἰσοτιμίας εἶναι καὶ μὴ ἀπᾴδειν Ἑλληνικοῦ γάμου ὁμονοίας τε καὶ σωφροσύνης.

Ἀφίκετο οὖν τοῦ εἰς Ἀσπασίαν ἔρωτος καὶ εἰς Ἰωνίαν τὸ κλέος καὶ εἰς τὴν Ἑλλάδα πᾶσαν. πεπλήρωτο δὲ καὶ ἡ Πελοπόννησος τῶν ὑπὲρ Κύρου τε καὶ ἐκείνης λόγων, ἀλλὰ καὶ εἰς βασιλέα τὸν μέγαν ἧκεν ἡ δόξα· πεπίστευτο γὰρ δὴ ὅτι γυναικὸς ἄλλης μετ' αὐτὴν οὐκ ἠξίου πειραθῆναι Κῦρος. ἐκ δὴ τούτων εἰσῄει τὴν Ἀσπασίαν μνήμη τῶν ἀρχαίων φασμάτων, περιστερᾶς τε ἐκείνης καὶ τῶν ἐξ αὐτῆς λόγων καὶ ὅσα προεῖπεν ἡ θεός· καὶ ἐπίστευεν αὐτὴν ἐξ ἀρχῆς μελεδωνὸν αὐτῆς γεγονέναι καὶ ἔθυε τῇ Ἀφροδίτῃ τελεστήρια καὶ χαριστήρια. πρῶτον μὲν οὖν εἴδωλον χρυσοῦν ἀρκούντως μεγέθους ἔχον αὐτῇ κατεσκεύασεν. ἐνενοεῖτο δὲ τὸ ἄγαλμα τοῦτο Ἀφροδίτης εἶναι, καὶ πελειάδα αὐτῇ παρέστησε

shout and said he would regret such actions. Cyrus was delighted. As she got up and tried to leave because he had touched her breasts, the son of Darius was then, contrary to Persian custom, exceedingly pleased with her nobility. He turned to the man who had brought her and said: "This is the only free and uncorrupted girl you have brought. The others simply sell their good looks, and their manners even more." From that time on Cyrus had a greater liking for her than any of the other women he had had dealings with. Later he fell very much in love with her, and she returned his affection. The love of the pair reached such a point that they were near to being equals and did not fall short of the harmony and morality of a Greek marriage.

His love for Aspasia was celebrated in Ionia and the whole of Greece; the Peloponnese was full of reports about the love of Cyrus and Aspasia, and their fame even reached the Great King. It was really believed that after her Cyrus would not wish to have anything to do with any other woman. At this point Aspasia remembered her old dreams: the dove, its utterances, and the prophecies of the goddess. She was confident that the goddess had been looking after her, and she set about making a sacrifice of thank offerings out of gratitude to Aphrodite. First of all she prepared for the goddess a golden statue of fair size; intending that this statue should represent Aphrodite, she

---

[1] ἀγοραστὴν] σατράπην Per.

[2] ἔτι huc traiecit Per.: post εἴδους praebent codd.

[3] suppl. Slothouwer

λιθοκόλλητον· καὶ ἀνὰ πᾶσαν ἡμέραν θυσίαις τε ἱλεοῦτο καὶ εὐφημίαις. ἀπέπεμψε δὲ καὶ Ἑρμοτίμῳ τῷ πατρὶ δῶρα πολλὰ καὶ καλά, καὶ πλούσιον αὐτὸν ἀπέφηνε.[1] σωφροσύνῃ τε διέζη, ὡς αἱ Ἑλληνίδες γυναῖκες λέγουσι καὶ αἱ Περσίδες.

Ὅρμος ἐκομίσθη ποτὲ Κύρῳ ἐκ Θετταλίας, πέμψαντος τὸν ὅρμον Σκόπα τοῦ νεωτέρου (τῷ δὲ Σκόπᾳ κεκόμιστο ἐκ Σικελίας τὸ δῶρον). ἐδόκει δὲ ὁ ὅρμος θαυμαστῇ τινι τέχνῃ καὶ ποικιλίᾳ ἐξειργάσθαι. πάντων οὖν, οἷς ἔδειξεν αὐτὸν ὁ Κῦρος, θαυμαζόντων, ὑπερησθεὶς τῷ κειμηλίῳ, παραχρῆμα εἰς Ἀσπασίας ἀφίκετο, μεσούσης ἡμέρας, καὶ καταλαβὼν αὐτὴν καθεύδουσαν, ὑποδὺς ὑπὸ θοἰμάτιον καὶ παρακλιθεὶς ἠρέμα, ἀψοφητὶ ἔμενεν αὐτὸς μὲν ἀτρεμῶν, ἐκείνη δὲ ἐκάθευδεν. ἐπεὶ δὲ διυπνίσθη καὶ ἐθεάσατο τὸν Κῦρον, περιπλακεῖσα αὐτῷ κατὰ τὸν συνήθη τρόπον ἐφιλοφρονεῖτο αὐτόν. ὁ δὲ ἐξελὼν ἐκ τοῦ κιβωτίου τὸν ὅρμον ἔδειξεν, ἐπειπὼν ὅτι ἄξιός ἐστιν οὗτος ἢ θυγατρὸς βασιλέως ἢ μητρός. τῆς δὲ ὁμολογούσης "ἰδού, δίδωμί σοι τοίνυν" φησὶν "αὐτὸν ἔχειν κτῆμα· καί μοι ὡς ἔχεις περιθεμένη δεῖξον τὸν τράχηλον." ἡ δὲ οὐχ ἡττήθη τοῦ δώρου, ἀλλ' εὖ μάλα σοφῶς καὶ πεπαιδευμένως ἀπεκρίνατο· "καὶ πῶς" ἔφη "τολμήσω Παρυσάτιδος δῶρον ἄξιον τῆς τεκούσης σε περιθέσθαι αὐτή; ἀλλὰ τοῦτον μὲν ἀπόπεμψον ἐκείνῃ, Κῦρε· ἐγὼ δέ σοι καὶ ἄνευ τούτου παρέξω καλὸν τὸν τράχηλον." Ἀσπασία μὲν οὖν μεγαλοφρόνως καὶ ὑπὲρ τὰς γυναῖκας βασιλικῶς τὰ

set a dove alongside it, studded with jewels, and every day she sought her favour with sacrifice and prayer. She sent many fine presents to her father Hermotimus and made him a wealthy man. And she lived a restrained life, as both Greek and Persian women say.

One day a necklace was brought to Cyrus from Thessaly. It was sent by Scopas the Younger, and Scopas had acquired it from Sicily. The necklace appeared to have been produced and ornamented with amazing skill. Everyone to whom Cyrus showed it admired it, and he, delighted with this treasure, at once went to Aspasia. It was in the middle of the day, and he found her asleep. He got under the bedcover, lay down by her quietly, and waited calmly without a sound while she slept. When she woke and saw Cyrus she embraced and kissed him in the usual way. He took the necklace out of its box to show her and remarked that it was worthy of a king's daughter or mother. When she agreed he said: "Well then, I will give it to you, to be your property; show me how it looks when you put it round your neck." But she was not overwhelmed by the gift, and replied in a very witty and cultivated way: "How can I make so bold as to wear a gift worthy of your mother Parysatis? Instead you should send it to her; I will display to you the beauty of my neck even without it." Aspasia thus did the opposite of what women tend to do, as they are extremely fond of jewellery; it was

---

[1] ἀπέφηνε Gesner: ὑπ- codd.

ἐναντία ἔδρασεν ἤπερ εἰώθασι γυναῖκες δρᾶν (φιλόκοσμοι γάρ εἰσι δεινῶς)· ὁ δὲ Κῦρος ἡσθεὶς τῇ ἀποκρίσει τὴν μὲν Ἀσπασίαν κατεφίλησεν, αὐτὰ δὲ ἕκαστα καὶ τῶν πραχθέντων καὶ τῶν λεχθέντων εἰς ἐπιστολὴν ἐγγράψας, ἀπέπεμψε πρὸς τὴν μητέρα σὺν τῷ ὅρμῳ. καὶ ἡ Παρύσατις λαβοῦσα τὸ δῶρον οὐδὲν ἔλαττον ἥσθη τοῖς ἐπεσταλμένοις ἢ τῷ χρυσῷ· καὶ ὑπὲρ τούτων ἠμείψατο τὴν Ἀσπασίαν μεγάλοις δώροις καὶ βασιλικοῖς· ηὔφρανε γὰρ αὐτὴν μάλιστα ἐκεῖνο, ὅτι καίτοι πάνυ σφόδρα εὐδοκιμοῦσα παρὰ τῷ παιδὶ αὐτῆς ἡ Ἀσπασία, ὅμως ἐν τῷ φιλεῖσθαι ὑπὸ Κύρου ἐβούλετο τῆς Κῦρον τεκούσης ἡττᾶσθαι. ἐπῄνεσε μὲν οὖν Ἀσπασία τὰ δῶρα, οὐ μὴν ἔφατο αὐτῶν δεῖσθαι, ἐπεὶ[1] καὶ χρήματα ἧκεν αὐτῇ μετὰ τῶν δώρων πάμπολλα, ἀπέστειλε δὲ Κύρῳ εἰποῦσα· "πολλοὺς ἀνθρώπων τρέφοντί σοι γένοιτο ἂν ταῦτα λυσιτελῆ· ἐμοὶ δὲ σὺ ἀρκεῖς φιλούμενος καὶ κόσμος μοι εἶναι." καὶ ἐκ τούτων οὖν, ὥσπερ εἰκός, τὸν Κῦρον ἐξέπληξε καὶ ἀναμφιλόγως ἐθαυμάζετο ἥδε ἡ γυνὴ καὶ διὰ τὸ κάλλος τὸ τοῦ σώματος καὶ ἔτι μᾶλλον διὰ τὴν εὐγένειαν τῆς ψυχῆς.

Ὅτε δὲ ἀνῃρέθη Κῦρος ἐν τῇ πρὸς τὸν ἀδελφὸν μάχῃ καὶ ἑάλω τὸ στρατόπεδον τοῦ Κύρου, μετὰ [καὶ][2] τῶν ἄλλων λαφύρων καὶ αὐτὴ ἑάλω, οὐκ εἰκῇ καὶ ὡς ἔτυχεν ἐμπεσοῦσα εἰς τοὺς πολεμίους, ἀλλ' ἀνεζήτησεν αὐτὴν σὺν πολλῇ τῇ φροντίδι ὁ βασιλεὺς Ἀρταξέρξης· ᾔδει γὰρ αὐτῆς τὸ κλέος καὶ τὴν

a noble and royal act beyond the reach of other women. Cyrus was charmed by her reply and kissed Aspasia. He recorded what she had said and done in a letter, and sent it to his mother with the necklace. When Parysatis received the gift she was as much delighted by the contents of the letter as by the gold, and in return she heaped great royal gifts upon Aspasia. What had given her particular pleasure was that although Aspasia enjoyed very great favour with her son, still she wished, while being loved by Cyrus, to take second place to Cyrus' mother. Aspasia was complimentary about the gifts but said that she had no need of them, as she had also received a great deal of money with the gifts, and she sent them back to Cyrus with the message: "As you support many men these may come in useful; for me it is a sufficient distinction to love you." By those words, as was natural, she impressed Cyrus. This woman was unreservedly admired both for her physical beauty and even more for her nobility of character.

When Cyrus was killed in the battle against his brother,[a] and Cyrus' camp was captured, she too was captured along with the other booty. She did not fall into enemy hands by chance or as a result of luck; king Artaxerxes sought her out quite deliberately, because he was

[a] The battle of Cynaxa, described by Xenophon in the *Anabasis*, 1.8.

---

[1] ἐπεὶ <δὲ> Per., δὲ post ἀπέστειλε deleto
[2] del. Her.

ἀρετήν. ἐπεὶ δὲ αὐτὴν ἤγαγον δεδεμένην, ἠγανάκτει καὶ τοὺς μὲν τοῦτο δράσαντας εἰς δεσμωτήριον ἐνέβαλε, προσέταξε δὲ αὐτῇ δοθῆναι κόσμον πολυτελῆ. ἡ δὲ ἄκουσα[1] καὶ ποτνιωμένη καὶ δακρύουσα ἐπὶ πολλοῖς ἐβιάσθη τὴν ἐκ βασιλέως στολὴν ἐνδῦναι· ἐθρήνει γὰρ ἰσχυρῶς τὸν Κῦρον· ἐνδῦσα δὲ ἐφάνη καλλίστη γυναικῶν, καὶ παραχρῆμα ὁ Ἀρταξέρξης ἐφλέγετο καὶ κατετήκετο, καὶ πρώτην γε τῶν γυναικῶν ἦγε, καὶ εἰς ὑπερβολὴν ἐτίμα δι' ὧν ἔσπευδεν αὐτῇ χαρίζεσθαι, θαρρῶν ὅτι Κύρου μὲν ἀναπείσει ἐπιλαθέσθαι αὐτήν, διδάξει δ' οὖν αὐτὸν φιλεῖν οὐδὲν ἐκείνου ἧττον. καὶ ἔτυχε μὲν τῆς ἐλπίδος, ὀψὲ δὲ καὶ βραδέως· δεινὴ γὰρ ἡ εἰς Κῦρον εὔνοια ἐντακεῖσα τῇ Ἀσπασίᾳ δυσέκνιπτον ὡς ὅτι[2] μάλιστα τὸ φίλτρον ἐνείργαστο αὐτῇ.

Χρόνῳ δὲ ὕστερον Τηριδάτης ὁ εὐνοῦχος ἀποθνῄσκει, κάλλιστος τῶν ἐν τῇ Ἀσίᾳ καὶ ὡραιότατος γενόμενος· κατέστρεψε δὲ ἄρα οὗτος τὸν βίον μειρακιούμενος καὶ ἐκ τῆς παιδικῆς ἡλικίας ἀνατρέχων, ἐλέγετο δὲ αὐτοῦ ἐρᾶν ὁ βασιλεὺς ἀνδρειότατα. ἐκ δὴ τούτων ἐπένθει βαρύτατα καὶ δριμύτατα ἤλγει καὶ δημοσίᾳ κατὰ πᾶσαν τὴν Ἀσίαν πένθος ἦν, χαριζομένων ἁπάντων βασιλεῖ τοῦτο. ἐτόλμα τε οὐδεὶς αὐτῷ προσελθεῖν οὐδὲ παραμυθήσασθαι· καὶ γὰρ ἐπίστευον ἀνιάτως αὐτὸν ἔχειν ἐπὶ τῷ συμβεβηκότι πάθει. τριῶν δὲ ἡμερῶν διελθουσῶν, στολὴν ἀναλαβοῦσα ἡ Ἀσπασία πενθικήν, ἀπιόντος τοῦ βασιλέως ἐπὶ λουτρόν, ἔστη δακρύουσα καὶ ὁρῶσα

aware of her fame and virtues. When they brought her before him in chains, he was angry with the men who treated her in this way and put them in prison, while issuing orders that she be given expensive jewellery. Unwillingly, protesting and in tears—for she deeply mourned the loss of Cyrus—she was finally obliged to wear the dress sent by the king. When she put it on she seemed to be the most beautiful of women, and Artaxerxes was at once fired and melted with love. He treated her as his senior wife, and showed her exceptional respect by his devoted attentions. He was confident of persuading her to forget Cyrus and that he would teach her to love him just as much. His hopes were realised, but slowly and after a long time, because Aspasia's loyalty to Cyrus was deeply rooted and made her love very difficult to eradicate.

Some time later the eunuch Tiridates died. He had been the most handsome and attractive man in Asia. He ended his days still a youth, emerging from childhood, and the king was said to be greatly in love with him. As a result he lamented bitterly and was in great distress; there was public mourning throughout Asia as a gesture to the king from all his subjects. No one dared to approach or console him, since they believed the grief caused by the loss he had suffered was incurable. When three days had passed, Aspasia put on mourning and, as the king departed to the baths, stood weeping, her gaze fixed on

[1] ἄκουσα Leopardus: ἀκούσασα codd.
[2] ὡς ὅτι Her.: ὥσπερ codd.

εἰς γῆν· ὁ δὲ ἰδὼν αὐτὴν ἐξεπλάγη καὶ ἤρετο τὴν αἰτίαν τῆς ἀφίξεως. καὶ ἐκείνη φησί· "λυπούμενόν σε, βασιλεῦ, καὶ ἀλγοῦντα ἀφῖγμαι παραμυθήσασθαι, εἴ σοι βουλομένῳ ἐστίν· εἰ δὲ χαλεπαίνεις, ἀπαλλάττομαι ὀπίσω." ὑπερήσθη τῇ κηδεμονίᾳ ὁ Πέρσης καὶ προσέταξεν εἰς τὸν θάλαμον ἀνελθοῦσαν ἀναμεῖναι αὐτόν· ἡ δὲ ἔδρασε ταῦτα. ἐπεὶ δὲ ἐπανῆλθε, τὴν τοῦ εὐνούχου στολὴν ἐπὶ τῇ μελαίνῃ περιῆψε τῇ Ἀσπασίᾳ· καί πως ἔπρεψεν αὐτῇ καὶ τὰ τοῦ μειρακίου, καὶ ἔτι μᾶλλον τὰ τῆς ὥρας αὐτῇ πρὸς τὸν ἐραστὴν ἐξέλαμψεν. ἐπεὶ δὲ ἅπαξ ἐχειρώθη τούτοις ἐκεῖνος, ἠξίωσεν αὐτήν, ἔστ' ἂν ἀπομαρανθῇ τοῦ πένθους αὐτῷ ἡ ἀκμή, οὕτως ἐσταλμένην ὡς αὐτὸν παριέναι [αὐτήν].[1] καὶ ἐκείνη χαριζομένη ἐπείσθη αὐτῷ· καὶ μόνη τῶν κατὰ τὴν Ἀσίαν οὐ γυναικῶν μόνον, φασίν, ἀλλὰ καὶ τῶν τοῦ βασιλέως υἱῶν καὶ τῶν συγγενῶν παρεμυθήσατο Ἀρταξέρξην, καὶ τὸ ἐκ τῆς λύπης ἰάσατο πάθος, εἴξαντος τοῦ βασιλέως τῇ κηδεμονίᾳ καὶ τῇ παραμυθίᾳ πεισθέντος συνετῶς.

2. Οὐδεὶς οὔτε πλάστης οὔτε γραφεὺς τῶν Διὸς θυγατέρων τὰ εἴδη παρέστησεν ἡμῖν ὡπλισμένα. ὁμολογεῖ δὲ τοῦτο ὅτι δεῖ τὸν ἐν Μούσαις βίον εἰρηνικόν τε ἅμα καὶ πρᾶον εἶναι.

3. Ἐπαμεινώνδας ὅτε ἐτρώθη ἐν Μαντινείᾳ καιρίαν, εἰς τὴν σκηνὴν κομισθεὶς ἔτι ἔμπνους Δαΐφαντον ἐκάλει, ἵνα ἀποδείξῃ στρατηγόν· οἱ δὲ ἔφασαν τεθνάναι τὸν ἄνδρα. εἶτα Ἰολαΐδαν καλεῖν διὰ

the ground. When he saw her he was amazed and asked why she had come. To which she replied: "I have come to console you in your grief and pain, Your Majesty, if it is your wish; if it annoys you, I will go away." The Persian was greatly encouraged by her sympathy and asked her to go to the bedroom and wait for him, which she did. When he came back he put the eunuch's cloak over Aspasia's black dress. Somehow the young man's clothing suited her, and her beauty struck her lover even more powerfully. Once overcome by this sight, he asked her to visit him in this attire until the severity of his grief waned. In order to please him she did so, and alone of all the inhabitants of Asia, not just the women, they say, but even the king's sons and relatives, she gave consolation to Artaxerxes and cured the suffering caused by his grief, as the king yielded to her sympathy and wisely accepted her consolation.

2. No sculptor or painter has portrayed for us the daughters of Zeus in armour. This proves that life among the Muses must be peaceful and gentle.[a]

3. When Epaminondas was fatally wounded at Mantineia but had been carried back to his tent still alive, he summoned Daiphantos, to appoint him commander. But they told him the man was dead; so he asked them to call

[a] This ch. is repeated in a fuller form below at 14.37. These repetitions are a sign that the *V.H.* is unfinished.

---

[1] del. Her.

ταχέων[1] ἠξίου. ἐπεὶ δὲ καὶ αὐτὸς ἐλέχθη τεθνάναι, συνεβούλευσε διαλύσασθαι πρὸς τοὺς πολεμίους καὶ φιλίαν θέσθαι, ὡς μηκέτι στρατηγοῦ καταλελειμμένου ἐν Θήβαις.

4. Φασὶν Αἰγύπτιοι Σέσωστριν παρ' Ἑρμοῦ τὰ νόμιμα ἐκμουσωθῆναι.

5. Ὅτι Λαῒς ἡ ἑταίρα, ὥς φησιν Ἀριστοφάνης ὁ Βυζάντιος, καὶ Ἀξίνη ἐκαλεῖτο. ἤλεγχε δὲ αὐτῆς τὸ ἐπώνυμον τοῦτο τὴν τοῦ ἤθους ἀγριότητα.

6. Ὅτι γελᾶν ἔξεστιν ἐπὶ τοῖς μέγα[2] φρονοῦσι διὰ τοὺς πατέρας, εἴ γε ἐν Ῥωμαίοις μὲν Μαρίου τὸν πατέρα οὐκ ἴσμεν, αὐτὸν δὲ θαυμάζομεν διὰ τὰ ἔργα· Κάτωνος δὲ τοῦ πρεσβυτέρου[3] καὶ αὐτοῦ τὸν πατέρα ἀναζητεῖν χρή.

7. Ὅτι Ἀλέξανδρος τὸν Ἀχιλλέως τάφον ἐστεφάνωσε καὶ Ἡφαιστίων τὸν τοῦ Πατρόκλου, αἰνιττόμενος ὅτι καὶ αὐτὸς ἦν ἐρώμενος τοῦ Ἀλεξάνδρου, ὥσπερ Ἀχιλλέως[4] ὁ Πάτροκλος.

8. Κλεομένης ὁ Λάκων τῶν ἑταίρων τῶν αὐτοῦ παραλαβὼν Ἀρχωνίδην κοινωνὸν ἐποιεῖτο τῶν πραγμάτων. ἐπώμνυεν οὖν, εἰ κατάσχοι <τὴν ἀρχήν>,[5] πάντα σὺν τῇ αὐτοῦ κεφαλῇ πράττειν.

[1] ταχέων Kor.: -έως V: -έος x
[2] μέγα Her.: μεγάλως codd.
[3] πρεσβυτέρου Kor.: πρεσβύτου codd.
[4] Ἀχιλλέως Peruscus: -εῖ codd.
[5] suppl. Her.

for Iolaidas quickly. When he too was reported dead, Epaminondas advised negotiation with the enemy to establish peace, as there was no general left in Thebes.

4. The Egyptians say Sesostris was instructed by Hermes in matters of law.[a]

5. Note that the courtesan Lais, as Aristophanes of Byzantium says [fr. 366 S.], was also called Axine. This nickname proved her cruelty of character.[b]

6. Note that one may laugh at men who are proud on account of their fathers, considering that among the Romans Marius' father is unknown to us, but Marius himself we admire for his achievements; and as to Cato the Elder, one again has to make inquiry to find out about his father.[c]

7. Note that Alexander laid a wreath on Achilles' tomb and Hephaestion on Patroclus', hinting that he was the object of Alexander's love, as Patroclus was of Achilles.[d]

8. Cleomenes the Laconian chose Archonides from among his friends to share in his activities. He swore that if he acquired power, he would do everything with the aid

[a] Chs. 4–6 are essentially the same as 14.34–36 below.

[b] *Axine* means "battleaxe." The great scholar Aristophanes of Byzantium was one of a number of ancient scholars who wrote about prostitutes. This fragment is also included in FGrH 347 F 2.

[c] In Sallust's *Jugurtha* 85 there is a speech by Marius in which he pours scorn on men who trade on the reputation of their ancestors. Aelian had probably read it.

[d] The tradition that the relationship of Achilles and Patroclus was erotic may have been started by Aeschylus in his lost play *Myrmidons;* it is the subject of some critical comment in Plato, *Symposium* 179 e–180 a.

κατασχὼν οὖν τὴν ἀρχήν, ἀποκτείνας τὸν ἑταῖρον αὐτοῦ καὶ ἀποκρίνας[1] τὴν κεφαλὴν καὶ μέλιτι ἐν σκεύει[2] ἐμβαλών, ὁπότε μέλλοι τι πράττειν, τῷ ἀγγείῳ προσκύψας ἔλεγεν ὅσα ἔπραττε, λέγων μὴ παρασπονδεῖν μηδὲ ἐπιορκεῖν, βουλεύεσθαι δὲ μετὰ τῆς Ἀρχωνίδου κεφαλῆς.

9. Τιμησίας ὁ Κλαζομένιος καλῶς ἐξηγήσατο τῶν Κλαζομενίων· ἦν γὰρ τῶν ἀγαθῶν ἀνδρῶν. ὅς γε μὴν εἴωθε κατισχύειν τῶν τοιούτων φθόνος, καὶ τοῦ Τιμησίου κατεκράτει. καὶ τὰ μὲν πρῶτα ὀλίγον ἔμελε φθονουμένῳ αὐτῷ, τῆς δὲ πατρίδος αὐτὸν ἐξελάσαι ἐκεῖνό φασι. παρῄει διὰ διδασκαλείου· οἱ δὲ παῖδες ἀφεθέντες ὑπὸ τοῦ διδασκάλου ἔπαιζον. γίνεται δὲ δύο παίδων ὑπὲρ γραμμῆς φιλοτιμία,[3] καὶ ὁ εἷς ἐπώμοσεν· "οὕτω ἐγὼ Τιμησίου τὸν ἐγκέφαλον ἐξαράξαιμι." τοῦτο ἐκεῖνος ἀκούσας καὶ ὑπολαβὼν ἀκρατῶς ἔχειν φθόνου καὶ δεινῶς ὑπὸ τῶν πολιτῶν μεμισῆσθαι, εἴ γε καὶ οἱ παῖδες αὐτὸν μισοῦσι, μήτι γοῦν οἱ ἄνδρες, ἑκὼν ἀπῆλθε τῆς πατρίδος.

10. Αἰγινῆταί ποτε ἐδυνήθησαν τὰ μέγιστα ἐν τοῖς Ἕλλησιν, εὐφορίαν[4] τινὰ φόρων[5] καὶ εὐκαιρίαν λαχόντες· δύναμιν γὰρ ναυτικὴν ἔσχον καὶ ἦσαν μέγιστοι. ἀλλὰ καὶ ἐν τοῖς Περσικοῖς ἀγαθοὶ ἐγένοντο, καὶ διὰ ταῦτα καὶ τῶν ἀριστείων ἠξιώθησαν.

[1] ἀποκρίνας] fortasse ἀποκείρας (Russell) vel ἀποκόψας
[2] ἐν σκεύει del. Scheffer [3] φιλοτιμία] φιλονικία Cobet
[4] εὐφορίαν] εὐπορίαν Her. [5] φόρων dubitanter scripsi: χρόνων codd.: χρημάτων Her.

of his friend's head. When he came to power he killed his friend, cut off his head and preserved it in honey. Before taking any action he would bend over the pot, to announce what he was doing, and so he claimed not to be in breach of his oath or undertaking, because he was consulting with Archonides' head.

9. Timesias of Clazomenae was a fine leader of his fellow citizens, because he was one of their best men. Yet jealousy, which has a habit of overpowering such men, had its effect on Timesias as well. At first he was not much concerned at being the target of such sentiments, but they say this is what forced him into exile. He walked through a school where the children had been let out by the master to play. Two of the children had an argument about a line[a] and one of them exclaimed: "I wish I could brain Timesias like that." Having heard that and realised he could not control the jealousy felt against him, and was deeply hated by his fellow citizens, because even the children disliked him, let alone the adults, he left the country of his own free will.

10. The Aeginetans at one time were the most powerful Greek state, as fortune gave them wealth of income and favourable circumstances. They had a fleet and great power. But they also performed well in the Persian Wars and consequently received an award for their prowess.

[a] An obscure reference to a game, perhaps a tug-of-war, as at Plato, *Theaetetus* 181 a, or a board game like drafts. But there is a more serious difficulty in this ch.: if the Timesias mentioned is the founder of Abdera in ca. 655 B.C., the reference to a school may well be an anachronism.

καὶ πρῶτοι νόμισμα ἐκόψαντο καὶ ἐξ αὐτῶν ἐκλήθη νόμισμα Αἰγιναῖον.

11. Ὅτι Ῥωμαῖοι ὑπὸ τῷ λόφῳ τῷ Παλλαντίῳ Πυρετοῦ καὶ νεὼν καὶ βωμὸν ἱδρύσαντο.

12. Ὅτι ἐν Κρήτῃ ἐν Γορτύνῃ μοιχὸς ἁλοὺς ἤγετο ἐπὶ τὰς ἀρχὰς καὶ ἐστεφανοῦτο ἐρίῳ ἐλεγχθείς. τὸ δὲ στεφάνωμα κατηγόρει αὐτοῦ ὅτι ἄνανδρός ἐστι καὶ γύννις καὶ εἰς γυναῖκας καλός. καὶ ἔτι ἐπράττετο[1] δημοσίᾳ εἰς στατῆρας πεντήκοντα καὶ ἀτιμότατος ἦν καὶ οὐδενός οἱ μετῆν τῶν κοινῶν.

13. Ἀφίκετο ἐξ Ἑλλησπόντου παρὰ τὴν ἑταίραν τὴν Ἀττικὴν τὴν Γνάθαιναν ἐραστὴς κατὰ κλέος αὐτῆς. παρὰ πότον οὖν πολὺς ἦν λαλῶν καὶ ἐδόκει φορτικός. ὑπολαβοῦσα οὖν ἡ Γνάθαινα "εἶτα οὐ σὺ μέντοι λέγεις" εἶπεν "ἥκειν ἐξ Ἑλλησπόντου;" τοῦ δὲ ὁμολογήσαντος, "καὶ πῶς" εἶπεν "οὐκ ἔγνως τῶν ἐκεῖ πόλεων τὴν πρώτην;" τοῦ δὲ εἰπόντος· "καὶ τίς ἐστιν;" ἡ δὲ ἀπεκρίνατο· "Σίγειον" καὶ ἐμμελῶς διὰ τοῦ ὀνόματος κατεσίγασεν αὐτόν.

14. Ἐρασμιώτατον καὶ ὡραιότατόν φασιν Ἑλλή-

[1] ἔτι ἐπράττετο J. Gronovius: ἐπιπράσκετο codd.

---

[a] Aegina was an important power in the sixth century B.C. The excellent performance of its contingent at Salamis is noted by Herodotus 8.93. It had also been the first city in Greece to mint currency, before 600 B.C.

[b] Malaria was a serious problem in the ancient world, so it is not surprising to find this personification. In fact, there was not

They were the first to coin money and a currency was named Aeginetan because of them.[a]

11. Note that the Romans established a temple and altar in honour of Fever under the Palatine hill.[b]

12. Note that on Crete at Gortyn an adulterer when caught was brought before the magistrates and after conviction was made to wear a garland of wool.[c] The garland amounted to accusation that he was depraved and effeminate, and had looks appealing to women. Furthermore he was obliged to pay the state fifty staters, suffered complete loss of rights and took no part in public affairs.[d]

13. A lover attracted by her reputation came from the Hellespont to visit the Athenian courtesan Gnathaena. He was very talkative over drinks and seemed vulgar. Gnathaena interrupted him, saying: "Now don't you claim to come from the Hellespont?" And when he agreed, she asked: "How could you fail to know the leading city in those parts?" When he said: "Which is it?" she replied: "Sigeum," and neatly silenced him with this name.[e]

14. They say that among the Greeks Alcibiades was the

one temple of Febris in Rome, but three according to Valerius Maximus 2.5.6, and inscriptions have been found with dedications to Quartana and Tertiana. See K. Latte, *Römische Religionsgeschichte* (Munich, 1962), p. 52.

[c] Presumably it was considered women's work to spin and weave.

[d] The famous extant inscription known as the Gortyn Code contains provisions similar to those outlined by Aelian; but they are not identical, and it is to be presumed that Aelian reflects later developments; see R. F. Willetts, *The Law Code of Gortyn* (Berlin, 1967), p. 28.

[e] The name Sigeum permits a play on the word for silence, *sigē*.

νων μὲν γενέσθαι Ἀλκιβιάδην, Ῥωμαίων δὲ Σκιπίωνα. καὶ Δημήτριον τὸν Πολιορκητὴν λέγουσιν ὥρας ἀμφισβητῆσαι. Ἀλέξανδρον δὲ τὸν Φιλίππου ἀπραγμόνως ὡραῖον λέγουσι γενέσθαι· τὴν μὲν γὰρ κόμην ἀνασεσύρθαι αὐτῷ, ξανθὴν δὲ εἶναι· ὑπαναφύεσθαι δέ τι ἐκ τοῦ εἴδους φοβερὸν τῷ Ἀλεξάνδρῳ λέγουσιν. ὁ δὲ Ὅμηρος ὅταν τοὺς καλοὺς θέλῃ εὐλογῆσαι,[1] δένδροις αὐτοὺς παραβάλλει·

ὁ δ' ἀνέδραμεν ἔρνεϊ ἶσος.

15. Τὸν Ἡρακλῆ λέγουσι τὰς ἐν τοῖς ἄθλοις σπουδὰς διαναπαύειν ταῖς παιδιαῖς. ἔπαιζε δὲ ἄρα ὁ Διὸς καὶ Ἀλκμήνης μετὰ παιδίων πάνυ σφόδρα. τοῦτό τοι καὶ ὁ Εὐριπίδης ἡμῖν ὑπαινίττεται, ποιήσας τὸν αὐτὸν τοῦτον θεὸν λέγοντα·

παίζω· μεταβολὰς γὰρ πόνων ἀεὶ φιλῶ.

λέγει δὲ τοῦτο παιδίον κατέχων.

Καὶ Σωκράτης δὲ κατελήφθη ποτὲ ὑπὸ Ἀλκιβιάδου παίζων μετὰ Λαμπροκλέους ἔτι νηπίου.

Ἀγησίλαος δὲ κάλαμον περιβὰς ἵππευε μετὰ τοῦ υἱοῦ παιδὸς ὄντος καὶ πρὸς τὸν γελάσαντα εἶπε· "νῦν μὲν σιώπα, ὅταν δὲ γένῃ πατὴρ αὐτός, τότε ἐξαγορεύσεις [πρὸς τοὺς πατέρας]."[2]

Ἀλλὰ καὶ Ἀρχύτας ὁ Ταραντῖνος, πολιτικός τε καὶ φιλόσοφος ἀνὴρ γενόμενος, πολλοὺς ἔχων οἰκέτας, τοῖς αὐτῶν παιδίοις πάνυ σφόδρα ἐτέρπετο μετὰ τῶν οἰκοτρίβων παίζων· μάλιστα δὲ ἐφίλει τέρπεσθαι αὐτοῖς ἐν τοῖς συμποσίοις.

most charming and handsome, among the Romans Scipio. It is also said that Demetrius Poliorcetes claimed to be handsome. Alexander the son of Philip is reported to have possessed a natural beauty: his hair was wavy and fair. They say there was something slightly alarming about Alexander's appearance. When Homer wishes to praise the handsome he compares them to trees [*Iliad* 18.56, 437]: "he grew like a sapling."

15. Heracles is said to have played games to relax from his labours. The son of Zeus and Alcmene apparently played a great deal with children. We get a hint of this from Euripides [fr. 864 N.], who made this very god utter the verse "I play, because I always like a change from work."[a] As he says this he holds a child by the hand.

Socrates too was once found by Alcibiades playing with Lamprocles, who was still an infant.[b]

Agesilaus, sitting astride a pole, played at riding with his small son, and when someone laughed at him he replied: "Keep quiet now. When you become a father, then you can express your thoughts [to other fathers]."

Even Archytas of Tarentum, statesman and philosopher, and owner of many slaves, very much enjoyed playing with their children, and indulged in games with the children born in his household. He particularly enjoyed their company at dinner parties.

[a] A verse from an unidentified play.

[b] The oldest of Socrates' three sons.

---

[1] εὐλογῆσαι scripsi: ἐλέγξαι codd.

[2] del. Kor. num ἄλλους pro τοὺς?

16. Ὅτι ἀπήχθετο Περδίκκᾳ Ἀλέξανδρος ὅτι ἦν πολεμικός, Λυσιμάχῳ δέ, ἐπεὶ στρατηγεῖν ἀγαθός, Σελεύκῳ δέ, ὅτι ἀνδρεῖος ἦν. Ἀντιγόνου δὲ αὐτὸν ἐλύπει τὸ φιλότιμον. Ἀντιπάτρου[1] δὲ τῷ ἡγεμονικῷ ἤχθετο, Πτολεμαίου δὲ τῷ δεξιῷ.

17. Ὅτι Δημήτριος τοσούτων ἐθνῶν ἡγεμονεύων ἐφοίτα εἰς Λαμίας τῆς ἑταίρας σὺν τοῖς ὅπλοις καὶ φορῶν τὸ διάδημα. αἴσχιστον μὲν οὖν ἦν αὐτῷ καὶ οἴκαδε μεταπέμψασθαι τὴν ἄνθρωπον· ὁ δὲ παρ' ἐκείνην ἐφοίτα φανερῶς.[2] ἀλλ' ἔγωγε Θεόδωρον <ἂν>[3] τὸν αὐλητὴν προτιμήσαιμι τοῦ Δημητρίου, ἐπεὶ τὸν Θεόδωρον μετεπέμπετο ἡ Λάμια, ὁ δὲ ὑπερεῖδε τὴν κλῆσιν.

18. Τὸν Φάωνα κάλλιστον ὄντα ἀνθρώπων ἡ Ἀφροδίτη ἐν θριδακίναις ἔκρυψε. λόγος δὲ ἕτερος ὅτι ἦν πορθμεὺς καὶ εἶχε τοῦτο τὸ ἐπιτήδευμα. ἀφικνεῖται δέ ποτε ἡ Ἀφροδίτη διαπλεῦσαι βουλομένη, ὁ δὲ ἀσμένως ἐδέξατο, οὐκ εἰδὼς ὅστις ἦν, καὶ σὺν πολλῇ <τῇ>[4] φροντίδι ἤγαγεν ὅποι ποτὲ ἐβούλετο. ἀνθ' ὧν ἡ θεὸς ἔδωκεν ἀλάβαστρον αὐτῷ, καὶ εἶχεν αὐτὴ[5] μύρον, ᾧ χριόμενος ὁ Φάων ἐγένετο ἀνθρώπων κάλλιστος· καὶ ἤρων γε αἱ γυναῖκες αὐτοῦ αἱ Μιτυληναίων. τά γε μὴν τελευταῖα ἀπεσφάγη μοιχεύων ἁλούς.

[1] Ἀντιπάτρου Per.: Ἀττάλου codd.
[2] φανερῶς Her.: φιλοφρόνως x (deest V)
[3] suppl. Kor. [4] suppl. Her. [5] αὐτὴ] αὔτη Her.

---

[a] Chs. 12–16, 22, and 29 are to a large extent repeated below at 14.46 a–d, 47 ab, and 48 a.

16. Note that Alexander hated Perdiccas because he was bellicose, Lysimachus because he was a good general, and Seleucus because he was brave. Antigonus' ambition annoyed him. He disliked Antipater for his leadership and Ptolemy for his cleverness.[a]

17. Note that Demetrius,[b] the ruler of so many nations, visited the courtesan Lamia in full armour and wearing his crown. It was a disgrace for him even to call the woman to his house, yet he went openly to visit her. I would have greater respect for the aulos player Theodorus than for Demetrius, because when Lamia sent for him he disregarded the summons.

18. Aphrodite hid Phaon, the most handsome man on earth, in a lettuce field. Another story is that he was a ferryman and earned his living in that way. One day Aphrodite arrived and wished to cross; he welcomed her with pleasure, not knowing who she was, and guided her most attentively where she wished to go. In return the goddess gave him an alabaster pot. This contained myrrh, and when Phaon rubbed this on himself he became the most handsome of men. The women of Mytilene fell in love with him. But in the end he was caught *in flagrante* and executed.[c]

[b] Demetrius Poliorcetes, king of Macedon 294–287 B.C. Aelian gives the impression that he ruled over a vast empire, which is not the case. [c] The story of Phaon is similar to that of Adonis, another handsome young man loved by Aphrodite; C. M. Bowra, *Greek Lyric Poetry* (2nd ed., Oxford, 1961), p. 213, suggested that Phaon was another name for Adonis. Athenaeus 69 BD cites various texts which show that the ancients thought of the lettuce as inducing impotence. The story has been analysed in detail by M. Detienne, *Les Jardins d'Adonis* (Paris, 1972), pp. 133–138 (English translation: *The Gardens of Adonis*, Hassocks, Sussex, 1977, pp. 68–71).

19. Τὴν ποιήτριαν Σαπφώ, τὴν Σκαμανδρωνύμου θυγατέρα, ταύτην καὶ Πλάτων ὁ Ἀρίστωνος καλὴν[1] ἀναγράφει. πυνθάνομαι δὲ ὅτι καὶ ἑτέρα[2] ἐν τῇ Λέσβῳ ἐγένετο Σαπφώ, ἑταίρα, οὐ ποιήτρια.

20. Λέγει Ἡσίοδος τὴν ἀηδόνα μόνην ὀρνίθων ἀμοιρεῖν[3] ὕπνου καὶ διὰ τέλους ἀγρυπνεῖν, τὴν δὲ χελιδόνα οὐκ εἰς τὸ παντελὲς ἀγρυπνεῖν, καὶ ταύτῃ[4] δὲ ἀπολωλέναι τοῦ ὕπνου τὸ ἥμισυ. τιμωρίαν δὲ ἄρα ταύτην ἐκτίνουσι διὰ τὸ πάθος τὸ ἐν Θρᾴκῃ κατατολμηθὲν τὸ εἰς τὸ δεῖπνον ἐκεῖνο τὸ ἄθεσμον.

21. Αἱ Λακεδαιμονίων μητέρες, ὅσαι ἐπυνθάνοντο τοὺς παῖδας αὐτῶν ἐν τῇ μάχῃ κεῖσθαι, ἀλλὰ αὐταί γε ἀφικόμεναι τὰ τραύματα αὐτῶν ἐπεσκόπουν τά τε ἔμπροσθεν καὶ τὰ ὄπισθεν. καὶ εἰ μὲν ἦν πλείω τὰ ἐναντία, αἱ δὲ γαυρούμεναι καὶ σεμνὸν ἅμα[5] καὶ βλοσυρὸν ὁρῶσαι τοὺς παῖδας εἰς τὰς πατρῴας ἔφερον ταφάς· εἰ δὲ ἑτέρως εἶχον τῶν τραυμάτων, ἐνταῦθα αἰδούμεναι καὶ θρηνοῦσαι καὶ ὡς ἔνι μάλιστα λαθεῖν σπεύδουσαι ἀπηλλάττοντο, καταλιποῦσαι τοὺς νεκροὺς ἐν τῷ πολυανδρίῳ θάψαι, ἢ λάθρᾳ εἰς τὰ οἰκεῖα ἠρία ἐκόμιζον αὐτούς.

22. Τιτόρμῳ φασὶ τῷ βουκόλῳ περιτυχεῖν τὸν Κροτωνιάτην Μίλωνα, μεγαλοφρονοῦντα διὰ τὴν

[1] καλὴν e Platone Her.: σοφὴν codd. [2] ἑτέρα Peruscus: ἑταίρα codd. [3] ἀμοιρεῖν Duker: ἀμελεῖν codd. [4] ταύτῃ Kor.: -ην codd. [5] ἅμα Kor.: ἄρα codd.

---

[a] According to a tradition preserved by Athenaeus 596 E it

19. The poet Sappho, daughter of Scamandronymus, is described as beautiful by Plato son of Ariston [*Phaedrus* 235 c]. I learn that there was another Sappho on Lesbos, a courtesan, not a poet.[a]

20. Hesiod [fr. 312 M.-W.] says the nightingale is the only bird to take no sleep and remain perpetually awake, whereas the swallow is not always awake but loses half its sleep. This is the penalty they pay for the misdeeds they dared to commit in Thrace at the notorious and monstrous banquet.[b]

21. Every Spartan mother who learned of her son's death in battle would go in person to inspect the wounds both on the front and the back of the corpse. If the majority were on the front the mother carried her child to the family cemetery proudly and with a solemn and serious demeanour. But if the wounds were elsewhere, then she was ashamed, lamented, and did her best to depart unseen, leaving the body to be buried in a mass grave or secretly bringing it back to the family's burial place.

22. Milo of Croton, who was proud of his physical strength, met the cowherd Titormus, they say. Seeing that

was this other Sappho who fell in love with Phaon, whereas most sources claim that it was the poet who did so. One might expect Aelian to include that story here; has the text been abbreviated? Bowra, *Greek Lyric Poetry,* thought that a confusion arose because the poet wrote a song in which Aphrodite declared her love for Phaon, and this was misunderstood as Sappho's love for a living man. [b] An allusion to a myth well known in antiquity. Procne and her sister Philomela were metamorphosed into a nightingale and a swallow after they had taken revenge on Tereus, Procne's husband, by serving up his child for dinner. Tereus' offence had been to seduce Philomela and cut out her tongue.

ῥώμην τοῦ σώματος. θεασάμενος οὖν μέγαν τὸν Τίτορμον τὸ σῶμα ἰδεῖν, ἐβούλετο λαβεῖν αὐτοῦ ἰσχύος[1] πεῖραν. ὁ δὲ Τίτορμος ἔλεγε μηδὲν μέγα ἰσχύειν, καταβὰς δὲ εἰς τὸν Εὔηνον καὶ θοἰμάτιον ἀποδὺς λίθον λαμβάνει μέγιστον, καὶ πρῶτον μὲν ἕλκει αὐτὸν πρὸς ἑαυτόν, εἶτα ἀπωθεῖ, καὶ δὶς καὶ τρὶς τοῦτο ἐποίησε, καὶ μετὰ ταῦτα αὐτὸν ἦρεν ἕως εἰς τὰ γόνατα, καὶ τέλος ἀράμενος ἐπὶ τῶν ὤμων ἔφερεν ὅσον ἐπ᾽ ὀργυιὰς ὀκτὼ καὶ ἔρριψεν· ὁ δὲ Κροτωνιάτης Μίλων μόλις τὸν λίθον ἐκίνησεν.[2]

Εἶτα δεύτερος ἆθλος τοῦ Τιτόρμου· ἐπὶ τὴν ἀγέλην ἦλθε καὶ στὰς ἐν μέσῳ τὸν μέγιστον ταῦρον ἄγριον ὄντα λαμβάνει τοῦ ποδός· καὶ ὁ μὲν ἀποδρᾶναι ἔσπευδεν, οὐ μὴν ἐδύνατο. παριόντα δὲ ἕτερον τῇ ἑτέρᾳ χειρὶ συναρπάσας τοῦ ποδὸς ὁμοίως εἶχε. θεασάμενος δὲ ὁ Μίλων εἰς τὸν οὐρανὸν τὰς χεῖρας τείνας ἔφατο· "ὦ Ζεῦ, μὴ τοῦτον Ἡρακλῆ ἡμῖν ἕτερον ἔσπειρας;" ἐντεῦθεν ῥηθῆναι λέγουσι τὴν παροιμίαν· "ἄλλος οὗτος Ἡρακλῆς."

23. Ἀνθρώπων ἐγὼ ἀκούω φιλοκινδυνοτάτους εἶναι τοὺς Κελτούς. τῶν ᾀσμάτων γοῦν[3] ὑποθέσεις ποιοῦνται τοὺς ἀνθρώπους τοὺς ἀποθανόντας ἐν τῷ πολέμῳ καλῶς. [καὶ][4] μάχονται δὲ ἐστεφανωμένοι, ἀλλὰ καὶ τρόπαια ἐγείρουσιν, ἅμα τε ἐπὶ τοῖς πεπραγμένοις σεμνυνόμενοι καὶ ὑπομνήματα αὐτῶν τῆς ἀρετῆς ἀπολείποντες Ἑλληνικῶς. οὕτως δὲ αἰσχρὸν νομίζουσι τὸ φεύγειν, ὡς μηδὲ ἐκ τῶν

[1] <τῆς> ἰσχύος Her. [2] ἐκίνησεν V: ἐκύλισεν x

Titormus was a big man he felt inclined to test his strength. But Titormus claimed to have no great strength; he went down to the Evenus, took off his cloak, and laid hands on a very large stone. First he pulled it towards him, then pushed it away. He did this two or three times, after which he lifted it to knee height, and then finally raised it to his shoulders, carrying it for about fifty feet and throwing it down. But Milo of Croton could scarcely move it.

Then Titormus performed a second feat. He approached his herd, stood in the middle and took hold of the largest bull by the hoof. It tried to run away but was unable to. As another bull passed by he grabbed it with his other hand and held it in the same way. At this spectacle Milon held up his hands towards the sky and said: "O Zeus, have you fathered another Heracles on us?" This is said to be the origin of the proverb "Here is another Heracles."[a]

23. I gather that the Celts face danger more boldly than other races.[b] Certainly they make heroic death in war the subject of their poems. In battle they wear garlands on their heads and they put up victory monuments; they take pride in their achievements and leave behind them memorials of their bravery, in Greek style. To run away is held to be so shameful that they often will not

[a] A shorter version of this ch. appears at 14.47b.

[b] Descriptions of Celts living in Gaul are found in Greek authors from the first century B.C. They include references to singers of epic poetry who were called *bardoi.*

---

[3] *γοῦν* Her.: *οὖν* x: om. V [4] del. Her.

οἰκιῶν κατολισθαινουσῶν καὶ ἐμπιπτουσῶν πολλάκις[1] ἀποδιδράσκειν, ἀλλὰ μηδὲ πιμπραμένων αὐτῶν περιλαμβανομένους[2] ὑπὸ τοῦ πυρός. πολλοὶ δὲ καὶ ἐπικλύζουσαν τὴν θάλασσαν ὑπομένουσιν. εἰσὶ δὲ καὶ οἳ ὅπλα λαμβάνοντες ἐμπίπτουσι τοῖς κύμασι καὶ τὴν φορὰν αὐτῶν εἰσδέχονται, γυμνὰ τὰ ξίφη καὶ τὰ δόρατα προσείοντες, ὥσπερ οὖν ἢ φοβῆσαι δυνάμενοι ἢ τρῶσαι.

24. Σμινδυρίδην τὸν Συβαρίτην λέγουσιν ἐπὶ τοσοῦτον τρυφῆς ἐξοκεῖλαι, ὡς εἰς Σικυῶνα αὐτὸν ἀφικέσθαι μνηστῆρα Ἀγαρίστης τῆς Κλεισθένους καὶ ἐπάγεσθαι χιλίους μὲν μαγείρους, τοσούτους δὲ ὀρνιθευτὰς καὶ ἁλιεῖς χιλίους.

25. Ὤνηντο ἄρα καὶ Ὀδυσσεὺς Ἀλκινόου καὶ Ἀχιλλεὺς Χείρωνος καὶ Πάτροκλος Ἀχιλλέως καὶ Ἀγαμέμνων Νέστορος καὶ Τηλέμαχος Μενελάου καὶ Ἕκτωρ Πολυδάμαντος, ἐν οἷς αὐτῷ προσεῖχε,[3] καὶ οἱ Τρῶες Ἀντήνορος. καὶ οἱ Πυθαγόρειοι μὲν ὁμιληταὶ Πυθαγόρου ὤνηντο, οἱ Δημοκρίτειοι δὲ συγγενόμενοι Δημοκρίτῳ πολλῶν ἀπέλαυσαν. Σωκράτει δὲ εἰ προσεῖχον οἱ Ἀθηναῖοι, πάντα ἂν ἐγένοντο εὐδαίμονες καὶ[4] ἐφιλοσόφουν. καὶ Ἱέρων δὲ ὁ Δεινομένους Σιμωνίδου τοῦ Κείου ἀπέλαυσε καὶ Πολυκράτης Ἀνακρέοντος καὶ Ξενοφῶντος Πρόξενος καὶ Ἀντίγονος Ζήνωνος. ἵνα δὲ [μοι][5] καὶ τῶν ἐμοὶ προσηκόντων οὐδὲν ἧττον ἤπερ καὶ οἱ Ἕλληνες προσήκουσι μνήσωμαι[6] (διαφέρει δέ μοι καὶ τούτων, εἴ γε

[1] πολλάκις del. Her. [2] περιλαμβανομένους Kühn: παρα-

even escape if a house collapses and falls on them, nor if the house is on fire and they are caught by the flames. Many of them stand firm as the sea washes over them. Some pick up weapons, rush into the waves, and feel their impact, brandishing naked swords and spears, as if these could frighten or wound them.

24. Smindyrides of Sybaris is said to have degenerated into such extravagant habits that, when he arrived in Sicyon as a suitor for Agariste the daughter of Cleisthenes, he brought with him a thousand cooks, equal numbers of birdcatchers, and a thousand fishermen.[a]

25. Odysseus benefited from Alcinous, Achilles from Chiron, Patroclus from Achilles, Agamemnon from Nestor, Telemachus from Menelaus, Hector from Polydamas, when he was willing to listen to him, and the Trojans from Antenor. Pythagorean disciples benefited from Pythagoras, Democriteans who spent time with Democritus gained a great deal. If the Athenians had listened to Socrates they would have enjoyed complete happiness and practised philosophy. Hieron son of Dinomenes gained from Simonides of Ceos, Polycrates from Anacreon, Proxenus from Xenophon, Antigonus from Zeno. If I may mention persons just as close to me as the Greeks are—since I am a Roman I have an interest in

[a] The marriage of Agariste is a famous episode in Herodotus 6.126–131; but the fanciful details given by Aelian are embellishments of the tale. The account in Athenaeus 273 C is very similar.

codd. [3] προσεῖχε Kühn: -ον codd. [4] καὶ Kühn: εἰ codd. (εἰ ἐφιλοσόφουν del. Scheffer) [5] del. Gesner
[6] μνήσωμαι scripsi: μεμνήσομαι x: om. V

Ῥωμαῖός εἰμι), καὶ Λεύκολλος Ἀντιόχου τι ὤνητο τοῦ Ἀσκαλωνίτου καὶ Μαικήνας Ἀρείου καὶ Κικέρων Ἀπολλωνίου καὶ ὁ Σεβαστὸς Ἀθηνοδώρου. Πλάτων δὲ ἐμοῦ καίτοι σοφώτερος ὢν λέγει ὅτι καὶ Ζεὺς εἶχε σύμβουλον· τίνα δὲ καὶ ὅπως, παρ᾿ ἐκείνου μανθάνωμεν.[1]

26. Ποτίστατοι γεγόνασιν ἄνθρωποι, ὥσπερ[2] φασί, Ξεναγόρας ὁ Ῥόδιος, ὃν ἐκάλουν Ἀμφορέα καὶ Ἡρακλείδης ὁ πύκτης, καὶ Πρωτέας ὁ Λανίκης μὲν υἱός, Ἀλεξάνδρου δὲ τοῦ βασιλέως σύντροφος. καὶ αὐτὸς δὲ Ἀλέξανδρος λέγεται πλεῖστον πιεῖν ἀνθρώπων.

27. Ἡμερώτατά φασι τὸν Ἡρακλῆ προσενεχθῆναι τοῖς ἑαυτοῦ πολεμίοις· πρῶτον γὰρ τῶν ἐξ αἰῶνος νεκροὺς ὑποσπόνδους ἀποδοῦναι ταφησομένους, εἰωθότων τῶν τότε ὀλιγωρεῖν τῶν ἀνῃρημένων καὶ ἀπολείπειν αὐτοὺς κυνῶν δεῖπνον εἶναι. καὶ Ὅμηρος·

ἑλώρια τεῦχε κύνεσσι

καὶ

κυσὶν μέλπηθρα γενέσθαι.

28. Λεωκόριον Ἀθήνησιν ἐκαλεῖτο τὸ τέμενος τῶν Λεὼ θυγατέρων Πραξιθέας καὶ Θεόπης καὶ Εὐβούλης. ταύτας δὲ ὑπὲρ τῆς πόλεως τῆς Ἀθηναίων ἀναιρεθῆναι λόγος ἔχει, ἐπιδόντος αὐτὰς τοῦ Λεὼ εἰς

them as well—Lucullus derived some advantage from Antiochus of Ascalon, Maecenas from Areius, Cicero from Apollonius, and Augustus from Athenodorus.[a] Plato [*Epist.* 2, 311 ab], a wiser man than myself, says that even Zeus had an adviser; who that was and how he acted, let us learn from him.[b]

26. The greatest drinkers on record, they say, were Xenagoras of Rhodes, who was called Amphora, the boxer Heraclides, and Proteas son of Lanice and childhood companion of king Alexander. Alexander himself is said to have drunk more than any other man.

27. Heracles is reported to have treated his enemies very gently. He was the first person in recorded history to return corpses for burial under a truce, whereas men of that time were in the habit of despising the dead and leaving them to make a meal for dogs, as in Homer [*Iliad* 1.4] "He made them the prey of dogs" and [*Iliad* 17.255] "to become the plaything of dogs."

28. Leocorium was the name at Athens for the temple in honour of the daughters of Leos, Praxithea,[c] Theope, and Euboule. The story tells how they died on behalf of the city of Athens when Leos gave them up in accordance

[a] A list of Greek and Greek-speaking scholars attached to prominent figures in Rome is given by J. P. V. D. Balsdon, *Romans and Aliens* (London, 1979), pp. 54–58.

[b] Plato, *Letter* 2 311 ab, says that the earliest generations of mankind thought of Prometheus as standing in this relation to Zeus. Many scholars think this text spurious.

[c] In the *Suda* lexicon s.v. *Λεωκόριον* the name of Praxithea is given as Phrasithea.

---

[1] *μανθάνωμεν* Per.: *-ομεν* codd. [2] *ὥσπερ*] *ὥς* Her.

τὸν χρησμὸν τὸν Δελφικόν. ἔλεγε γὰρ μὴ ἂν ἄλλως σωθῆναι τὴν πόλιν, εἰ μὴ ἐκεῖναι σφαγιασθεῖεν.

29. Πλάτων ὁ Ἀρίστωνος ἰδὼν Ἀκραγαντίνους καὶ οἰκοδομοῦντας πολυτελῶς καὶ ὁμοίως δειπνοῦντας εἶπεν ὅτι ἄρα οἱ Ἀκραγαντῖνοι οἰκοδομοῦσι μὲν ὡς ἀεὶ βιωσόμενοι, δειπνοῦσι δὲ ὡς αὔριον[1] τεθνηξόμενοι. λέγει δὲ Τίμαιος ὅτι καὶ ἀργυραῖς ληκύθοις καὶ στλεγγίσιν ἐχρῶντο καὶ ἐλεφαντίνας κλίνας εἶχον ὅλας.

30. Ταραντίνοις ἐν ἔθει ἦν πίνειν μὲν ἐξ ἑωθινοῦ, μεθύειν δὲ περὶ πλήθουσαν ἀγοράν. εἰς τοσοῦτον δὲ ἄρα Κυρηναῖοι τρυφῆς ἐξώκειλαν, ὥστε Πλάτωνα παρεκάλουν, ἵνα αὐτοῖς γένηται νομοθέτης. τὸν δὲ ἀπαξιῶσαί φασι διὰ τὴν ἐξ ἀρχῆς ῥᾳθυμίαν αὐτῶν. ὁμολογεῖ δὲ καὶ Εὔπολις ἐν τῷ Μαρικᾷ ὅστις[2] αὐτῶν[3] εὐτελέστατος σφραγῖδας εἶχε δέκα μνῶν. παρῆν δὲ θαυμάζεσθαι καὶ τοὺς διαγλύφοντας τοὺς δακτυλίους.

31. Φέρε οἴνων Ἑλληνικῶν διὰ σπουδῆς ἰόντων ἐν τοῖς πάλαι ὀνόματα καταλέξω ὑμῖν. Πράμνειόν τινα ἐκάλουν, ἱερὸς δὲ ἦν ἄρα οὗτος[4] τῆς Δήμητρος, καὶ Χῖος οἶνος ἐκ τῆς νήσου, καὶ Θάσιος ἄλλος, καὶ

[1] αὔριον e Diog. L. 8.63 Per.: ἀεὶ codd.
[2] ὅστις] ὅτι A. Gronovius [3] αὐτῶν <ὁ> Her.
[4] ἱερὸς . . . οὗτος Gesner: -ον . . . τοῦτο codd.

[a] A similar tale was told about king Erechtheus of Athens—that he needed to sacrifice his daughter, as ordered by the oracle, in order to save the city.

with the Delphic oracle. It had said there could be no safety for the city unless they were sacrificed.[a]

29. When Plato the son of Ariston saw that the inhabitants of Acragas built lavish homes and dined in equally lavish style, he remarked that they built as if they were to live for ever and dined as if they would die tomorrow. Timaeus [FGrH 566 F 26c] says they used oil flasks and scrapers of silver and had couches made entirely of ivory.[b]

30. At Tarentum the custom was to drink from dawn and to reach a drunken state by the time the market was active. The men of Cyrene lapsed into such extravagance that they called in Plato to give them a constitution. But he is said to have declined because of their persistent frivolity. Eupolis in the *Marikas* [fr. 202 K.-A.] agrees that the most ordinary man among them wears rings worth ten minae.[c] Even the engravers of the rings could be admired.[d]

31. Let me give you the names of Greek wines that were taken seriously by the ancients. They had one called Pramnian,[e] which was apparently sacred to Demeter, a Chian from the island, another from Thasos, and a

[b] Timaeus of Tauromenium (ca. 356–260 B.C.) was a historian who lived most of his life in Athens. His work, in 38 books, concentrated on Sicilian affairs.

[c] Eupolis' lost play *Marikas* was produced at the Lenaea of 421 B.C.

[d] The precise meaning of the last sentence in the Greek is not easy to establish.

[e] This adjective is found as early as *Iliad* 11.639 and *Odyssey* 10.235; but even the ancients could not explain it (see Athenaeus 30 D).

Λέσβιος. καὶ ἐπὶ τούτοις Γλυκύς τις ἐκαλεῖτο, πρέπων τῷ ὀνόματι τὴν γεῦσιν, καὶ Κρὴς ἄλλος. καὶ ἐν Συρακούσαις Πόλλιος· ἐκλήθη δὲ ἀπό τινος ἐγχωρίου[1] βασιλέως. ἔπινον δὲ καὶ Κῷον οἶνον, καὶ οὕτως αὐτὸν ἐκάλουν· καὶ Ῥόδιον, κατὰ τὰ αὐτὰ ὀνομάζοντες. τί δέ; οὐκ ἐκεῖνα[2] τοῖς Ἕλλησι τρυφῆς ἀπόδειξις; μύρῳ γὰρ οἶνον μιγνύντες οὕτως ἔπινον, καὶ ὑπερησπάζοντο[3] τὴν τοιαύτην κρᾶσιν· καὶ ἐκαλεῖτο ὁ οἶνος Μυρίνης.[4] μέμνηται δὲ αὐτοῦ Φιλιππίδης ὁ τῆς κωμῳδίας ποιητής.

32. Πυθαγόρας ὁ Σάμιος λευκὴν ἐσθῆτα ἤσθητο καὶ ἐφόρει στέφανον χρυσοῦν καὶ ἀναξυρίδας. Ἐμπεδοκλῆς δὲ ὁ Ἀκραγαντῖνος ἁλουργεῖ ἐχρήσατο καὶ ὑποδήμασι χαλκοῖς. Ἱππίαν δὲ καὶ Γοργίαν ἐν πορφυραῖς ἐσθῆσι προϊέναι διαρρεῖ λόγος.

33. Κινέας ὁ Πύρρου ἰατρός, φασι, πρὸς τὴν βουλὴν τῶν Ῥωμαίων ἔγραψε δι' ἀπορρήτων καὶ ᾔτει χρήματα καὶ ὑπισχνεῖτο ἀποκτενεῖν[5] φαρμάκοις τὸν Πύρρον. οἱ δὲ οὐ προσήκαντο τὴν ὑπόσχεσιν· δι' ἀρετῆς γὰρ ἴσασι Ῥωμαῖοι ἀγαθοὶ εἶναι,[6] οὐ μὴν διὰ τέχνης καὶ πανουργίας καὶ ἐπιβουλῆς καταγωνίζεσθαι[7] τοὺς ἐχθρούς. ἀλλὰ καὶ αὐτῷ τῷ Πύρρῳ τὴν γνώμην τοῦ Κινέου ἐξέφαναν.[8]

[1] ἐγχωρίου Peruscus: χωρίου g: ἐγχώρας da: ἐγχώρ V
[2] ἐκεῖνα] -νο Her.
[3] ὑπερησπάζοντο J. Gronovius: -ηναγκάζοντο codd.
[4] Μυρίνης e Poll. Onom. 6.2 Her.: μυρ(ρ)ινίτας codd.
[5] ἀποκτενεῖν Kor.: -κτείνειν codd.

Lesbian. Apart from these one was called Sweet, its name fitting the taste, and another from Crete. In Syracuse they had Pollios, named after a local king. They also drank wine from Cos, and named it accordingly, and some from Rhodes, naming it in the same way. Furthermore, the following facts are surely proof of Greek extravagance. They put perfume into wine and then drank it, taking great delight in the mixture; the wine was called *myrines.*[a] The comic writer Philippides [fr. 40 K.-A.] mentions it.

32. Pythagoras the Samian put on white clothing and wore a golden garland and trousers.[b] Empedocles of Acragas wore a purple cloak and bronze shoes. Tradition records that Hippias and Gorgias went about in purple clothes.

33. Pyrrhus' doctor Cineas (so they say) wrote a secret letter to the Roman senate, asking for money and promising to kill Pyrrhus with poisons. The proposal was not accepted; the Romans know how to behave honourably, and do not overcome their enemies with craft, guile, and intrigue. In fact they revealed Cineas' plan to Pyrrhus himself.

[a] Many ancient wines had additives; a few of these were intended to have a medicinal effect.

[b] The wearing of trousers has been interpreted as a sign of connections with Persia or Scythia; so W. Burkert, *Lore and Science*, pp. 112, n. 16; 165.

---

[6] ἀγαθοὶ εἶναι del. Nauck

[7] καταγωνίζεσθαι Kor.: -ίσασθαι codd.

[8] ἐξέφαναν] -ηναν Gesner

34. Ἔρωτες ἡμῖν τῶν ἀρχαίων πολλοὶ μὲν καὶ ἄλλοι εἰς μνήμην ἐδόθησαν, καὶ οὗτοι[1] δὲ οὐχ ἥκιστα. Παυσανίας μὲν γὰρ ἤρα τῆς ἑαυτοῦ γυναικός, Ἀπελλῆς δὲ τῆς Ἀλεξάνδρου παλλακῆς, ᾗπερ ὄνομα ἦν Παγκάστη, τὸ δὲ γένος Λαρισαία ἦν. ταύτῃ καὶ πρώτῃ, φασίν, ὁ Ἀλέξανδρος ὡμίλησεν.

35. Ὅτι δύο Περίανδροι, ὁ μὲν σοφὸς ἦν, ὁ δὲ τύραννος. καὶ Μιλτιάδαι τρεῖς, ὁ τὴν Χερρόνησον κτίσας καὶ ὁ Κυψέλου καὶ ὁ Κίμωνος. Σίβυλλαι τέτταρες, ἡ Ἐρυθραία ἡ Σαμία ἡ Αἰγυπτία ἡ Σαρδιανή. οἱ δέ φασι καὶ ἑτέρας ἕξ, ὡς εἶναι τὰς πάσας δέκα, ὧν εἶναι καὶ τὴν Κυμαίαν καὶ τὴν Ἰουδαίαν. Βάκιδες τρεῖς, ὁ μὲν Ἐλεώνιος,[2] ὁ δὲ Ἀθηναῖος, ὁ δὲ Ἀρκάς.

36. Ἐοίκασιν οἱ ἀρχαῖοι ὑπὲρ τοῦ ἀριθμοῦ τῶν τῆς Νιόβης παίδων μὴ συνᾴδειν ἀλλήλοις. Ὅμηρος μὲν ἓξ λέγει[3] καὶ τοσαύτας κόρας, Λᾶσος δὲ δὶς ἑπτὰ λέγει, Ἡσιόδος δὲ ἐννέα καὶ δέκα, εἰ μὴ ἄρα οὐκ εἰσὶν Ἡσιόδου τὰ ἔπη, ἀλλ' ὡς πολλὰ καὶ ἄλλα κατέψευσται αὐτοῦ. Ἀλκμὰν <δὲ>[4] δέκα φησί, Μίμνερμος εἴκοσι, καὶ Πίνδαρος τοσούτους.

37. Ἀλέξανδρος ὅτε Βῆσσον ἐδίωκεν, ἐν[5] ἀπορίᾳ γενόμενος τροφῶν, αὐτός τε ἥψατο τῶν καμήλων καὶ ὑποζυγίων ἄλλων καὶ οἱ σὺν αὐτῷ. τῶν τε ξύλων

[1] οὗτοι Kor.: -ος codd. [2] Ἐλεώνιος Scheffer: Ἕλλην codd. [3] λέγει <ἄρρενας> Her. [4] suppl. Page
[5] ἐν Kor.: ἐπ' codd.

34. Many instances of love among the ancients have been recorded for us, among them the following prominent cases. Pausanias was in love with his wife, Apelles with Alexander's mistress—she was called Pancaste and came from Larisa. She is said to have been the first woman Alexander slept with.

35. Note that there were two men called Periander, one a sage, the other a tyrant;[a] three called Miltiades, the founder of the Chersonese, the son of Cypselus, and the son of Cimon;[b] and four Sibyls: the Erythraean, the Samian, the Egyptian, and the one from Sardis. Some people say there were six more, making ten in all, including the Cumaean and the Jewish. There were three people called Bacis, from Eleon, Athens, and Arcadia.[c]

36. The ancients seem to disagree about the number of Niobe's children. Homer says [*Iliad* 24.603] there were six, all girls, Lasus [fr. 5 P.] says fourteen, Hesiod [fr. 183 M.-W.] nineteen, unless indeed the verses are not by Hesiod, but falsely attributed to him like many others. Alcman [fr. 75 P.] gives the figure ten, Mimnermus [fr. 19 W.] twenty, and Pindar [fr. 52 n Sn.] the same.[d]

37. When Alexander was pursuing Bessus,[e] he became short of food, and both he and his men ate camels and pack animals. As their stock of wood gave out they ate

[a] Aelian here agrees with a tradition recorded in Diogenes Laertius 1.98. [b] Aelian appears to be in error when he makes a distinction between Miltiades the son of Cypselus and the coloniser of the Chersonese. [c] Bacis like Sibyl is the title applied to a class of inspired prophets. See E. Rohde, *Psyche* (London, 1925), p. 292. [d] This ch. gives a notable proof of the fluidity of Greek myths. [e] Bessus was one of the assassins of Darius III and satrap of Bactria.

αὐτοὺς ἐπιλιπόντων ὠμὰ τὰ κρέα ἤσθιον. ἐπεκούρει δὲ αὐτοῖς τὸ σίλφιον πολὺ ὂν ὥστε τὰς σάρκας συνεκπέττειν.

Ἐν δὲ τῇ Βακτριανῇ οἱ στρατιῶται αὐτόθεν[1] τὰς κώμας κατελάμβανον, ὅτι οἰκοῦνται ἐκ τοῦ καπνοῦ συνιέντες,[2] καὶ τὴν χιόνα ἀφαιροῦντες τῶν θυρῶν.

38. Οἱ Σακῶν ἵπποι, ἐὰν ἀποβάλῃ τις τὸν δεσπότην, εἰς τὸ ἀναβῆναι αὐτὸν[3] παρέστηκεν. ἐὰν δέ τις γῆμαι βούληται παρθένον, μονομαχεῖ τῇ παιδί. καὶ κρατήσασα μὲν αἰχμάλωτον ἄγεται καὶ κρατεῖ αὐτοῦ καὶ ἄρχει· ἐὰν δὲ νικηθῇ, ἄρχεται. μονομαχοῦσι δὲ ἄχρι νίκης, οὐ μέχρι θανάτου. πενθοῦντες δὲ οἱ Σάκαι εἰς οἴκους τινὰς ὑπάντρους καὶ κατασκίους ἀποκρύπτονται.

39. Περδίκκας ὁ Μακεδὼν ὁ συστρατευσάμενος Ἀλεξάνδρῳ οὕτως ἄρα ἦν εὔτολμος, ὥς ποτε εἰς σπήλαιον παρελθεῖν ἔνθα εἶχεν εὐνὴν λέαινα μόνος· καὶ τὴν μὲν λέαιναν οὐ κατέλαβε, τούς γε μὴν σκύμνους αὐτῆς κομίζων προῆλθε καὶ ἔδοξεν ἐπὶ τούτῳ θαυμάζεσθαι[4] ὁ Περδίκκας.

Πεπίστευται δὲ οὐ μόνον παρὰ τοῖς Ἕλλησιν ἀλκιμώτατόν τε καὶ δυσμαχώτατον εἶναι θηρίον ἡ λέαινα, ἀλλὰ καὶ παρὰ τοῖς βαρβάροις. φασὶ γοῦν καὶ Σεμίραμιν τὴν Ἀσσυρίαν <ὅτι> οὐκ, εἴ ποτε εἷλε λέοντα ἢ πάρδαλιν κατέκτανεν ἢ ἄλλο τι τῶν

[1] *αὐτόθεν* dubitanter scripsi: *αὐτὰς* codd.: del. Cuper
[2] *συνιέντες* Gesner: -*όντες* codd.

the meat raw. They were helped by having plenty of silphium to tenderise the meat.[a]

In Bactria the soldiers at once identified the villages because they saw smoke as a sign of habitation, and they cleared the snow away from the doors.

38. Among the Sacae, if a horse loses its rider it waits for him to mount again. If a man wishes to marry a girl he fights a duel with her; if the girl wins she takes him off as a captive, and has power and control over him. But if she is defeated she is under his control. They fight to win but not to the death. When the Sacae are in mourning they retreat into sheltered cave dwellings.

39. Perdiccas the Macedonian who accompanied Alexander on his expedition was apparently so courageous that he once went alone into a cave where a lioness had her lair. He did not catch the lioness, but he emerged carrying her cubs. Perdiccas won admiration for this feat.

Not only Greeks, but barbarians as well, are convinced that the lioness is an animal of great bravery and very difficult to contend with. They say that the Assyrian Semiramis had her spirits raised, not if she killed a lion or

[a] This is one of the few texts that give us information about the use of the silphium plant. It yielded a resin similar to asafoetida, much valued for medicinal use and in the kitchen as an ingredient for sauces. For centuries the main source of supply was Cyrene, but the variety grown there ceased to be produced on a commercial scale by the first century A.D. Recently it has been suggested that silphium was used as a contraceptive; see J. M. Riddle, *Archaeology* 47 (issue no. 2 of 1994): 29–35.

---

[3] fortasse scribendum <αὖθις> αὐτὸν
[4] malim <ἄξιος> θαυμάζεσθαι

τοιούτων, ἀλλ' εἰ λεαίνης ἐγκρατὴς ἐγένετο, μέγα ἐφρόνει.

40. Τά τε ἄλλα ἐφόδια εἵπετο τῷ Ξέρξῃ πολυτελείας καὶ ἀλαζονείας πεπληρωμένα, καὶ οὖν καὶ ὕδωρ ἠκολούθει τὸ ἐκ τοῦ Χοάσπου. ἐπειδὴ ἔν τινι ἐρήμῳ τόπῳ ἐδίψησεν, οὐδέπω τῆς θεραπείας ἡκούσης, ἐκηρύχθη τῷ στρατοπέδῳ, εἴ τις ἔχει ὕδωρ ἐκ τοῦ Χοάσπου, ἵνα δῷ βασιλεῖ πιεῖν. καὶ εὑρέθη τις βραχὺ καὶ σεσηπὸς ἔχων. ἔπιεν οὖν τοῦτο ὁ Ξέρξης καὶ εὐεργέτην τὸν δόντα ἐνόμισεν,[1] ὅτι ἂν ἀπώλετο τῇ δίψῃ, εἰ μὴ ἐκεῖνος εὑρέθη.

41. Πρωτογένης ὁ ζωγράφος τὸν Ἰάλυσον, φασίν, ἑπτὰ ἔτεσι διαζωγραφῶν ἐξετέλεσεν. ὃν Ἀπελλῆς ἰδὼν τὸ μὲν πρῶτον ἔστη ἄφωνος, ἐκπλαγεὶς ἐπὶ τῇ παραδόξῳ θέᾳ, εἶτα ἀπιδὼν[2] ἔφη· "καὶ ὁ πόνος μέγας καὶ ὁ τεχνίτης· ἀπολείπεταί γε μὴν τῆς χειρουργίας ἡ χάρις, ἧς ὁ ἀνὴρ εἰ τύχοι, ὁ πόνος αὐτοῦ τοῦ οὐρανοῦ ψαύσει."

42. Κῦρον τὸν Μανδάνης[3] ἔθρεψε, φασί, κύων, Τήλεφον δὲ τὸν Αὔγης[4] καὶ Ἡρακλέους ἔλαφος, Πελίαν δὲ τὸν Ποσειδῶνος καὶ Τυροῦς ἵππος· ἀλλὰ καὶ τὸν Ἀλόπης. Ἀλέξανδρον τὸν Πριάμου ὑπὸ

[1] ἐνόμισεν] ὠνόμασεν Struve
[2] ἀπιδὼν] ἀπιὼν Scheffer: ἐπιδὼν Kor.
[3] Μανδάνης Bongars: -άλης codd.
[4] Αὔγης Rhodiginus: Ἀγαύης codd.

---

[a] The Choaspes ran through Susa, the Persian capital; according to Herodotus 1.188 the king of Persia always insisted

leopard or another animal of that kind, but if she captured a lioness.

40. Xerxes was followed by a train of supplies marked by luxury and pretension, and he even brought water from the Choaspes with him.[a] When he felt thirsty in a lonely spot and his servants had not arrived, it was announced in the army that anyone who had water from the Choaspes should give it to the king to drink. Someone was found who had a little of it, and stale. Xerxes drank it and reckoned the man was a benefactor, as he would have died of thirst had the donor not been found.

41. The painter Protogenes (they say) spent seven years working on his Ialysus.[b] When Apelles saw it at first he was at a loss for words, surprised at the unexpected exhibit. Then he looked closer and said: "Both the labour and the artist are great, but charm is missing from his production. If the man could achieve it, his work will reach celestial heights."

42. Cyrus (they say) was nursed by Mandane's dog, Telephus the son of Auge and Heracles by a deer, Pelias the son of Poseidon and Tyro by a horse, as was the son of Alope.[c] Alexander son of Priam is said to have been fed by

that his drinking water should be drawn from this river.

[b] Ialysus was a grandson of Helius and believed to be the founder of the city in Rhodes which bore his name. Protogenes was the great rival of Apelles in the second half of the fourth century B.C. According to Pliny, *Natural History* 35.102, this painting was on display in Rome at the Templum Pacis, but by Plutarch's day (*Demetrius* 22) it had been destroyed by fire. One wonders whether Aelian was aware of its fate.

[c] The son of Alope was Hippothoon, founder of an Athenian tribe. *Alope* was the title of a play by Euripides.

ἄρκτου φασὶ τραφῆναι, Αἴγισθον δὲ τὸν Θυέστου καὶ Πελοπίας ὑπὸ αἰγός.

43. Δαρεῖον ἀκούω τὸν Ὑστάσπου φαρετροφόρον Κύρου γενέσθαι. ὁ δὲ τελευταῖος Δαρεῖος, <ὁ>[1] ὑπὸ Ἀλεξάνδρου νικηθείς, δοῦλος ἦν. Ἀρχέλαος δὲ ὁ Μακεδόνων βασιλεὺς δούλης υἱὸς ἦν τῆς Σιμίχης. Μενέλαος ὁ Φιλίππου πάππος εἰς τοὺς νόθους ἐτέλει. ὁ δὲ τούτου υἱὸς Ἀμύντας ὑπηρέτης Ἀερόπου καὶ δοῦλος ἐπεπίστευτο. Περσεὺς δέ, ὃν καθεῖλε Παῦλος ὁ Ῥωμαῖος, Ἀργεῖος μὲν γένος ἦν, ἀδόξου δέ τινος υἱός. Εὐμένης δὲ πατρὸς ἀπόρου καὶ τυμβαύλου πεπίστευται γενέσθαι. Ἀντίγονος ὁ Φιλίππου, ὁ καὶ ἑτερόφθαλμος καὶ ἐκ τούτου Κύκλωψ προσαγορευθείς, αὐτουργὸς ἦν. Πολυσπέρχων δὲ ἐλῄστευε. Θεμιστοκλῆς δέ, ὁ τοὺς βαρβάρους καταναυμαχήσας καὶ μόνος συνεὶς[2] τὰς τῶν θεῶν ἐν τοῖς χρησμοῖς φωνάς, Θρᾴττης υἱὸς ἦν, καὶ ἐκαλεῖτο ἡ μήτηρ αὐτοῦ Ἁβρότονον. Φωκίων δὲ ὁ Χρηστὸς ἐπικληθεὶς πατρὸς μὲν δοίδυκας ἐργαζομένου ἦν, Δημήτριον δὲ τὸν Φαληρέα οἰκότριβα γενέσθαι λέγουσιν ἐκ τῆς οἰκίας τῆς Τιμοθέου καὶ Κόνωνος. Ὑπερβόλου δὲ καὶ Κλεοφῶντος καὶ Δημάδου, καίτοι προστατῶν γενομένων τοῦ δήμου τῶν Ἀθηναίων, οὐδεὶς ἂν εἴποι ῥᾳδίως τοὺς πατέρας. Καλλικρατίδας γε μὴν καὶ Γύλιππος καὶ Λύσανδρος ἐν Λακεδαίμονι μόθακες ἐκαλοῦντο. ὄνομα δὲ ἦν ἄρα τοῦτο τοῖς τῶν εὐπόρων <συντρόφοις>,[3] οὓς συνεξέπεμ-

[1] suppl. Kor. [2] συνεὶς Kor.: συνιεὶς codd.

a bear, Aegisthus the son of Thyestes and Pelopia by a goat.

43. I hear that Darius the son of Hystaspes carried the quiver for Cyrus. The last Darius, who was defeated by Alexander, was a slave.[a] Archelaus the king of Macedon was the son of the slave Simiche. Menelaus the grandfather of Philip was classified as illegitimate; his son Amyntas was believed to be a servant of Aeropus and a slave.[b] Perseus, who was defeated by the Roman Paulus, was born in Argos, the son of an undistinguished man.[c] Eumenes is thought to have been the child of a poor father who played music at funerals. Antigonus the son of Philip, who had one eye and consequently was known as Cyclops, was a peasant. Polysperchon was a bandit. Themistocles, who defeated the barbarians at sea and was the only man to understand the messages of the gods in oracles, was the son of a Thracian slave woman, and his mother was called Habrotonon. Phocion nicknamed the Good was the child of a man who made pestles, while they say that Demetrius of Phalerum [fr. 2b W.] was born a slave in the household of Timotheus and Conon. Although Hyperbolus, Cleophon, and Demades became champions of the Athenian democracy, no one could easily say who their fathers were. Furthermore, Callicratidas, Gylippus, and Lysander were called "inferiors" at Sparta, this being the term for the slaves of rich men sent by the

[a] In fact Darius III was the nephew of Artaxerxes II.

[b] On Menelaus and Amyntas see *SIG*[3] 135 n. 1.

[c] Aemilius Paullus Macedonicus, victor at Pydna in 168 B.C., where he put an end to the power of Macedonia.

---

[3] supplevi ex Athenaeo 271 E et Plut. *Cleom.* 8

που[1] τοῖς υἱοῖς[2] οἱ πατέρες συναγωνιουμένους ἐν τοῖς γυμνασίοις. ὁ δὲ συγχωρήσας τοῦτο Λυκοῦργος <συνεχώρησε καὶ>[3] τοῖς ἐμμείνασι τῇ τῶν παίδων ἀγωγῇ πολιτείας Λακωνικῆς μεταλαγχάνειν.[4] καὶ Ἐπαμεινώνδας δὲ πατρὸς ἦν ἀφανοῦς. Κλέων δὲ ὁ Σικυωνίων τύραννος καταποντιστὴς ἦν.

44. Αἱ ἐν Σικελίᾳ λιθοτομίαι περὶ τὰς Ἐπιπολὰς ἦσαν, σταδίου μῆκος, τὸ εὖρος δύο πλέθρων. ἦσαν δὲ ἐν αὐταῖς[5] τοῦ χρόνου τοσοῦτον διατρίψαντες ἄνθρωποι, ὡς καὶ γεγαμηκέναι ἐκεῖ καὶ παιδοποιῆσαι. καί τινες τῶν παίδων ἐκείνων μηδεπώποτε πόλιν ἰδόντες, ὅτε εἰς Συρακούσας ἦλθον καὶ εἶδον ἵππους ὑπεζευγμένους καὶ βόας ἐλαυνομένους, ἔφευγον βοῶντες· οὕτως ἄρα ἐξεπλάγησαν. τὸ δὲ κάλλιστον τῶν ἐκεῖ σπηλαίων ἐπώνυμον ἦν Φιλοξένου τοῦ ποιητοῦ, ἐν ᾧ, φασι, διατρίβων τὸν Κύκλωπα εἰργάσατο τῶν ἑαυτοῦ μελῶν τὸ κάλλιστον, παρ' οὐδὲν θέμενος τὴν ἐκ Διονυσίου τιμωρίαν καὶ καταδίκην, ἀλλ' ἐν αὐτῇ τῇ συμφορᾷ μουσουργῶν ὁ Φιλόξενος.

45. Φρύγιοι καὶ ταῦτα ᾄδουσι λόγοι· Μίδου τοῦ Φρυγὸς ἔτι νηπίου καθεύδοντος μύρμηκας εἰσέρπειν εἰς τὸ στόμα καὶ πάνυ φιλοπόνως καὶ φιλέργως εἰσφέρειν τοὺς πυρούς. Πλάτωνος δὲ μελίττας εἰς τὸ στόμα κηρίον ἐργάζεσθαι. καὶ Πινδάρῳ τῆς πα-

[1] συνεξέπεμπον Scheffer: συνεισ- codd.
[2] τοῖς υἱοῖς Scheffer: αὐτοῖς codd.
[3] suppl. Jens

father of a family to share in exercise at the gymnasium. It was Lycurgus who made this concession and granted citizenship at Sparta to those who adhered to the rules for the education of children. Epaminondas was also the son of an undistinguished father. Cleon the tyrant of Sicyon was a pirate.

44. The Sicilian quarries were at Epipolae,[a] one stade long and two furlongs wide. Men remained in them long enough to marry and have children; and some of those children, having never seen a city before, when they came to Syracuse and saw horses harnessed and cattle being driven, ran away screaming because they were so frightened. The finest of the caves there was named after the poet Philoxenus,[b] where (they say) he lived while composing the best of his poems, *Cyclops*, in utter disregard of the vengeance and punishment imposed by Dionysius; in the midst of disaster Philoxenus [fr. 4d P.] devoted himself to the Muses.

45. Phrygian traditions celebrate these facts: when as a small child the Phrygian Midas was sleeping ants came up to his mouth and with care and industry carried into it ears of corn. Bees made their wax on Plato's lips.[c] Pindar,

[a] This district of Syracuse is still called Epipoli.

[b] Philoxenus of Cythera (435/4–380/79 B.C.) was the author of many dithyrambic poems, the most famous being *Cyclops or Galatea,* which was parodied by Aristophanes in his *Plutus*. Ancient sources give differing accounts of the reason for his punishment.

[c] For a similar tale about Plato see 10.21 above.

---

[4] μεταλαγχάνειν Jens: -νει codd.

[5] αὐταῖς Faber: -τῷ codd.

τρῴας οἰκίας ἐκτεθέντι μέλιτται τροφοὶ ἐγένοντο, ὑπὲρ τοῦ γάλακτος παρατιθεῖσαι μέλι.

46. Διονύσιον δὲ τὸν Ἑρμοκράτους λέγουσι ποταμὸν διαβαίνειν· ἔφερε δὲ αὐτὸν ἵππος. καὶ ὁ μὲν ἵππος κατὰ τοῦ τέλματος ὠλίσθανεν,[1] ὁ δὲ ἀποπηδήσας τῆς ὄχθης ἐλάβετο καὶ ἀπῄει, ὡς οὐκέτι τὸν ἵππον ὄντα αὐτοῦ ἀπολιπών. ὁ δὲ ἠκολούθησε καὶ χρεμετίσας ἐπέστρεψεν αὐτόν. καὶ ἐκεῖνος ἐλάβετο αὐτοῦ τῆς χαίτης καὶ ἔμελλεν ἀναβαίνειν, καὶ τῇ χειρὶ αὐτοῦ περιπίπτει μελιττῶν πλῆθος. ἔφασαν οὖν οἱ Γαλεῶται πρὸς τὸν Διονύσιον ἐρόμενον ὑπὲρ τούτων, ὅτι ταῦτα μοναρχίαν δηλοῖ.

47. Διονύσιος ἐλαύνει τῆς Σικελίας Δίωνα, τὴν δὲ γυναῖκα αὐτοῦ Ἀρήτην[2] καὶ τὸν ἐξ αὐτοῦ παῖδα ἐφύλαττεν. ὕστερον δὲ τὴν γυναῖκα ἄκουσαν δορυφόρῳ αὐτοῦ <τῷ>[3] πάντων μάλιστα θεραπευτῇ Τιμοκράτει[2] γυναῖκα δίδωσι· Συρακούσιος δὲ τὸ γένος ἦν. Δίων δὲ παραλαβὼν Συρακούσας, ἀποδράντος εἰς Λοκροὺς Διονυσίου, ἐνταῦθα ἡ μὲν Ἀριστομάχη ἡ τοῦ Δίωνος ἀδελφὴ προσεῖπεν αὐτόν. ἡ δὲ Ἀρήτη[2] εἵπετο δι᾿ αἰδοῦς ἐγκαλυπτομένη καὶ οὐ τολμῶσα προσειπεῖν ὡς ἄνδρα, ἐπεὶ βιασθεῖσα τὸν θεσμὸν τῆς πρὸς αὐτὸν εὐνῆς οὐ διεφύλαξεν. ἐπεὶ δὲ ὑπὲρ αὐτῆς ἀπελογήσατο ἡ Ἀριστομάχη,[2] τὴν ἐκ τοῦ Διονυσίου ἀνάγκην καταλέξασα, ὁ Δίων προσηγάγετο τὴν γυναῖκα καὶ τὸν παῖδα καὶ εἰς τὴν οἰκίαν ἔπεμψεν.

exposed outside his father's house, was fed by bees, who gave him honey instead of milk.

46. They say Dionysius son of Hermocrates was crossing a river.[a] He was riding a horse. The horse slipped on the mud, but he jumped off, grabbed hold of the bank and went away, leaving the horse as if it were no longer his.[b] But it followed him, neighed and called him back. He took hold of its mane and was on the point of mounting, when a swarm of bees covered his hand. When he asked the Galeotae about this they told Dionysius that it was a sign of monarchy.[c]

47. Dionysius[d] drove Dion from Sicily but kept control of his wife Arete and her child by him. Later he gave the woman against her will to his most devoted bodyguard Timocrates, to be his wife. This man was from Syracuse. When Dion captured Syracuse Dionysius fled to Locri, and Dion was approached by his sister Aristomache. Arete followed, wearing a veil out of modesty and not daring to speak to him as her husband, since she had been compelled to renounce her legitimate marriage with him. When Aristomache pleaded her case and cited the compulsion used by Dionysius, Dion accepted his wife and child and sent them to his house.

[a] This is Dionysius I (430–367 B.C.).

[b] The Greek is ambiguous and could also be translated "leaving it there as if it were dead." [c] The Galeotae were priests at Hybla in Sicily. The name means "lizards," and these animals were sometimes believed to have value for making prophecies. [d] Dionysius II, tyrant 367–344 B.C.

[1] ὠλίσθανεν] ὤλισθε Her. [2] nomina e Plut. *Dione* restituit Scheffer [3] suppl. Her.

48. Ὅτι Ἰνδοὶ τῇ παρά σφισιν ἐπιχωρίῳ φωνῇ τὰ Ὁμήρου μεταγράψαντες ᾄδουσιν οὐ μόνοι[1] ἀλλὰ καὶ οἱ Περσῶν βασιλεῖς, εἴ τι χρὴ πιστεύειν τοῖς ὑπὲρ τούτων ἱστοροῦσιν.

49. Φωκίων ὁ τοῦ Φώκου πολλάκις στρατηγήσας κατεγνώσθη θανάτῳ, καὶ ἦν ἐν τῷ δεσμωτηρίῳ καὶ ἔμελλε πιεῖσθαι τὸ κώνειον. ἐπεὶ δὲ ὤρεξεν ὁ δήμιος τὴν κύλικα, οἱ προσήκοντες ἤροντο εἴ τι λέγοι πρὸς τὸν υἱόν. ὁ δέ· "ἐπισκήπτω αὐτῷ μηδὲν Ἀθηναίοις μνησικακεῖν[2] ὑπὲρ τῆς παρ' αὐτῶν φιλοτησίας, ἧς νῦν πίνω." ὅστις δὲ οὐκ ἐπαινεῖ καὶ ὑπερθαυμάζει τὸν ἄνδρα, δοκεῖ μοι μέγα ὁ τοιοῦτος ἐννοεῖν οὐδέν.

50. Λακεδαιμόνιοι μουσικῆς ἀπείρως εἶχον· ἔμελε γὰρ αὐτοῖς γυμνασίων καὶ ὅπλων. εἰ δέ ποτε ἐδεήθησαν τῆς ἐκ Μουσῶν ἐπικουρίας ἢ νοσήσαντες ἢ παραφρονήσαντες ἢ ἄλλο τι τοιοῦτον δημοσίᾳ παθόντες, μετεπέμποντο ξένους ἄνδρας οἷον ἰατροὺς ἢ <καθαρτὰς>[3] κατὰ Πυθόχρηστον. μετεπέμψαντό γε μὴν Τέρπανδρον καὶ Θαλήταν[4] καὶ Τυρταῖον καὶ τὸν Κυδωνιάτην Νυμφαῖον καὶ Ἀλκμᾶνα (Λυδὸς[5] γὰρ ἦν). καὶ Θουκυδίδης δὲ ὁμολογεῖ ὅτι μὴ ἐσπουδασμένως περὶ παιδείαν εἶχον, ἐν οἷς λέγει περὶ

[1] μόνοι <δ'> Kor. [2] μνησικακεῖν e Plutarcho Kor.: -ήσειν codd. [3] suppl. Kor. [4] Θαλήταν Simpson: -ῆτα codd. [5] Λυδὸς Kor. post Per.: αὐλώδης codd.: αὐλωδὸς Scaliger

---

[a] The source of this intriguing and probably false assertion may be Dio Chrysostom 53.6–7, who says that the Indians had translated Homer into their own language, and Dinon of

48. Note that the Indians transcribe the poems of Homer into their own language and recite them. They are not alone; the Persian kings do so as well, if we are to believe writers on these subjects.[a]

49. Although he had often served as general Phocion son of Phocus was condemned to death. He was in prison and about to drink the hemlock. When the executioner handed him the cup, relatives asked if he had any message for his son, and he said: "I instruct him not to bear any grudge against the Athenians on account of their loving cup, from which I now drink."[b] Anyone who does not praise and enormously admire the man seems to me to have no concept of greatness.

50. The Spartans had no experience of the arts. They were concerned with sporting exercise and arms. If they ever needed the help of the Muses, either for illness or mental disturbance or some other public misfortune of that kind, they sent for foreigners, who might be doctors or exorcists suggested by the Delphic oracle. They also summoned Terpander, Thaletas, Tyrtaeus, Nymphaeus of Cydonia and Alcman (he was a Lydian). Thucydides [4.84.2] too confirms that they were not seriously interested in culture when he describes Brasidas. What he says

Colophon, a historian of ca. 360–330 B.C. quoted at Athenaeus 633 D, who records that epic poetry was a feature of barbarian culture. An alternative is to accept the suggestion of Perizonius in his edition of 1701 that Ctesias was Aelian's source.

[b] The aphorism is recorded twice by Plutarch (*Phocion* 36 and *Moralia* 189 AB). It was given an unexpected interpretation by no less a figure than Jacob Burckhardt in his *Griechische Kulturgeschichte* (2.1): "this is not necessarily a proof of his nobility of character; it was his intention to protect his son from persecution in future."

Βρασίδου. λέγει γοῦν ὅτι ἦν <οὐδὲ>[1] ἀδύνατος εἰπεῖν ὡς Λακεδαιμόνιος οἷον ὡς ἂν ἰδιώτης.[2]

51. Μενεκράτης ὁ ἰατρὸς εἰς τοσοῦτον προῆλθε τύφου, ὥστε ἑαυτὸν ὀνομάζειν Δία. ἀπέστειλε[3] δέ ποτε ἐπιστολὴν Φιλίππῳ τῷ Μακεδόνων βασιλεῖ τοιαύτην· "Φιλίππῳ Μενεκράτης ὁ Ζεὺς εὖ πράττειν." ἀντέγραψε δὲ καὶ ὁ Φίλιππος· "Φίλιππος Μενεκράτει ὑγιαίνειν. συμβουλεύω σοι προσάγειν σεαυτὸν ἐπὶ τοὺς κατὰ Ἀντίκυραν τόπους."[4] ᾐνίττετο δὲ ἄρα διὰ τούτων ὅτι παραφρονεῖ ὁ ἀνήρ.

Εἱστία ποτὲ μεγαλοπρεπῶς ὁ Φίλιππος, καὶ δὴ καὶ τοῦτον ἐπὶ θοίνην ἐκάλεσε, καὶ ἰδίᾳ κλίνην αὐτῷ ἐκέλευσε παρεσκευάσθαι, καὶ κατακλιθέντι θυμιατήριον παρέθηκε, καὶ ἐθυμιᾶτο αὐτῷ· οἱ δὲ λοιποὶ εἱστιῶντο, καὶ ἦν μεγαλοπρεπὲς τὸ δεῖπνον. ὁ τοίνυν Μενεκράτης τὰ μὲν πρῶτα ἐνεκαρτέρει καὶ ἔχαιρε τῇ τιμῇ· ἐπεὶ δὲ κατὰ μικρὸν ὁ λιμὸς περιῆλθεν αὐτὸν[5] καὶ ἠλέγχετο ὅτι ἦν ἄνθρωπος καὶ ταῦτα εὐήθης, ἐξαναστὰς ἀπιὼν ᾤχετο καὶ ἔλεγεν ὑβρίσθαι, ἐμμελῶς πάνυ τοῦ Φιλίππου τὴν ἄνοιαν αὐτοῦ ἐκκαλύψαντος.

52. Ἰσοκράτης ὁ ῥήτωρ ἔλεγεν ὑπὲρ τῆς Ἀθηναίων πόλεως ὁμοίαν εἶναι ταῖς ἑταίραις. καὶ γὰρ νεανίσκους[6] τοὺς ἁλισκομένους ὑπὸ τῆς ὥρας αὐτῶν

[1] e Thucydide suppl. Kor. [2] οἷον . . . ἰδιώτης del. Her.
[3] ἀπέστειλε] ἐπ- Faber [4] τοὺς . . . τόπους Kor.: τοῖς . . . τόποις codd. [5] αὐτὸν Kor.: -τῷ codd.
[6] νεανίσκους J. Gronovius: ἐκείνους x: ἐκεῖναι V

is that Brasidas was not incompetent as a speaker, given that he was a Spartan, so to speak an amateur.[a]

51. The doctor Menecrates became so arrogant that he called himself Zeus. One day he sent Philip of Macedon a letter in the following terms: "Menecrates Zeus greets Philip." Philip replied: "Philip wishes Menecrates good health. I advise you to take yourself off to the region of Anticyra."[b] By this he hinted that the man was mad.

Philip was giving a grand banquet, and he invited this man to the feast. He ordered a separate couch for him, and when Menecrates had settled in his place Philip put an incense burner close to him, and lit the incense for him. Everyone else was feasting, and it was a splendid occasion. At first Menecrates was able to hold out and he enjoyed the honour paid to him; but when hunger gradually overcame him and he was shown up to be the mortal he was, and a naive one at that, he got up and walked away, saying he had been insulted. Philip had very artfully brought his insanity into the open.

52. The orator Isocrates [fr. 3,1 Bl.] said of the city of Athens that it behaved like courtesans. Young men captivated by their beauty want to make love to them, but no

[a] Modern scholars take the view that in the years 650–550 B.C. Sparta was one of the leading centres of art, literature, and music; see e.g. N. G. L. Hammond in the *Cambridge Ancient History* vol. III 3 (Cambridge, 1982), pp. 357–358.

[b] Anticyra was the name of two places in central Greece, both of which produced the plant hellebore, believed to be a remedy for madness. For this anecdote compare Plutarch *Moralia* 191 A, 213 A; and Athenaeus 289 D.

βούλεσθαι <μὲν>[1] συνεῖναι αὐταῖς, ὅμως δὲ μηδένα ἐντελῶς[2] οὕτω παραφρονεῖν,[3] ὡς ὑπομεῖναι ἂν συνοικῆσαί τινι αὐτῶν. καὶ οὖν καὶ τὴν Ἀθηναίων πόλιν ἐνεπιδημῆσαι μὲν εἶναι ἡδίστην, καὶ κατά γε τοῦτο πασῶν τῶν κατὰ τὴν Ἑλλάδα διαφέρειν, ἐνοικῆσαι δὲ ἀσφαλῆ μηκέτι εἶναι. ᾐνίττετο δὲ διὰ τούτων τοὺς ἐπιχωριάζοντας αὐτῇ συκοφάντας καὶ τὰς ἐκ τῶν δημαγωγούντων ἐπιβουλάς.

53. Ἐμὲ δὲ οὐ λέληθεν ὅτι τῶν μεγίστων πολέμων αἱ ἀρχαὶ δοκοῦσί πως εὐκαταφρόνητοι γεγονέναι. τὸν μὲν γὰρ Περσικὸν ἐκ τῆς Μαιανδρίου τοῦ Σαμίου πρὸς Ἀθηναίους διαφορᾶς τὴν ἀρχὴν λαβεῖν φασι, τόν γε μὴν Πελοποννήσιον διὰ τὸ <κατὰ>[4] Μεγαρέων πινάκιον, τὸν δὲ ἱερὸν καλούμενον ἐκ τῆς εἰσπράξεως τῶν δικῶν τῶν Ἀμφικτυόνων, τὸν δὲ κατὰ Χαιρώνειαν, φιλονεικησάντων Ἀθηναίων πρὸς Φίλιππον καὶ λαβεῖν οὐ θελησάντων <τὸν Ἁλόννησον, ἀλλ᾽ ἀπολαβεῖν>.[5]

54. Ἀλέξανδρον Ἀριστοτέλης ὀργιζόμενον πραῧναι βουλόμενος καὶ παῦσαι χαλεπαίνοντα πολλοῖς, ταυτὶ πρὸς αὐτὸν γέγραφεν· "ὁ θυμὸς καὶ ἡ ὀργὴ οὐ

[1] suppl. Her. [2] ἐντελῶς Koen: εὐ- codd.
[3] παραφρονεῖν Kühn: περι- codd.
[4] suppl. Kühn [5] suppl. Per.

---

[a] Although no such tactless remark can be found in the extant writings, it may still be authentic. [b] A rather similar ch. on the causes of war can be found in *N.A.* 11.27. [c] The statement about Maeandrius is not confirmed by other sources.

one is so completely off his head that he could bear to live with them.[a] Just so the city of Athens was a delightful place to visit, and in this respect superior to every city in Greece, but it was no longer safe to live in. By this he alluded to the informers, who were a regular feature of its life, and to the intrigues of the demagogues.

53. It has not escaped my notice that the causes of the greatest wars somehow seem trivial.[b] The Persian War is said to have had its origin in the disagreement between Maeandrius of Samos[c] and the Athenians, the Peloponnesian War because of the small tablet about the Megarians,[d] the so-called Sacred War[e] as a result of enforcing a verdict given by the Amphictyones,[f] and the Chaeronean War because the Athenians were at odds with Philip and did not wish to accept <Halonnesus, but to recover it from him>.[g]

54. When Aristotle [fr. 659 R.] wished to soothe Alexander's anger and check his annoyance with many people, he wrote to him as follows: "Temper and anger

[d] But the so-called Megarian decree excluding Megarian products from the markets of the Athenian empire is well known as a contributory factor to the outbreak of the Peloponnesian War.

[e] The Sacred War of 356–346 B.C. arose from the enforcement of a judgement in a case of alleged sacrilege, concerning the cultivation of land sacred to Apollo.

[f] The Amphictyones were delegates from the cities who cooperated in maintenance of a temple cult, as at Delphi.

[g] At the end of the ch. the text as transmitted does not give the required meaning; but there appears to be a reference to an incident from the years 343–342 B.C. concerning a former Athenian possession, the small island of Halonnesus near the Thracian coast.

πρὸς ἥττους,[1] ἀλλὰ πρὸς τοὺς κρείττονας γίνεται· σοὶ δὲ οὐδεὶς ἴσος."

Ἀριστοτέλης τὰ δέοντα συμβουλεύων Ἀλεξάνδρῳ πολλοῖς ὠφέλημα γέγονεν, ἐξ ὧν καὶ τὴν πατρίδα κατῴκισε κατεσκαμμένην ὑπὸ τοῦ Φιλίππου.

55. Τοὺς ὑπὸ τῶν ἐλεφάντων ἢ ἐν ταῖς θήραις ἢ ἐν ταῖς μάχαις ἀποθανόντας οἱ Λίβυες θάπτουσι διαπρεπῶς καὶ ὕμνους τινὰς ᾄδουσιν. ἔστι δὲ τοῖς ὕμνοις [ἡ][2] ὑποθήκη ἐκείνη· ἀγαθοὺς ἄνδρας εἶναι [λέγει][3] τοὺς ἀντιπάλους γενομένους θηρίῳ τοσούτῳ· λέγουσι γὰρ καὶ τὸ ἐνδόξως ἀποθανεῖν ἐντάφιον εἶναι τῷ θαπτομένῳ.

56. Διογένης ὁ Σινωπεὺς ἔλεγε πολλά, τὴν ἀμαθίαν καὶ τὴν ἀπαιδευσίαν τῶν Μεγαρέων διαβάλλων, καὶ <ὅτι>[4] ἐβούλετο Μεγαρέως ἀνδρὸς κριὸς εἶναι μᾶλλον ἢ υἱός. ᾐνίττετο δὲ ὅτι τῶν θρεμμάτων ποιοῦνται πρόνοιαν οἱ Μεγαρεῖς, τῶν παίδων δὲ οὐχί.

57. Ἡνίκα Ἀλέξανδρος ὁ Φιλίππου ἐπὶ τὰς Θήβας ἦγε τὴν δύναμιν, οἱ μὲν θεοὶ σημεῖα αὐτοῖς καὶ τέρατα ἀπέστελλον, προσημαίνοντες τὰς περὶ αὐτῶν ὅσον οὐδέπω τύχας· οἱ δὲ ὡς ᾤοντο ἐν Ἰλλυριοῖς Ἀλέξανδρον τεθνάναι, πολλὰ καὶ βλάσφημα εἰς αὐτὸν ἀπερρίπτουν. ἡ μὲν γὰρ ἐν Ὀγχηστῷ λίμνη φοβερὸν ἦχον ἀνέδωκε καὶ συνεχῆ καὶ ταύρου μυκήματι[5] ἐῴκει· ἡ δὲ παρὰ[6] τὸν Ἰσμηνὸν καὶ αὐτὰ τὰ τείχη ῥέουσα κρήνη καλουμένη Δίρκη καθαρῷ

are not displayed to inferiors but to superiors; and no one is equal to you."

Aristotle gave essential advice to Alexander and benefited many people. Among other things he resettled his home town, which had been razed by Philip.[a]

55. To men killed by elephants, either hunting or in warfare, the Libyans give honourable burial and sing certain hymns. The substance of the hymns is this: men who faced such a large animal were brave. In fact they say that a glorious death is the proper shroud for the deceased.

56. Diogenes of Sinope said a great deal in disparagement of the ignorance and vulgarity of the Megarians, and that he would rather have been a ram belonging to a Megarian than his son.[b] He meant that the Megarians look after their animals, but not their children.

57. When Alexander the son of Philip led his forces against Thebes the gods sent them signs and portents presaging their imminent fate; but the Thebans thought Alexander had died in Illyria and they made many rude remarks about him. The marsh at Onchestus made a continuous frightening noise which seemed like a bull roaring. The spring called Dirce, running parallel to the

[a] Philip did in fact destroy Stagira in 349 B.C.

[b] The aphorism recurs in Plutarch, *Moralia* 526 C, Diogenes Laertius 6.41, and the Gnomologium Vaticanum 191. See also J. van Leeuwen on Aristophanes, *Clouds* 1001.

---

[1] ἥττους Rutgers: ἴσους codd. [2] del. Kor.
[3] del. Her. [4] suppl. Cuper
[5] ταύρου μυκήματι Rutgers: τὰ ὁρμήματα codd.
[6] παρὰ Hermann: περὶ codd.

καὶ ἥδει ῥέουσα ὕδατι παρὰ πάντα τὸν πρόσθεν χρόνον, ἄφνω καὶ παρ' ἐλπίδα αἵματος ἀνεπλήσθη. Μακεδόσι δὲ ἐπίστευον Θηβαῖοι ἀπειλεῖν τὸ δαιμόνιον. ἐν δὲ τῷ κατὰ πόλιν ναῷ τῆς Δήμητρος ἀράχνη κατὰ τοῦ προσώπου τοῦ ἀγάλματος ἐξύφαινε[1] τὴν ἑαυτῆς τέχνην καὶ τὸν ἱστὸν ὃν εἴωθεν ἐργάζεσθαι. τὸ δὲ τῆς Ἀθηνᾶς τῆς καλουμένης Ἀλαλκομενηΐδος ἄγαλμα αὐτομάτως κατεφλέχθη, πυρὸς μὴ προσαχθέντος, καὶ ἄλλα πολλά.

58. Διώξιππος Ὀλυμπιονίκης ἀθλητὴς ὁ Ἀθηναῖος εἰσήλαυνεν εἰς τὰς Ἀθήνας κατὰ τὸν νόμον τῶν ἀθλητῶν. συνέρρει τοίνυν τὰ πλήθη καὶ ἄλλος ἀλλαχόθεν ἐκκρεμαννύμενος ἐθεῶντο αὐτόν· ἐν δὲ τοῖς καὶ γυνὴ κάλλει διαπρέπουσα ἀπήντησε τῇ θέᾳ. ἰδὼν δὲ αὐτὴν ὁ Διώξιππος παραχρῆμα ἡττήθη τοῦ κάλλους καὶ διετέλεσεν ἀποβλέπων τὴν[2] ἄνθρωπον καὶ ἐπιστρεφόμενος καὶ εἰς πολλὰς τὸ πρόσωπον ἀλλάττων χροιάς. ἐκ δὴ τούτων πολλοῖς ἐγένετο κατάφωρος μὴ ἀργῶς ἰδὼν τὴν ἄνθρωπον. μάλιστα δὲ αὐτοῦ τὸ πάθος κατέγνω [χρυσοῦν κάτοπτρον Κορινθιουργὲς ἐπιπράσκετο][3] Διογένης ὁ Σινωπεύς, καὶ πρὸς τοὺς πλησίον "ὁρᾶτε" εἶπε "τὸν ἀθλητὴν ὑμῶν τὸν μέγαν ὑπὸ παιδίσκης ἐκτραχηλιζόμενον."

59. Πυθαγόρας ἔλεγε δύο ταῦτα ἐκ τῶν θεῶν τοῖς ἀνθρώποις δεδόσθαι κάλλιστα, τό τε ἀληθεύειν καὶ τὸ εὐεργετεῖν· καὶ προσετίθει ὅτι καὶ ἔοικε τοῖς θεῶν ἔργοις ἑκάτερον.

Ismenus and the walls themselves, which had always previously had clear and pure water, was suddenly and unexpectedly filled with blood. The Thebans were sure the gods threatened the Macedonians. In the city at the temple of Demeter a spider began to cover the face of the cult statue with its handiwork and weave its usual product.[a] The statue of Athena known as Alalcomeneïs caught fire spontaneously, though no light was set to it; and much else.

58. Dioxippus the Athenian athlete[b] victorious at Olympia was driving into Athens as the athletes used to. A crowd collected from all directions and watched him intently. In it was a woman of great beauty who came to enjoy the spectacle. On seeing her Dioxippus was immediately struck by her beauty; he could not keep his eyes off her, turning to look at her and changing colour, so that many people realised he was not gazing idly at the woman. First to detect his feelings was Diogenes of Sinope, who said to his neighbours: "Look at your great athlete held in the grip of a little girl."

59. Pythagoras said these were the two finest gifts from the gods to men: to tell the truth and to do good to others. He added that both resemble activities of the gods.

[a] For the spider see Pausanias, *Periegesis* 9.6.6.

[b] Mentioned above at 10.22. The story recurs in Plutarch, *Moralia* 521 B.

---

[1] *ἐξύφαινε* x: -*ηνε* V

[2] <*εἰς*> *τὴν* Cobet

[3] del. Her.

60. Συνουσία ποτὲ ἐγένετο Διονυσίῳ τῷ δευτέρῳ καὶ Φιλίππῳ τῷ Ἀμύντου. πολλοὶ μὲν οὖν ὡς τὸ εἰκὸς καὶ ἄλλοι λόγοι ἐπέρρευσαν, ἐν δὲ τοῖς καὶ ἐκεῖνο· ἤρετο ὁ Φίλιππος τὸν Διονύσιον πῶς τοσαύτην παρὰ τοῦ πατρὸς λαβὼν ἀρχὴν εἶτα οὐ διεσώσατο αὐτήν. ὁ δὲ ἀπεκρίνατο οὐκ ἔξω μέλους ὅτι "τὰ μὲν ἄλλα μοι κατέλιπεν ὁ πατήρ, τὴν δὲ τύχην, ᾗ ταῦτα ἐκτήσατο καὶ διεφύλαξεν, οὐκέτι."

61. Θουρίοις ἐπέπλει Διονύσιος καὶ τριακοσίας ἦγεν ἐπ' αὐτοὺς ναῦς ὁπλιτῶν πεπληρωμένας· βορρᾶς δὲ ἀντιπνεύσας τὰ σκάφη συνέτριψε καὶ τὴν δύναμιν αὐτοῦ τὴν ναυτικὴν ἠφάνισεν. ἐκ δὴ τούτων οἱ Θούριοι τῷ Βορρᾷ ἔθυσαν καὶ ἐψηφίσαντο εἶναι τὸν ἄνεμον πολίτην καὶ οἰκίαν αὐτῷ καὶ κλῆρον ἀπεκλήρωσαν καὶ καθ' ἕκαστον ἔτος ἐπετέλουν αὐτῷ. οὔκουν Ἀθηναῖοι μόνοι κηδεστὴν αὐτὸν ἐνόμιζον, ἀλλὰ καὶ Θούριοι εὐεργέτην αὐτὸν ἐπέγραψαν. Παυσανίας δέ φησιν ὅτι καὶ Μεγαλοπολῖται.

62. Νόμος καὶ οὗτος Περσικός· ἐάν τις μέλλῃ τι τῶν ἀπορρήτων καὶ τῶν ἀμφιλόγων συμβουλεύειν βασιλεῖ, ἐπὶ πλίνθου χρυσῆς ἕστηκε. καὶ ἐὰν δόξῃ παραινεῖν τὰ δέοντα, τὴν πλίνθον λαβὼν ὑπὲρ τῆς συμβουλῆς μισθὸν ἀπέρχεται· μαστιγοῦται δὲ ὅμως, ὅτι ἀντεῖπε βασιλεῖ. ἀνδρὶ δὲ ἐλευθέρῳ, κατά γε τὴν ἐμὴν κρίσιν, οὐκ ἀνταξίαν ἀντικρίνειν δεῖ ὑπὲρ τοῦ μισθοῦ τὴν ὕβριν.

---

[a] This campaign took place in 379 B.C.

[b] The Athenian connection with Boreas was that he had car-

60. Dionysius II and Philip son of Amyntas met one day. Naturally there was a long and flowing conversation, and it included the following exchange. Philip asked Dionysius how it was that having inherited such a powerful state from his father he had not maintained it. The other replied, not without point: "My father left me everything else, but not the luck by which he obtained those possessions and kept them."

61. Dionysius attacked Thurii with his fleet, bringing three hundred ships manned with hoplites.[a] A headwind from the north damaged the vessels and destroyed his armada. As a result Thurii offered sacrifice to Boreas, decreed rights of citizenship to the wind, allocated to it a house and plot of land, and established an annual festival. So the Athenians were not alone in claiming kinship with him;[b] the Thurians also declared him to be a benefactor. Pausanias [8.36.6] says the men of Megalopolis did the same.[c]

62. Another Persian custom. If someone is about to advise the king on secret or difficult matters, he stands on a gold brick. If his proposal is thought to be necessary, he takes the brick as the reward for his advice and leaves. But he is nevertheless whipped for having contradicted the king. In my opinion a free man should not judge it worth accepting an outrage in order to achieve a reward.

ried off Orithyia, daughter of king Erechtheus, to be his wife. Herodotus 7.188–189 reports how the Athenians set up a temple to Boreas in gratitude for his dispersal of the Persian fleet. Other questions arising from this ch. are discussed by A. Jacquemin in *Bulletin de correspondance hellénique* 103 (1979): 189–193.

[c] Some scholars, from Faber onwards, have doubted the authenticity of the last sentence of this ch.

63. Ἀρχεδίκης τις ἠράσθη τῆς ἐν Ναυκράτει ἑταίρας. ἡ δὲ ἦν ὑπερήφανος καὶ δεινῶς φορτικὴ καὶ ἁδροὺς ᾔτει μισθούς, καὶ λαβοῦσα πρὸς ὀλίγον ἂν ὡμίλησε τῷ δόντι, εἶτα ἀπέκλινεν. ἐρασθεὶς οὖν ὁ νεανίσκος αὐτῆς καὶ τυχεῖν μὴ δυνάμενος, ἐπεὶ μὴ πάνυ ἦν πλούσιος, ὄναρ αὐτῇ συνεγένετο καὶ παραχρῆμα ἐπαύσατο τῆς ἐπιθυμίας.

64. Ὁ μὲν Φιλίππου καὶ Ὀλυμπιάδος Ἀλέξανδρος ἐν Βαβυλῶνι τὸν βίον καταστρέψας νεκρὸς ἔκειτο, ὁ τοῦ Διὸς εἶναι λέγων. καὶ στασιαζόντων περὶ τῆς βασιλείας τῶν περὶ αὐτόν, ταφῆς ἄμοιρος ἦν, ἧς μεταλαγχάνουσι καὶ οἱ σφόδρα πένητες, τῆς φύσεως τῆς κοινῆς ἀπαιτούσης τὸν μηκέτι ζῶντα κατακρύψαι. ἀλλ' οὗτός γε τριάκοντα ἡμέρας καταλέλειπτο ἀκηδής, ἕως Ἀρίστανδρος ὁ Τελμισσεύς, θεόληπτος γενόμενος ἢ ἔκ τινος ἄλλης συντυχίας κατασχεθείς, ἦλθεν εἰς μέσους τοὺς Μακεδόνας καὶ πρὸς αὐτοὺς ἔφη [τὸν][1] πάντων τῶν ἐξ αἰῶνος βασιλέων εὐδαιμονέστατον Ἀλέξανδρον γεγονέναι, καὶ ζῶντα καὶ ἀποθανόντα· λέγειν γὰρ[2] τοὺς θεοὺς πρὸς αὐτὸν ὅτι ἄρα ἡ ὑποδεξαμένη γῆ τὸ σῶμα, ἐν ᾧ τὸ πρότερον ᾤκησεν ἡ ἐκείνου ψυχή, πανευδαίμων τε ἔσται καὶ ἀπόρθητος δι' αἰῶνος.

Ταῦτα μαθόντες πολλὴν εἰσεφέροντο φιλονεικίαν, ἕκαστος εἰς τὴν ἰδίαν αὑτοῦ βασιλείαν τὸ ἀγώγιμον τοῦτο ἄγειν ἐπιθυμῶν, ἵνα κειμήλιον ἔχῃ βασιλείας ἀσφαλοῦς καὶ ἀκλινοῦς ὅμηρον. Πτολεμαῖος δέ, εἴ τι χρὴ πιστεύειν, τὸ σῶμα ἐξέκλεψε[3] καὶ μετὰ σπουδῆς

63. A man fell in love with Archedice, the courtesan from Naucratis. She was domineering and dreadfully vulgar. She would ask a very high price, and having got her money make love briefly to the man who paid it, then dismiss him. The young man who fell in love with her and could not obtain her favours, because he was not very rich, dreamt he was lying in bed with her and immediately ceased to have any desire.

64. Alexander, son of Philip and Olympias, lay dead in Babylon—the man who said he was the son of Zeus. While his followers argued about the succession he lay waiting for burial, which even the very poor achieve, since the nature common to all mankind requires a funeral for those no longer living. But he was left unburied for thirty days, until Aristander of Telmissus, whether by divine inspiration or for some other reason, entered the Macedonian assembly and said that of all kings in recorded history Alexander was the most fortunate, both in his life and in his death; the gods had told him that the land which received his body, the earlier habitation of his soul, would enjoy the greatest good fortune and be unconquered through the ages.

On hearing this they began to quarrel seriously, each man wishing to carry off the prize to his own kingdom, so as to have a relic guaranteeing safety and permanence for his realm. But Ptolemy, if we are to believe the story, stole the body and hurriedly made off with it to Alexandria in

---

[1] del. Kor. [2] γὰρ Her.: ἄρα codd.
[3] ἐξέκλεψε Freinsheimius: ἐξεκάλυψε codd.

εἰς τὴν Ἀλεξάνδρου πόλιν τὴν κατ' Αἴγυπτον ἐκόμισε. καὶ οἱ μὲν ἄλλοι Μακεδόνες τὴν ἡσυχίαν ἦγον, Περδίκκας δὲ αὐτὸν διώκειν ἐπεχείρησεν. οὐ τοσοῦτον δὲ ἔμελε τούτῳ τῆς εἰς Ἀλέξανδρον πολυωρίας καὶ τῆς εἰς τὸν νεκρὸν ὁσίας, ὅσον τὰ προλεχθέντα ὑπὸ τοῦ Ἀριστάνδρου ἀνέφλεγεν αὐτὸν καὶ ἐξῆπτεν. ἐπεὶ δὲ κατέλαβε τὸν Πτολεμαῖον, ὑπὲρ τοῦ νεκροῦ μάχη [καρτερὰ] πάνυ σφοδρὰ[1] ἐγένετο, ἀδελφὴ τρόπον τινὰ τῆς ὑπὲρ τοῦ εἰδώλου τοῦ ἐν Τροίᾳ, ὅπερ Ὅμηρος ᾄδει λέγων ὑπὲρ Αἰνείου τὸν Ἀπόλλωνα εἰς μέσους ἐμβαλεῖν τοὺς ἥρωας. ἀνέστειλε δὲ τὴν ὁρμὴν τοῦ Περδίκκα ὁ Πτολεμαῖος· εἴδωλον γὰρ ποιησάμενος ὅμοιον Ἀλεξάνδρῳ κατεκόσμησεν ἐσθῆτι βασιλικῇ καὶ ἐνταφίοις ἀξιοζήλοις. εἶτα τοῦτο ἀναπαύσας ἐπὶ μίαν τῶν Περσικῶν ἁμαξῶν, τὸ ἐπ' αὐτῆς κατεσκεύασε φέρτρον μεγαλοπρεπῶς ἀργύρῳ καὶ χρυσῷ καὶ ἐλέφαντι· καὶ τὸ μὲν ὄντως Ἀλεξάνδρου σῶμα λιτῶς καὶ ὡς ἔτυχε προὔπεμψε κρυπταῖς ὁδοῖς καὶ ἀτρίπτοις. ὁ δὲ Περδίκκας καταλαβὼν τὸ τοῦ νεκροῦ φάσμα καὶ τὴν διασκευασθεῖσαν ἁρμάμαξαν ἀνεστάλη τοῦ δρόμου, οἰόμενος ἔχειν τὸ ἆθλον· ὀψὲ δὲ ἔμαθεν ἀπατηθείς, ἡνίκα διώκειν οὐκ εἶχε.

[1] delevi et σφοδρὰ pro σφόδρα reposui

Egypt. The other Macedonians did nothing, whereas Perdiccas tried to give chase. He was not so much interested in consideration for Alexander and due respect for his body as fired and incited by Aristander's prediction. When he caught up with Ptolemy there was quite a violent struggle over the corpse, in some way akin to the one over the phantom at Troy, which Homer [*Iliad* 5.449] celebrates in his tale, where Apollo puts it down among the heroes to protect Aeneas. Ptolemy checked Perdiccas' attack. He made a likeness of Alexander, clad in royal robes and a shroud of enviable quality. Then he laid it on one of the Persian carriages, and arranged the bier sumptuously with silver, gold, and ivory. Alexander's real body was sent ahead without fuss and formality by a secret and little used route. Perdiccas found the imitation corpse with the elaborate carriage, and halted his advance, thinking he had laid hands on the prize. Too late he realised he had been deceived; it was not possible to go in pursuit.

ΙΓ

1. Λόγος οὗτος Ἀρκαδικὸς ὑπὲρ τῆς Ἰασίωνος Ἀταλάντης. ταύτην ὁ πατὴρ γενομένην ἐξέθηκεν· ἔλεγε γὰρ οὐ θυγατέρων ἀλλ' ἀρρένων δεῖσθαι. ὁ δὲ ἐκθεῖναι λαβὼν οὐκ ἀπέκτεινεν, ἐλθὼν δὲ ἐπὶ τὸ Παρθένιον ὄρος ἔθηκε πηγῆς πλησίον· καὶ ἦν ἐνταῦθα ὕπαντρος πέτρα καὶ ἐπέκειτο συνηρεφὴς δρυμών. καὶ τοῦ μὲν βρέφους κατεψήφιστο θάνατος, οὐ μὴν ὑπὸ τῆς τύχης προὐδόθη· ὀλίγῳ γὰρ ὕστερον ὑπὸ κυνηγετῶν ἀφῃρημένη τὰ ἑαυτῆς βρέφη ἄρκτος ἧκε, σφριγώντων αὐτῇ τῶν μαζῶν καὶ βαρυνομένων ὑπὸ τοῦ γάλακτος. εἶτα κατά τινα θείαν πομπὴν ἡσθεῖσα τῷ βρέφει ἐθήλασεν αὐτό, καὶ ἅμα τὸ θηρίον ἐκουφίσθη τῆς ὀδύνης καὶ ὤρεξε τροφὴν τῷ βρέφει. καὶ οὖν καὶ αὖθις ἐπαντλοῦσα τοῦ γάλακτος καὶ ἐποχετεύουσα ἐπεὶ τῶν ἑαυτῆς μήτηρ οὐκ ἔμεινε, τῆς μηδέν οἱ προσηκούσης τροφὸς ἐγίνετο. ταύτην οἱ κυνηγέται παρεφύλαττον οἱ καὶ[1] ἐξ ἀρχῆς ἐπιβουλεύσαντες τῷ θηρίῳ εἰς τὰ ἔγγονα αὐτῆς, καὶ αὐτὰ ἕκαστα τῶν δρωμένων κατασκεψάμενοι, ἀπελθούσης κατὰ συνήθειαν κατά τε ἄγραν καὶ νομὴν τῆς ἄρκτου, τὴν Ἀταλάντην ὑφείλοντο, καλουμένην τοῦτο

BOOK THIRTEEN

1. Here is a story from Arcadia about Atalanta the daughter of Iasion.[a] At birth her father exposed her; he said he wanted sons, not daughters. But the man who took her to be exposed did not kill her, and instead went to mount Parthenium and put her down near a spring. At that point there was a cave in the rocks, and close by it a dense wood. The child was under sentence of death, but she was not betrayed by fortune, for shortly afterwards arrived a bear, deprived of her cubs by hunters, her breasts bulging and weighed down with milk. Moved by some divine inspiration she took a fancy to the child and suckled it. In this way the animal simultaneously achieved relief from pain and gave nourishment to the infant. And so, still full of milk and supplying nourishment though she was no longer mother to her cubs, she nursed the child who was not her own. The hunters who had originally attacked her young kept an eye on her. They watched all her movements, and when the bear made her usual journey to hunt and feed, they stole Atalanta, who was not yet

[a] For the story of Atalanta see Apollodorus, *Bibliotheca* 3.9.2, with Frazer's notes (Loeb Classical Library).

---

[1] οἱ καὶ Gesner: καὶ οἱ codd.: οἱ Toup

οὐδέπω· αὐτοὶ γὰρ ἔθεντο αὐτῇ τὸ ὄνομα. καὶ ἐτρέφετο ἐν αὐτοῖς [ἐν][1] ὀρείῳ τῇ τροφῇ. κατὰ μικρὸν δὲ αὐτῇ τὰ τοῦ σώματος μετὰ τῆς ἡλικίας ἀνέτρεχε· καὶ ἤρα παρθενίας καὶ τὰς τῶν ἀνδρῶν ὁμιλίας ἔφευγε καὶ ἐρημίαν ἐπόθει, καταλαβοῦσα τῶν ὀρῶν τῶν Ἀρκαδικῶν τὸ ὑψηλότατον, ἔνθα ἦν καὶ αὐλὼν κατάρρυτος καὶ μεγάλαι δρῦς, ἔτι δὲ καὶ πεῦκαι[2] καὶ βαθεῖα ἡ ἐκ τούτων σκιά.

Τί γὰρ ἡμᾶς λυπεῖ καὶ ἄντρον Ἀταλάντης ἀκοῦσαι, ὡς τὸ τῆς Καλυψοῦς τὸ ἐν Ὁμήρῳ; καὶ ἦν ἐν κοίλῃ τῇ φάραγγι σπήλαιον μέγα[3] καὶ βαθὺ πάνυ, κατὰ πρόσωπον δὲ βαθεῖ κρημνῷ ὠχύρωτο. κιττοὶ δὲ αὐτὸ περιεῖρπον, καὶ ἐνεπλέκοντο οἱ κιττοὶ μαλακῶς <τοῖς>[4] δένδροις καὶ δι' αὐτῶν ἀνεῖρπον. κρόκοι τε ἦσαν περὶ τὸν τόπον ἐν μαλακῇ φυόμενοι καὶ βαθείᾳ τῇ πόᾳ. συνανέτελλε δὲ αὐτοῖς καὶ ὑάκινθος καὶ ἄλλη πολλὴ χροιὰ ἀνθέων οὐ μόνον εἰς ἑορτὴν ὄψεως συντελεῖν δυναμένων, ἀλλὰ καὶ ὀσμαὶ ἐξ αὐτῶν τὸν ἀέρα τὸν κύκλῳ κατελάμβανον· καὶ παρῆν τῇ τε ἄλλῃ πανηγυρίζειν καὶ κατὰ τὴν εὐωδίαν ἑστιᾶσθαι. δάφναι τε ἦσαν πολλαί, φυτοῦ διὰ τέλους ἀκμάζοντος ἡδεῖαι προσιδεῖν κόμαι, καὶ ἄμπελοι δὲ πάνυ σφόδρα εὐθενούντων βοτρύων πρὸ τοῦ ἄντρου τεθηλυῖαι τὸ φιλεργὸν τῆς Ἀταλάντης ἐπεδείκνυντο. ὕδατά τε διατελῆ καὶ εἰσρέοντα[5] καὶ καθαρὰ ἰδεῖν καὶ ψυχρά, ὅσον γε[6] ἁψαμένῳ τεκμήρασθαι καὶ καταγνῶναι πιόντι, χύδην καὶ ἀφθόνως ἐπέρρει· τὰ δὲ αὐτὰ ταῦτα καὶ εἰς ἀρδείαν τοῖς δέν-

so named, for it was they who gave her the name. She was brought up by them in the mountains, and slowly her body grew with age. She was committed to virginity, avoided contact with men, and longed for solitude. She established herself in the highest mountains of Arcadia, where there was a well-watered glen with big oak trees, also pines with their deep shadow.

What harm does it do us to hear of Atalanta's cave, like Calypso's in the *Odyssey* [5.56]? At the bottom of the defile was a large and very deep cave, at the entrance protected by a sheer drop. Ivy encircled it, the ivy gently twined itself around trees and climbed up them. In the soft deep grass there crocuses grew, accompanied by hyacinths and flowers of many other colours, which can not only create a feast for the eye; in fact their perfume filled the air around. In general the atmosphere was of festival, and one could feast on the scent. There were many laurels, their evergreen leaves so agreeable to look at, and vines with very luxuriant clusters of grapes flourished in front of the cave as a proof of Atalanta's industry. A continuous stream of water ran by: pure in appearance and cold, judging by the touch and the effect of drinking it; it flowed in generous and lavish quantity. This very stream served to water the trees already mentioned,

---

[1] del. Her.

[2] πεῦκαι A. Gronovius: πνεῦμα codd.

[3] μέγα ex Homero Kor.: ἓν codd.

[4] μαλακῶς <τοῖς> Kor.: μαλακοῖς codd.

[5] εἰσρέοντα] ἀεὶ ῥέοντα Kor.

[6] γε Her.: τε codd.

δροις τοῖς προειρημένοις ἦν ἐπιτήδεια, συνεχῶς ἐπιρρέοντα καὶ εἰς τὸ ἔμβιον αὐτοῖς συμμαχόμενα. ἦν οὖν τὸ χωρίον χαρίτων ἀνάμεστον, καὶ σεμνότατόν τε ἅμα καὶ σώφρονα παρθενεῶνα ἐδείκνυεν.

Ἦν δὲ ἄρα τῇ Ἀταλάντῃ στρωμνὴ μὲν αἱ δοραὶ τῶν τεθηραμένων, τροφὴ δὲ τὰ τούτων κρέα, ποτὸν δὲ τὸ ὕδωρ. στολὴν δὲ ἤσθητο ἀπράγμονα καὶ τοιαύτην οἵαν μὴ ἀποδεῖν[1] τῆς Ἀρτέμιδος· ἔλεγε γὰρ ζηλοῦν αὐτὴν καὶ ἐν τούτῳ καὶ ἐν τῷ παρθένος εἶναι διὰ τέλους ἐθέλειν. πεφύκει δὲ ὠκίστη τοὺς πόδας καὶ οὐκ ἂν αὐτὴν διέφυγεν οὔτε θηρίον οὔτε ἐπιβουλεύων αὐτῇ ἄνθρωπος· φυγεῖν <δ'>[2] ἐθέλουσαν, ἀλλ' ἐνταῦθα μὲν οὐκ ἄν τις αὐτὴν κατέλαβεν. ἤρων δὲ αὐτῆς οὐχ ὅσοι μόνον αὐτὴν εἶδον, ἀλλ' ἤδη καὶ ἐκ φήμης ἠρᾶτο.

Φέρε δὲ καὶ τὸ εἶδος αὐτῆς, εἴ τι μὴ λυπεῖ, διαγράψωμεν· λυπεῖ δὲ οὐδέν, ἐπεὶ καὶ ἐκ τούτων προσγένοιτ' ἂν λόγων τε ἐμπειρία καὶ τέχνη. μέγεθος μὲν γὰρ ἔτι παῖς οὖσα ὑπὲρ τὰς τελείας ἦν γυναῖκας· κάλλει[3] δὲ ἤνθει[4] ὡς οὐκ ἄλλη τῶν ἐν Πελοποννήσῳ παρθένων τῶν τότε. ἀρρενωπὸν δὲ καὶ γοργὸν ἔβλεπε, τοῦτο μὲν [καὶ][5] ἐκ τῆς θηρείου τροφῆς, ἤδη δὲ κἀκ τῶν ἐν τοῖς ὄρεσι γυμνασίων. ἐπεὶ δὲ θυμοειδὴς ἦν,[6] κορικόν τε καὶ ῥαδινὸν οὐδὲν εἶχεν· οὐ γὰρ ἐκ θαλάμου προῄει, οὐδὲ ἦν τῶν ὑπὸ μητράσι καὶ τίτθαις τρεφομένων. τὸ δὲ ὑπέρογκον τοῦ σώματος οὐδὲ τοῦτο εἶχε καὶ μάλα γε εἰκότως, ἅτε ἐν τοῖς κυνηγεσίοις καὶ περὶ αὐτὰ τὰ γυμνάσια τὸ πᾶν

with an unfailing current contributing to their vigour. The spot was full of charm, and suggested the dwelling of a dignified and chaste maiden.

Atalanta slept on the skins of animals caught in the hunt, she lived on their meat and drank water. She wore simple clothes, in a style that did not fall short of Artemis' example; she claimed the goddess as her model both in this and in her wish to remain a virgin. She was very fleet of foot, and no wild animal or man with designs on her could have escaped her; and when she wanted to escape, no one could have caught her. It was not just those who saw her that fell in love with her; by now her reputation won her lovers.

Now let us describe her appearance, if that is not unwelcome—and it is not, since from it one might gain experience and skill in writing. While still a girl she was bigger than a full-grown woman, and more beautiful than any young woman from the Peloponnese in those days. She had a fiery, masculine gaze, partly the result of having been nurtured by an animal, but also because of her exercise in the mountains. But since she was full of spirit, there was nothing girlish or delicate about her; she was not the product of the women's apartments, not one of those brought up by mothers and nurses. Nor was her body overweight, not surprisingly, since she exercised every limb in hunting and physical exercise. Her hair was

---

[1] ἀποδεῖν] ἀπᾴδειν Valckenaer
[2] suppl. Muretus [3] κάλλει Vx: καλὴ Φ
[4] ἤνθει Jacoby: ἦν codd. [5] del. Her.
[6] ἐπεὶ . . . ἦν huc revocavi: post τροφῆς praebent codd.

σῶμα ἐκπονοῦσα. ξανθὴ δὲ ἦν αὐτῆς ἡ κόμη οὔ τί που πολυπραγμοσύνῃ γυναικείᾳ καὶ βαφαῖς ἅμα καὶ φαρμάκοις, ἀλλ' ἦν φύσεως ἔργον ἡ χροιά. πεφοίνικτο δὲ καὶ ὑπὸ τῶν ἡλίων αὐτῇ τὸ πρόσωπον καὶ ἐρυθήματι ἐῴκει ἄντικρυς. τί δὲ οὕτως ὡραῖον <ἂν>[1] γένοιτο ἄνθος, ὥσπερ οὖν καλὸν ἦν[2] τὸ πρόσωπον αἰδεῖσθαι πεπαιδευμένης παρθένου; δύο δὲ εἶχεν ἐκπληκτικά· κάλλος ἄμαχον, καὶ σὺν τούτῳ καὶ φοβεῖν ἐδύνατο. οὐδεὶς ἂν αὐτὴν ἰδὼν ἠράσθη ῥᾴθυμος ἄνθρωπος, ἀλλ' οὐδ' ἂν ἐτόλμησεν ἀντιβλέπειν[3] τὴν ἀρχήν· τοσαύτη μετὰ τῆς ὥρας κατέλαμπεν [ἡ][4] αἴγλη τοὺς ὁρῶντας. δεινὴ δὲ ἦν ἐντυχεῖν τά τε ἄλλα καὶ τῷ σπανίῳ. οὐ γὰρ ἂν αὐτὴν εὐκόλως οὐδεὶς εἶδεν· ἀλλ' ἀδοκήτως καὶ ἀπροόπτως ἐπεφάνη[5] διώκουσα θηρίον ἢ ἀμυνομένη τινά, ὥσπερ ἀστὴρ διᾴττουσα <δ'>[6] ἐξέλαμπεν ἀστραπῆς δίκην. εἶτα ἀπέκρυπτεν αὐτὴν διαθέουσαν ἢ δρυμὼν ἢ λόχμη ἤ τι ἄλλο τῶν ἐν ὄρει δάσος.

Καί οἵ ποτε οἱ τὴν ὅμορον οἰκοῦντες, μεσούσης τῆς νυκτός, ἐρασταὶ θρασεῖς καὶ κωμασταὶ βαρύτατοι, ἐκώμασαν[7] δύο τῶν Κενταύρων, Ὑλαῖός τε καὶ Ῥοῖκος. ἦν δὲ ἄρα ὁ κῶμος αὐτῶν οὔτε αὐλητρίδες οὔτε αὐτὰ[8] δήπου τὰ τῶν μειρακίων τῶν κατὰ πόλιν, ἀλλὰ πεῦκαι μὲν ἦσαν, καὶ ταύτας ἐξάψαντες καὶ ἀναφλέξαντες ἐκ τῆς πρώτης τοῦ πυρὸς φαντασίας ἐξέπληξαν ἂν καὶ δῆμον, μήτι γοῦν μίαν παρθένον. κλάδους δὲ πιτύων νεοδρεπεῖς ἀποκλάσαντες, εἶτα τούτους ἑαυτοῖς διαπλέξαντες εἰργάζοντο στεφά-

golden, not due to feminine sophistication, dyes, or applications, but the colour was natural. Exposure to the sun had reddened her face and it looked just as if she was blushing. What flower could be so beautiful as the face of a young woman taught to be modest? She had two astonishing qualities: unrivalled beauty, and with it a capacity to inspire fear. No indolent man would have fallen in love on looking at her, nor would he have had the courage to meet her gaze in the first place; such radiance with beauty shone over those who saw her. To meet her was remarkable, especially since it happened rarely; no one would have easily spotted her. But unexpectedly and unforeseen she would appear, chasing a wild beast or fighting against one; darting like a star she flashed like lightning.[a] Then she raced away, hidden by a wood or thicket or other mountain vegetation.

One day her neighbours, audacious lovers and very tiresome revellers, burst in upon her noisily at midnight; they were two of the Centaurs, Hylaeus and Rhoecus. Their noisy interruption was not done with flute players or in the style of young men from the city; there were pine torches, which they lit and made to burn fiercely; the first sight of fire would have terrified even the population of a city, let alone a solitary young woman. Breaking fresh branches off the pines they wove them together and made

[a] The wording of the Greek here suggests an allusion to tragedy (registered in TrGF adespota 14 a).

---

[1] suppl. Kor. [2] ἦν Kor.: ᾖ VΦ: ἢ x [3] ἀντιβλέπειν Gesner: -έψειν codd. [4] del. Her. [5] ἐπεφάνη Her.: -φηνε V: -φαινε x [6] suppl. Per. [7] ἐκώμασαν d in margine: om. cett. [8] αὐτὰ] δεταὶ van Leeuwen

νους. συνεχῶς δὲ καὶ θαμινὰ ἐπικροτοῦντες ταῖς ὁπλαῖς[1] διὰ τῶν ὀρῶν, συνεκκαίοντες καὶ τὰ δένδρα ἐπὶ τὴν παῖδα ἔσπευδον, κακοὶ μνηστῆρες, σὺν ὕβρει καὶ οἴστρῳ τὰ ἕδνα τῶν γάμων προεκτελοῦντες. τὴν δὲ οὐκ ἔλαθεν ἡ ἐπιβουλή· ἰδοῦσα δὲ ἐκ τοῦ ἄντρου τὸ πῦρ καὶ γνωρίσασα οἵτινές ποτε ἄρα ἦσαν οἱ κωμασταί, μηδὲν διατραπεῖσα μηδὲ ὑπὸ τῆς ὄψεως καταπτήξασα τὸ μὲν τόξον ἐκύκλωσεν, ἀφῆκε δὲ τὸ βέλος καὶ ἔτυχε τοῦ πρώτου μάλα εὐκαίρως. καὶ ὁ μὲν ἔκειτο, ἐπῄει δὲ ὁ δεύτερος οὐκέτι κωμαστικῶς ἀλλ' ἤδη πολεμικῶς, ἐκείνῳ μὲν ἐπαμῦναι θέλων ἑαυτοῦ δὲ ἐμπλῆσαι τὴν ὀργήν.[2] ἀπήντησε δὲ ἄρα καὶ τούτῳ τιμωρὸς ὁ τῆς κόρης οἰστὸς ὁ ἕτερος. καὶ ὑπὲρ τῆς Ἰασίωνος Ἀταλάντης τοσαῦτα.

2. Μιτυληναῖος ἀνήρ, Μακαρεὺς ὄνομα, ἱερεὺς τοῦ Διονύσου, ὅσα μὲν οὕτως[3] ἰδεῖν πρᾶος ἦν καὶ ἐπιεικής, ἀνοσιώτατος δὲ ἀνθρώπων τὰ μάλιστα. ξένου δὲ ἥκοντος παρ' αὐτὸν καὶ δόντος αὐτῷ παρακαταθήκην χρυσίου πλῆθος, ἐν τῷ μυχῷ τοῦ ἀνακτόρου τὴν γῆν διασκάψας ὁ Μακαρεὺς κατώρυξε τὸ χρυσίον. χρόνῳ δὲ ἀφικόμενος ὁ ξένος τὸ χρυσίον ἀπῄτει. ὁ δὲ εἰσαγαγὼν ἔνδον ὡς ἀποδώσων κατέσφαξε, καὶ τὸ χρυσίον ἀνώρυξεν, ἀντ' αὐτοῦ δὲ τὸν ξένον κατέθετο· καὶ ᾤετο, ὥσπερ τοὺς ἀνθρώπους, λανθάνειν οὕτω καὶ τὸν θεόν. πλὴν οὐκ ἀπήντησε ταῦτα ταύτῃ· πόθεν; χρόνου δὲ ὀλίγου διεληλυθότος, αἱ μὲν τοῦ θεοῦ τριετηρίδες ἀφίκοντο, ὁ δὲ ἔθυε μεγαλοπρεπῶς. καὶ ὁ μὲν περὶ τὴν βακχείαν εἶχεν,

garlands for themselves. The incessant, continuous sound of hooves was heard in the mountains; they burned trees and made towards the young woman, evil suitors who in a violent and over-excited state brought gifts for the wedding in advance. But she saw through their plan. From the cave she caught sight of fire and realised who the revellers were; not flinching or cowed by what she saw she bent her bow, shot her weapon, and hit the first of them directly. He lay there, and the other advanced, no longer in the mood of a reveller but with hostile intent, wishing to defend his companion and vent his anger. But he too was punished, by the young woman's other arrow. So much on the subject of Atalanta, daughter of Iasion.

2. A man from Mytilene called Macareus, who was a priest of Dionysus, though to all appearances a mild and reasonable person, was the most unscrupulous of men. When a visitor arrived and deposited with him a quantity of gold, Macareus dug a hole in a corner of the temple and buried the gold. Later the visitor came to ask for its return. Macareus took him in as if about to hand it back, murdered him and dug up the gold, putting the visitor's body in its place. He thought that in this way he could escape divine as well as human attention. But matters did not turn out that way. How so? A short time elapsed, and the biennial festival of the god took place. He made opulent sacrifices. While he was occupied with the bacchic

---

[1] ταῖς ὁπλαῖς Röhl: τοῖς ὅπλοις codd.
[2] ὀργήν Kor.: ὁρμήν codd.
[3] οὕτως Faber: οὗτος codd.

οἱ δὲ παῖδες αὐτοῦ, δύο ὄντες, ἔνδον ἀπελείφθησαν ἐν τῇ οἰκίᾳ καὶ μιμούμενοι τὴν τοῦ πατρὸς ἱερουργίαν τῷ βωμῷ τῷ πατρῴῳ προσῆλθον ἔτι καιομένων τῶν ἐμπύρων· καὶ ὁ μὲν νεώτερος παρέσχε τὸν τράχηλον, ὁ δὲ πρεσβύτερος ἠμελημένην εὑρὼν σφαγίδα τὸν ἀδελφὸν ἀπέκτεινεν ὡς ἱερεῖον, οἱ δὲ κατὰ τὴν οἰκίαν ἰδόντες ἀνεβόησαν. ἀκούσασα δὲ ἡ μήτηρ τῆς βοῆς ἐξεπήδησε, καὶ θεασαμένη τὸν μὲν νεκρόν, τὸν δὲ κατέχοντα ἔτι τὴν σφαγίδα ᾑμαγμένην, σχίζαν ἁρπάσασα τῶν ἐκ τοῦ βωμοῦ ἡμίκαυτον, ταύτῃ τὸν παῖδα ἀπέκτεινεν. ἧκε δὲ ἀγγελία πρὸς τὸν Μακαρέα, καὶ ἀπολιπὼν τὴν τελετὴν ὡς εἶχε, σὺν ὁρμῇ[1] καὶ θυμῷ εἰσεπήδησεν εἰς τὴν οἰκίαν καὶ τῷ θύρσῳ ᾧ κατεῖχε τὴν ἑαυτοῦ γυναῖκα ἔκτεινεν. ἔκπυστα οὖν ἐγένοντο τὰ τολμηθέντα εἰς πάντας, καὶ συλληφθεὶς ὁ Μακαρεὺς καὶ στρεβλούμενος ὡμολόγησεν ὅσα ἐν τῷ ἀνακτόρῳ ἔδρασεν· ἐν αὐταῖς δὲ ταῖς κολάσεσι τὴν ψυχὴν ἀπέρρηξεν. ὁ δὲ παρανόμως σφαγεὶς διὰ τιμῆς ἦλθε δημοσίᾳ καὶ ἐτάφη τοῦ θεοῦ προστάξαντος. ἔτισεν οὖν ὁ Μακαρεὺς οὐ μεμπτὴν τὴν δίκην τοῦτο δὴ τὸ ποιητικὸν σὺν τῇ ἑαυτοῦ κεφαλῇ καὶ τῇ τῆς γυναικὸς καὶ οὖν καὶ τῇ τῶν παίδων προσέτι.

3. Ξέρξης ὁ Δαρείου παῖς, τοῦ Βήλου τοῦ ἀρχαίου διασκάψας τὸ μνῆμα, πύελον ὑελίνην εὗρεν, ἔνθα ἦν κείμενος ὁ νεκρὸς ἐν ἐλαίῳ. οὐ μὴν πεπλήρωτο ἡ πύελος, ἐνέδει δὲ ἀπὸ τοῦ χείλους εἰς παλαιστὴν ἴσως. παρέκειτο δὲ τῇ πυέλῳ καὶ στήλη βρα-

celebrations his two sons were left at home. Imitating their father's sacrificial ritual they approached the family altar while the offerings were still burning. The younger exposed his neck, the elder found a knife lying unused and killed his brother as a sacrificial offering. Members of the household who witnessed this raised a cry of horror. Hearing the shouts their mother jumped up, and seeing that one son was dead, while the other still held the blood-stained knife, she snatched from the altar a half-burnt log and with this killed her son. The news reached Macareus. He left the ceremony with the utmost haste and anxiety, burst into the home, and killed his own wife with the thyrsus he was carrying. The outrageous acts became generally known; Macareus was arrested and tortured; he confessed to what he had done in the temple, and during the ordeal he expired. The victim of his injustice received public honours and burial at the demand of the god. So Macareus paid no contemptible penalty, as the poets have it,[a] with his own life, that of his wife and furthermore those of his sons.

3. Xerxes son of Darius dug his way into the monument of the ancient god Belus[b] and found a glass sarcophagus, in which the body lay in olive oil. The sarcophagus was not full, the oil was perhaps an inch short of the rim. Nearby lay a small stele with the inscription: "For the

[a] Aelian paraphrases *Iliad* 4.161–162.

[b] This monument was an enormous pyramid, the tomb of Marduk, an agrarian divinity whose death and resurrection were celebrated annually. Strabo 16.1.5 (738) says that Alexander the Great contemplated rebuilding it.

[1] ὁρμῇ] ὀργῇ Kühn

χεῖα, ἔνθα ἐγέγραπτο· "τῷ ἀνοίξαντι τὸ μνῆμα καὶ μὴ ἀναπληρώσαντι τὴν πύελον οὐκ ἔστιν[1] ἄμεινον." ἀναγνοὺς δὲ ὁ Ξέρξης ἔδεισε καὶ προσέταξεν ἐπιχέαι ἔλαιον τὴν ταχίστην· οὐ μὴν πεπλήρωτο. ὁ δὲ πάλιν προσέταξεν ἐπιχέαι. αὔξησιν δὲ οὐκ ἐλάμβανεν, ἕως ἀπεῖπε μάτην ἀναλίσκων τὸ ἐπιχεόμενον. κατακλείσας δὲ τὸν τάφον, ὀπίσω[2] ἀπηλλάγη ἀδημονῶν. οὐ διεψεύσατο δὲ ἡ στήλη ὅσα προεῖπεν· ἀθροίσας γὰρ ἑβδομήκοντα μυριάδας ἐπὶ τοὺς Ἕλληνας, κακῶς ἀπήλλαξεν, εἶτα ἐπανελθὼν αἴσχιστα ἀνθρώπων ἀπέθανεν, ἀποσφαγεὶς νύκτωρ ἐν τῇ εὐνῇ ὑπὸ τοῦ υἱοῦ.

4. Ἀρχέλαος ὁ βασιλεὺς ἑστίασιν παρεσκεύασε πολυτελῆ τοῖς ἑταίροις. προϊόντος δὲ τοῦ πότου ζωρότερον πιὼν Εὐριπίδης ὑπήχθη πως κατ' ὀλίγον εἰς μέθην· εἶτα συγκλιθέντα αὐτῷ Ἀγάθωνα τὸν τῆς τραγῳδίας ποιητὴν περιλαβὼν κατεφίλει, τετταράκοντα ἐτῶν που γεγονότα. τοῦ δὲ Ἀρχελάου πυθομένου εἰ καὶ νῦν ἔτι ἐρώμενος αὐτῷ δοκεῖ εἶναι, ἀπεκρίνατο· "ναὶ μὰ Δία· οὐ γὰρ μόνον τὸ ἔαρ τῶν καλῶν κάλλιστον, ἀλλὰ καὶ τὸ μετόπωρον."

5. Ἐρασθῆναι πρῶτον γενναίων παιδικῶν λέγουσι Λάιον, ἁρπάσαντα Χρύσιππον τὸν Πέλοπος. καὶ ἐκ τούτου τοῖς Θηβαίοις ἓν τῶν καλῶν ἐδόκει τὸ τῶν ὡραίων ἐρᾶν.

6. Ἐν Ἡραίᾳ τῆς Ἀρκαδίας ἀκούω πεφυκέναι ἀμπέλους, ἐξ ὧν γίνεται οἶνος, ὃς τοῦ λογισμοῦ

man who opens the tomb and does not fill the sarcophagus things will not improve." When Xerxes read this he was afraid and gave orders to pour in oil at once. But the sarcophagus did not fill up. He gave the order to pour once again. But the level did not rise, and he gave up after wasting to no avail what was poured in. Closing the tomb, he retreated in dismay. The inscription did not fail in its prediction: for having assembled 700,000 men against the Greeks he came off badly, and on his return he suffered a most shameful death, murdered one night in bed by his son.

4. King Archelaus gave a lavish banquet to his companions. As the drink flowed Euripides drank wine very little diluted with water, and gradually became drunk. Then, as the tragic poet Agathon sat down beside him, he embraced and kissed him, even though Agathon was about forty. When Archelaus inquired if Agathon still seemed suitable to be the object of his love, he replied: "Yes, by Zeus, it is not just spring that is excellent in handsome men, there is also autumn."[a]

5. They say Laius was the first lover of a noble boy; he made off with Chrysippus, son of Pelops. As a result the Thebans thought it a good thing to love the handsome.[b]

6. At Heraea in Arcadia I hear that vines grow from which wine is produced that causes Arcadians to lose

[a] The anecdote is registered in TrGF 39 T 22 a.

[b] The punishment which overtook Laius and his son Oedipus might have been expected to discourage this attitude.

---

[1] ἔστιν] ἔσται Faber

[2] ὀπίσω huc revocavi: ante τὸν τάφον praebent codd.

παράγει καὶ ἔκφρονας τοὺς ἄνδρας[1] ποιεῖ, τὰς δὲ γυναῖκας τεκνοποιοὺς τίθησιν.

Ὅτι ἐν Θάσῳ δύο γένη φασὶν γίνεσθαι οἴνων· καὶ τὸν μὲν ἕτερον πινόμενον εἰς ὕπνον κατάγειν εὖ μάλα βαθὺν καὶ διὰ ταῦτα ἡδύν, τὸν δὲ ἕτερον ἀντίπαλον εἶναι τοῦ βίου καὶ ἀγρυπνίαν ἐμποιεῖν καὶ ἀνιᾶσθαι παρέχειν.

Ἐν δὲ Ἀχαΐᾳ περὶ Κερυνείαν[2] οἶνος γίνεται, ὃς ταῖς βουλομέναις γυναιξὶν[3] ἀμβλῶσαι συμμάχεται.

7. Ὅτε εἷλε τὴν Θηβαίων πόλιν Ἀλέξανδρος, ἀπέδοτο τοὺς ἐλευθέρους πάντας πλὴν ἱερέων. ἀφῆκε δὲ τῆς πράσεως καὶ τοὺς τοῦ πατρὸς ξένους (ὡμήρευσε γὰρ παρ' αὐτοῖς ὁ Φίλιππος ἔτι παῖς ὤν), καὶ τοὺς συγγενεῖς δὲ τούτων ἀφῆκεν. ἐτίμησε δὲ καὶ τοὺς ἐγγόνους τοὺς τοῦ Πινδάρου, καὶ τὴν οἰκίαν αὐτοῦ μόνην εἴασεν ἑστάναι. ἐφόνευσε δὲ τῶν Θηβαίων εἰς ἑξακισχιλίους, αἰχμάλωτοι δὲ ἐλήφθησαν τρισμύριοι.

8. Λύσανδρον τὸν Λακεδαιμόνιον ἐν τῇ Ἰωνίᾳ διατρίβοντα τὰ Λυκούργου φασὶ νόμιμα ῥίψαντα ἐπίπονα ὄντα διατεθρύφθαι τὸν βίον. 9. Λάμια γοῦν ἡ Ἀττικὴ ἑταίρα εἶπεν· "οἱ ἐκ τῆς Ἑλλάδος λέοντες ἐν Ἐφέσῳ γεγόνασιν ἀλώπεκες."

10. Ἐν μιᾷ ἡμέρᾳ δύο γυναῖκας ἠγάγετο Διονύσιος, Δωρίδα τὴν Λοκρίδα καὶ Ἀριστομάχην[4] τὴν

[1] ἄνδρας ex Athenaeo Joh. Meyer: Ἀρκάδας codd.

[2] Κερυνείαν Her.: Κεραυνίαν codd.

[3] γυναιξὶν <εἰς τὸ> Her.

their reason and makes them mad, while it brings fertility to their women.

Note that in Thasos there are said to be two types of wine. One when drunk leads to very deep and therefore agreeable sleep, the other is an enemy of life, causing insomnia and bringing pain.

But in Achaea near Cerynia a wine is made which helps women to miscarry if they wish.[a]

7. When Alexander captured Thebes, he sold into slavery all free citizens except priests. He also exempted from sale his father's hosts—Philip as a boy had been a hostage there—and released their relatives. He paid honour to the descendants of Pindar, and allowed his house alone to stand. He executed about 6,000 Thebans, and 30,000 were taken prisoner.

8–9. When Lysander the Spartan lived in Ionia he is said to have rejected Lycurgus' rules of behaviour, which were burdensome, and to have adopted very luxurious habits.[b] The Attic courtesan Lamia remarked: "The lions of Greece turn into foxes at Ephesus."[c]

10. Dionysius married two women in a single day, Doris from Locri and Aristomache daughter of Hippari-

[a] Athenaeus 31 EF may well be the source of this ch.; see also Theophrastus, *Historia plantarum* 9.18.11.

[b] See n. on 3.20 above.

[c] Lamia's remark looks like an adaptation of a proverb, to judge from Aristophanes, *Peace* 1189–90. (Chs. 8–9 are really only one, the division being an oversight on the part of an early editor.)

---

[4] Ἀριστομάχην e Plutarcho Scheffer: Ἀρισταινέτην codd.

Ἱππαρίνου, Δίωνος δὲ ἀδελφήν· καὶ παρ' ἑκατέρᾳ ἀνεπαύετο ἐν τῷ μέρει. καὶ ἡ μὲν ἠκολούθει στρατευομένῳ, ἡ δὲ ἐπανιόντα ὑπεδέχετο.

11. Λόγος τις εἰς ἐμὲ ἀφίκετο λέγων αἴτιον Ἰσοκράτην γενέσθαι τὸν ῥήτορα τοῖς Πέρσαις καταδουλώσεως, ἧς[1] ἐδουλώσαντο αὐτοὺς Μακεδόνες. τοῦ γὰρ πανηγυρικοῦ λόγου, ὃν Ἰσοκράτης ἐν τοῖς Ἕλλησιν ἐπεδείξατο, εἰς Μακεδονίαν ἐλθοῦσα ἡ φήμη, πρῶτον μὲν Φίλιππον ἐπὶ τὴν Ἀσίαν ἀνέστησεν· ἀποθανόντος δὲ ἐκείνου, Ἀλέξανδρον τὸν υἱὸν αὐτοῦ <τῶν> πατρῴων[2] κληρονόμον τὴν ὁρμὴν τὴν τοῦ Φιλίππου διαδέξασθαι παρεσκεύασε.

12. Μέτων ὁ ἀστρονόμος, μελλόντων ἐπὶ τὴν Σικελίαν πλεῖν τῶν Ἀθηναίων ἤδη[3] [τῶν στρατευμάτων],[4] καὶ αὐτὸς εἷς ἦν τοῦ καταλόγου. σαφῶς δὲ ἐπιστάμενος τὰς μελλούσας τύχας τὸν πλοῦν ἐφυλάττετο, δεδιὼς καὶ σπεύδων τῆς ἐξόδου ἑαυτὸν ῥύσασθαι. ἐπεὶ δὲ οὐδὲν ἔπραττεν, ὑπεκρίνατο μανίαν· καὶ πολλὰ μὲν καὶ ἄλλα ἔδρασε πιστώσασθαι τὴν τῆς νόσου δόξαν βουλόμενος, ἐν δὲ τοῖς καὶ τὴν συνοικίαν τὴν αὑτοῦ κατέπρησεν· ἐγειτνία δὲ αὕτη τῇ Ποικίλῃ. καὶ ἐκ τούτου ἀφῆκαν αὐτὸν οἱ ἄρχοντες. καί μοι δοκεῖ ὁ Μέτων ἄμεινον ὑποκρίνασθαι τὴν μανίαν τοῦ Ὀδυσσέως τοῦ Ἰθακησίου·

[1] ἧς] ἣν Russell
[2] <τῶν> πατρῴων Kor.: πατρῷον codd.
[3] ἤδη x: om. V [4] del. Kor. possis <καὶ> ἤδη <συλλεγομένων> τῶν στρ. (Russell)

nus, sister of Dion. He slept with each in turn. One went with him on his campaigns, the other received him on his return.[a]

11. A story has reached me according to which Isocrates the orator was the cause of the enslavement which the Persians suffered at the hands of the Macedonians. The *Panegyricus*, which he delivered before the Greeks, became known in Macedonia, and first inspired Philip to attack Asia.[b] When he died, it caused his son Alexander, as heir to his father's estate, to continue Philip's enterprise.

12. When the Athenians were on the point of sailing to Sicily, the astronomer Meton was one of those enlisted.[c] Knowing full well what was going to happen he was wary of making the voyage. Though afraid and making efforts to save himself from the expedition, he had no success, so he pretended to be mad. He did a great deal in his attempts to strengthen the impression that he was ill, and among other things burned down his own apartment house. This was near the Stoa Poikile.[d] As a result the archons released him. In my opinion Meton feigned madness better than Odysseus of Ithaca; the latter was

[a] Plutarch, *Dion* 3, also describes the bigamy of Dionysius I, without suggesting that it was a source of grave scandal.

[b] Isocrates published the *Panegyricus* in 380 B.C. Aelian speaks as if he delivered it in person, attempting to rally panhellenic sentiment at the Olympic festival, but this is not correct.

[c] On Meton see 10.7 above. The story recurs in Plutarch, *Alcibiades* 17 and *Nicias* 13.

[d] "Multi-coloured," so called because of the fresco paintings on it. Zeno made it the location of his philosophical school.

ἐκεῖνον μὲν γὰρ ὁ Παλαμήδης κατεφώρασε, τοῦτον δὲ Ἀθηναίων οὐδείς.

13. Πτολεμαῖόν φασι τὸν Λάγου καταπλουτίζοντα τοὺς φίλους αὑτοῦ ὑπερχαίρειν. ἔλεγε δὲ ἄμεινον εἶναι πλουτίζειν ἢ πλουτεῖν.

14. Ὅτι τὰ Ὁμήρου ἔπη πρότερον διῃρημένα ᾖδον οἱ παλαιοί. οἷον ἔλεγον Τὴν ἐπὶ <ταῖς>[1] ναυσὶ μάχην καὶ Δολώνειάν τινα καὶ Ἀριστείαν Ἀγαμέμνονος καὶ Νεῶν κατάλογον καὶ [που][2] Πατρόκλειαν καὶ Λύτρα καὶ Ἐπὶ Πατρόκλῳ ἆθλα καὶ Ὁρκίων ἀφάνισιν. ταῦτα ὑπὲρ τῆς Ἰλιάδος, ὑπὲρ[3] δὲ τῆς ἑτέρας· Τὰ ἐν Πύλῳ καὶ Τὰ ἐν Λακεδαίμονι καὶ Καλυψοῦς ἄντρον καὶ Τὰ περὶ τὴν σχεδίαν <καὶ>[4] Ἀλκίνου ἀπολόγους <καὶ> Κυκλώπειαν καὶ Νέκυιαν καὶ Τὰ τῆς Κίρκης <καὶ> Νίπτρα <καὶ> Μνηστήρων φόνον <καὶ> Τὰ ἐν ἀγρῷ <καὶ> Τὰ ἐν Λαέρτου.

Ὀψὲ δὲ Λυκοῦργος ὁ Λακεδαιμόνιος ἀθρόαν πρῶτος εἰς τὴν Ἑλλάδα ἐκόμισε τὴν Ὁμήρου ποίησιν· τὸ δὲ ἀγώγιμον τοῦτο ἐξ Ἰωνίας, ἡνίκα ἀπεδήμησεν, ἤγαγεν. ὕστερον δὲ Πεισίστρατος συναγαγὼν ἀπέφηνε τὴν Ἰλιάδα καὶ Ὀδύσσειαν.

15. Φασὶ παχύτατον γενέσθαι τὴν διάνοιαν οἱ τῆς κωμῳδίας ποιηταὶ τὸ δέρμα ἔχοντα[5] ἀδιακόντιστον[6] Πολύδωρόν τινα καὶ ἄλλον Κοικυλίωνα ὄνομα, ὅσπερ τὰ κύματα ἠρίθμει ὑπὸ τῆς ἄγαν μανίας. λόγος δέ τις καὶ Σαννυρίωνα τοιοῦτον γενέσθαι,

[1] ex Eustathio ad *Il.* 915.22 supplevi [2] del. Kor.
[3] ὑπὲρ . . . ὑπὲρ] μέρη . . . μέρη Lehrs

detected by Palamedes, but no Athenian detected Meton.[a]

13. Ptolemy son of Lagus (they say) took great pleasure in enriching his friends. He said it was better to make others rich than be rich oneself.

14. Note that the ancients originally recited Homer's poems separately. For instance they spoke of The battle by the ships, The Doloneia, The aristeia of Agamemnon, The catalogue of ships, The Patrocleia, The ransoming, The games for Patroclus, The breaking of the oaths. That concerns the *Iliad*. For the other poem they had: Pylos, Sparta, Calypso's cave, The raft, Alcinous' tales, The Cyclops story, The Necyia, The story of Circe, The bath, The murder of the suitors, In the countryside, and At Laertes' house.

At a late date Lycurgus of Sparta was the first to bring Homer's poems to Hellas. He introduced them from Ionia, where he had been staying. Later Pisistratus put them together and produced the *Iliad* and *Odyssey*.[b]

15. The comic poets [fr. com. adesp. 72 K.-A.] say a certain Polydorus, who had a skin that could not be pierced, was very slow-witted. So was a man called Coecylion, who was completely mad and counted the waves. A tradition has it that Sannyrion was the same; he

[a] According to a story found in the early epic poem *Cypria* but not in Homer, Odysseus feigned madness in the hope of avoiding participation in the Trojan War. Palamedes exposed him by placing his infant son in front of his plough (Hyginus, *Fabulae* 95). [b] Compare 8.2 above.

---

[4] *καὶ* sexies suppl. Her. [5] *ἔχ<ειν λέγ>οντα* Marcovich
[6] *ἀδιακόντιστον* König: *-νιστον* codd.

ὃς ἐν τῇ ληκύθῳ τὴν κλίμακα ἐζήτει. καὶ Κόροιβον δὲ καὶ Μελιτίδην καὶ ἐκείνους ἀνοήτους φασίν.

16. Ἀπολλωνιᾶται πόλιν οἰκοῦσι γείτονα Ἐπιδάμνου ἐν τῷ Ἰονίῳ κόλπῳ. καὶ ἐν τοῖς πλησίον αὐτῆς χωρίοις ἄσφαλτός[1] ἐστιν ὀρυκτὴ καὶ πίττα[2] τὸν αὐτὸν ἐκ τῆς γῆς ἀνατέλλουσα τρόπον, ὃν καὶ αἱ πλεῖσται πηγαὶ τῶν ὑδάτων. οὐ πόρρω δὲ καὶ τὸ ἀθάνατον δείκνυται πῦρ. ὁ δὲ καιόμενος τόπος ἐστὶν[3] ὀλίγος καὶ οὐκ εἰς μέγα διήκει καὶ ἔχει περίβολον οὐ πολύν, ὄζει δὲ θείου καὶ στυπτηρίας. καὶ περὶ αὐτόν ἐστι δένδρα εὐθαλῆ καὶ πόα[4] χλωρά· καὶ τὸ πῦρ πλησίον ἐνακμάζον οὐδὲν λυπεῖ οὔτε τὴν τῶν φυτῶν βλάστην οὔτε τὴν τεθηλυῖαν <πόαν>.[5] καίεται δὲ τὸ πῦρ καὶ νύκτα καὶ μεθ' ἡμέραν, καὶ διέλιπεν οὐδέποτε, ὡς Ἀπολλωνιᾶται λέγουσι, πρὶν τοῦ πολέμου τοῦ πρὸς Ἰλλυριοὺς συμβάντος αὐτοῖς.

Ὅτι Ἀπολλωνιᾶται ξενηλασίας ἐποίουν κατὰ τὸν Λακεδαιμόνιον νόμον, Ἐπιδάμνιοι δὲ ἐπιδημεῖν καὶ μετοικεῖν παρεῖχον τῷ βουλομένῳ.

17. Πτήσσει Φρύνιχος ὥς τις ἀλεκτρυών· παροιμία ἐπὶ τῶν κακῶς τι[6] πασχόντων. ὑποκρινομένου

[1] ἄσφαλτός Gesner: -άλτου x: -αλέστερ. V
[2] πίττα ex Arist. *Mirab.* 842 b 14 Kor.: πιμπλᾷ codd.
[3] τόπος ἐστὶν ex Arist. Her.: ἐστι λόφος codd.
[4] πόα Kühn: πολλὰ codd. [5] suppl. Her.
[6] κακῶς τι] melius κακόν τι (Her.) vel κακῶς (Nauck)

[a] This ch. is discussed by W. M. Calder III, *Philologus* 117 (1973): 141–142, and M. Marcovich, *Živa antika* 26 (1976): 49–51. The name Polydorus should perhaps be given as Poly-

looked for a ladder in his oil flask. Coroebos and Melitides are also said to have been stupid.[a]

16. The city of Apollonia is a neighbour of Epidamnus on the Ionian gulf.[b] In its territory bitumen is dug up, and pitch comes out of the ground in the same way as most springs of water. Not far away the everlasting flame is pointed out; the area burned is small, not extensive and with a small perimeter, and there is a smell of sulphur and alum. Around it trees flourish and the grass is green; the fire nearby does no damage to the growing plants or the luxuriant grass. The fire burns night and day, and the men of Apollonia say it never went out before the war they fought against the Illyrians.

Note that Apollonia banished foreigners, using the Spartan law,[c] while Epidamnus allowed anyone who wished to visit or settle.

17. "Phrynichus cowers like a cock" is a proverb applied to those who suffer misfortune.[d] For when Phry-

orus, as in Eustathius, *In Odysseam* 1669.55; see also M. J. Osborne and S. G. Byrne, *A Lexicon of Greek Personal Names* II (Oxford, 1994), s.v. [b] Apollonia and Epidamnus, now Poian and Durazzo in Albania, were both colonies of Corcyra, itself a colony of Corinth. [c] There are several recorded expulsions of foreigners in Spartan history; but it is not obvious why a city founded from Corcyra should have felt the need to adopt a Spartan practice. [d] The opening words of this ch. (registered as TrGF 3 T 14) are almost identical with line 1490 of Aristophanes, *Wasps* and may already have been proverbial in his day. The Phrynichus in question was the early tragedian whose play about the capture of Miletus in 494 B.C. annoyed the Athenian public so much that they fined him; the story is in Herodotus 6.21. At that date it was probably still the rule that the poet himself took the leading role in the performance.

γὰρ Φρυνίχου τοῦ τραγικοῦ τὴν Μιλήτου ἅλωσιν οἱ Ἀθηναῖοι δακρύσαντες ἐξέβαλον δεδοικότα καὶ ὑποπτήσσοντα.

18. Διονύσιος ὁ τῆς Σικελίας τύραννος τραγῳδίαν μὲν ἠσπάζετο καὶ ἐπῄνει καὶ οὖν καὶ δράματα ἐξεπόνησε τραγικά, ἀλλοτρίως δὲ πρὸς τὴν κωμῳδίαν διέκειτο, ὅτι οὐκ ἦν φιλόγελως.

19. Ἔλεγεν ὁ Κλεομένης λακωνικῶς[1] κατὰ τὸν ἐπιχώριον τρόπον τὸν Ὅμηρον Λακεδαιμονίων εἶναι ποιητὴν ὡς χρὴ πολεμεῖν λέγοντα· τὸν δὲ Ἡσίοδον τῶν Εἱλώτων, λέγοντα ὡς χρὴ γεωργεῖν.

20. Ἀνὴρ Μεγαλοπολίτης ἐξ Ἀρκαδίας, Κερκιδᾶς ὄνομα, ἀποθνήσκων ἔλεγε πρὸς τοὺς οἰκείους ἐνθυμούμενος[2] ἡδέως ἀπολύεσθαι τοῦ ζῆν· δι' ἐλπίδος γὰρ ἔχειν συγγενέσθαι τῶν μὲν σοφῶν Πυθαγόρᾳ, τῶν δὲ ἱστορικῶν Ἑκαταίῳ, τῶν δὲ μουσικῶν Ὀλύμπῳ, τῶν δὲ ποιητῶν Ὁμήρῳ. καὶ ἐπὶ τούτοις, ὡς λόγος, τὴν ψυχὴν ἀπέλιπεν.

21. Ὅτι ἐν Κελαιναῖς τῇ δορᾷ τοῦ Φρυγὸς ἐὰν προσαυλῇ τις τὴν ἁρμονίαν τὴν Φρύγιον, ἡ δορὰ κινεῖται· ἐὰν δὲ εἰς Ἀπόλλωνα, ἀτρεμεῖ καὶ ἔοικε κωφῇ.

[1] λακωνικῶς x: om. V: ὁ Λάκων Φ: del. Her.
[2] ἐνθυμούμενος] εὐ- Kühn: παραμυθούμενος Nairn: παραμυθουμένους Russell

---

[a] Although no more than a few lines of his poetry survive, it is known that Dionysius won a prize when he had a play produced at Athens in 367 B.C. (TrGF 76).

nichus the tragedian was acting in *The Capture of Miletus* the Athenians wept and expelled him from the theatre in his state of fear and terror.

18. Dionysius the tyrant of Sicily appreciated tragedy; he praised it and went so far as to compose tragedies himself.[a] But his feelings about comedy were different, as he was no lover of humour.

19. Cleomenes the Laconian made the typically Spartan remark that Homer was a poet for Spartans, as he instructed men to fight; Hesiod was for helots, as he tells men to farm.[b]

20. A man from Megalopolis in Arcadia called Cercidas[c] told his friends when dying that on reflection he was pleased to be released from life, because he hoped to meet the sage Pythagoras, the historian Hecataeus,[d] the musician Olympus,[e] and the poet Homer. And with that, as the story goes, he expired.

21. Note that at Celaenae if someone plays a Phrygian tune in the vicinity of the Phrygian's skin, the skin moves. But if one plays in honour of Apollo, it is motionless and seems deaf.[f]

[b] Cleomenes was king ca. 525–488 B.C. The anecdote is also found in Plutarch, *Moralia* 223 A. [c] Rather strangely Aelian fails to tell us that Cercidas was a politician and the author of satiric poems called *Meliambi.* An Oxyrhynchus papyrus, no. 1082, contains some of them. [d] Hecataeus (fl. ca. 500 B.C.) was one of the earliest prose writers; his works were historical and geographical. See FGrH 1 T 8. [e] Olympus was believed to be one of the founders of Greek music. [f] The Phrygian satyr Marsyas was supposed to have challenged Apollo to a musical contest, in which the winner would be allowed to do whatever he liked to the loser. Apollo flayed Marsyas and the skin was preserved at Celaenae. See Herodotus 7.26.

22. Πτολεμαῖος ὁ Φιλοπάτωρ κατασκευάσας Ὁμήρῳ νεών, αὐτὸν μὲν καλῶς ἐκάθισε, κύκλῳ δὲ τὰς πόλεις περιέστησε τοῦ ἀγάλματος,[1] ὅσαι ἀντιποιοῦνται τοῦ Ὁμήρου.

Γαλάτων δὲ ὁ ζωγράφος ἔγραψε τὸν μὲν Ὅμηρον αὐτὸν ἐμοῦντα, τοὺς δὲ ἄλλους ποιητὰς τὰ ἐμημεσμένα ἀρυομένους.

23. Λυκοῦργος ὁ Λακεδαιμόνιος ὁ Εὐνόμου παῖς δικαίους βουληθεὶς ἀποφῆναι Λακεδαιμονίους, ὑπὲρ τούτου γε οὐ καλοὺς τοὺς μισθοὺς ἠνύσατο.[2] ἀπήντησε γὰρ αὐτῷ τὸν ὀφθαλμὸν ἐκκοπῆναι ὑπὸ Ἀλκάνδρου, ὡς μέν τινές φασιν, ἐξ ἐπιβουλῆς λίθῳ βληθείς, ὡς δὲ ἄλλος διαφοιτᾷ λόγος, βακτηρίᾳ παθὼν τὸ πάθος. λέγει δὲ Ἔφορος αὐτὸν λιμῷ διακαρτερήσαντα ἐν φυγῇ ἀποθανεῖν.

24. Λυκοῦργος ὁ ῥήτωρ ἔγραψε μὴ ἐλαύνειν τὰς γυναῖκας ἐν τοῖς μυστηρίοις ἐπὶ ζευγῶν ἢ τῇ δρώσῃ τοῦτο ἐπηρτῆσθαι ζημίαν, ἥν γε ᾤετο <ὁ>[3] τάξας ἀποχρῶσαν. πρώτη τῷ ψηφίσματι ἠπείθησεν ἡ τούτου γυνή, καὶ τὴν ζημίαν ἐξέτισε καταδικασθεῖσα. λέγεται δὲ ὁ λόγος πρὸς τοὺς ἄλλα <μὲν>[4] θελήσαντας, ἄλλων δὲ τυχόντας.[5]

Καὶ Περικλῆς ἔγραψε μὴ εἶναι Ἀθηναῖον, ὃς μὴ ἐξ ἀμφοῖν γέγονεν ἀστοῖν. εἶτα ἀποβαλὼν τοὺς γνησίους παῖδας ἐπὶ τῷ νόθῳ Περικλεῖ κατελέλει-

[1] τοῦ ἀγάλματος] τῷ -ατι Dilts [2] ἠνύσατο Cobet: ἠρύσατο codd. [3] suppl. Kühn [4] suppl. Her. [5] λέγεται . . . τυχόντας huc revocavi; post πάθος in c. 23 praebent codd.

22. Ptolemy Philopator built a temple to Homer.[a] He set up a fine statue of the poet, and around it in a circle all the cities which claim Homer as theirs.

The painter Galaton depicted Homer being sick, with the other poets drawing upon his vomit.

23. Lycurgus of Sparta, son of Eunomus, wanted to instil justice into the Spartans, but did not receive a good reward for this. He suffered the loss of an eye at the hands of Alcander; some say a stone was deliberately thrown at him, but another widely current account [FGrH 596 F 19(b)] is that he suffered a blow from a stick. But Ephorus says [FGrH 70 F 175] that after a long struggle against hunger he died in exile.

24. Lycurgus the orator proposed a law that women should not ride in chariots during the festival of the mysteries; if anyone did, a fine was to be imposed which he as the legislator thought sufficient.[b] The first woman to disregard the law was his wife, and she was convicted and paid the fine. The story is aimed at those who try for one thing and achieve another.

Pericles proposed that whoever was not the child of two citizen parents should not be an Athenian citizen. Then he lost his legitimate children and was left with his

[a] On the temple of Homer in Alexandria see P. M. Fraser, *Ptolemaic Alexandria* (Oxford, 1972), vol. 1 p. 611, vol. 2 p. 862, and the epigram now published as item 979 in H. Lloyd-Jones and P. J. Parsons, *Supplementum Hellenisticum* (Berlin, 1983). The site is not known. Homer's birthplace was a subject of debate in antiquity; see e.g. *Greek Anthology* 16.297, 298.

[b] The Greek of the last clause is obscure and the translation approximate.

πτο. δῆλα δὲ ὅτι καὶ Περικλῆς ἐβούλετο μὲν ἕτερα, ἔτυχε δὲ ἑτέρων.

Κλεισθένης δὲ ὁ Ἀθηναῖος τὸ [δεῖν][1] ἐξοστρακίζεσθαι πρῶτος εἰσηγησάμενος αὐτὸς ἔτυχε τῆς καταδίκης πρῶτος.

Ζάλευκος ὁ Λοκρῶν νομοθέτης προσέταξε τὸν μοιχὸν ἁλόντα ἐκκόπτεσθαι τοὺς ὀφθαλμούς. ἃ τοίνυν μηδὲ προσεδόκησε, ταῦτα ὁ δαίμων αὐτῷ παρὰ τὴν δόξαν καὶ τὴν ἐλπίδα ἐπήγαγεν· ὁ γάρ τοι παῖς ἁλοὺς ἐπὶ μοιχείᾳ εἶτα ἔμελλε πείσεσθαι τὰ ἐκ τοῦ πατρῴου νόμου. ἐνταῦθα ἵνα μὴ διαφθαρῇ τὸ ἅπαξ κεκυρωμένον, ὑπέμεινεν αὐτὸς ὁ εἰσηγησάμενος ὑπὲρ τοῦ ἑτέρου τῶν τοῦ παιδὸς ὀφθαλμῶν ἀντιδοῦναι τὸν ἑαυτοῦ, ἵνα μὴ ὁ νεανίσκος τυφλωθῇ τελέως.

25. Πίνδαρος ὁ ποιητὴς ἀγωνιζόμενος ἐν Θήβαις ἀμαθέσι περιπεσὼν ἀκροαταῖς ἡττήθη Κορίννης πεντάκις. ἐλέγχων δὲ τὴν ἀμουσίαν αὐτῶν ὁ Πίνδαρος σῦν ἐκάλει τὴν Κόρινναν.[2]

26. Διογένης ὁ Σινωπεὺς ἔρημος ἦν καὶ μόνος ἀπέρριπτο, καὶ οὔτε τινὰ δι' ἀπορίαν ὑπεδέχετο, οὔτε τις αὐτὸν ἐξένιζε, τὸν ἄνδρα ἐκτρεπόμενος διὰ τὸ τοῦ τρόπου ἐλεγκτικὸν καὶ ὅτι ἦν πρὸς τὰ πραττόμενα καὶ λεγόμενα δυσάρεστος. ἠθύμει οὖν ὁ Διογένης <καὶ μᾶζαν>[3] καὶ φύλλων ἄκρα ἤσθιε· ταῦτα γάρ οἱ παρῆν. τοῖς δὲ ἀποπίπτουσι τοῦ ἄρτου θρύμμασι μῦς ἐχρῆτο ἐπιφοιτῶν. ὁ οὖν Διογένης φιλοπόνως κατεσκέψατο τὸ πραττόμενον, καὶ μειδιάσας καὶ

[1] del. Her. [2] σῦν . . . Κόρινναν] ἔφη· σῦς αἰκάλλει

illegitimate son Pericles. Clearly in his case as well policy was one thing, the outcome another.

Cleisthenes the Athenian, who first suggested the necessity of ostracism, was the first to suffer this punishment.

Zaleucus the lawgiver at Locri ordained that adulterers should be blinded. But fate brought upon him, against expectation and hope, a fate which he did not anticipate, for his son was convicted of adultery and was on the point of suffering under his father's law. In order that a measure once ratified should not be invalidated, Zaleucus himself, the author of the law, in place of one of his son's eyes agreed to sacrifice one of his own, so that the son should not be completely blinded.

25. The poet Pindar, competing in Thebes, was exposed to an ignorant public and defeated five times by Corinna. Criticising the public's lack of taste Pindar called Corinna a sow.[a]

26. Diogenes of Sinope lived alone and rejected by the world. He was too poor to entertain anyone, and no one invited him. He was avoided because of his carping manner and his dissatisfaction with everything that was said or done. So Diogenes was miserable and ate barley-bread and green shoots—that was what he had. A mouse used to come and take crumbs of his bread. Diogenes watched closely what was happening, smiled and became more

[a] Pindar's remark is not entirely logical; C. Charitonides, *Mnemosyne* 49 (1921): 139–140, proposed to make him say instead "The pig flatters the crow," which would be a way of attacking both Corinna and the public.

κορώνην Charitonides [3] suppl. Scheffer

ἑαυτοῦ γενόμενος φαιδρότερός τε καὶ ἵλεως εἶπεν· "ὁ μὲν μῦς οὗτος τῆς Ἀθηναίων πολυτελείας δεῖται οὐδέν, σὺ δέ, ὦ Διόγενες, ἄχθῃ [φησὶ][1] ὅτι μὴ συνδειπνεῖς Ἀθηναίοις."[2] καὶ ἐπόρισεν ἑαυτῷ εὔκαιρον εὐθυμίαν.

27. Ὅτι τὸ Σωκράτους σῶμα πεπίστευτο κόσμιον καὶ σωφροσύνης ἐγκρατὲς γεγονέναι καὶ ταύτῃ. ἐνόσουν Ἀθηναῖοι πανδημεί, καὶ οἱ μὲν ἀπέθνῃσκον, οἱ δὲ ἐπιθανατίως εἶχον, Σωκράτης δὲ μόνος οὐκ ἐνόσησε τὴν ἀρχήν. ὁ τοίνυν τοιούτῳ συνὼν σώματι τίνα ἡγούμεθα ἐσχηκέναι[3] ψυχήν;

28. Διογένης ἡνίκα ἀπέλιπε τὴν πατρίδα, εἷς αὐτῷ τῶν οἰκετῶν ἠκολούθει ὄνομα Μάνης, ὃς οὐ φέρων τὴν μετ' αὐτοῦ διατριβὴν ἀπέδρα. προτρεπόντων δέ τινων ζητεῖν αὐτὸν ἔφη· "οὐκ αἰσχρὸν Μάνην μὲν μὴ δεῖσθαι Διογένους, Διογένην δὲ Μάνους;" οὗτος δὲ ὁ οἰκέτης εἰς Δελφοὺς ἀλώμενος ὑπὸ κυνῶν διεσπάσθη, τῷ ὀνόματι τοῦ δεσπότου δίκας ἐκτίσας ἀνθ' ὧν ἀπέδρασεν.

29. Ἔλεγεν ὁ Πλάτων τὰς ἐλπίδας ἐγρηγορότων ἀνθρώπων ὀνείρους εἶναι.

30. Ὀλυμπιὰς ἡ Ἀλεξάνδρου πυθομένη ὅτι πολὺν χρόνον ὁ παῖς αὐτῆς ἄταφος μένει, βαρὺ ἀναστένουσα καὶ θρηνοῦσα εὖ μάλα λιγέως "ὦ τέκνον," εἶπεν, "ἀλλὰ σὺ μὲν οὐρανοῦ μετασχεῖν βουλόμενος καὶ τοῦτο σπεύδων, νῦν οὐδὲ τῶν κοινῶν δήπου καὶ ἴσων πᾶσιν ἀνθρώποις μετασχεῖν ἔχεις,

[1] del. Her. [2] notam interrogationis apposuit Blake
[3] ἐσχηκέναι scripsi: εἶχε codd.: ἔχειν Cobet

cheerful and contented than he had been, remarking: "This mouse does not need any of the luxuries of the Athenians, but you, Diogenes, are annoyed at not dining with Athenians." And he provided himself with timely comfort.

27. Note that Socrates' constitution was believed to be well balanced and capable of moderation for the following reason. The Athenians suffered an epidemic;[a] some died, others were close to death, while Socrates alone was not ill at all. What kind of soul do we suppose inhabited that body?

28. When Diogenes left his own city, one of his slaves called Manes went with him, but then ran away because he could not endure to live with him. When some people urged Diogenes to look for him he said: "Wouldn't it be shocking that Manes has no need of Diogenes while Diogenes needs Manes?" This slave reached Delphi in his wanderings and was torn to pieces by dogs, paying the penalty for his action in a manner appropriate to his master's name.[b]

29. Plato used to say that hopes are the dreams of men awake.[c]

30. When Alexander's mother Olympias learned that her son lay unburied for a long time, she groaned deeply and cried in a high-pitched voice: "My child," she said, "you wanted to reach heaven and made it your aim, but now you do not enjoy even what are surely common rights

[a] A reference to the plague which devastated Athens in 429 B.C.

[b] The anecdote is one of many to exploit the derivation of "cynic" from the word for "dog."

[c] This remark cannot be traced in the Platonic corpus, but is attributed by Diogenes Laertius 5.18 to Aristotle.

γῆς τε ἅμα καὶ ταφῆς," καὶ τὰς ἑαυτῆς τύχας οἰκτείρασα καὶ τὸ τοῦ παιδὸς τετυφωμένον ἐλέγξασα.

31. Ξενοκράτης ὁ Χαλκηδόνιος, ὁ ἑταῖρος Πλάτωνος, τά τε ἄλλα ἦν φιλοικτίρμων καὶ οὐ μόνον φιλάνθρωπος, ἀλλὰ καὶ πολλὰ τῶν ἀλόγων ζῴων ἠλέει. καὶ οὖν ποτε καθημένου ἐν ὑπαίθρῳ, διωκόμενος βιαίως στρουθὸς ὑπὸ ἱέρακος εἰς τοὺς κόλπους αὐτοῦ κατέπτη. ὁ δὲ ἀσμένως ἐδέξατο τὸν ὄρνιν καὶ διεφύλαξεν ἀποκρύψας, ἔστε [ἂν][1] ὁ διώκων ἀπῆλθεν. ἐπεὶ δὲ ἠλευθέρωσεν αὐτὸν τοῦ φόβου, ἁπλώσας τὸν κόλπον ἀφῆκε τὸν ὄρνιν, ἐπειπὼν ὅτι μὴ ἐξέδωκε τὸν ἱκέτην.

32. Φησὶ Ξενοφῶν ὅτι Θεοδότῃ τῇ ἑταίρᾳ εἰς λόγους ἀφίκετο[2] Σωκράτης, καλλίστῃ γυναικὶ οὔσῃ. ἀλλὰ καὶ τῇ Καλλιστοῖ ἦλθεν εἰς λόγους, ἣ ἔλεγεν· "ἐγὼ μέν, ὦ <παῖ>[3] Σωφρονίσκου, κρείττων εἰμί σου· σὺ μὲν γὰρ οὐδένα τῶν ἐμῶν δύνῃ ἀποσπάσαι, ἐγὼ δέ, ἐὰν βούλωμαι, τοὺς σοὺς πάντας." ὁ δέ· "καὶ μάλα γε εἰκότως· σὺ μὲν γὰρ ἐπὶ τὴν κατάντη αὐτοὺς πάντας ἄγεις, ἐγὼ δὲ ἐπὶ τὴν ἀρετὴν ἥκειν βιάζομαι· ὀρθία δὲ ἡ ἄνοδός ἐστι καὶ ἀήθης τοῖς πολλοῖς."

33. Ῥοδῶπίν φασιν Αἰγυπτίων λόγοι ἑταίραν γενέσθαι ὡραιοτάτην. καί ποτε αὐτῆς λουομένης ἡ τὰ παράδοξα καὶ τὰ ἀδόκητα φιλοῦσα ἐργάζεσθαι τύχη προὐξένησεν αὐτῇ οὐ τῆς γνώμης ἀλλὰ τοῦ κάλλους ἄξια. λουομένης γὰρ καὶ τῶν θεραπαινίδων τὴν ἐσθῆτα φυλαττουσῶν, ἀετὸς καταπτάς, τὸ

shared by all men, the right to earth and to burial." Thus she lamented her own fate and criticised her son's arrogance.

31. Xenocrates of Chalcedon, the friend of Plato, was compassionate and not only kind to men but showed pity for many brute animals. One day when he was sitting out of doors a sparrow pursued hotly by a hawk flew into his lap. He welcomed the bird and hid it in order to protect it until its pursuer went away. When he had calmed its fear he opened his cloak and let the bird go with the comment that he had not betrayed the suppliant.

32. Xenophon says [*Memorabilia* 3.11] that Socrates had a conversation with the courtesan Theodote, a most beautiful woman. He also talked to Callisto, who said: "Son of Sophroniscus, I am superior to you. You cannot detach any of my people from me, but I, if I wish, can detach all yours." "Of course," he replied, "because you lead everyone on the downward path, and I force them to move in the direction of virtue. The ascent is steep and most people are not used to it."

33. The Egyptian tradition is that Rhodopis was a very beautiful courtesan.[a] Once when she was taking a bath fate, which is so fond of bringing about the strange and unexpected, acted in a way appropriate not to her intelligence but to her beauty. As she washed and the maids looked after her clothes an eagle flew down, snatched one

[a] The same story is told by Strabo, 17.1.33 (808), which may be Aelian's source.

---

[1] del. Kor. [2] ἀφίκετο Her.: ἀφῖκτο codd.
[3] suppl. Russell

ἕτερον τῶν ὑποδημάτων ἁρπάσας, ἀπιὼν ᾤχετο· καὶ ἐκόμισεν εἰς Μέμφιν, δικάζοντος Ψαμμητίχου, καὶ εἰς τὸν κόλπον ἐνέβαλε τὸ ὑπόδημα. ὁ δὲ Ψαμμήτιχος θαυμάσας τοῦ ὑποδήματος τὸν ῥυθμὸν καὶ τῆς ἐργασίας αὐτοῦ τὴν χάριν καὶ τὸ πραχθὲν ὑπὸ τοῦ ὄρνιθος προσέταξεν ἀνὰ πᾶσαν τὴν Αἴγυπτον ἀναζητεῖσθαι τὴν ἄνθρωπον, ἧς τὸ ὑπόδημά ἐστι· καὶ εὑρὼν γαμετὴν ἠγάγετο.

34. Ὅτι τὸν Λέοντα ὁ Διονύσιος μετὰ τὴν πρόσταξιν τὴν κατ' αὐτοῦ ἀνευρὼν εἰς τρὶς τοὺς δορυφόρους[1] ἐκέλευσεν ἀπάγειν, καὶ μετέγνω τρίς, καὶ καθ' ἑκάστην μεταπομπὴν κατεφίλει κλαίων καὶ καταρώμενος ἑαυτοῦ,[2] ὅτι [ὅτε][3] ἔλαβε[4] τὸ ξίφος. τελευτῶν ἥττηται τῷ φόβῳ,[5] καὶ προσέταξεν ἀποσφαγῆναι εἰπὼν ὅτι "οὐκ ἔστιν, ὦ Λέον, σοι ζῆν."

35. Λέγουσι φυσικοὶ ἄνδρες τὴν[6] ἔλαφον καθάρσεως δεομένην[7] σέσελιν[8] ἐσθίειν, φαλαγγίων δὲ κνήσμασιν ἐχομένην καρκίνους.

36. Ὀλυμπιὰς τῇ Φιλίππου θυγατρὶ Εὐρυδίκῃ (ἦν δὲ ἄρα αὐτὴ ἐξ Ἰλλυρίδος γυναικὸς τῷ Φιλίππῳ γενομένη) προσέπεμψε κώνειον καὶ βρόχον καὶ ξίφος· ἡ δὲ αἱρεῖται τὸν βρόχον.

[1] τοὺς δορυφόρους Russell: τοῖς -οις codd. [2] ἑαυτοῦ] αὑτῷ Her. [3] del. Kühn [4] ἔλαβε] expectares ἔδωκε vel ἔβαλε (Russell) [5] τῷ φόβῳ] τοῦ φόβου Russell [6] τὴν Scheffer: τὸν codd. [7] δεομένην . . . ἐχομένην Her.: -νον . . . -νον codd. [8] σέσελιν Scheffer: σέλινα codd.

---

[a] As transmitted by the MSS. this story is unclear, but the

of her shoes, and made off with it. It carried the shoe to Memphis, where Psammetichus was judging cases, and threw it into his lap. Psammetichus was amazed by the design of the shoe, the beauty of its workmanship, and by the action of the bird. He gave orders for the woman who owned the shoe to be searched for throughout Egypt, and when he found her he married her.

34. Note that Dionysius made an order against Leon and caught him. Three times he gave his bodyguard instructions to lead him away to execution, and three times he changed his mind. Each time he brought him back he embraced him with a tear and a curse for having picked up his sword. Finally he was overcome by fear and gave the order for execution saying: "Leon, it is not possible for you to live."[a]

35. Scientists say that deer eat hartwort when they need a purge and crabs when they have been bitten by the tarantula.[b]

36. Olympias sent Philip's daughter Eurydice—she was the child of Philip and an Illyrian woman—hemlock, a noose, and a dagger.[c] Eurydice chose the noose.

fault may not lie with Aelian, as the ch. begins with the formula used for abbreviation. Cicero, *Tusculan Disputations* 5.60, gives a clearer version: Dionysius I handed his sword to one of his favourites called Leon, and another person present remarked "You can certainly entrust your safety to him." Leon laughed, and Dionysius ordered that both be executed. In Cicero's version the name Leon is not given. [b] Compare 1.8 above. [c] It was often suggested in antiquity that there were three ways to commit suicide; the idea first appears in Aristophanes, *Frogs* 118–135, where they are: hanging, hemlock, and throwing oneself from a height. See E. Fraenkel, *Philologus* 87 (1932): 470–473 (= *Kleine Beiträge zur klassischen Philologie* I (Rome, 1964), pp. 465–467.

37. Γέλων ὁ τῶν Συρακουσίων τύραννος τὴν τῆς ἀρχῆς κατάστασιν πραότατα εἶχε· στασιώδεις δέ τινες ἐπεβούλευον αὐτῷ. ἃ πυθόμενος ὁ Γέλων, εἰς ἐκκλησίαν συγκαλέσας τοὺς Συρακουσίους εἰσῆλθεν ὡπλισμένος [ὁ Γέλων],[1] καὶ διεξελθὼν ὅσα ἀγαθὰ αὐτοῖς εἰργάσατο, καὶ τὴν ἐπιβουλὴν ἐξεκάλυψε καὶ ἀπεδύσατο τὴν πανοπλίαν, εἰπὼν πρὸς πάντας· "ἰδοῦ τοίνυν ὑμῖν ἐν χιτωνίσκῳ γυμνὸς τῶν ὅπλων παρέστηκα, καὶ δίδωμι χρῆσθαι ὅ τι βούλεσθε." καὶ ἐθαύμασαν αὐτοῦ τὴν γνώμην οἱ Συρακούσιοι, οἱ δὲ καὶ τοὺς ἐπιβουλεύοντας παρέδοσαν αὐτῷ κολάσαι καὶ τὴν ἀρχὴν ἔδωκαν. ὁ δὲ καὶ τούτους εἴασε τῷ δήμῳ τιμωρήσασθαι. καὶ εἰκόνα αὐτοῦ οἱ Συρακούσιοι ἔστησαν ἐν ἀζώστῳ χιτῶνι· καὶ ἦν τοῦτο τῆς δημαγωγίας αὐτοῦ ὑπόμνημα καὶ τοῖς εἰς τὸν μετὰ ταῦτα αἰῶνα μέλλουσιν ἄρχειν δίδαγμα.

38. Ἰσχυρῶς Ὅμηρον ἐθαύμαζεν Ἀλκιβιάδης, καί ποτε διδασκαλείῳ παίδων προσελθὼν ῥαψῳδίαν Ἰλιάδος ᾔτει. τοῦ δὲ διδασκάλου μηδὲν ἔχειν Ὁμήρου φήσαντος, ἐντρίψας αὐτῷ κόνδυλον εὖ μάλα στερεὸν παρῆλθεν, ἐνδειξάμενος ὅτι ἐκεῖνος ἀπαίδευτός ἐστι καὶ τοιούτους ἀποφαίνει τοὺς παῖδας.

Οὗτος ἐπὶ κρίσιν καλούμενος θανατικὴν ἐκ Σικελίας ὑπὸ τῶν Ἀθηναίων οὐχ ὑπήκουσεν εἰπών· "εὔηθες τὸν ἔχοντα δίκην ζητεῖν [μὴ][2] ἀποφυγεῖν, ἐνὸν φυγεῖν." εἰπόντος δέ τινος· "οὐ πιστεύεις τῇ πατρίδι

[1] del. Her. [2] del. Leopardus

37. Gelon, tyrant of Syracuse, established a very mild regime. But some conspirators began plotting against him. Learning of this Gelon summoned the Syracusans to an assembly and entered in full armour. He detailed all the benefits he had brought them, revealed the plot, and took off his armour, saying to the assembled company: "Here you are, I stand before you lightly dressed and with no weapons, and you may do what you like with me." The Syracusans admired his decision, and some of them handed over the conspirators to him to punish, and gave him command of the city. But he left it to the people to deal with the conspirators. The Syracusans set up a statue of him wearing a tunic without a belt; this was a memorial to his popularity with the public and a lesson to future rulers.[a]

38. Alcibiades was a great admirer of Homer. One day he went into a school and asked for a book of the *Iliad.* When the master told him he had nothing of Homer's, he punched the man violently and walked off, demonstrating that the teacher was uneducated and was producing pupils of the same kind.[b]

When recalled by the Athenians from Sicily to stand trial on a capital charge[c] he refused, saying: "It is silly, when one has right on one's side, to aim at acquittal, if one can escape altogether." When someone said: "Don't

[a] Compare 6.11 above.

[b] The anecdote occurs also in Plutarch, *Alcibiades* 7 and *Moralia* 186 D.

[c] Thucydides 6.27–29 reports that Alcibiades was summoned back from Sicily to face charges of having parodied the mysteries of Eleusis and being involved in the mutilation of the Hermae.

τὴν περὶ σοῦ κρίσιν;" ὁ δὲ εἶπεν· "οὐδὲ τῇ μητρί·[1] δέδοικα γὰρ μὴ ἀγνοήσασα καὶ σφαλεῖσα τοῦ ἀληθοῦς εἶτα τὴν μέλαιναν ἐμβάλῃ ἀντὶ τῆς λευκῆς ψῆφον." πυθόμενος οὖν ὅτι θάνατος αὐτοῦ κατεγνώσθη ὑπὸ τῶν πολιτῶν, "δείξωμεν οὖν" εἶπεν "ὅτι ζῶμεν," καὶ ὁρμήσας πρὸς τοὺς Λακεδαιμονίους τὸν Δεκελεικὸν ἐξῆψε πόλεμον ἐπὶ τοὺς Ἀθηναίους.

Ἔλεγε δὲ μηδὲν παράδοξον ποιεῖν Λακεδαιμονίους ἀδεῶς ἐν τῷ πολέμῳ ἀποθνήσκοντας· τὴν γὰρ ἐκ τῶν νόμων ταλαιπωρίαν ἀποδιδράσκοντας θάνατον ὑπὲρ τῶν πόνων <ὧν>[2] ἔχουσι προθύμως ἀλλάττεσθαι.

Εἰώθει δέ, φασιν, ἐπιλέγειν ταῖς ἑαυτοῦ πράξεσιν ὅτι τὸν τῶν Διοσκούρων ζῇ βίον παρ' ἡμέραν τεθνηκώς τε καὶ ἀναβιούς· εὐημερήσας γὰρ ἐν τῷ δήμῳ ἴσος θεοῖς νομίζεσθαι, κακῶς δὲ ἀπαλλάξας τῶν νεκρῶν μηδὲ ὀλίγον διαφέρειν.

39. Ἐφιάλτης, στρατηγοῦ ὀνειδίσαντος αὐτῷ τινος[3] <τὴν>[4] πενίαν, "τὸ δὲ ἕτερον" ἔφη "διὰ τί οὐ λέγεις, ὅτι δίκαιός εἰμι;"

40. Στρεπτῷ κειμένῳ ἐπὶ τῆς γῆς χρυσοῦ Περσικοῦ[5] ὁ Θεμιστοκλῆς παρεστὼς <τῷ>[6] παιδὶ εἶπεν· "οὐκ ἀναιρήσει, ὦ παῖ, τὸ εὕρεμα τόδε;" δείξας τὸν στρεπτόν· "οὐ γὰρ σὺ Θεμιστοκλῆς εἶ δήπου."

Ὅτι ἠτίμασαν αὐτόν ποτε Ἀθηναῖοι, εἶτα ἐπὶ τὴν ἀρχὴν αὖθις παρεκάλουν· ὁ δέ· "οὐκ ἐπαινῶ τοὺς

[1] *μητρί* Michael Apostolius, *Proverbia* 8.63 (qui etiam *βάλῃ* pro *ἐμβάλῃ* praebet): *μητρίδι* codd. [2] suppl. Boivin

you trust your country to try you?" he replied: "No, nor my mother. I am afraid she might fail to recognise me, miss the truth, and then vote to condemn instead of acquit." When he heard he had been condemned to death by his fellow citizens he said: "So let's prove we are alive," went off to Sparta, and started the Decelea campaign against the Athenians.

He said the Spartans who died fearlessly in war were not doing anything strange. They were escaping the misery imposed on them by their laws and gladly accepted death in place of their troubles.

They say he used to describe his career as the life of the Dioscuri, alive and dead on alternate days. If he was successful the public treated him as a god; if he failed, he was no better than a dead man.

39. When one of the generals criticised Ephialtes for being poor he replied: "Why don't you mention the other fact, that I'm honest?"

40. Themistocles stopped near a necklace of Persian gold that lay on the ground. He pointed to it and said to his slave: "Boy, won't you pick up this find? After all, you are not Themistocles."[a]

Note that the Athenians on one occasion disfranchised him and then invited him to take office again. He

[a] For the first paragraph of this ch. compare Plutarch, *Themistocles* 18 and *Moralia* 808 F, for the third *Themistocles* 11 and *Moralia* 185 B.

---

[3] τινος Scheffer: τινα codd. [4] suppl. Kühn

[5] χρυσοῦ Περσικοῦ Her.: -ῷ -ῷ codd.

[6] suppl. Kor.

τοιούτους ἄνδρας, οἵτινες τὴν αὐτὴν ἀμίδα καὶ οἰνοχόην ἔχουσι."

Πρὸς Εὐρυβιάδην τὸν Λακεδαιμόνιον ἔλεγέ τι ὑπεναντίον, καὶ <ὃς>[1] ἀνέτεινεν αὐτῷ τὴν βακτηρίαν. ὁ δέ· "πάταξον μέν, ἄκουσον δέ." ᾔδει δὲ ὅτι ἃ μέλλει λέγειν τῷ κοινῷ λυσιτελεῖ.

41. Ὀδυρομένου <τινὸς>[2] τῶν μετὰ Φωκίωνος μελλόντων ἀποθνήσκειν, εἶπεν ὁ Φωκίων· "εἶτα οὐκ ἀγαπᾷς, Θούδιππε, μετὰ Φωκίωνος ἀποθνήσκων;"

42. Ἐπαμεινώνδας ἔφευγε δίκην θανάτου ἐπανελθὼν ἐκ τῆς Λακωνικῆς, ὡς ἐπιβαλὼν[3] τῇ βοιωταρχίᾳ τέτταρας μῆνας παρὰ τὸν νόμον. τοὺς μὲν οὖν συνάρχοντας ἐκέλευσεν εἰς αὑτὸν τὴν αἰτίαν ἀναφέρειν ὡς ἐκβιασθέντας [ἄκοντας],[4] αὐτὸς δὲ παρελθὼν εἰς τὸ δικαστήριον οὐκ ἔφη βελτίονας ἔχειν τῶν ἔργων τοὺς λόγους· εἰ δὲ μή, ἠξίου ἀποκτείνειν αὐτόν, ἐπιγράψαι μέντοι τῇ στήλῃ ὅτι μὴ βουλομένους Θηβαίους ἠνάγκασεν Ἐπαμεινώνδας τὴν μὲν Λακωνικὴν πυρπολῆσαι πεντακοσίοις ἐνιαυτοῖς ἀδῄωτον οὖσαν, οἰκίσαι δὲ Μεσσήνην δι' ἐτῶν τριάκοντα καὶ διακοσίων, συντάξαι δὲ καὶ συναγαγεῖν εἰς ταὐτὸν[5] Ἀρκάδας, ἀποδοῦναι δὲ τοῖς Ἕλλησι τὴν αὐτονομίαν. καὶ ἀφῆκαν αὐτὸν αἰδεσθέντες οἱ δικασταί. ἐπανελθόντα δὲ αὐτὸν ἐκ τοῦ δικαστηρίου Μελιταῖον κυνίδιον ἔσαινε. διὸ πρὸς τοὺς παρόντας εἶπε· "τοῦτο μὲν ἀποδίδωσιν εὐεργεσίας μοι χάριν,

[1] suppl. Kor. [2] ὀδυρομένου <τινὸς> Kor.: -μένῳ codd.
[3] ἐπιβαλὼν e Plutarcho Kühn: ὑπολαβὼν codd.

observed: "I cannot approve of men who use the same vessel as chamber pot and wine jar."

He made some rather hostile remark to Eurybiades the Spartan, who raised his stick to strike. Themistocles said: "Hit me, but listen." He knew that what he was about to say was of value for the common enterprise.

41. When one of the men due to die with Phocion lamented Phocion said: "So you are not content, Thudippos, to die with Phocion."[a]

42. Epaminondas returned from Laconia to face a capital charge, that he had extended illegally the term of office of the Boeotian leaders by four months. He told his fellow commanders to lay the blame on him, as if they had been under duress. He appeared in court and said that he had no better case than his achievements. If this failed, he invited them to execute him, but to inscribe on the pillar by the grave that Epaminondas had obliged the Thebans, against their will, to burn Laconia, which had been untouched for five hundred years; to settle Messenia after an interval of two hundred and thirty years; to organise and unite the Arcadians in a single location; and to give the Greeks autonomy. The jury were shamed into acquitting him. When he returned from the court his little Maltese dog greeted him with a wag of the tail. This led him to say to those who were present: "This dog thanks

[a] For this story compare Plutarch, *Phocion* 36 and *Moralia* 189 A.

---

[4] del. Her.

[5] ταὐτὸν e Plut. Kor.: αὐτὸν codd.

Θηβαῖοι δὲ πολλάκις ὑπ᾽ ἐμοῦ εὖ παθόντες ἔκρινάν με θανάτου."

43. Ὅτι Τιμόθεος ὁ στρατηγὸς Ἀθηναίων ἐπιστεύετο εὐτυχὴς εἶναι· καὶ ἔλεγον[1] τὴν τυχὴν αἰτίαν εἶναι, Τιμόθεον δὲ οὐδενός, κωμῳδοῦντες ἐπὶ τῆς σκηνῆς.[2] καὶ οἱ ζωγράφοι δὲ καθεύδοντα ἐποίουν αὐτόν, εἶτα ὑπὲρ τῆς κεφαλῆς ἀπηώρητο ἑστῶσα ἡ Τύχη ἕλκουσα εἰς κύρτον τὰς πόλεις.

Πυνθανομένου Θεμιστοκλέους τινὸς κατὰ τί μάλιστα ἥσθη ἐν τῷ βίῳ, ὁ δὲ ἀπεκρίνατο· "τὸ θέατρον ἰδεῖν Ὀλυμπίασιν ἐπιστρεφόμενον εἰς ἐμὲ εἰς τὸ στάδιον παριόντα."

44. Τοὺς αὐτοὺς ἐπιτρόπους ἔσχε Θεμιστοκλῆς καὶ Ἀριστείδης ὁ Λυσιμάχου, καὶ διὰ ταῦτά τοι καὶ συνετράφησαν καὶ συνεπαιδεύθησαν <ὑπὸ>[3] κοινῷ διδασκάλῳ. ἐστασιαζέτην δὲ ὅμως καὶ ἔτι παῖδες ὄντες, καὶ παρέμενεν[4] αὐτοῖς ἡ φιλονεικία ἀπὸ τῆς πρώτης ἡλικίας καὶ εἰς ἔσχατον γῆρας.

45. Ὅτι Διονύσιος τὴν μητέρα διέφθειρε φαρμάκοις· Λεπτίνην δὲ τὸν ἀδελφὸν σῶσαι δυνάμενος ἐν τῇ ναυμαχίᾳ περιεῖδεν ἀπολλύμενον.

46. Πόλις ἐστὶ τῆς Ἀχαΐας αἱ Πάτραι. παῖς παρ᾽ αὐτοῖς[5] δράκοντα μικρὸν ἐπρίατο καὶ ἔτρεφε

[1] ἔλεγον Kühn: ἔλεγε codd. [2] κωμῳδοῦντες . . . σκηνῆς huc revocavit Kor.: post αὐτὸν praebent codd.
[3] suppl. Her. [4] παρέμενεν Her.: -μεινεν x (deficit V)
[5] αὐτοῖς Cuper: -αῖς codd.

me for my favours; the Thebans, after the benefits I conferred on them, tried me on a capital charge."[a]

43. Note that the Athenian general Timotheus was reckoned to be fortunate. People said fortune was responsible, and Timotheus had no part in it. They ridiculed him on the stage, and painters portrayed him asleep, with Fortune hovering above his head and pulling the cities into her net.

Someone asked Themistocles what he had most enjoyed in his life, and he replied: "To see the public at Olympia turning to look at me as I enter the stadium."[b]

44. Themistocles and Aristides the son of Lysimachus had the same guardians, and so they were brought up and educated by the same teacher. Nevertheless, even as children they quarrelled, and their rivalry lasted from an early age until their last years.

45. Note that Dionysius poisoned his mother with drugs, and when he could have saved his brother Leptines in the sea battle he left him to die.[c]

46. Patrae is a city in Achaea. A boy living there bought a small snake and reared it with great care. When

[a] The main part of this ch. is close enough to the version given by Plutarch, *Moralia* 194 AC, to make it likely that Aelian used Plutarch as his source.

[b] Judging by the version of the story found in Plutarch, *Themistocles* 17, Themistocles was given a hero's welcome at the first Olympic games held after the battle of Salamis.

[c] Plutarch, *Moralia* 338 BC, reports that Dionysius I killed his mother by strangling her, and adds that Dionysius in one of his tragedies had written "Tyranny is the mother of injustice." Dionysius' brother Leptines was a successful admiral, and died in 375 B.C.

μετὰ πολλῆς τῆς κομιδῆς. αὐξηθέντος δὲ αὐτοῦ ἐλάλει πρὸς αὐτὸν ὡς πρὸς ἀκούοντα καὶ ἤθυρε μετ' αὐτοῦ καὶ συνεκάθευδεν αὐτῷ. εἰς μέγιστον δὲ μέγεθος ἐλθὼν ὁ δράκων ὑπὸ τῶν πολιτῶν εἰς ἐρημίαν ἀπηλάθη.[1] ὕστερον δὲ ὁ παῖς νεανίας γενόμενος ἀπό τινος θέας ἐπανιών, λῃσταῖς περιπεσὼν μετὰ τῶν συνηλίκων, βοῆς γενομένης ἰδοὺ ὁ δράκων· καὶ τοὺς μὲν διεσκόρπισεν, οὓς δὲ ἀπέκτεινεν, αὐτὸν δὲ περιεσώσατο.

[1] ἀπηλάθη Her.: ἀπελύθη codd.

it grew he spoke to it as if it could hear, played with it and slept with it. When it became very big the city had it sent to an uninhabited spot. Later, when the child, now a young man, came back from an entertainment, he and his companions were set upon by brigands. There was a commotion, and the snake appeared. It dispersed some of the attackers and killed others, saving the young man.[a]

[a] A rather similar story about a pet snake is told in *N.A.* 6.63, but there the owner is an Arcadian.

ΙΔ

1. Ἀριστοτέλης ὁ Νικομάχου, σοφὸς ἀνὴρ καὶ ὢν καὶ εἶναι δοκῶν, ἐπεί τις αὐτοῦ ἀφείλετο τὰς ψηφισθείσας αὐτῷ ἐν Δελφοῖς τιμάς, ἐπιστέλλων πρὸς Ἀντίπατρον περὶ τούτων φησίν· "ὑπὲρ τῶν ἐν Δελφοῖς ψηφισθέντων μοι καὶ ὧν ἀφῄρημαι νῦν οὕτως ἔχω ὡς μήτε μοι σφόδρα μέλειν ὑπὲρ αὐτῶν μήτε μοι μηδὲν μέλειν." οὐκ ἂν δὲ εἴη[1] φιλοδοξία ταῦτα, οὐδ' ἂν καταγνοίην ἔγωγε τοιοῦτόν τι Ἀριστοτέλους, ἀλλ' εὖ φρονῶν ᾤετο μὴ ὅμοιον εἶναι ἀρχήν τινα[2] μὴ λαβεῖν καὶ[3] λαβόντα ἀφαιρεθῆναι. τὸ μὲν γὰρ οὐδὲν μέγα, τὸ μὴ τυχεῖν· τὸ δὲ ἀλγεινόν, τὸ τυχόντα εἶτα ἀποστερηθῆναι.

2. Ὅτι τοὺς παραβάντας ὅρκους τῶν βαρβάρων ἐπῄνεσεν Ἀγησίλαος, ὅτι τοὺς θεοὺς ἑαυτοῖς ἐχθροὺς ποιησάμενοι ταῖς ἐπιορκίαις, αὐτῷ φίλους καὶ συμμάχους κατεπράξαντο.

[1] εἴη Kor.: ἦν codd. [2] τινα] τι Düring
[3] καὶ Faber: ἢ codd.

---

[a] These honours are recorded in a surviving inscription from Delphi dating from 334–332 B.C. (*SIG*[3] 275). Aristotle and Callisthenes had published a work on the Pythian games, and the

BOOK FOURTEEN

1. Aristotle, son of Nicomachus, a wise man in reality as well as by repute, was deprived of the privileges he had been granted at Delphi,[a] and wrote to Antipater on the subject as follows [fr. 666 R.]: "About the privileges voted to me at Delphi and now taken away from me, my feeling is that I neither care about them very much nor disregard them entirely." This is not the remark of a man anxious to be well known, and I would not accuse Aristotle of such sentiments; on the contrary, he sensibly thought there was a difference between not receiving in the first place and being stripped of what one had acquired. Not to receive was no great blow; but to acquire and then be deprived was painful.

2. Note that Agesilaus had kind words for the barbarians who broke their oaths, because they brought upon themselves the hostility of the gods by perjury, and so made the gods friends and allies of his cause.[b]

local authorities had gratefully ordered that the list of victors be inscribed on a stele. The quotation from Aristotle's letter given in this ch. may well be genuine; see I. Düring, *Aristotle in the Ancient Biographical Tradition* (Gothenburg, 1957), p. 339.

[b] This story appears to concern Agesilaus' dealings with the Persian Tissaphernes, narrated in Xenophon, *Agesilaus* 1.12.

3a. Ὅτι Τιμόθεος πρὸς Ἀριστοφῶντα ἄσωτον ὄντα πικρότατα καθικόμενος αὐτοῦ εἶπεν· "ᾧ ἱκανὸν οὐδέν, ἀλλὰ τούτῳ γε αἰσχρὸν οὐδέν."

3b. Τιμόθεος ὁ Κόνωνος πρὸς Ἀριστοφῶντα τὸν Ἀζηνιέα πάντων ἄριστα ἔχοντα λόγον εἶπεν. ἐπεὶ γὰρ ἄσωτος ἦν ὁ Ἀριστοφῶν, πικρότατα αὐτοῦ καθίκετο ὁ Τιμόθεος εἰπών· "ᾧ ἱκανὸν οὐδέν, τούτῳ γε αἰσχρὸν οὐδέν."

4. Ὅτι Ἀριστείδης ὁ Λοκρὸς ὑπὸ Ταρτησσίας γαλῆς δηχθεὶς καὶ ἀποθνήσκων εἶπεν ὅτι πολὺ ἂν ἥδιον ἦν αὐτῷ δηχθέντι ὑπὸ λέοντος ἢ παρδάλεως ἀποθανεῖν, εἴπερ οὖν ἔδει τινὸς τῷ θανάτῳ προφάσεως, ἢ ὑπὸ θηρίου τοιούτου, τὴν ἀδοξίαν, ἐμοὶ δοκεῖν, ἐκεῖνος τοῦ δήγματος πολλῷ βαρύτερον φέρων ἢ τὸν θάνατον αὐτόν.

5. Οὐ μόνοις τοῖς ἀστοῖς ἐχρῶντο Ἀθηναῖοι πρὸς τὰς ἀρχὰς καὶ τὰς στρατηγίας <τοῖς>[1] ἐπιτηδείοις, ἀλλὰ γὰρ καὶ ξένους προῃροῦντο καὶ τὰ κοινὰ αὐτοῖς ἐνεχείριζον, εἴπερ οὖν αὐτοὺς ἀγαθοὺς ὄντας κατέγνωσαν καὶ ἐπιτηδείους εἰς τὰ τοιαῦτα. Ἀπολλόδωρον <γοῦν>[2] τὸν Κυζικηνὸν πολλάκις στρατηγὸν εἵλοντο ξένον ὄντα, καὶ Ἡρακλείδην τὸν Κλαζομένιον· ἐνδειξάμενοι γὰρ ὅτι ἄξιοι λόγου εἰσίν, εἶτα οὐκ ἔδοξαν ἀνάξιοι τοῦ Ἀθηναίων ἄρχειν εἶναι. καὶ ὑπὲρ μὲν τούτων ἐπαινεῖν χρὴ τὴν πόλιν μὴ καταχαριζομένην τἀληθὲς τοῖς πολίταις, ἀλλὰ νέμουσαν καὶ τοῖς γένει μὲν μὴ προσήκουσι, δι' ἀρετὴν δὲ ἀξίοις τιμᾶσθαι.

3a. Note that Timotheus made a very bitter attack on the rake Aristophon, saying: "A man who is not satisfied with anything is not shamed by anything."[a]

3b. Timotheus son of Conon made the best possible remark to Aristophon of Azenia. Since Aristophon was a rake, Timotheus attacked him very bitterly by saying: "A man who is not satisfied with anything is not shamed by anything."

4. Note that Aristides of Locri was bitten by a Tartessian weasel, and his dying words were that he would much rather have died from the bite of a lion or leopard, if there had to be some reason for dying, than of such a lowly beast. He felt the indignity of the bite, it seems to me, much more than death itself.[b]

5. It was not only citizens that the Athenians found suitable to act as magistrates and generals; they could prefer foreigners and entrust affairs of state to them, if their worth and suitability for office had been recognised. They frequently appointed as general the foreigner Apollodorus of Cyzicus, and Heraclides of Clazomenae. As they had demonstrated their qualities these men were thought worthy to have command over Athenians. On this score one should congratulate the city which, rather than misrepresent the truth to its citizens, assigned honours to outsiders whose merits deserved them.[c]

[a] Another example of a ch. fully preserved by Stobaeus, whereas the MSS. of Aelian offer a perfectly intelligible but abbreviated version. [b] This mysterious figure may be the man named as a friend of Plato in Plutarch, *Timoleon* 6.

[c] This ch. is inspired by Plato, *Ion* 541 cd.

[1] suppl. Russell post Kor. [2] suppl. Russell

6. Πάνυ σφόδρα ἐρρωμένως ἐῴκει λέγειν ὁ Ἀρίστιππος παρεγγυῶν τοῖς ἀνθρώποις μήτε τοῖς παρελθοῦσιν ἐπικάμνειν μήτε τῶν ἐπιόντων προκάμνειν· εὐθυμίας γὰρ δεῖγμα τὸ τοιοῦτο καὶ ἵλεω διανοίας ἀπόδειξις. προσέταττε δὲ ἐφ' ἡμέρᾳ τὴν γνώμην ἔχειν καὶ αὖ πάλιν τῆς ἡμέρας ἐπ' ἐκείνῳ τῷ μέρει, καθ' ὃ ἕκαστος ἢ πράττει τι ἢ ἐννοεῖ. μόνον γὰρ ἔφασκεν ἡμέτερον εἶναι τὸ παρόν, μήτε δὲ τὸ φθάνον[1] μήτε τὸ προσδοκώμενον· τὸ μὲν γὰρ ἀπολωλέναι, τὸ δὲ ἄδηλον εἶναι εἴπερ ἔσται.

7. Λακεδαιμόνιος οὗτος ὁ νόμος· ὁ δὲ νόμος ἐκεῖνα λέγει· μηδένα Λακεδαιμονίων ἀνανδρότερον ὁρᾶσθαι τὴν χροιὰν ἢ τὸν ὄγκον τοῦ σώματος ἔχειν ὑπὲρ τὰ γυμνάσια· ἐδόκει γὰρ τὸ μὲν ἀργίαν ὁμολογεῖν, τὸ δὲ οὐχ ὁμολογεῖν ἄνδρα. προσεγέγραπτο δὲ τῷ νόμῳ [καὶ][2] διὰ δέκα ἡμερῶν πάντως τοῖς ἐφόροις τοὺς ἐφήβους παρίστασθαι γυμνοὺς δημοσίᾳ. καὶ εἰ μὲν ἦσαν εὐπαγεῖς καὶ ἐρρωμένοι καὶ ἐκ τῶν γυμνασίων οἱονεὶ διαγλυφέντες καὶ διατορευθέντες, ἐπῃνοῦντο· εἰ δέ τι χαῦνον ἦν αὐτοῖς τῶν μελῶν ἢ ὑγρότερον, ὑποιδούσης καὶ ὑπαναφυομένης διὰ τὴν ῥᾳθυμίαν πιμελῆς, ἀλλ' ἐνταῦθα μὲν[3] ἐπαίοντο καὶ ἐδικαιοῦντο. ἐτίθεντο δὲ καὶ φροντίδα οἱ ἔφοροι καθ' ἑκάστην πολυπραγμονεῖν τὰ περὶ τὴν στολήν, ἵνα[4] ἕκαστα αὐτῆς μὴ ἀπολείπηται τοῦ κόσμου τοῦ δέοντος. ἔδει δὲ ὀψοποιοὺς ἐν Λακεδαίμονι εἶναι κρέως μόνου· ὁ δὲ παρὰ τοῦτο ἐπιστάμενος ἐξηλαύνετο τῆς Σπάρτης, ὡς τὰ τῶν νοσούντων καθάρσια.

6. Aristippus [fr. 208 M.] was thought to have made a very sound observation when he advised mankind not to fret about the past or worry about the future.[a] Such advice was a sign of confidence and the proof of a happy disposition. His instruction was to concentrate one's mind on the day, and indeed on that part of the day in which one is acting or thinking. Only the present, he said, belongs to us, not the past nor what is anticipated. The former has ceased to exist, and it is uncertain if the latter will exist.

7. This law is a Spartan one. The wording is as follows: no Spartan is to be seen with an effeminate complexion or a heavier body than exercise will produce—the one was a confession of idleness, the other of effeminacy. It was also provided in the law that every ten days the ephebes should without fail appear naked before the ephors. If they were well-built and strong, emerging from the gymnasium as if they had been sculpted or chiselled, they were complimented. But if there was anything flabby or soft in their limbs, any swelling of fat arising from idleness, they were beaten and punished on the spot. The ephors also made a point of reviewing their dress every day, to ensure that in each detail the proper style was maintained. Spartan cooks were expected to know about meat only; anyone with other skills was banished from Sparta, as if this were the purging of a sick element.

[a] For Aristippus see 7.3 above.

---

[1] *φθάνον*] *φθάσαν* Kor.
[2] del. Her. [3] *μὲν*] *γε* Her.
[4] *ἵνα* scripsi: *εἰ* codd.

Οἱ αὐτοὶ Ναυκλείδην τὸν Πολυβιάδου ὑπερσαρκοῦντα τῷ σώματι καὶ ὑπέρπαχυν διὰ τρυφὴν γενόμενον εἰς τὴν ἐκκλησίαν[1] τῶν θεωμένων κατήγαγον καὶ ἠπείλησαν αὐτῷ φυγῆς προστίμησιν,[2] ἐὰν μὴ τὸν βίον ὃν ἐβίου τότε ὑπαίτιον ὄντα καὶ Ἰωνικὸν μᾶλλον ἢ Λακωνικὸν τοῦ λοιποῦ μεθαρμόσηται· φέρειν γὰρ αὐτοῦ τὸ εἶδος καὶ τὴν τοῦ σώματος διάθεσιν αἰσχύνην καὶ τῇ Λακεδαίμονι καὶ τοῖς νόμοις.

8. Δύο εἰκόνας εἰργάσατο Πολύκλειτος κατὰ τὸ αὐτό, τὴν μὲν τοῖς ὄχλοις χαριζόμενος, τὴν δὲ κατὰ τὸν νόμον τῆς τέχνης. ἐχαρίζετο δὲ τοῖς πολλοῖς τὸν τρόπον τοῦτον· καθ' ἕκαστον τῶν εἰσιόντων μετετίθει τι καὶ μετεμόρφου, πειθόμενος τῇ ἑκάστου ὑφηγήσει. προὔθηκεν οὖν ἀμφοτέρας· καὶ ἡ μὲν ὑπὸ πάντων ἐπῃνεῖτο, ἡ δὲ ἑτέρα ἐγελᾶτο. ὑπολαβὼν οὖν ἔφη ὁ Πολύκλειτος· "ἀλλὰ ταύτην μὲν ἣν ψέγετε ὑμεῖς ἐποιήσατε, ταύτην δὲ ἣν θαυμάζετε ἐγώ."

Ἱππόμαχος ὁ αὐλητὴς ἐπεὶ αὐτῷ μαθητὴς αὐλῶν ἥμαρτε μὲν[3] κατὰ τὸ αὔλημα, ἐπῃνέθη δὲ ὑπὸ τῶν παρόντων, καθίκετο αὐτοῦ τῇ ῥάβδῳ καὶ ἔφη· "κακῶς ηὔλησας· οὐ γὰρ ἂν οὗτοί σε ἐπῄνουν."

9. Ξενοκράτης ὁ Χαλκηδόνιος ὑπὸ τοῦ Πλάτωνος εἰς τὸ ἄχαρι σκωπτόμενος οὐδέποτε ἠγανάκτησε, φασίν,[4] ἀλλὰ καὶ πρὸς τὸν παροξύνοντα αὐτὸν ὑπὲρ τούτου, ἵνα τι ἀποκρίνηται τῷ Πλάτωνι, ὁ δὲ καὶ

[1] εἰς τὴν ἐκκλησίαν ex Athenaeo Scheffer: ἐκ τῆς ἐκκλησίας codd.

[2] προστίμησιν Gesner: προ- codd.

The same authorities brought Nauclides son of Polybiades before the assembled inspectors. He was overweight and had become fat through luxurious living. They threatened him with the additional punishment of exile if he did not for the future change his habits, which were the subject of criticism and Ionian rather than Spartan. They claimed his appearance and physical condition brought disgrace on Sparta and its laws.[a]

8. Polyclitus made two sculptures of the same subject, one of which satisfied popular taste, and the other the rules of his art. He satisfied popular taste in this way: he made alterations and adjustments to suit each visitor, following all their suggestions. He then exhibited both pieces. One was universally praised, the other ridiculed. Polyclitus responded by saying: "But you have made the one you criticise, and I the one you admire."

When a pupil of the aulos player Hippomachus made a mistake in playing but was complimented by his auditors, Hippomachus struck him with his cane and said: "You played badly; otherwise these people would not have complimented you."[b]

9. Xenocrates of Chalcedon [fr. 103 H.] was often criticised by Plato because of his gauche manner but never showed any anger—so they say—and when someone urged him to respond in some way to Plato, he very

[a] This ch. is very close to Athenaeus 550 CD, which may be Aelian's source.

[b] At 2.6 above Hippomachus was a gymnastics trainer.

---

[3] μὲν <μηδὲν> Per.

[4] φασίν Per.: φησίν codd.

πάνυ ἐμφρόνως κατασιγάζων τὸν ἄνδρα ἔφατο· "ἀλλὰ τοῦτο ἐμοὶ συμφέρει."

10. Προείλοντο τοῦ Φωκίωνος Ἀθηναῖοι τὸν Δημάδην στρατηγεῖν. ὁ δὲ προτιμηθεὶς καὶ μέγα φρονῶν, προσελθὼν τῷ Φωκίωνι "χρῆσόν μοι" ἔφη "τὴν ῥυπαρὰν χλαμύδα, ἣν εἰώθεις φορεῖν παρὰ τὴν στρατηγίαν." καὶ ὃς "οὐδέποτε" εἶπεν "οὐδενὸς ῥυπαροῦ σὺ ἀπορήσεις, ἔστ' ἂν ᾖς[1] τοιοῦτος."

11. Φίλισκος πρὸς Ἀλέξανδρον ἔφη ποτέ· "δόξης φρόντιζε, ἀλλὰ μὴ ἔσο λοιμὸς [καὶ μὴ μεγάλη νόσος],[2] ἀλλὰ [εἰρήνη καὶ][2] ὑγεία," λέγων τὸ μὲν βιαίως ἄρχειν καὶ πικρῶς καὶ αἱρεῖν πόλεις καὶ ἀπολλύειν δήμους λοιμοῦ εἶναι, τὸ δὲ ὑγιῶς,[3] προνοεῖσθαι τῆς[4] σωτηρίας τῶν ἀρχομένων· εἰρήνης ταῦτα ἀγαθά.

12. Ὅτι ὁ Περσῶν βασιλεὺς ὁδοιπορῶν, ἵνα μὴ ἀλύῃ, φιλύριον εἶχε καὶ μαχαίριον, ἵνα ξέῃ τοῦτο. καὶ τοῦτο εἰργάζοντο αἱ χεῖρες αἱ βασιλικαί· πάντως γὰρ οὐκ εἶχεν οὐ βιβλίον, οὐ διάνοιαν, ἵν' ἢ σπουδαῖόν τι καὶ σεμνὸν ἀναγινώσκῃ ἢ γενναῖόν τι καὶ λόγου ἄξιον βουλεύηται.

13. Πολλοῖς καὶ πολλάκις χρῆται τοῖς ἀντιθέτοις ὁ Ἀγάθων. ἐπεὶ δέ τις οἷον ἐπανορθούμενος αὐτὸν ἐβούλετο περιαιρεῖν αὐτὰ τῶν ἐκείνου δραμάτων, εἶπεν· "ἀλλὰ σύ γε, γενναῖε, λέληθας σεαυτὸν τὸν Ἀγάθωνα ἐκ τοῦ Ἀγάθωνος ἀφανίζων." οὕτως

[1] ᾖς Kor.: εἶ codd.

sensibly silenced the man by saying: "But this is to my advantage."[a]

10. The Athenians preferred Demades to Phocion for the office of general. Demades, proud to be given preference in this way, approached Phocion and said [fr. 44 de F.]: "Lend me the grubby coat you used to wear on campaign," to which the other replied: "You will never be short of grubby articles, so long as you are like that yourself."

11. Philiscus once said to Alexander: "Take care of your reputation; don't become a plague [or a great disaster], bring [peace and] health." By plague he meant violent and savage rule, the capture of cities, the destruction of populations; by health, care for safety of subjects; that is the benefit of peace.

12. Note that when travelling the Persian king took with him, in order not to be bored, a small block of lime wood and a little knife to scrape it. This was the activity of the royal hands. He certainly did not take with him a book or serious thoughts, in order to be able to read something important and improving or meditate on a noble and worthwhile subject.

13. Agathon used a lot of antitheses in many of his works. When someone with the idea of correcting him wanted to remove them from his plays he said: "My good friend, you have failed to notice that you are destroying the Agathon in Agathon." Such was his pride in these

[a] For Xenocrates see 2.41 above.

---

[2] del. Her. [3] ὑγιῶς Dilts: ὑγείας codd.
[4] τῆς Per.: καὶ codd.

ἐκόμα ἐπὶ τούτοις ἐκεῖνος, καὶ ᾤετο τὴν ἑαυτοῦ τραγῳδίαν ταῦτα εἶναι.

14. Στρατόνικον τὸν κιθαρῳδὸν ὑπεδέξατό τις ἀμφιλαφῶς· ὁ δὲ ὑπερήσθη τῇ κλήσει· καὶ γὰρ ἔτυχεν οὐκ ἔχων καταγωγήν, ἅτε εἰς ξένην ἀφικόμενος· ὑπερησπάζετο γοῦν τὸν ἄνδρα διὰ τὸ πρόχειρον τῆς κοινωνίας τῆς κατὰ τὴν στέγην. ἐπεὶ δὲ καὶ ἄλλον εἶδεν εἰσιόντα καὶ ἄλλον, καὶ τρόπον τινα ἄκλειστον αὐτοῦ τὴν οἰκίαν πᾶσι τοῖς καταλύειν προῃρημένοις, ἐνταῦθα ὁ Στρατόνικος ἔφη πρὸς τὸν ἀκόλουθον· "ἀπίωμεν ἐντεῦθεν, ὦ παῖ· ἐοίκαμεν γὰρ ἀντὶ περιστερᾶς ἔχειν φάτταν, ὑπὲρ οἰκίας εὑρόντες πανδοκεῖον."

15. Λόγος τις διεφοίτα λέγων τοὺς Σωκράτους λόγους ἐοικέναι τοῖς Παύσωνος γράμμασι. καὶ γάρ τοι καὶ Παύσωνα τὸν ζωγράφον ἐκλαβόντα[1] παρά τινος γράψαι ἵππον καλινδούμενον, τὸν δὲ γράψαι τρέχοντα. ἀγανακτοῦντος οὖν τοῦ τὸ πινάκιον ἐκδόντος ὡς παρὰ τὰς ὁμολογίας γράψαντος, ἀποκρίνασθαι τὸν ζωγράφον ὅτι "στρέψον τὸ πινάκιον καὶ [ὁ][2] καλινδούμενος ἔσται σοι ὁ τρέχων." καὶ[3] τὸν Σωκράτην μὴ σαφῶς διαλέγεσθαι. εἰ γοῦν τις αὐτοῦ τοὺς λόγους[4] στρέψαι, ὀρθότατα ἔχειν. οὐκ ἐβούλετο δὲ ἄρα ἀπεχθάνεσθαι τούτοις, πρὸς οὓς διελέγετο,

[1] ἐκλαβόντα Struve post anonymum (1733): ἀκούσαντα codd. [2] del. Per.

[3] malim <ὡσαύτως δὲ> καὶ vel <οὕτω> καὶ (Russell)

[4] αὐτοῦ τοὺς λόγους Gesner: αὐτοὺς codd.

passages; and he felt that they made his tragedies.[a]

14. Stratonicus the cithara player was given generous hospitality. He was very pleased by the invitation as he was travelling abroad and had no lodging to go to. So he was very grateful to his host for the prompt offer of hospitality under his roof. But when he saw a second and then a third guest arrive, and that the house was more or less open to anyone who chose to stay in it, Stratonicus said to his servant: "Boy, let's leave; we seem to have found a ring dove instead of a pigeon,[b] a boarding house instead of a home."

15. A tradition was current according to which Socrates' statements were like Pauson's paintings. The story is that Pauson the painter received a commission to paint a horse rolling on the ground, and he portrayed it running. The man who had commissioned the picture was annoyed at the breach of contract, but the artist replied: "Turn the panel upside-down and the running horse will be rolling on the ground." Similarly Socrates was not clear in his conversations, but if one turned them on their head they would be perfect. He apparently did not wish to get on bad terms with the people he conversed with, and for

[a] In the few surviving fragments of Agathon antithesis is prominent; it is also parodied by Aristophanes, *Thesmophoriazusae* 146–147. This ch. is registered as TrGF 39 T 24.

[b] This expression goes back to Plato, *Theaetetus* 199 b; it recurs in Aelian's *Epistulae rusticae* 19 and (in a slightly different form) in Libanius, *Epistula* 1594; see D. A. Tsirimbas, *Sprichwörter und sprichwörtliche Redensarten bei den Epistolographen der zweiten Sophistik: Alciphron–Cl. Aelianus* (Munich, 1936), p. 73. See also Artemidorus Daldianus 2.20 for the significance of these birds in dreams.

καὶ διὰ τοῦτο αἰνιγματώδεις αὐτοὺς παρείχετο καὶ πλαγίους.

16. Ἱππόνικος ὁ Καλλίου ἐβούλετο ἀνδριάντα ἀναστῆσαι τῇ πατρίδι ἀνάθημα. ἐπεὶ δέ τις συνεβούλευσε παρὰ Πολυκλείτῳ κατασκευάσαι τὸ ἄγαλμα, οὐκ ἔφη προσέξειν[1] τοιούτῳ ἀναθήματι, οὗ τὴν δόξαν οὐχ ὁ ἀναθεὶς ἀλλ᾽ ὁ ποιήσας ἕξει. δῆλον γὰρ ὡς οἱ ὁρῶντες τὴν τέχνην ἔμελλον τὸν Πολύκλειτον ἀλλ᾽ οὐκ ἐκεῖνον ἄγασθαι.

17. Σωκράτης ἔλεγεν Ἀρχέλαον εἰς τὴν οἰκίαν τετρακοσίας μνᾶς ἀναλῶσαι, Ζεῦξιν μισθωσάμενον τὸν Ἡρακλεώτην, ἵνα αὐτὴν καταγράφοι, εἰς ἑαυτὸν δὲ οὐδέν. διὸ πόρρωθεν μὲν ἀφικνεῖσθαι σὺν πολλῇ <τῇ>[2] σπουδῇ τοὺς βουλομένους θεάσασθαι τὴν οἰκίαν· δι᾽ αὐτὸν δὲ Ἀρχέλαον μηδένα εἰς Μακεδόνας στέλλεσθαι, ἐὰν μή τινα ἀναπείσῃ χρήμασι καὶ δελεάσῃ, ὑφ᾽ ὧν οὐκ ἂν αἱρεθῆναι τὸν σπουδαῖον.

18. Ἀνὴρ Χῖος ὀργιζόμενος τῷ οἰκέτῃ "ἐγώ σε" ἔφη "οὐκ εἰς μύλην ἐμβαλῶ, ἀλλ᾽ εἰς Ὀλυμπίαν ἄξω." πολλῷ γὰρ ᾤετο πικροτέραν, ὡς τὸ εἰκός, εἶναι τιμωρίαν ἐκεῖνος ἐν Ὀλυμπίᾳ θεώμενον ὑπὸ τῆς ἀκτῖνος ὀπτᾶσθαι ἢ ἀλεῖν μύλῃ παραδοθέντα.

19. Ἀρχύτας τά τε ἄλλα ἦν σώφρων καὶ οὖν καὶ τὰ ἄκοσμα ἐφυλάττετο τῶν ὀνομάτων. ἐπεὶ δέ ποτε ἐβιάζετό τι εἰπεῖν τῶν ἀπρεπῶν, οὐκ ἐξενικήθη, ἀλλ᾽ ἐσιώπησε μὲν αὐτό, ἐπέγραψε δὲ κατὰ τοῦ τοίχου, δείξας μὲν ὃ εἰπεῖν ἐβιάζετο, οὐ μὴν βιασθεὶς εἰπεῖν.

this reason made his remarks enigmatic and oblique.

16. Hipponicus son of Callias wanted to dedicate a statue as an offering to his country. When someone suggested having the statue made by Polyclitus, he said he would not have a high regard for a statue the reputation of which depended on the artist, not the donor. Clearly those who saw it would have admired Polyclitus and not him.

17. Socrates said Archelaus had spent 400 minae on his house, hiring Zeuxis of Heraclea to paint it, and nothing on himself. So people came from far afield, very keen to see the house. But no one travelled to Macedonia purely on Archelaus' account, unless he persuaded someone with financial inducements and enticed him in ways that a serious person would not yield to.[a]

18. A man from Chios was annoyed with his servant and said: "I will not put you in the treadmill, but I'll take you to Olympia." He thought it a much more severe penalty, in all probability, to watch at Olympia under the baking heat of the sun than to be sent to the mill to grind corn.

19. Archytas was in general well-behaved and certainly avoided bad language. Once, when he was compelled to use an unbecoming expression, his resolution was not defeated: he did not utter the word but wrote it on the wall, thus demonstrating what he had to say but without being forced to say it.

[a] The most celebrated guests of Archelaus were Euripides and Agathon.

---

[1] textus vix sanus; fortasse προσ<ηνῶς> ἕξειν

[2] suppl. Her.

20. Συβαρίτης ἀνὴρ παιδαγωγός (καὶ γὰρ οὖν μετὰ τῶν ἄλλων Συβαριτῶν καὶ αὐτοὶ ἐτρύφων), τοῦ παιδὸς ὃν ἦγε διὰ τῆς ὁδοῦ ἰσχάδι περιτυχόντος καὶ ἀνελομένου, ἐπέπληξεν αὐτῷ ἰσχυρότατα· γελοιότατα δὲ αὐτὸς τὸ εὕρημα παρὰ τοῦ παιδὸς ἁρπάσας κατέτραγεν. ὅτε τοῦτο ἀνελεξάμην ἐν ἱστορίαις Συβαριτικαῖς, ἐγέλασα· ἔδωκα δὲ αὐτὸ εἰς μνήμην, μὴ βασκήνας διὰ φιλανθρωπίαν γελάσαι καὶ ἄλλον.

21. Ὅτι Οἴαγρός[1] τις ἐγένετο ποιητὴς μετ' Ὀρφέα καὶ Μουσαῖον, ὃς λέγεται τὸν Τρωϊκὸν πόλεμον πρῶτος ᾆσαι, μεγίστης οὗτος ὑποθέσεως λαβόμενος καὶ ἐπιτολμήσας ταύτῃ.

22. Ὅτι Τροιζήνιός[2] τις τύραννος βουλόμενος ἐξελεῖν τὰς συνωμοσίας καὶ τὰς κατ' αὐτοῦ ἐπιβουλὰς ἔταξε τοῖς ἐπιχωρίοις μηδένα μηδενὶ διαλέγεσθαι μήτε κοινῇ μήτε ἰδίᾳ. καὶ ἦν τὸ πρᾶγμα ἀμήχανον καὶ χαλεπόν. ἐσοφίσαντο οὖν τὸ τοῦ τυράννου πρόσταγμα, καὶ ἀλλήλοις ἔνευον καὶ ἐχειρονόμουν πρὸς ἀλλήλους, καὶ ἐνεώρων δριμὺ καὶ αὖ πάλιν γαληναῖον καὶ βλέμμα[3] φαιδρόν· καὶ ἐπὶ τοῖς σκυθρωποῖς καὶ ἀνηκέστοις ἕκαστος αὐτῶν συνωφρυωμένος ἦν δῆλος, τὸ τῆς ψυχῆς πάθος ἐκ τοῦ προσώπου τῷ πλησίον διαδεικνύς. ἐλύπει τὸν τύραννον καὶ ταῦτα, καὶ ἐπίστευε τέξεσθαί τι αὐτῷ πάντως κακὸν καὶ τὴν σιωπὴν διὰ τὸ τῶν σχημάτων ποικίλον. ἀλλ' οὖν ἐκεῖνος καὶ τοῦτο κατέπαυσε. τῶν τις οὖν ἀχθομένων τῇ ἀμηχανίᾳ καὶ δυσφορούντων καὶ τὴν μοναρχίαν καταλῦσαι διψώντων[4] ἀφίκετο εἰς

20. A slave acting as tutor at Sybaris—they too shared in the luxury of the other Sybarites—gave a very severe beating to the boy in his charge who had found a fig in the street and picked it up; and then, quite ridiculously, he snatched it from the child and ate it. When I read of this in a book about Sybaris, I laughed; but I put it on record as a kindness to my fellow men, because I do not wish to deprive others of a laugh.

21. Note that a certain Oeagrus became a poet after Orpheus and Musaeus.[a] He is said to have been the first to compose after the Trojan War, addressing a grandiose theme and bold enough to tackle it.

22. Note that a tyrant of Troezen, who wanted to eliminate plots and conspiracies against himself ordered people not to speak to each other in public or private. The situation was impossible and grave. But they got round the tyrant's order, by nodding and gesturing to each other, and by giving sharp or peaceful or cheerful looks. Every man obviously frowned at unwelcome news or hopeless situations; his face showed his emotions to anyone nearby. This too vexed the tyrant, and he felt sure that even silence accompanied by a wealth of gestures was bound to create trouble for him. So he put a stop to it. One of the men irritated by the impossible situation, in his annoyance and desire to end the tyranny, arrived in the

[a] Oeagrus was usually identified as the father of Orpheus.

---

[1] Οἴαγρός König: Σύαγρός codd. [2] Τροιζήνιος Per.: Τρύζος codd. [3] βλέμμα del. Cuper [4] ἀχθομένων . . . δυσφορούντων . . . διψώντων Kor.: -νος . . . -ρῶν . . . -ψῶν codd.

τὴν ἀγοράν, εἶτα ἔκλαε στὰς πολλοῖς ἅμα καὶ θαλεροῖς[1] τοῖς δακρύοις. περιέστησαν οὖν αὐτὸν καὶ περιῆλθον τὸ πλῆθος καὶ ὀδυρμῷ κἀκεῖνοι συνείχοντο. ἧκεν ἀγγελία παρὰ τὸν τύραννον ὡς οὐδεὶς αὐτῶν χρῆται νεύματι οὐκέτι, δάκρυα δὲ αὐτοῖς ἐπιχωριάζει. ὁ δὲ ἐπειγόμενος καὶ τοῦτο παῦσαι, μὴ μόνον τῆς γλώττης καταγινώσκων δουλείαν μηδὲ μόνον τῶν νευμάτων ἀλλ' ἤδη καὶ τοῖς ὀφθαλμοῖς τὴν ἐκ φύσεως ἀποκλείων ἐλευθερίαν, ᾗ ποδῶν εἶχεν ἀφίκετο σὺν τοῖς δορυφόροις, ἵνα ἀναστείλῃ τὰ δάκρυα. οἱ δὲ οὐκ ἔφθασαν ἰδόντες αὐτὸν καὶ τὰ ὅπλα τῶν δορυφόρων ἁρπάσαντες τὸν τύραννον ἀπέκτειναν.

23. Κλεινίας ἀνὴρ ἦν σπουδαῖος τὸν τρόπον, Πυθαγόρειος δὲ τὴν σοφίαν. οὗτος εἴ ποτε εἰς ὀργὴν προήχθη καὶ εἶχεν αἰσθητικῶς ἑαυτοῦ εἰς θυμὸν ἐξαγομένου, παραχρῆμα πρὶν ἢ ἀνάπλεως αὐτῷ ἡ ὀργὴ καὶ ἐπίδηλος γένηται ὅπως διάκειται, τὴν λύραν ἁρμοσάμενος ἐκιθάριζε. πρὸς δὲ τοὺς πυνθανομένους τὴν αἰτίαν ἀπεκρίνετο ἐμμελῶς ὅτι "πραΰνομαι." δοκεῖ δέ μοι καὶ ὁ ἐν Ἰλιάδι Ἀχιλλεύς, ὁ τῇ κιθάρᾳ προσᾴδων καὶ τὰ κλέα τῶν προτέρων διὰ τοῦ μέλους εἰς μνήμην ἑαυτῷ ἄγων, τὴν μῆνιν κατευνάζειν· μουσικὸς γὰρ ὢν τὴν κιθάραν πρώτην ἐκ τῶν λαφύρων ἔλαβε.

24. Χρημάτων κατεφρόνησαν καὶ μεγαλοφροσύνην ἐπεδείξαντο ὁρῶντες ἐν πενίᾳ τοὺς πολίτας ὄντας πλουτοῦντες αὐτοὶ ἐν μὲν Κορίνθῳ Θεοκλῆς

main square and stood there weeping profusely. A crowd arrived and stood around him, sharing in his grief. News reached the tyrant that no one was using gestures any longer, but tears were the convention. Anxious to stop this as well, abolishing not only freedom of speech, not only freedom of gesture, but also the natural freedom of the eyes, he arrived quickly with his bodyguard to put an end to the tears. But the crowd on seeing him at once seized the guards' weapons and killed the tyrant.

23. Clinias was a man of serious character, of the Pythagorean school. If he was ever provoked into anger and had a perception that his temper was coming out, at once he would tune his lyre and play, before his anger reached its full force and the state of his feelings became apparent. When people asked him the reason he replied appropriately: "I am calming myself." I think Achilles in the *Iliad* [9.186], who plays the cithara and with songs reminds himself of the great deeds of former ages, is soothing his wrath. As he was musical he chose the cithara as his first object to take from the booty.[a]

24. Theocles and Thrasonides of Corinth and Praxis of Mytilene, when they saw their fellow citizens in poverty, while they personally were rich, disregarded money and

[a] The source of this ch. may be Athenaeus 624 A (compare Chamaeleon, fr. 4 W.). The booty in question came from Eetion of Imbros, a friend of Priam; he had paid the ransom for Priam's son Lycaon, captured by Achilles.

---

[1] θαλεροῖς Gesner: θολ- codd.

καὶ Θρασωνίδης, ἐν δὲ Μιτυλήνῃ Πρᾶξις. καὶ οὖν καὶ ἄλλοις συνεβούλευον ἐπικουφίσαι τῆς πενίας τὴν ἀνάγκην τοῖς ἀπορουμένοις. ἐπεὶ δὲ οὐκ ἔπειθον, ἀλλ᾿ αὐτοί γε τὰ ἑαυτῶν ἀφῆκαν χρέα, καὶ ὤνηντο οὐκ εἰς ἀργύριον, ἀλλ᾿ εἰς αὐτὴν τὴν ψυχήν· οἱ γὰρ μὴ ἀφεθέντες ἐπιθέμενοι τοῖς δανείσασι, προβαλόμενοι τῆς ὀργῆς τὰ ὅπλα καὶ εὐλογωτάτην χρείαν τὴν ἄμαχον καὶ τὴν[1] ἐκ τῶν ἐπειγόντων ἀνάγκην, ἀπέκτειναν τοὺς δανειστάς.

25. Ἐστασίασάν ποτε πρὸς ἀλλήλους οἱ Χῖοι, ἀνδρειότατα νοσήσαντες νόσον ταύτην βαρυτάτην. ἀνὴρ οὖν ἐν αὐτοῖς πολιτικὸς τὴν φύσιν πρὸς τοὺς σπουδάζοντας τῶν ἑταίρων πάντας[2] ἐκβάλλειν τοὺς ἐναντίους "μηδαμῶς" ἔφη· "ἀλλ᾿ ἐπεὶ κεκρατήκαμεν, ὑπολειπώμεθά τινας, ἵνα μὴ τοῦ χρόνου προϊόντος, οὐκ ἔχοντες ἀντιπάλους, ἡμῖν αὐτοῖς ἀρξώμεθα πολεμεῖν." καὶ εἰπὼν ἔπεισε· καὶ γὰρ ἔδοξε καλῶς λέγειν, ἐπεὶ οὕτως ἔλεγεν.

26. Ἀρκεσίλαον τὸν ἐξ Ἀκαδημίας Ἀνταγόρας ὁ ποιητὴς ἐλοιδορεῖτο προσφθαρεὶς αὐτῷ, καὶ ταῦτα ἐν τῇ ἀγορᾷ· ὁ δὲ σφόδρα μεγαλοφρόνως, ἔνθα ἑώρα μάλιστα συνεστῶτας πολλούς, ἐνταῦθα ἐπορεύετο διαλεγόμενος, ἵνα ὁ λοιδορῶν ἐν πλείοσιν ἀσχημονῇ. οἱ γοῦν ἀκούοντες ἀπεστρέφοντο καὶ μανίαν ἐπεκάλουν τῷ Ἀνταγόρᾳ.

27. Ἐγὼ δὲ ἐπαινῶ μάλιστα ἐκείνους, ὅσοι τὰ ὑποφυόμενα τῶν κακῶν φθείροντες[3] ἀεί, ταῦτα ἐκ-

[1] καὶ τὴν del. Her. malim εὐλογώτατα τὴν χρείαν τὴν ἄμαχον <προφασισάμενοι> vel sim.

showed a noble spirit. In fact they advised others to lighten the burden of poverty on the poor. When the advice was rejected, they at least remitted debts owed to them, which brought them benefit, not financially but in saving their lives. Those who had not been let off their debts attacked the moneylenders, their anger supported by weapons, by imperative need which has all reason on its side, and by the compulsion of necessity. They killed the moneylenders.

25. There was once civil strife on Chios, a very bad case of this most destructive plague. A man of political skill said to some of his companions, who wanted to expel all members of the opposition: "No; now that we have won, let's leave ourselves some opponents, in case with the passing of time, we begin to fight each other." He convinced them; it was thought that by this remark he had made a good suggestion.[a]

26. The poet Antagoras had an unfortunate encounter with Arcesilaus of the Academy, whom he abused, and in the main square at that. Arcesilaus was quite unperturbed; he walked, conversing, in the direction where he saw the largest number of people collected, so that the author of the insults should misbehave before a larger public. Those who heard turned away and called Antagoras a madman.

27. I am full of praise for anyone who regularly eliminates evil in its early stages, nipping it in the bud before it

[a] This anecdote is also found in Plutarch, *Moralia* 91 F–92 A. There a certain Demus is the speaker.

---

[2] *πάντας*] *πάντως* Faber
[3] *φθείροντες*] *φθάνοντες* Faber

κόπτουσι πρὶν ἢ δυνάμεώς τινος ἐπιλαβέσθαι. Ἀγησίλαος γοῦν[1] συνεβούλευσεν ἀκρίτως ἀποκτείνειν[2] τοὺς συνιόντας νύκτωρ ὑπὸ τὴν τῶν Θηβαίων εἰσβολήν.

28. Ὠνείδισέ τις τῷ ῥήτορι Πυθέᾳ ὅτι κακός ἐστιν. ὁ δὲ οὐκ ἠρνήσατο· τὸ γὰρ συνειδὸς οὐκ ἐπέτρεπεν αὐτῷ. ἀπεκρίνατο δὲ ἐκεῖνο, ἐλάχιστον χρόνον τῶν πεπολιτευμένων Ἀθήνησι γενέσθαι κακός· μέγα φρονῶν δῆλον ὅτι μὴ διὰ τέλους ἦν τοιοῦτος, καὶ ἡγούμενος μὴ ἀδικεῖν, ἐπεὶ μὴ τοῖς πονηροτάτοις παρενεβάλλετο. εὔηθες δὲ τοῦτο τοῦ Πυθέου· οὐ γὰρ μόνον ὁ ἀδικήσας κακὸς ἀλλὰ καὶ ὁ ἐννοήσας ἀδικῆσαι, παρά γε ἐμοὶ κριτῇ.

29. Ὅτι Λύσανδρος ἐκόμισεν εἰς Λακεδαίμονα χρήματα καὶ ἐδίδαξε τοὺς Λακεδαιμονίους παρανομεῖν εἰς τὸ πρόσταγμα τοῦ θεοῦ τὸ κελεῦον ἄβατον εἶναι χρυσῷ καὶ ἀργύρῳ τὴν Σπάρτην. τῶν οὖν φρονούντων[3] τινὲς διεκώλυον, φρόνημα ἔτι κεκτημένοι Λακωνικὸν καὶ Λυκούργου καὶ τοῦ Πυθίου ἄξιον· οἱ δὲ προσέμενοι[4] διεβλήθησαν καὶ ἡ ἐξ ἀρχῆς αὐτῶν ἀρετὴ κατὰ μικρὸν ὑπέληξεν.

30. Ἄννων ὁ Καρχηδόνιος ὑπὸ τρυφῆς ἐν τοῖς ἀνθρώπων ὅροις οὐκ ἠξίου διαμένειν, ἀλλ᾽ ἐπενόει

[1] γοῦν Her.: οὖν codd. [2] ἀποκτείνειν Peruscus: -κτένειν codd. [3] <εὖ> φρονούντων Faber [4] προσέμενοι V: προέμενοι x

[a] This is an episode in the siege of Sparta by Epaminondas in

acquires strength. As an example, Agesilaus advised summary execution of all those who congregated at night before the Theban invasion.[a]

28. Someone criticised the orator Pytheas for being dishonest.[b] He did not deny it, since his conscience would not let him,[c] but he made the famous reply, that he had been dishonest for a shorter time than any of the other Athenian politicians. Evidently he was proud of not having been dishonest throughout his career, and reckoned he had not committed injustice because he could not be listed as one of the worst politicians. This was silly on the part of Pytheas; in my judgement at least, not only the man who commits injustice is evil; so too is the man who plans it.

29. Note that Lysander introduced currency to Sparta and taught the Spartans to disobey the instruction of the god which ordered that Sparta should be closed to silver and gold.[d] Some sensible people tried to prevent him, because they still retained the Spartan spirit in the tradition of Lycurgus and the Pythian god. Those who welcomed the change were criticised and their original virtues gradually ebbed away.

30. Hanno the Carthaginian in his arrogance was not prepared to accept the limitations of humanity; he

370/69 B.C., and is known also from Plutarch, *Agesilaus* 32.

[b] Pytheas (mentioned in 7.7 above) was a minor politician who supported Demosthenes and then changed sides.

[c] In Aelian's day the notion of conscience was no longer so rare as it had been in the classical age of Greece. For the history of the idea see H. Chadwick's article "Gewissen" in *Reallexikon für Antike und Christentum.*

[d] For Lysander see 3.20 above. Sparta did not in fact mint currency until 280 B.C.

φήμας ὑπὲρ ἑαυτοῦ κατασπείρεσθαι κρείττονας ἢ κατὰ τὴν φύσιν, ἥνπερ οὖν ἔλαχεν. ὄρνιθας γάρ τοι τῶν ᾠδικῶν παμπόλλους πριάμενος ἔτρεφεν ἐν σκότῳ αὐτούς, ἓν διδάσκων μάθημα λέγειν· "θεός ἐστιν Ἄννων." ἐπεὶ δὲ ἐκεῖνοι μίαν φωνὴν ταύτην ἀκούοντες ἐγκρατεῖς ταύτης ἐγένοντο, ἄλλον ἄλλοσε διαφῆκεν, οἰόμενος διαρρεῦσαι[1] τῶν ὀρνίθων τὸ ὑπὲρ ἑαυτοῦ μέλος. οἱ δὲ τὸ πτερὸν ἀπολύσαντες ἅπαξ καὶ ἐλευθερίας λαβόμενοι καὶ εἰς ἤθη τὰ σύντροφα αὐτοῖς ἐλθόντες, τὰ οἰκεῖα ᾖδον καὶ τὰ ὀρνίθων ἐμουσούργουν, μακρὰ χαίρειν εἰπόντες Ἄννωνι καὶ μαθήμασι τοῖς ἐν τῇ δουλείᾳ.

31. Πτολεμαῖος ὁ Τρύφων (τοῦτο γὰρ αὐτὸν ἐκάλουν ἐκ τοῦ βίου), γυναικὸς ὡραίας ἐντυχεῖν αὐτῷ βουλομένης, ὁ δὲ ἔφη· "ἀπηγόρευσέ μοι ἡ ἀδελφὴ παρὰ γυναικὸς καλῆς λόγον δέξασθαι." ἡ δὲ ἀτρέπτως πάνυ καὶ ἐμμελῶς "παρὰ καλοῦ δ' ἂν λάβοις;" εἶπε. καὶ ἐκεῖνος ἀκούσας ἐπῄνεσε.

32. Λακεδαιμόνιος ἀνὴρ Τιμανδρίδας ὄνομα ἀποδημήσας τὸν υἱὸν ἀπέλιπε μελεδωνὸν τῆς οἰκίας. εἶτα ἐπανελθὼν χρόνῳ ὕστερον καὶ εὑρὼν τὴν οὐσίαν ποιήσαντα ἧς ἀπέλιπε πλείω, ἔφη πολλοὺς

[1] διαρρεῦσαι] -εύσειν Her.

---

[a] This Hanno is probably the man mentioned by Pliny, *Natural History* 8.55, as the first lion tamer; see also *N.A.* 5.39. He is sometimes dated to the third century B.C.; but note that

planned to have reports of himself spread abroad which would represent him as superior to the human condition that was his.[a] He bought a large number of song birds and kept them in the dark, teaching them to say one thing: "Hanno is a god." When they had mastered this one sentence by listening to it, he sent them off in all directions, thinking to broadcast the birds' cry about himself. But once they stretched their wings and found their freedom they headed for their native haunts, sang their natural song and made music as birds do, without the slightest regard for Hanno or the lessons received in captivity.

31. Ptolemy the voluptuary,[b] who was so called because of his habits, when a beautiful woman wanted to meet him, said: "My sister forbade me to converse with a beautiful woman."[c] Quite undeterred, the woman replied wittily: "But would you converse with a handsome man?" On hearing that he complimented her.

32. A man from Sparta called Timandridas went abroad and left his son in charge at home. When he returned later and found the son had made the family property more substantial than it had been at his departure, he declared that injustice was being done to many:

Isocrates, *Antidosis* 213, seems to presuppose that lions were already being tamed.

[b] Ptolemy VIII Euergetes II became king in 145 B.C. He is notorious for the expulsion of intellectuals and artists from Alexandria in 144 B.C.; they included the famous critic Aristarchus, who according to Athenaeus 71 B had been one of his tutors. The name Tryphon could have been taken in a good or a bad sense, "splendid" or "extravagant"; but he also had a nickname "Physcon" = "pot-belly."

[c] His sister, Cleopatra II, was also his wife.

ἀδικεῖσθαι ὑπ' αὐτοῦ θεούς τε καὶ οἰκείους καὶ ξένους· τὰ γὰρ περιττὰ τῶν ὄντων[1] εἰς ἐκείνους ἀναλίσκεσθαι ὑπὸ τῶν ἐλευθέρων. τὸ δὲ ζῶντα μὲν φαίνεσθαι πένητα, τελευτήσαντα δὲ καταφωραθῆναι πλούσιον, ἀλλὰ τοῦτο τῶν ἐν ἀνθρώποις ἐστὶν αἴσχιστον.

33. Διελέγετο ὑπέρ τινων ὁ Πλάτων, παρὼν δ' ὁ Διογένης ὀλίγον αὐτῷ προσεῖχεν. ἠγανάκτησεν οὖν ἐπὶ τούτοις ὁ Ἀρίστωνος καὶ ἔφη· "ἐπάκουσον τῶν λόγων, κύον." καὶ ὃς οὐδὲν διαταραχθεὶς "ἀλλ' ἐγὼ" εἶπεν "οὐκ ἐπανῆλθον ἐκεῖσε[2] ὅθεν ἐπράθην, ὥσπερ οἱ κύνες," αἰνιττόμενος αὐτοῦ τὴν εἰς Σικελίαν ἐπάνοδον.[3] εἰώθει δέ, φασιν, ὁ Πλάτων περὶ Διογένους λέγειν, ὅτι μαινόμενος οὗτος Σωκράτης ἐστίν.

34. Αἰγύπτιοί φασι παρ' Ἑρμοῦ τὰ νόμιμα ἐκμουσωθῆναι· οὕτω δὲ καὶ ἕκαστοι[4] τὰ παρ' ἑαυτοῖς σεμνύνειν προῄρηνται. δικασταὶ δὲ τὸ ἀρχαῖον παρ' Αἰγυπτίοις οἱ ἱερεῖς ἦσαν. ἦν δὲ τούτων ἄρχων ὁ πρεσβύτατος, καὶ ἐδίκαζεν ἅπαντας. ἔδει δὲ αὐτὸν εἶναι δικαιότατον ἀνθρώπων καὶ ἀφειδέστατον. εἶχε δὲ καὶ ἄγαλμα περὶ τὸν αὐχένα ἐκ σαπφείρου λίθου, καὶ ἐκαλεῖτο τὸ ἄγαλμα Ἀλήθεια. ἐγὼ δὲ ἠξίουν μὴ λίθου πεποιημένην καὶ εἰκασμένην τὴν Ἀλήθειαν περιφέρειν τὸν δικαστήν, ἀλλ' ἐν αὐτῇ τῇ ψυχῇ ἔχειν αὐτήν.

35. Ὅτι Λαῒς καὶ Ἀξίνη ἐκαλεῖτο. ἤλεγχε δὲ

[1] τῶν ὄντων J. Gronovius: τούτων codd.
[2] ἐκεῖσε Gesner: ἐκεῖθεν codd.

the gods, his family, and their circle—because it is to them that free men dispose of what is surplus to their own needs. If a man during his lifetime gives the impression of poverty and on his death is found to be rich, that is the most shameful thing that can happen.

33. Plato was discussing various subjects in the presence of Diogenes, who paid little attention to him. The son of Ariston was annoyed and said: "Listen to what I have to say, dog." Diogenes, unruffled, replied: "But I have not returned to the place where I was sold, as dogs do," alluding to Plato's second journey to Sicily.[a] Plato used to say of Diogenes, according to reports, that he was a mad Socrates.

34. The Egyptians are supposed to have been instructed in their laws by Hermes.[b] Each nation makes a practice of claiming superiority for their own institutions in this way. In ancient times the priests were judges in Egypt. The most senior of them was in charge, and had jurisdiction over everyone. He had to be exceptionally honest and rigorous. Round his neck he wore a statuette carved from lapis lazuli, and the stone was called Truth. I would have the judge not carry around an image of truth made from stone, but possess truth in his soul.

35. Note that Lais was also called Axine.[c] This nick-

[a] The reference is to the story that after his first visit to Sicily Plato was sold into slavery and had to be ransomed; see e.g. Diogenes Laertius 3.18–23.

[b] Compare 12.4 above, and note also FGrH 665 F 104.

[c] Compare 12.5 above.

---

[3] ἐπάνοδον Kor.: ὁδόν codd.

[4] ἕκαστοι] -τα Scheffer

αὐτῆς[1] *τὸ ἐπώνυμον τοῦτο τὴν τοῦ ἤθους ἀγριότητα καὶ ὅτι πολὺ ἐπράττετο, καὶ ἔτι μᾶλλον παρὰ τῶν ξένων, ἅτε ἀπαλλαττομένων θᾶττον.*

36. *Γελᾶν δὲ ἔξεστιν ἐπὶ τοῖς μέγα φρονοῦσι διὰ τοὺς πατέρας καὶ τοὺς ἄνω τοῦ γένους, εἴ γε Μαρίου μὲν τὸν πατέρα οὐκ ἴσμεν, αὐτὸν δὲ θαυμάζομεν διὰ τὰ ἔργα, καὶ Κάτωνα δὲ καὶ Σέρβιον καὶ Ὀστίλιον καὶ Ῥωμύλον.*

37. *Φιλῶ δὲ μήτε τὰ ἀγάλματα, ὅσα ἡμῖν ἡ πλαστικὴ δείκνυσι, μήτε*[2] *τὰς εἰκόνας ἀργῶς ὁρᾶν· ἔστι γάρ τι τῆς χειρουργίας*[3] *σοφὸν καὶ ἐν τούτοις. καὶ πολλὰ μὲν καὶ ἄλλα δύναταί τις καταγνῶναι ἔχοντα ταύτῃ, ἐν δὲ τοῖς καὶ ἐκεῖνο· τῶν Μουσῶν οὐδεὶς οὐδέποτε οὔτε γραφικὸς ἀνὴρ οὔτε πλαστικὸς οἷός τε ἐγένετο ψευδίστατα καὶ κίβδηλα καὶ ἀλλότρια τῶν Διὸς θυγατέρων τὰ εἴδη παραστῆσαι ἡμῖν. ἢ τίς οὕτως νεανικῶς ἐμάνη δημιουργός, ὥστε ὡπλισμένας ἡμῖν ἐργάσασθαι; ὁμολογεῖ δὲ τοῦτο ὅτι δεῖ τὸν ἐν Μούσαις βίον εἰρηνικόν τε ἅμα καὶ πρᾶον εἶναι καὶ ἄξιον ἐκείνων.*

38. *Ἐπαμεινώνδου τοῦ Θηβαίου πολλὰ μὲν καὶ ἄλλα καλὰ οἶδα, ἐν δὲ τοῖς καὶ τόδε· ἔλεγε πρὸς Πελοπίδαν μὴ πρότερον ἀπαλλάττεσθαι τῆς ἀγορᾶς [ἡμέρᾳ]*[4] *πρὶν ἢ φίλον τοῖς ἀρχαίοις τινὰ προσπορίσαι*[5] *νεώτερον.*

[1] *αὐτῆς* Kor.: *αὐτῇ* x (deficit V)

[2] *μήτε . . . μήτε* Her.: *μηδὲ . . . μηδὲ* codd.

[3] *τῆς χειρουργίας* Faber: *ταῖς -αις* codd.

name showed her aggressive character and her high charges, especially to foreigners, as they were leaving the country sooner.

36. One can laugh at people who take great pride in their fathers and ancestors, considering that we know nothing of Marius' father but admire the son for his achievements, and the same is true for Cato, Servius, Hostilius, and Romulus.[a]

37. I do not care to look idly at pictures or the statues that sculptors produce.[b] Part of the craftsman's wisdom is actually in these works. Many examples of this fact can be recognised, and in particular the following: no one, whether painter or sculptor, has ever succeeded in giving us utterly untrue images of the Muses, false and alien to the nature of the daughters of Zeus.[c] What artist has been so irresponsibly stupid as to depict them for us wearing armour? The fact proves that life dedicated to the Muses must be at once peaceful, gentle, and worthy of them.

38. I know of many other fine acts of Epaminondas, in addition to the following. He told Pelopidas not to leave the marketplace before adding one new friend to those he already had.

[a] Compare 12.6 above. But here Servius Tullius, the sixth king of Rome (578–525 B.C.), Tullus Hostilius, the third king (673–642 B.C.), and Romulus are included.

[b] A few wealthy Romans had private picture galleries; see Vitruvius 6.5.2. Lucullus' gallery attracted visitors (Varro, *De re rustica* 1.2.10).

[c] Compare 12.2 above.

---

[4] del. Faber

[5] προσπορίσαι] -ίσασθαι Kor.

39. Ὁ Περσῶν βασιλεὺς (βούλομαι γάρ τι ὑμῖν καὶ φαιδρὸν εἰπεῖν) στέφανον εἰς μύρον βάψας (διεπέπλεκτο δὲ ῥόδων ὁ στέφανος) ἔπεμψεν Ἀνταλκίδᾳ πρεσβεύοντι ὑπὲρ εἰρήνης πρὸς αὐτόν. ὁ δὲ "δέχομαι μὲν" ἔφη "τὸ δῶρον καὶ ἐπαινῶ τὴν φιλοφροσύνην, ἀπώλεσας δὲ τὴν ὀσμὴν τῶν ῥόδων καὶ τὴν τῆς φύσεως εὐωδίαν διὰ τὴν ἐκ τῆς τέχνης κιβδηλίαν."

40. Ἀλέξανδρος ὁ Φεραίων τύραννος ἐν τοῖς μάλιστα ἔδοξεν ὠμότατος εἶναι. Θεοδώρου δὲ τοῦ τῆς τραγῳδίας ποιητοῦ[1] ὑποκρινομένου τὴν Ἀερόπην[2] σφόδρα ἐμπαθῶς, ὁ δὲ εἰς δάκρυα ἐξέπεσεν, εἶτα ἐξανέστη τοῦ θεάτρου. ἀπολογούμενος δὲ ἔλεγε τῷ Θεοδώρῳ ὡς οὐ καταφρονήσας οὐδὲ ἀτιμάσας αὐτὸν ᾤχετο, ἀλλ' αἰδούμενος εἰ τὰ μὲν ὑποκριτοῦ πάθη οἷός τε ἦν[3] ἐλεεῖν, τὰ δὲ τῶν ἑαυτοῦ πολιτῶν οὐχί.

41. Ὅτι Ἀπολλόδωρος πλεῖστον ἀνθρώπων πίνων οἶνον οὐκ ἀπεκρύπτετο τὸ ἑαυτοῦ κακόν, οὐδὲ ἐπειρᾶτο περιαμπέχειν τὴν μέθην καὶ τὰ ἐξ αὐτῆς κακά, ἀλλὰ καὶ ἐκ τοῦ οἴνου ὑπαναφλεγόμενος καὶ ὑπεξαπτόμενος ἐγίνετο φονικώτερος, πρὸς τῇ φύσει καὶ τὸ πῶμα[4] ἔχων ἐνδόσιμον.

42. Ξενοκράτης ὁ Πλάτωνος ἑταῖρος ἔλεγε μηδὲν διαφέρειν ἢ τοὺς πόδας ἢ τοὺς ὀφθάλμοὺς εἰς ἀλλο-

[1] ποιητοῦ] ὑποκριτοῦ Nauck

[2] Ἀερόπην] Μερόπην Valckenaer: Ἑκάβην e Plut. *Pelop.* 29 et *Mor.* 334 A Per.

39. The Persian king—I want to tell you something cheerful—dipped a garland in perfume—the garland was made up of roses—and sent it to Antalcidas, who had come on a diplomatic mission to discuss peace.[a] "I accept the gift" said the recipient, "and I appreciate your kindness, but you have destroyed the perfume of the roses and their natural scent by an artificial disguise."

40. Alexander[b] the tyrant of Pherae was regarded as exceptionally savage. When the tragic poet Theodorus played the part of Aerope with great emotion, Alexander burst into tears and left the theatre.[c] By way of apology he told Theodorus that he had not left out of scorn or contempt, but shamed by the fact that he could pity suffering portrayed by an actor and not the suffering of his citizens.

41. Note that Apollodorus[d] drank more than anyone else and did not hide his fault or try to cover up his drunkenness and the problems resulting from it. In fact when he was inflamed and excited by wine, he became more bloodthirsty because drink added a stimulus to his natural character.

42. Plato's friend Xenocrates used to say [fr. 95 H.] it made no difference whether one cast eyes on another

[a] The negotiations led to the Peace of Antalcidas in 386 B.C.

[b] Tyrant of Pherae in Thessaly 369–358 B.C.

[c] Though Aelian calls Theodorus a poet, he is perhaps to be identified with a famous actor; see TrGF I no. 265.

[d] Tyrant of Cassandreia in northern Greece in the third century B.C.

---

[3] ἦν Kor.: ᾖ codd.

[4] πῶμα Her. post Kor.: σῶμα codd.

τρίαν οἰκίαν τιθέναι· ἐν ταὐτῷ γὰρ ἁμαρτάνειν τόν τε εἰς ἃ μὴ δεῖ χωρία βλέποντα καὶ εἰς οὓς μὴ δεῖ τόπους παριόντα.

43. Ὁ μὲν Πτολεμαῖος, φασίν, (ὁπόστος δὲ αὐτῶν, ἐὰν δεῖ) καθήμενος[1] ἐπὶ κύβοις καὶ πεττεύων διετέλει· εἶτά τις αὐτῷ παρεστὼς ἀνεγίνωσκε τῶν κατεγνωσμένων τὰ ὀνόματα καὶ τὰς καταδίκας αὐτῶν προσεπέλεγεν, ἵνα ἐκεῖνος παρασημήνηται τοὺς ἀξίους θανάτου. Βερενίκη δὲ ἡ γαμετὴ αὐτοῦ λαβοῦσα τὸ βιβλίον παρὰ τοῦ παιδὸς εἶτα οὐκ εἴασε διαναγνωσθῆναι[2] τὸ πᾶν, "οὐκ ἔδει"[3] φήσασα "πάνυ σφόδρα προσέχοντα τὴν διάνοιαν ὑπὲρ ἀνθρώπου ψυχῆς λογίζεσθαι[4] καὶ μὴ πρὸς παιδιᾷ γινόμενον;" οὐ γὰρ ὁμοίαν εἶναι τὴν πτῶσιν τὴν τῶν κύβων καὶ τὴν τῶν σωμάτων. πρὸς ταῦτα ὁ Πτολεμαῖος ἥσθη καὶ οὐδέποτε κυβεύων μετὰ ταῦτα ὑπὲρ [τῆς][5] ἀνθρώπου κρίσεως ἤκουσεν.

44. Λακωνικὸν μειράκιον ἐπρίατο χωρίον ὑπερεύωνον, εἶτα ἐπὶ τὰς ἀρχὰς ἤχθη καὶ ἐζημιώθη. τὸ δὲ αἴτιον τῆς καταδίκης ἐκεῖνο ἦν, ἐπεὶ νέος ὢν τὸ κερδαίνειν ὀξύτατα ἑώρα. ἦν δὲ Λακεδαιμονίων ἐν τοῖς μάλιστα ἀνδρικὸν καὶ τοῦτο, μὴ πρὸς μόνους πολεμίους παρατετάχθαι ἀλλὰ καὶ πρὸς ἀργύριον.

45. Γυναῖκας τῶν Ἑλλήνων ἐπαινοῦμεν Πηνελόπην Ἄλκηστιν καὶ τὴν Πρωτεσιλάου, Ῥωμαίων

[1] καθήμενος scripsi: καθῆστο codd.
[2] διαναγνωσθῆναι Faber: διαγ- codd.
[3] οὐκ ἔδει Rutgers: οὐκέτι codd.

man's house or intruded into it. It was equally wrong to look where one should not and to enter where one should not.

43. Ptolemy, they say—which one of them, is a question to leave aside[a]—would sit down for a game of dice and regularly played draughts. Then someone stood by him to read the names of persons found guilty and add a word about the convictions, so that he could indicate which of them deserved the death penalty. His wife Berenice took the document from the slave and would not allow the rest of it to be read out, saying "When one is making calculations about a man's life ought one not to apply the faculties fully instead of playing a game?" The fall of dice and the collapse of a body were not the same. Ptolemy was pleased with this and from that time onwards never conducted hearings involving human life at the same time as playing dice.

44. A young man from Sparta bought a piece of land exceptionally cheap, but was hauled before the authorities and fined. The reason for his conviction was that as a young man he had a very sharp eye for profit. This was one of the Spartans' most characteristic forms of courage, to stand firm not only against the enemy but also against money.

45. Among Greek women we admire Penelope, Alcestis, and the wife of Protesilaus; among Romans Cornelia,

[a] In fact this is Ptolemy III (284–221 B.C.).

---

[4] λογίζεσθαι V: διαλογίζεσθαι x: δεῖν λογίζεσθαι Her.
[5] del. Her.

Κορνηλίαν καὶ Πορκίαν καὶ Κλοιλίαν.[1] ἐδυνάμην δὲ εἰπεῖν καὶ ἄλλας, ἀλλ' οὐ βούλομαι τῶν μὲν Ἑλλήνων εἰπεῖν ὀλίγας, ἐπικλύσαι δὲ τοῖς τῶν Ῥωμαίων ὀνόμασιν, ὡς ἂν μή μέ τις δοκοίη χαρίζεσθαι ἐμαυτῷ διὰ τὴν πατρίδα.

46. Οἱ Μαιάνδρῳ παροικοῦντες Μάγνητες Ἐφεσίοις πολεμοῦντες ἕκαστος τῶν ἱππέων ἦγεν αὑτῷ συστρατιώτην θηρατὴν κύνα καὶ ἀκοντιστὴν οἰκέτην. ἡνίκα δὲ ἔδει συμμῖξαι, ἐνταῦθα οἱ μὲν κύνες προπηδῶντες ἐτάραττον τὴν παρεμβολήν, φοβεροί τε καὶ ἄγριοι καὶ ἐντυχεῖν ἀμείλικτοι ὄντες· οἱ δὲ οἰκέται προπηδῶντες τῶν δεσποτῶν ἠκόντιζον. ἦν δὲ ἄρα ἐπὶ τῇ φθανούσῃ διὰ τοὺς κύνας ἀταξίᾳ καὶ τὰ παρὰ τῶν οἰκετῶν δρώμενα ἐνεργῆ. εἶτα ἐκ τρίτου ἐπῄεσαν αὐτοί.

46a. Μοιχὸς ἐν Γορτύνῃ ἁλοὺς ἐπὶ τὰς ἀρχὰς ἤγετο, εἶτα ἐλεγχθεὶς ἐστεφανοῦτο ἐρίῳ. ἐνόει δὲ τοῦτο τὸ στεφάνωμα κατηγορεῖν αὐτοῦ ὅτι ἄνανδρός ἐστι καὶ γύννις καὶ εἰς γυναῖκας καλός. καὶ ἔτι ἐπράττετο[2] δημοσίᾳ καὶ ἀτιμότατος ἦν ἀπὸ τούτου καὶ οὐδενός οἱ μετῆν τῶν κοινῶν.

46b. Ἀφίκετο ἐξ Ἑλλησπόντου παρὰ τὴν Ἀττικὴν ἑταίραν <τὴν>[3] Γνάθαιναν ἐραστὴς ἀνὴρ κατὰ κλέος αὐτῆς. παρὰ πότον οὖν πολὺς ἦν λαλῶν καὶ ἐδόκει φορτικός. ὑπολαβοῦσα οὖν ἡ Γνάθαινα πρὸς αὐτὸν ἔφατο· "εἶτα σὺ μέντοι λέγεις ἥκειν ἐξ Ἑλλησπόντου;" τοῦ δὲ ὁμολογήσαντος, "καὶ πῶς" εἶπεν "οὐκ ἔγνως τῶν ἐκεῖ πόλεων τὴν πρώτην;" τοῦ

Porcia, and Cloelia.[a] I could mention others, but I do not wish to mention just a few Greeks and swamp them with Roman names, lest someone think I am indulging myself for patriotic reasons.

46. The Magnesians living by the Maeander were at war with Ephesus.[b] Each of the cavalry took as his companion on campaign a hunting dog and a slave javelin-thrower. When battle was due to begin the dogs, which were fearsome, aggressive and ferocious to encounter, rushed forward and disturbed the enemy formation; the slaves jumped out in front of their masters and threw javelins. After the disorder already caused by the dogs the activity of the slaves also had its effect. Finally in their place the masters attacked.

46a. Cf. 12.12.[c]

46b. Cf. 12.13.[d]

[a] The three Greek ladies are all figures from myth who displayed outstanding devotion to their husbands (the third is Laodamia). As to the Romans, Cornelia was the daughter of Scipio Africanus and mother of the Gracchi; Porcia the daughter of Cato Uticensis, who became one of the conspirators against Julius Caesar; and Cloelia (if the name is correctly restored) was sent as a hostage to the Etruscan king Porsenna in 508 B.C. but escaped to Rome by swimming across the Tiber.

[b] This ch. appears to refer to a war mentioned by Strabo 14.1.40 (647), to be dated before the middle of the seventh century B.C.

[c] This ch. repeats 12.12 above, but omitting the detail of the 50 staters.

[d] A repetition of 12.13 without significant variation.

---

[1] *Κλοιλίαν* Per.: *Κεστιλίαν* x: om. V [2] *ἔτι ἐπράττετο* J. Gronovius: *ἐπιπράσκετο* V (deficit x) [3] suppl. Her.

δὲ εἰπόντος· "καὶ τίς ἐστιν αὕτη;" ἡ δὲ ἀπεκρίνατο· "Σίγειον." καὶ ἐμμελῶς διὰ τοῦ ὀνόματος κατεσίγασεν ἄρα αὐτόν.

46c. Ὡραιότατοι καὶ ἐρασμιώτατοι λέγονται γενέσθαι Ἑλλήνων μὲν Ἀλκιβιάδης, Ῥωμαίων δὲ Σκιπίων. λέγουσι δὲ Δημήτριον τὸν Πολιορκητὴν ὥρας ἀμφισβητῆσαι. Ἀλέξανδρον δὲ τὸν Φιλίππου ἀπραγμόνως ὡραῖον γενέσθαι λέγουσι. τὴν μὲν γὰρ κόμην ἀνασεσύρθαι αὐτῷ, ξανθὴν δὲ εἶναι· ὑπαναφύεσθαι δέ τι ἐκ τοῦ εἴδους φοβερὸν τῷ Ἀλεξάνδρῳ λέγουσιν.

46d. Ὅτι κάλαμον περιβὰς[1] Ἀγησίλαος ἵππευε μετὰ τοῦ υἱοῦ. καὶ πρὸς τὸν γελάσαντα "νῦν μὲν σιώπα" εἶπεν, "ὅταν δὲ γένῃ πατήρ, τότε ἐξαγορεύσεις." καὶ τὸ Εὐριπίδου δὲ οὕτως ἔχον·[2]

παίζω. μεταβολὰς γὰρ πόνων ἀεὶ φιλῶ

φιλεταιρίας δόξαν ἠνέγκατο.

47. Ὅτι Ζεῦξις ὁ Ἡρακλεώτης ἔγραψε τὴν Ἑλένην. Νικόμαχος[3] οὖν ὁ ζωγράφος ἐξεπλήττετο τὴν εἰκόνα καὶ τεθηπὼς τὸ γράμμα δῆλος ἦν. ἤρετο οὖν τις αὐτὸν προσελθὼν τί δὴ παθὼν οὕτω θαυμάζοι τὴν τέχνην. ὁ δὲ "οὐκ ἄν με ἠρώτησας" εἶπεν "εἰ τοὺς ἐμοὺς ὀφθαλμοὺς ἐκέκτησο." ἐγὼ δ' ἂν φαίην τοῦτο καὶ ἐπὶ τῶν λόγων, ἀλλ' εἴ τις ἔχοι πεπαιδευμένα ὦτα, ὥσπερ οὖν οἱ χειρουργοὶ τεχνικὰ ὄμματα.

47a. Λέγεται Ἀλέξανδρος ὁ Φιλίππου ζηλοτυπώτατα πρὸς τοὺς ἑταίρους διατεθῆναι καὶ βασκαίνειν

46c. Cf. 12.14.[a]

46d. Note that Agesilaus rode on a broomstick with his son. When someone laughed at him he replied: "Keep quiet now. When you become a father you can express your thoughts." And there is the Euripidean verse [fr. 864 N.] which runs: "I play because I always like a change from work"—admired as a sign of friendship.[b]

47. Note that Zeuxis of Heraclea painted Helen. The painter Nicomachus was amazed at the picture and obviously admired it. Someone approached to ask him why he so admired the artistic quality. To which he replied: "You wouldn't have asked me if you had my eyes." I would say the same thing about the spoken word, provided one had a trained ear in the way that craftsmen have trained eyes.[c]

47a. Alexander son of Philip is said to have been very jealous of his friends and envious of them all, though not

[a] A repetition of 12.14 above, omitting the quotation from Homer.

[b] This ch. combines two elements of 12.15 above.

[c] One may suspect that this ch. has been abbreviated, or that it reflects some critical controversy which Aelian has not explained to us. (The recurrence of the anecdote in Plutarch fr. 134 = Stobaeus 4.20.34, does not solve the puzzle.)

---

[1] περιβὰς Bevegni: παρα- V (deficit x)

[2] ἔχον Per.: ἔχει V

[3] Νικόμαχος Per.: Νικόστρατος codd.

μὲν πᾶσιν, οὐ μὴν διὰ τὰς αὐτὰς αἰτίας. ἀπήχθετο γὰρ Περδίκκᾳ μὲν ὅτι ἦν πολεμικός, Λυσιμάχῳ δὲ ἐπεὶ στρατηγεῖν ἀγαθὸς ἐδόκει, Σελεύκῳ δὲ ἐπεὶ ἀνδρεῖος ἦν· Ἀντιγόνου δὲ αὐτὸν ἐλύπει τὸ φιλότιμον, Ἀντιπάτρου[1] δὲ ἤχθετο τῷ ἡγεμονικῷ, Πτολεμαίου δὲ τὸ δεξιὸν ὑφωρᾶτο,[2] Ἀταρρίου[3] ἐδεδίει τὸ ἄτακτον, τό γε μὴν νεωτεροποιὸν Πείθωνος.

47b. Ὅτι μέγαν τὸ σῶμα καὶ ἰδεῖν τοιοῦτον οἷον ἐκπλῆξαι γενέσθαι λέγεται Τίτορμον, γενναῖον δὲ οὕτως ὡς ἐλθόντα εἰς ἀγέλην ἀτιμαγέλην ταῦρον καὶ ὑβριστὴν λαβεῖν[4] τοῦ ποδὸς ὡς μὴ ἀποδρᾶναι δύνασθαι βουλόμενον, καὶ παριόντα ἕτερον τῇ ἑτέρᾳ χειρὶ συναρπάσαι. ἅπερ οὖν θεασάμενος Μίλων ὁ Κροτωνιάτης ἀνατείνας εἰς τὸν οὐρανὸν τὰς χεῖρας "ὦ Ζεῦ," ἔφατο "μὴ καὶ τοῦτον Ἡρακλῆ ἡμῖν ἔσπειρας;" ἐντεῦθεν τὸ τῆς παροιμίας· "ἄλλος οὗτος Ἡρακλῆς."

48. Ὅτι Φίλιππος τῶν ἐν Μακεδονίᾳ δοκιμωτάτων τοὺς υἱεῖς παραλαμβάνων περὶ τὴν ἑαυτοῦ θεραπείαν εἶχεν, οὔτι που, φασίν, ἐνυβρίζων αὐτοῖς οὐδὲ διευτελίζων, ἀλλ' ἐκ τῶν ἐναντίων καρτερικοὺς αὐτοὺς ἐκπονῶν καὶ ἑτοίμους πρὸς τὸ τὰ δέοντα πράττειν ἀποφαίνων. πρὸς δὲ τοὺς τρυφῶντας αὐτῶν καὶ εἰς τὰ ἐπιταττόμενα ῥᾳθύμως ἔχοντας διέκειτο, φασί, πολεμίως. Ἀφθόνητον γοῦν ἐμαστίγωσεν, ὅτι τὴν τάξιν ἐκλιπὼν ἐξετράπετο τῆς ὁδοῦ ὡς[5] διψήσας καὶ παρῆλθεν εἰς πανδοκέως. καὶ Ἀρχέδαμον ἀπέκτεινεν, ὅτι προστάξαντος αὐτοῦ ἐν τοῖς ὅπλοις συν-

for identical reasons. He disliked Perdiccas for being a born soldier, Lysimachus because he had a good reputation as a general, and Seleucus for his bravery. Antigonus' ambition pained him, he disliked Antipater's quality of leadership, was suspicious of Ptolemy's adroitness, and feared Atarrius' insubordination, not to mention Pithon's revolutionary instinct.[a]

47b. Note that Titormus is reported to have been of enormous stature, so as to be frightening; he was so vigorous that he approached a herd of cattle, took hold of a solitary recalcitrant bull by the foot so that it could not run away even though it wished to, and as another came by grabbed it with his other hand. When Milo of Croton saw this he raised his hands towards the sky and said: "O Zeus, is he too a Heracles you have created for us?" Hence the proverb "This man is a second Heracles."[b]

48. Note that Philip took the sons of the leading Macedonian families into his personal service, not intending (so they say) to insult or demean them, but on the contrary training them to be fit and ensuring that they would be ready for action. He took a hostile view (they say) of any who were self-indulgent and slack in obeying orders. So he whipped Aphthonetus for breaking ranks, leaving the road because he was thirsty, and entering an inn. And he executed Archedamus because when he personally

[a] This is a full version of 12.16 above.
[b] An abridgement of 12.22 above.

---

[1] Ἀντιπάτρου Per.: Ἀττάλου V (deficit x) [2] ὑφωρᾶτο] -εωρᾶτο Her. [3] Ἀταρρίου Scheffer: Ἀρρίου V
[4] λαβεῖν Per.: λαβὼν V (deficit x) [5] ὡς V: om. x

ἔχειν ἑαυτόν, ὁ δὲ ἀπεδύσατο·[1] ἤλπισε γὰρ διὰ τῆς κολακείας καὶ ὑποδρομῆς χειρώσασθαι τὸν βασιλέα, ἅτε ἀνὴρ ἥττων τοῦ κερδαίνειν ὤν.

48a. Ὅτι Πλάτων ἰδὼν Ἀκραγαντίνους οἰκοδομοῦντας πολυτελῶς καὶ ὁμοίως δειπνοῦντας εἶπεν· "Ἀκραγαντῖνοι οἰκοδομοῦσι μὲν ὡς ἀεὶ βιωσόμενοι, δειπνοῦσι δὲ ὡς αὔριον τεθνηξόμενοι."

[1] ἀπεδύσατο Kor.: ὑπελύσατο codd.

ordered the man to stay in his armour, he took it off. Archedamus was unable to resist thoughts of gain and had hoped to win over the king by flattery and wheedling.[a]

48a. Cf. 12.29.[b]

[a] An obscure passage; perhaps Archedamus had been tempted to plunder the enemy camp before the danger of a counterattack was past.

[b] An abridgement of 12.29 above.

FRAGMENTS

1. Stob. 3.17.28 (SVF 469)

Χρύσιππος ὁ Σολεὺς ἐποιεῖτο τὸν βίον ἐκ πάνυ ὀλίγων, Κλεάνθης δὲ καὶ ἀπὸ ἐλαττόνων.

2. Stob. 4.25.38

πρώτῃ καὶ ὀγδοηκοστῇ Ὀλυμπιάδι φασὶ τὴν Αἴτνην ῥυῆναι, ὅτε καὶ Φιλόνομος καὶ Καλλίας οἱ Καταναῖοι τοὺς ἑαυτῶν πατέρας ἀράμενοι διὰ μέσης τῆς φλογὸς ἐκόμισαν, τῶν ἄλλων κτημάτων καταφρονήσαντες, ἀνθ' ὧν καὶ ἀμοιβῆς ἔτυχον τῆς ἐκ τοῦ θείου· τὸ γάρ τοι πῦρ θεόντων αὐτῶν διέστη καθ' ὃ μέρος ἐκεῖνοι παρεγίνοντο.

3. Stob. 4.55.10

ὁ Σωκράτης ἐπεὶ τὸ κώνειον ἔμελλε πίεσθαι, τῶν ἀμφὶ τὸν Κρίτωνα ἐρομένων αὐτὸν τίνα τρόπον ταφῆναι θέλει, "ὅπως ἂν ὑμῖν" ἀπεκρίνατο "ᾗ ῥᾷστον."

FRAGMENTS

1. Stob. *Ecl.* 3.17.28

Chrysippus of Soli lived off very little, Cleanthes from even less.[a]

2. ibid. 4.25.38

They say Etna erupted in the 81st Olympiad, when Philonomus and Callias the Catanians picked up their fathers and carried them through the flames, paying no attention to their other possessions. For this they received a reward from the gods: as they ran the fire parted at their approach.[b]

3. ibid. 4.55.10

When Socrates was on the point of drinking the hemlock, Crito's companions asked him how he wished to be buried, and he replied: "In whatever way is easiest for you."[c]

[a] Chrysippus (281 or 277–208 or 204 B.C.) and Cleanthes (331/0–232/1 B.C.) were eminent Stoic philosophers. The latter's *Hymn to Zeus* is still extant.

[b] A story of this kind is told in variant forms by many classical authors. It also features on some coins of Catania and on a Roman denarius issued by M. Herennius in 108/7 B.C. See F. Wilhelm, *Philologus* 80 (1924): 106–109.

[c] Compare 1.16 above.

4. Stob. 2.31.38

Σωκράτης ὁ γενναῖος ᾐτιᾶτο τῶν πατέρων ἐκείνους, ὅσοι <μὴ> παιδεύσαντες αὐτῶν τοὺς υἱεῖς, εἶτα ἀπορούμενοι ἦγον ἐπὶ τὰς ἀρχὰς τοὺς νεανίσκους καὶ ἔκρινον αὐτοὺς ἀχαριστίας, ὅτι οὐ τρέφονται ὑπ' αὐτῶν. εἶπε γὰρ ἀδύνατον ἀξιοῦν τοὺς πατέρας· μὴ γὰρ οἵους τε εἶναι τοὺς μὴ μαθόντας τὰ δίκαια ποιεῖν αὐτά.

5. Suda α 4140

πολὺς δὲ καὶ ἀσελγὴς τίκτεται ἐκεῖθι (ἄνεμος)· γένεσις δὲ αὐτῷ αὐλῶνες βαθεῖς καὶ φάραγγες, δι' ὧν ὠθούμενος ἐκτείνει λαβρότατος.

6. Suda δ 1478

αἳ δεξάμεναι παρὰ Πύρρου τὰ δῶρα ἔφασαν ἡ δὼς αὐταῖς πρέπειν καὶ ἀξία εἶναι τοῦ πέμψαντος Πύρρου· ἀνόσιον δὲ αὐταῖς εἶναι φορεῖν.

7. Suda φ 445

ἐπ' ἐλευθερίᾳ τινὲς Ῥωμαίοις φιλωθέντες, εἶτα μέντοι τὴν πίστιν, ἥπερ οὖν δεσμός ἐστι φιλίας, οὐκ ἐτήρησαν.

8. Suda κ 146

οὐδεὶς οἰκέτης μνημονεύεται κάκῃ εἴξας προδοῦναι τὸν δεσπότην.

4. ibid. 2.31.38

The admirable Socrates criticised fathers who did not educate their own sons and then, when in financial difficulty, brought the young men before the magistrates, accusing them of ingratitude because they as parents were not maintained by them. He thought that the fathers were asking for something impossible, because people who had not learned about justice could not behave justly.[a]

5. Suda α 4140

A powerful and uncontrollable wind is created there; its origin is in deep defiles and ravines, through which it is propelled and blows very violently.

6. Suda δ 1478

They received the gifts from Pyrrhus and said that the offering suited them and was worthy of the man who had sent it; but it was sinful for them to wear it.

7. Suda ϕ 445

Some were made friends of the Romans with the condition that their freedom was preserved; but then they failed to maintain their loyalty, which is certainly the bond creating friendship.

8. Suda κ 146

No slave is recorded to have betrayed his master by yielding to cowardice.

[a] The obligations of children to parents are much emphasised in Greek literature, especially tragedy.

190. Stob. 3.29.58

Σόλων ὁ Ἀθηναῖος Ἐξηκεστίδου παρὰ πότον τοῦ ἀδελφιδοῦ αὐτοῦ μέλος τι Σαπφοῦς ᾄσαντος, ἥσθη τῷ μέλει καὶ προσέταξε τῷ μειρακίῳ διδάξαι αὐτόν. ἐρωτήσαντος δέ τινος διὰ ποίαν αἰτίαν τοῦτο ἐσπούδασεν, ὁ δὲ ἔφη "ἵνα μαθὼν αὐτὸ ἀποθάνω."

190. (= 187 Her.) Stobaeus 3.29.58
Solon the Athenian, son of Execestides, when his nephew sang a lyric by Sappho at a drinking party, enjoyed the song and asked the young man to teach it to him. When asked why he was so keen to do this he replied: "So that I can learn it and then die."

INDEX